QUEEN
of CAMELOT

MORE PRAISE FOR *QUEEN OF CAMELOT*

"A lovely story, a wonderfully human retelling of the Arthur and Guinevere legend, one touched with passion and enchantment."
—JENNIFER BLAKE

"A love story like no other. You will be charmed. . . . Sit back and enjoy, for who of us would not wish to return to Camelot?"
—ELAINE COFFMAN

"Powerful . . . Establishes Ms. McKenzie as a formidable presence in speculative fiction."
—*Romantic Times*

"McKenzie brings immediate freshness to her entertaining reworking of an often-told story by focusing on the girl destined to be queen."
—*Publishers Weekly*

"I couldn't put it down."
—*Feminist Bookstore News*

QUEEN

of CAMELOT

NANCY McKENZIE

BALLANTINE BOOKS

NEW YORK

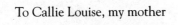
To Callie Louise, my mother

A nyone who has ever read any one of Mary Stewart's Merlin trilogy (*The Crystal Cave*, *The Hollow Hills*, *The Last Enchantment*) will know how much I owe to her vision of fifth-century Britain. These books, among others, inspired me to create my own tale about Guinevere, Arthur, Lancelot, and the real world these legendary people inhabit. I am indebted to many who have contributed to the Arthurian tradition, historians, and storytellers alike. As I have built upon the works of others, so I hope some future writer might build upon mine. After all, that is the ultimate compliment— to be considered even a small part of the tradition surrounding this ancient, time-tested tale.

Special thanks are due to several people whose help and encouragement are directly responsible for the publication of this book. Meg Affleck, my sister and first reader, went to a lot of trouble to convince me to find an agent; Bruce McKenzie, my husband, gave me the courage to try; Virginia Kidd, my agent, supplied good advice and dealt patiently with my questions; and Deborah Hogan, my editor, worked long and hard to give my story shape.

I thank also my friend Kate Delaney for her gift of Xenophon's *On Horsemanship*, and John Downey of the Andrus Planetarium, The Hudson River Museum, for his prompt answers to astronomical questions. Karen Kramer gave me invaluable support and advice about writing and editing; Caroline McKenzie helped me research White and Malory; Marsha Gorelick and Lydia Soifer provided me a constant source of excited and enthusiastic support, and Joellen Finnie listened patiently to hours of proposed interpretations of Arthurian tales.

Finally, my thanks to Shelly Shapiro, editorial director of Del Rey Books for republishing *The Child Queen* and *The High Queen* in a single volume, which is how I originally submitted these stories. This version of my Guenivere tale is much more faithful to the original manuscript in both structure and format. Many changes that were made to enable a single story to be published as two seperate books have been eliminated in this volume, making *Queen of Camelot*, like a prodigal child, dearer to my heart than either of its predecessors.

—Nancy Affleck McKenzie,
September 2001

Arthur's Britain

PICTS

LOTHIAN
Dunpelder
LOTHIAN

STRATHCLYDE

North Sea

Eden River
Caer Eden
RHEGED
Galava

Irish Sea
Caer Garton
Isle of Mona
Pellinore's Castle
GWYNEDD
NORTHGALLIS
POWYS

ELMET
York
Caer Mord

ANGLES

BRITAIN

ANGLES

EAST SAXONS

DYFED
Caerleon
Ynys Witrin
Camlann
GUENT
Severn River
Amesbury
Guan's Dance
BRITONS
Camelot
WEST SAXONS
Winchester
Mt. Badon
Potter's Bayn
Castle Doare
Seal's Bay

Thames River
Rutupiai
SOUTH SAXONS

Tintagel
DUMNONIA
CORNWALL

Narrow Sea

CLODO·MIR'S
FRANKS

FRANKS

CHILDEBERT'S
FRANKS

Benoic

BRITTANY
LANASCOL
LESS
BRITAIN

BURGUNDIANS

Kerrec
Aatan

IRELAND

GAUL

Map by S.T. Palmer

BOOK I

THE CHILD QUEEN

♔ PROLOGUE

I was alone in my cell when the abbess came for me. For hours I had been trying to pray, but I could not stay on my knees. The darkening sky and freshening breeze among the willows by my window broke in upon my peace. And then I thought I caught the thud of a horse's canter from the road beyond the monastery walls. When the abbess finally knocked, I was half expecting her and stood serene before her hasty curtsy. Kind woman, she had never learned the art of dissembling and her weathered face betrayed her disapproval and her fear.

"My lady Queen."

"Please, Mother," I murmured as a small thrill of terror shook me. If the rumors that had flown about the land the past weeks were true, I was no longer Queen, and whoever had come for me might well have come to take me to my fate. Indeed, it was hard to image another reason for a visitor, or for the Mother's fear. But I had heard only one horse.

"My lady," she began again. "You have a visitor in the garden."

I waited. With lowered eyes, she seemed to seek guidance from the polished stones of the floor. "I told him you do not receive visitors. He bade me give you this and ask you to come."

I gasped. In her hand she held his ring, the great ruby with the Dragon of Britain carved small. I took it from her, trembling. It was warm, as if it had just come from his finger. My knees shook and for a moment I feared I might fall.

"Mother!" I cried. "Is it the King?"

Then her sad eyes met mine, her compassion overcoming her fear. "No, my lady. It is not the King, but a king's messenger. Her has ridden hard but will not tarry long. Time presses upon him."

"I will go at once," I replied, and with her help adjusted the white veil of mourning over my face. She walked with me as far as the garden entrance and then, with a quick obeisance, left me.

I did not see him at first. The garden was small and private, surrounded by high walls. Pear trees stood silent, slowly turning color in the autumn light; the herbs of summer were gone; the roses recently pruned; only golden chrysanthemums blazed at the corners of the walks. A last ray of sun escaped the approaching storm clouds and lit the smooth alabaster of the Virgin's statue.

Then I saw him. He was kneeling before the statue, head bent in prayer, a weary knight, the dust of travel still upon his clothes. But I would know that back anywhere, among thousands, and in spite of myself, my heart leaped within me.

The Mother's disapproval was now clear to me, and her fear as well. She would never fear for my death—what was that but going home to God? But she feared mightily for my soul.

I walked slowly toward him. He rose and turned, and I lifted my veil. He had washed his face and his hair and his hands. We looked at one another a long time. Then he went on one knee, took my hand and pressed it to his lips. I caressed his black head, wondering desperately why I should feel so pained by the silver threads I found there. He led me to a bench and we sat silent, looking at one another in a kind of quiet desperation, because we had said good-bye forever long ago.

"Gwen," he said at last. There were new lines in his face and a weariness in his soul, an admission of defeat that was new to me. I did not need to ask what it was. I opened my hand and looked at the King's ring.

"It is true, then," I whispered, daring the words for the first time. "Arthur is dead."

"I helped to bury him," he said in a low voice. "Niniane took him to Ynys Witrin. The priestesses prepared him. The monks dug his grave on the Tor. It was—it was dreadful."

"And you were hurt?"

Light leaped to his face, and he quelled it. "Yes. But it's better. I accompanied him. There was no one left."

"What? Did none survive?"

"None. Gwen, they are all gone." His voice shook and he bowed his head.

I sat stunned. "Kay? Ferron? Gereint? Galahantyn?" I whispered. "Even Bedwyr?"

He nodded, head down.

"And—and Mordred?" That steadied him. He looked up, the old dislike in his eyes.

"Mordred killed him. It was Mordred's hand that struck the blow, cursed be his name forever! Mordred opened his head. He fulfilled his fate, as Merlin predicted. You backed the wrong horse, Gwen."

I took both his hands. The pain between us was unbearable.

"God called Arthur home. God guided Mordred's hand. It had to happen. If we don't believe that, we shall go mad." I felt the bitter tears on my face, and I felt his eyes on them. "You have been away a long time. You have heard rumors. But, my dear, this you must believe. There was never any King for me but Arthur."

He kissed my fingers. "I never doubted *you*, Gwen. But I have always doubted Mordred. He was ambitious."

"*Was?*" My voice broke. "Oh, dear God! Is he dead then? By whose hand?"

"By Arthur's," came the cruel reply. "Arthur slew him in the same instant he received his death blow."

The truth was so plainly written on his face that I burst into tears and had to hide my face in my hands. Angrily he paced the garden walk.

"S'trewth! I never thought to see more tears shed for a traitor and a King-slayer than for the King!"

I prayed God for the strength to recover myself—this was a grievous blow indeed. I had believed, in spite of the rumors, in my heart of hearts, that Mordred must be ruling as High King, biding his time until the remnants of Arthur's army would rally to him, and he could ratify his precious treaty with Cerdic the Saxon and secure Britain's borders forever. My dear Arthur! My poor Mordred, who fought so hard against his fate! Whatever was the future to hold for us Britons now? Were we, in fact, still a nation at all? Or was I a Welsh princess once more, and Lancelot a Breton, as we had been in the dark days before Pendragon?

"Are we in the hands of the Saxons, then?" I cried, and he turned to me in surprise.

"The Saxons? No, not yet. Constantine is King. Who else?" He came back to me and sat down. "I thought you grieved for Mordred. I know you loved him, though I will never fathom why."

"Dear God, I loved him too much. But not as you and others think, you who should know better."

"I never—"

"Yes, you did. In your heart you have doubted even me."

He bowed his head. He would never understand what had been between me and Arthur's son, who had fought so hard and cared so much. To Lancelot he would always be a traitor. To Lancelot, and to all of Britain.

"I have grieved for Arthur this fortnight past," I said slowly. "In my heart I am with him, as he is with God. But Mordred is gone from me forever. That devil's spawn Merlin was right. His name will be dragged through mud for centuries to come. No one but I will ever know his goodness."

There was silence between us, but thunder rumbled far off and Lancelot stirred.

"I have not yet told you why I came. Three things I have to tell you. Then I must be off." He glanced sideways at the door and suddenly I was afraid.

"Are you pursued?"

"Of course. By both Constantine and Cerdic. For different reasons. The last of the Companions. Never mind. Before Arthur died, as Morgaine held his head in her lap, he spoke of you."

I bowed my head, not knowing what was coming. The dying words of a King were powerful by every magic known to man. But I knew that since it was Arthur, they would be merciful.

"He blessed you, Gwen, and he expressed the wish that when your time comes, you be buried with him. In the same grave."

The tears ran freely down my face as I felt the love of that strong heart reach out to me, even from death.

"I have left instructions for this with the abbess, or her successor. She has promised upon the Book of God that it shall be done." He paused, and by the strength of his control I knew what was coming next. "I am on my way home to Less Britain. My lands are divided, my troops scattered. If my sons are to have any birthright, I must go back and put things straight. If Constantine wants me badly enough, he can come find me. But he will not. Cerdic will be watching his back."

I smiled inwardly. Here we were, finally alone and unobserved at this singular time in our lives, and we talked of affairs of state. It was fitting, I thought. See how far we had come. But I smiled too soon.

"If you would do me the honor, my dearest Queen, my only love, I would take you with me, and you should spend the rest of your days with me. Come out of your fastness, Gwen. Come with me. This is our chance at last. There will never be another. Come with me now."

His heart was in his eyes, and I knew well that nothing had changed between us since the first moment we had met; we had waited all our lives for this. He desired this, and yet he feared it. He was reluctant, and yet his eagerness was like the flame of youth. For so many years I had loved him but had been held by stronger vows. And now, at last, we were free.

I looked up at the swirling sky, where dark thunderclouds piled against one another in oncoming fury, and felt again the bitter agony of deep desire. I saw Ygraine and Uther, bound in a powerful passion that held a kingdom together but lost them their son. I saw Merlin, with his damning eyes, all his powers focused on Britain and her preservation, who let no one, man or woman, stand in his way. And I saw Arthur, sober and patient and kind, waiting for my decision, waiting to see if at the last, and for such a reason, I would betray his memory, his work, his Kingdom. I thought of Elaine, who had struggled once with such a passion, and I forgave her, after all these years. Last, I am afraid, I thought of my promise to God.

"Thank you, sweet Lancelot, for the invitation. God knows I have waited many years to hear it. But I cannot, my love. It is too late."

He kissed me then, and in his touch I felt both joy and sorrow. In a perverse way he was glad I had chosen to stay. He knew it was impossible and wrong, but it had been impossible not to ask. He relied, as he had so long ago, on my judgment. Only I knew how close I had come to giving in.

"My precious Gwen," he whispered, going down on one knee. "You are steadfast and unchanging, the only virtue in a wicked world." He drew my hand to his cheek and kissed my palm. "There is one thing more. I had a vision on Ynys Witrin after we buried Arthur."

I stared at him. "*You* had a vision?"

He nodded fervently. "I do not know if it was God who sent it, or Mithra, or Niniane, or even Merlin. They all spoke to me. I was to come to you when it was safe, bearing a message."

For half a second I both hoped and feared he would command me to go with him, quoting divine direction, but he had never been a subtle man.

"You are to write it down, Gwen. The story of your life. Of Arthur's deeds. Of the times."

If he meant to shock me, he succeeded. "Me? Write it down? A woman's words? Whatever for?"

"Merlin spoke with his voice of power. He commanded you to do it, and not to question—"

"That sounds like Merlin."

"—and to be faithfully honest, as you are. Those were his words, Gwen. 'Faithfully honest.' And you used to think he disliked you. Do it, and tell the world the truth about us, and the truth about Mordred, if you like. There's no harm in it, is there?"

I thought about this awhile, holding his hand and letting his head rest in my lap, knowing that this time it would truly be the last time.

"No one will listen to a woman. And there is no one alive now who would believe a word I said. It wouldn't suit their purposes."

"Then perhaps it shan't be read by those alive now. Perhaps it will come to light when times have changed and the people of Britain wish to know the truth about their King and Queen."

Like Arthur, Lancelot knew how to win me over. "The people of Britian" never failed. And suppose he really had seen a vision?

"All right," I said. "I suppose I might try it. It will give a purpose to the years I have left."

He rose and took my arm as the first few raindrops splashed on the warm, gray stone of the garden walls. I walked him to the gate, but there we lingered, the postern guard eyeing us, reluctant to come to our final parting. Suddenly I remembered the ring, which I had held in my hand all this while.

"Am I to keep this ring or are you to take it home to Lanascol?"

"It is yours. I took it from his finger."

"Did he bid you bring it me?"

"He was beyond speech."

My throat ached suddenly but I persisted. "And his Sword? Where is that?"

He cleared his throat uncomfortably. "When I heard his death sigh, I became enraged with grief," he said in a low voice I had to strain to catch. "I took the Sword out of his very hand and threw it into the Lake of Avalon. You could say it has disappeared."

I gazed at him in frank astonishment. "Why did you do that?"

He braved himself for his reply, standing stiffly. "I heard Merlin's voice telling me to do it. 'From the deeps of the Underworld has it come, and so shall it go home.' "

Merlin's words sounded strange on Lancelot's lips, but I believed them nonetheless. Arthur had believed that Merlin died, but Merlin's spirit was alive in the world after his passing. This was fact.

"If Excalibur has gone, then Britain is forsaken," I whispered. "We are dead, Lancelot. Our time is past."

He nodded heavily, and that weariness of spirit which I had first noted in him returned once more. "Yes. It is over. I shall disappear into Less Britain, and you shall vanish within this fastness. Forever. Unless you leave our tale behind you."

The breeze blew up suddenly, cold on the back of my neck. I gripped his hand. "Lancelot."

"Sweet love, I must go."

"Now?"

He kissed me formally, courtier to Queen, for eyes were watching.

"Go with God," I managed.

"Good-bye, Guinevere."

The storm broke.

1 ♕ GISELDA'S PROPHECY

The night of my birth the famed witch Giselda, the ugliest woman in all Britain, came to see my father, the King of Northgallis. It was the last night in April, cold and blowing a fine, icy rain. My father and his drinking companions, such nobles and petty lords as could leave their lands in the hands of others, sat in the hall before a great log fire while the women attended my mother and brought him tidings as the night wore on.

The guard let her in, not knowing who she was. She was old and bent, her hands were crippled and swollen, and my father's hospitality to the poor and infirm was well known. But she would not stay to warm herself before the peat fire in the kitchen, where the cooks were heating water for the queen's birthing. She made for the hall and the king. When the guard would have stopped her, she lifted her hood and glared at him. The very sight of her face froze him to the spot where he stood, and she passed by.

Likewise, when she came into the hall, and the company turned to her in surprise and then protest, she silenced them all when she uncovered her head.

"King Leodegrance!" she cried.

My father faced her. He was always the bravest man among brave men. "I am he, witch. State your business and be gone. You come at a time of celebration, and we would not be interrupted! Know you not my young queen gives birth this night?" His companions cheered him, and he even smiled at the old witch. He was the father of five sons of fighting age and the new husband of the loveliest woman in Wales. He could afford to be magnanimous.

But the witch stared at him, trancelike, until the room was quiet and all eyes were on her. "Beware, King! Laugh not until the night is over! It is a night of wonders! The queenstar in the east has fallen in a hail of light. And in its place burns a new star of wondrous brightness! The fairest in the heavens! These are portents of things to come. There is magic in the air this night. In this house."

My father was not a Christian, nor were the others in the room. He worshipped Mithra, the Bull-Slayer, when he was at war, along with all the other men who fought under the High King Uther Pendragon, and the Great Goddess when he was at peace. Yet he also believed in the ancient gods of his ancestors, the gods of roadways and rivers, of the storm winds, the low forests and the high hills, gods whom men had worshipped before ever the Romans came to Britain. To speak to him of magic was to touch him near the heart, and he was afraid.

"What do you mean, woman?" he demanded, hiding his fear in anger. "Where in this house?"

The witch grinned, showing black and broken teeth. Her voice fell into a low and vibrant monotone, and all strained to hear her words. "This night shall be born a daughter who shall rule the mightiest in the land." Her words fell on silence. "She will be the fairest beauty the world has known and the highest lady in all the kingdoms of Britain. Her name will live on in the minds of men for ages to come. Through her will you reach glory." Here she paused and passed her tongue over dry, cracked lips. Someone handed her a cup of spiced wine, and she drank. "But she will bring you pain, King, before ever she brings you joy. Beloved of kings, she shall betray a king and be herself betrayed. Hers will be a fate no one will envy. She will be the white shadow over the brightest glory of Britain." Here she stopped, shook herself awake, and, doing my stunned father a low curtsy, hurried out of the house before any man had sense enough to stop her.

The room was at once alive with voices. Each man asked his neighbor what she had meant. Each man thought he knew what the prophecy foretold. All of them took it as wonderful news for my father, except my father himself. He sat frowning in his great chair, saying over and over "the white shadow. White shadow." He used the Celtic word the witch had spoken: *gwenhwyfar*.

Just before dawn the weather broke and the wind softened. It was the first of May, a day sacred to the ancient Goddess, and the queen's labors were over. My father, asleep over his wine like his fellows, awoke with a start of premonition to find his chamberlain trembling at his elbow. He was charged with a dolorous message. The good Queen Elen had brought forth a daughter, but had died thereof. With her last breath she had kissed me and named me: Guinevere.

2 👑 NORTHGALLIS

My seventh year was my last one at home. It was not customary in those days for boys and girls of noble birth to spend their youth as pages and ladies-in-waiting in strangers' castles. Those were troubled times. The land was not at peace, and men did not trust one another. The law lay in the strongest sword. Outlaws lived among the hills, making travel treacherous. Even warriors undertook journeys only upon necessity, and that usually meant war.

And to tell truth, there were not many real castles in Wales. Our strongest buildings were fighting fortresses, where the king's troops slept on straw strewn over dirt flooring, and the walls of dressed stone were unadorned by the tapestries and weavings that kept the wind from our cozy rooms at home in the king's house. Caer Narfon, on our northern border, was the biggest fortress in Wales. It had been built by the Romans and then left to decay with the passing of centuries, but it was still in use as a fighting fortress and was our securest defense against the Irish raiders. With Y Wyddfa, the Snow Mountain, at its rear, and the Western Sea under its guarding eye, it was considered impregnable and was the pride of all Wales.

Nowadays, every petty king has a wonderful castle of quarried stone and plenty of tapestries and fine silks and cushions and carpets to adorn it, for the land has been at peace for twenty years and we have all had time, blessed time, to devote to the arts of peace. But in my childhood the king's house was a simple enough dwelling. Welshmen have a devilish pride, and even the king's house could not outshine his soldiers' homes by much, else he have trouble on his hands.

My father's house at Cameliard was of wood and wattle, with a large meeting and drinking hall that had a hole cut in the roof to let out the firesmoke. Beautiful hangings adorned the walls, keeping out the winter winds, and beneath the fresh rushes on the floor were real Roman tiles. Cracked and faded as they were, the designs were still discernible. I remember a crouching panther, birds with bright feathers and long necks, and a golden lion, seated and serene, which was just in front of my chair, next to my father on the dais. He kept me by him all the time; I believe he was very lonely. During long audiences and even meetings with his men, I was beside him and amused myself by watching the animals on the floor and imagining that they moved and spoke. The men never bothered about me. They assumed I could understand nothing of their schemes and worries, and I never undeceived them.

Indeed, growing up without a mother had a few definite advantages. Instead of spending all my time with the queen's women, learning needlework and the weaving of war cloaks, I was allowed to go where I would, with either my nurse Ailsa or some page of the king's as companion. I rode everywhere. In my youth horses gave me freedom and independence; later, they were my comfort and solace. I have taken this to be a sign from God, that I should live in close harmony with these most honored of his creatures. With sturdy Welsh mountain ponies as my friends and teachers in childhood, I grew bold and free and as wild, they said, as any boy. Which is how, in the autumn of my seventh year, I caused trouble, lost my best friend, and learned an important lesson about friendship and power.

The king my father and all his sons and all their attendants were away on a boar hunt. Every year at the change in seasons the king took his sport, and the men brought back venison and boar to be salted away for palace feasts all winter.

In the village women gathered the harvest of their gardens and small plots, foraged for berries and late herbs, prepared flax for winter's weaving and dyes for winter dyeing. Men went hunting, from the king and his courtiers down to the lowliest peasant; all the animals of the forests throughout Wales took heed; waterfowl fell to men's nets in the marshes, and fish to nets in the lakes and hill ponds. Everyone was busy, even the children. But as royal children, my cousins and I had it easier than most. We collected windfalls from the palace orchards, and when the gardeners were done with their other duties, we scrambled into the trees and shook off the ripening fruit into their woven baskets.

I speak of my cousins, who were my playmates in these early days, but actually they were my nephews. My father's sons by his first wife, Gwella, were grown men with children of their own. My eldest brother, Gwarth-gydd, was seven and twenty, a thick, powerful man with a thatch of black hair on his head and a mat of hair nearly as thick on his body. Most children feared him for his temper, but he had a ready smile and kind heart and was always good to me. His youngest son, Gwillim, was only a year older than me and was my best friend. There were not many girls in our family, and none of them was kind to me, for I did not look much like them, but took after my mother. Gwill's two older sisters were my chief tormenters. They insulted the memory of my mother, the affection of my father, whom I adored, the frailty of my body, which was not thick and dark and sturdy like their own, even the pale color of my hair, as if I could change it of my will. In my innocence, I did not understand it.

On a fine autumn day in the month of the Raven, Gwillim and I could not resist the chance to sneak away from work, to play in the wooded hills that encircled our valley. We pretended we were hunters, tracking our prey along the winding banks of a brook that led up through the hills to a spring in a mossy clearing. There we would flop on our stomachs to rest, drinking the clear water and pouring a small libation for the god of the place, for everyone knew that springs were holy. We could see the white shoulders of Y Wyddfa, the highest mountain in Wales, from that clearing. Its peak was always shrouded in mist, for gods lived there.

Sometimes, when I beat Gwill to the clearing, he would complain that I was cheating, for I was a girl and shouldn't have been there at all. Instead of a gown, I wore soft doeskin leggings better than his own, and as I was taller and my legs were longer than his, I ran faster and was more adept. He didn't really hold these things against me—he liked the challenge. But he disliked being taunted by his brothers and cousins that he played with girls and would grow up to be one. I don't blame him; they were cruel taunts, and I loved him more because he defended me and took abuse for my sake.

This day he reached the clearing first and was already on his knees pouring the libation when I arrived. We knelt together, mumbled our thanks to the god, and drank. Then we sat side by side and gazed at the distant heights of Y Wyddfa, which sparkled in the afternoon sun.

"Gwen, do you think anybody has ever seen a god?" he asked suddenly.

"Of course," I replied in surprise. "Holy men talk with them. Magicians and witches command them. They are everywhere, all about."

"Yes," he said slowly, his eyes on the mountain. "So men say. But if they are everywhere, why can't we see them?"

I was puzzled by his obtuseness. "Because you need special powers to see them," I patiently explained. "That's what makes holy men holy."

"Exactly," he said, turning to me eagerly. "What makes them holy is that they can see and talk to gods. But they can't see and talk to gods unless they are holy. You see?"

"See what?"

"Who's to prove or disprove it? It's their claim to be holy that makes them so. If I claim to be a wizard, it's my claim that makes me powerful, for no one can disprove that I talk to spirits."

"Gwill, do you mean that you don't—you don't believe in gods?"

"No. Of course not. Didn't we just pray to one? I mean, well—my mother fears a witch's curse because she believes the witch has power, and it's her believing that the witch has power that gives her the power she fears. Do you see?"

I was very impressed with his reasoning. But I had a more practical mind. "What witch has cursed her? What did she say?"

He looked a little embarrassed, and I guessed that he was not supposed to tell anyone.

"Swear by Mithra the foul fates," he commanded, and I solemnly swore by Mithra to bring devastation upon myself and my family and my descendants if ever a word that Gwill confided to me should pass my lips.

"Well," he said more easily, "Haggar of the Hills came by in the guise of a beggar as my mother and sisters were washing at the brook. She begged a drink of honey mead that they carried in their flask, for she was thirsty and dusty. Mother pointed out that the brook water was good enough for such as she, and that common folk would fall ill drinking the mead of the royal house."

I grinned. Gwillim thought his mother insufferably snobbish about her connection to the royal house. Glynis had been the daughter of one of my father's minor nobles and not a good match for Gwarthgydd, but she had been lovely when young, and he had stood by her and married her when she got with child. In return for his kindness, she lorded her position over everyone around her and made everyone's life miserable if she could. Someday, no doubt, if Gwarth lived, she would be queen, and she let no one forget it. But for all that, Gwill was devoted to her, and often rose well before dawn to fish the stream for speckled trout, which she adored.

"Then Haggar revealed herself and called upon the powers of the air. My sisters say the sky darkened, but I do not believe this. I was not far away that day, and I saw nothing. She cursed my mother's vanity, saying that the highest shall be brought low and the least valued made high; that all my mother's hopes should come to naught, and her line should dwindle. That her home should be destroyed, and her husband die in a far-off land." He gulped and continued. "And that the Kingdom of Northgallis should be swallowed by a great dragon and disappear from the face of the earth forever."

I stared at him in horror. "Northgallis disappear?" I whispered. "Oh, Gwillim, no! What does it mean? Saxons?"

He shook his head. He was clearly more worried about the fate of his family than about the Kingdom of Northgallis. "Don't you see what my mother has done? She made the old woman mad, and now she believes every word she said. But what if the old woman isn't really a witch? I mean, what if everybody just thinks she is? Nothing need come to pass unless we make it so by believing it will."

I gazed at him with wonder and respect. "You are the bravest boy I know! To think you can save Northgallis simply by believing you can—it's wonderful. Does this mean that the witch has no power over you?"

He flushed with pleasure and smiled. "She doesn't determine my future, Gwen, unless I believe that she does. That's what I think."

"And—and is this true also of other witches? And enchanters? What about the High King's enchanter? What about Merlin?"

He shivered at the name of the great wizard, but bravely stuck to his belief. "Yes, it is also true of Merlin. But—but perhaps I might believe Merlin," he admitted, frowning. "He is wise as well as powerful. He is not afraid of kings."

The air around us had gone very still. Fleecy clouds hung motionless in the sky, and the birds fell silent in the trees. I realized suddenly that we were talking in whispers, and a thrill of foreboding ran up my spine.

"And the gods?" I breathed, wide-eyed. "Are they the same? Have they power only over those who worship them, so that Mithra has power over warriors, and the Elder spirits over the common people and the hill people, and the new *Kyrios Christos* over the Christians?"

He stared at me. We hardly dared to breathe in the awful silence.

"You understand me," he whispered, and we were filled with terror at our sacrilege.

Suddenly we were not alone in the clearing; we felt the new presence before we heard or saw anything. For an instant time stood still, and we saw in each other's eyes the everlasting terror of perdition. Then I saw behind him, at the edge of the clearing, the soft brown eyes and pink nose of a wild mountain pony, and I exhaled with relief. We were not to be claimed by spirits after all! A small band of ponies had come to the spring to drink, that was all. Gwill turned slowly, flushing scarlet when he saw them, four of them, edging daintily toward the spring pool. We sat still, and they gathered courage and came forward, three of them lowering their pretty heads to drink, while the fourth eyed us warily.

Gwill was ashamed of his terror and needed to feel brave.

"They're very fine," he said softly. "And the leader is black. That's very rare. Let's see if we can catch two."

I was entranced. Ever since my father had placed me himself on a fat little pony at the age of three, I had loved horses. They spoke a language I somehow understood, and riding came effortlessly to me. At seven, I was already as good a rider as boys of eleven and twelve, who were ready for war training. And while Gwill was only slightly less skilled than I, catching wild ponies was a very different thing from riding trained ones and was a job for a group of mounted men and not for two children.

Nevertheless, I assented immediately and drew from my belt the windfalls I had brought along for our hunter's meal. Keeping movement to a minimum, I approached the nearest pony, a white one, offering the apple. While the other ponies scented danger and backed away, this one was overcome by curiosity. I fed him the apple and stroked his neck, lifting the heavy mane and scratching his withers. His eyes closed with pleasure, and Gwill whispered "Now!" In a single leap I was astride. The pony snorted in fear, spun around, and tore off through the woods. I buried my fists in his mane and clung to him for dear life, lying low on his back as we crashed through the brush, and branches whipped at my face and hair. I had a vague picture of Gwill grappling with the black one, his belt around its neck, but I could hear nothing behind me. The other ponies had bolted, too, but whether Gwill was with them I had no idea. I spoke to the terrified pony in a low singsong, hoping he could hear me over the clatter of his hooves. Eventually he slowed, either calmed by the song or tired from his fruitless efforts. He cantered, then trotted, then came to a trembling halt. I stroked and comforted him but did not dismount. I let him feel my legs against his sides, gently, and then I sat up. As he got over his fear he seemed to understand the messages my legs and body sent him. It is magic of a sort, speaking to horses, and a thrill I have never outgrown. We walked along a woodland track until he was calm and had got his breath back. Then, crooning to him all the while, I headed him back the way we had come, as well as I could judge. He was lathered with fear and sweat, his sides were slippery. So when, as we neared the spring, I heard my name suddenly shouted from the top of the ridge and the pony reared in fright, I slipped off as quickly as a raindrop from a downspout and fell hard against a tree. The last thing I remembered was the cry "Guinevere!" echoing among the hills, and then the world went black.

I began to hear voices dimly, as if from a distance. I was warm and protected deep in my darkness, and the voices washed over me in gentle swells, gently rolling me this way and that. I was tired, too tired to move, so I lay still and listened to the coming and going of the voices.

Gradually I floated nearer the bright surface, and the voices came more clearly. There was a kind, deep voice that spoke in quiet desperation, and a higher-pitched voice that spat in angry whispers.

"It's not fair!" cried the angry voice. "He has no right to kill the boy!"

"He has the right of the king," the deep voice replied slowly, wearily. "And he will not do it if she lives. So do your job and nurse her, Glynis. Enough of this argument."

"You listen to me, Gwarth! This girl is a curse to your house, to your family, and to your line. She was cursed on the night of her birth by the most powerful witch in Wales, do you not remember?"

"Hush, woman!"

Glynis lowered her voice, but her spite intensified. "She has brought nothing but trouble to Northgallis since that day. She killed her mother the queen with her birth. We had drought in her first year of life and a killing frost in her second. She is spoiled and petted by all the king's courtiers and servants. Even you! Yes, even you, with fine children of your own, are kinder to her than to them. She is a young witch, I tell you—"

"Woman, I will put you away! Hold your tongue!"

"She has woven a spell around Gwillim. He is enchanted, I tell you! He follows her everywhere! And now, a week after the hill witch's curse—"

"By the Bull! I am tired of hearing about that hag—"

"She said my house would be destroyed and my line diminished! And now this! This—this brazen witch leads my son into the hills, gets herself hurt, and now the king your father will take his life in vengeance! If that isn't diminishing my line, what is! Gwarth, he is your son, too! Can't you stop it?"

The deep voice came nearer; it was very kind. "Glynis. Calm yourself. Do your duty and poultice the girl. She is only a child. This was an accident, my dear. Children are heir to them. She can do you no harm unless she dies. You have seen your own children recover from worse falls than this."

"Yes," Glynis continued, her fury unabated, "but they were strong children, not dainty and pampered like this one. If it were not for Gwillim, I would not try to save her! Oh, gods!" she cried, choking. "Tell me, why does everyone love her so much?"

Gwarth was silent while Glynis sobbed noisily. "She is ugly!" she blurted. "Such fairness—such pallor—is ugly! Her bones are too small! She cannot work; she is useless! My daughters are more worthy to be princesses of Northgallis! They are strong, and—and . . . they are brown and healthy . . . I hate her! I hate her!"

She must have sensed she had gone too far, for she began to mumble an apology and flung a cloth across my brow.

For a long time Gwarthgydd said nothing. Then he spoke with the voice of command. "*You* have destroyed your house. *You* will diminish your line. I put you away. Take your brown daughters with you, Glynis, and go."

The woman screamed, and pain shot through my head. I pulled the quiet darkness around me with thanks and sank into its depths.

When I awoke it was early evening. I was in my own bedchamber, where a wood fire burned in the grate. The king's physician sat by my side, watching me eagerly. I was wrapped in warm furs, and my head was bound in cool cloth. When I looked about me, the outlines of things were murky, but soon my sight cleared, and the physician uttered a prayer of thanks to Mithra.

I knew what I must do.

"Where is my father?" I asked him. "Is the king near? Bring him to me."

The physician nodded and patted my hand soothingly. "King Leodegrance is but waiting for word of your awakening." He snapped his fingers, and the page by the door hurried out. The physician poured some warm broth into a flat bowl and supported my head while I drank of it. It tasted of herbs and medicines, but it was warming and steadied my head.

"Please help me to sit up," I begged, but the physician insisted I lie quietly.

"If my father is coming, I will sit up," I commanded, using the voice I had heard Gwarthgydd use, and the physician obeyed immediately. I was dizzy and my head felt several sizes too large, but I could hold myself erect.

"How long have I been here?"

"Since yesterday, my lady. You were brought to me in the evening."

"Please tell me what happened before the king comes. I remember nothing of it."

He hesitated, but gave in to me. "When the king's hunting party returned, the palace was in an uproar because you could not be found. No one remembered having seen you since midday. In fear of their lives, the gardeners and house servants took to the hills to look for you."

"And Gwillim," I added, but he averted his eyes. "Yes, my lady. Ailsa fell down in a fit with brain fever. She is delirious still." Ailsa, my nurse, was a loving but lazy soul, who had attended me from birth. It was during one of her illicit naps in the garden that I had stolen away.

"I expect she will recover when she finds out I am all right."

The physician was doubtful. "It appears to be a serious case, my lady."

"Never mind. I will cure her. How did you find me? What of Gwillim?"

He looked uncomfortable when I said his name, and I began to be afraid.

"The king's son Gwarthgydd and his men found you, coming down from the hills across the back of a white pony, led by Gwillim," the physician said, frowning. "The lad was frantic. He thought you were dead. He told King Leodegrance he had led you away from the orchard and taken you to play with him in the hills. He said you had seen some wild ponies, and he dared you to catch one. He blamed himself for what happened. He said it was punishment for evil thoughts."

"Did the king believe him?"

"We all believed him, my lady."

"And where is he now? Pray, quick! I hear the guards!"

"He is—he is in the king's dungeon, my lady. His family is disgraced."

"It was not his fault!" I cried hotly, but cut off my speech, for the door swung open, and my dear father strode into the room.

"Gwen!" He took me gently into his arms, and I hugged him and kissed his rough cheek. "Praise Mithra you are alive! How do you feel? Shouldn't you be lying down?"

"Not yet," I said, to forestall the physician. "I must speak with you first, dear Father. May I see you alone?"

A wave of his hand sent the others out of the room, although the physician did not like to go.

"Father," I said, looking right into his eyes. "I owe my life to Gwillim. He saved me when I fell, and he brought me home. If it were not for Gwillim, I would be with Mother now. Can you send him to me, that I may thank him?"

The reference to my mother diffused his rising anger, and he grumbled a bit. "That is not what Gwillim says. He admits that he endangered your life. He didn't claim he saved you."

I managed a blush and took his big, brown, callused hand between my own small white ones. "Well, what would you expect him to say? That your daughter behaved like an Irish hooligan? That she enticed him away from his chores and ran off to the hills to enjoy the day, knowing he would be forced to escort her? That she bragged she could catch and ride a wild pony, although he begged her not to risk it? And that when she was thrown and lay senseless, he found her and managed to tame the wild pony himself and bring her home upon its back? Would you have believed such a story?"

He glowered at me. "No, I would not. And I do not believe it now."

I sighed and inwardly took a deep breath. "Well, my dearest father, it is near the truth. I have behaved very badly. I ask your forgiveness. Gwillim lied to defend my honor, and I am ashamed."

He looked at me searchingly, but I withstood him. His uncertainty gave way at last to resignation. "Do you swear by the blood of the Bull this is the truth?"

"I swear it."

"Well," he said at length, "I am both grieved and relieved to hear it. I will send Gwillim to you after I have spoken to him, and when the physician says I may. You should be punished, Guinevere; but it is not in me to do it. And indeed, I believe Mithra will see to it in His own way, and in His own time."

"There is one other thing." He was getting up to go, and he turned warily, scenting deception. I put on the most guileless face I could summon. "May I also have my nurse back? I dislike this physician near me. In my illness, I remember a light touch that comforted me. Would it be possible to send her back to me?"

He looked confused, but could not resist my supplication. "If you mean Glynis, she is gone from the house." As the ranking woman, after me, of the royal house, Gwarthgydd's wife would be appointed nurse to any royal patient.

"If she is gone because of Gwillim, can it not be put right?"

The king stood and looked down full upon me. "Guinevere, are you asking me to send you that jealous shrew? Do you really want her with you? Are your wits about you? You needn't— Gwillim is safe without that."

Safe, perhaps, but miserable and forever shamed without his mother. I trembled with the effort it cost me, but I lied. "She is a good nurse."

He stared at me and then shook his head. "All right. She is yours. But when you are well, my girl, you and I must talk about your future."

"Yes, Father," I said meekly.

Glynis returned the next morning. Her face was rough and blotched with the marks of blows and tears, and I guessed that Gwarth had lost his temper once again. There was no love in her face, no understanding, no gratitude; only fear. I was a witch; she was beholden to me, and she was afraid. I did not speak to her, but let her tend me and feed me with what tenderness she could muster, and we got along tolerably well.

In the evening Gwillim was brought to my door. Glynis would have embraced him, but Gwillim kept his eyes on the floor, and she crept out without a word.

I lay on the pillows and looked at Gwillim. He was newly washed and dressed in clean clothes, but there were red marks on his wrists where they had bound him. Bound him! What he had been through in the last two days, I could not guess. But what confounded me was his fear. He, too, was afraid of me and averted his eyes from my face.

"Gwillim," I whispered. "Kneel down so we can talk." He obeyed and waited. "Gwillim, I take responsibility. I am sorry they put you in prison. It wasn't fair." He said nothing.

"Gwillim, tell me what happened." It was a command, and he obeyed.

"I tried to come after you, but I lost the black pony. So I followed on foot. I could see where you went clearly enough, because the branches were bent and the undergrowth trampled. After a while I realized that if I followed you, I would never catch up. I figured you would circle back to the clearing. I knew you would be able to speak to him. I knew you would not come off unless—unless something scared you." So that was it. It was his voice that had startled the pony. "When at last I saw you returning, I—I—Gwen—I mean, my lady—I shouted. For joy, but—"

"I know about that part. Never mind. I'd have done the same. What happened after that? How on earth did you get me back on the pony?"

The ghost of a grin swept his face and was instantly supressed.

"I didn't know what to do. You were bleeding, my lady. There was lots of blood around your head. I thought you were dying. I sat down beside you and cried. And then—" His hushed voice sank so low I had to strain to hear it. "—then *the pony came back to you*. I was sitting there, and he came right out of the forest, right up to you, and nuzzled you. He let me put my belt around his neck. He let me lay you across his back. He let me lead him down the mountain, and he walked so carefully over the stones, you never even slid." There was awe in his voice, and in his face, and I realized with a shock of despair that Gwill had changed.

"The soldiers came and rescued you. They let me put the pony in the paddock before they took me to the king. He is there still. He didn't even try to get away." Suddenly his shyness fled, and he spoke eagerly. "Don't you see, Gwen? It's a sign. After the evil things we thought about by the spring, we were both punished, you immediately and me later on, and then the pony's coming all by himself. It's a sign from the god."

"From which god, Gwill?"

He looked pained. "Does it matter, my lady? It's the proof, you see."

"Proof of what?" My throat ached so it was hard to speak.

"I blasphemed," he said humbly, "and was given a sign. I have no doubts any longer."

"You believe because you saw a sign, but you saw the sign only because you believed."

"Don't," he said quickly. "Please, my lady. Don't say those awful things. You will be punished again."

"I am being punished now," I retorted. "Why do you address me as 'my lady'? I'm 'Gwen' to you, remember?"

He lowered his eyes, and I was instantly sorry I'd said it. I understood, of course. It was the risk I'd had to take to save his honor, but it was a bitter pill to swallow for a proud, brave boy.

"You are the king's daughter," he said slowly, addressing the coverlet. "And I am your servant. A word from your lips saved my mother and sisters from a cruel fate. For this I thank you. Even my father must be obedient to your command and take back what he had put away. The honor of our house is in your hands, my lady."

"Yes, w—well," I stammered, fighting back tears. "I saw no other way. You'd better go."

He rose with dignity, bowed, and turned away. I turned my face to the wall and wept.

3 👑 GWYNEDD

On my eighth birthday I left my home forever.

My father called me to him one wretched night that winter and, with tears streaming unchecked into his beard, told me that come spring and my eighth birthday, he would send me away. It felt like death. Nothing he said could comfort me. I was not going far away, only into the next kingdom, by the Western Sea, to the house of my mother's sister, whose husband was lord of that land. But in those days, and at that age, it was across the world.

The reason was, he said, that it was the only place I would be safe.

I did not understand at first. He would not tell me that he had felt the first touch of the hand of Death. I thought he meant we should have war.

Wales had been quiet enough. Winter had closed the seas, and the Irish raiders kept to their own coasts. Of the inland fighting to the east and south against Angles and Saxons, news filtered in from time to time. But the names of the strange places and kings, of Cornwall, Strathclyde, Rheged, Lothian, of Cador, Ector, Urien, and Lot—these were foreign words, foreign lands, foreign princes. For the Kingdom of Northgallis was my country and Wales the limit of the civilized world.

When my father fell ill that winter, he called his sons to him. To the eldest, Gwarthgydd, he bequeathed the major part of his kingdom and the king's house at Cameliard. To the others he gave lands of their own to keep independently, provided, and he made this condition clear, that they follow and fight for the High King Uther Pendragon against his enemies.

For the king my father believed very strongly that the safety and, indeed, the future of Wales depended on the High King's desperate efforts to contain the Saxon invasions on eastern coasts. And he knew whereof he spoke. He had been a young man when the High King Vortigern had invited Saxons to Britain's shores to help him quell the rebellious Picts who threatened from the north. These Picts, a fierce and primitive race of thieves and bandits, had badgered the country incessantly and for generations, since the last Roman legions had left the land. But the Saxons were worse. At least the Picts had no organization and never stayed in the land they conquered, but retreated to their own homes to sing their victory paeans. The Saxons stayed. Vortigern found that, once he had invited them in, he could not make them leave and was forced to reward them with land in return for their service against the Picts. He gave them small plots along the southeastern shores and thought, the shortsighted fool, that that should content them. But within five years their families and all their relations had come to join them, and the Saxon colonies grew.

As everyone knows, their numbers increased until their lands could not hold them, and their war leaders Hengist and Horsa were a greater threat to King Vortigern than ever the Picts had been. Vortigern even married a Saxon queen, Hengist's daughter. After that no true Celt would follow him, and he lost his power to the Saxon horde. It was Ambrosius who saved us. Aurelius Ambrosius, brother of the rightful king whom Vortigern had murdered, invaded from Less Britain with an army of twenty thousand and fought Vortigern to a bloody victory. My father fought in that battle, where the old wolf and his Saxon queen were smoked out of their hill fort and burned alive. And he fought in the battle at Caer Konan, where Hengist was beaten, when Merlin himself appeared out of thin air to predict Ambrosius' victory. Had it not been for Ambrosius, we should all have been as degenerate as the Picts.

The great Ambrosius and his younger brother Uther gathered the many British kings together, from Lothian and Rheged to Dyfed and Dumnonia, and bound them with oaths of loyalty to the High King of Britain. Fighting together under a strong war leader was our only hope of stemming the Saxon tide, so my father was wont to exhort his warriors on cold winter nights, when war looked distant and glorious. But this my father deeply believed, even when he was called upon to take arms and fight in Uther's army. And he saw to it that his sons should follow his example.

Now, after fifteen years of vigilance and fighting constant small battles to hold the kingdoms together and give the people peace, Uther was getting old. I thought my father foresaw war coming closer to home and was sending me temporarily to the coastal kingdom of Gwynedd to live under the care of King Pellinore and Queen Alyse, until Northgallis should be safe for me once more.

It was a sad leave-taking. I adored my father. He had not held my mother's death against me, and I think he loved me more tenderly because I reminded him of her. He was a good king and a strong one, but he never used his sword unnecessarily, nor took joy in killing. The worst I can say of him is that he spoiled me and knew it. I worshipped him.

"My little Gwen," he said, hugging me tightly as the escort made ready to leave early on the first of May. "I will come visit you at summer's end, the gods willing. You must make a place for yourself in your mother's family. You have a cousin for company, and they will give you book learning, which I cannot do here. You should know more than I do, my dear, if the witch is to be believed. King Pellinore is a wise man and has a scholar in his house. There are fine horses there, too, my sweet. You will not be without your favorite entertainment. Now dry those pretty eyes and be a brave princess. And always remember," he said under his breath, "always remember who you are and what you will be."

I was used to his references to the hag's prophecy and nodded obediently. Ever since the fortelling at my birth I was held to be a wonder by the Welsh. On more than one occasion I heard fantastic stories told about me that bore no relation to the truth, but that the people willingly believed. Thanks to Giselda, they expected me to bring them honor. This is a hard thing to live with, even now.

Thus I left Northgallis, but I never saw his dear face again, for he died when summer came and was buried before the news reached me.

My cousin Elaine was a gossip, even at seven. She befriended me on sight and made me feel at home from my first moment. She was eager to have a companion near her own age to talk to and play with, as her mother and the nurses were busy with three younger sons. I loved her for this. She was gay and warm-hearted, bold where I was shy, open and loving where I was reserved. I have never forgotten her sweetness to me at that time when it mattered most. For remembrance of this, I have struggled to forgive her cruel betrayal, for without her love and friendship in my childhood, I should not have had the courage to face what the fates have brought me.

While Ailsa unpacked my trunk and scant belongings in Elaine's room, Elaine took my arm and gave me a tour of her home. She showed me everything, from basement scullery to the turrets on the western tower, where the sentries kept watch all year for Irish pirates. She never stopped talking. She knew everything: reports of Saxon fighting to the east; which queens were witches, and which kings coveted another's land; who in the village was engaged to whom, and which of the kitchen slaves had given birth to an illegitimate child. I laughed to hear her tales, told with a gleam in her sky-blue eyes and a light in her happy face. Indeed, within an hour of my arrival, it was possible to forget, at least for a while, the hard two days' journey and my dear father's parting kiss.

When she took me to the sentry tower I had my first sight of the sea. It seemed to stretch on forever, away in the distance, low and gray, empty and immensely sad. Elaine was delighted at my amazement.

"Have you never seen the sea, then? Why, we ride upon the shore on holidays, or when Iakos gives us the day free. I have even been upon it in a golden ship with silver sails! Well, it was pretty fancy, anyhow. My father sailed to Caer Narfon last September, and he let me come aboard before they departed. It was wonderful—the very floor I stood upon rolled this way and that, like a cradle, almost! I should love to have an adventure at sea!"

I smiled at her. "I would be afraid to feel the floor beneath me move so," I said. "But I should love to ride along the shore."

"Oh, yes! I have heard how you love horses. Let's go down to the stable, and I'll show you my pony. That is"—with a doubtful look at me—"if you're not too tired. Grannic says I mustn't tire you. She says we must take special care of you. Are you sickly, or something?"

"No, of course not. I think she means because I am your mother's sister's daughter, and kin to you. That's all."

But Elaine still looked uncertain. "But you're different from other people, aren't you?"

I seemed to feel a cold hand upon my neck. "Whatever do you mean?"

"Oh, now you're mad, Gwen. I'm really sorry. It's just something I overheard once. Nobody told me anything. I don't know anything about it."

"What did you overhear?"

"Promise that you won't be angry with me?"

"Elaine, I will not be angry with you. I promise."

"Well, didn't a witch put a spell on you at birth?" I gasped, but she went on. "Not a bad spell, a good spell. Aren't you going to marry a great king and rule over all of us someday?"

A cold shiver ran through me. I found myself furious that the prophecy had followed me even here. I wondered in sudden despair if there was anyone in all of wide Wales who had not heard it.

"Of course not. You believe in old wives' tales, and you a Christian? I thought your God frowned on magic."

Elaine was undaunted. "But *everybody* knows there are witches. And wizards, as well. Have you never heard of Merlin the Enchanter? He can see the future in a raindrop and vanish into thin air! All the world knows this."

"And many people who have no such power pass themselves off as witches with skill and luck. I am not different, Elaine. As my father is a king, no doubt in time he will marry me off to the finest Welsh lord he can -

find, but the rest is nonsense. Truly it is. Rule the land, indeed! I shall never rule over you, Elaine. Of that I am quite sure."

She grinned in relief. "Good, because I like being first."

If I gave her ease, I am glad, but I was frightened. It was the first time I had voiced my own beliefs about the prophecy, and I was stunned to find how vehemently I resented old Giselda's interference. I was more unhappy to learn that people here knew and believed her words. It occurred to me for the first time, as I stood on the turret beside Elaine, looking out at the strange sea, that I might live under that cloud my whole life. I had insisted I was not different. But if everyone thought that I was, did that not make me so?

In the stables I forgot my fears. King Pellinore had many fine animals, all the sturdy mountain horses that breed freely in the hills of Wales. And Elaine had a pretty fat pony with a fine, dry face and great, dark eyes.

"His name is Petros. It means 'rock.' Iakos says it is a good name for a princess' pony. He's very lazy and does not like to move. This makes him safe to ride!" She laughed gaily at her jest and let me pat his warm neck and stroke the glossy coat. "Mother says you know how to ride already. Did you have your own pony in Northgallis?"

"Yes, a lovely white one. I found him running wild in the hills, and he let me ride him."

Elaine looked put out. "Did you bring him with you?"

"No, I—before I left, I let him go back into the hills. He belonged there."

She brightened again. "Well, Mother said you may take your pick of the next batch they bring in, as long as he gets along with Petros. That's a rare honor, you know. It's because she heard you were skilled."

I felt my face flush with pleasure. Perhaps having oneself talked about wasn't such a bad thing, after all. "I must thank her for the offer. And who is Iakos?"

"Iakos is my tutor—I mean *our* tutor. He is teaching me Latin and writing and figures, although not too much of that because I hate it. Also music. Leonora, the queen's woman, will teach us stitchery and weaving, and also housekeeping when we are older. There's a lot to learn to be a good queen, isn't there?"

She cocked her head sideways and looked up at me shrewdly. She seemed to me to be ready for anything, full of confidence and willing to try whatever came to her hand. I envied her enormously. I was completely untutored in any feminine skills. My childhood had been spent with my doting father and my rough, grown half-brothers. I could run, ride, shoot with bow and arrow, and hawk as well as any youth my age. For my fifth birthday Gwarth had given me a young falcon, fallen from his nest and saved just in time, to raise for my own. He had helped me to train it, and I learned to fashion jesses from worked leather and had made my own glove. But I instinctively kept these accomplishments a secret from Elaine, who I feared might despise them. Of embroidery and the weaving of war cloaks, tasks every woman of even moderate birth must learn in order to marry, I knew nothing.

And of her religion, the worship of the Christian God, I knew very little. But there was a priest among the household staff, and I knew I would be instructed in the new ways. This had been my father's only reservation in sending me to my mother's people. They had been Christians for two generations, ever since an Irish martyr landed upon their coast and with wit and charm persuaded them to turn their backs on the Elder spirits. Whether my father had thought it an inevitable consequence of his plans for me, or whether he recognized that the tide of change was sweeping the land, he had consented to my instruction. So I was brought into the fold of the jealous Christian God, my feet were set upon the True Path, and the little deities of hill and stream, rock and high place, were left behind.

It was a busy summer. Elaine's mother, Queen Alyse, kept us to our tasks and allowed us little time for mischief-making. As I was to find, her word was law. To her credit, she believed her daughter deserving of the same education she gave her sons and made no excuses to Iakos on our behalf. I tried my best to please her in everything, but it was not easy to accomplish. She was not unkind, but neither was she warm. Tall and beautifully featured, with the family's fairness and a majestic bearing, she did not welcome confidences from children. Even Pellinore was half afraid to cross her.

At our first meeting she looked me over carefully, placing her hand on my chin and turning my face toward the light.

"So you are Elen's daughter," she said thoughtfully, after I had made my speech of thanks for taking me in. "I pray you will be as well behaved. We will teach you manners here, Guinevere, and make a princess of you." I was tempted to retort that I was a princess already and that my father had taught me manners, but I held my tongue, afraid that to speak would give the lie to my assertion. "You would do well," she said coolly, "to follow Elaine in everything." It was advice I learned to take.

That summer the old High King, Uther Pendragon, who had held the kingdoms of Britain together for nearly fifteen years, began to fail. Messengers rode into the castle every week with news. It was said he could no longer sit a horse, but had to be carried to battle in a litter, like a woman. Some of the men scoffed at the rumor, denying that any soldier of mettle would follow an invalid war leader. But King Pellinore himself believed it, saying that Uther was the best warrior in the kingdoms, afoot, astride, or abed, and only a fool would be too proud to follow him. So the dissenters kept their grumbling quiet, sharpened their spears, polished their swords, and waited.

The Saxons were massing, they said, clogging the shores in the south-east, and Colgrin their leader was making alliances with the petty kings there, gathering strength for an attack on the High King. But weeks wore on, and no royal messenger came to summon King Pellinore and his men. What came instead were the rains. We had had drought all winter, and now, after a warm, dry spring, the skies opened over all Wales and drowned the fertile valleys. Crops rotted where they stood, the rich soil was scoured from the land by raging rivers, and sheep and horse foundered in the mired pastures. Ailsa muttered charms under her breath against evil spirits; the miller's boy went mad and threw himself in the sea; the queen's garden was spoiled, and the cooks complained bitterly; even the priest was seen to cross himself whenever the clouds grew black.

Every day brought news of some sort: local news of local catastrophes; distant news of discontent, uprisings, invasions, and assaults. A blight lay upon the land. Some said God was displeased that ignorant souls persisted in the worship of Mithra and would give no victories to pagan soldiers. But Elaine and I scoffed at that. Colgrin and his Saxons worshipped gods far more barbarous than Mithra! Some said the land was failing as the High King failed and that we would not recover until we had a new King. This argument was no longer whispered in corners between nervous warriors; it was spoken aloud at the king's supper table, after the women had left. Elaine and I heard it ourselves.

Of course, we were not in the hall. We were eavesdropping. Elaine showed me this secret in my first week there. Along the parapet between the east and south turrets was a smallish crack in the stone, and through this crack we could peer down into the smoky hall. This fissure was protected by the guardhouse wall from the east wind, else it would have been discovered when the rain blew in. But if we covered ourselves in our dark, hooded cloaks and crept up past the guardhouse when the sentries were warming themselves by the fire, or standing at their posts at either turret, we could crouch unseen by the crack and learn of the high matters young maids were never allowed to know.

To do the guards justice, they were good men and loyal to the king, but it never occurred to them that the young princesses were not abed past dark, or would be curious about what rough soldiers said in the drinking hall. But we were always curious and never afraid to listen when we knew a courier had come. Only the very worst weather could keep us away. Ailsa and Grannic, Elaine's nurse, slept outside our door, it is true. But they were loud snorers and deep sleepers, embarrassingly easy to deceive.

Thus we learned of the country's discontent, and the threat of war that loomed on the horizon, a war that would change our lives, whatever the outcome. All of King Pellinore's men were loyal to the Pendragon banner, and trained almost daily in the courtyard. But as the summer wore on and the crops and animals died, and men went mad from hunger and lack of sun, they were called to their lands to put down unrest among the farmers and oversee the care of their own families, so that the king's fighting force was scattered. There were barely enough men at court to get up a hunt, and no one cared to hawk when the gloom lay so heavy on the land. Talk at dinner invariably returned to one theme: would not the High King at last recall his only son Arthur from his secret fastness and reveal him to the lords and set him to lead us against the Saxons?

Everyone in Britain knew this tale. I had been raised on it. Indeed, it was the one tale, in my father's country, which was better known than mine. When Uther Pendragon was crowned High King of Britain, he had fallen desperately in love with Ygraine, wife of Gorlois, Duke of Cornwall. She was only twenty, and Gorlois a grizzled warrior of fifty. Some said Merlin the Enchanter had put a spell on the King at his coronation feast, so that as soon as he saw her, he had no peace of mind, but planned how he could take her and yet not wreck the Kingdom by so doing. Remembering stories of my dear father's infatuation for my mother, I did not think that sudden love needed any supernatural explanation, but I believed with the rest of the world, that the famous enchanter had been responsible for the clever plan that brought Uther his heart's desire. Gorlois removed his wife from the High King's reach as soon as etiquette permitted and brought her to the impregnable fortress of Tintagel on the Cornwall coast. He and his fighting men repaired to a fine fighting fortress that guarded the route, in case the High King should follow. As soon as the official feasting was over, Uther, and Merlin with him, came with a large army and camped just out of bowshot. It looked like the fragile kingdom would soon be split by war. But Merlin changed the King by magic arts into the very likeness of Gorlois, and thus disguised, he rode along the track to Tintagel and was admitted by the guard, all unknowing. Men believe that the young duchess was also deceived, but no woman I know believes this. It is a known fact that Ygraine was a faithful and loving wife to King Uther, obedient to his every wish to the end of their days, as if the flame of love never died in her heart. During the night they were together, when Arthur was conceived, Gorlois led his troops in a surprise attack against the High King's army, which is treason, and the old duke was killed in the fighting. Uther married Ygraine as soon as he decently could, before her pregnancy began to show. But out of guilt for the death of Gorlois, he refused to acknowledge the son that was born, and three nights after his birth handed him to Merlin to safeguard and raise. Since then the boy had been in Merlin's keeping, but no one knew where. Some said even Uther did not know.

King Uther and Queen Ygraine had no other sons in all the years of their marriage. And now, with Uther ill and the Saxon power growing in the east, men said it was time for the Prince to be brought forth and for Uther to acknowledge him. Wales would rise for him, that was clear. But there were lands in the east, already menaced by the Saxons, that were less certain. King Lot of Lothian had met with Colgrin, and no one knew if he would support Uther when the time came or try to supplant him. Ambrosius' fragile kingdom might be split forever, if Prince Arthur did not soon appear.

Elaine and I were careful never to let slip any comment that would reveal how much we knew about events. But when news came, at midsummer, of my father's death, and Queen Alyse gave me a new pony of my own as a comfort gift, Elaine and I would ride along the shore, ahead of the escort, and have long conferences. Elaine could talk of little else but Arthur. No one had seen him, no one really knew if he even existed, but Elaine knew all about him. She even knew what he looked like.

"He's dark," she confided. "Black hair and blue eyes, the true Celt. And stronger than any man his age."

"Which is all of thirteen," I pointed out, grinning. We were five and six years younger, but girls could be married off at twelve, while boys had to wait until fifteen to be made warriors. Elaine was undaunted.

"He's a Christian, too, so the men will follow him."

"How can he be Christian if Merlin the Enchanter has raised him? Everyone knows Merlin is a pagan and a powerful one. It is said he speaks to the gods directly and has seen Mithra himself slaying the Bull."

Elaine crossed herself quickly, then made a sign against the ancient evil spirits that was not Christian at all. "Hush, Gwen, don't say such things! You're blaspheming, I know it! Have you no fear? Anyway, Queen Ygraine is a Christian, even if the High King is not, and she wouldn't have him raised by a pagan household. And how can he lead Christian soldiers if he isn't one himself?"

"King Uther does. I don't think soldiers care so much, as long as their leader is successful. And I don't know about Queen Ygraine. I mean, she can't be much of a mother if she was content to give her firstborn son away three days after she bore him. She may not care how he is raised." I saw I had hurt Elaine, who adored her image of Prince Arthur, and I was ashamed of myself. "Never mind, Elaine. You are probably right. I'm sure he's a devout Christian like Father Martin and handsome, as well." But as her humor was restored, I fell to teasing her again. "But perhaps he is fair. King Uther was red-headed in his youth, they say, although now he is gray."

Elaine was unmovable on this point. "You forget his descent. Uther's

line is dark. Uther's brother Ambrosius was dark, and Constantius, their father, was dark, and so on back to the Emperor Maximus, founder of the line."

"Who was Iberian, and not Celt," I reminded her. "And black-eyed, to
boot."

Elaine sniffed. "Dark hair can be Celt, too, and blue eyes certainly are.
Maximus married a Welsh princess from our own country, Princess Elen,
and she had blue eyes. She's famous for it. Dark, brilliant blue, like the sea
in a summer storm. She's my kin." Then she stopped, remembering that she
was related to the famous Elen through her mother's line, and therefore I
was descended from her, too. She looked at me cautiously. I knew already
what she saw, because the color of my eyes had been compared to the
Princess Elen's all my life.

"Well," I said quickly, "it's no wonder we think so much of Prince
Arthur, since we are both kin to him, if you go far enough back."

Elaine looked delighted. This was the kindest thing I had ever yet said
about Arthur, and she took it as a victory. The truth was, I disparaged him
only to tease Elaine; but the skeptical attitude, once adopted, stuck. From
that summer on, I was always finding fault with him, if only because Elaine
thought him so perfect.

The sun returned when September came, but it was too late. The smell of
rotting growth and mud stank in the river valleys, and men and beasts died
from mysterious fevers. Water lay everywhere on the ground, breeding in-
sects and disease. We could not bury our dead for the mud, and burned
them instead on funeral pyres like the dead of the Saxon savages. The
queen kept us to the castle and forbade our rides upon the shore, fearing we
would catch noxious vapors and fall ill. Indeed, the youngest of Elaine's
brothers fell to the fever in September, and the queen was prostrate with
grief. Men muttered under their breaths of omens and witchcraft; women
wore charms against ancient evils, the Christian women secretly and others,
like Ailsa, actually jingled and clicked as they walked from the jumble of
talismans they carried. Small offerings were made daily at the wayside
shrines. The village folk had not forgotten the Elders. King Pellinore, saddened and restless, called in his men from their homes and drilled them
mercilessly in preparation for action, any action, to keep their minds from
dwelling on the death and stagnation that enveloped Britain.

And then finally, toward the end of that interminable month, the royal
courier arrived. Elaine and I were on the eastern wall when he rode up the
valley on his tired horse, spattered with mud and so exhausted he could
barely stay in his saddle. We knew who he was by the leather pouch at his
belt, and we exchanged glances behind the sentry's back, knowing we
would creep out that night to overhear the king's conference.

The news was thrilling indeed. King Uther Pendragon was gathering his forces at Caer Eden, a week's march north, and all loyal Britons were called to arm and join him there to meet the Saxon attack. The time had come. Cheering filled the hall. The men sounded wild with happiness, as if the courier were bringing them tidings of great joy. The king proposed a toast, and as the men turned to their tankards and the noise died down, we heard Arthur's name.

"Will Arthur be there?" "Yes, will the great Enchanter reveal him now?" "Will Uther acknowledge him, I wonder, and give him a command?" "He's just a boy—how could he?" "Ah, but he's the royal heir, with black magic behind him, and we'll follow him anywhere."

King Pellinore hushed them, looking fierce under his bushy black eyebrows, but the courier fidgeted nervously. He was not charged with any official message about the prince, but rumor had it—rumor, mind you—that Merlin had been sent for. And where Merlin was . . .

This was the best news to come to Wales in years, and within two days every able-bodied fighting man had marched north to fight the Saxons, confident in the certain victory that the fabled Arthur would bring. Elaine was beside herself with excitement, but I felt the loss of the men keenly. There was no more news, no more eavesdropping, no more feeling a part of events. We had shrunk to a household of women, and our chief occupations were putting the castle to rights, getting in what little harvest there was, weaving and sewing against the inevitable winter cold, and for me and Elaine, uninterrupted lessons with Father Martin and Iakos.

We did not hear about the battle for two whole months, when it was long over and the glory of the battlefield had faded in the minds of the wounded and maimed, who were the first to come home.

4 👑 KING ARTHUR

Queen Alyse organized a primitive hospital in the castle outbuildings. It was not primitive by the standards of the day, only by comparison to what I have seen since, for there were no learned men of healing in Gwynedd, no army physicians, no Merlin. We were a community of women with skill to heal minor wounds such as men get hunting. Those soldiers who made it back to us were grateful for our attentions, but they were halfway to recovery before ever setting foot in the sickrooms. The worst wounded had died in the field hospital at Caer Eden, and more on the road home.

Elaine and I were not allowed to treat the men directly on account of our youth, and I was grateful for this. Nursing repelled me; I had not the stomach for maimed limbs and open sores and the stench of sickness. We were happy to help the washing women hang the clean linens to dry and fold them away, sweet-smelling and herb-scented, until they were needed again. We helped to change the bedding on the pallets that lined the floor and were allowed to bring around cool water for the men to drink.

One day, as Elaine and I stood outside the sickrooms, folding linens, I began to hum, and then sing, an old Welsh song I had learned in North-gallis about the beauty of Wales, her fertile meadows where sheep grazed in summer, her shining ponds and white-frothed streams, her cool forests full of game, and the crown of her glory, glittering Snow Mountain, where the gods walked among the clouds. Elaine loved the song and begged me to teach it to her, so I repeated it for her sake. Then we brought our folded linens to Cissa, the queen's lady-in-waiting who was in charge of the washing. To my amazement, she curtsied low before me.

"The queen's compliments, Lady Guinevere," she said softly, "and would you be pleased to continue singing, for the men were quiet and restful just now, and seemed relieved of pain. The queen tells me they had tears in their eyes, and indeed, my lady, it was beautiful to hear."

I stared, astonished that the queen favored me with such attention, and assured Cissa I would be delighted to sing. From that day forward, singing to the men was my chief duty, and Queen Alyse had a cushioned chair brought for me and set just inside the door, so that all could hear the song, and yet I was not overcome by the sickroom vapors. To show their gratitude, the men began to call me the Lark of Gwynedd.

As men healed and were allowed to sit outside in the afternoon sun and take exercise on the grounds, Elaine and I learned from them all we wanted to know about the great things that had happened in the north. To be sure, King Pellinore had sent his queen a messenger bearing news of the glorious victory over Colgrin and his Saxon hordes, of Uther's death and of young Arthur's succession. With the kings of Britain united behind him, the new King pursued the Saxons eastward, and Pellinore went with him, leaving Gwynedd in the capable hands of Queen Alyse.

But these were dry facts, and we sought among the convalescing soldiers for those who could tell us what we really wanted to know. Finally we found Corwin, a twenty-year-old foot soldier who had suffered a broken leg. He was lucky that the bones had not pierced the skin. Merlin himself, he said, had splinted the leg and prophesied that it would knit cleanly and straight. He had since fashioned himself a pair of crutches and got about easily enough. He had a ready tongue, a bard's gift for exaggeration, and a lazy nature. He spun us tales by the hour, and we believed them all.

"Tell us about the battle!" Elaine cried, settling down at his feet, her face aglow. "Did Prince Arthur fight?"

"Did he indeed!" Corwin exclaimed, grinning. "Why, he won it for us, you may be sure, and proclaimed himself by the deed, even if he was the last to know it."

"What do you mean, the last to know it?"

Corwin laughed. "When he came to Caer Eden with Sir Ector of Galava, he was more a body servant to Ector's son Kay than a warrior. By rights, he's a year or two short of making a soldier. He'd no more idea of who he was than Kay did himself, or I, or any man there, excepting only Ector, King Uther and that sly fox Merlin. And as far as anyone could see, Merlin was there alone, standing silently with his arms folded into his sleeves and a face as dark as stormclouds, watching everything, saying nothing, keeping his own counsel. No one gave a second glance to Ector's fosterling."

"Ector's fosterling?" I wondered.

"Oh, never mind that now!" Elaine cut in. "Go on, Corwin, tell us about the battle!"

Corwin settled himself among the cushions we had brought him. He had a Welshman's love of a good tale, and this had all the earmarks of an afternoon's work. "It was midmorning when we saw them coming across the river plain. You should have seen them—thousands of Saxons—blond giants with four-foot moustaches, whirling their two-headed axes over their heads in a mad frenzy of noise. Wild men, they were, screaming uncouth paeans—I don't mind admitting it to you girls, but my bones were shaking."

Elaine giggled. "You're no soldier, then. Soldiers are never afraid."

"Aren't they, my lady? Well, that's as may be. I can only speak for myself. And yet I'll wager there wasn't a man on the field who saw them coming who didn't wish he were safely home in bed."

Elaine was scandalized. "You call Prince Arthur a coward? And King Uther? And Pellinore, my father?"

Corwin shook his head quickly. "Certainly not, little princess. Brave men, all of them. But if a man has no fear to face and overcome, where is bravery? He is a fool, that's all."

"Oh, stuff and nonsense. You're just making excuses. Go on with the battle!"

"He was, until you interrupted," I pointed out, and was rewarded with a bold retort and an angry shake of her head.

"I'll tell you this," Corwin cut in. "They almost took us. We were all looking about for Prince Arthur when the trumpets sounded, but no one saw him anywhere. Half the men watched Uther, half watched Merlin. But Uther lay abed upon his litter, with his own guards in attendance, and Merlin busied himself in the field hospital, paying no attention to anyone.

Men began to doubt the prince had come. When the Saxons attacked, we gave up hope and followed the High King's litter onto the field."

Corwin's voice fell into the singsong lilt of the storyteller, and we hugged our knees and listened, enraptured.

"The Saxons attacked at the center of the line, where the High King's litter was. So savage they were, we could not hold them, and fell back against the onslaught. They pressed hard, eager to get to Uther, a sick king, and have it over early. Now, Sir Ector of Galava led the right flank, and saw his chance to cut the Saxons off. Good soldier that he is! If Lot, who led the left, had had the sense to do the same, the villainous dogs would have been swallowed up and surrounded. But Lot stood his ground and looked the other way."

"I hope he was hanged for his treachery!" Elaine exclaimed hotly.

Corwin laughed. "On the contrary, brave lass, he rides at the side of the young King as they chase Colgrin toward the sea."

Elaine objected violently, but I said, "Since he is alive, it is the best place for him, where Arthur can keep an eye on him."

Corwin regarded me thoughtfully. "So many have said, my lady, and Merlin one of them, if rumors be true."

"Well, I'd have killed him myself if I were king!" Elaine cried emphatically. "But go on, Corwin, what happened next? Don't take all day."

"For God's sake, Elaine—" I began, but Corwin raised a hand.

"Bide a bit, young ladies, and let me tell the tale. You will know it all, in time. Well, there we were, face to face with the stinking Saxon hordes. Had Lothian grown roots in the hill, that he could not move? Was he waiting, as some were saying, to see which way the battle went? If the Saxons got to the King, he could join them from the flank and cut *us* off—the lines wavered, uncertain. Good Ector led the charge from the right and drove deep, with his son Kay right at his side. But an ax got his leg and he lost his sword; he had to withdraw. Young Kay tried to take his place—he fought hard, he's a valiant soldier—but he had no sense of the battlefield, of the flow of things, of where he was. He was pushing too hard in the wrong place, and the seasoned warriors all knew it. The charge began to waver, the lines began to weave, the Saxons scented the kill; for a moment it seemed that all was lost—the charge, the Briton positions, the field, the day, the High King, the Kingdom. For a moment—the same moment—every man on the field knew it, wherever he was. It was one of those moments when time stops, when the balance between two futures—defeat and victory, death and life, evil and good fortune—lies on a thin edge of chance." Corwin paused. We could have heard a leaf fall in the silence. "But it was no chance the unknown boy rode forward, raised his sword, gave the orders in a voice that brooked no hesitation, and saved the day. Out of nowhere he came; but he knew what to do, and every man there followed him. I followed him myself, and I don't know why. I'd never seen him before. But he'd a cool head on his shoulders, and he fought a damned smart fight. Before old Colgrin knew what had happened, he found himself pushed hard against the hill where Lothian waited, and King Lot, forced to choose and seeing a new commander bidding fair to take his place at the King's right hand, cast his future with the British and attacked. That was the end of it, really. It was all over but the mopping up."

"And then?" Elaine asked excitedly. "Surely everyone knew by then? Surely King Uther proclaimed him?"

"No, my lady. It's a busy time, after battle, with the field to clear and the wounded to tend. We all found our own camps and took stock of who was left."

"But you must have wondered who he was," I said, "and where he had come from."

"Oh, he was the talk of the army, of course. Who was the new commander? No one knew his name or had seen his badge. The word went round he was a child, a dogsbody, a nameless lad who tagged along in Kay of Galava's wake. Ector's fosterling, they said, meaning Ector's bastard, born on the wrong side of the blanket and good only for errands and hard labor."

"No! How did they dare!"

"Who was to know? A few bright souls wondered if it might be Prince Arthur in disguise—such a disguise!—but no one knew, and no one liked to wager on such a long shot. All that long night we carried the dead from the field, dug the grave pits, sorted their belongings, and tended to our wounds. That's when I broke my leg, in a scuffle with a half-dead Saxon who attacked me when I took his armband. In the field hospital I saw my cousin Durwen—the bardling, we called him, because he wanted to be a bard, he had a gift for it. He was delirious with pain from a slice across his thigh, but he had already made a song about the battle. 'The Wrath of the Nameless Prince' he called it. He had sung it for Merlin, he claimed, as he stitched his leg, and Merlin had smiled."

Elaine wrinkled her nose. "Ector's fosterling? No, Corwin, it's too ignoble. Tell us rather that Merlin raised him in the Magic Isles across the Western Sea and brought him forth just in time to save us from the Saxons!"

"I'm telling you what happened, if you'll be polite like your cousin and wait for me to get there." Corwin winked at me and took another pull from his flask. "When the work was done, the men who were well and whole caroused till dawn. There were plenty of girls in Caer Eden to toast our victory. Ah, those lovely northern lasses—" He stopped, recollecting where he was, and cleared his throat. "Beg pardon. But I cursed the misfortune of my leg, I can tell you that. At daybreak we gave thanks to Mithra in a formal ceremony, with King Uther in attendance, pale as a nether spirit. And that night there was to be a formal victory feast. Rumor had it he was going to bring forth the prince at last and name his heir—he was dying on his feet, anyone could see it. Men looked all about for Prince Arthur but could not find him. Meanwhile, Ector's fosterling was in the hospital with Merlin, visiting the wounded and offering his arm to Ector so the man could walk. By daylight you could see he was only a beardless boy, and hopes fell." Corwin paused. "These things I saw and can swear to. The rest I know only because the camp was alive with rumors, and I spoke with men who had been at the victory feast, and—and at what came after."

Elaine and I looked at each other. He was making the sign against enchantment behind his back, and we wondered why. We had certainly heard no rumors of magic from the men, only bragging about the battle itself.

"Then suddenly, toward sunset, talk began to go through camp that the King was dying. Everyone fell still. The guard was doubled around Uther's tent, and all the lords gathered inside, including Ector with Kay and the fosterling, and Merlin, and the kings of Rheged, Strathclyde, Cornwall, Elmet, Lothian, and Gwynedd. I can't tell you just what happened, because I wasn't there, but word went round that Uther, on his deathbed, proclaimed the fosterling to be his own son by the queen Ygraine, named him his heir, and bade the kings follow him. The lords took it as well as they might: Ector pleased as punch; Cornwall, Rheged, Strathclyde, and our own good King Pellinore cheered the lad and swore him faith. But Lothian was furious. Lot had schemed for years to become High King, betrothing Uther's bastard daughter for the purpose. She was there, you know, the beautiful Morgause, to persuade her father to the choice. But they reckoned without Arthur, those two." He turned to spit, then recollected his audience and contented himself with a gruff rumble in his throat. "There might have been a brawl, except that in the middle of the fracas, Uther died. And that put an end to the celebrations." The sadness in Corwin's face bespoke his loyalty to Uther. I was moved to see it. "It's an uncommon bad omen, victory or no victory, the High King dying while the Saxons still lay encamped across the river. Why, the smoke from their funeral pyres kept us up coughing half the night. A new King had to be chosen, and fast. And while young Arthur had been proclaimed, no one felt easy about making a child a King with such a deadly enemy so near. In the interim, King Lot took charge."

"Traitor!" Elaine cried.

"No, my lady. It needed the strong hand of an experienced warrior the soldiers trusted. It was best for everyone. And who else to turn to? Merlin might have stepped forward, but he did not. He returned to the field hospital, and young Arthur with him, looking dazed and grim. Lot announced we would hold the victory feast as planned, in Uther's honor, and that afterward a council of commanders could discuss the wisdom of Uther's recommendation and choose the next High King."

"Recommendation!" Elaine bristled. "How dare he! It is treason!"

"Nonsense," I retorted, tired of her interruptions. "We are not Roman yet. Kings are still chosen by the lords who must serve them."

"If the king's son or his nephew are not worthy!" Elaine cried, beside herself. "But *Arthur* is the King's son! He *is* worthy! Were they blind? Hadn't he just won the battle for them?"

"Yes," I replied calmly, "it is easy enough to sit here safe in Wales and say so, but imagine being a soldier in the field. What Corwin says makes sense to me. They were all grown men, kings and lords and warriors; they did not want to serve a boy."

"Exactly so, my lady," Corwin said sadly. "It is ever the way of men not to see what is before their noses."

"What happened at the victory feast?" I asked.

Corwin frowned. "Well, they fell to arguing as soon as the wine went round. I have this from Durwen, who dragged himself from bed to accompany Pellinore. There were lords in the hall who were in league with Lothian and objected that a boy not yet fourteen was too young to lead a troop of seasoned warriors, much less a kingdom. Some argued long and loud on Lot's behalf: Cyndeg of Gore, the snake Aguisel, a few others. Lot himself said nothing. Be sure he had paid them well beforehand for their speeches. They said the High King's dying in the face of Saxons was an omen, and that Britain itself would die if we did not change the line."

"Had they already forgotten who brought them victory? What better omen could there be than that?" Elaine was shouting.

"Soldiers are superstitious," Corwin replied, "as you very well know. Black Celts from the hills of Wales are the worst of all. There was many a man in that hall who took it as a sign from the gods that Uther's line ended with Uther's death. There were cries of 'Lothian! Lot for High King!' from one side of the hall, and cries of 'Arthur!' from the other. And then, when the hall was near to erupting into open warfare, Merlin the Enchanter arose before the crowd. One look from him froze the wagging tongues, and when it was quiet, he spoke. It did not matter, he told them, what choice men made. This King had been ordained by gods a hundred years before his birth. He was the Light of Britain; his time had come. That day he had proved his prowess before them all. He was Chosen, and the gods that made men would prove it so that very night. Lot stood up and objected—he has more courage than I have, to face Merlin in the midst of a pronouncement, I grant him that—Lot stood up and objected that an army of men needed a man to lead them, not a boy, and talk about gods and magic and foretelling was so much stuff and nonsense, to borrow my lady's phrase. Merlin, cool as ice, gestured toward the unarmed boy and said that Arthur stood before them without a sword for a reason. It was not Uther's sword that would bring him into Kingship, but one given by the gods themselves. That very night, in the presence of them all, they would give the Sword into his hand, the Sword that would protect Britain from her enemies for as long as Arthur held it." Corwin paused. "Now, Merlin, besides having power from the gods, besides being wise beyond the wisdom of men, Merlin is also a showman of the first class. He let the questions run through the hall like wind through a hayfield, and then he let the murmuring die down until all was still. And then, when he commanded every eye and every ear, he told the history of the Sword. It was, he said, the Sword of the Emperor Maximus."

Elaine and I gasped. All Welsh children were brought up on the story of Macsen Wledig, as the Welsh called Maximus, but the tale of the Sword was new to us. Magnus Maximus had been the last Roman commander in Britain; when the Romans pulled out, Macsen stayed with his Welsh princess Elen and forged the hill tribes of Britain into a Kingdom. It was the Sword of Maximus that turned aside the Saxons, the Picts, and the Irish in the dark time men call the Flood Year. Romano-British civilization teetered on the edge of extinction then, but Maximus' disciplined troops beat back the savages and won for Britain a breathing space of peace. He was acclaimed Emperor of Britain by the people and kept the peace in the Roman way.

But at length his ambitions outstripped his judgment, and he declared war on the emperor in Rome. He led his loyal British troops across the Narrow Sea into Gaul and across Gaul into Italy. Some say he defeated the Emperor of Rome, some say he was defeated by him; whatever happened, he died there in Aquilea, and his remaining troops brought home his armor and his Sword. Many men stayed in Gaul and settled along the edge of the Narrow Sea in what men call Less Britain. The rest returned to Wales. His son Constantius ruled after him and was the ancestor of Constans, who was murdered by Vortigern, and of Ambrosius, who was the first to reunite the kings of Britain, and of Uther, who just managed to hold the Saxons at bay, until Arthur should come.

"It was written in the stars, Merlin said in a soft voice that carried to every corner of the hall, that in the dark hour the Light of Britain should blaze forth with a Sword of wondrous brilliance: Maximus' own Sword, hidden in darkness for a hundred years, waiting for the hand of Britain's greatest King to lift it once again into the light."

He stopped and let the silence hang.

"Corwin," I whispered, "you should be a bard."

He laughed. "I may have to be, unless my leg heals straight. Anyway, those are Merlin's words about the Sword. Durwen told me, and he was there with King Pellinore. He *was* studying to be a bard and had learned how to get things by heart in one hearing."

"Was?" I asked quickly.

Corwin sobered. "Yes, my lady. The poor lad died on the way home of his wound. It was stitched, but he opened it again by sitting a horse too soon, and against orders."

"But the Sword!" Elaine cried impatiently. "What can you tell us about that? Where was it? How did Prince Arthur get it? And when did they proclaim him King?"

"Merlin claimed the Sword lay under Lluden's Hill, where it had been left by Maximus' chief captain. He had brought it north from Wales when Elen, in her grief, banished it from her sight. It lay in darkness, Merlin said, protected by the god of the place, to be raised into the light by him who was born the rightful King of Britain. He invited all the lords present to ride there that very night and witness its lifting. What could Lot do? Every lord in the hall, from king to count to troop captain, would have given years off his life to witness Merlin's powers in person. Lot had no hope of being acclaimed King in that hall; his only hope was to join the throng on Lluden's Hill and hope that Arthur or Merlin would fail." He laughed and then slowly sobered. "King Pellinore took only Durwen with him, because, according to Durwen, he felt that the anointing of a new king should be witnessed by a bard. Now, I suppose, it is left to me to tell it."

He paused again and, closing his eyes, spoke softly. "So they took to horse and rode upstream along the river Eden. In the dark hours of the morning they came to the black island that sits hard by the ford. Lluden's Hill, the locals call it; it has been a sacred place time out of mind. Merlin led them up the slope to an old tunnel, hidden by undergrowth, and through it into a gigantic cave. So large it was, none could see its roof, nor its ending. Their torches shed a dim and smoky light, enough to glimpse the cold immensity of the place and feel the weight of dark shadows pressing down." Elaine and I shivered in spite of ourselves and made the sign against enchantment, although we were Christians. "Forty men had followed Merlin, and they all stood within the cave, shuffling and whispering, hearing their own voices speak back to them from the living rock; a place haunted, Durwen swore, with the spirits of the Elder past. Merlin stood up before them, a black shadow in the darkness. 'Look before you,' he cried, 'and see the Sword of Maximus!' And there it was, in the middle of the vast cavern, stuck into the cleft of a huge rock. There it was; where a moment before they had seen nothing, now they saw the split rock, the dark shaft rising, the dim glow of the hilt seeming to float in the very air. Merlin beckoned, they moved closer, the bravest among them trembling. The scabbard was of some ancient silken fabric, embroidered with the crude marks of the Old Tongue that Britons spoke before the Romans came. Merlin raised high a torch that all might see the writing carved into the rock below the sword: 'WHOSO LIFTS THIS SWORD FROM THE STONE IS RIGHTWISE BORN KING OF ALL THE BRITONS.' He read it out in a voice of dread, and the echoes circled, chilling the soul. '*rightwise born . . . rightwise born . . . King of all the Britons.*' "

"Corwin!" Elaine quavered, gripping my arm.

His eyes were closed. He did not even hear her. "No one dared to breathe. The Sword stood in its dark sheath, dull and cold, and all around the air stank with the sweat of fear. 'Let him who dares touch the Sword,' Merlin called out. But no one moved. At last King Lot stepped forward. 'I am fitter than any man here to be High King,' he proclaimed, 'but I distrust magicians.' Merlin folded his hands into his sleeves. 'Sir,' he said, 'there is no magic in this place but what the gods have bestowed in the Sword itself. I am powerless before it. If the Sword is yours, take it.' The lords held their breath as Lot reached out, put his hand to the hilt, and pulled."

Corwin opened his eyes and stared at us. "Then was the sacred silence rent with a mighty yell, for the Sword did not budge an iota, but Lot's hand was burned, the flesh seared across the palm where it had held the hilt. He withdrew his hand, white-faced with pain, and cursed Merlin for a lying, two-faced bastard." Elaine and I both gasped at such outrageous foolhardiness, but Corwin hardly paused for breath. "The company shrank back, afrighted. Someone called out, 'Let the boy try! Where's Ector's fosterling?' Arthur was pushed forward, and seeing that there was no way out of it, he stood straight as a spear before Merlin the Enchanter. 'Is it for me?' he asked the great magician. 'If you tell me to, I shall try it.' "

"Oh, how brave he is!" Elaine cried.

"How so," I countered, "when he has known Merlin his entire life? If there is not trust between them yet—"

"Oh, shut up, Gwen! You ruin everything!"

"Merlin told him," Corwin went on, ignoring us both, " 'it is yours, my lord King. It was made for your hand, even before it was made for Maximus.' So the lad went forward and put his hand to the hilt, and the great Sword slid as sweetly out of the sheath as a knife through butter. Torchlight caught the blade, setting it aglow; as he lifted it into the light, the great jewel in the hilt blazed into life. A huge emerald, hidden in the dark, struck its green fire into every soul and brought them all to their knees. Life! it signaled. Victory! As Arthur held it aloft he seemed to grow taller before their eyes. His face shone in the reflected glory of the Sword, a face full of pride and fierce determination. 'I shall call it *Excalibur*,' he said, which in the Old Tongue means 'unconquered.' Then every lord came and knelt before him to pay homage and receive his blessing. Lot was last, but he spoke well and promised faithful service. So they made young Arthur their King in that sacred place, King of all the Britons, and carried him outside as dawn broke in the east. And behind in the cavern the rock lay split in two halves, and the scabbard crumbled into dust, when the Sword was freed."

Elaine's eyes were as large as goose eggs. The magnificence of her hero had been amply confirmed.

"That's not the end." Corwin smiled. "While Durwen was busy spinning phrases in his head to recite to me, others among the lords, including Cyndeg and Aguisel, were grumbling that the whole thing had been planned by Arthur's allies. Merlin had done nothing but lead them to the Sword. They might have sworn to follow the boy who held that Sword, but they wanted proof that Merlin's powers were behind him. The lifting of the Sword was not enough; they wanted more."

"What fools men are!" I breathed.

"And Merlin heard them. As they made ready to depart, with the new King at their head, Merlin turned around in the saddle and raised his arms. A thunderous crack rent the sky, a flash of fire burst forth, and the hillside above the cave came down. Trees bent double, horses bolted and men bellowed in fear, but Merlin sat and calmly watched Lluden's Hill slide into a mountain of rubble. When the last stone had tumbled to a stop at Merlin's feet, he coolly turned and surveyed the doubters, who shook before his gaze. Then he reined in and rode behind Arthur back to camp."

We brought Corwin a flask of honey mead and thanked him sincerely for his tale. Elaine was speechless for a while, but soon she found her tongue.

"And what does King Arthur look like?" she asked eagerly. "Do tell us." Corwin looked a little blank. "What do you mean, my lady?"

"I mean, is he dark or fair? Tall or short? Lean or heavy?"

Corwin smiled and said to me, "It seems the young princess is not without ambition." I winked at a scarlet Elaine as he continued. "Well, from what I saw of him, he is tall for his age and slender for a warrior, but he is young yet. He is an excellent swordsman, near the best I have seen. What else? Let me see, brown hair, brown eyes, a clear skin with a serious expression, well featured, with a look of Uther about him, and when he was young Uther was considered handsome by all the ladies of the land." Then Corwin's gaze grew distant, and his voice pensive. "But I think what is most impressive about him is something that I cannot put into words. Men call it poise, or inner peace, or wisdom, or strength, or grace of bearing, but it is all those and more; he is a man in harmony with himself. He has a mission. He knows who he is."

"He must be a born leader," I said thoughtfully, "for the men he commands are seasoned warriors and kings in their own right. Sword or no sword, men like King Pellinore and my brother Gwarthgydd would not follow a mere boy."

"Indeed," Corwin agreed. "And it isn't due to Merlin's magic, either. For Merlin disappeared after the lifting of the Sword and hasn't been seen since. Yet the army is off after Colgrin, with King Arthur at its head."

"He will beat the Saxons," Elaine said confidently, "and drive them from our shores forever."

"It will be a miracle indeed if he does that," Corwin replied. "The Saxons have been living on the Shore since Vortigern first invited them, fifty years ago. There are children your age, my young lady, whose grandfathers were born in Britain. Small wonder they consider it their home."

"But we were here first," Elaine objected.

"We Welsh?" I asked her. "Or we British? We are led by a descendant of Maximus, who was a Roman and a foreigner. The Celts were here before the Romans, and the Ancients before the Celts. No one knows who was here before the Ancients. Perhaps the Saxons are next."

"That's treason!" Elaine cried, tears springing to her eyes. "Gwen, I will never forgive you unless you take it back! How can you say such a thing?" Even Corwin looked shocked.

"If it isn't possible to drive the Saxons out—and where, indeed, can they go? —then it will be necessary to treat with them. Yes, I know the old saying: A treaty with a Saxon is as lasting as smoke in the wind, but it seems to me it's the strongest sword that prevails. Perhaps what Merlin said is true and that Arthur's Sword is the strongest. Then we shall have peace with the Saxons." I could see that they both were calmer, and Elaine was on the verge of forgiving me. "Who knows? In two hundred years perhaps even the Saxons will be British."

Elaine gasped in horror and began to berate me; Corwin looked afraid.

"My lady Guinevere, it is not my place to say so, but these are not matters that should concern young maids. These are high matters, and beyond such as me; they are better left to the king's council chamber. You have a mind, my lady, which may bring you grief if you give it tongue. Such thoughts are better left unspoken."

It was good advice. I did not tell him that it was talk in the king's council chamber that had given rise to these thoughts, voiced here for the first time. I accepted his rebuke, apologized to Elaine, and kept my thoughts to myself thereafter. It was twenty years before I found a mind receptive to these thoughts: a man who accepted them and went beyond them, who believed in compromise and in the value of other cultures besides his own, a man who envisioned the entire civilized world as one community. That man was Mordred.

5 ♛ THE SIN

During the next five years King Pellinore was often from home while
Arthur's new Kingdom fought for its fledgling life. The Saxons had
been soundly defeated at Caer Eden, and Colgrin their leader had died of
wounds received on that field. But there were other war leaders eager to fill
Colgrin's place. Caelwin, Colgrin's second-in-command, organized the East
Saxons, treated with the Angles, and with their combined forces fought to
establish a new beachhead along the eastern shores. If Lot of Lothian
treated with them, it would split Britain in two.

And along the Saxon Shore arose a youth who dared to call himself
King of the West Saxons: Cerdic the Aetheling, Eosa's son, who promised
his people freedoms and rule by law, should they conquer Britain. I wondered at his temerity—was not Roman law good enough for the likes
of him?

But Arthur led his troops to victory after victory, with great losses on
the Saxon side and few on his own. Young as he was, older men granted him
their respect, and hardened warriors deferred to his opinions, for there is
no talisman luckier than victory, and he did not seem able to lose. Everywhere they were attacked, Britons fought bravely, from king to foot soldier,
knowing that the High King would come to their aid with his invincible
Sword, Excalibur, and his companion force of trained warriors.

Without fail Arthur came and conquered. By the time I was ten he was
already a legend in his own land. He never lost so much as a skirmish. His
name was a password for victory, and men said he had only to appear on the
horizon for the Saxons to turn and flee.

Elaine believed every word she heard about him, and I was forced to
stop my teasing under the pressure of her adoration. She even fasted the
whole day of his coronation, while everyone else feasted. He was no longer
our hope, she told me with earnest passion, he was our savior. And truly, I
could not in good grace quarrel with her, for the kings of Britain hastened to
unite behind this fearless warrior, and for the first time in men's memories
Wales, Cornwall, Rheged, Lothian, and scores of lesser kingdoms felt a kinship with one another—we were all part of one realm.

This took time to achieve. Indeed, for the first year of his reign, Arthur
was busy fighting stop-gap battles in the east, north, and southeast. He had
been High King for over six months before the Saxons left him enough

breathing space to get himself crowned. It was a Christian ceremony, and he was anointed by a Christian priest at Pentecost, but it was held in the old fighting fortress of Caerleon with a minimum of ceremony, because, in the King's own words, there was little time. Most of his attendants were his troops and nobles, although all the lords and ladies of the land had been invited. King Pellinore and Queen Alyse attended, for Caerleon, lying on a hill above the River Usk, was but four days' journey south. It was April, and spring was early that year, so the roads were clear and they made good time. According to Elaine, Pellinore had intended to take only his soldiers with him, but the queen refused to be left behind. She claimed she didn't care if she had to sleep in a tent; she wanted to see the young High King crowned.

When she returned, she was the center of all our attention, and one afternoon, in an expansive mood, she gathered us all around her: her waiting women, Elaine and me, and our nurses, and she told us all about it.

It was not grand, she said, more a meeting among war leaders than a social event, but the High King's mother, the lady Ygraine, had come up from Cornwall and had spent much time with Alyse, one of the few queens to attempt the journey. Ygraine still grieved for her lost Uther and looked pale and wasted. Her physician traveled with her, but it was Merlin who concocted her a brew that brought color to her cheeks and allowed her to attend the ceremony without exciting her son's attention.

"Merlin!" Elaine cried. "Was he there? Did you really see Merlin the Enchanter, Mother? Were you in the room with him? What does he look like?"

Queen Alyse laughed gently. "You young ones grew up on the tales of his doings, I see, and to you he is a creature of fable. But he is real enough, I assure you. And free of arrogance, for such a powerful man. Without him, young Arthur would not now be King."

"Saints preserve us!" Grannic cried, crossing herself, and Ailsa clutched the amulet at her breast.

"Is he very fearful, Mother?" Elaine whispered. "Did you see him use magic?"

"No, child. He came often to visit Ygraine. They are old friends. But he used no magic except what he put in the broth that gave her the strength to see her son crowned."

"Is he ugly, Mama?"

"Goodness, no. He is tall, of course, and dark. Black hair and eyes. You would think him old, but I do not. He is slender and quiet and does not say much. He listens to everything. They say the young King loves him as a father and depends upon him greatly. Not for fighting, of course. By his own admission Merlin is no swordsman. But for matters of state, I should imagine he is the wisest advisor a king could have."

"What was the coronation like, Mother? Did you have to stay in a tent? Did you get to see King Arthur? Is he handsome and fierce? Tell us!"

Alyse laid a gentle hand on Elaine's head, and I watched her eyes. They looked through Elaine to something beyond. "We were lodged in a house next to Ygraine's. It was a high honor, for there are few private dwellings there yet, although I hear the High King has plans for the place. Yes, I saw the High King at the ceremony and afterward, when he greeted his guests. He is just fourteen, but already an experienced war leader. You could see it in his eyes, his bearing, his sureness. He is—he is—" she paused, searching for the words to describe the youth she saw in her mind's eye. "He is tall, but not too tall, he is handsome, but not to swooning point. He has a look of Uther about him, but not his temper, God be praised. And by all accounts he is moderate in his habits." No one needed to remind us of Uther's reputation for womanizing. It was a saying that he had never slept alone. "But one doesn't see him in that way. What you see is singleness of purpose, of youth and strength and joy. He was born for this, Merlin said to Ygraine, and it seems he knows it." She sighed and smiled gently. "As a mother, I would want him for my son. Were I a girl again, I would want him for my husband."

Elaine caught my eye and sighed in deep satisfaction. Alyse continued her account of her visit and the nobles she saw, but for Elaine the rest was chaff. She had her fantasy of Arthur confirmed and was happy to bursting point.

Those were good years, those early ones. While Elaine and I studied Latin and Greek and figuring, learned stitching and weaving and housekeeping, raced along the rocky beaches on our ponies, and listened in on the king's councils when we could, Arthur was busy repairing the Kingdom's defenses, building roads and fortresses, setting up communication links of signal fires from hilltop to tor top, refurbishing ransacked towns and castles, restoring life and trust to the land. He traveled constantly from kingdom to kingdom, renewing treaties and helping lords with their local problems in return for their pledge to come to his call. Around him he gathered the young men of the kingdoms, nobles' sons, and forged them, through friendship, into a close-knit group. With the help of a king's son from Less Britain, who was a consummate horseman, Arthur sent to Gaul for fine, swift horses and crossed them with the strong, native breeds to get warhorses unsurpassed in power, speed, and intelligence. Arthur's mounted Companions became a swift, mobile cavalry and one of his deadliest weapons.

But as they say in Wales, every sun has its shadow. No one is immune from slander, and one day I heard a tale that wove a dark thread of evil into the fabric of the new King's glory. I was in my horse's stall, rubbing him down after a ride and grooming his silken coat, a job I preferred to do myself than leave to a groom, when I heard men talking.

One of Pellinore's men spoke carelessly as he handed over his sweated horse; I had lingered long after my ride and no doubt they thought I had returned to the castle with Elaine.

"Ho there, Stannic, how goes it?"

"Well, young master, thank you kindly. You made good time. We weren't expecting you before sundown."

"I hurried from York," the trooper replied, and then their voices became muffled as they went together into the horse's stall. I was about to straighten up and slip out, when I caught the High King's name and the word "massacre." Quickly I crouched in the corner of the box and kept as still as I could. The trooper came out and lounged nearby in the aisle, speaking with the voice of one who delights in bearing bad news.

"They are talking about it all over York," he gloated. "Two hundred babies, they say, all boys, all newborns, set adrift in a fishing craft with the sail lashed to the tiller and the course set for the rocks. I got it from a man who got it from his sister, and she lives in Dunpeldyr."

Dunpeldyr! The capital of Lothian. Lot's city.

"Oh, he was in a rare fury was King Lot. Put yourself in his shoes, Stannic. You're away campaigning with the High King, your bride of eight months tucked safely away in your castle, with guards aplenty. You have left her with child, but what do you find when you return for her lying-in? A slender wife, an empty crib, a thin tale of an early birthing and a quick death. And all the while the place is buzzing with the rumors of a strong boy born six weeks ago, looking no more like Lot than a dragon does an eagle!"

Stannic mumbled something, and the trooper laughed. I wondered what this common little tale had to do with the High King.

"Yes, there was a child, all right. But she hid him well. She's a witch, you know, a proper sorceress as well as a beauty. I'd say she was capable of anything. Seduction and deception would come as natural as breathing to Queen Morgause. Oh, it's not Lot's child, that's for certain. Lot beat her till she was well nigh senseless but could get no truth from her. All York is full of the news."

"Is that why he killed the children?" Stannic asked. "To find the boy?"

"Did I say it was Lot's doing? The babe had other enemies. Can't you guess whose child it was?"

"Her bath slave? The captain of the guard?"

The trooper paused, and I feared he would leave his tale unfinished, but he had only stopped to drain his hip flask, for I heard him push the stopper in and belch.

"Listen, Stannic," he continued, but very softly, and a curious, stealthy quality in his voice sent a shiver of fear down my spine; I crept to the front of the box to hear. "Can't you guess the reason for Lot's fury? No, no, if it had just been the queen's bastard, he'd have tossed it out, not sought to kill it. You never heard the rumors then? There was talk after Caer Eden about them. Morgause and Arthur, I mean. Before she was married to Lot, and before he was proclaimed King Uther's son." His voice fell to a hoarse whisper, and I strained to catch it. "The young prince shared her bed there, they say, his first woman, the night of his victory. And that she carried his child within her when she wed Lot soon after. You can be sure Lot had heard the rumors and wanted no dragon chick in his nest, bastard or not."

"Does the High King know?" Stannic asked, coming out of the box.

"Well, that's the question of the hour, isn't it? Someone's troops invaded the city and slayed every newborn male child. Every house was searched. Babies dragged from their mothers' breasts, lifted sleeping from their cradles, and thrown into an open boat. They said you could hear the cries of those babies for hours after the boat was out of sight, and of course the wailings of the mothers for days on end . . . No, none survived. The bodies all came in on the tide three days ago."

"Are you suggesting—" Stannic's voice was shaking, "—are you suggesting they were *royal* troops?"

"Who knows? They wore no badge. And it stands to reason the King would want to kill the child. What a hostage to his future that would be, a bastard son raised by the Witch of Lothian!"

"Not this King," Stannic whispered. "He's but a youth yet. He's no evil in him."

"And who stands behind him at his right hand but Merlin the Enchanter, master of the black arts? Don't tell me, my man, it isn't possible. With kings, anything is possible. The north country is already laying the blame at Arthur's door. York is divided. In the south, they'll probably blame Lot."

"I blame the Witch herself!" Stannic cried, and the trooper laughed.

"Well, no doubt, she is the root of all the trouble. So beautiful, they say, she turns men's wits. But would she give the order to murder innocent children?"

"She might, to safeguard the boy. Bastards have come to power before now. Didn't you say Lot had beaten her in a temper? Well, I've known women who would do any evil thing to cover the tracks of a lie. If she'd hidden the baby well, as you said, she could slay the city's children and keep her dangerous son safe. That would cool the king's anger and still the wagging tongues."

"Hmmm. Perhaps, if you think a woman capable of murdering children. I don't know. But it was a terrible, black deed, and the blame for it must settle somewhere."

"I pray the Goddess it does not settle on the young King."

"Even if it doesn't, he will suffer for it. How would you like a crafty wolf like Lot murdering a host of innocents just to kill yours? Leave you with a bad taste in your mouth, wouldn't it? Leave you feeling a little unclean?"

I believe I screamed in horror, but my hands were over my mouth, and they were walking away together, so they did not hear me. The trooper left, but Stannic came back and walked down the aisle, checking the horses. I was pressed frozen into the corner, and he did not see me. He doused the oil lamp, closed the door, and went out. I went to my dozing horse and wrapped my arms around his neck, burying my face in his rough mane to hide my tears.

I knew, as the trooper told the story, that there was more to it than he was telling, or perhaps than he knew, and when he said the word "unclean" I knew suddenly what it was. Morgause was Uther's bastard daughter, born before he married the Queen Ygraine. *She was Uther's daughter. Arthur's sister.* I crossed myself quickly as I thought the unclean thought. It had been a sin time out of mind. Could it be true? Could the High King have done such a thing? I thought back to the Battle of Caer Eden. I remembered the tales that had circulated among the returning wounded at that time, that the prince was kept ignorant of his birth, at Uther's wish, until Uther proclaimed him on his deathbed. That was the day after the battle, when they celebrated the victory. Was it possible, then, that when he went to Morgause he did not know who he was?

But if he sinned in innocence, he must have realized the truth the next day, when Uther acknowledged him. Hadn't Corwin described him as dazed and grim soon after the announcement? Here was a motive for murder stronger than any the trooper had named. Such a son would be a blight upon his honor, a smear across his good name, as well as a threat to his power.

I found myself shaking badly. There seemed no way out of the dilemma. Arthur was guilty either of incest or of murder, and perhaps of both. Our new King, our stainless, shining hope, would bear forever the taint of evil, once the news got out.

I realized suddenly that the trooper had come home to tell the news at the council table, and I straightened and stilled my trembling. I would dampen my clothing in the horse's trough and feign illness, so Elaine could not persuade me to go out on the parapet and eavesdrop tonight. Someday she might find out, and if the story of the massacre was spreading across Britain with the speed it was spreading across Wales, then it was likely she would hear it from someone, but it wasn't going to be me. Elaine was my only friend, and I was going to keep her Arthur untarnished for her.

6 ♕ THE GIFT

Queen Alyse and her ladies-in-waiting sat stitching and dozing in the queen's garden, enjoying the soft sea breeze and the warming sun of midmorning. The winter had been a hard one, and more than one of the women nursed a lingering cough. It was luxury to spend the day outside the cold castle walls, delighting in the sun, the smells of new growth, and the early birdsong.

It was the first of May and my thirteenth birthday. Father Martin released us early from our lessons, praising our progress and pretending he didn't know it was my birthday. There were celebrations in the village, where maids plaited wildflowers into their hair and danced with the young men, and the smoke from their feast fires drifted up the hill to our castle. This was Beltane, a day sacred to the Goddess, and while King Pellinore and Queen Alyse kept a Christian household, most Welshmen honored the Mother as well as Christ and observed Her holy days.

I had been looking forward to this day for a long time, because I was sure that on this day God would make me a woman. I had prayed so hard and tried so earnestly to keep all His commandments, obeying even the most stringent of the rules set down by Queen Alyse for ladylike behavior.

And more than that, I had learned, at great cost to my pride, to take my appointed place in Elaine's shadow. When she was willful I did not thwart her, but found some politic way, if I could, to temper her headstrong ways and yet avoid her anger. When I failed, and her silly schemes ended in disaster, I learned to hold my tongue when I was blamed. Once when Elaine and I sneaked down to the buttery to steal the new cream from jugs just set out, the cook caught us and scolded us roundly for our greed. Knowing from long experience whose idea it was, she chided Elaine for her appetite and threatened to tell the queen. That very morning Alyse had lectured Elaine about her fondness for sweets and cream, so Elaine turned around and blamed the adventure on me. Because I knew I would pay for it well if I denied it, I confessed, and from then on Alyse concluded that it was I who was responsible for every lump of sugar that went missing from the storerooms.

When there was punishment, I took it. Afterward, Elaine would give me a sweet apology and a promise of better behavior. And if Alyse frowned and scowled and called me a young fool, I could always rely on Pellinore's forgiveness. He could not bear to see me out of temper and would tease me back to good humor with all the good-hearted boisterousness in his generous nature.

For these sacrifices, I was sure God would answer my prayer. Although Elaine was a year younger than I, she had already grown round breasts and hips and had passed her menarche. All I had done was grow taller. I was taller now than Queen Alyse, but straight as a boy, with no sign that my body would ever change. But I was sure God had heard my prayers. Father Martin said He paid special attention to the requests of virgins.

Queen Alyse and her ladies had made us each a new dress to celebrate the day, and we hurried to change into them. Elaine's was made of a sky-blue cloth, soft and fine, that matched her eyes exactly. It had a high belt and rounded throat, accentuating her budding figure. She looked beautiful. Mine was a soft, spring green, the color of new leaves, cut out of silk that must have come from the warm lands far to the south. The lace at the throat was a sign of love and honor, for lace was rare in Britain and very costly. But the dress fit like a glove and could not hide the straightness of my frame. Next to Elaine, I looked like one of Alyse's garden scarecrows.

"Gwen!" Elaine gasped. I turned to find her staring at me in distress.

"What's the matter?"

She shook her head angrily. "You have no right to outshine me!" she blurted. "Change your dress!"

"What? What are you talking about?"

"You know full well what I am talking about! You have been admiring yourself in the bronze half the morning! I mean it, I will not be outdone!"

"Outdone, indeed!" I retorted. "It ill becomes you to mock me, Elaine. Just because you look like a woman of twenty, and I—I—I will grow a shape someday and find a husband, just wait and see!"

"Too soon for me!" she cried, in tears.

"Good heavens, Elaine! Are you blind? Come and look at yourself! You look fit to be courted by one of the High King's Companions!"

This was the highest compliment I could think of, for the King's Companions were the finest men in all the land. But it did not please her; she scowled and turned away. I did not dream, then, of Elaine's ambition.

"Fat chance I shall have of ever courting anybody, Gwen, until you are married. Who will look at little Elaine, standing in Guinevere's shadow?"

I grabbed her arm. "What nonsense is this? You are Pellinore's daughter! Have some sense, Elaine!"

But she pulled away angrily. "Leave me alone! You'd just better leave me alone!" And she fled out the door and down the corridor before I could stop her.

"What have I done?" I cried to Ailsa, who bent to retrieve the comb Elaine had thrown aside. "What did I say? Do you know what is the matter?"

"Indeed"—she smiled—"but pay it no mind, my lady. It's an illness without a cure."

"Well, whatever is amiss?" I demanded. "Tell me!"

She looked up slowly, her eyes narrowing in laughter. "If you don't know yet, time will tell you. Go on down to her now and be kind to her. You can bring her around, if you try."

I composed myself as best I could and went down to the garden, where I knew the queen was waiting for us. Elaine was there before me, but she kept her eyes in her lap and did not greet me. The conversation centered on the big event of the day, which was Pellinore's return from King Arthur's court. He was bringing me a special birthday gift, the messenger had said, but it was a great secret. Not even Alyse knew what it was.

Pellinore had been gone three months with his troops of fighting men, helping the High King repair the defenses along the Saxon Shore. Rumor had it they had been with Arthur when they defeated a Saxon force newly landed in longboats. The Saxons had been many in number, and the High King's force small, only Pellinore's foot soldiers and those of two lesser lords of the Summer Country, but the Saxons had been without horses, and Arthur's Companions had demolished them. The young knight from Less Britain, Lancelot of Lanascol, who had bred and trained the horses, had been honored at the victory feast. The High King graciously gave him credit for the victory and made him first among the Companions, his second-in-command. This he already was in all but name, for having no kin in Britain, he of necessity lodged and traveled with the High King, and they had become close friends.

Now the King had moved north to York, and Pellinore was coming home for what we all hoped was a long stay, bringing with him a surprise.

I picked up the piece of stitchery I was working on and listened almost absentmindedly to the women talking, my thoughts full of womanhood and distress at Elaine's sudden temper. Would she never cease her childish sulking and be my friend again?

"Melwas is King of the Summer Country," Alyse was saying, "although they say it is his sister Seulte who rules there. She claims to be a witch, but those who live there on Ynys Witrin say her foul temper is only bitterness at her inability to find a husband." Leave it to Alyse, I thought, to touch unerringly on Elaine's sorest spot.

"Isn't there a shrine to the Good Goddess on Ynys Witrin?" Elaine asked swiftly, to divert her mother. "I'm sure I heard it somewhere, but I thought there was a monastery there, too. How can there be both?"

"My goodness, Elaine, how do you get your information? You have never been to the Summer Country, and I am sure I did not know anything about it until Pellinore spent so much time there in the last year."

Of course we had got the information by eavesdropping. I caught

Elaine's quick, warning glance and hid a smile. She turned an innocent face to her mother. "I don't know, Mother, I must have picked it up at the stables, I guess. Sometimes the men talk when they don't know young maids are about."

A chill of horror shot through me, and I almost gasped, reminded of the trooper from York. Was it possible Elaine knew the wretched tale, or had it merely been an arrow in the dark? I bent low over my work to hide my face.

"Ah, well, little pitchers have big ears. Yes, Avalon lies on Ynys Witrin below Melwas' fortress, the Christian monastery farther up the Tor. The monks and the Ladies of the Lake get along well enough. They are all in the service of the Divine. The priestesses are skilled in the healing arts, as the monks are in prayer and meditation. There has been no trouble there, at any rate. The trouble has all come from Melwas. He is young and handsome and is a likable enough fellow, I gather, but he has rather an eye for the girls in training. I understand he has ruined more than one pretty acolyte, and he is only twenty."

"Perhaps," one of her ladies said, "it is time for him to marry."

"No doubt it is, Cissa. But his sister stands in his way. No one is good enough for the lady Seulte, although I daresay Melwas himself is not so choosy. But he will not cross his sister, who feeds him full of praise and ambition, and so he bides by her will. Pellinore fears there will be more trouble in that quarter for some time."

"But at least it's only woman trouble," Leonora said.

"Perhaps," said Cissa, "he should look farther north for his bride." She turned and smiled at Elaine, who colored. I shot Elaine a triumphant glance, but she ignored me.

Alyse paused and looked at both of us thoughtfully. "Perhaps," she said, "but there is time yet. And I haven't told you the big news." She put down her work and gathered our attention. "I expect we will hear the details when King Pellinore comes home tonight, but I don't see why I can't tell you now what I know of it. As you know, the High King has been looking to build a fortress for his troops for some time. Caerleon, reinforced though it is, is not big enough. He has collected many men who follow him, not to mention the horses, and there are no hill forts large enough to accommodate his household. So a month ago they broke ground at a new site."

This set the ladies chattering with delight. At last the kingdom would have a center, a court that did not have to migrate from kingdom to kingdom, a place Arthur could call his own.

"It is in the Summer Country, which is what made me think of Melwas," Alyse continued. "On a high tor, flat-topped and long-sloped, within sight of the signal fires on Ynys Witrin. It sits near the river Camel, and there is a spring near the summit. It is rumored that before winter the fortifications will be complete, and lodging for the troops and horses ready. The castle, of course, will take longer."

What need had Arthur of a castle, I thought to myself, if he had good fortifications and lodgings for troops and horses? For five years he had done without either consistently and was still victorious wherever he raised his Sword.

"This is good news indeed, my lady," Cissa cried. "And perhaps, in two or three years, when he has built a home to bring a bride to, the High King will marry at last." It had long been a worry among my lady's maids, and I suspect among many of the ladies of the land, that the young King had not yet given a thought to marriage. He was now eighteen, well grown, well favored, war-hardened, and beyond all doubt the most eligible bachelor in the land.

Queen Alyse laughed in delight. "Cissa, my dear, you anticipate me. The new court at Caer Camel was but half my news. Hear this. The High King is betrothed and will wed come September."

I happened to be looking at Elaine and saw her blanch. She bent her head quickly, but I had seen tears forming in her eyes. With the swiftness of a lightning flash, I understood at last.

"Who is it, my lady?" the ladies were asking with eagerness. "Who backed her? What is her family?"

Queen Alyse took time to hush them, and Elaine struggled valiantly to compose her features. "She is the daughter of the Earl of Ifray, who was killed in battle at Duke Cador's side four years ago. Her mother died at her birth, and she has been raised in Cador's household since her father's death. Remember that the High King made Cador of Cornwall his heir until a prince should be born. And Cador is on excellent terms with his stepmother, the queen Ygraine." The women nodded solemnly to one another. There were no stronger backers in the land than the High King's mother and his heir-apparent, excepting only Merlin.

"She is sixteen," the queen continued, "and quite pretty, by all accounts. She has had speech once or twice with the High King. At least they know one another." Alyse had married Pellinore for love, which was almost unheard of at that time, and firmly believed that young maids should not be given in marriage to strangers. "And her name," Alyse said, "is Guenwyvar." They all gasped in surprise and then looked at me sidelong, as if I had lost by a near miss.

"Lord be praised," Leonora murmured. "At last we shall have a Queen and Arthur's line shall be established."

"Yes," the queen continued. "And it has been in my mind, that after the building at Caer Camel is finished, the High King and his Queen will want company at court, and his Companions may want wives, if the wars allow. It may be we shall move to the Summer Country in two years' time." The ladies looked at us and smiled knowingly.

Elaine's misery was heartbreaking to see, but no one seemed to notice it but I. As soon as I could, I made some excuse to leave, and Elaine followed me willingly. We fled to our room, and Elaine burst into sobs upon her bed. I sat beside her and stroked her fair hair. It was the color of ripe grain, dark gold and glowing. Much lovelier, to my mind, than my white-gold hair, a childhood color I had yet to outgrow, and which always made strangers stare.

"I'm sorry, Elaine. I had no idea. I knew you idolized him; he has been your hero since tales about him first started to go round. But I never knew you really—expected to—"

"Oh, stop!" Elaine sobbed. "I knew it was hopeless, but I couldn't help it! I knew this would happen! And now Mother thinks to marry us off to his Companions!"

"Would that not be an honor?" I asked her. "Surely any maid chosen by the Companions would be among the first in Britain."

"I don't care! Oh, Gwen, it would be too awful! To be there in the High King's court and married to someone else. I couldn't stand it! And I don't *want* to marry anyone else! I shall never marry! Never!"

I tried to soothe her and calm her, but she so enjoyed her weeping fit that she ceased to fight for control and grew hysterical. It took Grannic and Ailsa both to calm her, with cold cloths to her head and warm blankets on her body. This was Elaine at her most tiresome; she often enjoyed the complete release of her emotions, always suffering dreadfully for it afterward, with headaches that could last days, but in a strange way I did not understand, she enjoyed the suffering, too.

I left her to the nurses, who calmed her to sleep, and went to the stables. My brown gelding Peleth was beyond his best years, which is why King Pellinore had taken him from a trooper and given him to me. But he was willing and had been an athlete in his prime, and I had taught him a new skill in his old age: I had taught him to jump. We had begun with natural barriers on the woodland trails: downed trees, rain-washed boulders, low walls, but these became easy with practice, and lately I had secretly built obstacles from branches, rocks, and greens, some wide and some tall, and he learned to take them all with ease. It was a wonderful feeling, flying through the air with the wind whipping my hair, and Peleth loved it.

I was not yet a woman; I checked before I went out, but the day was only half spent, and there was still time. We practiced jumping until Peleth took all his fences perfectly, and then went for a gallop along the beach.

The day was mild and clear, and the sea spray cold. We returned as the sun dipped toward the hilltops, splashed with seawater, sand, and mud, and very tired and happy. I did not go in the stable, but left him with the groom, for I knew I was late and had probably been missed.

Ailsa was in a panic. "My lady, where in the name of all the saints and devils have you been? King Pellinore has returned, and we are bidden to dinner! And look at you! You've torn your tunic, God knows on what"— she crossed herself quickly—"and your leggings are filthy!"

I laughed as she tugged the tunic off. "This is nothing, Ailsa. You should see Peleth!"

"What will become of you!" she wailed. "You're as wild as an Irish elf and shall never find a husband!"

She had touched inadvertently on my innermost fear, and I felt the gaiety drain from my body.

Ailsa saw it and began to croon lovingly. "That's just my way of talking, my lady. Don't pay any heed to a silly old woman. You're as lovely as a summer's eve, and as soon as the Good Lady blesses you with your monthlies, there's not a prince in the land who won't be knocking at King Pellinore's door for your hand. Mark my words, my lady. Remember what the witch foretold. First in the land will you be."

A sob rose in my throat, but I swallowed it back. Giselda's prophecy! It was clear to me now. The witch had been right. I might be flat-chested forever, a spinster and a burden in my old age, but no matter. The first in the land bore my name.

I had missed King Pellinore's arrival, and remembering that the feast tonight was held in my honor, I lifted my skirts and raced down to the greeting hall. I was surprised to see that Elaine had recovered enough to join the ladies seated about the great log fire. Usually she was long abed after such weeping. I supposed she had been made to join the birthday celebration; she looked pale and unhappy.

King Pellinore stood beside the queen's chair, holding Alyse's hand. His affection for her was a true one, and he never strove to hide it. He had two visitors with him, a man and a youth, but they stood with their backs to me, facing the fire, so I came upon them unawares.

"Ah, here's Gwen!" the king cried, smiling kindly at me.

I curtsied low before him. "Please forgive me, gracious king. We are so happy to see you safely returned to us, and I did not mean to be late. It was—"

He laughed and raised me, hugging me warmly. "The horses, no doubt. What else? Come, see who I have brought back with me from court."

I turned and faced two tanned, black-haired warriors, no taller than myself, with thick, strong bodies and dark pelts of hair along their arms. The younger of the two, after a wide-eyed glance at me, studied the floor; the elder grinned at me, his black eyes sparkling.

"Gwarthgydd!" I gasped, throwing myself into his arms. "Oh, Gwarthgydd, my brother!"

He laughed and swung me around. "Little Guinevere, I'd not have known you! Look at you, taller than me, by Mithra! You are a beauty, Gwen, there's no denying it." He turned to the youth beside him. "This will be something to tell your mother, Gwillim, won't it?"

"Gwillim!" I cried, staring at him. I had not recognized him at all. He was fourteen, had grown a beard and moustache, and looked at me with the eyes of a stranger. But I hugged him nevertheless. We had been playmates once. He stiffened and nearly fell to one knee, but restrained himself.

"Oh, Gwillim, I am so glad to see you! Have you been with the High King? Did you not stop at Northgallis? Did you come on to see me?"

Gwillim was clearly speechless, so Gwarthgydd replied. "To see you, dear sister, and to honor King Pellinore, who invited us most kindly. And to show Gwillim his first sight of the sea." His glance flicked ever so slightly toward the moody Elaine, and I noticed that Pellinore was smiling at Alyse. "And the beauties of Gwynedd," he finished politely. I understood instantly. They had come to inspect Elaine.

King Pellinore was clearly delighted, but Queen Alyse did not return his smiles. After the conversation in the garden I understood she had much higher ambitions for her daughter than marriage to a Welsh lord. Everyone was polite, of course, and conversation never lagged. King Pellinore's table was unlike any other I had heard of—it was round. The beauty of this arrangement was that it allowed everyone to see and talk to everyone else. There were long trestle tables and benches, as well, which were used to feast troops after victories of importance, or on high holy days, but always the family sat at the round table.

There was much toasting my health, and conversation about the Saxon wars, which was supposed to be above the ladies' heads, but which I listened to avidly. Elaine kept her eyes on her plate like any shy, young maid being courted for the first time. But I knew it was not modesty but misery that was blanketing her high spirits. And Gwillim, who should at least have shown some interest, if only curiosity, about the girl his father offered for, either looked at his own plate or looked at me. Try though I might, I could not engage him in conversation. He only responded "Yes, my lady" or "No, my lady" or, when I referred to the time we had found the wild ponies, "I pray you won't mention it, my lady." What could one do? At least Gwarthgydd had news of home. He and all his brothers were in the High King's service now, and he had nothing but praise for Arthur. What a leader! Calm, wise, purposeful, never a hasty move or an unplanned foray; gentle with women, just with men, ruthless with his enemies. He was full of laughter and good humor; men feared his rare anger; he fought not with heat but with unswerving, cold purpose.

When I could get him off the subject of Arthur, he told me of home. He had married two of his daughters off and seemed glad to be rid of them. His brothers had large families, more than the King's house at Cameliard could hold, and lived on their own lands. That left him with Glynis, two young daughters, Gwillim and his two older sons, who took turns soldiering and tending the kingdom of Northgallis. I was still remembered there, he said. Never had the black Celts of our family produced anyone so fair. I nodded toward the blond Alyse, my mother's sister, and her daughter, the fair Elaine. Gwarth smiled. Yes, he said, everyone knew where it came from, and he wouldn't mind at all having another fair maid in Northgallis. I felt obliged to tell him it looked unlikely. He glanced unhappily at Gwillim and agreed.

"King Pellinore seems pleased with the match, though."

"Probably because it means his precious daughter would be next door," I told him. "But I assure you, Gwarth, the queen feels strongly that her daughter will not be forced into a marriage against her will—and the lady Elaine has a strong will."

"Hmmmm. Well, I expect you're right. I can't say Gwill cares at all. Perhaps it's just as well. He won't look at anyone but you, Gwen. He never has."

I blushed. It was absurd. Gwillim was my nephew! I told Gwarth how happy I was to see them both and that King Pellinore could not have brought me a better birthday present.

He laughed aloud. "We're not your present, Gwen. King Pellinore has brought you a rare gift, more precious than any Welsh prince could ever be to you."

Pellinore heard him and rose. "I confess that the High King Arthur has done me a great honor. In return for my services in the last battle, he asked me to name anything I wished, and if it was in his power to give it me, he would." I saw heads turn and nod at this extraordinary generosity. King Pellinore smiled. "I thought of the young lass I keep in my care and told the High King I wished to bring a birthday gift to my ward. I asked him for a mare from his own stables."

I gasped, and everyone stared. Such a gift was unheard of! All of the fine horses Lancelot imported from Gaul, and their colts and fillies, were kept for training or for breeding stock. None had ever left the High King's stables. And mares were prized above all. I stared at Pellinore in amazement.

"Did—did he agree?" I whispered.

Pellinore laughed. "The mare is in the stables now. The High King keeps his promises."

I could barely contain my excitement. If she'd been stabled as soon as Pellinore arrived, she must have been in the barn when Peleth and I returned from our ride! I berated myself for not having gone in to tend the horse myself—I could have seen her then. As it was, I would not be allowed to go out until morning.

"Oh, dearest Pellinore!" I cried, jumping from my seat and running into his arms. "How can I ever thank you enough! What is she like? Her color, her stride, her spirits? Did anyone ride her on the journey home? Where is he, that I may ask?"

King Pellinore laughed and sat me on his lap, just the way my father had been wont to do when I was small. "No one rode her, young lady. She is yours. She's a filly, but two years old, and a dark dappled gray. But she will be as white as the High King's charger one day, you may be sure. She is not fully trained—I leave that to you—but what lessons she has had, she has had from the best. Young Lancelot bred her and trained her himself, and a finer hand with a horse I never hope to see. He hated to part with her and was sure I was exaggerating your skill." He pinched my cheek. "I told him you rode bareback, as he does himself, and flew like the west wind over whatever lay in your path." I blushed violently; I had thought my jumping a secret. "He said to me, 'There's a maid after my own heart' and let me take the mare. You may see her in the morning, Gwen. Happy birthday."

I was beside myself with joy and anticipation. When dinner was over, I kissed Gwarth and Gwillim good night, paid my respects to Queen Alyse, and flew upstairs to my room. Elaine was sullen, whether with jealousy over my great gift or with a headache from her weeping, I knew not, and I cared not. A mare from the High King's stables! It was too wonderful to be true! I said my evening prayers in a hurry. God had not made me a woman that day, after all, but now I hardly cared.

I was up at dawn, dressed quietly in my doeskin leggings, crept out without waking Elaine or the nurses, and raced to the stables.

Stannic was up, and he grinned to see me, not surprised. "This way, my lady. I gave her the corner box. It's the biggest and she can look out over the meadow."

I stopped at the door and held my breath. She was a beauty! Tall, slender, straight legs, long, arched neck, flat croup, tail held high. She was looking out her window when I came up but, hearing my step, swung around to see me. Her face was lovely: broad in the forehead but narrow in the muzzle, with fine, large dark eyes.

"Sweet Mary," I whispered, opening the door a crack and slipping in. She was taller than I was, much taller than the Welsh mountain ponies I had grown up on, but lighter and finer than Peleth. Her coat was a dark dappled gray, with black legs, black mane and tail, and dark muzzle. I spoke to her softly, crooning an old Welsh tune, and held out my hand. She was nervous at first, but then stood calmly and let me approach. When I was near, she lowered her head and put her soft muzzle in my hand. Clearly, she had been brought up with no fear of men, which meant she had been well treated always. I stroked her gently, and she nuzzled me in return.

I slipped a halter on her and led her from the stall. She moved daintily, careful where she put her feet. I guessed she would be surefooted on rough ground. She did not look heavy enough to carry a soldier, but she must at least have carried Lancelot, so I was not afraid to mount her. I refused the bridle Stannic proffered, although it was very fine, with silver worked on the browband. She was only two, and likely tender-mouthed.

"Give me a leg up, Stannic."

"My lady," he protested, "surely you're not going to try her without a bridle. You'll not have control!"

"I have the halter and the rope. I can spin her in a circle if she looks to bolt. Have no fear."

My eagerness made me impatient, and I was ready to climb the fence to mount her, but Stannic helped me against his better judgment.

How can I describe what it felt like to be astride of her? She was light and quick, she felt every shift of my seat, every touch of my leg. She quivered with eagerness, but when I stroked her neck and talked to her, she calmed under my touch. I let her walk around the stableyard and then onto the track that led down the gentle valley toward the sea road. It was a lovely spring morning, with dew on the grass and a cool mist rising. The sun was up, rose pink through the haze, and the hills were alive with birdsong. The filly danced along the track, swinging this way and that, pulling at the rope, wanting her head. I denied it to her, and she did not fight me, but bent her neck gracefully and walked on. She had been handled, I could see, with consummate gentleness; she responded to the lightest touch. When we reached the valley floor, the track widened, and I let her move out a bit. What a fluid, ground-covering canter she had! It was easier to sit than the queen's chair that rocked back and forth on curved braces. She tossed her head and snatched again at the rope, but I held her, and she obeyed. But I felt the power in her hindquarters and the desire to run that coursed through her. I had not intended to run her at all, not the first time, but she was convincing me. Before I could do it, I had to know if she would stop. I sat up and pulled back on the rope, squeezing my leg. She came back to me at once, slowed to a trot, and stopped. But she trembled in frustration.

"Oh, good girl, my beauty, my pretty, my love. For that you shall have your gallop on the beach."

We trotted down the sea road and turned off along a woodland path that ran down to the shore. Suddenly, as the trees thinned out, the filly shied, screamed, and reared. I grabbed her mane to keep from sliding off, she whirled and tried to bolt back the way we had come, but I turned her and made her stand, facing the sea. She must never have seen the sea before! It must be as amazing to her as it was to me the first time I saw it. I stroked her neck, wet with the sweat of fear, and gradually she calmed.

I turned her away, and we rode along the dry shingle, where the sand is firm.

"All right, my lovely one, now let's see what you can do." And I gave her her head. She exploded out from under me so swiftly, I'd have fallen if I hadn't buried my hands in her whipping mane. I clung there, bent over her withers, as the ground flew by and the salt spray stung my cheeks and the west wind brought tears to my eyes. She fairly flew over the ground—I felt nothing but speed, like a spear flying. She raced past the place where Peleth always slowed down, winded, and past the last trail up from the beach. I pulled the rope in vain; when she felt the pressure, she leaned against it, increasing her speed. The trees became blurs, the sea a pounding accompaniment to her hooves. There were treacherous rocks ahead, I knew, sharp, black boulders that protruded from the soft sand like wolf's teeth—The Fangs they were called—and there was no way around them. They were a natural boundary. Fighting my panic so the mare would not sense it, I sang to her again, steadying my gulping breath, and straightened up as much as I could. Whether it was my song or the motion of my body I know not, but at last she slackened her pace, and by the time The Fangs came into view she was cantering easily, tossing her head, enjoying herself.

I brought her to a halt and turned her around. Her nostrils were flared wide, and her sides heaved, but she did not seem tired. She was not even lathered; any other horse I knew would have been dead.

"Well, my pretty one," I said, patting her neck and her rump as we started the walk back, "you are in wonderful condition. You have been loved by someone who loves horses, that is easy to see. I think I must make it a goal of mine to meet someday this knight who raised you and thank him for this gift. Yes, when Elaine goes to Caer Camel, I shall go with her, to thank him. For while you are the High King's gift, it was Lancelot who made you what you are. And I have a name for you now. I will name you Zephyr, after the west wind, for you fly as swiftly as the wind and yet are as gentle as the sea breeze. Someday I shall meet this great Sir Lancelot and thank him for my Zephyr."

7 ♛ MERLIN

Gwillim's visit was the first of many by Welsh princes. We had one or two a month, I believe, come to offer for Elaine's hand. Alyse and Pellinore were proud and happy but they were guided by Elaine's decision, and she always refused her suitors. At first she was barely polite, but as time wore on she, too, was flattered by the attention and grew condescendingly courteous. No one offered for me and in time Elaine passed from gloating into a genuine sorrow for my condition. I did not much mind the absence of suitors; my head was much too full of Zephyr to have room for men.

But Elaine's pity nearly drove me to distraction. "I am ten times the rider she is," I railed at Ailsa when we were alone, "and twice the seamstress! I can do figures in my head and read as well as anyone, and speak better Latin than most! And even though she is beautiful, she is vain about it, as if her beauty were something she had earned herself and not a gift of God! How can she be so cruel to me? In her eyes I am a poor, impoverished orphan—like Cam, the cripple—just because she has grown a bosom and I have not!"

Good Ailsa hugged me and calmed my weeping and told me, in her motherly way, that things would change as the wheel of time went round. The last would become first, she crooned, and the low made high. I frowned and looked at her askance: I never found Giselda's prophecy comforting.

In the month of the Raven near the autumn equinox, almost five years to the day after his victory at Caer Eden, King Arthur wed Guenwyvar of Ifray. There had been much fighting during the summer, but the High King managed to find three weeks of peace in which to marry. Then, with his bride bedded and the elders satisfied, he went back to war. His young Queen was left in Caerleon, protected by his soldiers, with all the people daily watching her waistline to see if the High King had bred his heir in her. Elaine envied her, but I cannot say that I did.

King Arthur's victories continued, and work continued on the new fortress of Caer Camel. One Gaius Marcellus, grandson of Ambrosius' chief engineer, designed it—the fortifications, the groundwork, the buildings, and the open places. He had even given directions for the quarrying of the stone. The fortress was to be the biggest, strongest, and best defended in all the kingdoms, a gathering place for Britons, a warning to Saxons, a symbol to all of the High King's power. And after the bishop of Caerleon had blessed the cornerstone, it was whispered behind doors, Merlin the En-chanter, in a ceremony of his own, had looked into the flames, foreseen a glorious future, and sanctioned its building. After that, Arthur gave the or-ders to proceed.

Merlin was at Caerleon for the High King's wedding and stayed behind when Arthur and his troops rode north. He was the most trusted member of Arthur's household, and the most feared, as well. The King's sister Morgan was promised in marriage to Urien of Rheged, and since fighting in the east near Elmet required the High King's presence, Merlin was left to escort the princess and her train to Rheged for her wedding. They left on a hot day in October and traveled north through Wales.

King Pellinore and Queen Alyse had attended the High King's wed-ding but had not taken Elaine and me, much as we had begged to go. As a guilt gift, perhaps, they agreed to let us accompany them to meet the princess Morgan's train and pay homage to her. Elaine and I were beside ourselves with excitement. Elaine and Queen Alyse were going to ride in a litter, and they thought it only right that I should, too, but I begged and pleaded with good King Pellinore to be allowed to ride my new mare. It was not unknown for ladies, especially when young, to travel on horseback; I was sure the only reason Elaine chose the litter was because she did not have a mount as fine as mine. When she had complained to her father that she had outgrown Welsh ponies he had given her Peleth, but she could barely handle him, old though he was. Pellinore at last gave in and said I could ride, but only if I rode Peleth. With tears of frustration, I begged him to allow me to ride Zephyr. He thought her too young, too flighty, but I con-vinced him by giving him a demonstration. In five months she had learned a lot and would do anything I asked. At the end of my demonstration, he was silent for a while, stroking her neck and looking up at me. At last he nodded.

"Use a saddle, for form's sake," was all he said.

We started out on a brilliant, crisp day, with sixty troopers in our party and twelve pack mules with all the tents, gear, and bridal gifts. I rode be-tween King Pellinore and the litter, where he thought I was safest. In obedi-ence to his wishes, I had on my best tunic of a dark, forest green, with a light-green mantle for warmth. I had woven threads of green and blue into Zephyr's bridle and into her braided mane. I wondered if there would be anyone in the princess' party who had known the filly. If so, I wanted to make sure a good report reached the knight who had trained her.

With the cool weather and the crowd of horses, she was very excited, and harder to sit than I expected. King Pellinore shot me a look from under his bushy brows, but I only smiled in return and quietly sang to the mare. She settled down, as I knew she would, and by midday was perfectly calm and well behaved. On the evening of the third day we reached the meeting of the roads from Caerleon and Glevum. We had been there only an hour when the royal escort came in sight. From our tent, we watched them set up camp, admiring the fine horses and trying to see if we could distinguish any of the royal party. Elaine and I shared a tent with Ailsa, Grannic, Leonora, and Cissa—we were all in a fever, as eager to catch a glimpse of Merlin the Enchanter as of the princess Morgan. But it was many hours before we were called to audience. We changed into our finest gowns and followed King Pellinore and Queen Alyse through the crowd of troopers, courtiers, and guards, to the royal tent. The servants followed, bearing our gifts.

The princess Morgan, daughter of King Uther and Ygraine his Queen, sat on a gilded chair, dressed in a heavy red gown. Her hair was dark brown and decked with a circlet of red gold; around her neck and wrists hung jewels of every color, and on her fingers she wore rings of ruby, pearl, and sapphire. She was only fifteen—she looked twenty. Her eyes were a golden brown that did not suit her coloring; she was not pretty, really, but rather proud and distant. Now she was about to wed a major king, a man with lands wider than Lot's or Pellinore's, but a man old enough to be her father. No doubt her future had been a matter of negotiation among Arthur, Urien, and Queen Ygraine. I wondered if she dreaded going to it. I shuddered involuntarily. It was not fair that happiness in a woman's life should depend so completely upon a man.

Courtiers crowded around her at a respectful distance while the servants laid our gifts at her feet, and King Pellinore performed the introductions. She smiled as Elaine made her curtsy, but at me she only stared and barely nodded. I flushed with embarrassment—it was almost a slight! What had I done?

Among the gifts we had brought, goblets and carved platters, thick warm blankets woven from good Welsh fleece, and ornaments of beaten silver from the mines near Snowdon, were several silken hangings for the new queen's chamber. Alyse and her ladies had sewn them and then we all had stitched decorative patterns in different colors of thread. One of these, of white silk with a mare's head in the center and colts frolicking in fields of green at each corner, caught her attention. She motioned for the servant to hold it up to the light.

"This one is most unusual," she said. "The stitching is very fine and the use of color shows an eye for beauty. I thank you, Queen Alyse, I shall use this for my bridal bed."

Queen Alyse curtsied low.

"Thank you, gracious Princess. But I cannot take credit for the workmanship. That silk was done by my ward, Guinevere of Northgallis."

Princess Morgan turned to stare at me, and her eyes grew cold. The smile left her lips, but her breeding held. "This is fine work indeed, for so young a maid. Thank you, Guinevere. I shall remember it."

Something moved in the darkness behind her stool—I felt eyes on me suddenly, and my flesh crept on my bones. There was a man behind her, come from nowhere it seemed, although I suppose the truth was that I simply had not noticed him before. He was tall and thin, with black hair and beard, skin as ageless as oak bark and much the same color, and black, fathomless eyes that glared at me with intense, unwavering, malignant hatred. I began to tremble violently, trapped like an insect in the web of his gaze; conversation went on around me, it seemed no one noticed. He was wrapped in a black cloak from shoulder to boot and clutched a staff in his left hand. I knew him at once. He was Merlin.

Elaine took my arm and drew me away, as Pellinore and Alyse moved off. I was shaking so hard I could barely walk and tears stung my eyes.

"Gwen! What's wrong? Why are you shaking so?"

"Why does he hate me, Elaine? What have I done?"

"Whatever are you talking about? Who hates you?"

"Merlin."

She gasped. "Merlin! How do you know? What makes you think so?"

"Didn't you see the way he looked at me?"

She stopped and stared at me, looking puzzled and a little frightened.

"Yes, I saw him," she said finally in a halting voice, "but he wasn't looking at you. He was just watching us present the gifts. He looked kindly, I thought."

Now it was my turn to stare. I thought she was teasing me at first, but then I understood her astonishment was genuine. No one, not Pellinore, Alyse, Cissa, or Leonora, had noticed anything unusual. Was it possible I had imagined it? But I knew I had not.

I kept my thoughts to myself and did not tell Ailsa. For Merlin was perhaps the most powerful man in all Britain, and an enchanter, as well. It would not do to have him as an enemy, and my dear, superstitious nurse would die a thousand deaths, yes, and clutch her amulets forever, if I shared my fears with her. I composed myself for sleep that night as usual, but sleep did not come. I lay awake, uneasy and full of fear, until the dark time at moonset. Then I seemed to feel a heaviness come upon my spirit, and I sank into sleep. Almost at once I saw Merlin's face again—not angry this time, but sorrowful. His black eyes bored through me with urgency and feeling, with beseeching, almost, but I knew not for what. I sensed longing, desperation, and then a breath, a cat's-paw touch of deep love. At last, his quest unsatisfied, he seemed to sigh with a sorrow from the depths of the earth. He nodded kindly, as if in benediction, and turned sadly away. As I drifted into forgetfulness, I knew even in my sleep that it was not a dream; I knew that Merlin's power had reached me where I lay, that he had seen something in me that had broken his heart and left him desolate.

In the morning, everything was packed and made ready for departure, but no one could leave until the royal party left first. I was ill with fatigue and fear and would have remained in the tent until all the farewells were said, but the tents were struck early and I had nowhere to hide. Elaine kept near Queen Alyse and Leonora, but I slipped away when no one was looking. It was very busy, with servants and soldiers bustling everywhere, everyone wanting to get an early start. I went to the horse lines and took an apple to Zephyr. She nickered a greeting and daintily took the fruit from my hand. The grooms had already saddled her. I rebraided her mane, crooning to her all the while and keeping well out of sight. But I knew that I could not hide from a magician. Magic was in the air that morning, all about me, the still, awful dread I had known by the spring pool in Northgallis. I was amazed that no one else seemed to notice it. Everyone was bustling about his chores, calling out morning greetings, exchanging bawdy jokes, laughing and grunting, moving and working. Only I, it seemed, was caught in this bright web of stillness, where the very air I breathed was alive with the whisperings of phantoms.

Quite suddenly, he was beside me. I had not heard a footfall of his approach. He was plainly dressed; only the gold and red enamel Dragon brooch at his shoulder gave a clue to his identity. I believe I gasped as I sank to my curtsy.

"My lord Merlin."

He reached out and took my hands, raising me quickly. To my surprise, his flesh was warm and comforting. He did not let go of my hands, but held them in his own and looked at me with kind, deep eyes. I was shaking, and the air around me positively sang with voices, but he stilled them. I saw him do it. He gave his head a quick shake, and the world went quiet.

"Do not be afraid," he said simply.

I could not speak. Neither could I take my eyes from his face.

"Your heart's desire will be granted in six months," he said. "After that, it is with the gods. You cannot change your fate, my dear, and neither can I."

"You—you don't hate me, my lord?"

Something flashed in the eyes then, and the corners of his thin mouth moved. "For his sake, I cannot. Glory and greatness are built on love. What will be, will be. Let it be so."

He dropped my hands then, as pounding filled my ears, and he actually bowed to me before he left. The last thing I heard as the world went dark was a groom calling out in panic, "The lady Guinevere has fainted!"

King Pellinore made me ride home in the litter with Elaine, convinced I was ill. Of course I told Elaine all about it, and her eyes went wide with astonishment that Merlin the Enchanter should single me out to speak to.

"But is that all he said? What does it mean?"

"I have no idea what it means."

"But it was a blessing, wasn't it, and not a curse?"

I went cold inside at the thought. "I don't know, Elaine. Would he have held my hands while he cursed me? Would he have bowed? Why did he come to find me in the midst of the bustle of departure, just to tell me not to be afraid? How could he possibly think I would not be afraid?"

"But you are brave, Gwen. I've seen you—flying through the air with Zephyr. It makes me weak with fear to watch you!"

"Nonsense. I'm not afraid of Zephyr. I think you have to be afraid in order to be brave. And I am truly afraid of Merlin. Do you believe—a pagan enchanter has power over a Christian?" I was reminded of my conversation with Gwillim, long ago. Did he command real powers, or just my thoughts and dreams? If I did not believe he had power over me—but that was the trouble. Christian or not, I did believe it. I knew it.

"Ask Father Martin," Elaine advised. "He will know. He speaks to God."

When we were home, and I had convinced Queen Alyse that I had recovered from my faintness, I sought out Father Martin. He was a robust and comely man of about thirty who enjoyed the company of peasants and low folk as much as that of Pellinore's nobles. He was not a scholar like Iakos, but he was warm and approachable. I found him in his garden, surrounded by a group of dirty, brown-skinned children in ragged clothing. They were listening open-mouthed to the story of Jonah and the Whale. I wondered if any of them were sons of fisher-folk and what would happen when they next went out upon the sea.

Father Martin rose when he saw me and smiled. The children filed out, eyes downcast, and then we heard them running down to the village, hollering and shouting, and Father Martin laughed.

"To have such energy! I would I could be young again. Well, my lady Guinevere, to what do I owe the honor of this visit?"

"I wish to know the answer to a question, Father, and I think only you can answer it."

He paused and led me to a stone bench among the pear trees. "I will certainly answer it if I can, my lady."

"Do pagan enchanters have powers over spirits, or only God?"

I don't know what he was expecting, but it wasn't that. He stared a moment and then almost smiled. "Are you referring to any pagan enchanter in particular, my lady?"

"Yes. To Merlin."

He cleared his throat then, and looked away. "Ahhh. Merlin." He studied the clouds for a while and then turned to me. "May I know what brought this on, my lady? Has something happened that concerns Merlin?"

"Y—yes, Father. I met him. He spoke to me."

"And he frightened you."

"He told me not to be afraid. But he—he did frighten me."

Father Martin took both my hands, as Merlin had done, but the effect was not the same. There was nothing in them. They were human hands.

"You know, Guinevere, that the Lord God is the True God. He loves His children, especially the innocent. He protects you, child, He protects you daily. You have nothing to fear from Merlin while God's Hand is over you."

"Then Merlin has no power? Or is it that God's is stronger?"

Father Martin looked uncomfortable. "There are many kinds of power, child. There is the kind of power the High King wields against his enemies. There is the kind of power the soothsayers and hill witches have over the minds of simple folk. But the kind of power God grants is greater than all of them. It is the power of love."

I did not understand him. "Do you class Merlin with the soothsayers, then? Does he only have power over those who believe in him? Is it so with God, also?"

Father Martin crossed himself quickly, shocked. "Hush, my sweet child, it's blasphemy to say such a thing. That God's holy power could depend on something as frail as the will of a human! No, no, never think it. No matter what you believe, my dear girl, God will love you and protect you. His love is everlasting."

"Forgive me, Father. I did not mean to blaspheme. It's only—I want to know if Merlin has power or not."

Father Martin sighed and struggled with his words. "I do not know the man myself," he said at last. "But I have heard of his many doings. I will not deny that he has power. But they say his power has always been used for the good, for building and making. It is God's power, though even Merlin may not know it."

I wanted to believe him, but I did not. Jesus had never come to me in my sleep the way that Merlin had.

"What, if I may ask, my lady, did Merlin say to you?"

Now it was my turn to look away and feel nervous. "He—he spoke of the future, I think, but it was very unclear. I mean, I didn't understand him. He said what will be, will be. He said glory and greatness are built on love.

But he seemed very sorry about it. It was the way he said it. As if he could see my future and it broke his heart."

Father Martin looked relieved and a little awed. Merlin's words, even secondhand, could strike awe into the heart of a Christian priest.

"He has told you the truth about the power of love," Father Martin said. "It is a thing a wise man knows. And if Merlin the Enchanter is concerned about your future, Lady Guinevere, it must be a mighty future indeed."

I rose. I had learned what I came to learn. Father Martin believed every word out of Merlin's mouth. He was even staring at me with wonder. I wanted to cry.

"Thank you for your time, Father Martin," I managed, gulping. "I must—I must get back. The queen—" I choked on the words and turned away.

He rose hastily. "Whatever happens, my lady, God will protect you. Do not be afraid."

I shook my head as I hurried toward the gate, brushing tears from my eyes.

Poor Father Martin tried again. "Merlin cannot hurt you, now or ever."

I turned as I opened the gate and looked up into his worried face. "Perhaps not. But he will never forgive me, either, for whatever it is I am to do."

In bed that night, I told Elaine everything that had passed. It did not surprise her that Father Martin believed in Merlin's powers. Only a fool would not believe in them, so well known were they. I was the one she found puzzling.

"But what did you expect, Gwen? You never doubted Merlin's power. You felt it yourself, you said so. So why do you think Father Martin has let you down? What does God have to do with Merlin?"

"Can Merlin see the future, Elaine? Truly, do you think he can?"

"Of course. He sees what he wills to see. If he has seen yours, you may be sure it is important somehow." She paused. "If your future is important, it must mean you will be a great lady someday. Perhaps you will follow me to the High King's court. Perhaps you will marry one of the Companions."

"Elaine, you must know by now that is not my ambition."

Elaine smiled slyly. "What about the other thing he said? What is your heart's desire, Gwen? To marry a prince?"

"No, by Mithra. Just to be a woman, like you. The older I get the less I think I ever want to be married."

Elaine was scandalized. "You can't mean you want to be a spinster! And you shouldn't swear by Mithra now that you've been baptized. Gwen, what's the matter with you? Don't you want to be a queen someday and have lands of your own?"

"They won't be lands of my own. They'll be my husband's lands. I'll be the keeper of his house. He won't even discuss what's going on in the world because 'it's not a fit subject for young maids.' Whether I'm happy or not will depend completely upon him, and not at all upon me. I tell you, Elaine, I hate the thought of it."

"Well, you don't have to marry anyone like that. Mother says so. She's let me refuse all the young men, even when Father is so furious, because she says it's only right that both husband and wife should want the same thing. And she'll do the same for you. I'm sure she will."

"Oh, Elaine, do you really think she would? Even though Gwarthgydd and Pellinore might want it differently? Would she really require my consent? I tell you now, I don't think I ever want to go near Caer Camel, or see the King's Companions. Not if Merlin is nearby." And I shivered.

Elaine put her arms around me and hugged me warmly. "You will come with me. I will protect you. You are meant for someone special, that much is clear. One of the Companions, without a doubt, cousin. Perhaps that young knight with the foreign name who trained your horse. Just wait and see. You'll love it at court."

Two weeks later Merlin disappeared. Princess Morgan had married King Urien, the wedding feast had lasted a week, the guests had departed. Merlin stayed on in conference with the aging bridegroom, discussing defense strategy. Lot's queen, Morgause, Morgan's half-sister, stayed on waiting for a fair wind to sail back to the Orkney Isles. While her body had grown thick with childbearing, she was still the most beautiful woman at the wedding and far outshone the bride. With her was a red-headed boy of three, Lot's firstborn son, Gawaine. She had other sons at home in Orkney; one of them, the whispers went, was older than Gawaine, "the dark prince" she had left at home, but I did not believe the talk. Lot, of all people, surely would not allow the Queen to raise her bastard side by side with his own sons. At any rate, on the day Morgause sailed for Orkney, Merlin disappeared. No one could explain it. He was gone, and he left no trace.

People laughed at first and said the King's enchanter was up to his old tricks again, but as time went on faces grew sober. Always before when Merlin disappeared in one place, he reappeared somewhere else; the people always knew the enchanter was there when Arthur wanted him. But this time even Arthur could not find him. The King's troops scoured the wood where he had vanished, visited his cold hilltop cave in south Wales, hunted around Caer Camel and anywhere else they could think of, but Merlin was not there. Winter winds closed the seas, early snows blanketed the land, covering the woodland tracks, and the search parties were called off. Now King Arthur was alone.

News came from Caerleon that the young Queen was with child of the royal heir, and bonfires were lit throughout the land in celebration. King Pellinore held a feast on All Hallow's Eve in honor of the event. Elaine was green with envy, but I told her what a dreary life it would be, married to the High King.

"You'd only be a broodmare to him," I said. "That would be your foremost duty. Bear his children as fast as you could and see that they're all sons. Forget having a companion, he would never be there. Even Alyse only sees Pellinore six months of the year, and he's a homebody compared to the High King. He must always travel about the Kingdom. You would never really know him. There wouldn't be time. You would be miserable." I succeeded only in convincing myself. I never convinced Elaine. She was completely and thoroughly in love with Arthur, and there seemed to be nothing anyone could do about it.

Then, as the first snows fell, the High Queen began to ail. All Caerleon was thrown into confusion. Priests, physicians, witches, and enchanters passed in a steady stream through the young Queen's chamber. Arthur promised gold to any who could stay her bleeding and turned no one away who offered help. King Pellinore went to court to see what he could do, but, as he told us later, there was nothing anyone could do. Neither Mithra, nor Christ, nor Bilis, Eroth, Llyr nor Lluden, nor the Great Goddess of Avalon could prevent the horror that followed. Merlin might have saved the child, it was thought, but Merlin was not there. Arthur was beside himself with grief. And that poor girl, only seventeen and still a bride, died on Arthur's birthday in desperate agony, with the High King weeping at her bedside. When it was over Arthur shut himself away and for three weeks spoke to no one. Finally his officers threatened to beat down his door. Word had reached the Saxons of the King's grief, and they were massing for an attack along the great river Thames, as far west as Amesbury. This news aroused the King, but he came out from his fastness a changed man. Gone was the gaiety and exuberance of youth; this was a man quick to anger and dangerous to cross. The Saxons retreated before his fury as before a wall of flame.

The entire Kingdom of Britain grieved with Arthur, all except Elaine. Elaine alone was serene, at peace again. He was free once more, and she was biding her time. She tired me with her fantasies and her ambition, or perhaps it was the long, dreary winter days and nights within the castle that tired me. When the midwinter thaw finally came, I spent all the daylight hours out riding. It felt so wonderful to be free again! I pitied the High King, if he could not find joy in the freedom of a horse.

One clear, bright January morning I rose early, slipped into my doeskin leggings and a warm cloak, and took Zephyr down to the shore. Her favorite run was along the beach, and afterward she was relaxed and ready for practice jumping fences. Her prowess amazed me; she could fly over any obstacle I put before her with plenty of room to spare, and she seemed to love it. She was eager that morning, tossing her head and snatching playfully at the bit, urging me to hurry. But she came back to my hand the instant I asked her and obediently walked down the track to the sea. It was a fine morning, cold and clear, the last traces of dawn painted pink streaks on the gray sea. I caressed the mare, who trembled in anticipation, and, hooking a fist in her mane, gave her her head. She shot forward, and the shore sped past in a blur. I loosened my hair with my free hand and let it whip in the wind. I felt free of everything then—the Kingdom with its constant wars, Wales with its jealous lords, and castle routine with daily lessons and strictures—all were left behind me at that moment. I was as free as the seabirds, and as wild. The future lay before me, unknown and therefore bright and beckoning. As icy air filled my lungs, I shouted aloud with joy. Zephyr responded by quickening her thundering pace, and we flew up the beach, only slowing when The Fangs came into view. As we turned and trotted back, I hugged the mare in exhilaration.

"Oh, my proud beauty, what happiness you bring me! I shall never part with you, my Zephyr. We shall always ride together!"

She nodded her head exactly as if she understood, and we cantered slowly back the way we had come. I headed her toward a track that left the beach toward the jumping field, when suddenly she started, shying violently, and almost threw me. I grabbed her mane, and only just kept her from whirling and bolting. She was shaking like a leaf in an autumn storm, and though I sang and spoke to her, she did not settle.

The beach was deserted, the sea quiet. I saw no movement anywhere. But the mare was frantic and would not advance. I slid off her back and held her head close to my body. When I wrapped her nostrils in my cloak, she calmed a little, and I knew then it was something she had smelled. The light land breeze still blew at that hour, so I looked inland, up the track, searching the sparse gorse bushes that grew in the sand, toward the line of bare hardwoods that marked the edge of the woods. And I saw something. Underneath our own footprints the sand had been disturbed. It looked like something heavy had been dragged up the track, and something small and white fluttered ahead under the bushes, just short of the trees.

"Come on, my sweet, let's find out what it is." Frightened as she was, the filly followed me up the track, but as we neared the trees she snorted once and screamed. A low moan answered from the bushes, and to my amazement, the filly blew once and was quiet. The mystery was solved for her: it was human, and therefore a friend. I tied her to a sapling and left her standing peacefully while I went to see who lay half concealed and moaning in the sand.

He was a stranger. There was dark blood caked in his bright hair, and his left leg was bent at an unnatural angle. His tunic was torn, but the cloth was fine. I saw no cloak anywhere. His face was blue with cold and pain, and his eyes were closed. I drew off my cloak and covered him. He shivered violently. I laid a hand to his forehead. He was very cold. The light touch seemed to revive him, for his eyes fluttered open and he looked right at me. His eyes were a brilliant green in color, with honey-colored flecks around their dark centers; I found it impossible to look away as he stared at me.

"Forgive me my sins," he mumbled, and then he sank into senselessness.

I ran to the filly, beginning to shiver myself, and jumped on her back. His speech had been in Latin, but his accent was foreign. I was sure he was not Welsh, perhaps not even British. He lay on the sand by the Irish Sea. My heart pounded in time with the filly's galloping strides as we raced back to the castle. Was he one of the Irish devils all good Welsh children had been taught to fear?

I roused the castle with the news, and King Pellinore sent troops with a litter down to fetch the stranger, but he would not let me show them the way. He ordered the grooms to care for Zephyr, and he roused Leonora, who took one look at me and threw me into a hot bath. Queen Alyse scolded me for parting with my cloak and made me go back to bed with hot bricks at my feet. I was furious with frustration, for I felt perfectly fine, only cold, and I wanted news of the stranger.

Thank goodness Elaine was adept at eavesdropping, for she tripped in and out of my room all day with whatever news she picked up. When they found the stranger he was delirious and half dead with cold. He was not expected to live, so they did not put him in the dungeon, but in a guest chamber near the guard tower. They bathed him and placed hot bricks wrapped in herb-soaked towels around his body. King Pellinore's physician set his leg and bandaged his head, and Father Martin gave him the last rites, for it was clear he was a Christian. In his delirium he called upon the Christian God and his angels to save him. But most of the time he rambled in a tongue no one could understand.

By nightfall he was hot with fever and still delirious. An Irish kitchen slave, captured in a thwarted raid upon our shores eight years before, was brought into the room to see if he could understand the stranger's delirious speech. The man broke into tears at hearing once more the lilting Gaelic of his homeland.

"And so," Elaine announced, perched on my coverlet, "he is Irish, just as you thought, Gwen. If he lives he will be a prisoner, and if he is a lord of some kind, a hostage, which could bring Father some Irish gold. They say he is young, not over twenty. What does he look like?"

I saw again the white, drawn face with the matted gold hair and the mesmerizing eyes. "He's the handsomest man I've ever seen."

Elaine giggled. "You'd better not fall in love with an Irish prince, Gwen. I don't think Mother would let you go to Ireland for all the gold in Rome. She saw his clothes, you know, and said they were of good quality. So he might be someone important. Isn't it exciting?"

"But how did he come to be lying on our beach?"

"I don't know yet. But I'll know before dinner is over."

I was not allowed up for dinner, but Ailsa brought me a meal in bed and fixed me a hot posset. I did not protest this care, for my throat was beginning to feel raw, and I knew I would be abed for two days with the usual winter chills. But Elaine was as good as her word and had all the news by bedtime.

"There was a raid last night," she confided, eyes shining. "The thaw has opened the seas, and Father has had the beach patrolled for the last five days. Last night a ship was sighted, and four boatloads of ruffians came ashore, led by a young hothead, or so the soldiers say. They didn't get far, and most of them escaped back to their ship, but the fighting was fierce, and many were wounded. The soldiers rounded them up and they're in the dungeon now, but I guess they missed this one. I wonder if he's the leader."

"From your description of the raid, he can't be much of a leader."

Elaine laughed. "Well, he's no Arthur. But the Irish aren't thinking fighters. They never have been. They fight from passion. Show them cold steel, and they turn and flee."

I grinned at her. "If he lives, I'll be sure to let our stranger know your good opinion of him."

"I don't care what he thinks of me," she retorted. "He will always be an Irishman, and I'm going to be a British queen."

At least, I thought later, as I drew the covers around me and fell towards sleep, she didn't say "Queen of Britain."

8 ♛ FION

I lay abed a week with fever and chills. I was nursed and cosseted, but given no news and forbidden to ask questions. An air of secrecy seemed to envelop the castle. Elaine was with me often, but turned the conversation from any topic of interest except King Arthur and his doings. He was doing much, it seemed, even in the winter snows. Tales of courageous deeds and of murderous rages were told and retold; he was no longer referred to as a youth. He was nineteen now and a man. Wherever he raised Excalibur in the defense of Britain he was victorious. Ten major battles and thousands of skirmishes lay behind him; he had never received so much as a scratch from a Saxon weapon. Yet in the midst of his glory he grieved for his lost wife, his lost child, and his lost friend, the great enchanter. His tread was heavier; his smiles were rarer. He got on with the business of defeating his enemies and unifying the kingdoms with a cold determination that made his own men afraid of him.

Of the Irish stranger, Elaine would say nothing except that he still lived. But her eyes sparkled, and she winked at me when Ailsa's or Grannic's back was turned. Finally my strength returned, and I grew weary of convalescence. I insisted on getting up to sit by the fire or to take short walks on Ailsa's arm. When after two weeks I was fully recovered, the wild winter weather set in, and we were snowbound. I couldn't even get out to visit Zephyr. I had to spend my days with the rest of the women in the weaving room, spinning, weaving, sewing, talking. We joined the men at meals in the dining hall, but otherwise we were cloistered together. It was the dreadful winter routine. People got fractious without exercise in the sun, and personalities began to rub one another into irritation. All this I knew and expected, but this winter was better than most. The Queen's ladies were often in buoyant spirits, teasing each other and laughing, singing new songs, even weaving new patterns—and all because of our stranger.

His name was Fion. He was, it seemed, quite a catch. He was certainly an Irish prince, and if the kitchen slave who served as translator was to be believed, he was *the* Prince of Ireland, son of Gilomar the King. He had lived through a three-day fever, survived two leechings and the setting of his leg, and was fast recovering from a chest cold. He ate like a young wolf and sang like a bard. He had already picked up enough Welsh to carry on a conversation, and he flirted with the ladies, even Queen Alyse, from dawn until dusk.

He showed no fear and bore no grudge against his captors. He was a hostage, and he knew it. But he appeared to be in no hurry to return to his native land. As long as there was a woman in his room, he spouted poetry, sang songs, teased, admired, cajoled, and flirted. He had captivated every woman in the palace, from queen to cook, and although he was rapidly recovering his health, there was no talk of moving him into the dungeon with his fellows. The queen's ladies waited upon him themselves. King Pellinore seemed glad they had the diversion; everyone was in a better temper.

"Saints be praised," Cissa said as she sat spinning, "if the rascal didn't pinch me again this morning! And me old enough to be his mother!"

"He's a handsome rascal, to be sure," Leonora added. "And an amorous young devil. Do they breed them so in Ireland on purpose, to conquer our hearts?"

Queen Alyse laughed. "If he is on a mission to subdue Wales by winning its women, he is very likely to succeed. I have seen the way he looks at my daughter when he thinks I do not observe him."

Elaine blushed and I grinned. So this was what she had been hiding from me! She had an admirer, and this one, it seemed, she did not object to.

"Mother, please," Elaine protested. "He's a hooligan. A foreigner."

"Well, my dear," Alyse said smoothly as she bent over her stitching, "Welsh princesses have married foreigners before now. To be Queen of Ireland would be a great honor, would it not?"

I glanced quickly at Elaine. It was written on her face as clearly as the writing on any scroll that she wished only to be Queen of Britain.

"Mother!" Elaine cried. "I am British! I will never leave my homeland! I would rather be a British spinster than an Irish queen!"

All the ladies laughed and nodded approvingly, and I saw it had just been a leg-pull. Alyse had been teasing—indeed, I thought, she would be the last one to want to send her daughter across the sea where she might never see her again.

"Such poetry!" Cissa exclaimed. "And such good Latin he speaks. He's an educated man, you may be sure of it. This morning when I brought him his willow tea, he was on about the angel again."

"The Angel from Heaven who feeds his soul?" Leonora asked. "He is on about her day and night. You would think a man lying half frozen on a winter beach would see devils and monsters, not angels. He has a vivid imagination."

"What is this about angels?" I asked. "I have not heard this story before. Is it an Irish tale?"

"No, my lady. The young man had a dream as he lay upon the shore. He claims he saw an Angel of God, a vision of loveliness with hair of white fire, who touched him just as life was about to expire and brought him back from the jaws of death." She smiled benevolently as my heart began to sink. "He claims he saw a halo of light around her head, the stars of Heaven in her eyes, and the joy of everlasting life in her smile. Oh, he has a way with words, that one. He had Cissa and me believing him, he did."

Elaine looked at me suddenly and made a face. "He's probably talking about Gwen. He's just dressing it up. After all, she saved him."

"Yes, and in addition to all our thanks, Prince Fion would like to thank you, Guinevere, when you have regained your strength," Alyse said. "But I warn you, he thinks we are playing upon his credulity. He does not believe a child could save his life. And he certainly does not believe any king or queen in their right minds would allow a ward of such tender years to venture forth alone on a frosty winter morning along a beach where raiders had been slain the night before."

It was meant as a rebuke, so I bowed my head and said nothing, but I resented it. How was I to know there had been a raid? They told us nothing, because we were young maids. If the weather had been warm, Elaine and I would have sneaked up to the tower wall and learned of the news ourselves, but I did not see how I was to be held responsible for my ignorance as things were. One thing was clear—gone was my freedom with Zephyr.

When Elaine and I went up to our room to change for dinner, we walked in silence. I was hurt that Queen Alyse had referred to me as a child, and here I was only three months short of fourteen. It was the old wound again, and sore still from constant bruising. It was not until we were in our chamber and half undressed that Elaine spoke to me.

"Gwen, if you take him from me, I will never forgive you."

I simply stared at her. "What on earth are you talking about?"

"Mother will take you to see Fion, and once he looks at you he will never again look at me."

"Oh, please be sensible, Elaine. Do not start this again. You are Pellinore's daughter. You're a woman, and I'm a child. Your own mother said so."

Elaine was smiling, but her eyes were unhappy. "Mother hasn't seen you in your undergarments recently." She came up to me; she was a full head shorter. "Your shape is changing. Didn't you even know it?"

She led me to the polished bronze we kept by the window, and I looked at my reflection in some astonishment. I had not known it. I had not felt it. But there it was. My breasts were swelling, and my waist looked smaller because my hips, always as narrow as a boy's, were widening ever so slightly. At last I looked like a young girl on the verge of womanhood, the way Elaine had looked at ten.

"Elaine!" I cried, and hugged her, as the tears streamed down my cheeks. "Oh, Elaine, perhaps old Merlin was right, God rest his soul. Perhaps I shall be a woman at last!"

Elaine did not return my embrace.

"You will be too beautiful to bear when it happens," she said slowly. "I know already what will happen. Every man who looks at you will love you."

"Nonsense," I said, taking her hand. "You underestimate youself. You are the king's daughter. I am an orphan. Anyway, I don't want Fion. You don't, either, if it comes to that. Why should it matter what he thinks?"

Elaine would not look at me. "I'm not talking just about Fion."

But I did not understand her. "Come, I will guarantee you that after I have met him, his admiration for you will be undiminished. Shall we place a wager on it?"

"I am not such a fool as that."

Her good humor had vanished, but mine simply grew and expanded like a giant bubble, filling all the space between us and gradually, as it enveloped her, she acquiesced to its power and joined me, at least outwardly, in my happiness.

I did not forget Merlin the Enchanter in my prayers that night. Whether he was alive or dead, I prayed to God to be merciful to him, to save his soul, for what he had foretold was coming to pass, and in three swift months I should have my heart's desire.

"Come, Guinevere, and bring the basket of new bread." Obediently I fell into the train of waiting women burdened with clean linens, fine silks, and bowls of dried fruit and nuts, who followed Queen Alyse up the staircase to the prisoner's chambers.

The guard at the door smiled and shook his head when he saw us and, bowing to Queen Alyse, let us pass.

The chamber was large, with a narrow window facing the sea, and a log fire burning merrily in the grate. Fion sat on the window seat, bathed and dressed in a fine linen shirt, loose leather leggings, and wrapped in a warm, russet cloak. His splinted leg he held straight before him, and as we entered he rose, leaning on a stout staff.

"Welcome, my fair ladies, my morning nymphs." He spoke Welsh with a charming lilt to his voice and put a softness to the rough word-sounds that were foreign, and yet pleasing, to our ears. He was tall and handsome, standing there in his dark cloak with his bright hair falling across his brilliant eyes. He made me want to smile, and my heart beat faster. I pulled the hood of my cloak around my face and turned away with the others to place my basket upon the table. Queen Alyse was greeting him formally, as her husband's prisoner, but she used the tone of voice she might have used for a son. One by one the waiting women curtsied to him and left, until only Leonora and I remained. Queen Alyse signaled me to come forward, and as I rose from my curtsy my hood fell back, and I looked up into his eyes.

He gasped and fell back on the window seat, wincing with pain.

"Dear Lord in Heaven!" he cried in Latin. "Angel of God! 'Tis thee in the flesh! O Lord, have mercy upon my soul!" And he crossed himself reverently.

"My dear prince Fion," Alyse began smoothly, "may I present my ward, my sister's daughter Guinevere of Northgallis. Guinevere, Prince Fion, son of Gilomar of Ireland."

I smiled at him and extended my hand. He took it between both of his and gazed into my face. Finally, as the silence began to be awkward, he spoke in Welsh. "You are real, my lady? You are flesh and blood, as I am? May the blessed saints be praised! An Angel of God and real to the touch." He lifted my hand to his lips, and from the corner of my eye I saw the queen's eyebrows rise.

"It was Guinevere," she said, "who found you on the beach and sent my husband's troops to find you. It is she you must thank for your life."

Fion turned to her in amazement. "My beautiful Alyse, I thought you said a child had found me." And his brilliant eyes traveled from my face slowly down my gown and back up again, while I turned scarlet, and he held my hand firmly in his own.

Queen Alyse smiled. "She is at an age when every day makes a difference in a maid. It seems I have not been paying close enough attention."

She turned away, and I hastily withdrew my hand and followed, but at the door she stopped.

"Leonora," she said, "stay with the lady Guinevere awhile. I am sure our foreign prince would like to ease his conscience and thank her for the gift of life. Come to me in an hour." And she left us there.

I was dumbfounded. Leonora, with a secret smile, settled herself before the fire and began stitching a silk shirt, no doubt for Fion. I whirled around. The Irishman had risen, clutching his staff, and held out his hand to me. It was all too, too clear. He was not good enough for Elaine, of course. The mother's ambition lagged not far behind the daughter's. But he was perfect for me. She had waited until I had my health and color back before she brought me to him, for *his* sake, not for mine. By leaving us alone with only Leonora for chaperone, she was giving her consent to his courtship as clearly as if she had spoken it aloud. Alyse was no fool. It would suit her purposes very well to see me married and settled in Ireland. Pellinore would have friends across the Irish Sea, and they could stop worrying that I would somehow cast a shadow across Elaine's future.

Poor Fion seemed unaware of all that had passed. He simply stared at me with his glorious eyes and blessed aloud the luck that had brought him to Wales. I walked demurely to settle on the other side of the fire and took up some embroidery.

"We are pleased to see you looking so well, Prince Fion," I said, in just the tone Alyse had used. "Our clean Welsh air seems to do you good."

He hobbled over to the hearth and stood with his back to the fire, looking from one of us to the other.

"The air here is very fine indeed, my lady. And I have been nursed by the loveliest gentlewomen in all Britain, I am sure. How could I not return swiftly to health under such care?" His tone was very cool. I glanced up. His face, before so expressive, was masked like a courtier's, and he nodded gravely to me. "I would know, if my lady would not think it impertinent of a stranger, and a hostage one at that, where Northgallis is? And what fortunate king names you as his daughter?"

I put down my needlework and looked up at him. "Sir, I am an orphan. My mother died at my birth. My father was King Leodegrance of Northgallis, who sent me here to live with my kin before he died. Northgallis lies a day's hard ride eastward, a small kingdom in North Wales."

He smiled gently. "My sympathies for such misfortune. And I? Do you wish to know what manner of hooligan, as I think you Welsh call it, you have in your midst?"

I smiled back. "If you are a hooligan, my lord, at least you are an educated one, a Christian one, and at the moment, a tamed one."

He grinned, and his face lit. Leonora raised an eyebrow.

"Indeed," he replied. "Tamed and caged. And completely at your service, Guinevere of Northgallis." He bowed deeply and made it look graceful, although it was obviously difficult with his splinted leg. "If my good Leonora will permit me to sit at her side?" He made an obeisance to Leonora, who blushed and hastily made room for him on the bench.

"You don't fool me, my young lord. You sit here not for my company, but so you may better see young Guinevere."

He laughed and kissed her cheek quickly. "And could you blame me now? Is there a lass in all the Northern Isles to match her? Would she not grace any king's hall?"

I bowed my head as he jabbered on and picked up my stitching. But I noted that his position on the bench enabled him to stretch his injured leg out straight upon it, and this seemed to afford him some relief. It had not occurred to me before, but he must have been all the time in some pain. I decided to be direct.

"And now, Fion, son of Gilomar. What manner of man are you? Did I do my foster father a disservice by bringing you into our midst? You came to raid us—are you now a spy?"

He looked up swiftly and with new interest. "I have been here three weeks. You are the first person to ask me a serious question." He paused. "My father calls himself King of Ireland. But if you know aught of Ireland you know we have ten or twenty such kings with ten or twenty such claims. We are a proud race and like not to bend the knee. Thus we waste our strength in petty quarrels and cannot unite. The rest of the known world thinks of us only as pirates." He paused, and I struggled to keep the truth of his statement from showing on my face. "I am Gilomar's youngest son, and the last living. All my brothers were hotheads, like my father, who threw themselves at the first foe they could find. When my father was my age, and the great Ambrosius lay dying, Merlinus came to Ireland to find the standing stones to bedeck his grave. He was protected by a small force led by Uther Pendragon. My father had five hundred men at his back, but it took Uther only three hours to repel his attack and send him fleeing. You have not heard this story? It is true. I tell it to illustrate the great difference between you British and we Irish. My father has not changed. My brothers were just like him. I am not. When my father insisted that I show my mettle and lead a raid upon your shores, I resolved to do it for one reason only. I wanted to see Britain. I want to meet this son of Uther's who knows how to rule men. Whether I go as a hostage or as a free man, I wish to see Arthur Pendragon and judge him for myself." He was looking into the fire as he spoke, and the passion of his feeling gave strength to his face. "If he is a true man, I will pledge my allegiance to him. And then perhaps in time my Ireland may become part of the civilized world."

In the silence the snapping of the burning logs was the only sound. I was moved. He had dealt straight with me and had spoken to me as if I were his peer. "I am sure you will get your wish, my lord."

He slowly came out of his deep thoughts and smiled again. "That's as may be. Being a hostage can be chancy. You must stay on the good side of your host and not wear out your hospitality. Pray let me recite you a poem from one of our famous bards."

He regaled us for a long time. He had a lovely speaking voice and an accurate memory. Leonora warmed willow bark tea for us at the hearth, and we all partook of the fruit we had brought him. At length he touched Leonora's arm.

"Your hour is up, good Leonora, and your duty done. Take the queen's ward away and the light out of my life."

Leonora did not know what to say. "Good sir, I beg your pardon. We may stay as long as we will, I am sure, unless we tire you."

"Heard you not the queen's orders? They struck fire in my young princess. I have no wish to force myself upon you longer than I must. You are free to go."

Leonora turned to me beseechingly.

"Fion." I rose. "It is true I was angry. But I am no longer. Time passes quickly with you, and I was pleased. If this is to be daily repeated—" I glanced at Leonora, who nodded, "—then I pray you will not dread it on my account, for I assure you that I am content to be here. That is—" I fumbled suddenly and looked away from him, "—that is, if you understand."

"I understand, Guinevere." His voice was very gentle as he slipped into Latin. "Thou art not for me."

I looked up at him gratefully and was surprised to catch him gazing at me with longing. To cover, he added hastily, "Please, my lady, if there are any books in the place, bring them that I may read aloud to you."

"I'll bring them and read them aloud to you, Prince Fion."

He stared in amazement. "What! You know your letters? Can you write, as well?" He came close to me then, his back to Leonora and grasped my hands. "For whom are you being groomed?" he demanded softly.

My bewilderment must have shown, for he released me at once and stepped back.

"Queen Alyse believes all young ladies of breeding should know reading and writing," Leonora stated, bundling up her needlework. "The lady Elaine and Guinevere have studied with a Greek scholar right along with Pellinore's sons. Someday they will make good wives to the High King's Companions, if God wills."

Fion looked thoughtful. "I see," he said. "Perhaps."

He kissed my hand before we left and begged me to give his love, his undying devotion, and his limitless admiration to the lady Elaine.

"Be sure you bring her tomorrow," he whispered. "The applecart must not be upset."

It occurred to me, as I followed Leonora down the hall, that in three weeks he had learned a great deal more about us than we had learned about him.

I went daily to see him at the queen's direction, and as often as she could manage it, Elaine accompanied me. She was determined to come every day, but Alyse preferred that the prince spend as much time alone with me as propriety would allow. I did not mind, for Fion and I were friends, and if Leonora chose to take our conversations as flirting and report to the queen that everything was progressing nicely, no harm was done. But Elaine could hardly bear it and was always cross when she was kept from him. She dared not face her mother with her displeasure, so instead she grew angry and sullen with me. At bedtime, when we used to share our thoughts and hopes and secrets, she either berated me for my brazen attempts to attach Fion or refused to speak to me altogether.

"Who do you think you are?" she would snap as Ailsa brushed out my hair. "What right have you to take up all his time? He must be sick to death of all your pestering!"

"Elaine, you know perfectly well it is your own mother who commands it—"

"Fah! Don't give me that! You're disobedient enough whenever it suits you! Who went riding on the beach the morning after the raid, against orders? Who—"

"How was I to know there had been a raid on the beach? No one—"

"You're a guest in this house, Gwen, don't forget it! You can tell her no, you can feign illness, you can insult Fion, you can do a thousand things to prevent it!"

In the end, I had to apologize for my forwardness, for there was no winning an argument with Elaine. But apologies did little to improve her temper. The only time she was happy was when she went to see Fion.

Usually when Elaine was with us, Fion asked for the Story of Arthur, because she told it with such feeling. This was not a tale they told in Ireland, I suppose for obvious reasons, although they tell it now. He got the tale by heart, then retold it to us one day, with some embellishments of his own. I thought it well done, but Elaine was shocked.

"But, Fion, it is a true tale. The bits you have added are make-believe, of course, and you mustn't do it. The tale is true."

Fion looked amused. "Indeed? Dragons flying over Tintagel, King Uther changed by magic arts into the very Duke Gorlois? The prince hidden in the Enchanted Isles?" Elaine nodded, and he turned to me. "Do you believe this, Guinevere?"

It was awkward, for I had not expressed doubts about Arthur to Elaine for a long time, and I did not wish to arouse her temper, but I told Fion the truth. "It is a manner of speaking, my lord. I believe it was Merlin's plan and that he disguised King Uther and the disguise worked. I believe he protected Prince Arthur throughout his youth, and no one knows where, so one tale will do as well as another."

Fion nodded. "And that while Merlin may be a wise man, he is not—"

"Sir, make no mistake about Merlin." I met his eyes squarely. "He is an enchanter of the first order. He has power. Believe the tales you hear of Prince Merlin."

Fion's eyes widened. "*You* believe, my lady?"

Elaine jumped to my defense. "She knows it for a fact. Prince Merlin singled her out to speak to."

Fion looked thoughtful. "Did he indeed? And what did he say, if I am permitted to ask?"

"Why, nothing much," I replied, suddenly flustered because he was so intent. "He spoke about the future, but he didn't say anything specific. He told me not to be afraid."

"And right after that he disappeared," Elaine continued, "and no one has seen him since. Not even the High King. And although King Arthur has needed him desperately, he has not returned. Why, even the Saxons know and have attacked all winter, thinking King Arthur vulnerable without him, but—"

But Fion was hardly listening. He leaned upon his staff and stared thoughtfully into the fire. Elaine ended with the most recent account of Arthur's victory and of his decisive revenge. She spoke of him proudly, as if he were already her husband. I blushed for her boldness, and I thought Fion noticed it, too. He turned to her.

"And what does this prove, my pretty Elaine? Either that Merlin's magic is working still, or that he is a very wise man."

She misunderstood and tossed her head impatiently. "It proves King Arthur does not need a magician at his back to win battles or hold power."

"Precisely," Fion agreed, smiling benevolently. "He is a man now. And would the world ever have known that, had not Merlin disappeared?"

Elaine looked puzzled. Fion turned to me. "What say you, Guinevere?"

"It is true. Whether it is magic or wisdom, I know not, but I believe that Merlin's disappearance, at least in this respect, has done the Kingdom good."

"This confirms me in my desire to meet the High King. Tell me, how old is he?"

"Nineteen last Christmas Eve," Elaine supplied. Fion looked shocked.

"Nineteen! I am twenty myself!" He laughed then, at himself, and shook his head. "He has led a Kingdom for six years already, and what have I done? Studied poetry and music until my father threatened to disown me, and got myself shipwrecked upon Arthur's coast."

"Pellinore's coast," Elaine corrected. Again Fion looked surprised.

"And is not Pellinore Arthur's servant? Is this Britain or Wales? You surprise me, my lady. I thought Britain was a Kingdom and a civilized land."

Elaine squirmed, aware she had erred, but not caring to demote her father.

"It is both," I replied. "This is Wales, part of Britain. These are Pellinore's ancestral lands, but he holds them for Arthur. You may ask him yourself."

Fion smiled and bowed to me. "You are a born diplomat, my lady. I knew I was in a civilized land. I must meet your King."

Elaine glanced at Leonora, who was fast asleep and snoring gently, lulled by the heat of the fire. "You may as soon as you are ransomed, whenever that will be," she said softly, tilting her head and looking coyly up at him. "But perhaps there is a quicker way."

Fion grinned. "I'm much too well bred to escape."

I giggled, but Elaine ignored me. "Offer for the hand of a maiden. If she is highborn, Pellinore must free you to avoid dishonor, and he must have the High King's consent, seeing who you are, I think."

Fion stood quite still, looking at neither of us. I glared at Elaine. How bold! How foolishly direct! It was clear she referred to herself, although she did not want him for a husband. And I knew from the careful way he guarded his expression that he was thinking of me, not of her. Merlin's words came back to me: "What will be, will be." Would it be so bad to have this handsome prince for a husband, even if it were in Ireland? He was amusing, educated, and he spoke to me about important matters, and he valued the things I valued. I could do much worse very easily. Perhaps this was my future. I did not mind. But I knew, as Fion turned toward me with a grave tenderness on his face and desire in his luminous eyes, that I did not love him.

"Perhaps," Fion said softly, "you have hit upon the solution, Lady Elaine."

Elaine flushed angrily, watching his face. Her ruse had backfired; against her will she had played into her mother's hands. A knock came at the door, and Cissa stuck her head in.

"Lady Elaine, the queen your mother requires your presence in the weaving room."

"Leave me, Cissa!" Elaine retorted. "I am not at leisure!"

"Nonsense, you know very well I'd never take such a message to your mother. You're doing naught but flirting with Prince Fion, and that can certainly wait until later. Come, my lady, she dislikes to be kept waiting."

Elaine shrugged gracelessly. Her manners always left her when she was out of temper. She stalked past Cissa, who leaned toward me with a sly wink and whispered, "The queen's orders, my lady, to stay with the prince awhile. No need to wake up Leonora." She closed the door firmly behind her.

I studied the floor tiles carefully, my heart pounding fearfully as Fion stepped close to me. He placed his hand on my waist and drew me closer. "Guinevere, look at me." Obediently I raised my face to him, and he kissed me. Then he sighed most dolefully and backed away.

"Fion, I cannot marry you—"

"I know."

I was about to finish "because I am not yet a woman" but stopped in midbreath, astonished.

·He smiled a thin, bitter smile. "I would fall to one knee if I were able, Guinevere, and beg your forgiveness for my forwardness. But, you see, I love you. I thought if I did not kiss you, I would perish of the desire." He motioned me to sit, and I collapsed gratefully into the chair. My knees were jelly. Leonora was still asleep.

"I am not a fool," he said after a long silence. "I can see your future plain enough, even if you cannot. Queen Alyse sees it, too, you know. That's why she throws you to me every day, hoping my hothead heritage will overcome my civilized veneer, and I will take you, willingly or not—"

"No!" I gasped. "She would not!"

"And then," he continued, "you would be forced to come to Ireland. And you are mistaken about the queen. She would. Do you think she would entrust her precious daughter to a chaperone who sleeps? Whenever Elaine is alone with me, there are three of them, at least."

I buried my face in my hands. "What are you talking about, Fion? You sound like Merlin, so sure and so garbled. What do you see for me? Why should they fear me so?"

"Ah. Merlin. It takes no magician's eyes to see your promise, Guinevere." He took my hand and raised me, walking me to the door. "You will come to fame and glory, as surely as the stars wheel about the heavens. In two years' time—well, I only hope I shall see it." He kissed my hand and pressed it to his cheek. "Come again tomorrow. Can you sing? Let me teach you a song. And now leave me here with Leonora and let me spin her a yarn when she awakes."

I left him, but so troubled that I slept not at all that night, and felt ill the next day. And although my illness kept me from him, Elaine did not speak to me for almost a week. Finally I tired of her sulks and faced her. "Elaine, for heaven's sake, try to remember who you are. This behavior becomes a scullery drudge better than Pellinore's daughter."

"How dare you speak to me so!" she retorted. "You forget yourself! Your father was naught but a petty lord, a black Celt whose forefathers were hill men!"

"How dare you insult my father! He was wise and brave and kindhearted, and besides, there's not a Celt in Wales, including Pellinore, who is not descended from the Ancients, and you are a pin-headed hussy to think otherwise!"

Elaine screamed in fury and stamped her foot. "Stop this instant! I forbid you to speak to me ever again! I hate you, Gwen! I wish—I wish—Oh! How I wish you were ugly!" She burst into tears and threw herself upon the bed. I stood silent, stunned into speechlessness by her unexpected words.

"But, Elaine," I ventured lamely, "this is foolishness. I do not want Fion. And he does not want me. Why do you fear me so?"

"He does! He does!" She sobbed into her pillows. "It's plain as day—if you take him from me, I will kill you—I will have you turned out—sent back to your black brothers—I will—" She blubbered on unintelligibly and her distress confused me. Fighting anger, I stood looking down at her shaking body.

"Do you want him? Truly? To marry? Come, Elaine, control yourself just for the smallest second. Tell me your heart. Is Queen of Ireland your ambition?"

But she did not answer and shrugged away my hand. She did not want him. All she wanted was his undivided admiration. Her weeping was hideous, and she did not strive to control it. Grannic hurried in, clucking and fussing, with Ailsa behind her.

"Oh, Lady Guinevere, what have you done to distress her so? Oh, dear, the poor child! Come, Ailsa, help me with her. Oh, dear!"

"Poor child indeed." I snorted in contempt. "She loves weeping better than sense, that's all."

"Guinevere!"

"I will not take insults from her any longer!"

"The lady Elaine would not insult you," Grannic protested, stroking Elaine's hair with tenderness.

"Of course not," I said bitterly. "Within the hour she will have you all believing it was *I* who insulted *her*. I don't care. Elaine, you are an ass."

"Guinevere!" they shrieked, as Elaine howled in rage, but I had already closed the door behind me.

Eventually we were made to apologize to one another, and at length we were allowed to return to Fion, but he must have guessed the trouble, for he never spoke personally to me again. When he discovered I could sing, he was delighted and taught me songs and ballads, sang with me, or just sat by the window, looking out at the Irish Sea and listening as I sang to him. And I sang to him often, to spite Elaine, who had not the voice for it.

So winter passed, and the spring rains came and washed the woods of snow. Messengers arrived from Ireland demanding ransom for the prince, and negotiations took place, week upon week, while the sun warmed the earth into bud and green grass sprang from the mud. Zephyr and I went out daily, but the beach was forbidden us now. Queen Alyse, thinking Fion's courtship progressed nicely, was graciousness itself toward me. She reminded me of a cat preening. Elaine could be no more than civil, but she was pleased that he no longer singled me out for his admiration.

Of the High King we heard only that he still grieved for his lost queen and that he still grieved for Merlin. The anguish of his grief had settled into a kind of grim despair, which worried his Companions. But his judgment of men, his justice, and his prowess as a warrior never faltered. The building on Caer Camel was nearly finished, and he planned to take possession of the fortress by midsummer. But the Saxons would not give him rest. Every time a leader fell, a younger, more eager, more bloodthirsty one rose to take his place, and the attacks continued.

A royal messenger arrived near the end of April. There were Angles and Saxons in the Caledonian Forest. Lot was marching to hem them in from the north; King Arthur was riding north and would pass through Wales in two days. Pellinore was summoned to gather troops and join him.

Negotiations for the return of Fion were nearly completed. It was time, Alyse said, he made his move.

We feasted the royal courier that night at the round table, and Elaine and I were allowed to stay and listen as the men talked about the wars. King Pellinore seemed delighted to be escaping the confines of the castle and taking to horse. He spoke eagerly of the upcoming action, and also of the Irish gold he expected to help finance the expedition. This was the first the courier had heard of an Irish prisoner, and he listened attentively as Pellinore told the story of his capture and convalescence. Of course Pellinore left women out of the story and, in so doing, missed most of what had actually happened. Elaine and I kept our faces straight, but her eyes were bright with merriment.

At the end of the story, the king's chamberlain approached and announced that the hostage, Prince Fion, begged audience of the king in the presence of the royal messenger. Pellinore was surprised and looked over at Alyse for advice. She nodded complacently, and he shrugged.

"Very well. Bring him. Let's see what he wants."

Fion entered in his best clothes. There was the fine, white blouse of Irish linen Elaine and I had repaired for him, new leggings of soft leather, and a dark-green mantle of good Welsh wool. He walked without a splint now, and the leg had knit straight, although it pained him to wear a boot on it for long.

He bowed low before King Pellinore, and then before the ladies, and last before the royal courier.

"Good King Pellinore, I have been a prisoner and hostage in your home for three months now, and I have been treated like an honored guest. Such hospitality is amazing to one such as I, bred in a less sophisticated land, especially as I know well I have done nothing to deserve it. I feel I must do something for you, my lord, besides allow my relations to send you gold." He paused, to judge how it was going. King Pellinore seemed pleased and the courier stunned. Queen Alyse waited expectantly.

"There is not much that is in my power to do, I admit. But I am young, I am unwed, and promised to no woman. I am my father's only heir. It would please me, and I hope do you honor, to make one of your household my wife and future Queen of Ireland."

King Pellinore's jaw dropped, and then he grinned broadly. "I call that a handsome offer, lad. Which one of them do you want?"

Fion bowed low. "Sir, with humble respect, I ask for the hand of your daughter, the beautiful Elaine."

Elaine gasped. Alyse looked scandalized. With an effort, I made my face an expressionless mask—it was best; everyone expected me to look hurt, while I could barely contain my laughter. King Pellinore had opened his mouth to accept him when Alyse cut in.

"Pellinore, this is not a thing to be taken lightly, nor discussed in public. It is up to Elaine to decide, and she should be given time. She is young to leave home. I—I would have thought, sir," she addressed herself coolly to Fion, "that there are those among the king's household of a riper age for marriage than my daughter. Honor would still be conferred."

"Perhaps so, gracious lady," Fion replied with a glint in his eye, "but none but Princess Elaine could I ask to be my wife." He left it at that, and there was nothing Alyse could say. But Pellinore was slower to catch on. He motioned Fion over to him and lowered his voice until he thought I could not hear him.

"If she's too young, what about my ward, Guinevere? She's as pretty as the other, if I do say it myself, and a mite older. Wouldn't she do as well, my lord?"

"With all due respect for yourself, sire, and with all respect and admiration for your ward, whose beauty has not passed unnoticed, I assure you, I can only offer for the Lady Elaine. I would be false to my heart to do otherwise."

"Well, well," Pellinore grumbled, pleased as punch at his reply, and tickled pink, I could see, at the thought of Elaine's being Queen of Ireland, "I'll not stand in your way. But it's up to my daughter, you know, and the queen seems not to favor it. Let me speak with them awhile."

"Thank you, my lord. There is—one more thing. I wonder if you would present me to King Arthur."

"If my daughter accepts you, you may be sure I shall. If not, on what grounds? You are my hostage, not his."

"So I am aware, my lord. But as I am to be King of Ireland, it is meet I should know the man with whom I shall have to deal. It matters not to me whether I come to him as hostage or free man, and I can't see that it would matter to him."

"Hmmm. I shall consider it. There is something in the suggestion. I leave day after tomorrow to join him; perhaps I shall discuss it with him then, if the Saxons give us leave."

Dinner ended swiftly after Fion left, and Alyse called us both into her chamber for a conference.

"Did you know about this, Guinevere?" she asked angrily.

"No, madam, indeed I did not."

"Why are you angry with Gwen, Mother? She has done nothing but been publicly spurned," Elaine protested, slipping an arm around my waist. "How can you blame her? She is to be pitied. Oh, Gwen, I'm so sorry I was jealous. All this time I thought he loved you, not me."

I shrugged. "There's no need for pity."

Alyse paced furiously across the chamber.

"I don't believe it for a minute," she snapped. "It's a clever plot, very clever. I've harbored a viper in my nest. The scoundrel! How dare he?"

Leonora and Cissa backed against the drapes. I kept my eyes on the floor.

"Mother!" Elaine cried. "Are you insulted at his proposal? You act so, and yet you want it for Gwen. I thought you would be proud."

Alyse shook her head. "Oh, Elaine, my dear. You cannot understand. It was an honorable enough proposal. I accuse him of being insincere. He offered for you because he knows you will reject him." A wave of fear swept her face. "You *will* reject him, Elaine."

"Yes, Mother."

"Had he offered for Gwen, he might have been accepted."

"I would not have accepted," I said quietly, to the floor.

"You are my ward. I might have accepted for you," Alyse replied, stiffening.

I looked up then. So she would not allow me my choice, after all. I think I had suspected it all along. I met her eyes squarely, and the relationship between us subtly changed and hardened into battle lines. "You could not have accepted for me."

Alyse bristled. "I am queen and your guardian. Tell me why I could not have accepted for you. It is the best you could ever do."

"Because," I said, the words dropping into the silence like stones into a still pool, "I am not yet a woman."

Alyse stared, then threw up her hands in resignation.

"Then perhaps it is just as well. You are old enough to be betrothed, and marriage could wait six months or longer. It cannot be that far off, at the rate you are growing. But as it stands, he has not offered, so I cannot accept."

"If you had accepted, I would not go."

The women gasped and held their breaths as Alyse flushed darkly. "You would go. Else you would be horsewhipped."

"I shall not leave Britain." I spoke with certainty, although it was only a blind faith in Fion's visions.

Alyse came up to me. I noticed that I was taller by a handspan and that there were gray hairs among the gold on her head. "Until you come into womanhood, niece, you will do exactly as I tell you. And when that blessed day arrives, I shall marry you off to the very first lord who looks at you twice. See if I don't. You are dismissed."

Back in our chamber, Elaine embraced me. "Gwen, I apologize for my mother. And I apologize for all my rude behavior. I have said things—you know which things—I did not mean. But I thought, all this time, that he loved you."

I lowered my eyes. "Thank you, Elaine. But he has not hurt my feelings, as everyone thinks. I knew he would not offer for me. So you see, I have lost nothing by it. And you have gained much. You have turned down the King of Ireland!"

She brightened and hugged me again. "Let's make a pact. We will swear by the Virgin never to fall in love with the same man. Is it agreed?"

The mischievous glint in her eye made me laugh. "Whoever sees him first, you mean? If I am ever to find a husband with you about, Elaine, I see I must practice my sprints!"

We laughed together, but I knew in my heart what she meant. I must take care from now on to keep well away from anyone Elaine admired. I was never again to be first in anyone's eyes. She would not forgive me twice.

Alyse and Pellinore did not sleep at all that night, by the look of them in the morning. And their arguments continued for the next two days. Pellinore was heard to exclaim that he didn't give a——if Elaine liked the lad or not. Queen of Ireland was good enough for him, and therefore good enough for her. If she persisted in refusing every suitor who came to her door, he would take matters into his own hands and contract her, sight unseen, to a lord of his choosing. Queen Alyse got round him somehow, though, for he was resigned to it by the time he left to meet Arthur.

Fion was left behind to nurse his disappointment. What he really thought we did not know, for we were forbidden to visit him any longer. But when we rode beneath his window, sometimes we heard him singing.

9 👑 BETROTHAL

A week after my fourteenth birthday, Merlin's prophecy was fulfilled, and I began to bleed. I shared my excitement only with Elaine, and together, with Ailsa's help, we kept it secret from Alyse. For although her anger had passed, she was not kind to me any longer, and all of us who had heard her threaten me believed her. King Pellinore, her only master, was still away at war; while he was gone her power was absolute.

Fion was kept to his room, and I missed his company. Even when I was out with Zephyr, which was where I loved best to be, I thought of him, now a true prisoner, with pity and regret. I even toyed with the idea of telling Alyse I would marry him if he asked me—he was a good companion, I knew he cared for me, and Ireland could not be so bad. Almost anything was better than this tension at home. But I knew, in my heart, he would not take me. By some strange logic he had convinced himself I was meant for something else. It made me want to laugh, had it not been so sad.

Then in the month of the summer solstice we had a messenger from King Pellinore. The fighting was done, and the Saxons turned back in a great victory. King Lot of Lothian had received his death blow there, and Merlin the Enchanter had been found living in a cave in the Caledonian Forest within a stone's throw of the battleground. King Pellinore would be home with his troops in a week's time, and we were to send messages to Ireland to bring gold for Fion's ransom and take him away.

The palace was thrown into sudden activity. Everything was made ready at once. The castle was cleaned from top to bottom, a great feast was prepared, hunts were organized for fresh game, wild flowering herbs were gathered and fashioned into wreaths, which we hung in every room to sweeten the air. In all the bustle I managed to visit Fion twice without being noticed. The first time I went to thank him properly for his offer for Elaine. He kissed my cheek and replied it was the least he could do for the princess who saved his life. When I told him the great news, that the High King had been victorious and Merlin had been found alive, he replied that he had never doubted either event. The second time I went to see him was the day before Pellinore's return and his own departure. He was very solemn then, and excited, also. We said good-bye.

"I shall see you again, sweet Guinevere," he promised. "I shall come to your wedding."

I shuddered. "Don't talk about weddings, I pray you." And I told him what Queen Alyse had said.

He only smiled. "She can't do it. You will see. There are forces at work in this land that not even Queen Alyse can command. Open your eyes."

"What will you do when you are free?"

"To Ireland, I suppose, since the High King is away. And you?"

"What I always do in summer. Ride away from the castle as often as I can, on whatever excuse I can fashion."

"You should get yourself a falcon. That's all the excuse you need. Oh, Guinevere, this parting is more difficult than I expected."

He reached for me and pulled me up against him. He kissed my throat, and then my lips, and hugged me tightly. "Never forget you have a friend in Ireland. You need only send a word, and I will come to your aid."

His countrymen sailed in that evening and were reunited with him. King Pellinore arrived the next day with much fanfare. Everyone attended a great feast in the hall that night. The room was crowded with extra benches, and between the press of bodies and the flaring torches, it grew very warm.

The first piece of business was the ransoming of Fion. This was accomplished with great ceremony, and when it was done, and Fion was a free man, he was offered and accepted a seat of honor at the round table. Then King Pellinore gave an account of the battle against the Saxons and the finding of Merlin.

"He was wandering about the fringes of the battlefield, his wits quite gone, giving directions to the soldiers. One of the captains bound him to a tree to keep him out of harm's way, but at battle's end when they went back to release him, he was gone, although the rope was there, with all the knots still tied. The soldiers were convinced he was an apparition, but the captain was not so sure. He had been calling out the names of Ector, Kay, and Bedwyr, and Arthur's childhood name. When the High King heard this story, he left off his pursuit of Saxon stragglers and raced back to scour the forest."

The story Pellinore told of Arthur's reunion with his friend touched the heart of everyone in the hall. He found Merlin in a small, damp cave, dressed in skins, aged twenty years, gray-haired and feeble, and never left his side from the moment he arrived until the great enchanter opened his eyes and spoke his name, three days later. Then he wept and kissed him, and fed him broth with his own hands. Merlin recovered his wits, but had no recollection of what had happened to him last autumn, or of the time in between. Some said the rigors of the Caledonian winter had robbed him of his youth and vigor; some said it had to be the work of poison; others maintained this was just another shape that Merlin took, by his own choosing.

There followed many toasts to King Arthur and some to Fion, and the hall began to get rowdy. Queen Alyse rose to lead the ladies out. But before we left, I heard Pellinore advise Fion that the High King was traveling south to Caerleon before going on to invest Caer Camel and would be passing along the eastern border of Wales in the next day or two. Fion's features lit with joy, and he thanked Pellinore for ransoming him, that he might meet the High King of Britain as a free man. He left the next day to catch the King along the Glevum road. What he thought of our young King we did not learn that season, for he returned along the northern route to Caer Narfon and took sail from there. But I heard later that within a day of their meeting, Prince Fion had sworn the future allegiance of Ireland to Arthur, and Arthur had sworn the present friendship and protection of Britain to the Gaels.

Caer Camel was invested that summer, and at last Britain had a center, a fighting fortress for her King and his fighting men. It lay in the middle of the Summer Country, that land of gently rolling downs and soft breezes where sheep graze year round, the air smells faintly of the salt marshes, and the signal fires on hill and tor give long warning of an enemy's approach. The Saxon hordes were quiet that summer. Rumor had it they were finally defeated or, on the other hand, that they were regrouping for one last desperate attack. Arthur of the Eleven Battles was ready for them. He spent that year reinforcing his defenses, reestablishing contact with all his vassal lords, settling territory disputes, and gathering to his side young men of fighting age who wished to join the King's Companions.

I followed Fion's suggestion and persuaded Pellinore to let me hawk. I think he pitied me, after my public rejection by Fion, and sensing the queen's mistrust of me afterward, determined to do me a kindness. He was a soft-hearted man, though his speech was blunt and his manner gruff. His falconer found me a young bird, which I trained as Gwarthgydd had taught me. I fashioned its jesses myself out of soft worked leather and then, to my consternation, discovered that Zephyr was terrified of the thing. It took two whole months to get her to accept the bird and to get her accustomed to being ridden without reins and following leg signals only. But eventually we three worked as a team, and my young falcon Ebon provided many a fat dove for the queen's supper, whether she knew it or not.

The next time I saw Fion was in the autumn of my fourteenth year. Gilomar had died that summer, and Fion was now King. He was on his way to Caer Camel to a meeting of all of Arthur's nobles and his allies, called by the Companions for the purpose of finding Arthur a wife. Pellinore himself was going and stayed his departure to wait for Fion and travel down with him to the Summer Country. The news of this great meeting spread like wildfire throughout the kingdoms, and every king who attended carried instructions from his lady to propose his daughter, or his granddaughter, or his niece or whomever among his kin was the most eligible. Bards were hired to sing poems extolling the beauties of this maid and that. Family lineages were hunted up and extended back to Roman governors, or Maximus if it was possible. Bargains were made among families for backing; friendships of long standing were broken in the heat of competition.

The only two people in the Kingdom who stood aloof from this frenzy were, oddly, the High King and myself. By all reports Arthur had no desire to remarry, but was aware of the necessity to produce an heir, and thus yielded to the pressure brought by his Companions. He was content to let his subjects make the choice for him. All he required in a bride, he had said, was an honest tongue and a soft voice. As for myself, even if I had had Elaine's ambition, which I did not, there was no one to speak for me. My parents were dead. My brothers had daughters of their own. My guardians were the parents of one of the most eligible maidens in the land, and one who desired nothing more than the very position that needed filling. At last, it seemed, the world was marching to Elaine's tune. This, she told me in secret, as if it were news, was what she had been born for. She was sure of it.

Indeed, in the new gown she wore to Fion's welcome feast, she looked every inch a queen. With her dark gold hair bound with flowers, her dancing, sky-blue eyes, her milky skin, and willowy figure, she could have passed for a woman of twenty, although she was but thirteen. Even Fion stared. He was still unmarried, but it was too late to renew his suit for Elaine. The only topic at dinner that night was the searching of Britain for Arthur's bride, and Elaine positively glowed. When Pellinore announced his intention to propose Elaine to the High King, the hall stood up and cheered. Elaine squeezed my hand hard under the table, and although she cast down her eyes as a maid should, her look was triumphant. I kissed her cheek affectionately and caught Fion looking at us thoughtfully.

When the noise in the hall had abated somewhat, I turned to Fion. "My lord Fion, the last time we saw you, you were on your way to make your peace with our King. Pray tell us how you found him: Were you treated honorably? Did you get fair hearing?"

"I have never met a more honorable man," Fion replied solemnly. "Your King was graciousness itself. He heard me out until I had nothing more to say. He knew who I was, but he did not hold my father's sins against me. By the questions he asked, I saw he had a thorough knowledge of our shore defenses and knew something of the rivalries among our petty kings. I do not know how he gets his information, or how he has the time to think of Ireland with the Saxons at his back, but he understood how the land lay all about him, and he welcomed me most honorably. He made me feel like a brother." He paused. Pellinore was nodding with a broad smile on his face, and Elaine's eyes were shining. "He speaks to the lowliest of his servants with consideration. Every man has respect at Arthur's table. Were my heart not in Ireland, I would lay it at his feet."

Every man in the hall rose cheering, and there were many shouts of "Arthur!" and "Fion!" I was moved by his testimonial. Elaine was beside herself with excitement.

"You see, Gwen," she whispered to me, "he really is what he is supposed to be! I have known it my entire life!"

So she had. Elaine had never lost her faith in Arthur. She had believed every wondrous tale she had heard about him, and Fion's words were only fuel to her fire. I prayed hard that night that God would grant her her wish, even if it meant Alyse took us all to live at court.

———

Everyone knows what happened, of course. It is difficult to look back over the span of years and remember the uproar of those days. The meeting, which had been planned to last a week in order that everyone could speak, stretched to two weeks, and then three. There were too many candidates, and a consensus could not be found. Every leading family in the land had a daughter or a niece of marriageable age. Every maid had a flawless lineage, flawless complexion, flawless eyes of black, brown, blue, green, gray; flawless hair of gold, brown, black, red; features of surpassing beauty, an honest tongue and a lovely voice. Even Arthur wearied of it and went hawking. Feuds developed, powerful leaders backed one family and then another as the offers of gold increased. Happy was the man who had nothing to gain or lose by the King's decision. And throughout it all, Merlin sat by the High King's chair, old and frail, his black eyes watching it all, saying nothing.

At last, his patience near an end, King Arthur commanded the meeting to close. He would not divide his Kingdom over a woman, he said. He would rather die unwed. Only then did a young man rise from the rear of the Welsh delegation and, having received permission to speak, addressed the High King in a trembling voice. Just as silver was found threaded into black rock deep within the earth, he began, just as gold was sprinkled sparsely over pebbled sands, so all treasures worth pursuing did not come easy; the brightest jewel often lay buried in the darkest clay. As he overcame his fear, his voice fell into the sweet singsong of the storyteller, and the Welshmen in the hall settled back comfortably to hear his tale. It was, it seems, the tale of the emperor Maximus and how he found his Elen, the famous Welsh beauty with sapphire eyes whom Maximus wed and for whom he forswore allegiance to Rome. She was, he sang, fairer than the stars among the heavens, more constant than the sun in his course across the sky, sweeter than wildflowers that grace the summer meadows, and ever a true companion to the king. In all his endeavors she was beside him; she brought him luck and victory; he never lost a battle until he left Britain, where she could not follow. The singer paused—Welshmen were wont to attribute Maximus' prowess to the virtues of his Welsh wife, but it was unwise to expect this descendant of Maximus to believe it—he claimed, instead, that hidden in the dark Welsh mountains lay a jewel as bright as Elen, a girl as beautiful, as wise and steadfast, as Maximus' own bride. Like a vein of precious metal lying undiscovered in the hills, she awaited the High King's notice; a word from him could bring her gold to light. A king's daughter she was, descended from Elen, with hair of starlight and the voice of a nightingale. And Gwillim, for it was my old childhood companion who had risen to speak before them all, took a deep breath and held hard to his courage. The maiden's name, he said, was Guinevere.

There was a shocked silence. The Companions froze. Arthur's face was a mask. Merlin closed his eyes. Then the throng found their voices, and angry protests arose on all sides. "How dare the boy?" "What maid is this? I have heard no tell of her." "That he should mention the name before the King!" Then Gwarthgydd rose and clapped a hand on Gwillim's shoulder.

"My lords," he said, and his deep rumbling voice got their attention. "The lad speaks of my half-sister, Guinevere of Northgallis. In his later years, my father the King of Northgallis wed Elen of Gwynedd, a beauty of renown. She died giving birth to the lady in question, who was a childhood friend of Gwillim's here. She is now the ward of King Pellinore and Queen Alyse and lives in Gwynedd. Gwillim likes a good tale, but all he has said is true enough."

"Is that the Lark of Gwynedd?" someone asked. "I have heard of her."

"Isn't that the maid the old witch prophesied about, the night of her birth? You remember Giselda—"

"A curse, I thought it was, a spell—"

"Oh, no, she prophesied great beauty and great fame—"

"Has anyone seen her?" one of the Companions asked. "Where is Pellinore? Who can attest to the lad's claims?"

But Pellinore, weary of words, was out hunting. It was Fion who stood.

That winter lasted forever. Elaine lay abed with an illness born of disappointment and envy, and Alyse could barely tolerate the sight of me. Pellinore was proud and conscious of his new status in the High King's inner circle, but he never came to the women's quarters, wishing to avoid Alyse's cold fury at his betrayal, and I saw him only at dinner in the evenings. The queen's ladies kept aloof at the queen's wishes. Only Ailsa, of all the women in the castle, was thoroughly excited on my behalf.

"Just think of it! Wouldn't your dear mother be proud! Her little Gwen to be King Arthur's Queen! Why, I just pinch myself when I think of it! How lucky you are, my lady! How happy you will be!"

But I could not see how this unexpected event could make me happy. Already it seemed to have cost me Elaine's friendship, and she was the only real friend I had ever had. Proud as I was to be chosen out of all the maids in Britain, I could not envision happiness ahead. I was to be married to a man I had never met, and because he was who he was, there was no possible way out of it. I did not feel the thrill all Britain expected me to feel; I felt only apprehension and a nagging regret that I had not married Fion.

However much she suffered at the sight of me, Alyse knew her duty. She set all her ladies to work on my wardrobe, and we sat together all winter sewing my wedding clothes, fashioning new gowns, weaving bed linens and chamber hangings. Dear Pellinore ended up spending Fion's ransom on my bridegift. For if I did not go to Arthur surrounded by the most luxurious finery in the kingdom, I would shame Wales. We had the long winter to get ready, for in the spring the King would come himself to take me out of Wales.

I put this from my mind, for I shook with fear at the very thought of it. Wales was the only home I knew. I remembered every word I had ever spoken to Elaine about how dreadful it would be to be Arthur's Queen—well, I thought, I was justly served. That horrible witch had been proved right. And poor Gwillim, who I am sure thought he was doing me the finest service of his life, had been the unwitting instrument of my undoing. But there was nothing to do but face it. If I opened my mouth in complaint, I would shame Alyse and Pellinore, I would shame Northgallis, I would shame Wales. So I said very little and let the people take my silence for maidenly modesty if they chose.

In the month before the equinox Elaine finally rose from her bed. She was thin and pale and took the chair closest to the fire, but at least she joined us.

"Gwen," she said on our first night together in four months, "please forgive me for my grief. I wish you all happiness, you know that. I hated you for a while, but that was my unruly jealousy. I have remembered the prophecy at your birth, and also Merlin's prophecy, and I know that it is you who were born for this, and not I. Please forgive me."

"Oh, Elaine!" I threw my arms around her and we cried together for a long time. "Dear cousin, I would give anything in the world to change places with you and give you your heart's desire! Can you think for one moment I would not, knowing how you feel? Oh, Elaine, I do not want to leave Wales!"

"You will not have to go alone," she said. "Mother says we shall all accompany you to court and see you married."

"Bless you!" I cried.

"And although Mother must return, I will stay if you like. Surely you may have your own friends there, as the High King has his."

"Oh, thank you, Elaine. You warm my heart, truly. You would give up your home for *me*? Dear Elaine, marry one of his Companions and stay with me always!" But I should not have spoken of marriage. She went pale and trembled.

"I will never marry. Never."

A cold breath seemed to blow upon my neck, and I shivered. "You will not always feel so, I am sure. Listen, Elaine, once you see the King himself you will not be so enamored of him. He cannot be the dream you cherish any more than he can be the ogre I fear." But she did not answer.

Wedding gifts began to arrive in Gwynedd and Caer Camel. King Fion sent yards of the finest, snow-white linen—no one on earth makes finer linen than the Irish, and this must have been bleached and beaten two hundred times to get such softness and luster. Alyse declared it perfect for the marriage bed and would not let me touch it, but set her ladies to do the embroidery, although my needlework was finer. Fion also sent quantities of jewelry for Elaine and Queen Alyse as well as myself, all silver and enamel, worked in the intricate way of the Gaels, with interlocking vines and queer nested squares. And he sent me as his personal gift a pair of silver earrings worked around dark blue sapphires that caught the firelight and reminded one of the color of the sea in a summer storm. "To wear," said his note, "with sapphire eyes." I missed him dreadfully.

King Pellinore's carpenters were hard at work building wagons to carry all the gifts and all the luggage to Caer Camel. Horses had to be bought from neighboring lands and trained to pull them, and his stable had to be enlarged to hold them. Food had to be bought from other kingdoms, even from Less Britain, for the High King would stay with us a month, and everyone in his train had to be fed, yes, and housed. Barracks were erected, and more temporary stables. The place was a riot of feverish activity. Men worked through snow and frost, day and night; no one rested. I used to stand by my window and watch them, amazed that this was all for me. At such times I felt the crushing weight of Britain's expectation. I was the chosen of Arthur—I could be no less than perfect. Whatever flaw they found with me would be magnified a thousand times. And there would be many—all the relatives and friends of the maids he had not chosen—looking to find fault. I could take no wrong step, say no hasty speech, or I would cast a shadow across the glory of Britain. These fears usually sent me into a fit of weeping, but the women only nodded to one another and winked behind my back. Even Ailsa said once in my hearing that all I needed was a good bedding and my fears would take care of themselves. I fainted when I heard it, and after that the women were more careful in their speech.

The truth was, I had never stopped to think that I was marrying a man. At twenty, Arthur was already a legend, even among the Saxons. He was an idea, not flesh and blood. I should have to bear him princes, but exactly what that meant I had not considered. As the rains of April fell, and Elaine grew quieter, and the women stitched away madly at the King's wedding sheets, it began to be real to me. And I was terrified.

I escaped to the stables on dry days and took Zephyr out on the hills, or flew Ebon, or dallied on the beach. They let me go wherever I chose, although I had a chaperone of troopers. Nothing could be allowed to happen to me. I was no longer merely Guinevere; I was King Arthur's betrothed. It angered me sometimes that the word of a single man I had not even met could so change my life. And it frightened me, also. What was the High King expecting? An ornament to his court? A broodmare? Surely he must realize that Gwillim's words were poetry and never meant to describe a woman of flesh and blood! Suppose—suppose he frowned on women riding horses? Should I have to take to a litter, like Alyse? Oh, I wept in frustration and pounded my poor mare over the hills in desperate attempts to escape such thoughts, but they were always there when I returned.

Father Martin was useless as a confidant. He could barely hear my confession, so ready was he to bend the knee to me. I prayed to the Virgin, helpmate of women, to give me the strength to endure what was coming. But when I closed my eyes at night, all that came to me was Merlin's face and the gentle, ghostly voice repeating "what will be, will be."

My fifteenth birthday came and went, barely noticed in the frantic bustle, and three days later a royal courier arrived. Elaine and I gripped each other on the staircase as we strained to hear him give his message to Pellinore in the hall. Spring had brought new longboats to the eastern shores, and the northern kings could not hold their defenses against an attack of such numbers, should it come. King Arthur was required to show his face there and deal with them and could not come to take his bride to Caer Camel. But not wishing to delay the wedding, which was set for the summer solstice, he was sending in his stead three of his closest Companions and a troop of horses to take me to Caer Camel to await his arrival there.

Elaine and I turned to each other. On her face was writ her disappointment; on mine was sheer relief. The men would be arriving in three days and would stay until such time as we felt ready to depart. This was wonderful news! The building could cease, the cooks could rest, and everyone except the queen's ladies could be sure that the preparations they had already made would be sufficient. But a bridegift is never finished. There is always one more cushion to stuff, one more gown to stitch, one more slipper to line.

Elaine had made me a nightgown, entirely of her own design and working, of creamy linen lined with silk, and edged with costly laces. On the morning of the third day she bade me try it on for a final fitting. It was a lovely thing, with loose, flowing lines and a low throat. But Elaine was unhappy with the bodice, which she felt should be tighter. She gripped the cloth at the back until it was tight, and then placed her hand upon my bosom to get the shape. Then an odd thing happened. She hesitated and met my eyes. We both thought, at exactly the same moment, of where this gown would be worn, and that a man's large, brown hand would be where her small, white one lay, and she jumped away as I gasped, and we both turned scarlet.

"Oh, Gwen, I can't bear the thought of it!" she cried, tears welling in her eyes.

"Neither can I!" I wailed, as we fell weeping into each other's arms. This is but one illustration among many of the state we were in.

Unable to stand the castle any longer, I dressed in my doeskin leggings and soft boots and my old green mantle and went to the stable. I asked no one's permission. Today was the long-awaited day, and everyone was too busy to notice me. I took Ebon on my arm, hopped on Zephyr, and rode bareback up into the hills. The King's men were not expected until nightfall, and I should be back, bathed, perfumed, and gowned before they saw me.

It was a glorious day in May, golden and soft, and the forests were full of birds returning to their summer homes. We had a good gallop, and then we had wonderful hunting, one exciting chase after another, with five kills to Ebon's credit by midafternoon, when I hooded him because the pouch was full. He could have filled a saddlebag that magic day, had I brought one with me. We stopped at a stream for Zephyr to drink, and I felt it suddenly—the thrill of excitement, the throbbing expectancy of something marvelous that lay ahead and was coming. It was a wonderful day to be alive. For the first time in months my spirit lifted, and I felt like singing. We stood in the silence of the forest with dappled sunlight falling all about, while cool water dripped from the mare's muzzle and small creatures rustled in the underbrush. In the blessed stillness, the birds began to sing, tentatively at first, and then in full-throated song. The hawk sat hooded and quiet on my arm as the budding treetops came alive with music. I whistled in imitation and then joined in their chorus, and they let me.

The mare walked gently down the forest track while I sang to the birds, happy to be young and alive, glorying in the magic brightness of that special day. We came upon a clearing, and suddenly the mare stopped, threw up her head, and nickered. I looked about, but it was several moments before I saw the young man on the black horse. They stood under the trees where the track left the clearing, and he was staring at me. As I noticed him, he slid from his horse and took two steps forward. He cleared his throat, but no sound came out. He just stood in the clearing as if he had been there always, and my heart began to pound. He wore a strange device on his cloak, and his clothes were cut a little oddly, but that he was a knight there was no doubt. Black hair fell across his brow and shaded his eyes. His face had good lines and would have been handsome if his nose had not been broken and set slightly crooked. It gave an oddness to his face that set his features apart from those of other men. I could not explain why my spirit soared as I looked at him. He was a stranger, yet he set me trembling. He took another step forward and tried again to speak. I went weak inside, melting like butter in the sun.

"Are you—are you a vision or are you real?" he whispered. The question, spoken low and almost out of hearing, did not seem out of place, for I had wondered the same about him.

"I am no vision, my lord. Where—who—what badge is that you bear? You are no Welshman."

He bent one knee and sank down on the new grass. "I am a poor knight from foreign parts, and this badge is the badge of my homeland. My name is Lancelot."

10 ♛ LANCELOT

Your manners commend you, good Lancelot. Welcome to Gwynedd. My name is Guinevere. My guardian King Pellinore is lord of this land. We are not far from his castle. If there is aught that you require—food or rest or fodder for your horse, I—I am sure he would provide it."

His eyes widened. They were clear and cool and liquid gray. I stopped speaking. The silence around us seemed to breathe.

"Gracious lady," he said at last, his voice husky. "I have been there. It is you I seek, if you are Guinevere of Northgallis."

I was trembling so hard that Ebon shifted on my arm. The pressure of his grip brought me back to myself. "Please rise, my lord. I am the one you seek."

He stood and came toward me. Then Zephyr did an unexpected thing. She lowered her head and shoved him gently in the chest. He looked at the mare.

"Fina!" he cried. "Is it you, my girl? Dear God, it is!" Then he turned to me, and his smile robbed me of breath. "*You* are the one! Pellinore's ward! I remember it now!"

I feared lest he touch me, and I lose my seat on the horse. But he did not. He backed away a pace.

"You—you are the knight who bred and trained her? I—I had forgotten the name. I had always hoped to meet you and thank you for bringing so much pleasure into my life."

He flushed scarlet. "It gives me great joy to do you the smallest service."

His lashes were long and dark and lent his eyes a beauty that is usually a woman's gift. He was tall and slenderly built, with a sword hanging in a much-used, plain leather scabbard from his belt. As I looked at him, and he looked at me, the birds took up their interrupted song, and I knew in my soul that he was the magic behind the day. I believe I smiled at him; I know his face lit with happiness.

"What service may this humble maid perform for Lancelot, to repay the debt?" I asked him softly.

He caught his breath in surprise and then sobered suddenly, tapped on the shoulder by the finger of remembrance. He straightened and bowed. "My lady Guinevere, I have come to take you to Arthur."

It was a cloud across the sun; the cold shadow passed over, and the day darkened. Only then did I see two other horsemen in the trees behind him, waiting patiently. They wore swords and badges, and an indefinable air of self-importance. Of course. They were the King's Companions, they and Lancelot, who was foremost among them. As I watched, they rode forward into the clearing and, unsheathing their swords, touched the blades to their foreheads in salute.

"Princess Guinevere," Lancelot said formally, "these are two of the King's Companions, Kay of Galava, son of Ector, and Bedwyr of Brydwell, son of Boad. Gentlemen, Princess Guinevere of Northgallis."

They performed their formal greetings, as I did mine. Bedwyr looked worriedly at Lancelot, and Kay looked in some alarm at the hooded falcon on my arm.

"No doubt you could outride us at will," Lancelot said smiling, "so I beg you will lead us a decorous pace back to the castle, else we lose our way. We are supposed to be your escort."

I returned his smile, and for a moment there seemed to be only the two of us in the whole world. "Far be it from me to bring shame upon any who serve King Arthur. Have no fear. I shall be ladylike."

He grinned, and I could see the others were pleased by my response. Lancelot turned and whistled for his stallion, who trotted up and stood patiently while he mounted.

Zephyr nickered, and the stallion's ears shot forward.

"Not now, Nestor." Lancelot laughed. "Maybe next year." And he signaled me to take my place at his side for the ride back.

"That is a trick you must teach me, my lord," I said to him. "I can see that it would be useful."

"It would be an honor and a pleasure, my lady. But if my eyes deceive me not, there is not much I could teach you about a horse. You speak their language."

I was thinking the same about him. One can tell a born rider simply by watching the way he sits his horse. Lancelot's stallion was interested in the mare, but he controlled the animal effortlessly, without thought, with legs and seat and hand, as fluidly and as softly as the horse himself moved. It must give pleasure to the horse, I thought, to be ridden with such skill.

As we approached the castle, the woods gave way to fields, and I glanced mischievously at Lancelot. "Would my lord care to follow me? I know a shorter way back, but there are obstacles."

He hesitated, aware of the challenge. "Obstacles for a horse, my lady, or obstacles for a man?"

I laughed. "Follow me, my lord, and find out."

He glanced swiftly behind him and nodded. "Lead on."

I took them to my jumping field where I had, over time, fashioned a formidable series of obstacles. I settled Ebon on my arm and sang softly to him for reassurance, for this was new to him. Then I put Zephyr into a light gallop, and we flew over the obstacles. I gloried in the sensation of hurtling through the air, with the salt sea breeze in my face and my hair whipping behind me. I felt like a prisoner granted a last day of freedom before execution, and this was it—my last taste of girlhood. At the top of the field, I cantered the mare in a circle and then brought her to a halt. All three knights were standing where I had left them, watching me. I waited. It had been easy for us, we had done it before. But although the fences were new to them, the animals they rode were trained warhorses, stronger than Zephyr and as nimble, who knew maneuvers on a field of battle and could be a third weapon under a good rider. Lancelot was a horseman. We should see about the others.

Lancelot gathered his stallion and cantered toward the first fence. The stallion shied, but then obeyed and pushed himself over. At the next brush pile he took off too far out and barely missed landing upon it. By the third fence Lancelot had learned to judge the distance, and every obstacle thereafter was an improvement upon the one before. At length he drew up beside me, breathing hard, eyes shining.

"By heaven, that is a sport for kings! My compliments to Pellinore for building it, and to your own skill, my lady—the bird never stirred from your arm!"

"Pellinore had nothing to do with it," I retorted. "It was my own idea. I like to jump. And as for Ebon, he trusts me."

He stared. "My compliments to you, then, Lady Guinevere. But surely he built it for you."

"Certainly not. He disapproves of my jumping. I built it myself."

"By God!" he cried, his eyes dancing, "You are one woman in a thousand!"

I looked away to avoid looking into his eyes. "Am I odd, then? I do not wish to be."

"You are perfect! Perfectly suited to the High King, I mean." I was watching the others when he spoke, and heard in his voice the tenderness I had seen already in his face. I wished with all my heart that he would stop reminding me of Arthur. I did not know then that he was reminding himself.

Bedwyr made a good attempt. His horse refused the obstacle at first, but he persevered and got him over. All was then well until he came to the hen coop, where the stallion slid to a stop at the last moment and tossed Bedwyr over. Kay, who refused the challenge altogether, cantered over to him.

"What manner of man is Kay of Galava?"

Lancelot smiled. "He's old for his age and always has been. He's Arthur's seneschal. His place is at Caer Camel, and he misses it. He worries about it every minute he's away. Since he was injured at Caer Eden his sword arm is weak, and as he cannot take the field for Arthur, he holds his fortress in readiness. It is his service, and he is devoted."

It was clear from his tone of voice that Kay was valued for his devotion. "He frowns upon my hawking."

Lancelot shrugged. "He believes that women should ride litters, not horses, and should be rocking cradles, not hunting falcons. It is his way."

I plucked nervously at Zephyr's mane. "And the High King?"

"What about the High King?"

"Does he disapprove of women hawking?"

Lancelot turned toward me, amused. "Do I hear aright? Are you actually frightened of Arthur?"

I raised my chin in defiance. "Do you blame me, my lord? I have heard so much and know so little."

He laughed outright. "My dear Guinevere, Pendragon may be feared by Saxons, and rightly so, but you have no need to be afraid. Do you imagine him a cruel tyrant? He is the kindest man in all the kingdoms. Why, Arthur would no sooner keep you from hawking or doing whatever it was you pleased than he would cut off his nose to spite his face. He would laugh at the very idea!"

He filled me with relief. "Then I shall be allowed to keep Zephyr? Is this truth, Lancelot? It has worried me a long time."

He began to look astonished. "Of course you may keep her. He is not a monster, Guinevere. Your doubts disturb me. Is not the High King known among his people here in Wales?"

"How a King treats his people is one thing. How a man treats his—his wife may be quite another."

He grew instantly grave and nodded. "That is true. But with Arthur it is the same thing. The man and the King are one."

I looked into his face and saw his own devotion there. Clearly Arthur was a great leader to inspire love in such different men as Kay and Lancelot.

Bedwyr rode up then, with Kay behind him, and I apologized sincerely for putting them through my little game. It had been a long winter, I told them, with nothing for maids to do but sew and listen to women's gossip. The high spirits of spring had to be played out in some fashion. They forgave me like the gentlemen they were; no one reminded me of my promise to be ladylike; and we approached the castle yard as princess and royal escort, much to Kay's relief.

Elaine was aghast. "Oh, Gwen, how could you! All these months we have been preparing for this visit, and their first sight of you is bareback upon your horse, in those filthy leggings! And your hair is flying everywhere! Oh, what must they think?"

I grinned at her as Ailsa pulled the shift down over my head. "My leggings are not filthy. I brush them well after every ride."

"Oh, don't, Gwen. Think of the report will they send to King Arthur!"

Ailsa sat me on the stool and began to brush my hair. I took Elaine's hand.

"Forgive me. I see this affects you deeply. But truly," I said, smiling as I thought of Lancelot standing rooted in the clearing, "I am not worried about the report they will send to King Arthur."

She looked puzzled. "I see you are not. But for goodness' sake, why not?"

"Never mind. I am bathed and clean now, dear Elaine, and Ailsa will dress my hair, and I shall wear the blue gown you embroidered with wildflowers, and I promise I will be a lady and try to make a good impression."

"I should hope so," she said crossly. "It's important to Mother. And to me. You must be—that is, you must try to be—"

"Perfect," I finished for her, sadly. "As everyone says Arthur is."

She nodded. "I guess so. I suppose it's a lot to ask."

I fought off panic as the weight of responsibility descended upon me once again. "It's far too much to ask. And everyone in Britain expects it. But at least I shall not be alone." I was thinking of Lancelot, who had become my friend so quickly.

Elaine kissed my cheek. "I shall be there as long as you are, Gwen. Rely on it."

Startled, I thanked her, and covered my confusion with some question about the progress of the bridegift. She answered with eagerness and filled me in on all the things I had missed while I was out—principally the arrival of the King's men. I listened, but my thoughts drifted back to the clearing, and to the jumping field, and to a pair of clear gray eyes and serious black brows.

"Dress my hair with the little pearls and bluebells, Ailsa," I said suddenly. "I wish to look my best tonight."

Ailsa looked at me sharply, and Elaine smiled.

"Now I know what's different about you today," she said. "You are finally happy. You have been happy ever since you came in."

"Have I?" I avoided Ailsa's eyes. "Well, perhaps so. It was a glorious day."

Queen Alyse led us into the greeting hall, where Pellinore waited with the King's Companions. The mellow evening light filtered in through the open windows and picked out the jewels the men wore on shoulder, belt, and wrist. They were weaponless, for Pellinore followed the High King's practice of leaving all weapons outside the meeting hall, except for the short dagger needed to cut food. King Pellinore presented Queen Alyse and Elaine; the courtiers bowed low. Lancelot wore a dark blue tunic of plain, fine wool. The silver buckle on his belt was worked in the shape of a hawk with wings outspread. He stood half a head taller than Pellinore, who was not considered a small man. Even as I looked at him, he dipped one knee to the floor and kissed my hand.

"King Arthur's compliments, my lady," he said formally. "He has sent us poor soldiers in his stead, not because he did not want to come, but because he could not."

"So I understand, my lord."

"He has sent me with words of greeting and begs for your forgiveness of his most untimely absence."

"He is High King. My lord, I understand."

"He would rather be here in Wales with you, my lady, than riding north to look at Saxons. He told me this himself."

"Where Britain needs him most, there must the High King go," I replied. "My lord may tell him he is forgiven." At last, it seemed, I had said the right thing. Kay and Bedwyr were nodding, pleased.

"And he bade me present you with this gift," Lancelot continued, "in the hope that it might ease your anger toward him and incline you to look favorably upon him."

Lancelot proffered a small packet, wrapped in soft linen.

"Good Sir Lancelot. You speak as if Pendragon were one suitor among many. I do assure you, my lord, that I look with favor upon the High King so long as he holds the Saxons at bay. There is no cause for anger. He need send no gifts to win me. I know wherein my duty lies."

Kay and Bedwyr were positively beaming. Alyse looked at me in wonder, hardly able to credit me capable of a diplomatic word.

When he spoke, Lancelot's voice was low and gentle. "Will my lady not accept it, then, as a token of the King's esteem?"

I smiled at him. "I would be honored to accept a token of the King's esteem, my lord."

Lancelot opened the soft wrappings and lifted from them a single sapphire set in silver, the size of a robin's egg, and hung from a silver chain. It glowed in the evening light, dark blue and deep and clear. Lancelot came up to me and put his arms around my shoulders as he fastened it behind my neck. By sheer effort of will I stilled my trembling and stared hard past his shoulder at Kay, but I felt his breath on my skin, and then the warm touch of his hands as he struggled with the clasp. I felt it then for the first time—the hot lick of fire that set me ablaze with an emotion I did not then understand. He hesitated and leaned closer. "It is the color of your eyes," he whispered in my ear, and stepped back slowly. I sank to the floor in a low curtsy, shaking, which sent light glittering off the great sapphire.

"Please—please tell King Arthur I am overwhelmed," I managed.

Elaine and Alyse crowded round to view the stone and chatter in admiration. I was glad for their protection while I recovered my composure. I could not meet his eyes; it was like looking into flame. At last Pellinore offered me his arm and took me into dinner. Lancelot followed with Queen Alyse, and Kay with Elaine. At dinner, Pellinore placed me beside Lancelot, his foremost guest of honor.

As the wine was passed around, Bedwyr gave what news there was of the state of the Kingdom, but for once I was not attentive. I looked everywhere about me, at the troopers, Pellinore's and the High King's, eating together in the hall, at the bowl of jonquils and bluebells at the center of the round table, at the bodice of Elaine's yellow gown, which I had embroidered with stars. Look where I might, I was conscious only of the man beside me, of the grip of his long fingers around the winecup, the turning of his head toward the speaker, the stillness of his body in his chair.

King Pellinore was proposing a series of hunts for the Companions to keep them busy while we finished the bridegift. To this Kay and Bedwyr readily agreed.

Then Lancelot spoke. "I have one favor to ask of you, Pellinore. Give me two hours each day to spend with the young princesses. The High King appreciates that leaving home to marry a man one has never seen may be hard on a young maid and he does not wish to meet Lady Guinevere as a stranger. He has instructed me to tell her aught she wishes to know about him and the life we lead at Caer Camel. If the young ladies are willing, I beg your permission to fulfill the High King's desire."

Kay and Bedwyr looked surprised, and it made me wonder if Lancelot had made the whole thing up. But Elaine looked ecstatic, and Pellinore of course agreed, so it was settled.

As dinner progressed and conversation became general, I gathered my courage and turned to Lancelot. "Forgive my impertinence, my lord, but did you speak the truth about the High King just now?"

He smiled. "Does my lady suspect me of inventing ways to spend more time in her presence?"

I flushed scarlet, I could feel the heat in my face, but his look was tender.

"It was truth, my lady. He spoke so only to me, but it is truly his desire to ease what fears you have of him. And I know now that you have them." He lowered his gaze to his plate, and his voice went low. "But had he not said so, I would have invented it. Your suspicions are just."

I felt triumphant and weak all at once and struggled to keep my voice steady. "I am glad you included Elaine. She is a great admirer of Arthur's."

He raised his eyes to me then and looked at me long and directly. "And so will you be, Guinevere, in time."

I bowed my head.

Lancelot kept his word. Whatever the men were doing, hunting, hawking, drilling troops, he took time out every day to spend with Elaine and me. In the beginning all the queen's ladies crowded round him to hear him speak of Arthur, but eventually, as the day of departure grew near and the bridegift lay unfinished, they kept to the sewing room, and we had just Leonora for chaperone. Elaine was almost always with me. On the four or five occasions when Lancelot and I went riding, we took several of Pellinore's men along for escort and said very little to one another. And every time we spoke, Lancelot was careful to bring King Arthur between us, gently and firmly. In my mind's eye I saw him as our guardian, and in this I was not far off the mark.

When we sat together, usually in the queen's garden, it was always Elaine who asked about Arthur.

"What is the truth of his birth?" Elaine wanted to know. "Why did no one ever see him? Where did Merlin hide him?"

Lancelot smiled. "In spite of the rumors that I know run rampant, Merlin did not spirit him away to a far-off land, nor change him into an eagle. He grew up in Galava, with Sir Ector as his foster father and Kay his brother. No one noticed him because he was not specially treated. When he traveled with Ector, he went not as a prince of the land but as a minor noble's son in Ector's protection, with small escort and smaller fanfare. Ector, a brave soldier who fought with Ambrosius, and a kind man, took him into his household for fostering when he was just a baby. Arthur and Kay grew up as brothers." The source of Kay's devotion lay revealed, and also of his readiness to disapprove of me.

"But where was Merlin all this time?" Elaine wondered. "I thought he raised the King himself."

Lancelot smiled at her, but Elaine seemed unaffected. "So people say, but Merlin himself has never said so. And yet there is some truth in the claim. Behind the scenes, Merlin supervised the prince's education and kept track of him through the power of his Sight. He sometimes lived as a holy hermit in the forest above Count Ector's castle. There he would meet the boy and give him lessons and tell him the story of his begetting and his lineage, as if it all pertained to someone else. You might remember," Lancelot continued, "Uther Pendragon proclaimed throughout Britain that he would not acknowledge the son he begot at Tintagel. Thus neither Ector nor Merlin could in all fairness tell him who he was."

"But how was his true birth kept from him?" I asked. "I have always found that part of the tale difficult to believe. Sir Ector must have told him something."

"But it is true, my lady. He did not know. Ector told him his parents were of noble birth, but that they could not claim him. Arthur assumed he was the bastard of some petty lord, and Kay his superior in birth and breeding. He heard all the tales about Prince Arthur that you have heard, but he never once thought they might apply to him."

"But the name!" Elaine exclaimed. "And to have Merlin the Enchanter as a teacher! I'd have guessed, if it had been me!"

"Ah, but 'Arthur' was not his name." Lancelot turned to me and smiled. My breath caught in my throat. "Sometime when he is deep in thought and not attending, call 'Emreis' softly, and judge the truth yourself by the unthinking quickness of his response." I colored and looked down. "As for Merlin," Lancelot continued gently, "he is a master at disguise. He transformed himself so completely into a wild holy man that Ector himself barely knew him. As Arthur had never seen him, it really is no wonder he did not guess."

"Well, why is Merlin so dear to him, then," Elaine objected, with a shake of her bountiful curls, "if Sir Ector was his foster father?"

"Perhaps because he valued more the things that Merlin taught him." Lancelot shrugged. "Or perhaps it is just the chance agreement of two personalities." He shot me a swift glance and looked away. I blushed uncontrollably.

"It may have been so for his childhood," Elaine went on, "but surely, by the time he went to Caer Eden to fight for the High King, he must have guessed. Holy men are not so wise as Merlin and never stay so long in one place."

Suddenly I saw what lay ahead and attempted to steer the conversation another way, but Elaine would not have it. She pressed Lancelot to answer.

"Ah, but Arthur did not know that. Galava is a small place, and his experience of wandering holy men was limited to one."

"Then surely he must have guessed when Ector armed him for the battle. He was by rights too young to be a warrior."

Lancelot smiled, unaware of the bog ahead. "While it is true that Ector brought him on Uther's orders, it does not surprise me that Arthur did not guess. Think of the long years he had believed himself to be only a foster-ling. And Galava is not far from Caer Eden. Had the Saxons won, his 'homeland' would have been directly threatened. He would have thought it strange had Ector *not* taken every able-bodied man and boy at his command, especially as Arthur, even at thirteen, was the best swordsman in Galava."

Elaine sighed in resignation. "Then it's true, after all, that Uther waited until the last minute to declare him?"

Still Lancelot went on, unseeing. "I have heard it was Uther's intention to talk to the boy and reveal his identity to him before the battle, but the Saxons attacked unexpectedly, and there was no time."

I looked down at my hands, twisted together in my lap. "And when, my lord, did he learn the truth?"

There was a long silence, and at last I glanced up. Lancelot looked stricken, having seen the pitfall too late. Elaine, in her innocence, merely waited for his answer. He cleared his throat and spoke stiffly.

"Uther told him the next day he was his father, in a public declaration, as he lay dying." When it was too late, I thought bitterly, *after* he had lain with his half-sister. Lancelot's eyes met mine, and he saw that I knew the tale, and I saw that the tale was true. If I felt grief, it was nothing to what Lancelot felt, having brought it upon me. Elaine continued unawares.

"You speak as if you were there, my lord. Did you attend, or did you hear these things from King Arthur?"

"I—I was there, my lady. I was young for it, just fourteen. I accompanied my father. He was convinced that our future lay with Britain, and he brought me over to fight at his side for Uther. He was wounded in the battle and, when he recovered, went home. I stayed to serve the new King." He spoke absently, his attention focused on what he had not said.

The conversation lagged, for we had heard about the battle, and at length Elaine excused herself. Leonora sat nodding in the sun. I leaned toward Lancelot.

"These are heavy matters, Lancelot," I whispered. "What has the High King said to you about it?"

Lancelot took a deep breath. "He has never spoken about it to anyone at all. Unless to Merlin. It is a subject the whole court avoids. I—I did not know you knew."

"I have heard rumors only. I have told no one."

He met my eyes. "Can you forgive him this, Guinevere? It is a great sin. It would be within your right to refuse him for this. No one could hold it against you."

"But—then the whole Kingdom would know for certain," I said softly. He nodded and touched my hand. "Yes. But Arthur would survive it."

I rose unsteadily and went to the parapet. Lancelot followed. "Before I answer, there is another question I must ask you. Since you love him, I know what you will say. But you must, you *must* tell me the truth."

Lancelot took both my hands in his. "I will not lie to you. I swear it by most holy God."

My whole body shook with fear at the risk I took, but somehow I found the courage to ask him. "Did Arthur kill the children at Dunpelder?"

Lancelot went white and stepped back, but his grip upon my hands was firm. "No. Never."

"Everyone thinks he did."

"No one who knows him thinks so."

"That is not an answer. Perhaps you do not know him well enough."

Anger darkened his eyes. "I know him better than I know myself. It is not in him. He did not do it."

"Has he said so? To you?"

"Yes."

"Who did the deed, then?"

"He does not know. But it must have been either Lot or Morgause herself." He spoke the woman's name reluctantly, as if it left a bad taste in his mouth.

"Then why do the rumors persist, if he is innocent?"

Lancelot shrugged. His face was cold. "Blame must land somewhere. The Witch of Orkney has seen to it that it fell on him."

I struggled to hold back the final accusation, but it was a moment of truth between us, and it came out. "He stood to gain so much."

Lancelot's features twisted in revulsion; still, he held my hands. "No one ever gains by killing children. The crime itself leaves a stain upon the soul. Had Arthur done it, he would not be the man he is now."

I exhaled in relief, and warmth returned to his face. "But this other evil—you admit his guilt. Has that deed not left a mark upon his soul?"

Lancelot's hands tightened around my own. "Indeed it has. So deep a mark, he will never be healed of it. That is why he cannot bear to hear her mentioned, though she is his kin. If you dare, you can make him talk about the massacre at Dunpelder. But you will never hear him speak the name 'Morgause.'" Lancelot paused and dropped my hands. "You must decide, Gwen, if you can forgive him. You must decide now. If you wish to withdraw, I must get the word out soon."

I looked down, hopelessly torn. Lancelot had offered me a way out, had opened the door, and now stood aside like a gentleman to let me go through, if I would. But what was beyond that door, I could not see. A tarnished

Arthur, for certain. What would the people of Britain do when they knew the truth as I now knew it? What would Lancelot think of me if I refused? I felt a sob rise in my throat and squeezed my eyes shut. I knew what I must do.

I gathered my courage and met his eyes again, clear and gray and trusting. "It was done in ignorance," I whispered. "One should not be punished for ignorance. I know I feel it is unjust when it is done to me. So I should not be honest with myself if I held it against the High King."

Lancelot flung himself to his knees and clutched my hand, pressing it to his lips. "O noble heart!" he cried. "What forbearance is this in one so young and unworldly? May God in His Heaven bless you, I believe you are worthy of him!"

"What's this? What's this?" Leonora cried, waking suddenly. "What's happened here?"

Lancelot jumped to his feet, coloring, and bowed in her direction. "If I am out of turn, good Leonora, please forgive me. Lady Guinevere has just revealed her noble soul, and I have thanked her on the King's behalf."

Then he turned and fled. Leonora looked at me in bewilderment.

"Don't ask," I said wearily. "It's too much to tell. Come, let's get in out of this hot sun."

11 ♕ THE PARTING

The day of departure approached. I noted that Ailsa said very little to me and clutched her amulets a great deal. Even Elaine, whom I expected to show increasing excitement, watched me worriedly. I had no idea what about me concerned them.

On the last day of May I finished the bridegroom's gift. I had thought long and hard over what I could give a King who had gifts beyond counting, and finally decided that it must be something I made myself. I took some fine white wool, lined it with white silk, and fashioned it into a day robe, such as King Pellinore wore when illness or bad weather kept him indoors. But I wanted to make it finer and more comfortable, for surely warriors must enjoy a change from leather and mail. This was a plain shift, warm enough for all but the coldest days, with soft silk next to the skin. It could be worn loose or belted and was edged in dark blue so as not to show dirt. Over the left breast I embroidered a design of my own invention: interlocking squares in the Celtic pattern, stitched in blue, forming a square turned on end; and within, the Red Dragon of Britain standing on hind feet, clawing the air. And above it all, in the tiniest of stitches for which my work was best known, a silver star to represent the kingstar that had lighted in the west the night of Arthur's begetting. And that was all. The rest of the garment was without ornament, simple and fine. Elaine was after me for weeks to add some decoration to the sleeves, or along the hemline, but I refused. It would not be my gift, if it was not as I liked it.

I showed it to no one but Elaine and Ailsa. We packed it carefully in cloth wrappings, and then within a box, and it was placed with my traveling chests that were already in readiness. Then King Pellinore, who had been chuckling secretly for weeks, revealed his wedding gift to the High King. His carpenters had fashioned for Arthur another round table, three times as large as the one in Pellinore's hall. It broke down into sections for ease of transport and to enable it to be taken through doorways, but he displayed it proudly to us all before it was disassembled. It was made of white oak and sanded and polished until it shone like glass. It could easily seat thirty men and could do double duty as a dinner table, or in the council chamber. The Companions were impressed and complimented Pellinore until his poor head was swollen with pride. Alyse declared it would take months to get him back in line.

As the day of departure neared, I should have been nervous, but I felt instead both exhilarated and terrified. One evening Elaine and I took Lancelot up to the western tower to watch the sun set over the sea. The sky was aflame with light, and we watched in silence as the red streaks burned purple and the evening star blazed forth.

"I shall miss Wales," I said softly. Elaine turned to me, and I saw there were tears in her eyes.

"I've always lived in sight of the sea," she exclaimed. "I cannot imagine what life will be like without it."

"Caer Camel is not far from the sea," Lancelot offered. "You cannot see it from the towers, but you can see the signal fires on the tor of Ynys Witrin, which sits on the Lake of Avalon, which is fed by the sea tides."

It was not the same, but no one said so. Lancelot seemed subdued.

"Has there been any news from the north?" I asked.

"There has been no fighting, my lady. The High King and his allies have shown the Saxons a strong front. I believe they are working on a treaty and on strengthening the line of defenses."

"There is no new word on when—when—" I could not finish, so Lancelot finished for me.

"No. My instructions are to take you to Caer Camel and there await him."

I nodded. In the darkness, Lancelot took my hand. Elaine had her handkerchief to her face, and Leonora had not wished to make the climb. I breathed out slowly as excitement and longing filled me. I now understood what I had only felt on the first day of his visit. In a month's time he had become more precious to me than life. His touch inflamed me, his smile robbed me of breath. Each night I dreamed I stood in his embrace, and each morning I awoke yearning for his kiss. And I knew that he felt the same. It was exhilarating, agonizing, thrilling, almost overwhelming, but it also hurt more than daggers, and all at the same time. So we stood in silence, hand in hand, in the beauty of the long June evening, loving without hope, and thinking of Arthur.

In bed that night, Elaine put her arms around me and said, "I know now, Gwen. I know why you've been so happy and so sad, and why you are not nervous about leaving, and why you so dread Arthur. You love Lancelot."

"Please, Elaine—"

"I shall never tell a soul. I was angry with you, though, until I saw that you could not help it, any more than I could. But what are we to do, Gwen?"

I gripped her by the wrists. "There is nothing to be done."

"Is there no way to talk to them and come to some agreement? That you may take Lancelot, and I Arthur?"

"No!" I cried, the tears that had been kept back at such cost all day finally bursting forth. "No, there is not! Think, Elaine! Arthur is High King of Britain, and Lancelot his second-in-command. The honor of all Britain is in our hands!"

"But—but it seems so unfair!"

"Yes. It is unfair. To you, to me, to Lancelot; most of all, to the King himself. But I truly don't see what is to be done about it. We must bear it. That is all."

"And if I can't bear it?" Elaine cried in despair.

"Elaine, you must!" I had a sudden prevision that filled me with horror. "Elaine, attend me! You must make me a promise—when we get to Caer Camel, you must behave as if you care nothing about the King. You must pretend that you dislike him. Be polite but always, always cool. Don't follow him with your eyes, don't put yourself in his way—you know what I mean. Everyone's honor depends on it. Will you promise?"

Elaine wept. "What you ask is impossible and you know it!"

"It is no more than I must do toward Lancelot. I know it is hard, but we are strong. You *have* to do it. It is the only way."

"You ask too much. I cannot promise."

"Then," I said slowly, "you cannot come."

She gasped. "You cannot prevent me! Mother has given me permission!"

"I can send you home with her when the celebrations are over. I will be Queen then. Even your mother must be obedient to my command."

Elaine went suddenly still and silent. Her tears dried but her body trembled. For a long time she said nothing. I waited in wretchedness, remembering Gwillim kneeling at my bed, sacrificing his friendship to my power. But I had no choice—it was the Kingdom's honor.

"I see," she said at last in a different voice. "Very well. I promise."

"You will be discreet? And engage in no embarrassing display?"

"I promise."

"And you will stay out of his way, as much as is in your power, and never let him know what is in your heart?"

"I promise."

I exhaled slowly. "And I will hold you to it. I have sworn to do the same with Lancelot. If we break these vows, we shame ourselves, and Wales, and Britain. I know it makes the future bleak, when it should be bright. But somehow, the future must be borne."

Suddenly the day was upon us. The castle yard was filled with loaded wagons, servants scurried everywhere to fetch packages and search for last-minute, forgotten items. The troops stood by their mounts, surrounding the caravan. Goods and gifts were bundled onto pack mules. A stableboy held Zephyr's bridle in one hand and Nestor's in another, and he had his hands full. The women's litters were just behind, and from my window I saw Leonora taking charge of the women's arrangements, while Kay supervised the troops and the loading procedures. He was good at his job, patient and exacting, organized and able to keep track in his head of a thousand details. Everyone who needed information came to him, and he knew where everything was, or where it was headed, or when it would be needed, and whose responsibility it was to tend.

"Come, Guinevere," Alyse commanded. "It is time."

Lancelot appeared at the doorway and made a low obeisance to the queen. "The litters are prepared, my lady. King Pellinore is mounted and ready to be off."

"Thank you, Lancelot. We are ready. I suppose, Guinevere, you will choose to ride like a man again?"

Lancelot was shocked at her tone, but I was not. To Alyse, I was still her sister's daughter and her ward. I was not yet her Queen.

"No, madam. On this journey I shall ride in the litter with Elaine. But I should like to ride into Caer Camel when we get there."

And to everyone's surprise, I consented to be carried, while my mare walked alongside, unbridled. But I thought there might be people who would come out at crossroads to see the girl the High King had chosen to wed, and I wished to appear to them as they wished to see me. But once we got to Caer Camel, I wished to be myself. Before the people who would live with me, I wanted no false impressions. Also, to tell truth, I both dreaded and craved Lancelot's company. It was easier in the litter with Elaine, who knew my secret, than it would be riding by his side, with my face a mask and my heart in turmoil.

I was right about the people's interest in their new Queen. Not just at crossroads, but along every highway people stopped their labors and came out to watch the caravan go by. Elaine and I kept the sides of the litter open since the weather was fine, and people threw us flowers and called to us as we passed. As I got used to it, I waved to them, and they cried out their blessings and good wishes. It became a real procession, all the way through Wales, past Caerleon, across the Severn, and down into the Summer Country. Every night we stopped and set up tents, and for three hours or so received the good folk who lived round about, and accepted gifts of all kinds. I sat in a little gilded chair, with Queen Alyse on one hand, and Elaine on the other, Lancelot behind me, Bedwyr to one side, and Pellinore to the other. Kay stood at the door and let well-wishers in by twos and threes. They all brought gifts, from carved tools to woven stuffs, to trinkets to hens, vegetables and fresh eggs. One village maiden brought a yellow songbird she had trained to sing, and this caught my fancy. She kept it in a little cage of willow reeds, and it sang joyful melodies all day. Everyone who came was kind, and blessed me, and everyone seemed to go away pleased and satisfied. The farther south we went, the more people crowded to see us. Bedwyr, who was a quiet man with a shy manner, grinned at me one night as he handed me a goblet.

"My lady, you were born for this," he said proudly. "I wish Arthur could see it."

"You may be sure," Kay answered, "that he will hear about it."

Early in the mornings and very late at night I spent time with Zephyr, grooming her, crooning to her, occasionally riding her. Lancelot came with me for escort at these times, but he kept his distance. Eyes were upon us, it seemed to me.

On the tenth day we camped in sight of the signal fires of Ynys Witrin, the Isle of Glass, the Holy Hill, and knew that the next day would bring us to Caer Camel. Kay left us that night to ride on to the fortress, for he was frantic with worry that his lieutenant had not carried out his instructions, and he felt strongly that nothing should go amiss the day that Arthur's bride came to his home. Since we were so close to Caer Camel, messengers came and went constantly. The High King was still in the north, but expected well before the solstice. In his stead, I was to be welcomed by Melwas, King of the Summer Country. There was to be a ceremony, everything would be formal, stiff and endless, and I did not look forward to it. For one thing, it meant the end of Lancelot's company. For another, it meant the beginning of yet another period of preparation and waiting that would end only with the High King's arrival. All I could see ahead was one trial after another.

Hundreds of people came that night to pay their respects, and Bedwyr had to send to Caer Camel to have more carts brought up before morning to carry all the gifts the kind people brought. The people themselves truly amazed me. Arthur was a person to them, not just their war leader who kept their lands from the Saxons. He was more real to them than he was to me, and they were intensely curious about the girl he had chosen to marry. They came from every walk of life, not just lords' domains, many old and poor, some of them in good health, some in bad. Everyone wanted just a few minutes of my time, and when I saw that Bedwyr was ready to quit after three hours, I signaled him to continue. I excused Alyse and Elaine, since they were tired from the journey and wanted to rest, but I continued to see the people myself.

"My lady Guinevere," Lancelot murmured after four hours had passed, "are you not tired? Should you not take rest for tomorrow?"

"Yes, my lord, I am, and I should. But look at the people outside. Think of the distance they have come, and for what? Just to greet me and wish me good health and long life. How can I turn them away?"

Lancelot glanced at Bedwyr, who smiled and shrugged. "You can do nothing, Lancelot. It's just what Arthur would say." Lancelot nodded. The people kept coming.

The morning broke cool and cloudy, with a rose-pink haze across the sun, and the meadowlands swathed in fog. I was up early to tend Zephyr, whom I would ride today, and to have some time to myself for contemplation. I was alone in the horse lines, but people were up and about, for I heard the voices of grooms and cooks, although I could not see them. Zephyr did not like the fog, and it made her a little edgy. She moved restlessly and tossed her head while I tried to braid her mane. Then suddenly she calmed and stood quietly. My heart began to race. Lancelot's face appeared like magic in the mist across her shoulder.

"Lancelot!"

"Guinevere."

We stood and looked at each other.

"I came to tell you," he began, and then stopped. He cleared his throat. "How much I have enjoyed your company. I think you are the bravest woman I have ever known, and the kindest and the truest. I know you look at what is to come as a trial to be endured, but I want to assure you—Gwen, you will come to love him, as we all do. You won't be able to help it, any more than I was able to help—you know I love you, Guinevere, and I will always be at your service, whatever happens. But for Arthur's sake, we cannot—"

"Oh, Lancelot!" I whispered. "It will kill me to say farewell! And I couldn't help it, either! Lancelot, I will love you till I die." I gasped as the words came out; they were the last words I had meant to say! Lancelot ducked under the mare's head and took me in his arms. Thank God the mist lay heavy around us, for he kissed me with passion, and I returned his love. Then he was gone, and I collapsed breathless against the mare's body, shaken to my soul. How the future was to be borne, I did not know. I had no protection against Lancelot.

By midmorning the mist had lifted, and the sun shone forth in splendor. Lancelot rode at my side, stone-faced and silent, wearing his sword in its ceremonial scabbard of silver set with jewels. We rode slowly, for we still had litters, and I was content to walk along, wave to the crowds who lined the road, and let the time pass. It was lovely country we rode through, rolling green hills where sheep grazed, fertile farmland, thick woods full of game. In the west from Ynys Witrin the marsh birds came in flocks, wheeling overhead and calling, and then soaring back to the Lake of Avalon. It was a rich land compared to stony Wales, soft and green and full of life.

In early afternoon Caer Camel came into view. I caught my breath at the sight of it, and Lancelot finally smiled. "There it is, Guinevere. Your new home."

There were twelve turrets, each with a flag flying gaily in the summer breeze. The castle looked huge, even from this distance, and I knew from the soldiers' talk that there was a triple ring of fortifications around it. The sandstone walls shone golden in the sun, and it looked lovely set upon its green hill. The closer we got, the steeper I realized were the sides of this hill. Only the lower shoulders were forested. Most of it was sheep meadow and open, so as to see the enemy's approach. But the fortress itself was gigantic. At one end of the flat-topped hill stood the castle, at the other a sizable woodland, all within the ring of fortifications. A city would grow there in time, although in those days there were only workmen's huts outside the castle. As we approached along the western road, we saw the great, sweeping thoroughfare that ran up to the studded double gates: the entrance to Caer Camel. This road was wide enough for ten men riding abreast, and the steep sections were paved with rough stones so the turf would never wash away in the spring rains. This was the road down which Arthur's fearful cavalry flew at a moment's notice, swooping down upon the enemy almost before he had time to draw his sword.

"Will Merlin be there?" I asked Lancelot suddenly.

"No, my lady. Probably not."

"Why not?"

"He is old, Gwen. He has retired to a small house in the forest east of here, where he lives with an apprentice. Arthur rides out to visit him every now and again, but Merlin seldom comes to Caer Camel."

"Won't he come for the—the wedding?"

"If Arthur wants him, he will be there. But I shouldn't say it's likely."

"What has Merlin advised the King about this match?"

Lancelot eyed me warily. "It's odd that you ask. He was there when your name was proposed and said nothing. When Arthur asked him for his advice, he simply said 'what will be, will be.' No one knows how he truly feels."

I shuddered suddenly, remembering my audience with Princess Morgan. "I know how he feels."

Slowly the procession climbed the great roadway. Sentries saluted Lancelot, and he gave the word to open the fortress gates. Within stood King Melwas, a huge, blond man with hard, light eyes, and beside him, old white-robed Nimue of Avalon, Lady of the Lake, and Landrum, Caer Camel's Christian bishop, overdressed. A crowd of people stood behind them, and as we rode up, they broke into cheering and shouting.

Lancelot dismounted, then came around to help me down. I slid off the mare into his arms, and he recoiled as if he had been burned. We took up our positions, my hand upon his arm, and faced King Melwas. He bowed low, the Lady curtsied, the bishop nodded. They each made a speech, welcoming me to Caer Camel on King Arthur's behalf. Melwas was brief enough but the Lady went on at length, praising the Good Goddess, describing Arthur's virility and strength with a light in her eye, blessing me with fertility and talking hungrily about procreation until I began to blush. Melwas, who stood half the time staring at me open-mouthed, and the other half glaring at Lancelot, finally interrupted and brought her back to the subject at hand. I was most grateful for this. Beneath my hand, Lancelot's arm was trembling.

Then Bishop Landrum stepped forward, lavishly bedecked in gold and crimson robes, with an ornate jeweled cross hung on his breast. He began a long tirade upon the banishment of heathens and the anathema of pagan ways in a civilized land. Clearly he was enraged at the inclusion of the Lady in the welcoming ceremonies and was determined not to be outdone. But the old priestess had been included by Arthur's order, it was certain. I began to see an even-handedness here that without doubt was not shared by any of the participants.

At length, the bishop finished, and Lancelot and I both knelt to receive his blessing. Then Lancelot led me forward, followed by King Melwas and the Lady, and the bishop and Bedwyr, down the street of workmen's huts where swordsmiths, blacksmiths, armorers, coopers, carpenters, and tanners all stood outside and bowed as we went by. There was nothing there yet that was not devoted to the arts of war. At last we came to the marble steps that led to the doors of the castle. Kay was there, smiling proudly at me, and I was glad to see him. As Arthur's seneschal, the castle was his domain. He thanked Lancelot formally for bringing Arthur's bride safe and virgin from Wales, and Lancelot rather stiffly replied that anything done in the High King's service was his pleasure to perform. Then Kay took me into the castle and led me to my quarters. The halls were cool and dark after the bright June sunshine, and by the time my eyes adjusted to the dim light, we were at a wide oak door carved with the Dragon of Britain and guarded by two sentries.

Beyond this door were the Queen's quarters, which had never been occupied. At long last, after many thanks and assurances, Kay left and it was over. Alyse, Elaine, and I stood in the round foyer, with Leonora, Cissa, Grannic, and Ailsa huddled by the door, and we looked about us. The place was a fighting fortress, with smooth stone walls, narrow windows, dirt floors, and stone benches. Some attempt had been made to make it fit for women. Straw was strewn across the dirt, and tapestries, touched by moth around the edges, hung on the walls.

"Well!" Alyse exclaimed. "I am glad we brought so much with us from Wales. I thought before we were burdening ourselves needlessly, but now I wonder if we brought enough."

But I found the situation amusing and rather touching. "There have been no women here. We are the first." From this central foyer branched hallways with spacious rooms. My own chambers were somewhat more elaborately furnished. There were three rooms below: two sitting rooms and a maid's chamber with wide, glazed windows that looked out upon a terrace and a lovely, walled garden. From the maid's chamber rose a stairway to my sleeping chamber. The sitting rooms were floored with colored tiles in the Roman style, depicting animals and surrounded by flowers. The walls were hung with imported carpets in rich reds and blues. Blue and gold cushions adorned plain wood benches. Someone had gone to great lengths to make these rooms habitable for women, but that someone had most definitely been a man.

Alyse began to give orders to her women as to the hangings and coverings we would need. I turned to face her. "I will give the directions as to the furnishings of my home, Alyse."

She stopped, shocked. I saw the realization sink into them all, one by one. This *was* my home now, and not theirs. Within days I would be their sovereign Queen. And one by one they sank into a curtsy, even Elaine, and last Alyse.

I went alone up the stairs into the sleeping chamber. It was a large, octagonal room, opening on a terrace, flagged in stone, that overlooked the garden. The bed was large and made of carved fruitwood, hung with silk hangings of light blue with golden trimmings. It looked old, and the workmanship was very fine. I later learned it was Ygraine's and had come from Tintagel. It was the bed where Arthur himself was conceived and born, and where Ygraine had died. The floor tiles were blue and gold and white and covered with a soft carpet of blue, gold, and rose, so thick and rich I knew it must be one of those imported from the East. A bowl of roses sat on a slender-legged table by the window, and an old chest, made of pearwood and carved all over with flowers and vines, stood at the foot of the bed. It was a simple room, but the touches were fine; it was beautiful.

There was only one other doorway, and this was covered with a heavy leather flap. I lifted it tentatively and, hearing nothing on the other side, went in. It was another bedchamber, the twin of mine in shape and size, but plain and completely different in style and taste. The floor was polished wood, without coverings. The windows were unglazed. The bed was large, carved of some dark, shining wood I did not know, and covered with a thick blanket of stitched bearskins. There was an oak chest in one corner and a marble-topped writing table beside a triple-flamed lamp. The bed itself stood on a low dais, and on the wall at its head hung an old silk banner, much worn, of the Red Dragon of Britain clawing at a field of gold.

My heart thudded painfully in my chest, and my palms began to sweat. This was the High King's bedchamber. There could be no doubt of it. Why had I imagined that his rooms would be in another part of the castle? But they were not. This was his room, and it spoke to me about the man himself. It was a soldier's room, bare of all ornament except the banner. He wrote here, or read. He slept here, dressed here, and that was all. It was clean and quiet and calm. I went to the window. It looked west, as mine did, and in the far distance I fancied I could see the dim shadow of Ynys Witrin. Of course the King would want to be able to see the signal fires, just in case the sentry slept. Aside from the entrance to my own chamber, there was only one other door, and it led to a staircase. No doubt his chamberlain slept in the room below. I turned and walked slowly to the great bed. The bearskins were soft to my touch. I wondered about them until I recalled that his name came from "Artos," which meant "Bear." They were probably a gift. Under the bearskins the bed sheets were fine and white and clean, but not nearly so fine as the ones we had brought him. This lifted my spirits, and I looked around the room again in satisfaction. It was a restful place, and if it suited Arthur, it was a good sign.

I returned to my own chamber and sat upon the bed, thinking hard. I thought I could bear any kind of husband, even a slovenly or domineering one, provided he was fair. It would be impossible to live with a man whose respect could not be won. I was prepared to do anything the High King desired to make him think well of me and not regret his choice. If he was at all fair, the future might be endured. Somehow, seeing his room gave me hope. Next to his skill as a war leader, King Arthur was renowned for his fairness. "Arthur's justice" was a by-word for fair treatment. If so, perhaps Lancelot was right, and it might not be the trial I dreaded.

But how, dear God, how was Lancelot himself to be endured? He could not leave court—Arthur needed him—and I would die if he left. But how was I to stand it if he stayed? The utter hopelessness of it all swept over me in a wave, and at last I gave in and wept, burying my head in the cushions, sobbing like a child. I did not care. I was alone for the first time in months.

At least, I thought I was alone. But by and by I felt eyes upon me, and when I looked up, I saw a thin youth in a servant's tunic peeking in through the leather curtain.

He looked dreadfully frightened, and his eyes darted all about. He tried to look anywhere but at me.

"Is—is my lady all right?" he asked timidly. "Is there aught that I can do?"

I smiled, wiping my eyes. "There is nothing wrong that time will not heal. I am homesick."

"Ah." He plucked nervously at his shirt. "Would you care for honey mead, or perhaps wine?"

"Who are you?"

He bowed low, and kept his eyes down. "My name is Bran, my lady. I am the High King's body servant."

"If you are the King's body servant, why are you not with the King?"

He flushed hotly and stammered. "I—I—I am an apprentice, really. Varric is the chamberlain. He went with the King. I—I came up to straighten the room and set the coals in the grate. Then I heard weeping."

"Straighten the room?" I cried, incredulous. "There is nothing to straighten!" I gasped as I realized what I had revealed, as Bran looked up and grinned. I burst out laughing then, and he laughed with me. He was about my age.

"Please, Bran, apprentice chamberlain, do not tell the High King you found me weeping in here on the day of my arrival. The last thing he should have to worry about is a foolish, homesick girl."

"If I know my lord, he will understand it. I was homesick, too, when I first came here. He caught me weeping more than once."

"And what happened? Did you get a whipping?"

His jaw dropped and he stared. "A whipping? From the High King?" He did not know how to respond; clearly he took me for an idiot.

"Never mind. I see you did not. Does the High King never anger, then?"

"My lady, I have not seen it. But I have heard that he does not like his time wasted."

I smiled. "Who does? Where do you come from, Bran, and how long have you served King Arthur?"

"From Less Britain, my lady. I have been with him five years."

"You are content to stay? You don't miss your home?"

He straightened. "I wish to be nowhere else but here." Then he smiled. "You will get used to it in time. There's a lot going on. Kings and princes in and out, knights coming to offer service, knights riding out to adventures, priests and enchanters everywhere—" He stopped as I shuddered.

"And old Merlin lurking about the corridors, no doubt."

Bran looked sideways out of his eyes, and lowered his voice. "Do not let the High King hear you call him old, my lady. Merlin will not confess what it was that aged him, but the High King believes it was poison."

Now it was my turn to stare. "Surely your life will be longer if you keep such things to yourself, Bran."

"I can trust you, my lady," he said simply, with all the certainty in the world. "Would you like some mulled wine? We have a special way of making it here—"

"No, thank you, Bran. I would like a drink of water."

"I will bring you a carafe. We have a spring on Caer Camel with the sweetest water in Britain." He darted back through the curtain and then popped his head through once more.

"You might as well know, my lady. I came up here to set the room to rights because we have just had news. The High King is on his way and will arrive the day after tomorrow."

12 ♕ THE BRIDE

I had no time to be nervous. If we thought we had been busy packing, it was nothing to the unpacking. Good Kay lent us all the hands we wanted, and there was a constant flow of people, laden with furniture, hangings, cushions, and sundry necessities to and from the women's quarters.

Elaine's rooms rapidly became the most luxurious, and what excess trappings she could not use, she found use for in my sitting rooms. Ailsa established herself in the small sleeping chamber at the foot of my stair. My own bedchamber I left the way I found it except for two things. I hung the singing yellow bird in its willow cage in the corner by the window, and I brought up the small carved bench that I had brought with me from Northgallis when I went to Gwynedd. It had belonged to my mother, and she had covered the bench cushion with needlework of her own design, showing the blue sea, the white stag of Northgallis, and the gray wolf of Gwynedd, with snowcapped Y Wyddfa behind. This bench I set upon the little terrace, so that I could sit there of an evening and watch the setting of the sun as I used to do on the towers of Pellinore's castle.

The rest of the castle was also thrown into an uproar by the news of Arthur's coming. The wedding gifts were all laid out, the hundreds of gifts we had collected on our journey were displayed, along with those brought by the lords and nobles who daily arrived and set up tents upon the open fields, come to see the wedding. King Pellinore's round table was set up in the dining hall, which was the only room big enough for it. All these people who flooded into Caer Camel had to be fed, and there were daily hunting parties into the woodlands for game and to the salt marshes for fowl. All the horses that carried the good folk and pulled their wagons had to be housed and tended to. All these things Kay oversaw, and although he was pressed to fuming point, he never lost his temper or said an unkind word to anyone.

Lancelot kept to the stables, which was part of his responsibility as Arthur's Master of the Horse, and with Bedwyr he drilled the guard troops daily. I saw him once or twice from Elaine's window, exercising Zephyr, and it was a rare pleasure to watch my mare's elegant paces, which I had felt but never seen. Elaine was beside herself with joy and excitement. At long last she was going to see King Arthur in the flesh. She kept pinching herself to be sure that it was not a dream. She could not decide which gown to wear when we were presented to him. I sat upon her cushioned chair and stared out her window, which faced east toward the open meadows and beyond to the wood. The meadows were alive with tents of every description, with lords and ladies from every corner of Britain. I was thankful the weather was dry for there was no mud. As it was, the meadows were so trodden down I wondered if the grass would ever come back.

"Gwen, you're not attending! I've asked you three times if I should wear the yellow or the blue."

"Wear what pleases you, Elaine."

"But what are you wearing? I don't want to wear the same."

"I don't know. I haven't given it thought."

"But you must! He arrives tomorrow!"

It was an effort to turn away from the window and concentrate on clothing. "What is your mother wearing?"

"The gold." One should have expected it.

"Then wear the yellow, and I shall wear the blue. I must wear the sapphire, remember."

"Yes, and have Ailsa dress your hair with the seed pearls and bluebells again, as you did the night the Companions arrived. That was wonderful."

"There aren't any bluebells. It's June."

"Well, cornflowers then. I know I saw blue flowers in the meadows as we approached King's Gate. Send Kay to get some."

I sighed and turned back to the roiling throng that jammed the road from the valley below. "Poor Kay. I suppose I might ask Bran."

"Who's Bran?"

"The King's apprentice chamberlain."

Her eyebrows rose. "And how did you meet him?"

"Come sleep with me tonight, and I'll show you. Oh, Elaine, you will be with me tonight, won't you? Why didn't you come up to me last night?"

Elaine shook her head. "Mother forbids it. It's bad luck. The bride must sleep alone until—after you're married I can."

"But after I'm married—" I stopped, beginning to shake. The truth was, I had no idea what to expect. No one had ever spoken to me about what arrangements obtained between husband and wife. And everyone might be different. How was I to know what to do?

"I mean, when the King's away, of course," Elaine said hastily, coloring. It was too late. Arthur the man had intruded into the conversation, and we could not be comfortable with each other now. I left her shaking out the yellow gown and went to my rooms to help Ailsa unpack my wardrobe.

He came at sundown. The thundering of cavalry could be heard for miles, and I raced down from my chamber to Elaine's room and huddled with her by the window. Lancelot had troops lining the street from King's Gate, keeping back the crowds. I saw him sitting quietly on Nestor, and Bedwyr was there on his big chestnut, as twilight darkened to night. All the men had torches, and when the King came, he rode down a tunnel of light. His stallion was white and bunched his haunches to come to a sliding stop right at the castle steps. The King slid off in an easy motion as a groom stepped up to grasp the reins. He was too distant to see his features, but we could see his actions well enough. He went to Lancelot, who dismounted and saluted, but the King placed his hands upon his shoulders, said something, and then hugged him warmly.

"He is as tall as Lancelot," Elaine breathed in my ear. "But how broad his shoulders are!"

"Hush, Elaine."

He greeted Bedwyr likewise, then mounted the castle steps where Kay saluted at the door. Kay gave a long report and nodded in response to the King's questions. Then the King embraced him and slapped him on the back. He signaled to the guards, who moved to let the crowd of people into the forecourt, and they gathered at the steps. The King addressed them, but we could not hear his voice, for Elaine's window was glazed. Then the people raised a great cheer, which we heard even though the glazing, and the King turned and entered his castle. Lancelot glanced swiftly in our direction before he followed.

Elaine and I sat back and exhaled.

"Well!" Elaine exclaimed, glowing. "He's here at last! And every inch a warrior king. You don't suppose he would call an audience tonight, do you? After we are all dressed for bed?"

"I shouldn't think so. He's been away two months. There must be a lot to catch up on."

She raised an eyebrow. "I bet most of it's about you. He's probably grilling Lancelot right now."

I turned away, unable to bear the thought of it. "Won't you come up with me, Elaine? Just for a while?"

"Oh, Gwen, I'd love to! Just to peek into his chamber—but Mother would have my hide. I dare not do it. You'll be all right. Sit with Ailsa a while and have a hot posset."

I followed her advice. Ailsa and I sat together in her anteroom, talking about old times in Northgallis, and she sent for a warm drink, fragrant with spices. There must have been a sleeping potion in it, for soon I grew weary, and when she took me upstairs and tucked me into the great bed, I fell asleep instantly.

I awoke quite suddenly in the night to the sound of voices. I looked toward the leather curtain and saw the soft glow of lamplight around the edges. He was there. I clutched the coverlet about my throat and held my breath, listening. I could hear his heavy tread on the floorboards and heard him speaking to someone, probably Varric or Bran, but I could not hear the words. It was a warm voice, pleasant in tone and deep. I heard muffled responses, and quite suddenly the lamp went out, and all was quiet. I lay there for what seemed like a long time, but I heard nothing. At last, toward dawn, I drifted back to sleep.

I awoke with sunlight streaming in through the terrace doorway and knew that he was gone. I rose and donned my robe, then tiptoed to the curtain.

"Bran?" I called softly, hoping it was not Varric I heard stirring coals in the grate.

"My lady?" He came to the curtain and drew it aside. He looked tired but, in some indefinable way, satisfied. His King was back.

"Bran, were you up late last night?"

"Yes, my lady. We put the King to bed."

"Did—did he say anything about—"

Bran smiled. "Oh, yes, my lady. Of course he knew you had arrived safely. He got the full report from Sir Lancelot. But when he discovered I had met you—I did not tell him I heard you weeping, my lady. I said it was by accident."

"Oh, thank you, Bran. I am in your debt."

"Not at all, my lady. When he discovered I had met you, he asked me if I liked you."

"He did? Does he value your opinion so?"

"I could not say, my lady. But he knows that I am near your age, perhaps that was why he asked."

"What did you say?"

Bran's eyes widened. "Why, I told him the truth, of course. I said yes. He asked me why, and I told him you were without affectation. That seemed to please him."

I felt heat rise to my face. Bran looked suddenly shy and cast down his eyes, but I reached out and touched his arm. "Thank you, Bran. I think you have done me a great service."

"I told him the truth, my lady, as everyone does who knows him."

I drew back into my chamber and left him to his tasks. It boded well, that the High King was somewhat curious about me. It meant, perhaps, with luck, that he would treat me as a person. I did not want to hope too much; for if it were not so—and who could blame the High King of Britain if he had more important matters to think about than the thoughts and feelings of a girl?—I should be the more disappointed. I wondered how much Lancelot had told him. Had the King been able to see the truth behind his praise of me? I called Ailsa to me then, to occupy my mind with other thoughts.

Our audience was set for noon. People thronged all morning in the forecourt, waiting for the great doors to open. I sat with Elaine at her window, while Ailsa and Grannic dressed our hair, and watched them. Once again I noticed that people of every station were assembled, lords and ladies in fine clothes, knights and ladies-in-waiting, workmen, servants, peasants, and poor folk with only rags to wear. They all came, and they were all admitted.

Sometime later a page came to our door and brought the message that the High King was in court and waited upon our leisure. The time had come. Elaine and Ailsa put last-minute touches to my hair and gown. It was the smoke-blue gown Elaine had embroidered, and the High King's sapphire was round my neck, and Fion's earrings on my ears. Someone had gathered early cornflowers for my hair, which Ailsa dressed with seed pearls, braiding in the flowers to frame my face, and letting the long tresses hang loose down my back. In summer the sun turned my hair almost white, like a child's hair, much to my dismay. The gown itself was of heavy silk, and the day was warm, but I was shivering and my fingertips were ice.

Elaine gripped my arm, trembling. "Oh, Gwen, take care what you say! The honor of Wales is in your hands!"

As if I could forget it! With these helpful words ringing in my ears, I was led to the outer door. Lancelot was there, with Pellinore and Bedwyr, and I was never so glad to see him in my life. They led us through the long halls, where sentries snapped to attention at their posts, and slid their eyes sideways as we passed, watching. We came to the gilded doors of the Hall of Meeting and stopped. Lancelot looked down at me. My hand upon his arm trembled visibly.

"Courage, Gwen," he whispered, and I took a deep breath and stilled myself. He nodded to the guards, and the doors swung open. The babble of conversation stilled as the throng divided to let us pass, silent except for the occasional gasp and sigh. The High King's chair was on a dais at the end of the hall, and I gathered my courage and dragged my eyes off the tiles to look at him as we approached. He was standing, looking at me. It was a good face, of straight planes marked by dark brows, dark eyes, and straight lips. It was a rugged, handsome face, which one might expect of a warrior who was Uther's son. What caught me by surprise were his eyes. They were a rich, warm brown in color, glowing with a joyful light that seemed to come from within himself. He stood easily, waiting, not at all stiff or nervous, not shaking like a leaf in the winter wind, but calm and serene, and sure.

I dropped my eyes hastily and felt color rise to my face. I held on to Lancelot's arm for dear life and fought to collect my wits. The procession halted before the dais, and the High King came down the step to greet us.

"My lord Arthur," I heard Lancelot's voice dimly, "it is my pleasure to present to you the bravest, truest, loveliest maid in all Britain, Guinevere of Northgallis."

I sank helplessly into a curtsy at his feet. He extended a hand, brown from the sun, and raised me. He must have felt me shaking, for his voice was very kind.

"So this is the lass who has taken my Kingdom by storm." I glanced up quickly and saw he was smiling. "Since I left the north country, I have heard nothing but tales of your great beauty and your unflagging generosity to my

people. I thank you, Guinevere of Northgallis, for this service. You are welcome here."

I tried to speak, but could not. He gently squeezed my hand and
brought me to stand beside him, then turned to greet Queen Alyse and
Elaine. I never heard what he said to them, for my head was whirling. His
flesh was warm and dry and comforting somehow. He imparted strength and
ease of heart to me, I know not how. It was always so in his presence. It was
his gift.

When the greetings were over, King Arthur offered me his arm and led
me to the small, gilded chair that stood next his own. He bowed over my
hand, screening me for a moment from the throng.

"You need say nothing," he said softly. "We must greet all the people
who have come, but you may let me do the talking."

"My lord is kind," I whispered.

"Thou art young," was his reply, and then he straightened. It reminded
me suddenly of Fion, who had a habit of saying personal things in Latin.

It took hours. First the nobles came forward, lord and lady, and bowed
and curtsied and welcomed the High King home and looked me over from
head to toe and wished us well. Then came the common folk, and this took
longer, for they were mostly tongue-tied, but determined to say their piece.
Arthur was amazingly patient and kind, addressed some of them by name,
and knew their wives and kinfolk; others he met for the first time and took
time to inquire about their lives, the number of their cattle, and the success
of their crops, or the death of their elders. I had sense enough to realize that
there was military intelligence to be gleaned from these conversations, and
I was sure he was filing away new facts in the back of his mind, but he also
seemed genuinely interested in how his people lived and what they needed.

At last the greetings were over, but none made move to leave. Now the
petitioners lined up before him. The business of the High King's court was
about to begin. But first Arthur turned to me and looked somewhat anxiously into my face. "Are you tired, Guinevere? You need not stay for this. It
happens every day. You may leave when you will."

By this time I was able to manage a smile. "No, my lord. I am not tired.
Though it may happen every day, I have never seen it before. It would be
my pleasure to see the running of the Kingdom at firsthand."

He looked at me a moment, and his gaze was utterly direct.

"By Heaven," he said softly, "Lancelot was right." Then he grinned as I
colored. "You *are* one in a thousand."

So we sat for three hours while Arthur's justice was dispensed. He listened attentively to each case that was brought before him, and I thought
the questions he asked were to the point and clever. He was quick to smoke
out lies, and I began to understand why people told him truth. His decisions

were even-handed, and although not all parties went away pleased, I heard no grumbling. And after three hours had passed and everyone had been seen, he seemed as fresh and eager as he had at the start. At last he gave the signal that the meeting was ended and rose, extending a hand and raising me as well. He led me through a door behind the dais into a small ante-room. Lancelot was there, standing stiffly, waiting. Arthur stretched his arms and sighed. It was the first sign of weariness he had shown.

"I could do with a workout, Lancelot. Is there any chance of it?"

"Sword practice in the library," Lancelot said, his eyes lighting. "Or mud wrestling in the sties. There are crowds everywhere else." Arthur threw back his head and laughed. It was a deep, honest, joyful laugh, and I could not keep from smiling.

"What would I not give to be able to do it!" the King cried. Then he took my hand and raised it to his lips.

"You have been an angel, Guinevere. It bodes well. I wish we had more time to spend together. When is the solstice? Three days? Perhaps we could ride out together. Lancelot tells me you are accomplished. But I fear we may be too busy. Too many people about, and more are coming. I shall see you at dinner, at least." He inclined his head. "Till then."

I curtsied. "My lord." Lancelot offered his arm, and I took it.

The King paused at the door, suddenly looking almost shy. "I don't wish to be bold, or to instruct you in matters that are none of my concern," he began, and I froze, fearful of what was coming. "But I like you in blue," he finished, and disappeared.

I was so relieved I laughed out loud, though Lancelot was silent. He escorted me back to the women's quarters and stood solemnly by the door.

"You see," he said.

I nodded. "Yes."

I was awake late that night when the King came to bed. I saw the lamplight creep around the curtain, heard voices, the King's and one other, and then the light died. But the King did not sleep. Instead, he paced the chamber, back and forth, and I listened, amused, until I fell asleep to the steady sound of his measured tread.

We did not have time for riding. Two days were hardly sufficient to prepare for an event the Kingdom had waited so long to see. Thousands of people came to Caer Camel and camped upon the slopes outside the fortress walls. Their bonfires lit the night sky, their dancing and games and hunting cries filled the day with noise. I was taken to be examined by Bishop Landrum, a sour stick of a man, who questioned me at great length and at close quarters, with lust in his eyes and garlic on his breath, before pronouncing me fit to wed a Christian prince.

"I pray I will never have any sins to confess," I cried to Elaine when I returned, "for, most certainly, I would not tell that man!"

She quieted me somehow, and we both longed for friendly Father Martin. I was fretful and restless, much to the amusement of Alyse and her ladies. I could not ride out, for the crowds. I could only walk in the Queen's garden, for the palace was thick with strangers. So I paced there by the hour, much as Arthur paced his room at night, as the time crawled by. Whoever had designed the garden knew what he was about. There were pear trees set against the wall where the morning sun warmed them and creeping vines that flowered in many colors. Roses grew along the walks, and wildflowers and sweet herbs along the walls. It was peaceful there, when everyone would leave me alone, and I blessed the gardener, whoever he was. All it needed was a fountain for the birds to play in. As I paced, Elaine kept up a steady stream of chatter.

"He has fine, strong hands and a dexterous touch. Have you noticed how he holds his head when he is listening? His concentration is tremendous. He listens with every fiber of his body. No wonder grown men twice his age tremble before him! I'll bet he is skilled at bending other wills to his purpose. And such handsome features! His face should be stamped upon a coin. What joy it would be to see him wield a sword! With shoulders like that—who could stand against him? I've never known a man with such a bearing, such a presence. And his stride is twice the length of Lancelot's—"

"Heavens, Elaine!" I cried. "Have you looked at no one else besides the King? What have you been doing?"

"Don't worry," she said lightly. "I've been discreet. I'll wager a copper coin no one's seen me watching. And I'll wager another you could describe Lancelot from head to toe."

"I could. But I won't."

"Well," she said with a defiant toss of her head, "you were wrong about his falling short of my expectations. He is everything a king should be, and more. And he *does* have beautiful hands."

"Oh, Elaine!"

She came up to me and gripped my arm until it pained me. "Gwen," she whispered fiercely, "take care. You have never known a man like this. This is a powerful man."

"Well, of course, he is High—"

"I am not talking about kingship!" she said, leaning closer. "I am talking about the man himself. He has power of a kind you don't suspect. Take care you please him."

I felt heat rise slowly to my face as I trembled in her grip. I dared not ask her what she meant.

We took our meals in our quarters, by choice. But dinner was a public affair. The High King sat surrounded by his Companions, and I sat between Pellinore and Alyse, on his right hand. I was toasted every night and heard many speeches in my honor. Only Lancelot never looked my way. Every time I saw him he looked thinner and paler than the time before. Once or twice I saw Arthur look at him with compassion and felt a trickle of fear slide down my spine. I returned from this ordeal exhausted, for it was hot in the hall, what with the torches and the press of bodies. But sleep came hard. Ailsa mixed me potions, and on the night before the wedding, I sat on the floor with my head in her lap and cried. She stroked my hair and sang me songs as she had been wont to do in nursery days. But each night it was Arthur's restless pacing that lulled me finally to sleep.

The wedding day dawned cool and cloudy, with a fitful breeze. I knelt by my bed and prayed God to give me strength. I was up early, but Arthur was already up and about. Ailsa brought me tea, and we sat on my terrace and watched the morning mists rise off the distant meadows.

"It will clear," she predicted. "And be cool for the games. Never fear, my lady. 'Twill be a perfect day."

We were married at midmorning by the bishop in the church. King Pellinore was my escort, and as my guardian it was his right to give me to the King. I remember little of the preparations. My dress was white, and trimmed with laces. Arthur, too, was simply dressed in white. He wore a thin circlet of red gold on his head, and wonderful Excalibur hung from his jeweled belt. I remember the moment I first saw it, as King Pellinore led me down the aisle to where he stood. The scabbard was old, oiled leather, and very plain. But the hilt burned bright and deadly in the candlelight, while the dark emerald flashed once, as he turned toward me, and then lay quiet. It was a cold weapon, and dangerous, the Saxon-Slayer, and hugged his hip as if it were part of him. Kingship sat upon this man like a glowing mantle, and he wore it easily.

We were married while the mists lifted, and as I left the church on his arm, the sun broke through the clouds and the throng of people cheered.

I sat beside him at the wedding breakfast, for it was now my place, while Elaine sat weeping between her parents. Lancelot, straight and pale on the King's right, never glanced my way. All the people who could fit into the dining hall were given seats, rich and poor alike, and shared the same food and drink that was served to the King. I noticed that while wine was served to all, Arthur and I drank water only. The hall was loud with the babble of a hundred tongues, and at some tables the people sang and danced. The High King walked about the room, stopping at every table to say some word of thanks, or endure a humorous remark, or greet a friend. He did not seem to weary of it. I remarked to Bedwyr, who sat next me, that he had a talent for making friends.

"He loves his people," was Bedwyr's reply. And they, it seemed, loved him. As Lancelot continued to stare moodily at his plate, I kept talking to Bedwyr to keep nervousness at bay.

"And where is Merlin? I would have thought he would be here, to see the High King wed."

Bedwyr smiled and shook his head. "Merlin dislikes weddings, and he is getting old. He sent to beg to be excused, for he suffers from a chest cold. He will be here in a few days, however, for the High King has called a Council meeting. And Merlin is his chief counsellor."

This was good news and bad news. I was mightily relieved the old enchanter was not there, but uneasy about his coming. Sooner or later, I knew, I must face him.

King Arthur returned to his place, gathered the hall with a look, and raised a toast in praise of me. Everyone drank and cheered. Then I stood, to his surprise, and raised a toast in praise of Arthur, who brought glory and honor to Northgallis and all of Wales, by choosing a Welsh maiden as his bride. This brought the house down, and there were shouts of "Northgallis!" and "Pendragon!" as men slammed their goblets on the tables and stomped their boots upon the floor.

Arthur said nothing, but kissed my hand to the cheering of the crowd.

Then we returned to the church in grand procession, this time for my coronation. Arthur himself took the slender silver crown set with amethysts and set it on my head, while the bishop blessed me.

"It was my mother's," he said softly as he came close. "May you wear it in good health and have long life, as she did."

Wearing Ygraine's crown and feeling overwhelmed, I was led at last to the open fields by the woodlands, where flags waved gaily in the breeze and stands had been constructed for the King's guests. We spent the brilliant afternoon watching Arthur's Companions compete at various skills for the honor of his notice. There was wrestling, and swordplay, and foot races, and horseracing. There were even contests to see who could throw a spear the farthest and whose horse could pull the most tree trunks the greatest distance. Nowhere, although I looked for him, did I see Lancelot. But finally, as the shadows began to lengthen in the long, June twilight, I saw Nestor's head through the crowd and then heard the stallion scream. Lancelot rode out alone upon the field.

He gathered Nestor under him and began to canter in a circle. With a fluid change of lead they changed direction and circled the other way. Then he cantered away in a straight line, changing leads every four strides, every three, every two, *every stride*—it was like dancing! I held my breath in excitement. What skill was this! Then he galloped the horse down the field, gathering speed, till they raced by in a blur of motion and came to a full sliding stop, the stallion sitting on his haunches and the clods flying. The horse whirled and reared, striking out with his forelegs, and when Lancelot set him down, he began to canter sideways, bent around the rider's leg, first one way and then the other. It was breathtaking! How I longed to get astride Zephyr and teach her those things!

"I see you are a horseman in your soul," Arthur whispered, smiling.

"Yes, my lord," I breathed, unable to take my eyes from the field.

Then the stallion reared again, holding it, standing on two legs in arrested motion, then coming down and trotting smoothly forward. Suddenly he leaped into the air and kicked out with his hind legs, like a deer in full flight, and the crowds gasped. They did it three times, Lancelot landing lightly, never stirring from the horse's back, never tugging at the bit, hardly moving a leg. It was like magic. To wild applause, my own included, horse and rider came and stood before the King. Nestor ducked his proud head, as Lancelot touched his forehead with his sword.

Arthur was moved. He leaned over the railing and spoke to Lancelot. Above the roar of the crowd I could not hear what he said. Lancelot, white-faced, asked him something. The King paused and then assented. Lancelot saluted him once more, sheathed his sword, and rode away.

The competitions over, we all moved back indoors as dusk fell, to the great feast that awaited us. This time the wine that went around was not watered, and the men drank thirstily. Even the King partook of it, although I did not. Lancelot did not appear at dinner. When Bedwyr asked after him, the King replied without expression that he had asked to be excused, and after the demonstration he had given, he had not been refused.

"Is he ill?" Kay inquired, who overheard. "He looked well enough this morning. What ails him?"

Arthur turned slowly toward Kay. His eyes were dark and sorrowful, but his voice was hard. "It is something he has suffered from for weeks. He will be better in the morning."

Kay looked bewildered and shrugged. Bedwyr seemed to have lost something in his lap. The King could not mean what I thought he meant, I was certain, but I began to be uneasy. Suddenly Arthur downed the wine in his cup in a single gulp and signaled to bring on the bards.

Four bards sang for us that night, from the four corners of Britain. One of them was a Welshman with a melting tenor. We had all the King's favorite tales, and then the one about King Arthur that Merlin himself had devised. Several new tales had been composed for the occasion, one of them very lovely, accompanied by lap harp and flute. I enjoyed the music, and after the last bard had finished and been served his well-earned wine, I turned to Arthur to praise his choice.

I found him looking hard at me, seeing through me, in the way he had of judging men. It was a moment of testing, and I knew it even then. His color was high with the effects of wine, and his eyes were bright, but they pierced like a sword thrust and felt like cold steel. It took every ounce of courage I possessed to meet his gaze and hold it; this was in deadly earnest. There was no tenderness on his face. I saw suddenly that he knew everything, he who could judge a man's character to a hair's breadth and from whom few could keep secrets. He was wondering what manner of woman he had married. In that instant I felt his spirit reach out to me, and I felt his great need. I placed my hand upon his own as it rested in his lap.

"My lord."

"Art thou mine?" he asked in Latin, so low that only I could hear.

My throat ached, and I blinked back tears. I held onto his hand and from it drew strength. "King. I am thine."

He nodded and slowly lifted my hand to his cheek, where he held it resting against his face. At last he let me go and turned away. Released, I felt drained; strength had left me, and my hand shook as I reached for my water cup.

"Dearest Guinevere," Bedwyr whispered, leaning toward me and staring hard at his plate, "I bless you."

I shook my head, but I could not speak. There was no way to explain the turmoil of emotion I felt. The power of the man was real, and it was tremendous. And Elaine had known it before me.

Singers and jesters were circulating now, and the hour was growing late. Alyse kept looking at me expectantly. The songs grew bawdier and bawdier, and many of the men, who were drunk, started telling anecdotes and singing little ditties that reflected on the High King's prowess in more domestic fields of battle. Alyse's looks grew pointed, but she had never told me what to do. At last I turned to Arthur, who was laughing. He had recovered his good spirits and looked at me kindly.

"Yes, I think it's time you went. It's only going to get rougher, and I see Alyse is already embarrassed. Take the ladies away. We will be hours yet." Then he caught me by the hand as I rose and kissed my upturned palm. "But I shall come to you before midnight."

I fled back to my rooms, Elaine close behind me, and fell quaking into Ailsa's lap. She was tipsy herself and giggled at my distress.

But Elaine understood. "Oh, Gwen, dear Gwen, don't go! I can't stand it!"

I hugged her tightly in my terror. Too much was happening, and too fast. He knew, I kept saying to myself, and yet when he had asked me the question I dreaded, I had told him the truth. It had been dragged out of me without my will, and it was true. It was true, and I had not known it until I said it. What kind of man was this?

Ailsa tempted me with honey mead, but I refused.

"You'll need something to calm your nerves, dear," she advised. "Lady Elaine, see if the queen has any of that sherry left."

But Alyse, who was on her way in with it, smiled kindly at me. "Guinevere is Queen now, Ailsa." And she dipped a curtsy to me.

"Oh, Aunt Alyse!" I cried, using the name I had not used since childhood. "I am so afraid!"

"Of course you are," she said easily, pouring a small glass and putting it into my hand. "Every girl is. I was terrified of Pellinore. But it passes."

"Let's see your crown," Elaine interrupted hastily.

I took off the silver circlet and let her hold it. "He told me it belonged to Queen Ygraine."

Alyse confirmed it, for she had seen Ygraine wear it. This led to stories of King Uther and Queen Ygraine, and between the two of us, Elaine and I kept her going for a long while. But it could not last forever. She happened to glance out of the window and saw how high the stars stood and cried out in anguish.

"Dear God, what devil has possessed me, on this night of all nights! Come, Gwen, Ailsa. You must be ready. You must be waiting when he comes."

They dressed me in the gown Elaine had made for me. The bodice fitted me now to perfection, but neither she nor I could look at it. Ailsa slipped my blue robe over my shoulders, and we all climbed the steps to my chamber. The leather curtain had been pulled aside and fastened against one wall. The lamps were lit in my room and the King's. There was no one there but us, and Alyse heaved a sigh of relief.

"I shall do penance tomorrow," she said fervently. I sat down on my bed and looked at them all unhappily.

"No, no!" Alyse cried, smiling, "not here, Guinevere. In there." And she pointed to the King's bedchamber.

I paled and gritted my teeth to keep my voice from shaking. "What must I do?"

Alyse came over and took my hand gently between her own. "Simply get into his bed. He will expect to find you there. Go in and close the curtain. No chamberlain will come in. Once the bride is there, no one goes in but the bridegroom. Don't shake so, child. He seems a kind man. He will not be long. It is near midnight now." She kissed me tenderly, as a mother would, and I clung to her. She hugged me once, then led her women back down the stairs.

Elaine, struggling against tears, embraced me. "Be obedient and please him," she whispered. "Just remember, I would give half a lifetime to be in your place!" Biting her lip, she whirled and raced for the stairs. Ailsa waited until I had gone in and pulled the flap across the doorway. Then she left.

13 ⚜ THE KING

I stood in the center of the room, shaking. It was warm. A low coal fire burned in the grate, and the night breeze blew through the window, laden with scent. On one side of the bed stood a skin of wine hung over a low flame, and a small table with two silver goblets, one set with amethysts and one very plain. I went slowly to the bed and sat on the bearskins. They were soft and tickled my bare feet. I looked up at the Dragon of Britain above the bed and pinched myself on the arm. It was still there. I slipped out of my robe and folded it neatly, laying it on the oak chest in the corner. The thudding of my heart was the only sound. Tentatively I lifted the bearskins. The chamberlains had remade the bed with the sheets we had brought the King from Wales. I stroked the fine linen; it felt like silk. Holding my breath, I slipped in and pulled the bearskins tight around my chin.

Nothing happened. The lamp flared in the corner as the breeze passed, and then all was still. I tried closing my eyes, but it was pointless. It was so very quiet. There were no sounds from outside. I could not hear the rowdiness in the feasting hall. I knew they would give a great cheer when they finally sent the High King off to bed, but I did not hear it.

After what seemed like hours lying rigid on his sheets, I heard the King coming. There was laughter from the room below his stairs, and several voices wishing him good hunting. Then there were only two voices, his and Varric's. I heard the splash of water and the King's deep voice asking a question, and Varric's soft one giving an answer. Then there was silence. I heard no footfall on the stairs, but suddenly he was there, standing at the foot of the bed, watching me. He was wearing the day robe I had made him, and against his tanned skin it shone silver white. He came around to where I lay and sat down beside me. I had not realized I had a death grip on the bearskins until he gently pried my fingers loose, one by one. He had washed his face and hair and looked scrubbed clean and rather boyish.

"Guinevere, sit up." He took the skin of warmed wine and poured a little into the jeweled cup and handed it to me.

It smelled enticing, heavy with sweet spices I did not know.

"Try it," he said gently. "It's mulled wine. We have a recipe here that comes all the way from the East. That wonderful smell is cinnamon, and there are rare cloves in it, also. It is not strong." The shadow of a smile crossed his face. "But I think you need to relax a little."

I obeyed him and drank. It was very good, sweet and fragrant and warming. Slowly my joints began to thaw.

"I don't know how much young maids are told about wedding nights," he said, holding my eyes. "But there really isn't much to fear. I promise not to frighten you, Gwen. I know you are brave, but this should not need courage." He poured some wine into the plain cup, sipped, and put it down. He reached out and took a strand of my hair and ran it through his fingers, watching it as the white-gold threads crossed his rough palm.

" 'Hair like light,' Bedwyr told me. Bedwyr is a poet, did you know? He's a skilled musician, as well. But he has a gift for words . . . hair like light . . . I have never seen hair so light as yours, nor blue eyes so dark."

I sipped the wine and watched him over the rim of the goblet. He was not drunk. He was not in a hurry. He looked as if he had all the time in the world. Such was his patience.

"Do—do you like your robe, my lord?"

"Indeed I do. It is the most comfortable thing I have ever worn. It was a gift from you, I am told. Did you design it?"

"My lord, I made it."

He looked surprised. "Yourself? And the emblem here? You stitched that? The work is very fine, Guinevere. Then the gift is doubly dear to me. I like the way you have done the Dragon. I was thinking of having it copied for a new banner in the Council chamber I am building. Would that please you?"

"Yes, my lord."

"Guinevere," he said, drawing closer. "My name is Arthur."

"My lord Arthur," I repeated in a whisper. I did not mean to shrink back as he leaned forward, I simply could not help it. He sat up and looked at me thoughtfully. I expected him to be annoyed, but he was not.

"There are ways around it, you know," he said calmly, watching me steadily. "It needn't be done tonight. I have no desire to force you. I will await your sign."

I stared at him wide-eyed. "But—but what about—the proof—"

Something flickered in the dark eyes. "There are ways around that, too. I know a few tricks." With a flick of the wrist he whipped back the bearskins. A dagger leaped to his hand, I know not from where, and he cut his fingertip, squeezing three drops of blood onto the sheet. "There," he said, binding up his finger. "You see how easy it is?"

But I had jumped up and stood trembling beside him.

"No!" I cried. "I will not be shamed so! What you suggest is a disgrace to Wales and a disgrace to Britain!"

Arthur rose slowly, a look of great tenderness on his face. His shoulders were very broad. He took my face in his hands and kissed me.

"You pass every test with honor," he said softly, "and yet you fear me. I will not hurt you, Guinevere. Trust me for that. And I meant what I said. I will not take you against your will. I believe it's wrong. You must give the sign."

"I?" I quavered. "I do not know how."

"When you are ready, it will come to you. In the meantime—" He drew away and smiled down at me. "How much of the castle have you seen since you've been here?"

I think I gaped at him in shock. "The women's quarters."

"That's what I thought. Come on, put on your slippers. I want to show you something."

"What? Where are we going?"

He was already at the top of the stairs, whistling. "Varric! Get Kay! Send him here. Double march!"

He picked up my robe from the chest, fingering the fine cloth. "So soft. Will it keep you warm?"

"Is it cold where we are going?"

He laughed. "No. You'll be warm enough." He held out the robe, and I slipped it over my gown. He lifted my hair and held it in his hands a moment, then let it fall. As he took breath to speak we heard running footsteps, and Kay's panicked voice.

"Arthur! My lord Arthur! What's amiss?" Kay bounded up the steps and into the room and stopped dead, staring.

"I want you to clear the way to the northwest tower. Minimum sentries. No lights. No passwords. Double guards on the entrances."

Kay's eyes widened. "*Now*, my lord?"

Arthur grinned. "Yes. Now, Kay. No questions."

Kay turned on his heel and was gone.

"We'll give him five minutes. He's a good man."

"What's in the northwest tower?"

"A sight not to be missed. And some clean air. It will do us both good."

He took my hand, and the torch from the wall sconce, and we sneaked out through the castle corridors like a couple of errant children. His glee was infectious, and I found myself enjoying the adventure immensely. The whole castle thought we were abed, and instead we were tiptoeing through the dark, hand in hand. Kay had doused the torches in the hall, and the sentries on guard snapped to attention, eyes forward, and said nothing. Eventually we reached the tower door. Two soldiers stood there. Arthur brought the torch down to his face, and they sprang aside, eyes averted. Not a word was spoken. Inside the stairs wound upward, slowly circling. He led me up cautiously. I began to giggle, and Arthur squeezed my hand.

"I feel as if we're stealing something," I whispered.

"We are," he whispered back. "Privacy."

Up and up we went, stopping once or twice so I could catch my breath. Arthur was not even winded. At last we came to an unguarded door, and Arthur pushed it open. At once I smelled the salt air and felt the light sea breeze in my hair.

"Arthur!" I cried. "The sea!" The northwest corner of Caer Camel was the highest part of the hill, and from the turrets of that tower the view was fabulous, leagues in every direction. The full moon rode low in the western sky, and distant Ynys Witrin seemed close enough to touch.

Arthur stood beside me, leaning his arms on the parapet and pointing west.

"On a clear night when the moon is in the west, you can see the sea," he said. "Look for her reflection, that silver streak? That's the sea."

"It is? Oh, how wonderful! Are you sure it's not the Lake of Avalon?"

"I'm sure. I've checked it."

The wind blew steady like a sea breeze, and smelled of salt and salt marsh and new-mown hay. I breathed in great gulps of it, and felt at home.

"Have you ever sailed upon the sea?" he asked.

"No. I never have. But I have often wondered what it must be like, to be on a ship in the middle of the sea out of sight of land."

Arthur laughed softly. "It's heaven. I dream of it often." He was silent awhile. "I have been upon the sea three or four times as King, but the best time was the first time. I was six, I think. Ector took me. My guard let me spend time with the sailors when Ector was seasick. What a wonderful freedom that was! To be alone and unattended! I remember well standing in the bow and looking out upon the endless sea, rising and falling, all by myself."

"It must be hard to find ways to be alone as King."

He barked a short, bitter laugh. "It is impossible." He gazed back at the distant Tor. "I am never alone. Except in sleep." He turned to me quickly. "I beg your pardon, Guinevere. I did not mean—"

"No need, my lord. I know what you meant. It's one of the reasons I love to ride so much. When I'm on a horse, I am alone with my thoughts, and free."

He nodded. "Then you understand. Some people, I think, are only happy in the company of others. But I, I could sometimes give my Kingdom for an hour's solitude!" He spoke vehemently, and stared back out toward the sea.

"You were constantly guarded, then, even as a child?" I asked, to divert his thoughts. "Did everyone else in Galava know who you were?"

He shot me a swift glance and then smiled. "If you want to know whether it is true my birth was kept from me, the answer is yes. No one in Galava knew but Ector. He was as cautious as they come; he had Kay guarded as closely, so none guessed."

"When you were a boy, Arthur, did you not dream of being a king? I imagine it is a thing that boys do."

He sighed. "No. Not a king. That was out of my stars, I thought. But I wanted to be important. I felt it in my bones that there was something I must do. I could do so many difficult things more easily than other boys, I felt it was a sign. Not of anything so grand as kingship—you must believe me, Guinevere, it never crossed my mind it could be possible—but I wanted to make a difference."

His voice was tinged with melancholy again, and I did not understand it. I was not yet old enough to feel so, looking back upon youth. "Britain is whole," I said slowly. "And her enemies fear her power. That is a big difference from the way things were."

"But so many people have died," he said under his breath, bowing his head. "Because of me. So many lives laid to my account." He lifted a hand before his face and slowly formed a fist. "It's the curse of Kingship. I command, and men die." His voice tightened. "No one ever thinks of that in the heat of battle, while the banner is waving and paeans fill the air. No one thinks of it later, while we bury the dead and listen all night to the cries of the maimed and wounded. No one but I. And I grieve for every one of them." His hand dropped to his side and we stood together in silence.

Suddenly he straightened and turned towards me. "Whatever am I saying? My dear Guinevere, I beg your pardon. I did not bring you up here to listen to my sorrows. Forgive my bad manners—it is unpardonable!" He reached for my hand and lifted it to his lips. "What a wretched bridegroom I am making!"

"Oh no, Arthur! Not at all!" I faced him and placed my hands against his chest. "I understand you, my lord. But you are just the kind of man a soldier wants to fight for—he knows you value his life and will not carelessly discard it; he knows that if he dies, the King will weep for him. My lord, you treat them like they are beloved—I have heard them say so. Because you grieve, my lord, they are eager to offer you service and die in your cause. And the people who live, live in a new world. . . . A safe world. We are now one country. I remember when I was a girl I thought Wales the extent of the civilized world. We were Welsh. Others were Cornish, Bretons, Lowlanders,

Celts from the mountains of Rheged—now we are Britons, one and all. It is a miracle."

He looked down at me with tenderness on his face. "When you were a girl," he repeated softly, smiling. His arms came around me and he caressed my hair. "My sweet woman, I believe that you are jollying me back to good humor."

It was warm standing against him; the night breeze felt suddenly cold, and it was warm and safe in his arms. "Every word is true," I whispered, tentatively slipping my arms around his strong body. "If you will teach me how to please you, Arthur, I will try to keep you in good humor."

His smile broadened. "One in a thousand." He bent and kissed me very gently, and I felt the power of the man in his restraint. Excitement gripped me—pleasure at the feel of his lips and terror of the unknown merged into breathless excitement; I pressed closer and returned his kiss with sudden longing. His hands slid down my back and pulled me hard up against him as his lips moved on mine; my breathing quickened, my knees turned to jelly—so fast, so unforseen, like catching fire, my body spoke a language new to me, but that he understood at once. He sighed a great sigh and lifted me off my feet, carrying me in arms that felt like iron bands.

"I told you," he said huskily, "that it would come to you. Hang on." And he kicked open the tower door.

"Arthur! Who made this garden?"

It was the evening of our third day, and I stood on my terrace while Ailsa took down my hair and began unfastening my bodice. I could hear the King in his room, whistling.

He poked his head through the curtain, and Ailsa fell into a curtsy, eyes averted.

"Did you call me?" he asked.

"Who made this garden? It's so beautiful and done with such skill by a hand that knows plants. I would like to thank the gardener."

Arthur grinned, mischief in his eyes. He stepped into the room, and Ailsa, who had risen, flattened herself against the wall.

"You may meet him tomorrow. A master at his craft, as I should know better than anyone." He took the hairbrush from Ailsa's trembling hand and began brushing out my hair. He always loved to hold it in his hands. He bent and kissed my neck, and I looked sideways at poor Ailsa.

"You may go, Ailsa. I'll call you if I need you—if there's anything the High King finds he cannot do himself."

Ailsa fled, and Arthur laughed warmly. "Was that kind?"

I turned to face him and kissed him lightly. "Kinder than keeping her here, I should say. Now about this gardener. Where shall I find him?"

Again his face lit with mischief. "Most likely on an old bay gelding, with saddlebags full of herbs he has stopped to gather along the way, coming down the road at a snail's pace. He does not like riding."

"The *gardener?*"

"Yes. The gardener. Merlin."

"*Merlin? Merlin* is the gardener?"

"Guinevere, you are pale. Do not be frightened of Merlin. He is a good man. Wait until you meet him."

"I have met him."

"*What?*"

"Years ago. When King Pellinore took us to pay homage to the princess Morgan on her way to Rheged."

"Ah, yes. I sent him as escort because I could not go myself. But you only had sight of him, not speech. You can't know a man from that."

I wanted to tell him about it, but the words would not come. It was as if my lips were sealed upon any word against Merlin. I managed a smile.

"You are right, of course. But I have wondered about the garden—all my favorite plants are there, and some that I did not know, but which please me greatly. It is peaceful and sweet and beautiful. There are even songbirds in the trees. It is as if it were designed for me alone and exactly to my liking."

He paused and looked thoughtful. "I will not say it is impossible," he said slowly. "With Merlin, anything is possible. But you are asking me to believe that he knew, even then, you would be my Queen."

"My lord, is he not famous for seeing into the future?"

Arthur shifted uncomfortably. "He does not talk to me about magic," he said a little gruffly, and I could easily believe it. Arthur definitely lived in the world he could see and touch. "Well," he said at last, with a shift of his shoulders, "I shall ask him tomorrow, if you like. He will tell me."

"No, let it go. It does not matter. But I will thank him for the garden."

"I wonder," he said softly. "I wonder if it is true. It would explain why he was not surprised to learn that my first—that Guenwyvar died, when it was he who had foreseen a lasting marriage."

"Perhaps, but I do not think he wanted it to be me," I blurted suddenly, and he looked at me sharply.

"Why do you say that?"

But again my lips felt sealed, and I could only shake my head. "It was a feeling I had at the time, when I saw him."

"He lifted no hand to prevent it. He was there in the Council chamber when your name was raised."

"What will be, will be," I whispered.

Arthur gripped my arms. "What did you say? Never mind, I heard it. He has said it to me ten or twelve times, whenever I asked him for advice about you. I thought he was simply putting me off; he knows nothing about women. But perhaps he meant more by it. In the end he told me to follow my heart." He relaxed his grip, and I exhaled quietly.

"Why—why did you need advice, my lord? If Merlin knows nothing of women, you know a good deal more than he."

His eyes grew sad, and his lips thinned. "Because I feared another disaster."

"Ah." I sank onto the little bench and gently rubbed the places where his fingers had bruised me. "Arthur, will you talk about her? Can you? Was she pretty? Did—did you love her?"

He regarded me calmly and turned away, looking past the garden wall, past the fortress wall, to the distant darkness of the Tor.

"All right," he said gently, and then turned back to face me. "How odd that you should be the person I can tell." He took a deep breath. "She had not your beauty, Guinevere, but she was a pretty girl, and about your age. We had only three weeks together, a month perhaps. She was gay and bright and full of laughter. And in the end—she was so very brave." His jaw tightened, and the great vein in his neck stood forth. I reached for his hand. He sank to one knee, then, and took my hand between his own, holding hard. "The worst—the worst was the knowledge that I alone was responsible for her pain," he whispered. "Oh God, how she suffered! No soldier wounded in battle has endured what she endured. Dear Christ, there was so much blood!" He buried his face in my skirt, and his shoulders shook. That he, who was so strong, and from whom so many others drew strength, should reveal to me his weaknesses touched me near my heart. I stroked his head and spoke whatever words of comfort I could think of for a heart so burdened with woe. I sang softly a tune I had often sung to my mare, to calm her when she was frightened. It was an old Welsh melody, and the words had long been garbled beyond sense, but it had the power to comfort. He lifted his face to me, his eyes swimming, and I saw clearly his love, powerful and deep and uplifting, and my heart seemed to sing with joy. I sank to my knees beside him, clasped in his warm embrace.

"Oh, Arthur."

"My Guinevere."

"The King looks well, my lady," Bedwyr said. "It is the talk of the palace. He purrs like a well-fed cat."

I smiled at him. "He warned me you had a way with words, my lord Bedwyr."

He bowed and smiled shyly. "It is a fact that in the past three days he has not denied anyone whatever has been asked of him. Kay is hard put to it to see advantage is not taken. Merlin noticed at once—you should have seen the look! His eyebrows touched his hairline! You have done for him what no one else could do. He is happy."

I colored and dropped my eyes. "I pray you will not attribute all this happiness to me, good Bedwyr. Put some of it down to his homecoming, after two months away at soldiering."

He laughed, amused. "Oh, no, my lady. I put it down to love."

He was one of Arthur's closest friends; he had the right to speak so, but I blushed horribly and could not control it. We were walking to the Council chamber. It was dusk, and the Council had just ended. The wine was going around, and Arthur had sent Bedwyr to fetch me, since he knew I wished to speak to Merlin.

"Do not blush so, my lady Queen. There is no shame in it. And we are all so grateful to you. All of us." I knew what he was telling me.

We came to the door of the Council chamber.

"How is he?" I asked quickly, and he knew that I did not mean Arthur.

He looked at me straight with his black eyes. "He is as well as he is ever going to be."

"Some things," I said, my voice trembling, wishing him to understand, "some things cannot be helped."

Bedwyr smiled, very kindly. "If anyone knows that, my lady, I should say Lancelot does." And he opened the door.

The men were standing in clusters, mostly around Arthur, talking and laughing, while servants went around with skins of wine. I looked briefly for Merlin but did not find him. Heads turned toward me; Arthur looked up, the smile of welcome on his lips, when suddenly a horn sounded, loud and insistent, and all movement stopped. Within seconds a guard came flying down the corridor, nearly knocking me down as he threw himself, breathless, at Arthur's feet.

"The Tor!" he cried. "My lord, the Tor is lit! And the fire on Bekan's Hill, southward!" He gulped, pausing for breath. He did not need to go on. Every man in the room knew what it meant. "Saxons, my lord!" In the small silence that followed, Arthur's features hardened, and his eyes grew cold. I could see his swift calculations as the men around him began to shift and mutter. He spun on his heel and pointed.

"You and you, to the barracks. I want Lukan, Vasavius, Gereint, Galgerin, and Lamorak. All companies at the ready, armed, provisions for a week, at King's Gate in one hour. Lancelot!"

"Here, my lord!"

"Take charge of the Companions. We'll need double mounts for Caesar-speed. We'll get there first, and let the army come up later. I give you fifteen minutes. Bedwyr!"

"Here, my lord!"

"You've heard the orders. Inform Kay. We'll need to resupply by week's end. He can meet us at Uther's Ford. Then send to Melwas. I want every man he has at the Camel road by moonrise. He can fall in with Gereint."

Bedwyr bent his knee and asked the question on everyone's lips. "Where are we headed, my lord?"

Arthur's eyes narrowed. "Badon."

I saw the stunned surprise on all their faces. Whispers ran round the walls. The young men did not believe it. Badon? They would never dare Badon, it was too far inland. The peace was settled, everyone agreed. But if the Saxons got to Mount Badon, someone pointed out, there was nothing to stop them—no, no, it was too far west. They wouldn't dare, even with longboats. But with the King just wedded, perhaps they thought—the arguments eddied past me. They did not matter. The men would go where the High King led them.

I watched Arthur. His face was white, and his eyes—his warm, loving eyes—were as cold and dull as slate. I shivered to see them; so he must look to his enemies, I thought, before the steel goes home. But there was a glow about him, an excitement, an authority that I recognized immediately, though I had only known him a week. He was the Unconquered King, called to battle, and he was exultant.

"Cerdic has landed his longboats and is heading for Badon. We will meet the courier upon the road and discover their landing point. We must get to Badon first, or Britain is lost." He spoke with certainty, and the whispers stopped. "Get me my Sword."

Men charged away; I could hear shouts throughout the castle and within minutes the jingle of bridles and the scrape of hooves on the paving stones outside. A page came running in with Arthur's mail. A young knight spoke up timidly behind the King.

"What about the Queen?"

Arthur frowned, all his concentration on his far-off enemy as his fingers worked the buckles of his corselet. "What queen?" He looked up suddenly and saw me in the shadows near the door, but his look was the unseeing gaze of a man in sleep. "Benwic's company shall stay to guard her. And Merlin is here." He looked vaguely about. "Somewhere. She's safe with Merlin." Then he spun, belting on his great Sword as he strode for the door.

"See to it," he snapped, to no one in particular, and left. The young knight smiled nervously at me and shrugged. I waved him away, to show I understood and did not take offense, and he ran out after Arthur.

Outside in the forecourt the cavalry were gathered, and I heard Arthur's stallion scream as the spurs went home, and they all thundered away. They were gone, and in so short a time! The room so recently alight and warm with voices stood cold and empty, the candles guttered. I drew a trembling breath and went out into the dark corridor. Someone had taken all the lamps from the sconces, no doubt to light the troops upon their way. I was not sure I knew my way back to my chamber in the dark. But an icy fear was breathing on my back, and I hurried away in whatever direction seemed most likely. I had not gone twenty paces when a cold hand reached out of the dark and grabbed me.

I believe I shrieked, and suddenly there was light. Merlin himself stood before me, with an oil lamp in his hand. I covered my mouth with my hand, stifling a gasp, and tried weakly to do him a reverence.

"Guinevere."

"My lord Merlin. I—I—you frightened me!"

"I beg your pardon." He hung the lamp in its place and stood quietly before me. He was one of those men who seemed always in repose. If he ever felt a nerve, he never showed it. His stillness had no edge to it; his patience was unending.

"You wanted to see me." It was a statement of fact; I did not know whether or not Arthur had told him.

"Yes, my lord."

"And I you."

I gulped. "I am at your service, my lord."

"I wished merely to offer you my congratulations," he said lightly. "You see how it has come to pass, Guinevere of Northgallis. You are Queen."

"Yes, my lord."

"Does it please you?"

"Being Queen? I hardly know. I have no desire for power."

"What then do you desire?"

Although spoken lightly, it was not an idle question, and I gave it thought. I suspected that it mattered much what I answered him, and I knew for certain that he would know a truth from a falsehood. "My lord, I wish Britain to be whole, and safe, forever. I wish her borders to contain one nation. One people."

Not a muscle on his face moved, but I fancied his eyes softened. I sensed that he was pleased. "There will be Saxons on our shores beyond your lifetime." He said it flatly. It was a known fact to him.

"Perhaps so, my lord. Still—"

"Still?"

"Perhaps in time they will be British, also." His focus sharpened, and I hurried on. "I was Welsh once. It was the world to me. Now I am British, yet Wales is still a part of me. Could not the same be true someday of a Saxon maid?"

He took in a quick breath and let it out slowly.

"You dream of civilization," he said quietly. "Perhaps it will be so. I have not seen. But it is not in Arthur's destiny. Remember that. He shall hold Britain until the day he dies, but it will be the Britain that you know tonight."

I trembled before those penetrating eyes. "Be it so, my lord. I am content."

He paused for so long, I thought he was finished with me, but I dared not leave until he dismissed me. "What did you want with me?" he said suddenly. "You have not asked your question."

How did he know I had a question? My courage deserted me. "I came to thank you for my garden. It has brought me so much pleasure, and Arthur told me only yesterday it was you who built it."

He bowed gracefully. "You are welcome for the garden. It needs only a fountain to complete it."

I stared in amazement. "Then you did design it for me? You knew, when you spoke to me, that—Arthur did not believe it."

A glimmer of a smile touched his lips. "Visions do not sit easily in the same room with Arthur. It was likewise with his father. What is the other thing?"

"What other thing, my lord?"

"The other thing you came to say to me."

"Oh." I looked away, suddenly frightened. "My lord, you are so kind to me tonight. And yet when we met, two years ago, you were so angry. I—I wish to know why my lord was angry, and—and disappointed. What have I done? Or what am I to do?"

He considered this plea and frowned. "It is not a thing for a maid to know."

"Please, my lord. I am afraid—I am only afraid I may bring some dishonor upon the King. If I am to do something dreadful—if you have seen it in the stars—please tell me that I may take pains to prevent it, or take myself away where I cannot be a danger to him."

"You cannot prevent it," he said gently. "You are a noble child, and I was wrong ever to doubt it. But you would do better to go on your way unknowing."

"Oh, please, my lord! At least tell me if I shall somehow wound him! Tell me at least something of what you have seen!"

He paused, and when he spoke, his voice was very kind. "You will come to glory with Arthur. This I have seen. If you leave him, his glory will be less bright; his death will come sooner. Britain will suffer. If you stay, your name will live on the lips of men for beyond a thousand years. Do not ask me for more. There is suffering ahead for you; you will be torn two ways. You must live with that. I think perhaps you are brave enough."

"But my lord Merlin! You hated me once! Please, oh please, tell me why!"

"I was wrong to hate. Even to feel anger. You will fail the High King, Guinevere, although it will not be of your will, and it will grieve you more than it grieves him. I was hurt for Arthur's sake, and therefore angry. But what will be, will be. Perhaps it is for the best. He will stand alone in glory. Nothing will take from it."

I did not understand his words, but I could see that he had done his best to answer me. The gray hair upon his head trembled in the light.

"My lord, I thank you for your patience with me."

He smiled wearily. "No thanks are due me. Everything I do is done in Arthur's service." He lifted a long arm and pointed behind me. "Your chamber lies that way."

"Truly? Thank you. I fear I do not yet know my way about."

He handed me the lamp, and as I took it, the light shone fiercely upon his face. He looked human suddenly, like a grandfather doing a kindness for a child. The fear that had gripped me since the sounding of the horn found voice. "Will he live? Will he be injured? Will he return?"

Merlin smiled. "I have just prophesied a glory lasting past a thousand years, and you are afraid the Saxons will harm him. No, child. He will come back to you unblemished and, when he comes, will stay. This is the last battle. At Badon, he will break the back of the Saxon snake."

14 ♛ CAMELOT

All the world knows what happened at Badon Hill. The Saxons, pushed by the pressure of their growing numbers, made one last and desperately bloodthirsty attempt to take the south of Britain for their own. They landed in longboats in great number and pushed toward Badon with speed, murdering villagers and setting fire to the land as they went. But before they came to the hill itself, which would have given them command of the country roundabout, Arthur and his chosen troops swooped down on them in the darkness of early morning, completely unexpected, like a horde of murderous spirits from the Otherworld, silent and deadly, and destroyed them before they ever knew what happened. At dawn the signal fires flamed across Britain: the Saxon force was broken. For a generation after, Saxon children were raised on the stories of the Demon King, whose white steed could fly on silent wings and snatch them from their beds in the still predawn if they were naughty. As for the Saxon kings, they were resigned at last to peace behind the borders Arthur set them and turned their energies to the arts of peace: government, husbandry, and music.

It was a grand summer. After celebrating the great victory at Badon, Arthur gave himself time to honeymoon before the real building of his Kingdom began. No one could deny he had earned it. All Britain, it seemed, joined in the celebrations of his victory and his wedding. As for the King himself, he attended games and competitions among his knights and feasted with them nightly. He kept me near him always and seemed to enjoy my conversation. He never tired of my questions and gave me leave to explore the castle from towers to kitchens to stables. And when I willed, I could sit beside him in the audience chamber and listen to the petitions brought by the people. The first time that he asked for my opinion, I colored to the roots of my hair, unable to say a word. That he should care what I thought! The second time I was not so shy, and answered him. But the third time, I ventured my opinion when he had not yet asked me, for the cause concerned me. A villager sued for his wife's return from her mother's, whither she had gone when he had beaten her so badly she had lost the babe she carried. The King had heard the man's complaint with solemn face, and I feared in my heart that being after all a man, he might require the poor woman to be sent back to her husband, as was the law. I laid my hand upon the King's arm, and he turned to me at once, signaling the petitioners to fall back.

"My lord," I whispered urgently, "I know you are an honorable man and wish to keep the law, but consider this poor woman. You consign her to death if you return her to him. He has murdered her unborn child; if he had hate in his heart then, how much more will he have now, that she has fled from him? My lord, consider—what if I were in her place? I believe in the sacredness of the marriage vow, but this man has sinned against God in his treatment of his wife. Women should not stand outside the law, for we need its protection even more than men." I ended in a rush, amazed at my own temerity, and saw the faintest of smiles cross his lips. But his face remained solemn. After a moment, he took my hand in his and, facing the room, beckoned the villager closer. His voice, steady and low, never wavered, and all who attended that day were amazed by his words.

"Gilgarth, hear my judgment. The laws of my Kingdom are based on respect, honor, and trust. The vows of marriage are sacred. You have violated these vows by treating your own wife, who should be dearer to you than any in the land, as if she were a scoundrel. She is your wife; you may take no other. But you treat her not like a wife; therefore she need not share your house nor your bed. You have murdered your unborn child. For this you shall spend three months in my dungeons. The killing of children is a sin against God and a crime against Britain, whose future lies in her children's hands. When you are freed, you shall reform your life, else you will face my wrath. Your wife may return to you when and if she wills. She shall not be forced. And I tell you now, that all may know it, that in Britain we honor

women, and my laws shall protect them." He dismissed the stricken man
with a wave of his hand, and I slid from my chair and sank to my knees at
his feet.

"My lord Arthur!" There was silence in the hall.

He raised me quickly. "These are not tears of distress, Guinevere, I
hope."

"Oh no, my lord, I am—I am overcome by your generosity."

"Do not mistake me," he said softly. "I did not speak solely on your account. But you were right. And it would ill become me to deny it. As far as
women needing the protection of the law, it is only just. By setting an example, we shall make it so."

This was power, and I trembled to think of the magnitude of what I had
done.

"And I am pleased," the King continued with a glimmer of a smile, "to
hear that you value marriage vows as much as I."

One night at dinner Lancelot proposed a hawking party for the following
day, as the weather promised fair. Lancelot had seemed more at ease with
the King since the victory at Badon, in which he had played a major part. I
was glad to see their good fellowship restored, for it was clear to everyone
who knew them that their love was deep, if unspoken, and cherished by
them both.

The King readily assented, and they began to plan the outing. I waited
anxiously to see whether Arthur would think to include me in the party, but
they were deep into talk about horses and terrain. I recalled Kay's dislike of
what he called my "forwardness" and I remembered that Arthur had been
raised in Kay's household. Perhaps, I thought, Lancelot's assurances had
been more expressive of his own attitude than of the High King's. On the
thought, Arthur turned to me.

"And you, Guinevere, shall ride Zephyr and fly Ebon. Have you any
among your women who might attend you? We shall be out the entire day.
The best hunting is south and west of here."

I stared at him. "May I truly come? My lord is very kind to ask me. I—I
would love nothing more."

Arthur smiled. "I would not go without you. We will leave after breakfast, and Kay will send along a midday meal to Nob's Hill. Do you think the
lady Elaine might attend you?"

I looked at him in surprise, and I hope I kept my face straight. "I expect
so, my lord."

"Good," he said heartily. "Then Kay might come himself, who knows?"
And he turned back to Lancelot.

I was kept busy digesting this piece of news. So Kay was an admirer of

Elaine's! That a man so conservative and unchanging in his views should be interested in a willfull, headstrong girl like Elaine surprised me. I knew well she would never accept him. As I knew well she would come hawking, even though it meant riding the whole day, to be near the King.

I was up at dawn and in the stables before breakfast, grooming Zephyr myself and checking Ebon's jesses. The mare was happy to see me and greeted me with a soft nicker. If Lancelot was around, he did not come near. But one of the grooms, a boy named Petri, brought me a thick leather strap, well oiled and soft, and gave me to know that Sir Lancelot thought that, as I rode without a saddle, it might save the King worry if I made the mare wear it. I did not have to use it, Petri recited carefully, but as the High King had never seen me ride, it would be very natural if he feared for my safety. I laughed, taking the hint, and bade him thank Lancelot for the advice. I would use the neck strap.

I hurried back to my quarters to change into my doeskin leggings and my old green hunting mantle. Dear Lancelot! Encouraging me to be myself! He was right, of course. The pattern of our life together would be set in these few weeks, and it would be well to hide nothing from the King.

But Elaine, who was dressed down to her fingertips in fine cloth and trimmings, was furious at the sight of me in my old, comfortable hunting clothes.

"You just can't do it, Gwen! You can't go out like that! Think of who you are! You will shame King Arthur before all his Companions! You can't mean to ride bareback in those old leggings! Oh, Gwen! It isn't done!"

I wanted to laugh, but her distress was genuine, and it was, after all, on Arthur's behalf. "It will be done, Elaine, once I do it."

"But—but you are Queen, Gwen! You cannot!"

"It is because I am Queen," I said gently, "that I *can*. Who will say me nay?"

"The King himself, I'm sure!" she cried, in tears.

I shook my head. "I don't think so. Anyway, I mean to find out now. If he objects, I will simply change. There won't be any scandal. He will not be dishonored. Wait and see."

But as I sat bareback on Zephyr and waited with my women in the courtyard, I wondered if Elaine might not be right. Would the King be insulted, or his pride be hurt? I had to trust Lancelot, who knew him better than anyone. I had to rely on his honor, and not for the last time.

With a clatter of shod hooves on stone they came, the High King on a pretty bay mare, Lancelot, Bedwyr, Lamorak, Bellangere, Gereint, and some others behind him. He raised a hand in greeting and opened his mouth to speak; then he pulled up short: I saw him glance swiftly at Lancelot, who also rode bareback, and then he gave me that long, cool appraising stare for which he was known and feared. I sensed no anger in him, only concern. It was his duty, after all, as well as his right to protect me. It was an effort to meet those penetrating eyes, but I managed. At last he smiled.

"I yield, lady," he said, inclining his head. "Let us see what you can do." And we cantered out of King's Gate, side by side, followed by the host.

It was a glorious summer day and glorious country for hawking. The rolling downs promised fast galloping, the meadows were full of hare, and the woods to the south teemed with birds. We cantered along at a decorous pace down the long approach to Caer Camel and then let the horses out when we met the straight causeway south. It was along this road King Arthur had flown on his great war stallion countless times; now, pounding along beside me on the bay mare, he rode like a boy, relaxed and eager and full of the fun of life. To him horses were a tool of war or a means of transportation, nothing more. He acknowledged Lancelot the better horseman, just as he acknowledged Lancelot the finer swordsman. But this Lancelot disputed. While in sword play, man against man, Lancelot was the quicker, nimbler fighter, Lancelot himself maintained that in a real battle no one could touch Arthur. He had the great gift of calm in a heated fight. And, as everyone knew, he had the deadliest sword in the Kingdom. Wherever he raised Excalibur in the defense of Britain, he was victorious. So did Lancelot praise him to the young men who continually flocked to Caer Camel, hoping to be accepted into the High King's service.

As the King found I rode well, he increased his speed, and the party began to thin out, with some of the men reining in to keep pace with Elaine and the other women. The King was first to raise a hare and fly his hawk. The kill was swift and clean. Arthur honored me by offering it to me; I accepted it with thanks and had it stowed into my servant's pouch. Then Bedwyr flew his falcon at a hare. By this time the rest of the party had come up, and we all watched together. Elaine was looking breathless and unhappy, so I beckoned her to ride up next to me.

"Are you all right, Elaine? Isn't this exciting? Isn't it wonderful to be outside and free?"

She looked at me strangely and shrugged. "You always were wild as a boy. I don't see what's wrong with a cushioned seat in the garden and a piece of needlework. I have blisters on my leg, and I can prove it."

"That's what comes of saddles. The horse feels it more than you do, I assure you."

"Mmmm," she agreed absently, watching the King as he set his hawk free. "You seem to be enjoying yourself these days, Gwen, after all your fear. I suppose I ought not to ask you how you like married life."

I colored and said hastily, "Now that Alyse and Pellinore have returned to Wales, I know you must be very lonely. Let us spend time together every day from now on."

She turned toward me slowly. "But you are always with Arthur. Except in Council, you are always at his side or following him about. You don't even seem to see me, Gwen, and you ignore poor Lancelot. You are—it's as if you are dazzled by the sun."

I opened my mouth to speak, then closed it abruptly. It would serve no purpose to tell her that I was with Arthur because he wanted me there. He knew how short time was. Yet her remarks raised a host of emotions in me, and I could not speak of them. Ignore Lancelot! Could she not see that we looked away and kept apart on purpose? That we were always, always aware of each other's smallest movement, even in a crowd? I was certain the King knew it.

"Elaine, I don't mean to ignore anyone. But everything is so new. Once life settles into a routine again, things will be easier. Let some time pass."

Elaine's face grew stiff with the effort of control. She so seldom made the effort, I braced myself for what was coming. "Are you with child?"

My mouth dropped open. This was the last thing I expected. "How would I know, until I bleed?"

"How do you feel?"

"Fine."

Unless imagination deceived me, she was relieved. But this I did not want to believe, even of Elaine.

"I am sorry to hear it," she said flatly. "The whole court is waiting to hear the news."

I took a deep breath to steady my nerves. I should have known, I told myself bitterly, I should have known. Of course everyone was waiting for the prince to be conceived. It was, after all, why he had married me. Only I had been dazzled by the sun.

The silence grew heavy between us.

"Have you admirers among the Companions?" I asked finally, trying to think of something, anything to break the tension.

Elaine looked moodily away. "Five or six. Lamorak's all right. Kay's the worst."

"Well, be warned, then. The King has asked Kay to meet us at Nob's Hill for the midday meal."

"Oh, God," she groaned, watching as Arthur, Lancelot, and Bedwyr came galloping back to us, a pair of hares slung across the King's saddle.

But as the men approached, Elaine sat up straighter, and her eyes grew brighter, and color came back to her cheeks. The King's mare came to a sliding stop, and Arthur tossed the hares to a servant.

"Lady Elaine," he said politely, inclining his head.

Elaine's color deepened ever so slightly as she dropped her eyes. "My lord King."

"Guinevere." He turned to me, smiling. "That's five altogether. Shall we head toward the woodland and show Ebon some fat partridges?"

"Certainly, my lord, if we have enough hares to serve in hall tonight."

"We can always hunt for more on the way back. The game is so thick hereabouts it's hard not to trample it underfoot."

"Then by all means let's try the woods. Lancelot," I said, addressing him directly and seeing the startled look in his eyes, "perhaps you would fall back and ride with the lady Elaine?"

Lancelot bent from the waist. "Whatever my good Queen pleases," he replied, and obeyed. Arthur shot me a quick look but said nothing, and then we were off.

Hawking in woodland was difficult, but it was how I had learned in Wales. Everything I flew Ebon at, he killed, and he made us ride hard only once. Then, in a furious pursuit through the woodland tracks, Zephyr's training paid off. We flew over trees and brush in our path and landed both hawk and kill neatly. When Arthur, who had been close behind me until the last obstacle, came up, he found the falcon hooded on my arm and the partridge in my pouch, and Zephyr and I calmly awaiting him. He cantered up to me, took in the situation at a glance, and laughed aloud. Then he swung the mare's haunches into Zephyr's, threw an arm about my waist, and, half lifting me from the horse, kissed me.

"What a woman you are," he said roughly.

"My lord," I replied almost shyly, "it was nothing. We did it daily in Gwynedd, Ebon and Zephyr and I."

"You are a team, and no mistake. How did you teach your mare to jump so effortlessly? Could Lancelot teach our mounts, do you think?"

"I'm sure he could. I think all horses know how to do it; you just have to learn how to tell them, and then how to allow them."

"Is that all?" His smile was mischievous. Some way off we heard our closest followers fighting through the brush.

"Fly him again, Gwen! The escort can take care of themselves. How many can he take in a day?"

"Why, he caught five the day I met—" I stopped suddenly, frozen. "—the day your Companions came to Wales," I finished lamely, coloring deeply. I cast my eyes down, afraid to look at him. There was a long silence. I tried and tried to meet his eyes, but I could not. At length he spoke, and his voice was flat, without any anger, but without his warmth.

"Yes. Lancelot told me of your meeting."

My eyes flew up to his at that. "He did?"

His face was shuttered. I could read nothing in it, but it broke my heart to see it so.

"You sat in a clearing upon your white mare, with the black hawk hooded on your arm, your mantle thrown back, lovelier than a thousand springtimes, your eyes alight, and your cheeks glowing with youth and good health, and you sang to the birds in the trees, and they answered you."

He said it as if by rote, watching me steadily. The words were the words of a man in love, and the flat voice repeated that man's words, knowing them for what they were.

He waited. I seemed to feel his kiss still on my lips; I seemed to hear, beyond the realm of sound, a cry born of need. Then he spoke.

"He is my closest friend and first among the Companions. I made him knight. For me he has forsaken his home and his kin; he shall be by my side as long as I hold Britain. I shall not send him away."

I licked my dry lips and tried to keep my voice from shaking.

"My lord Arthur." It came out in a whisper. "I am no threat to the love you bear him, or that he bears you. I cannot come between you; do not fear it. I am but a woman."

I paused, and the King said, with a flicker of warmth, "Only a woman!"

"I would cut my wrist before I would bring dishonor to Britain. And what is a maid's life, or a man's, either, beside that?"

He moved at that; his chin lifted, the cold passed from his eyes. I moved Zephyr closer until we were knee to knee. Then I placed my hand upon his own and looked up into his eyes. "Arthur of Britain. I am thine."

He looked down at me, and his reserve left him suddenly. I was in his arms and he kissed me slowly, tenderly and long.

A horse nickered nearby, and he released me. I did not look up; I knew who it was. The escort was coming up, and I heard the King give the orders for moving off toward Nob Hill. Neither Lancelot nor Elaine could bring themselves to speak to me, so I rode beside Arthur, who wanted me near him. He knew, I thought helplessly, exactly what he was about. Again, I had been dazzled by the sun.

So life continued for six weeks, past midsummer. Every day brought a new adventure. Arthur's Companions accepted me, even Kay, and after the day of that first hawking party, there was even admiration in their bearing toward me. They drilled daily, held sword practice, tested their strength with wrestling and their aim with spears. As a group, they were a deadly fighting weapon in the King's hand, and the point had to be kept sharp.

Work on the Round Hall, which Arthur was building to hold the round table Pellinore had given him, went steadily forward. It was to be the Council chamber where all petitions would be heard and judgments given. I set my women to weaving a banner for the wall behind the King's chair, following the design upon his day robe. And I myself began work on a hanger for the King's great Sword.

I had twelve ladies-in-waiting by the time Arthur left. Now that there was a queen in Caer Camel, noble ladies from all over Britain sent their daughters to court to serve the Queen and to get husbands from among the Companions. Young men from the four corners of Britain came to take service with Arthur and trained rigorously, hoping to be accepted some day as one of the King's Companions.

So our population grew, and so did the town's. The city that came to be called Camelot was begun that summer, as tradesmen, artisans, physicians, musicians, and skilled workmen of every sort came flocking to the castle grounds, and brought their families. Arthur, or perhaps Merlin, had foreseen this, and had a plan for the city. That summer the foundations were laid.

And the King began that summer the long and difficult work of binding the kingdoms into one Kingdom and keeping the nation together with justice and laws, now that the Saxons no longer threatened. As he told me himself, this was in some ways harder than fighting battles.

"That, at least, I was born for," he said slowly, his gaze far away. "Once I took the Sword of Britain into my hand, I knew it. Fighting was always easy for me. As natural as drawing breath. But this," he said, his eyes coming to focus on the four walls of the chamber, "this will be the real test. Peace makes men fractious. Can I hold them together? Will they follow a king who no longer leads them into battle?"

"They will follow *you*," I replied with complete certainty. He smiled.

"So at least you and Merlin are agreed," he said.

Of the great enchanter I saw nothing, and Arthur said no more about him, though he rode out two or three times to his house in the nearby hills to visit. Rumor had it the old magician was failing and doted upon his assistant, Niniane, whom he was training to take his place. I was astonished that he chose a woman to replace him. Wasn't this the man who had said to me, "It is not a thing for a maid to know"? But Arthur seemed not to mind, and I could not ask.

The High King called a council of kings in York for the first week in September to settle a territorial dispute that had arisen and to cement the federation of the northern lords. The night before he left, he stayed late at council. It had been his custom during that peaceful, carefree summer to retire shortly after I and my ladies had left hall, and to come to me in my chamber where we would talk long on the terrace, or stroll in my garden, before he came to my bed. Not since that first night had I set foot in his own room. I assumed that this was how he wished it, and I did not think to change the pattern. But that night, although I was awake when he finally came upstairs, he did not come in. I heard him say good night to Varric, and I saw the lamp turned low, and then I heard his restless pacing across the room and back. I fancied he stopped once at the curtain, and I waited expectantly, but he resumed his pacing and did not come in.

Silently I slipped out of bed and tiptoed to the curtain. I did not know whether my interruption would be welcomed, but there was something in the cadence of his tread, in the fitful pace and hesitations, that made me think he was not working out some problem but some turmoil of heart.

I lifted the edge of the curtain. "Arthur?"

He stopped at once and turned. "Gwen?"

"My lord, may I come in?"

"Of course you may come in. You are always welcome here." He strode across the room and took me in his arms. "I thought you were asleep, but I am glad you are not. We leave at dawn, and I have things to say to you."

I nestled against his chest, and he hugged me, his hands caressing my hair. For a moment we stood so, and then he led me to the bed and sat me down upon it.

"I have not offended you, Arthur?"

He looked startled. "Offended me?"

"Why did you not come to me, but stayed in here, pacing?"

He laughed lightly. "My dear young Queen," he said, still smiling, "I thought you must be asleep. I have lain with you every night for six weeks. It is enough. I thought I ought not to wake you."

I stared at him, frankly astonished. "But, my lord, we are married!"

He looked puzzled and then, understanding, grinned broadly and knelt at my feet. Protesting, I reached out to raise him, but he just clasped my hands in his. The joy that lit his face delighted me.

"What innocence! No one has told you anything about it, have they? Do you imagine that Pellinore lies with Alyse every night?"

"I—I never thought of Alyse with—I never thought about it. But I thought it was what *you* do, my lord."

He kissed my palms, close to laughter. "And so it has been, my sweet. But I have so little time. We have each our own chamber because we are entitled to privacy, at least when we sleep. You are as free to come to me as I am to come to you, and we are both just as free to stay apart the night. There should be no offense in it. There might be many reasons why I would not come: If I were ill, or tired—"

"Or angry with me."

"Yes, it is possible. Should that happen, you may always come to me to charm me out of ill humor. It would not take you long."

I smiled at the compliment, and his eyes blazed.

"Would you—I should be afraid you might refuse me if I came in uninvited."

He took a deep breath and stilled himself. "Don't be afraid of me,

Guinevere. I might—it is not unheard of. But at this moment I find it hard to envision. And you, likewise, are free to refuse me."

I stared at him in wonder. I thought this to be against the law. "I would never refuse you, my lord!"

He groaned softly and laid his head in my lap. "I believe you mean that," he whispered. I stroked his hair, which sprang up thick and soft between my fingers.

"Of course I mean it. I shall miss you, Arthur."

Still on his knees, he raised his face to me and let his soul speak in his eyes. "Thou hast my heart," he said softly in Latin. "Know this and take care."

For answer, I took his upturned face between my hands, leaned down, and kissed him.

At length he arose, walked to the table, pouring water from the carafe there, and drank. When he returned, he sat down beside me and with a solemn face placed his hand gently against my belly.

"Guinevere, I must ask you this, though the gods know how little it matters to me. I have lain with you every night for these six weeks and have not known you to bleed. Is it possible you carry my child?"

"I know not, my lord. I have no sickness."

"But you have not bled."

"Oh, but that is nothing. My bleeding comes only once in six months."

He sat silent, and as he looked at me I saw shock, anger, fear, and relief cross his face.

"No one told me," he said slowly.

"Is it so important, my lord?" I asked. I had not known it was a matter for distress.

He shrugged. "In truth, I do not know. But I suspect so. No matter. For myself, I almost hope you are not with child. You are so young, and I could not bear—to be the cause of another disaster."

He looked in such pain that I leaned over to kiss his rough cheek. "What will be, will be, my lord."

But it was a mistake to remind him of Merlin. His face went white, and he rose quickly from the bed and took a turn about the room. At last, calmer, he came and stood before me, a very bitter smile upon his lips. "It is growing clearer," he said cryptically. "But let be. We shall know in time. As for more practical matters, I must tell you that, whereas before I was content to leave Caer Camel in Kay's hands whenever I left, he is my seneschal only, and not a fighting man. From now on I must leave in my place a knight who can protect you and who can represent me in council and hall alike. I have chosen Lancelot."

I saw it coming before he said it and schooled my face. Indeed, I knew not which was greater, my joy or my despair. "Has he consented to this, my lord?"

Arthur looked surprised and answered sharply. "I am his King. I did not ask for his consent."

"I meant—" I started, but he waved me silent.

"I know what you meant. He is the finest knight in all of Britain. In all truth, Guinevere, I could leave you in no safer hands. If you wish to know whether he is pleased or unhappy to be so appointed, I may tell you I think he is both. You are to sit at his side at table, and in the Hall of Meeting when you will. I have given orders that you are to be consulted if anything of importance arises, and in all cases of domestic disputes." The twinkle had returned to his eye, and I slowly let my breath out in relief.

"You are most generous, my lord."

"I hope," he said slowly, taking my hand and laying it against his cheek, "I hope I am also wise."

I met his eyes, then, and found them searching me once more. I rose and, going to the triple lamp, blew out the lights.

15 👑 MELWAS

The King was gone four months. At first it was awkward seeing Lancelot so often, sitting by his side at meals, sitting by his side in the meeting hall. Our conversation, to Elaine's amusement, was so stiff and formal that several of the Companions who had been left behind thought Lancelot disliked me, and I him.

We went riding often, always with an escort of armed guards, and usually with some of my women, as well. For the first two months the elders frowned and clucked as I rode out, but as it gradually became clear I did not carry the King's child, they let me be and awaited Arthur's return.

Lancelot obeyed Arthur's instructions to the letter. He shared with me the news of every courier who came, received every visitor in the King's name with me at his side, discussed with me the judgments he was asked to pass, and in general treated me as a trusted counsellor. If, when he looked at me, he let his eyes linger, or when he inclined his head to hear my speech, he stayed so a little long, no one noticed but I. And if my dreams were haunted by a pair of cool, gray eyes and a solemn, full-lipped mouth, it was no one's business but my own.

Every evening he took me to mass. He was, I discovered, a much more ardent Christian than Arthur. Ygraine had been devout, and she had had her son christened, but she had not raised him. Kay's household had been Christian, and as a boy Arthur had learned the ways of the Christian faith, but it was the pagan Merlin who had made him the man he was. I recalled his references to Mithra, the soldiers' god, the Light, and his calling upon older gods than that from time to time. But although he went to mass twice a week and worshipped no other God that I could see, and although for ceremony he wore an old enamel brooch of the Virgin set in copper Ygraine had bequeathed him, I did not know which god held his spirit. It seemed to me that Lancelot's faith, while perhaps stronger, gave him less ease of heart. He prayed most fervently as we knelt side by side in the chapel, but seemed to find little relief in it.

I spent nearly half of every day with my women and the other half with Lancelot. While the builders were at work on the Round Hall I asked Lancelot if I might have two to build a fountain for my garden, and he sent them without delay. He denied me nothing.

Gradually we slipped into an easier friendship, for our interests lay together, but there was always a watchfulness between us. We took great care to observe the courtesies between Queen and courtier and to be always attended. Only once did we find ourselves alone, and that was Elaine's doing. I had taken both Lancelot and Elaine to the top of the northwest tower to show them they could really see the sea from Caer Camel. It was near sunset, and we stood side by side on the turret as the sun dipped below the level of the land and painted the sky with broad strokes of color. Slowly the light faded, and night drew down.

"I love it up here." I sighed, drawing my cloak closer. "It reminds me so of home. Arthur brought me up here on our wedding night, to see the sea. To put me at my ease. I guess he thought I was nervous."

A strangled cry escaped Lancelot, and when I turned in surprise I found him several paces off, white as a sheet and trembling from head to foot. Elaine was gone.

"Lancelot!" I cried. "What ails you? Are you ill?"

He would not meet my eyes, but looked away. "Guinevere."

"What is it? What have I done?"

"I beg of you," he said in a choked voice, "if you value my sanity, please do not—do not speak to me about Arthur. He is my friend and my liege lord. I can bear it if I think of him as my King. I cannot bear it, Guinevere, if I think of him as your husband."

His words stabbed me to the heart. Suddenly the tissue veil of courtesy was rent; I saw the depth of his passion and the enormity of his suffering. For the first time I felt the deep pull of physical desire, and I shared his pain.

"Lancelot!" I whispered, and sank to my knees. "Oh, forgive me, do!"

He raised me quickly, but I clung to his hand.

"I forgive you. But do not speak of him again."

"Oh, my Lancelot, what has happened to us? Why can't it be the way it was?"

His grip tightened, and then he thrust himself away. "You know why. You have married the King."

"Did you want me to refuse him?" I cried, aghast.

"No," he whispered, running a hand through his hair in distraction. "No, of course not, Gwen. I only meant—where in God's name is Elaine?"

"Never mind Elaine." I reached for his hand and took it between my own. "Speak your mind. What did you mean?"

He went very still, although his breath came as fast as a runner's. "Only this," he said quietly. "We cannot be as we were because—you are not as you were. You have known a man. Now there is danger."

I stared at him and felt the heat rise to my face. I dropped his hand as if it burned my flesh. He was right. It made a difference. I no longer feared a man's touch; instead, I feared my own weakness. I tugged at the tower door, unable to see past my tears, and ran down the stairs away from him as fast as I could go.

The next day, as if by design, Arthur's courier arrived with orders to move the court to Caerleon for Christmas. We should be there by mid-December, and the High King would meet us there as soon as might be. Although we had ample time to prepare, this at least gave me an excuse to absent myself from some of the daily routine. But I discovered I could not absent myself for long, or the people began to wonder if I was ill. Illness in a bride meant to them only one thing, and to avoid renewing speculations of pregnancy, I had to show myself again.

Lancelot was perfectly behaved, and so I tried to be, that no one might suspect the turmoil in my soul. Only Elaine knew. She shared my bed, now that the King was away, and as I had in Wales, I shared with her my secret agony.

"Do not leave me alone with him again, Elaine!" I wept, holding her tightly. "It is too much for me to bear!"

"Why?" she asked quickly. "What happened?"

"Nothing. Only—it is so difficult to be near him!"

She gently stroked my hair and tried to soothe me. "You did not used to feel so, in Wales. Do you not love him anymore?"

"Oh, don't, Elaine! You know I do. But this is agony—we cannot, we *must* not dishonor the King!"

"Certainly you must not," she said calmly. "Did you feel tempted to?"

"Yes," I whispered, shaking. "Oh, yes."

"Well," she said after a moment. "I was only trying to give you joy."

Shortly before we made the move to Caerleon, King Melwas of the Summer Country invited me, and Lancelot as the King's proxy, to the Goddess' Harvest Festival celebrated at the Lady's shrine on Ynys Witrin. He was lord of the country thereabout, including the environs of Caer Camel, and since Arthur's ease of access to his own fortress depended upon good relations with Melwas, Lancelot did not like to refuse, although his Christian soul rebelled against the Mother's worship. I assured him that he would find nothing offensive in the ceremony; it was mainly an excuse for a feast. He was astounded to learn that I was familiar with the rites.

"Surely you know my father was a pagan. Wasn't it only a year ago my ancestry was publicly discussed in this very place?"

Lancelot flushed, and I placed my hand on his arm. He went very still.

"I meant only that I did not think it any secret. This used to be my favorite festival when I was a child, after Beltane, which was my birthday. I remember being disappointed when I went to Gwynedd that the Christians had no such celebration."

"Is there any part of the ceremony that requires my parting from you?" he asked, then added carefully, "I am responsible for your safety, my lady, even when I am not with you."

"There are rites that are sacred to the Goddess and that men may not attend. Actually, only initiates participate." I grinned at his worried expression. "I am not an initiate, Lancelot. I was eight when I last bent a knee to the Goddess. Have no fear for me."

"Could you not plead to be excused? You are a Christian Queen."

"And offend Melwas? It is likely that he remembers my ancestry, even if you do not!" He smiled and took my teasing in good part. "And Arthur attends the rites of Mithra when it serves his purpose. You knew that, surely. How would it look if I refused?"

"Then are there any among your women who could attend you?" he insisted. "You must be guarded, Gwen. Please do not be annoyed, but understand. As Arthur's Queen you are a valuable hostage. Your capture, may Heaven forfend, gives your captor a hold on the High King of Britain. Think of what that might mean."

"Arthur would never submit to—" I began hotly, and then stopped, as memory recalled moments of great tenderness.

"If you are dear enough to him," Lancelot said quietly, "he might. So must I protect you to protect Britain. Now, is there anyone who can attend these pagan rites with you?"

In the end I took a maiden named Alissa, sister to one Pelleas, King of the River Isles, and Ailsa, my own nurse, who believed in all gods as a matter of self-protection.

King Melwas received us royally. He was a big man, tall and tending to heaviness, with thick features and very light, cold eyes. Unlike Arthur and his Companions, who preferred clean-shaven faces, Melwas grew a short blond beard and moustache, which he kept neat and well combed. His palace was little more than a fighting fortress, for he was still unmarried, but he saw to it that we women were comfortably housed in the guest pavilion of the Lady's shrine. Melwas' sister, the lady Seulte, kept us company and ensured that we had everything we required. A hard-featured, proud woman, she spoke well of no one except her brother, but as I was polite to her, she took to me, and we got on well enough. Ailsa did not like her and told me that behind my back she came high and mighty with the servants, but of this behavior I saw nothing.

Lancelot was housed in Melwas' fortress with the escort, and with this he was not well pleased. Melwas' soldiers outnumbered the royal escort ten to one, but I told him not to be ridiculous. No one could get at me in the Lady's shrine. Her precincts were sacred, and the pain of violation was death. He did not like it, but in this he had no choice.

The ceremonies lasted most of the day. Melwas placed me at his left hand, next his sister, while Lancelot, representing the High King, he placed on his right. He thus stood between us at the public ceremonies and sat between us during the long feast that followed. There was much toasting and drinking and general good fellowship, and I took note that both King Melwas and his sister partook liberally of the unwatered wine. Melwas favored me with his attentions all evening, and he was scarcely intelligible by the time the bard came on. I had worn a gown of gold and blue, and Arthur's great sapphire, which seemed to bewitch Melwas. As his power of speech left him, he became unable to take his eyes off it, and seemed transfixed by its slow rise and fall upon my breast. I saw Lancelot getting restless, saw him color in annoyance, watched his anger slowly mount until I feared he would ruin everything by a display of temper. Quickly I turned to the lady Seulte, pleaded fatigue from the pleasures of the day, and begged to be excused with my women. She leered rather drunkenly at her brother, winked at him, and rose. All the women followed, and we escaped the hall. She led the procession back to the shrine, where men were forbidden to enter, but I sent a page to ask Lancelot to meet me outside the gate in an hour. It took me that long to disentangle myself from Seulte's oversolicitous care, and when I slipped out at length, cloaked and hooded, I found him awaiting me, pacing anxiously back and forth.

"My lady!" he cried, pressing my fingers to his lips. "I knew we should not have come!"

"Shhh! You will do our cause no good by shouting. What do you mean we shouldn't have come?"

"Melwas is enamored of you, Guinevere. Couldn't you see it? Dear God, I nearly strangled him, the fat oaf!"

"Lancelot!"

"Peering down your bodice and slobbering! Shall I never forget it!"

"Lancelot." I put out a hand to stop him and found it held hard between his own. "Do not let his subjects overhear you calling their king rude names," I whispered, smiling.

He shook his head impatiently.

"We are alone," he said. Then it was I who went still, but my heart was pounding.

"Let him look," I said at last. "The High King needs his friendship. If he admires the Queen, so much the better. It does not hurt me and furthers our cause."

"Ah," Lancelot said softly, "but it hurts *me*. You are his sovereign Queen, not one of the serving wenches he lusts after, to hear his soldiers talk. He will show you respect or he shall meet me on a field of honor."

"Good Lancelot, your words go to my heart. But he was in his cups. It is a compliment to the Bountiful Goddess to be so on this day. Everyone here understands. Do not fear for me so. You alone think I was insulted."

He looked at me, then, and I hoped he could not tell how I trembled. "Did you not feel insulted?"

"I—I did not like the way he looked at me," I admitted. "But I understand it."

"He wanted you."

"Yes."

"He had no right." Then I heard his quick intake of breath as he realized what he had said.

"It is no sin to want," I said slowly, "only to take."

He stood stiffly before me, pinned in place by his own spear.

"It is a sin to want," he said hoarsely.

I bowed my head and let the hood fall forward to hide my face.

"I asked you to come," I said desperately, "because I wish to leave at dawn. Make some excuse. I don't know what will be acceptable. If he presses you, tell him I have begun to bleed."

His hands gripped my shoulders firmly, for comfort. "Is this true, Guinevere?"

I raised my face to his, so near. "Oh, yes. He may verify it through his lady sister, if he doubts."

"I'll see him damned first," he whispered, and took me very gently in his arms, holding me lightly, while my tears welled up and my heart raced. "I am sorry," he said, and meant it. I shrugged and struggled to compose myself. Lancelot stepped away.

"I will send the escort at first light. Will you ride, or would you prefer a litter?"

"I would prefer to ride, but a litter is more diplomatic, surely. Have one prepared."

He inclined his head. "It will be done. Ought I—ought I to send a courier to the King?"

"No. I—I don't believe it will surprise him. Besides, anyone can wait three weeks to hear bad news."

So we left King Melwas in the morning. He saw us off with many smiles and gifts and protestations of goodwill, looking fully recovered from last night's debauch and ready to do it again. I don't know what excuse Lancelot made, but it wasn't the one I had given him, for Melwas' eyes were as hungry as ever, and I shuddered to think what must be in his heart.

We were at Caerleon only a week when the High King returned, four days before Christmas. After dinner I sat with Lancelot and several other knights before a log fire in the hall, waiting. Lancelot told us about his Breton boyhood, and his younger brother Galahantyn and his cousin Bors, and how he hoped to bring them both into Arthur's service in a few years' time. The words tumbled forth in a constant stream; this was so unlike him, I glanced at the other men, who watched Lancelot with compassion. Then I understood it was Arthur's coming that made him so anxious. As for myself, I dreaded the King's return. It wasn't that my daily visits with Lancelot were ended—for that, I was as thankful as I was sorry. But I felt ashamed of my failure as his Queen to conceive his heir. And this I had to tell him face to face. I rose abruptly, made my excuses, and retired to the company of Ailsa and Elaine.

The King's dwelling at Caerleon was the villa of some long-dead Roman governor, and it stood outside the walled fortress itself. This fortress had been maintained since Roman times, enlarged by Uther, and expanded to include the city without its walls by early in Arthur's reign. We were safe enough, for the place was always well guarded. But this arrangement meant that the King could receive guests, hold council, and go about his daily business at a far remove from his house. Thus when Bedwyr knocked upon the chamber door and begged to inform me that the King had been back three hours, had bathed, dined, and met with his advisors, and now had sent for me, I was shocked. What ill omen was this? I wondered. Arthur back three hours and no word sent to me? Ailsa had dressed me for bed and unbound my hair, but I threw a cloak over my nightdress and went out to Bedwyr.

"Good Bedwyr, what news? He is returned? Safely? Thank God for that. Where is he now?"

"In the library, taking Lancelot's report. He would like to see you, after."

"By all means. Let me dress, and I shall be with you."

But Bedwyr put out a hand to stop me. "No need, my lady. The page reported you had retired to bed, and the King gave me to understand that this is the request of a husband and not the command of a King." Bedwyr smiled gently as he bowed, and I exhaled in relief.

"Bedwyr, tell me truly. He is not angry with me?"

His eyes widened. "He did not seem so, my lady." He looked at me with curiosity, but said no more.

"All right. I am ready then."

He led me toward the King's quarters at the other side of the house. As we neared the library the door opened, and Merlin appeared, followed by a slender, dark-haired, beautiful young woman. I had not known he was even in Caerleon. As they passed us, Merlin inclined his head to me; his black eyes were cold and flat, and his face held no expression whatsoever. But the woman stared at me as if she would devour me, and the anger in her eyes set me shaking with fear.

Bedwyr felt it, for he stopped me at the door and took my hands. "What is it, my lady? Are you cold?"

"Who—who was that with Merlin?"

"His assistant, Niniane."

"Does she have the Sight?"

"Aye, and power, also, the King tells me."

Terror clutched at my bowels and I fought to keep my voice steady. "Bedwyr, I fear her."

"I see that, my lady. But why? She can do you no harm. You have Arthur's protection. She is his servant, and so must serve your ends. Where is the cause for fear?"

I shook my head. "She disapproves of me."

"If she does, she is the only one in all Britain," he replied gallantly. "Now come, compose yourself. Don't give the King cause to worry about you. He has enough on his mind."

Of course he was right, and for Arthur's sake I managed to still my trembling when Bedwyr pushed open the door.

Arthur and Lancelot stood before a great log fire, talking. They turned toward me as one, and I thought to myself as I sank into a deep curtsy, how welcoming they were, the brown eyes and the gray.

"My lord is welcome home," I said, as Arthur raised me.

"And glad to be here at last," he replied, smiling and looking at ease. "How have you been?" His very serenity calmed me, and I was suddenly extremely glad to see him.

"In perfect health, my lord."

He laughed and slipped an arm about my waist. "It is the gift of youth. I'm sorry to rouse you so late. Were you abed?"

"Not yet. Elaine and I were talking. We did not hear your arrival, or I would have been more ready to receive you."

"You're fine as you are. Thank you, Bedwyr." Bedwyr bowed and closed the door behind him. Arthur offered me a seat by the fire, and then stood, looking thoughtful.

"Lancelot has told me of your visit to King Melwas," he began, and I glanced swiftly at Lancelot, who kept his eyes on the flames.

"Yes, my lord?"

"I wish to know if your impressions of the king's behavior match his own."

I did not know how much Lancelot had told him, but it hardly mattered. One told Arthur the truth.

"He was very drunk, my lord. At the Harvest Feast it is acceptable, more so than at other times—"

"Yes. I know. Go on."

"And I think he wished for the old days when the festival sometimes led to—to—well, my lord, even in my father's day it led to orgies." I blushed, but the King was serious and intent.

"Yes. I know of it. Did Melwas suggest such a thing?"

"Oh, no, my lord! He was beyond speech."

One eyebrow lifted, and Lancelot shifted his weight to the other foot.

"Did he, by look, or gesture, indicate any such desire?"

The room was so still, the noise of the flames sounded like whip-cracks.

"Desire for an orgy? No, my lord."

A long pause.

"Desire for you, Guinevere. For your person."

I felt again Melwas' hot, sour breath on my cheek and neck, and his groping hand beneath the table. My lips felt dry and stiff, but there was no escaping the King's eyes and their demand.

"Yes, my lord. By look and gesture."

Lancelot looked up quickly at Arthur, triumphant and indignant. Arthur came over to me and took my hand. I could not meet his eyes, but I clung to him, and from his firm grip drew strength.

"For what you endured on my behalf, as my Queen, I sincerely thank you, Guinevere. Your going there served my cause, it is true. But I would not have it served thus, and it shall not happen twice. You will go there no more, even by invitation, and if he should come to Caer Camel, you will not receive him. Let Lancelot do it. I will deal with Melwas, in my own time." His voice, so gentle when he began, ended in a cold, flat tone that sent a shiver through me.

"Let me call him out!" Lancelot cried, hot with fury. "I will take him in three strokes!"

Arthur turned to him slowly, and, to my amazement, the cold was still in his voice. "On what grounds?"

Lancelot froze, then paled, then flushed.

"I will deal with him myself," Arthur repeated. It was a command.

"Perhaps he should marry," I ventured in a desperate attempt to ease the tension that fairly crackled between them. They both turned to me, Lancelot with a ghostly smile and Arthur with a warming of his features.

"No doubt you have put your finger on the problem," the King said. "But this I cannot do for him. We might have to wait until his sister dies or marries. She must have turned aside a hundred maids already, finding none good enough for her brother." He paused, then squared his shoulders in a familiar gesture half the Companions had copied. "At any rate, until he has said or done something publicly, I cannot come openly against him. But there are other ways."

He called for the servant to pour wine and handed me a goblet, and then Lancelot. They spoke together in low voices for some moments, and suddenly Lancelot lifted Arthur's hand and touched his lips to the great carved ruby on his finger. Arthur gripped his arm in the soldier's embrace, and then Lancelot left us.

The wine was warm and fragrant with spices, and I gladly yielded to its soothing powers. Arthur took a seat beside me and sat bent forward, his elbows upon his knees. "Are you tired, Gwen? Would you like to retire? It is past time, God knows."

I did not know if he meant this as dismissal or not, but I could not leave until I said what I had come to say.

"My—my lord Arthur." I sank to the floor at his feet and looked up into his face. "Please forgive me."

"Why, what is this?"

"My dear lord, I have—I have failed you."

He looked alarmed and set the wine aside to clasp my hands. "What is it, Gwen? What has happened?"

"Three weeks ago I bled," I blurted out.

He looked blank, and then comprehension came in a great rush of relief. "Dear Lord, you mean the heir! Oh, Gwen, don't look so tragic. I am in no hurry; there is time. What, did you think I would berate you?" He laughed at my expression and lifted me onto his lap. "Queen or no Queen, you're a girl yet," he said, and then grinned. "We are doing the best that we can, are we not? The rest is with God."

"But it is my duty," I whispered, feeling happy and safe in his arms, with my heavy burden lifted from me by his mere word.

"No. That is a broodmare's duty. Your duty is to be my companion. Stay at my side. Give me your company by day and the pleasure of your person at night, when you will. I am content."

I laughed for sudden joy. "Arthur, you are wonderful."

"The most welcome compliment I have ever had," he said gravely.

"And now, little Queen, what is your pleasure? Back to your bed with Elaine, or will you come with me and keep sleep at bay awhile longer?"
I went with him.

16 ♛ THE RAPE

I pulled my cloak tighter around me against the icy rain and paced back across the garden. It was a cold April morning and the wind blew in fitful gusts, tossing rain against the castle walls and hurling dark clouds across the pale gray sky. I desperately wanted a good gallop, a day hawking, anything to escape Camelot. I was sure the weather would clear. It had that smell, that keen edge of promise. Any excuse for an outing would do—if I could only be alone!

The garden extended the length of the women's quarters. At one end, beyond a locked door in a solid wall, was my own garden, accessible now only by steps from my terrace. When I had closed it off to create a little sanctuary, I had had the larger garden built, that my women might take the air and walk any time they chose and not disturb my privacy. Six of them sat now in a little curved bay with windows looking out upon my walk. They had just come from breakfast and worked upon the needlework I had set them. I could see them clustered around Elaine in the window seat, and they could all see me. Alissa was there, Kay's wife, heavy with her second child, and dear Ailsa, of course, with her brow furrowed in worry at my bad temper. The youngest was a girl of fifteen named Hanna, whose parents had sent her to court to find a husband among the Companions. It was the same old story. They came in droves, acquired manners and refinement, married the King's Companions, and were carted off to bear sons to fight in Arthur's service. I bit my lip hard against new tears and lifted my face to the rain. Sometimes they stayed, but usually they left. In five years I must have said good-bye to twenty at least.

I found myself at the foot of the garden and stood for a moment, pulling my hood closer, reluctant to head back. I knew what they were saying in there. The lady Elaine, favorite of the Queen, was holding court. She would be gently explaining to Hanna, in her kindest tones, why the Queen was so bad-tempered lately. It is not in her nature, she would begin, carefully laying the groundwork. Normally she is the gaiest, gentlest, sweetest-tempered woman in the Kingdom. And how not? There is not a man in the High King's service who does not adore her. She has the admiration of all Britain.

But you see, little Hanna, she cannot give the High King the one thing he most desires: a son of his body. It is the one thing her precious beauty cannot win for her. She has failed the High King Arthur as she has failed the people of Britain. She cannot conceive the heir.

If Hanna had courage, she might ask how it was known that the fault lay with the Queen and not with the High King himself. Elaine would remain composed and smile her sly, contented smile. Her reply, when it came, would be oversoft. It was known that the High King had fathered bastards here and there. He had acknowledged them and provided for the ones he knew about. There was a girl in Northumberland he had given a dowry to and had honored the knight who married her and gave a name to the child. He was, after all, away from court six to eight months out of the year, and even though he was known to be a man of moderate habits, well, if a pretty maid were willing, who could blame him? He saw to it she never suffered by it.

And then, if Hanna had any grasp of facts, she would ask Elaine if the High King meant to put the Queen away. Elaine would look slightly shocked, and afterward sorrowful, and take time to frame a reply. And in the meantime poor Hanna, who had only asked the question that lay on everyone's lips, would tremble in fear that she had overstepped the bounds of propriety.

One did not know, Elaine would answer gravely, what the High King might do. Whatever he did, it would be just, kind, and well thought out. He had spent four months with the High Queen this winter, at Caerleon and at Camelot, and when he left she had not bled and was feeling sickly. Everyone hoped that at last she might have conceived his child, but alas! Two weeks ago she bled, and afterward made herself ill with weeping. And now the High King was coming home; no one wanted to tell him the bad news; no one knew what he would do when he heard it.

I pressed my hands against my ears to stop the sound of words. This way lay madness. For five long years I had endured this humiliation before Arthur's subjects; had daily felt their eyes upon my waistline, daily heard their whispering behind my back. Even in my dreams they pursued me, with their frightful pity and their contempt. And everywhere I looked, I saw only bounty and increase. Camelot was growing; the streets were filled with pregnant women and the sound of infants crying. Among my own women, four had swollen bellies; in the last year, five had been delivered within my hearing. I, alone among them all, had failed to grow past childhood, was less than a woman and a wife. Alone among them all, I could not bear. And in failing, I failed the High King of Britain. I choked back a sob and wiped my eyes. I had to escape! Rain or no rain, I must get out. I was Queen. If I chose to go, I could go. None of them could stop me.

I ran back up the path and came in by the door that gave onto Elaine's rooms. I moved quietly, and they did not hear me. I meant to slip out into the hallway and so escape unnoticed to my own rooms, but when I came to the door I heard Lancelot's name.

"Do not worry, my dear. Lancelot will cure her. He always does. However low she is, he will make it right as rain. And only he can do it. We call it 'the Breton touch.' "

"Do you indeed?" I said coldly. Alissa gasped, and the others whirled, frightened. Elaine, who had spoken, did not even have the decency to blush.

"Yes, my lady, we do. It is intended as a compliment," she said airily.

I turned from her and addressed Alissa. "Send Kay to me. I will ride out this morning, and I wish to inform him of my plans."

Alissa was wise enough to keep her protests to herself, and she went at once. But the others had not acquired her wisdom.

"But, my lady, it's raining!"

"You'll catch your death of cold!"

"How can you go out in this storm?"

"Lancelot cannot accompany you. It is initiation for the new recruits." This last was from Elaine, and I turned back to her.

"I am aware of it. I will ride without him."

"He will not allow it." She was intent, excited about something but holding it in.

"I am his Queen," I told her angrily. "He cannot stop me." I knew she hated it when I pulled my rank, and I knew I would be ashamed of myself later, but at that moment it gave me great satisfaction to see her without an answer. "Breton touch, indeed," I muttered. Her curtsy was stiff, and I saw she was as angry as I.

"Any of you who wish may attend me," I said to the others, "but you need not come out unless you want to. There's a soaking rain now, but later it will clear."

No one volunteered. Kay was not pleased, but Alissa had briefed him, and he soon saw it was useless to argue. I told him where I was going, and he grunted, which was as close as he could come to an assent. Of course, he informed Lancelot, who showed sense and sent a message saying he would join me when he could and begging me to be careful. He knew better than to cross me in my moods.

We rode west, toward the low hills that sank into the marshlands surrounding Ynys Witrin. Marsh birds had been arriving in great flocks for a month now, and the wetlands were full of fowl. My new hawk Dakar was a wonderful hunter of marsh birds, and besides, the hills were low and the woods thin: It was great country for galloping.

And gallop we did. My horse Pallas was too light-boned for a war stallion, thus had he been gelded and given to me, but he ran like the wind. I had to wait every mile or so for the escort to catch up.

Toward midmorning the rain lightened and dispersed into mist, which hid the valley bottoms and sent thin tendrils of damp fog snaking up into the hills. The captain of the escort cleared his throat and looked at me pointedly. Clearly, they could not protect me in a fog, and it was time to go. But anger still bit at me, and I sought some excuse to delay. At that moment a young egret rose squawking from the fringes of Avalon and flapped noisily southward. The hawk stirred on my arm.

"One more, good Ferron, and we shall call it a day. The bird is slow. This will take moments only." I was right, of course, and I was also Queen. He had no choice but to agree. I loosed the hawk, who rose in graceful circles and, spotting the distant bird, took off. As I put leg to my horse, I had a sudden forboding. If, at that moment, I had changed my mind, or the hawk had lost the bird in the mist, or Ferron's native caution had exerted itself, how much might we all have been saved! I have thought of it often, since; how so many futures may hang on a single thread of circumstance; how long a shadow that day cast over so many lives!

Against all expectation, the egret headed into the woods. The road narrowed to a track, and we slowed our pace. I lost sight of the hawk in the thickening mist, and whistled to him at last to call him back. We all heard then a bird's cry and the crashing of some heavy animal through the bracken. My only thought was to recover my precious hawk.

"This way!" I cried, and sent Pallas straight into the woods in the direction of the cry. If the soldiers shouted, I did not hear them. All my senses were attuned forward, to the trees looming up suddenly out of the mist, to fallen logs that must be jumped, although the distances were difficult to judge, toward where I hoped my hawk stood patiently above his prey. We reached the bank of one of the slow-moving rivers that fed the marsh and pulled up. It was very quiet. I could see only the shadowed shapes of trees on the opposite bank twelve feet away. I heard no voices, no hoofbeats, no movement through the underbrush. I realized with a jolt of fear that I was lost, and without my escort. But we were only a few leagues from Camelot, and Pallas could find the way home. He stood easily, his nostrils wide and his small ears swiveling in every direction. I waited, calming myself, very sorry now that I had acted so arrogantly. I was framing a suitable apology to Ferron and to Kay, when Pallas' ears shot forward and his head lifted. He had heard something downstream. As he did not nicker, I feared it could not be the escort, but perhaps it was the hawk, caught in some tree by his jesses, or the injured bird in the brush. We went slowly along the bank, unable to see, feeling our way. The fog thickened as the land sloped lower and caught in the nostrils and mouth like a cold cloth over the face. My cloak was damp, and the horse's body slippery with wet. Which is why, when out of the white mist on the water a gigantic dark shape suddenly arose before our very eyes and shouted, Pallas spun, reared, leaped sideways, bucked twice—and I fell.

I awoke slowly to darkness, to pain in my back, and to gentle rocking. Had it not been for the pain, which grew steadily more insistent, I might have fallen back to sleep, for the rocking was very soothing and made my head feel heavy.

"Please," I cried, "my back!" but it came out the barest whisper, and when I opened my eyes I saw nothing, only whiteness. Frightened, I shut them. Strong hands supported and lifted me, and the pain eased. Even in my dazed state I felt relief, knowing I was not injured, but only lay on something hard and sharp. I was slowly let down upon some cushion or soft stuff. The hands that had held me did not leave me at once, but cupped my shoulders and then slowly slid down my arms to take my hands, before folding the cloak around me. It was a slow, sensuous gesture, and I shivered, a frisson of horror sliding up my spine. Discomfort was forgotten. There was danger here. I looked vainly about but could see absolutely nothing. I had no clue to where I was, or with whom, except that I was still surrounded by fog and the gentle sounds of river and marsh.

"Who are you?" I asked. "Who art thou?" I tried in Latin. No one answered. But someone was there. I sensed movement and breathing. "Where is my horse, good sir? What has become of the hawk? My escort must be about—if you call, they would be pleased to find me and to reward you for my rescue."

"Please be still," a male voice said softly. "All is well." I had heard the voice before, although I could not remember where. Perhaps he was a knight, or a nobleman who had been at Arthur's court.

"Good sir," I whispered, "I know you are a gentleman. Return me to the King and he will well reward you. For I am Guinevere, his Queen."

There was a rough bark of laughter, followed by a sliding, dipping motion as a shadow loomed above me in the mist. I realized suddenly that I lay on the bottom of a coracle and that we were well out in the marshes. Hands gripped my body, and a bearded face bent low to mine.

"I know who you are," a gruff voice said, "and now you are mine." Thick lips pressed against mine, and I smelled old mead upon his clothes and the sweat of fear upon his body. Mercifully I fainted. For I recognized him. It was Melwas.

When I awoke from the faint I had the wits to keep my eyes closed and let him think I still slept. It was warmer, and a breeze eddied against my cheek. I guessed that we were now on open water, for the boat rocked, water gurgled near my ear, and the splash of oars came steadily. I heard no other sounds, not of men, or of animals, not even of birds. My heart raced with terror, but I kept my breathing slow. All I could think of were Lancelot's words to me, long ago, about how valuable a hostage I would be, and how I had to let myself be guarded.

My poor Lancelot! In my mind's eye I could see the panicked ride of the messenger back to the palace, the fearful confrontation with Lancelot, the averted face and bent knee as the message was delivered, and the horror and anger and—most undeservedly—the guilt that would show on Lancelot's face. What would he do? He might take every man in Camelot to the spot where I had last been seen, if they could find it, but it would avail them nothing. They might find the horse and the hawk, but they could not find me.

I steadied myself and pushed the tears away. What, then, of Melwas? How dared he? Arthur would kill him. And then in a flash I understood. I was no longer so valuable as a hostage; once, perhaps, but a childless queen? Melwas did not think to gain some advantage over the High King, he thought only of me. He dared not kill me—no, that would touch the High King's honor and put his own life in jeopardy. But if he merely took me—I forced myself to face it—for his pleasure, and soiled me in the eyes of Arthur's subjects, and in the King's own eyes, as well, he could plead any excuse he liked and beg to take me formally from the King. It would solve Arthur's problem for him. He could put me away, give me to Melwas, binding his neighbor to him, and leaving himself free to marry a woman who could bear him sons. Against my will a tear slipped out, and I shuddered to hide a sob.

Melwas grunted, but said nothing and rowed on. Where on earth could we be going? Somewhere on the Lake of Avalon, no doubt, but where? Not to his palace, surely, where I was known. But wherever it was, clearly he had planned this. For the stuff I lay on was soft and sweet scented, not the normal outfit for a river craft. He had been expecting me.

The oars stopped suddenly, and we jolted gently against solid ground. I opened my eyes. Melwas was tying the boat to a wooden platform built out upon the water. The mist was thinning fast as the day advanced, and I saw him clearly. He was a huge man, thickset, dressed in hunting clothes. When he turned and found me awake he looked uncomfortable. I was glad to see it. I hoped he might be frightened at what he had done; but he was a brave man, and his face was set. He extended his hand to me.

"Come, my lady. We have arrived."

I allowed him to help me onto the platform, where I chafed my hands and arms to restore their use. "Where are we, King Melwas?"

He smiled, and I found his smile revolting. "In my kingdom. Safe from Arthur's lads. Come and see my house. It is prepared."

He referred to a small, wooden structure half hidden by willows, which stood on a low rise near the edge of open water. As he took my arm and led me up the rough path, he boasted about the isolation of his hideaway. We were on an island, he said, with marsh grasses all around that screened us from the shore a quarter mile away. No one could see us, he declared, chuckling, and no one could approach us, except by boat. At low water there was a land bridge at the far end of the island, which had tempted would-be thieves from time to time. Should anyone try to come that way to rescue me, they should find the sharp surprise the thieves had found. He laughed wickedly under his breath, as if pleased at some jest he had made. I shivered at the sound, and he turned to me, smiling.

"Don't worry your pretty head, my lady Queen. No one will come. You are safe with me."

Safe indeed! I struggled to keep my fear from my face as he handed me up the step and into the crude dwelling. Whatever it had been built for I could not guess, but its present purpose was clear enough. He had furnished it as luxuriously as he knew how, with soft skins and cushions and a low, Roman couch. A hearth stood stacked with logs, and skins of wine hung nearby. There was only one other door.

"Your clothing is damp," Melwas said nervously. "Please, my lady, change in here." And he opened the door to reveal a sleeping chamber containing a great bed hung with crimson hangings and piled with furs. "There is a robe ready for you," he hurried on. "Hand out your clothes to me, and I will dry them before the fire."

I said nothing but went into the room and closed the door behind me. There was no lock. I heard him moving about in the other room, and went to the window. It was barred and looked out toward the shore across acres of reeds and a stretch of open water. I put my hand to the window and saw how it shook. It looked small and cold and white, a hand that belonged to someone else. It seemed a poor frightened, delicate thing, trembling as it gripped the iron bars. It moved at my command, yet did not feel a part of me. I pulled against the bars with all my strength until I fell back, gasping, on the bed. I could not budge them. But even if I could, what then? I could not swim. I did not know how to handle the boat, supposing I could have got to it unseen. And I did not know where I was, or in what direction help lay.

I stared at the soft bed furs in rising panic. It was all too clear what Melwas wanted. My only chance was to play him fair, fend him off, and wait for rescue. But I did not hold out much hope of it. Even if the King's men could find me, they would never be in time.

I began to undress but it was slow work. My fingers were cold and stiff with fear and took minutes to manage a single knotted lacing. The robe he had set out was a good one of soft, combed wool, dark blue with a silver border. But it was too big, and there was only one belt. I shrugged. I thought nothing; I felt nothing. I seemed to be somewhere else, watching myself, wondering what I would do, wondering what it was possible to do, wondering if death might not be preferable to what Melwas had in mind, and wondering how I could come by it.

At length Melwas knocked upon the door and bade me come out. I obeyed him. He had a good fire going and two goblets of wine poured. He had not waited for me, but was on his second cup already. His greedy eyes ran over me with eagerness, and I blushed, turning away.

"My lord Melwas," I protested, surprised to hear my voice sounded natural as I handed him my damp riding clothes.

"Eh?" He looked up, fairly drooling, and it was all I could do to keep revulsion from showing in my face.

"You are a king, sir, and I a queen, and not the kitchen slave."

He seemed slightly embarrassed and licked his lips nervously. "Aye, madam. But you are the most beautiful woman I have ever seen. Such hair! Such eyes! Such skin!"

I lowered my eyes and took a seat on a stool by the fire. He hastily laid my garments near the hearth, but clearly he did not care whether or not they dried. "You are twenty, are you not? I have wanted you, Guinevere, since the day you came to Caer Camel at fifteen, and you now so far surpass in beauty that fifteen-year-old girl as a—as a full flower does an unopened bud. I tell you, I have been patient." He stopped for a gulp of wine.

"I belong to another," I said quietly. It was a mistake; his face grew dark with anger.

"Don't taunt me with that young pup! I'll not have it! For all his high and mighty ways, he's naught but a bastard of Uther Pendragon, and he's not master here!"

"No, my lord. Of course not. Pray forgive me. I will not mention him again."

He looked slightly mollified and poured himself another drink. "That's better. Where was I? Oh yes. I was patient, and do you know why? Because you are worth the wait, my beauty, and because I knew it would happen."

I looked up quickly, and he laughed loudly in delight. Clearly he did not worry about being overheard. I fed him his line. "How did you know?"

"The Lady of the Lake saw it in a vision. Not the witch that's there now. The old one. Nimue. She told Seulte about it years ago. That was why she would not let me marry. We were waiting for you."

I gasped and then tried to let my breath out slowly. "Your lady sister connived at this abduction?"

Melwas snorted rudely and then smiled. "I suppose it strikes you as abduction. I am only taking what I was meant to have. Your precious husband is finished with you. All the world knows that. You are to be mine. It is in the stars."

I was afraid if I shed tears he would try to comfort me, and the terror of it stopped their flow. Somehow I must try to keep him civilized until Lancelot—dearest Lancelot—he would leave no stone unturned! I glanced out the window. I could see the open waters of Lake Avalon and, in the far distance, the Tor. The veil of mist had lifted and it was, as I had known it would be, a clear day.

"Take what comes and live without complaint," I murmured. "Life is a woman's gift; death is God's. What will be, will be."

"What's that?" Melwas cried. "What are you saying about me?"

"Nothing about you, my lord," I replied wearily. "It's an old saying of Merlin's. And not very comforting."

"Forget Merlin. I fear him not. Drink up," he commanded, coming closer.

The cup I held shook horribly. I took a small sip, held hard to my courage, and faced him. "Are we to be married, sir?"

He stopped. Fair speech made him uncomfortable, I noted. I supposed he was well used to truculence.

"In time. Everything will be formalized in time."

I nodded and did my best to smile. "I knew you were a gentleman, King Melwas. See how you have prepared for all my wants. It shows forethought and consideration."

He glowed and preened under these shameless compliments like a young boy. He had no subtlety at all. "I am glad my lady is pleased. I promise you, Guinevere, I shall do my best to make you happy." The odd thing was, I believe he meant it.

"Do you have a book at hand, by chance?"

He gaped. "What for?"

What for, indeed, when he probably could not read! To hide my thought I smiled my sweetest smile. "That I might read to you, my lord, for your entertainment."

He snorted. "I've no use for reading, and as for entertainment, I've a much better idea—"

I moved quickly away as he came toward me and stood behind the supper couch. "Let me sing to you, then." I raised my winecup to him. "All things are better, my lord, if, like good wine, they are taken slowly."

He paused, astonished. I could see his thoughts run through his head. How much easier and more pleasant everything would be if I consented! And why not? He was a handsome enough man in middle years and king of a wide land. Not everyone would want Arthur's castoff. I could do much worse. As hope is ever the father of belief, no sooner had he thought it than he believed it. Complacently he settled his fat body on the couch and consented to be sung to.

At first, it was all I could do to open my throat, but after a while, my voice began to steady. I wondered if perhaps he was more frightened than he appeared. For all his brave talk, he must know that he had put his future in grave jeopardy. The High King was expected by week's end, and he did not take kindly to arrogance of any sort. But week's end would be too late. I would be this pirate's wife in all but name by then.

I sang him every song I knew, and some I made up on the spot. We had the best bards in Britain at Camelot, and I had learned something from every one of them. By midafternoon my throat was raw, and he was hungry. He brought out a tray of food he had prepared—soldier's rations with trimmings, little more—jerky, bread with honey, fruit, and pudding. And much more wine. I ate little, but I fed him everything, pretending all the while that I enjoyed thrusting biscuit and raisins into his mouth, and having my fingers kissed by sticky lips.

I made what small talk I could, as I had learned to do with visitors at Arthur's table. It seemed the old priestess of the shrine, who had made the prophecy about me, had died a year ago. The new Lady of the Lake was a young and powerful woman who disliked him. If she knew of Nimue's vision, she said nothing about it. Her allegiance, after the Goddess, was to Arthur. He and Seulte had planned secretly for twelve months how to take me; they had planned it all down to the last hair. That he feared and hated Arthur was clear, but I could not discover the reason.

He ate too much, of course, and drank more than most men did in a week. I bade him try the couch again, but he made me sit beside him, and held my hand. He looked at me like some adoring dog, but the greater beast was there, biding its time. Nevertheless, I sang to him, all the old Welsh lullabyes I had learned when I was young, and soon, as the afternoon turned golden and crept toward dusk, he slept. My clothes were dry; more than once I attempted to sneak away, but every time I moved my hand from his, he stirred and threatened to awaken. I dared not hazard a bold dash for the door. To flee or to fight him would only bring upon me the fate I dreaded. My best chance, I thought soberly, was to do as I had been doing, and string him along.

But a hooked fish cannot swim forever. At last he awoke and, grunting, rose and stretched his huge limbs. He lit candles and did not bother to close the shutter. With sinking heart I realized he felt perfectly safe from any detection.

"Come, Guinevere," he said, towering above me and extending a hand.

"It is time." My hand shook as he took it, and I found that I trembled so hard I could barely stand.

"King Melwas, I—I cannot give you children."

His great arms encompassed me, and he laughed. "I care not if you are barren. I do not want your children. It is you I want."

His lips sought mine and, held in his grip, I could not fight, but merely bore it. I dared not look ahead even to the next second.

"But, sir,—" I fumbled, my dazed thoughts running in circles. "—what will happen to your kingdom if you leave no sons behind you?"

He stood back for a moment, his eyes blazing. "Arthur will have it, the bitch's whelp! He is taking it from me now, what with harbor dues, raised every year, and road taxes. Your fancy boy, Lancelot, filled his head with lies about me, and he has set out to destroy me."

"Lancelot is not my fancy boy!" I cried hotly, but it was a great mistake to show resistance. His grip tightened, and his eyes filled with greedy lust.

"So," he said huskily, "that's how the land lies, does it? He will not find you here, my beauty." He released my belt and pressed his ugly lips to my neck, my shoulder, and, opening the robe, to my breasts. He made horrid noises, slurping and gurgling, and squeezed me with his big hands until he hurt me. But I would not give him the satisfaction of crying out. I simply wept, quietly and hopelessly. I could not stop the tears, once they started, but let them fall as he fondled me and sucked my flesh. He did not care that I could not respond, he was beyond any thought but the fulfillment of his desire. I looked over his shoulder, numbed, and in the blurred dimness beyond the window, I saw a light. It flickered and went out, then flashed on again.

"A light!" I gasped, pushing uselessly against his massive shoulders. His eager sighs and moans disgusted me, and I shuddered as his motions grew more frantic. "Sir, a light!"

He ignored me completely, and it was not until he straightened to whip off the thong that bound his leggings that he glanced out the window and saw it. He stared dumbly at the light and then broke into a stream of furious invective. I cowered against the wall as he pulled up his leggings and reached for his mantle. He got to the door and turned. I could not believe he was going. I could not imagine what the light meant.

"Don't bother trying to escape," he snarled. "I'm taking the only boat. And you'll never cross the bridge of swords alive." He paused, staring hungrily at me. "I'll be back," he said, and was gone.

I stood there, numbed and shaking and half dressed, while night descended and the fire burned low. I was aware of nothing. I reached for a cloth and began to wipe his slobber off my breasts. I wiped and wiped in a meaningless, steady motion without thought or feeling. I was dirty and feared I would never be clean. I don't know how long I stood there, dry-eyed and frozen in place, steadily wiping, but at length I heard a low grunt, the sound of gasping, and the hut began to shake. I believe I whimpered like a beast in pain, but I could not move. A loud thud, a cry of pain, an oath bitten off—the bedroom door flew open, and there stood Lancelot, dripping wet, bleeding from the knee and gripping a sword, white-fisted.

"Where is he?"

I stared dumbly at him, still wiping, and although I tried to speak, my lips made no sound. He turned left and right like a questing hound, and strode to the outer door, battering the bolt with his shoulder, kicking it down with his good leg, sword held ready.

"Melwas!" he shouted. He took a deep breath, collecting himself, and looked back at me. "Wait here," he said gently, as if I could have moved. I heard him outside, searching the little island, challenging Melwas in the King's name and, when he found the empty dock, calling him every sort of epithet. He returned with lowered sword.

"Is he gone? By boat?" I nodded, and began to shiver violently.

Lancelot came to me and took the cloth from my fingers. With the ut-most gentleness he rearranged the robe, covered my nakedness, and tied the belt around my waist. Then he poured wine and held it to my lips and threw a woolen blanket about my shoulders. He gripped me firmly and made me look into his face.

"What happened?" Panic stiffened his face as his beautiful eyes searched mine. "Dear Christ, am I too late?"

I fumbled hopelessly for words. At last my grief and terror found vent, and I burst into sobs, crying with an abandonment I could not help, while he held me tightly and kissed my hair. At last I found my voice. "Oh, Lancelot! Thank God! Thank God!"

"My sweet Guinevere," he whispered, his lips against my ear. "It doesn't matter, my dearest love. You are alive, that's all that matters."

I buried my face against his shoulder. "Lancelot, he—he—"

"Never mind it, now. It's over. You are safe."

"He almost—he started to—but—"

He pulled away and looked down into my face, hope lighting his fea-tures. "He did not take you?"

"No," I cried with a shudder, "no, but he was five minutes from it. Less. Then he saw the light. On the Tor. I—I don't know—he just left me—as you found me."

"Thank God," he murmured softly. "That makes things easier. But you are safe, that's what matters. Take heart, my love. Your cruel ordeal is nearly over. You must dress, and quickly, and then I will find some way to get you across the water. Once ashore, we can get you home."

"We?" I repeated blankly. "Is someone with you?"

He lifted my clothing from the hearth and held it in his hands. "Merlin is with me."

"Merlin!"

"He found you, Gwen, when we had been all day searching the woods and dragging the river, to no avail."

"You dragged the river?"

"Guinevere." He sounded impatient. "I love you. I would give my life for you. I feared you were dead—drowned, perhaps. I did everything I knew how to do in order to find you. When I saw it was beyond me, I sent for Merlin." I sat down slowly upon the stool and gazed at him unmoving. "He told me where to find you. In a vision he had heard your song." I gasped, and he reached for the winecup. "You were really singing?"

"Not—not for joy. I had to speak him fair," I whispered, "to keep him sweet. Every time I—I resisted, he—he—it was a challenge to him. He went mad." I swallowed hard, and Lancelot limped over to me and took my hand.

"I know the kind of man he is," he said gravely. "How you forestalled him an entire day I do not know."

"Lancelot, you are hurt! The blood on your leg!" Aghast, I saw suddenly a great pool of blood upon the floor. "It must be deep!"

"I have bound it. I will have it seen to. Listen, Gwen, we must hurry. I—"

"He isn't coming back?" I jumped to my feet, and he gripped my arms.

"No, he cannot. He must be at his palace to receive the King." I cried out, and he held me tighter. "What? Did you not know Arthur is back? His ships were sighted in the estuary three hours past. The light you saw must have been a signal to Melwas from some confederate on the Tor."

"The lady Seulte!" I whimpered, fighting rising panic.

"Truly?" He shook me gently. "Then both of them shall pay for this. Arthur will see to it. Hurry and dress, and I will take you to him. He will stay on Ynys Witrin tonight, with Melwas as his host."

"Dear God, no!" I cried. "So soon? Lancelot, no! I cannot do it! I cannot bear to face him!"

"Have you heard me, Gwen? Be still. No one knows what happened but Merlin and me. There will be no scandal. Your honor is unstained. And even so, you have nothing to fear from Arthur."

"What of his own honor? Have you thought of that? He will put me away."

"You do him an injustice."

"But I must tell him the truth. About what happened here."

"Yes."

"And after that? Oh, Lancelot, the—the monster touched me. He—he put his hands and lips on me. I am unclean."

Ever so gently, Lancelot kissed my lips and said, "I have done that, too." All at once it was more than I could stand, and I pressed against his wet and bleeding body and kissed him with passion. A sigh escaped him as his strong arms came around me and held me close. He bent my head back to kiss my neck, my throat, my breasts; his hands roamed my body with a deft and knowing touch, trailing fire. I clung to him, alive with excitement and desire.

"Lancelot! Oh, Lancelot!" I gasped. "Where is Merlin?"

He laughed shortly and pulled away from me, his face flushed, his gray eyes aflame. "My God, I had forgotten all about him." He passed a trembling hand across his face. "Take your clothes, Gwen, and dress in the other chamber."

"My dearest—"

"Hurry. We must both be there when Arthur hears Ferron's report."

One look at the bedchamber revealed how Lancelot had entered. The iron bars outside the window were bent wide, and the bedsheets all messed and bloody where he had fallen on them. It looked for all the world like the scene of a rape.

I felt much better back in my own clothing. Lancelot led me down a narrow path behind the hut toward the water.

"Is this how you came?" I asked him. "Over the land bridge?"

He grunted. "Over the bridge of swords, you mean? It is indeed."

"Swords! What swords?"

"Oh, he has set a neat trap in the middle of the bog. I was nearly caught, and I was expecting something of the sort. As it is, I got a blade in the leg. But there are bones about of others who were less nimble."

So that was Melwas' sharp surprise! "How then will we get back across?"

"Nestor will take us, if his training holds good."

At the water's edge he whistled for the stallion. We stood forty paces from the land bridge, now a bog in rising water. Within minutes we saw his dark head arrowing through the black water, swimming in a straight line toward us, safely past danger. He swam us both back, clinging to his mane. I was amazed at how little strength I had; twice my grip gave way. If Lancelot had not been holding me, I should have drowned.

Merlin sat on the bank, unmoving, on an old black horse. He nodded to me and spoke to Lancelot. "We have an hour, at most. Go quickly, and I will follow. Take her to Niniane."

I shivered. Lancelot bowed, holding me against his body with one firm arm.

"Sir," he said to Merlin, "on behalf of the High King, I thank you for the Queen's life."

I could see nothing of Merlin's face but black eyes glinting in moonlight.

"It is to Arthur she owes it," he said.

17 ♛ AVALON

I did not, in fact, face Arthur that night. The day's exposure to damp and the aftereffects of terror took their toll, and I fell into a fever. Lancelot delivered me to the Lady's shrine, where I was washed and put to bed, already delirious. They tell me Arthur came to see me the next morning and stayed at my bedside half a day before returning to Camelot, but in my fever I knew him not. I do not remember it.

After a week I was strong enough to sit in the garden and take short walks in the lovely orchards the women cultivate. I was well tended. Of the Lady of the Lake who had allowed the High King entrance to the shrine, I saw nothing until ten days had passed. I had said very little to anyone, since we were a stone's throw from Melwas' castle, and I did not know what had transpired between him and the King. But I was treated with respect, so I deduced that I must still be Queen.

Then on the tenth day the Lady came to me as I sat in the orchard, sunning. She wore the white robe of the Goddess' servant, but when she pushed back her hood to show her face, I found I knew her. It was Niniane, Merlin's pupil!

"Queen Guinevere." She made no obeisance, as I was not her sovereign. The Lady's shrine was under neither Arthur's protection nor Melwas', but belonged to itself, being an ancient sacred place. I inclined my head to her, for she was ruler here, and I her guest.

"Lady Niniane."

Her black eyes flickered. "You know me."

"I remember you."

"We have not met."

"No. But when I was a bride, I saw you once in Caerleon. With Merlin."

She looked down at me and paused. I could read no expression in her clear features. She was dark haired and light skinned, as slender as I was and a little older, but what distinguished her from ordinary beauty was an indefinable poise, a certainty, a wholeness. Arthur possessed it, and until now I had thought him to be the only one.

Because of this quality, the opening parry and thrust of our conversation filled me with dread. She did not like me, and she had power.

"Ahhhh, Merlin. My master and teacher. He has taught me everything he knows. And like every good pupil at training's end, I took flight. As you see." She glanced coolly about her. It occurred to me that in the year since she had become Lady of the Lake, we had not seen much of Merlin. "I do not recall seeing you in Caerleon. You have a good memory."

"I had occasion to remember it. You frightened me."

If I was not mistaken, the shadow of a smile touched her lips. "Did I? I beg forgiveness. It was not intentional."

"The fault was mine, Lady Niniane. I was very young."

She sat gracefully beside me on the bench. Introductions were over.

"You are recovered," she began. "In three days you will have your strength back."

"Thanks to the excellent care of your women," I murmured.

She accepted the thanks. "Yes. What do you wish to do when you are well?"

My eyes opened wide at that. What was she about? What had been going on? "I wish to go home, Lady, if it is permitted."

"To Camelot?"

"Of course. If—" The fear of it set me trembling. "—if it is still my home." There was no softening in her stern face. She accused me of some crime, yet I did not know what it was.

"Arthur is there."

I met her eyes. Here was the battleground. "I am glad to hear it. I wish to see him."

"He knows what happened."

"I should hope he does. It was not a small thing and affects him nearly. Please tell me, for I have heard nothing, what has become of Melwas?"

She regarded me closely, and I felt my thoughts probed by careful fingers. I was reminded of Merlin's visit in my sleep, years ago. That a woman could hold such power! On the thought, she spoke.

"Nothing yet."

"What! Is he not taken? Am I not believed?" I shook with fear and saw the first sign of compassion in her.

She placed her hand upon my arm. "No one has formally accused him yet but Lancelot, and he was largely incoherent with pain and fever."

I grew instantly still, and she noted it. Compassion fled, she withdrew her hand, and when she next spoke her voice was remote. "You do not ask after Lancelot?"

"How fares my rescuer?" I asked obediently. But it had been a week since he had ridden in with me, and if he still could not accuse Melwas it meant he was very ill indeed—or worse. That was instantly clear to me. My eyes were lowered, and I waited, barely breathing, for the blow.

"He lies gravely ill in our house of healing. The wound he received in his knee has festered. It might be necessary to remove the leg to save him."

"Dear God!" I covered my face with my hands.

"The King is held at Camelot by visitors of state, and he has asked—commanded—me to make a difficult request."

I steadied myself and looked up. Something was coming. Niniane looked strained.

"Difficult for me to make, I should have said. I doubt you will find it difficult to obey. The King commands me to ask you to go to Lancelot and stay by him through his illness, to whatever end comes."

I stared at her. It was all I could do to keep my seat. She sat there looking hard at me, and I barely kept myself from commanding her to take me to him that instant. She read the flow of my thoughts, and her expression grew cold. It was intolerable. Even Arthur did not judge me so.

"Lady Niniane!" I reached out and clasped her hand between my own. "Do not set traps for me, I pray. I know you see the truth. Why try to catch me in a falsehood? Merlin was there. I can hide nothing and do not wish to. I will tell my lord the truth. He needs to know it."

"The whole truth?" she asked.

"Ah," I said sadly, "he knows already. Can you doubt it? He has known it a long time." I paused, and Niniane said nothing, but looked sorrowful herself. "Have you led such a blameless life, Niniane, that you cannot conceive of being rent in twain by love?"

She gasped, and to my amazement I saw her disconcerted. I did not know, then, that as her old master neared his end, she had lost her heart to a handsome king in Arthur's service, one Pelleas, Alissa's brother. I knew none of this, yet God guided my arrow and sent it home.

She blushed faintly. "I love and honor Merlin," she whispered.

"Yes," I said calmly, meeting her eyes directly, "and I love the King."

She nearly protested, then looked at me a long time, searching, and finally nodded. "I did not know it."

"Know it now. His honor is safe with me."

The corners of her mouth twitched into a smile. "So he has told me many times."

"Why is he sending me to Lancelot? Is this some test you have devised?"

"No, my lady. He fears for Lancelot's life. He only hopes that your presence there may strengthen his will to live."

"I will go, then. Let us pray he is right."

"I advised him against it," she confessed.

"He is wiser than you," I said gently. "And I do not care who talks. Lancelot saved me, and I owe him this."

She shook her head. "The gods saved you, Guinevere, God, if you like, who sent the fair wind that blew Arthur's ships into the estuary two days early."

"As you say. But it was Lancelot who got me off that island. Whatever happens now, I am forever in his debt."

She turned away and gazed across the orchard to the distant shimmer of the Lake. I fidgeted impatiently, thinking of Lancelot, who lay near death for my sake.

"Will he live, Niniane?" The question escaped me against my will, and I bit my lip, afraid of her answer.

"Lancelot's fate I have not seen," she said apologetically. "The stars do not foretell everyone's destiny."

"Wait!" I cried, although she had made no move to go. "One thing more I would know. I—I am afraid of it. If it concerns Arthur, you will know it, will you not?" At the mention of his name her attention focused on me sharply, and my voice wavered. "Everyone thinks—he will put me away. God knows he has cause. I know it better than anyone. Will he do it, Niniane? Oh, please, tell me if you know!"

Her eyes grew cold once more and although she did not move, I felt her withdraw. "Should you care overmuch? You would be free. And Lancelot is still unwed."

I cried out and covered my face with trembling hands.

"I would rather die," I whispered brokenly. "I will kill myself first—I don't care if it means eternal damnation, I could not live with that shame, I could not, I could not. Oh, dear God, why must I bear this trial? Why can I not conceive the son he wants? What have I done to bring such shame upon him? I cannot bear it—"

At this point Niniane pressed her cool fingers against my temples and said some words in a low, calm monotone. My eyelids grew heavy and closed against my will.

"Rest, Queen Guinevere. I would help you if I could, but I do not know the answer to your question. Merlin has seen your end, but I have not. It is in Arthur's hands, and to him you shall go."

"May God have mercy upon my soul," I whispered.

"The gods have chosen you," she said quietly. "There is a reason. Perhaps you would do well to accept what life brings you."

"Take what comes and live without complaint," I said slowly. "What will be, will be."

"Life is a woman's gift; death is God's," she finished. "So you have heard Merlin's litany before."

I smiled and touched her hand. "Arthur says it to me every six months," I told her. "Thank you, Niniane. I feel better for your visit."

We rose together, and at last her smile was warm.

"You have great charm, Guinevere. All the world knows it, of course, but I thought—Arthur warned me I should not be proof against it. He was right."

I took her arm in mine. "Arthur is a very wise man."

I sat with Lancelot four days before the fever abated and he opened his eyes. As a nurse I was useless, except for applying cold compresses and fluffing pillows. I sat at his bedside holding his hand, and remembering my childhood role in the hospital of Gwynedd, I sang to him. I sang when the leeches were applied, I sang when they lanced an abscess and as it drained. I sang to keep myself from being sick and to ease my terror of the physician's art. I left his side only to eat and to sleep, and only then because Niniane insisted on it. A small service she would do Arthur, she said, if she allowed me to fall ill again. I obeyed her every command, and she seemed pleased with Lancelot's progress, although to me he looked deathly pale whenever he was not hot with fever.

That he was alive at all was something of a miracle. The night he brought me in, they told me, he had no sooner given me into the Lady's care than he had staggered into Melwas' fortress intent upon revenge. Hot with fever and so lame he could barely stand, he had burst in upon the kings at supper, sword drawn, and thrown himself at Melwas while the whole court sat frozen. Shouting accusations and half delirious, he had slipped in a pool of his own blood and missed his target, hit his head against the table and fallen senseless to the floor. Only Arthur's restraining hand on Melwas' arm had kept the two-faced coward from killing him then and there. While I had Arthur to thank that Lancelot lay struggling for life in the Lady's pavilion, Arthur was not there now.

On the fourth day Lancelot opened his eyes and knew me.

"Gwen!" he whispered.

"Hush!" I cried, and then, "Nurse!" The attendant lifted water to his lips, and he took it eagerly.

"Gwen, my beloved," he said, and slipped back into sleep. I pressed his hand to my cheek and cried for joy.

For two more weeks I stayed with him, and each day he improved. As he gained strength, he talked to me, and talked and talked, as if words could take the place of sweet caresses. He told me of his Breton boyhood, his harsh father, his loneliness, his dreams of honor and glory, and his finding in Arthur the answer to his prayers. I held his hand throughout and touched his brow, and wept and laughed as he moved me to it. It was as if his illness had dissolved the reserve that had always been between us, and he shared his thoughts freely with me. We were always attended and observed, but it mattered not to us. In the world we inhabited only we two existed. He did not mention Melwas, and neither did I. We grew so close during that time, and shared such happiness, that often we did not need to speak at all, but only touch. The memory of his brief passion burned in my thoughts, and in his, also. He would lay his hand upon my arm, and look at me with hot gray eyes, and we were back there in the cabin, alive and ready for surrender. Then one of us would look away and break the spell. It had happened; we could not deny it; but it was past.

At last, when Lancelot was on his feet and could put weight on his leg with the help of a stout staff, Niniane brought me news that the King desired my return and was sending an escort the following day to take me back.

I looked at her anxiously. "Is it a bad sign, Niniane, that he does not come himself?"

"I think rather it is a test for Melwas, who must give the escort passage," she replied kindly. "You are in no danger, Guinevere. Should Melwas try to prevent your going, the King's Companions would be down upon him within the hour." She smiled lightly. "I hear that many of them are beside themselves with eagerness for war, to avenge your honor. The King gives Melwas a chance to save his life."

I broke the news to Lancelot that evening, and he looked puzzled at my distress.

"I shall hate to lose your company, Guinevere, but you belong in Camelot with Arthur. When I am well enough to ride I will follow."

"It's—it's not so much leaving as arriving that I fear."

"Fear arriving? Whatever for?"

I paced the room nervously. The servant, flattened against the wall with wooden face, slipped out at my signal.

"I fear Arthur may—may see things as the world sees them and put me away. No one could blame him. Not even I. And now he has a perfect excuse."

"Guinevere." He spoke tenderly. I came to his bedside, and he took my hand. "Since I have known you, you have been afraid of Arthur. Has he ever given you cause?"

I shook my head. "I am not afraid, exactly. A little in awe, perhaps."

He smiled. "With Arthur, awe is easy. But I cannot believe you think he will do this. You are too entangled in your own fears. Think of how Arthur feels."

"But I am!" I cried. "How else could he feel, but betrayed by fate? He is High King, and he has no son."

Lancelot's face reflected only his loving kindness and his understanding.

"Gwen," he said gently, "think of the man you know. He would as soon part with a limb as part with you. As I would."

"He would part with a limb readily enough to save Britain, and no one knows that better than you, Lancelot."

He smiled and kissed my hand.

"True enough. But is this a matter of saving Britain or of pleasing her King?"

"Arthur's seed is Britain's future."

"Perhaps. That's with God, surely. But don't pretend to me that Arthur treats you like his broodmare, because I won't believe it."

His words were so like something Arthur had said to me once that I started in surprise. "You really think he will keep me?"

"Yes," Lancelot said. "I do."

I sat down next his bed and gripped his hand. "Dear God, I hope you are right."

18 ♚ FIDELITY AND BETRAYAL

The escort arrived with great pomp and flourish and not with a litter but with Pallas, dressed in a gilded bridle. The King had even sent new riding clothes so I could return to him in the style for which I had become well known.

Niniane's ladies dressed my hair, and Niniane herself as Lady of the Lake blessed me in public ceremony before I left the shrine. Outside, King Melwas' troops lined the road and saluted us as we rode by. Melwas himself was there, richly dressed and crowned, and, although I could scarcely credit it, still followed me with hungry eyes. I remembered he had spoken to me of visions fed him by the old Lady of the Lake. Perhaps, having come so close to his heart's desire, he could not bear to leave it and still had hope. I shuddered at the thought, and the captain of the escort, who rode beside me, guided his horse closer.

"Have no fear, my lady," he said in a low voice, "we shall be rid of Melwas soon."

I was surprised to recognize Ferron and saw in his very presence the touch of Arthur's hand. If the captain had been in disgrace as a result of my foolhardy behavior, he was being given the chance to redeem himself.

"Good Ferron," I greeted him, "how glad I am to see you here! I beg you will forgive my arrogance last time we met. I was wrong to ignore your good advice on that occasion and see now what it has cost us!"

He looked astonished and stuttered in reply. "Queen Guinevere, I—please do not—I beg you will not—the fault was mine, my lady. Were I half the horseman you are, I could have followed you in the fog!"

I laughed in delight, for his admiration was genuine and his compliment, so unlooked for, pleased me greatly. The bright May sun shone down upon us and my heart lifted.

"How does the King?" I asked him, knowing he had had an interview.

"The King is angry," he said stiffly, eyes straight ahead. And so he should be, I thought, but nonetheless I felt apprehension grip me. Soon after this we came to the end of the marshland causeway and met the open road to Caer Camel where, breaking into a gallop, we had no time for further talk.

The trumpets sounded at King's Gate as we drew nigh, and all of Arthur's troops came out to meet us. They lined the streets of Camelot and every man of them cheered as I rode past. I was overcome by such devotion, and when I dismounted in the castle forecourt, my eyes were blurry with tears. Ferron led me up the steps to the waiting party at the door. It was not until I sank into my curtsy that I realized with cold shock that Arthur was not there. Kay's hand raised me, and Kay's voice spoke the formal greeting.

"Welcome home, Queen Guinevere."

Trembling, I took his arm. "Where is my lord?" I whispered. "Kay, why is he not here? Take me to him!"

Kay grunted and led me inside. "My orders, lady," he said rather loudly, "are to take you to your rooms, where you may await the King's command. He will send for you when he is at leisure."

I glanced at him sharply, but his bland expression told me nothing. At leisure! What could he be doing now, with every one of his men on the streets of Camelot? Kay escorted me through the corridors to the door that gave onto the women's quarters. The nearest sentry stood a good ten paces off. When he bowed over my hand, he winked and said in a low voice, "He waits in your garden, but let no one know."

I thanked him swiftly and ran to my rooms. Ailsa and all my women were gathered in my sitting room, sunk in curtsies. I barely paused to greet them as I hurried by.

"My lady!" Ailsa cried in distress.

"Later!" I called over my shoulder. "I wish to be alone. Await my call." And I flew up the stairs to my bedchamber. Whether they thought I suffered from anger, fear, or humiliation, I cared not. I had to see Arthur. If he desired a private meeting he had chosen the place well. My garden could be approached from my bedchamber only, and no man could enter except through the King's apartments. As I stepped onto my terrace I stopped and took a deep breath to steady my nerves. So much depended on this interview!

Arthur stood at the end of the garden, half turned from me, watching the fountain play. I saw him suddenly as a stranger might, with that odd sight that is given to us at times to clear our senses and show us things anew. He was then in his twenty-fifth year, in the full flower of his manhood. He had been High King of Britain for eleven years, and kingship was part of the fabric of the man. He was tall and well made, with long limbs that moved with a natural grace. Clean shaven and clear-featured, he was a handsome man in a rugged, soldier's way. But what set him so apart from other men was something else: his inner light, his grace of bearing, his wholeness, his serenity. He knew who and what he was. He lived in his own time. This is what I saw that day, and it moved me deeply.

I came lightly down the stairway and crossed the garden toward him. The splash of the fountain hid the sound of my approach, and he did not see me until I was beside him. Thus I saw his true reaction and could judge his heart.

He turned and his face lit. "Guinevere!"

I sank to his feet and, taking his hand, pressed my lips to the great carved Pendragon ruby. "My lord Arthur!"

He lifted me with both arms and held me tightly, his hands in my hair, unbraiding it with practiced skill as he whispered endearments in my ear. "I have missed you so! Are you truly recovered from your ordeal? When you are able, I would like to hear everything you have to say."

"I shall tell you everything. But Arthur—"

He stopped my lips with his own, and I yielded to his ardor. I felt so safe in his arms. He was Britain, and my home.

"Ah, Gwen," he said at last, drawing away and allowing me breath, "can you forgive me for leaving you on Ynys Witrin? I've been through hell here, carrying on as if everything were normal, while you lay in Avalon surrounded by Melwas' troops. I wasn't sure he'd keep his promise to let you go. If I'd forced him—well, I'd have won the war, but risked losing the battle. I had to do what Merlin tells me you did and treat him like the gentleman he's not. If he thought I cared for nothing but your honor, he'd think he had less to lose by returning you. I had to sham indifference," he said with a touch of icy anger, "and give the coward hope."

I drew him to me and rested my head against his chest, where I closed my eyes and listened to the slow, strong beat of his heart.

"He told me," I said quietly, "that you would put me away. That all the world knew it." I felt his body tense, but I went on. "That was why he dared. That and some prophetic dream a priestess fed him. It matters not. But he is brave, Arthur. You were well advised to speak him fair and give him hope you would put me aside. Else I think he would have kept me and risked war."

He lifted my chin and looked down into my face. His eyes were dark and deep and warm. "Did you believe him?"

"I—I—I have feared it, my lord, before this. You have cause."

His face hardened, but his hand against my cheek was gentle.

"I shall not do it," he said roughly, holding my face in his hand and looking directly in my eyes. "I shall never do it, Guinevere. I swear it here before God. So long as I am King, you shall be Queen. At least I can spare you that horror."

Tears slid down my cheeks, and he kissed them, one by one. "Arthur," I whispered, choking back a sob, "I love you from my soul."

He closed his eyes at that and went quite still. "Mother of God!" he breathed. "That I should live to hear you say those words to me! And after what you have been through and where you have been!"

Then he laughed a joyous laugh and, sitting on the stone bench that flanked the fountain, pulled me onto his lap. "And how is Lancelot? I have had reports from Niniane, but you can tell me things that she cannot."

"He is impatient of return," I told him, "and furious that Melwas is still alive."

"Then he is nearly recovered. I do not worry about Lancelot with Melwas. There is not a man on Ynys Witrin who would willingly raise a sword against him. He is the finest swordsman in Britain."

I smiled at him. "He speaks highly of you, too."

"Besides, I brought his weapons home with me, for his own protection."

I laughed. "He did not tell me that."

"I think perhaps he owes you his life."

"But it was you who sent me to him. It was a noble gesture."

"It was a desperate one," he said gravely. "I wanted you here, but I cannot afford to lose him."

I slid my arms around his neck. "Arthur."

"Yes?"

"I must tell you. About Melwas."

"Ah, yes. Of what do you accuse him?"

"Of abduction."

"Is that everything? Not," he said, facing it, "of rape?"

"No. He did not take me. I escaped that fate—by minutes—but I escaped."

He let out a long, slow breath.

"Did no one tell you?" I cried. "Did they let you think—"

"No one knew, for certain. Lancelot lay senseless, and Merlin disappeared."

"But if you doubted—Arthur." I looked at him with awe. "Do you mean you vowed to keep me, even when you thought he had used me so?"

His face was grave, but his eyes were warm and comforting. "I do. Nothing Melwas could do could change what is between us. He would have to kill you to take you from me. As for the rest, it is simply fools' chatter. I have had, for years now, plenty of advice to put you aside—you know the reasons. But I cannot do it, Gwen. There is more to life than breeding children, and I do not wish to do without you." His arms about my waist tightened. "A King's life can be abominably lonely. I am away from home so often and so long, I feel I have the right to come back to the woman of my choice."

I kissed his throat and rested my head upon his shoulder. "You are the soul of generosity. You are the only man in Christendom to whom it would not make a difference."

"Oh, it makes a difference," he replied, with an edge to his voice. "But not to you. To Melwas. The difference between certain death and the chance to sue for mercy."

"What will you do to him?"

"I will charge him with the crime he has committed. We shall see how he responds. I have wanted to kill him, but it is not the best solution."

We sat silently awhile. I was wrestling with my conscience; Arthur looked at peace.

"My lord," I said at last. "There is more I should tell you about Melwas. Niniane told me you should hear it."

He waited. I could not tell from his face whether or not he already knew.

"I stalled him for as long as I could," I said slowly, forcing it out, "but eventually Melwas decided he could wait no longer. When it grew dark, he—he—Arthur, he put his hands and lips upon me, and half undressed me. Then he saw a light, a signal, from his confederate, and left. I should have covered myself, my lord, I know. But I was—frozen. I was so frightened I could not move."

"Yes," he said in a tight voice. "I have seen the same in men, after battle."

"I knew nothing. I did not feel time pass. I was still standing thus when—when Lancelot came in." My eyes were averted from his face, and I know I blushed. "He covered me, my lord, and took the unclean feeling from me."

His finger pressed against my lips to stop the words, and I was grateful. After a long silence, where neither of us looked at the other, he spoke. There was pain in his voice.

"He is my friend. He has done me a great service, and almost lost his life for my sake. If he—gave you ease of heart, Guinevere, I am glad of it."

Such generosity was beyond belief. I bowed my head and let the tears slip out. My heart ached for him.

"He told me," I whispered, "that you would not put me away."

"He knows me well."

I hugged him tightly and pressed my wet cheek to his face. "Sir, I would that it were not so. I would spare you this."

"Thank you, Gwen. But it cannot be helped. This we all three have known. It is the trust between us that matters."

"We shall never break it," I promised him, as I sat on his lap in the shaded garden with tears on my face and my heart too full for speech.

At length he lifted me and began his slow pacing to and fro before the fountain. I could not imagine what there was left to say.

"Guinevere," he said at last, "you have been brave and honest with me and told me things I did not like to hear. Now I am afraid that I must say such things to you."

"How so, my lord?"

"Recall I told you that I had to hide my anger from Melwas and feign indifference to your fate to give him hope, both by leaving you there so long, and by sending you to Lancelot."

"Yes."

"There was a double purpose in it. And in my sending Ferron in my place, and in my leaving Kay to greet you. I had to seem cold, not only to fool Melwas, but to fool his accomplice here in Camelot."

I gasped. "Accomplice?"

He glanced at me quickly, and he looked a different man. His eyes glinted hard and bright, and his face was set. I had never seen him so angry. "How else was Melwas there? He was not fowling in the fog. He had information that you would be riding that way. More than that, he had information that if he were successful he might keep you, for I might put you away. God knows the palace gossip has found little else to talk about this year past." He shrugged it off quickly and moved on. "A courier was seen leaving King's Gate before your party left, and after you had told Kay your plans."

"You don't suspect Kay!"

"I will not unless I have to. Who could have overheard your instructions to him?"

I thought back carefully. My answer might amount to accusation. "Six of my women," I said at last, and named them.

"Ah. So Elaine was there."

"Arthur!" I cried, gripping his arm. "You cannot suspect Elaine!"

His look was very gentle. "You feel about her as I do about Kay. You grew up together. She is your sister. But think closely on this, Guinevere. Is the trust between you strong?"

"My lord, I—I have always thought so."

"I am not sure that it goes both ways," he said. The very gentleness of his voice frightened me.

"Something has happened," I said suddenly. "Tell me."

He sat me down upon the bench and stood before me, holding both my hands. "Do you know why Elaine has refused all offers, even from the finest of my Companions, and never married?"

I gasped and met his eyes. "Yes, my lord. But—do you?"

He nodded, and I sat speechless, waiting for what was coming.

"I found her in my bed," he said simply, "when you had been two weeks away. For a moment only, I thought it was you. She has the trick of imitating your voice. For a brief moment I imagined you had escaped and come to me secretly somehow." He smiled, a little shamefaced. "A dream born of longing. It was a moment only. I knew, as soon as I touched her hair. But in that moment—" He hesitated and I felt my face grow red with shame. I stared miserably at the paving stones and clung to his hands. "—she revealed her soul. She said things to me that will not bear repeating. In truth, I think she is not well."

I shook my head. "No, Arthur. It is only infatuation. She has always been so. It is not new."

"You will keep her away from me!" It burst out of him with force, and then he sighed and sat down beside me. "I am trying to tell you, Gwen, that I suspect her of grave disloyalty to you. Whatever the cause, I think she betrayed you to Melwas."

I said nothing. It was possible; I saw that. But I did not want to believe it of Elaine. That she loved Arthur, yes. That she would actually try to supplant me, no. But if she had really gone to the King's bed—

"Are you certain it was Elaine?" I asked desperately.

"Yes," he replied with sadness. "I lit the lamp."

"And this happened when?"

"A week ago. After I had sent you to Lancelot. To all the world it looked as if I had given in to fate and cared no more about you, which, may God forgive such deceit, was the plan." He passed a hand across his brow. "I did not suspect her until this happened, but I do now. What I wish to know, Gwen, is whether you want to handle this yourself, or if you want me to do it. I leave the choice to you."

"If it is Elaine—she does not know that you have forgiven me?"

"Forgiven you?" He touched my cheek. "You have done naught to offend me."

"I mean—you have promised—she cannot know yet that you will not put me aside?"

"No. That has been one point of all this subterfuge, that the informer should not know my true feeling toward you. Thus I conspired to meet you privately, where not even Elaine could observe us."

"Then let me speak with her, my lord. I owe her that."

"I thought you might say that. It will not be pleasant, Guinevere."

I managed a smile. "Of a certainty. How was it left between you? Does she still feel as she did?"

For the first time I saw Arthur embarrassed. He did not know what to say. "It is my belief her feelings are unchanged," he admitted awkwardly. "For all that, she is angry with me."

"Of course she is, since you refused her. You need tell me no more. I know what line to take."

He rose then and took me in his arms, running his fingers through my loose hair. "Welcome home, my Queen. We missed your birthday. You are twenty now, and you are the most wonderful woman alive."

"Thank you, my lord."

"And you will be more careful of yourself from now on, for my sake, and not put my valuable captains through such tortures of soul?"

I smiled at him. "Yes, my lord."

"Whatever possessed you to take off that day, if I may ask?" I looked away, the smile gone. "Never mind," he said quickly. "I see it is as I thought."

"Take what comes and live without complaint, for what will be, will be," I said slowly, looking up at him again. "I will try to put it behind me, Arthur. I know I may never give you children. I can bear it, I think, if you can forgive it. Lend me your strength."

A deep sigh escaped him, as if something long held in had been freed at last.

"It is a day of miracles," he breathed, and kissed me. At length he loosed me and squared his shoulders.

"Let me leave first," he said, "that I may be in another part of the castle when you go to your quarters. Give me ten minutes. I shall see you at the feast tonight."

"What feast, my lord?"

His quick grin lit his face. "The Companions are throwing a great feast in the Queen's honor. You are their darling, did you not know? And there I shall publicly declare you my Queen for my life. In Council this afternoon I will charge Melwas. So you had better confront Elaine before that."

"As soon as you are gone, my lord."

"Brave woman." He saluted me, and left.

When I went in I called Ailsa to me and bade her shake out my blue gown, "for it is the King's favorite," and sat while she bathed me and brushed out my hair. She scented my gown with the jasmine scent the King had procured from southern lands and dressed my hair with seed pearls and a net of small sapphires, also the King's gift. When all these preparations were complete, I sat on my little needlepoint bench and bade Ailsa leave me, "for," I said, not untruthfully, "I await the King's command."

She had said very little to me, just chatted in the ordinary way, and asked no questions at all. But she looked pale and frightened, and I was sorry I could not relieve her fears. As she reached the door, I stopped her.

"Ailsa, if the lady Elaine is at leisure, and if she is so inclined, she may come to me. Keep everyone else away."

"Very good, my lady."

Elaine came up immediately. When she saw me sitting there in Arthur's favorite gown, dressed for a feast at midday, bathed and scented and waiting, her eyes lit, and my heart sank.

"Gwen!" she cried, running to me and hugging me lightly. "Oh, I am so glad you are back! Was it very horrible? Have you seen the King? Is he very angry?"

I had seated myself so my face was in shadow, and she put my nervousness down to fear of the King.

"I was hoping perhaps you could tell me that," I replied. "I—I have heard rumors."

"He is furious at Melwas, of course," she confided, seating herself upon a cushion at my feet. Light from the terrace doorway fell on her face, which was lifted to me. "It was an insult to his honor. But he shall be avenged." She paused. "What happened to you, Gwen? All we have heard here are rumors. That is, if you can bear to speak of it."

"What have you heard?"

"That Lancelot rescued you with Merlin's help, but that he was too late to save you from—the worst."

She watched me eagerly, and my flesh crept upon my bones.

"As far as it goes, that is true," I said, and the triumph on her face, quickly suppressed, was a knife in my heart. "But for Merlin's Sight and Lancelot's courage, I might still be—in that place. It was well hidden."

She had the grace to shudder. "And was Lancelot badly injured?" she went on. "They say he lay dying, until you went to his bedside and restored his will to live."

"They exaggerate," I replied.

"That must have been terribly hard, Gwen, to see him so near death, and for your sake."

"Yes. It was hard."

She took my hand to comfort me, and if she felt my trembling, she misconstrued it.

"Were you there when he regained his senses? Did you speak your heart?" she asked in a dreadful whisper. "It must have seemed like stolen time for both of you."

"Elaine," I said quickly, "what should I do? I have heard things about the King—that he is—that he might be ready to annul our marriage. Tell me it is not true! What can I do to regain his favor?"

She smiled. "You are off to a good start. It's well known he cannot resist you when you wear blue!" Then she rose and took a turn about the room. "Seriously, Gwen, I would be careful." She frowned. "I have had private speech with the King—" Here I stifled a gasp. "—and I tell you I think you are on dangerous ground. It is possible that he will put you away. He has spoken to the bishop about it."

It was a cool lie, and she told it without a flicker of hesitation.

"The bishop?" I whispered.

She turned to me. The excitement in her eyes belied the sorrow on her face. "Oh, Gwen, forgive me. I only meant—I don't know what will happen. I only tell you to prepare you. After all, what future has Britain unless the King has sons?" She came closer and reached for my hand. But I could not help myself, and I shrank from her touch.

"Are you so certain he has determined upon that course?"

"No. No one is sure. But Arthur indicated, when he spoke to me—" I blushed to hear her use his name so freely. "—that it was time to put the past behind him. Listen, Gwen." She sank to her knees and looked up at me earnestly. "Remember when we were girls in Wales? How happy you were with Lancelot, and how you longed to be his bride instead of Arthur's? It can be so—it can happen now with no disgrace! The King will charge Melwas with abduction and rape, and when he has avenged the slight to his honor, he will free you from this bond you never wanted. Lancelot will jump at the chance to wed you. Just think of it, Gwen! Your fondest dream can come true. You can marry your true love."

She came to a stop, breathless and excited, and I simply could not bear to look into her face. I rose and walked away, struggling to compose myself enough to speak.

"You have it all worked out, Elaine, do you not?" Her head went up at the tone of my voice, and she went suddenly still. "How did you make contact with Melwas? Was it after the Harvest Festival years ago when I told you how amorous he had been? Who was your go-between? The King will want to know."

She went white. "What are you talking about?"

"I have trusted you with secrets, Elaine, and loved you as a sister. What have you done to me?"

"Gwen," she whispered, "I am innocent."

I whirled and faced her.

"You should know," I said flatly, "that before I called you up here, I was with the King an hour."

She gasped. Then a subtle change came over her. Surprise left her features, along with every vestige of warmth and youth. She looked suddenly old and hard.

"Arthur made it clear to me, Elaine, very, very clear, that everything you have just said is false. You have made a grave mistake. He will not put me away. And he would not have you, even if he were free. Live with that."

It was cruel, and Elaine was never able to take a barb in silence.

"You do not deserve him!" she spat. "You are barren! Give him up and let him wed a fertile woman who will bear him sons!"

"That is his choice. But he will not do it. He has told me so."

"You are soiled!" she cried. "Do not stain his honor! Gwen, don't rob him of his future!"

"If I am soiled," I said levelly, "who set me up for it? How devoted to Arthur can you be, to conspire to defile his wife?"

"I have done nothing!" she screamed. "You can prove nothing!"

"I can ask Melwas, when he faces judgment, who his informer was."

Her face flooded with color, and she stood to face me. "You dare not do it! You dare not expose your shame to public view!"

I regarded her with heartfelt pity. "So that is what you counted on to save you. I wondered." I found myself near the foot of my bed and gripped the bedpost for support. "I suppose now is the time to tell you that Melwas did not rape me."

"Coward!" she shrieked, then clapped a hand over her mouth as tears started to her eyes.

"He tried, God knows, but was prevented by circumstance. I have told the King what happened. I tell you now so you may know how hopeless is your defense."

"I will not bother to defend myself!" she cried hotly, and I saw with dismay that the floodgates had opened, and her words and tears tumbled forth together. "Go ahead and accuse me! I do not care! You are so high and mighty, you who were taken in as orphan by my mother, always spoiled and pampered—oh, God!—past bearing! Nothing was denied you! You took everything away from me, even that God-forsaken Irishman! Everything I ever wanted was given to you! It was I who honored Arthur from my youth, not you. It is I who should be his Queen, not you! I can breed sons aplenty—I know it—as my mother did before me. It is not fair! You will destroy him! You—he loves you for your beauty, which you have done nothing to deserve, and you love that—that broken-nosed Breton who always stinks of stables! Oh, God! I cannot bear it! Kill me and have done!"

She flung herself to the floor, weeping horribly, while I stood by, numb, and waited. But as no one came to cosset and tend her, at length her sobs diminished and died into rhythmic whimpers.

I found my voice. "Is *that* what lies at the bottom of all this?" I took a deep breath. "Have you learned nothing? Beauty may be a gift from God, but I thought by now you would have learned this lesson: that it is as hard to bear and as welcome as a double-edged sword that turns in the hand. You are a beautiful woman, Elaine—how can you not know this? Only see the cost we pay—you, Melwas, Lancelot, and even Arthur! It is the first thing anyone sees, and few ever try to get beyond it. To half of Britain, man and woman, I am a mask, an ornament, a prized possession, no more, made for the King's pleasure, to dispose of as he wills! If Arthur regarded me so, or Lancelot, I should throw myself into the Lake of Avalon and have it over! Dear God! I have thought so often, if I were plain and men did not admire me, how simple and how easy life would be! Even you, Elaine, who have known me from childhood, do not know me. *And to find that this is why! Sweet Mary!* What I would not give to be judged by words and deeds and not by my face!" I stopped, gulping, forcing back the tears. Elaine had covered her ears and was not even listening.

"I have done nothing," I said slowly, "to deserve such treatment at your hands. I have loved you as a sister. You have shared my bed, Elaine, and shared my pillow talk. These things I cannot forget. For your treachery, which grieves me to my heart, I banish you from court. I will send you back to Alyse and Pellinore as soon as arrangements can be made, and perhaps you can find a husband in some corner kingdom of Wales."

"Guinevere." She looked up, and I saw her swollen, puffy face and reddened eyes. "Do you not love Lancelot?"

I sat suddenly upon the bed, trembling. "You know I do."

"Then why do you throw away the only chance you will ever have to wed him? I have done you a great service, if you but knew it."

"Because," I said slowly, "it would dishonor Arthur. I don't know if I can explain it to you, Elaine. Without Arthur, Lancelot and I would not be who we are. The love we bear each other is—is also love for the King. I can't say it any plainer. But I knew it—we both knew it—back in Melwas' cabin when he found me all alone, and we could so easily—how easily!— have been lovers. Don't you see, Elaine? You talk about honor, but I don't believe you know what it is."

She sank to the floor once more, utterly defeated. "You cannot have them both," she mumbled. "It isn't fair."

"I will send for your parents," I said at length.

"Please, Gwen," she cried piteously, huddled on the floor, "please let me stay until the solstice. My father will be so angry to learn I have displeased you! Let me stay at court just until then."

"Displeased me? Elaine, you have betrayed me."

She shivered but did not deny it any longer.

"I should have you whipped. Melwas, your dupe, must take his punishment publicly, like it or not. It is not fair that you should escape so lightly.

But—but you were once dear to me, Elaine, and I cannot forget it. You may stay until the solstice celebrations are over. The next day you must leave. But there is one condition." The sly smugness that had crept across her features slowly faded, and she waited in fear. She had some new plan afoot already, I saw, and my only thought was to protect the King.

"You will not come within sight or speech of the King or of myself. You shall take all your meals in your rooms. If either of us so much as sees your face, you are gone."

She blanched at that, but I saw relief in her face. "You are cruel," she whimpered, but she put no feeling in it. Her mind was already somewhere else.

"Go now. Tell Ailsa I will speak with Alissa."

So Elaine left, I thought forever. With Alissa I made arrangements for her confinement and surveillance.

Melwas was formally charged in the Round Hall with abducting the Queen and was bidden to show himself in three days' time in the Council chamber to answer the charge, else the High King would declare war against him and confiscate his lands.

I was worried about Lancelot's safety, but the King was not, which reassured me. When he met me before hall that night to take me into the feast, he asked after Elaine, and I told him what had happened and what I had done.

"My poor Gwen. I see you have suffered. I can imagine the kind of things she said."

"I did not know she had it in her."

"Sometimes those closest are the last to know. What will you do with her?"

"I will send her back to Wales after the solstice."

"Three weeks? That is generous indeed."

"She begged me so piteously to stay for that. And I could not forget what we have been."

He smiled. "You are kindhearted. Don't tell me she wants to celebrate our anniversary with us. She must have another reason. Look she does not take advantage of your lenience."

"In truth, my lord," I said slowly, "I do not want to send her back to Wales. It would break poor Pellinore's heart, and Alyse would never forgive her. If I know Elaine, in three weeks she will get herself a husband, and when she leaves, it will not be in disgrace. Pellinore and Alyse will be deceived, but you and I and Elaine will know the truth. I care not if she escapes public disgrace, so long as I never see her again."

He regarded me with approval. "A shrewd observation, Guinevere. Well done. Though but a girl, you are a diplomat."

"I am twenty, my lord!" I protested, grinning, pleased by his praise. "As old as you were when you married me. Did you think yourself a boy at this age, after six years as King?"

He laughed and slipped an arm about my waist. "But you are ageless, Gwen. Merlin says it is your fate. You will be as young at forty as you are to-day. You are my child Queen."

A childless queen was closer to the truth, I thought, but I did not speak it for Arthur's sake.

19 👑 THE TRAITOR

Three days later King Melwas of the Summer Country rode into Camelot with a force of armed men and Lancelot. He was received by Kay and escorted to the Round Hall where he sat in the Chair of Complaint oppo-site the King. Bedwyr later told me everything that happened, sparing no details, for I was wild to know.

In response to the King's accusation of abduction, Melwas said he had rescued me when my horse slipped on the muddy bank and, hearing no one else about, had taken me to a hunting cabin where he could attend me. He had had no servant, but had dried my wet clothing and fed me with his own hands, and was on his way to Avalon to fetch attendants and a barge when Arthur had sailed into the estuary.

"Liar!" Lancelot cried, struggling to his feet. "You were still on the is-land when the ships were sighted! Your confederate signaled you from shore!"

"What confederate?" Melwas demanded.

"And it was no hunting cabin, my lord," Lancelot persisted, who did not wish to accuse the lady Seulte without proofs of her guilt, "but furnished with furs and wine and gilded candlesticks! He had prepared the place, my lord! He had planned to bring her there!"

The Companions muttered among themselves, watching Arthur's stony face and waiting for Melwas' reply.

Melwas rose. "You lie, Lancelot. I never touched the Queen. And the place is a ramshackle cabin, nothing more. Come, my lords all, and I will show it to you."

"No doubt it is so now!" Lancelot shouted. "You have had plenty of time to put it back to rights! But it was not thus the night of your arrival, my lord King! I was there!"

"Yes," Melwas sneered, his voice gone dangerously soft. "Let us not forget that you were there." He lifted a hand and signaled to his servant, who brought up a canvas satchel. Melwas faced Arthur boldly. "While I was gone for help, my lord," he said coolly, "this ardent hothead broke in upon the Queen." He reached into the satchel and brought forth an armful of wrinkled sheets, foul with bloodstains and reeking with old wine. "I found these on the bed the morning after. I swear by Llyr, by Lluden, by Bilis, by the Great Goddess herself, that I was not the one between these sheets! But I can tell you who was." He turned to Lancelot and snarled, "If there was rape done, sir, you did it! You are the one who was wounded and bleeding—you are the one who was there when I was gone, all alone with the Queen!" He whirled toward Arthur. "He has loved her beyond all sense for years, my lord King. It's about time you knew it. And here is proof he has betrayed you!" He raised high the bloody sheets; the Companions sat stunned; Arthur shot to his feet, gray-faced. Lancelot's strangled shriek rent the silence. He threw himself across the Round Table at Melwas and caught him by the throat.

"Devil! Fiend! Liar! I shall have your life, you filthy blackguard!" Melwas crashed to the floor with Lancelot atop him, a wild man, raging incoherently, blind to his surroundings. Thank God Arthur banned all weapons from the Council chamber, or murder would have followed! The Companions came to their senses and pulled Lancelot away, holding Melwas back while the two men cursed and shouted at one another. Finally Arthur called for silence.

Lancelot fell to his knees, gasping in pain. "Arthur, Arthur, my most sovereign lord! I am innocent of his accusation! I swear it by the blood of Christ!"

Arthur came to where Lancelot knelt and extended his hand. "Rise, Lancelot. I know you are free of that sin. Neither you nor the Queen could hide it from me."

In the complete silence that followed his words, Melwas threw his glove upon the Round Table. "I will not be called a liar without redress! Arthur of Britain, I challenge you to make good your accusation! Meet me on a field of honor, on the day of your choosing. I will show you what justice is."

No one in the room dared to breathe. Lancelot kissed Arthur's ring and clutched his hand. "Let me fight him, Arthur! I can take him, wound and all! Oh, please, my lord! Let me clear her name!"

Arthur, as cold and pale as a stone carving, shrugged free of his grip. "On what grounds? The Queen's honor is mine to avenge." He turned to

Melwas. "I accept the challenge, Melwas. On the morrow I will meet you. The Queen accuses you of her abduction. And I accuse you of slandering her good name. Kay, see to it."

Melwas bowed, satisfied, and strode out of the Council chamber. Then pandemonium broke loose. The Companions crowded around Arthur, all talking at once, protesting against the outrageous suggestion that the High King should put his person in jeopardy to satisfy the honor of such a scoundrel. Each of them beseeched the King to let him fight in the King's place. When the bedlam passed its height, the King answered them.

"I thank all my brave Companions for your offers. But I ask you to think what you would do, if you were I. The Queen's honor is mine to avenge. And no one else's."

Bedwyr wrote two songs about this Council meeting and what came after. The true tale he wrote for Arthur; but the other he wrote for Lancelot. Lancelot could not forgive himself for Melwas' accusing me of adultery in public; he was certain that it was his injury which prevented Arthur from allowing him to fight. To soothe his tormented spirit, Bedwyr remade the story to his liking and sang of Lancelot's great rage in Council, and his great defeat of Melwas in single combat; how he split his brains with a sword-stroke and rid the Kingdom of an evil scourge. Lancelot delighted to hear it, and indeed, it was much the prettier song, although it was fancy. In later years I heard it retold by young men as if it were truth, but no one who ever knew Arthur thought so.

Everyone, myself included, was horrified that he should put himself at risk, but to Arthur it was a kind of a relief to be fighting again. His dislike of Melwas went deep, but more than that, he desired to show himself a warrior again after years of patient statesmanship as King. There were many young soldiers who had never seen the King's sword Excalibur lifted from its hanger in the Round Hall. To them the Sword of Britain was a symbol, for they could not remember the hard years of fighting, when Excalibur was raised against the Saxon terror, always victorious. So perhaps, I thought, it was a wise move. But it also brought the King joy.

The day dawned cloudy and cool, with the promise of rain. Every citizen of Camelot turned out to watch the King defend my honor; from the turrets I could see the press of people as they hurried through the streets, past closed shops and empty marketplace, to join the assembled throng at the Contest Field beyond the town. I spent the morning watching from the southeast tower, most of the time on my knees praying God to spare the life of my lord. What Britain would do without him I could not conceive. The banners that usually flew so gaily over Camelot hung limply in the still, unmoving air. I feared we would have a thunderstorm before the day was out. It was a good day to die, I thought suddenly, and then crossed myself quickly.

Shaken, I descended to my quarters to await escort to the field. All the women were going, except Elaine. Alone of my household, I did not wish to go. But I had no choice. I was the cause of this disaster and must show my face. "Sweet Mary," I prayed, "save me from such arrogance again! That I should put my lord in jeopardy!" It was unbearable.

Lancelot came for me at noon, in a black humor, followed by a group of Companions to escort the women. The ride from Ynys Witrin and his attack on Melwas had inflamed his leg, and he walked with a stout staff and leaned upon my arm, but he was determined to go. Slowly we filed out of the palace and through the streets of the town toward the field, while people stared openly at us and made reverences.

He stumped along beside me, muttering under his breath, making no attempt at civility.

"I owe you thanks for your defense of me in Council," I ventured. "Bedwyr told me of Melwas' denial and your quick response. I am grateful, Lancelot, and not for the first time, you hold my honor so dear."

"Do not speak of it, I pray you," he retorted. "It is my fault Melwas had the courage to accuse you. Had I caught the lying bastard, had I not blundered around so—"

"Blundered!" I cried. "Is that what you call it? You rescued me from a fate I could not have borne! You insult me to think so little of it!"

That startled him out of his selfish sulks, and he looked at me quickly. "I did not mean it that way, Gwen. Surely you know my heart. But Melwas accused me—boldly accused me before Arthur himself and all the Companions—of the one sin I dread committing—"

"Arthur knew it was a lie."

"Yes, but—" His voice sank to a whisper, "—it so nearly wasn't."

"Don't, I pray you. You are guiltless, and Arthur knows it."

"He accused me outright, and I cannot make him pay for it! Oh, God, I would give my right arm to fight him!" He clutched his sword hilt in distress. "But I must sit by helplessly while Arthur clears your name!"

"Lancelot," I said evenly. "He is my husband. It is his right."

"But—"

"Who do you think sent me to you on Ynys Witrin? Who has put your well-being first, at every step, before his own? He knows what he owes you."

"But I—"

"I pray you will be sensible! This public display is the best way to put things right between us all. He must do it."

"But, Gwen, I—"

"For the love of God!" I cried, clutching his arm. "Stop thinking about yourself and think of Arthur! King Melwas is twice his size!"

"Why, Guinevere!" Lancelot suddenly exclaimed. "You are shaking like a leaf in a storm! Surely you do not fear for the King?"

"Of course I do! Don't you?"

He looked amused. "Fear for Arthur? No, indeed. He cannot lose."

"How can you know that? He is mortal flesh like other men."

"He will not lose to Melwas." He spoke with certainty. "Melwas knows the truth behind his lies. In his heart he expects to be defeated. He expects to die."

"May his expectations be fulfilled."

"Amen to that." Lancelot grunted. "Besides, if today were Arthur's deathday, Merlin would know of it and be here. But as you see, he is absent, so all is well." As he spoke the word "death-day" he crossed himself, and I shivered.

"You believe in the magic of the Sword, then? Well, so you should, I suppose. You have seen it used enough."

"Aye, it has saved me more than once from a Saxon ax. But he will not wield Excalibur today."

"What!" I stopped so suddenly he almost lost his balance, and only just saved himself from falling. "Not Excalibur? What madness is this?"

Lancelot spoke with patience. "The Sword is meant to preserve Britain from her enemies. Melwas is a Briton himself. He—"

"He is an enemy of Arthur's," I said hotly, "and Arthur is Britain!"

Lancelot's mouth twitched in an effort to keep from grinning. "No one denies it. Relax just a little. Your fingers will leave bruises on my arm."

"I beg pardon," I said blushing, releasing my grip. "I am—not myself today. I had a premonition of disaster this morning and cannot shake the fear."

"Come, let us go on. We are holding up the others, and people are staring. Do not fear for Arthur, Gwen. He is twice the swordsman Melwas is, whatever sword he holds in his hand."

"And twice the rider, as well."

"Ahhh, well," Lancelot demurred, and I looked at him sharply.

"What are you going to tell me now?" I cried. "Will they not fight on horseback?"

"It is already arranged, Gwen, you can do nothing about it. Arthur knows Melwas has no horses that compare to his own. We have bred them for ten years, and he catches his loose in the hills."

"He felt it would be unfair," I finished bitterly. "What has fairness got to do with it? This is revenge. I am surprised he does not tie one hand behind his back to compensate for his greater skill."

Lancelot said nothing, and gradually my temper cooled and I saw the injustice of my protest. Lancelot read my thoughts perfectly.

"His victory must be earned," he said slowly. "It is important for his honor in the eyes of the people, as well as in his own eyes. To make use of all the advantages he has would ill become him. It must be a fair fight."

"But Melwas is so big. And he is brave. I heard him say things that let me know he was not afraid of Arthur."

"Bravado. It is easy to be brave with one's lips."

"Yet he dared to take me."

"His lust was greater than his fear." He looked quickly away, and I knew what he was thinking. He was ever quick to condemn himself.

"Love is not lust," I murmured softly.

"Thank you, Gwen."

We walked in silence until the field came into view. A small pavilion had been built at one end of the field, with a dais for chairs and an awning above. Here was where the King and his household sat to watch the contests during celebrations throughout the year. The steps up to the platform were narrow, and as Lancelot bade me precede him, I was first upon the dais. The crowds broke into wild cheering and stomping, raising their arms in the air. Vainly I looked about for Arthur, but could not see him.

Lancelot, come up behind me, said, "Gwen, they are cheering for you."

Amazed, I looked upon the people. "The Queen! The Queen!" they cried. Their faces were raised to me in joy, and their eyes were alight. I felt both uplifted and unworthy, and bowed my head and made them a deep reverence. The cheering only increased, and I turned to Lancelot helplessly.

"What do they want of me? I know not what to do."

"They just want to look at you. You are dear to them, and they nearly lost you. It is the way the King feels, too. And I."

I took my seat, my ladies filed in and sat on either side. Kay stood behind me, and Lancelot sat in the King's empty chair as his proxy while he was on the field. The Companions took their places guarding the pavilion. When all was ready, the noise gradually subsided. From opposite ends of the field the combatants suddenly appeared, each accompanied by his second, bearing arms. Arthur wore his fighting armor, thick leather leggings and boots, a heavy leather tunic studded with brass, and a leather helmet with a gold crown across the brow. That Melwas could look at him and not bend his knee defied belief. Melwas, who loved a rich display, was dressed as simply. He had come to fight.

Bedwyr and Arthur approached the center of the field. When Melwas and his second came up, the King spoke, but we were too distant to hear his words. Melwas' reply was short. Then he turned to his second and grasped his sword and short dagger. Arthur turned to Bedwyr and did the same. Then the seconds left the field, and Arthur faced Melwas alone.

A great roar went up from the assembled throng, and the two men began circling, like rival dogs over a bitch in heat. I gripped Lancelot's arm.

"Is there no way to stop this?" I whispered frantically.

He glanced at me swiftly. "He is your husband. It is his right."

"Damn you!" I gasped. "And may God protect him!"

"Amen. Relax, Gwen. See how they feint and dodge? He is taking Melwas' measure."

And Melwas was taking his, I thought, but did not say it. Growing up in a household among five brothers, I had seen plenty of fights, but none between such skilled swordsmen. Pellinore's men had been better trained, but their swordplay was only in practice. Never before had I seen two men face each other with the intent to kill. The difference in their styles was apparent before either scored a stroke. Arthur moved with grace and assurance and an inborn sense of timing. Melwas lunged with a boldness born of rage or desperation. He was nearly twice Arthur's size, and much the slower of the two, but any stroke that landed was capable of killing.

Each man gripped his sword, feinting, swinging, blocking each other's strokes. It was slow, this testing, getting a feel of the weapon and the opponent. It ended suddenly. Melwas feinted one way and lunged another. Arthur dodged but fell back. The crowd roared, and I gripped Lancelot's hand. Melwas pressed his attack, swinging ferociously, always advancing. Arthur sidestepped him, first one way and then another, but always retreating. They were getting farther from us, but I could hear Melwas' loud grunts of effort.

"What is he doing?" I cried.

"Watch now," Lancelot said, his eyes never leaving his King. "He will turn him in a minute. This is child's play."

Melwas raised his sword once more, and Arthur ducked under it and ran past. Melwas whirled in fury.

Lancelot chuckled. "Did you see that?"

"I see no humor in it. The man could kill him."

"He could, Gwen, but he won't."

I wished I had his calm. Immediately Melwas' tactics changed. He feinted toward the King's body, then chopped swiftly from the side, shortening his backstroke so his movements were harder to read. Arthur matched him stroke for stroke, blocking his thrust and being himself blocked. Once or twice they locked swords and came face to face. I saw Arthur's lips moving and could not guess what words he had to say to Melwas, there in the middle of the field. Melwas' sheer weight bore the King down, and they advanced toward us. Suddenly Melwas leaped sideways with surprising swiftness and swung upward. I gasped aloud. Arthur proved as agile, avoiding the stroke with a twisting of his body as he jumped toward Melwas and knocked the sword away just shy of his hip.

"Dear God," I whispered, but Lancelot was excited.

"Did you see that? I taught him that move, but he has never done it so well with me. He must have been practicing."

"Lancelot, this is not a game!" I cried in earnest, and for my sake he recovered his gravity. And so they went, back and forth and in circles around the field, with the people shouting encouragement, and Melwas always the aggressor. To ease my fears, Lancelot told me about the sword the King fought with, how it was made here in Camelot by a swordsman from the far north, a man of great skill who could fashion a living blade from cold iron in four days. But he had worked a month on the King's weapon. The blade was supple and strong, heated by the hottest fires and chilled in water just melted from ice blocks cut in midwinter and stored carefully in straw. The grip was made for the King's hand and none other. The smith swore if the blade ever chipped or cracked, the King might kill him with the remnant. Lancelot succeeded in distracting me for a while, and when I returned my attention to the fight, I noted that the pace had picked up considerably and that Melwas was getting angry.

"He thinks the King is playing with him," I said at a guess. Lancelot did not reply, and when I glanced at him I saw him looking worriedly at the leaden sky. "What's wrong?"

He shrugged. "I hope it does not rain."

"Why?"

"The footing will be slippery."

"Will that favor one or the other?"

"It often favors the heavier man. Oh, no, Gwen, forgive me! I should not have spoken. Look how Melwas is tiring. That is why he presses. Melwas is past thirty and fond of good living. The King is fit. Please don't worry."

But it was too late for reassurance. I watched in agony while the strokes got short and vicious. Arthur drew first blood, a glancing cut on Melwas' upper arm. Enraged, Melwas struck out blindly, and the very unpredictability of his attack made him dangerous. Blood flowed freely from his wound and wet the ground. Dodging, the King's foot slipped, and Melwas' sword came down. I believe I cried out. Lancelot half rose from his seat. The crowd gasped as one man. But Arthur rolled away, and the blow landed spent in the muddy grass, just grazing his arm. Melwas' sword stuck for a moment in the turf, pinned by the weight of his downstroke, and the King leaped to his feet, sword raised. The people roared, ready for the kill. But Arthur only pointed his blade at Melwas' heart and spoke to him.

"What is he about?" Lancelot cried, finally as fearful as I was. "Finish him, Arthur, before the rain!"

Melwas freed his sword and backed away, crossing the King's blade. He shouted something defiant, and I saw Arthur's shoulders stiffen. Then the King went on the attack, but Melwas gave no ground. Thunder rumbled menacingly, and the crowd grew uneasy. Arthur worked hard, but Melwas fought in fear of his life and was as quick. There was blood on the King's sleeve. "It's not his sword arm," Lancelot said, as if that should comfort me. Both men were tiring. Melwas used his weight to lean against the King, knowing he could not support it for long. I began to cry, silently, helplessly. Then Melwas tripped him. Lancelot leaped to his feet, shouting, and all the Companions drew their swords. It was the act of a coward, and base. Melwas had to be desperate. The King went down, but as he fell he kicked out at Melwas' sword hand, and his blade flew wide. Melwas drew his dagger and threw it.

"Bedwyr!" Lancelot yelled. "To him!"

Bedwyr was already running onto the field. The dagger caught Arthur in the shoulder, and as his blood soaked through his tunic, the people cried out in dismay. To the astonishment of all, including Melwas, Arthur pulled himself to his knees and pointed his sword at his attacker. The big man stepped back quickly, too quickly, and one foot slipped a pace in the bloody grass. In that moment the King was on his feet, his sword at Melwas' throat. Every person watching held his breath. But again the King forbore to kill him and spoke instead. Melwas was now weaponless, defeated, and he listened. When the King finished speaking, Melwas nodded slowly and sank to one knee. The crowd screamed wildly for an execution, but they were disappointed, for it was an act of submission to authority, and as such it was accepted. Arthur laid the flat of his blade upon Melwas' shoulders and spoke the ritual words that bound a vassal to his liege lord. The whole time he did this, the hilt of Melwas' dagger stuck out straight from his tunic, and I wept to see it. I did not know, having always had a horror of hospitals, that it was only safe to leave it thus; it was in the removal of the weapon that life was threatened.

The King put out a hand to Melwas and raised him, then suddenly staggered. Melwas lifted him in his great arms and carried him off the field. The crowd parted nervously and let them pass. Lancelot's face went white as Melwas approached the pavilion with the senseless King. The Companions surrounded him, swords drawn, but Melwas ignored them. He looked up at Lancelot.

"Where shall I take my lord?" he asked. "He needs attention."

The people who heard let out a great cheer, and others took it up. Lancelot's sigh of relief came from his soul.

"Follow Bedwyr, King Melwas. Kay will call the physicians." The clouds opened then, and the rain fell in a sheet, but no one noticed.

It is a fact that Melwas, having put the dagger in the King, waited by his bedside until he had recovered from its removal. Then he gathered his troops around him and went home in honor. From that day forward, he was Arthur's loyal ally, and his strongest supporter in the southwest. He would hear no word against the King, and men learned to watch their tongues in his presence. He never looked at me again.

Late that night, when the physicians were finished and the King lay wrapped in bandages and resting, Lancelot and I were allowed to go in to him. He had been given a posset of some healing drug with a sedative and was sleepy.

Instead of congratulating Arthur on his victory, Lancelot was hot with indignation. "Why did you let him off? You had him, three times, and let him go. He might have killed you."

Arthur grinned. "It's good to see you again, too." Lancelot threw up his hands and turned away to hide his emotion. But I did not have to hide mine.

"Arthur!" I knelt near his head, and he reached for me with his good arm.

"Hello, Gwen. You have been weeping."

I nodded and kissed his hand, unable to speak.

"Has she not!" Lancelot exclaimed. "All the world knows now where her heart lies." Then his expression softened, and he regarded Arthur with outright admiration. "What a King you are! With this day's work you have turned an enemy into an ally and set to rest the rumors that have been flying about the Kingdom. I congratulate you."

"It's about time." Arthur smiled, and yawned. "I made use of everything you taught me, did I not? And he never meant to kill me, or he would not have thrown so wide."

Lancelot shook his head, then came up to the bedside. "It was well done," he said gruffly.

They talked awhile about fighting strategy, while I held his hand and silently prayed my thanks to God. At length the King fell asleep, and Lancelot rose. He met my eyes.

"I will stay with him awhile," I said softly.

He nodded and went to the door, where he turned and looked back at Arthur, his eyes full of worship. "There is a King," he said.

20 ♛ THE SOLSTICE

Arthur's shoulder and Lancelot's knee healed together over the next weeks. By the solstice they were whole. All of Camelot was busy during this time, making preparations for the great day of celebration. The summer solstice had been a sacred day time out of mind, and the people of Britain had not given up this feast day as the Christian God drove out the worship of older deities. Since the King and I had been married on this day, the bishop sanctified it as a holy day, and now Christian and pagan alike joined in the celebrations. Lords and ladies from all over Britain came to Camelot, if they could, and set up their tents, or built pavilions, on the open fields.

There were to be contests of skill and daring among the men, a few knights who had earned it would be admitted to the ranks of the King's Companions, and of course there would be horseracing. Competition among the women was less formal, perhaps, but no less desperately waged. Married ladies displayed their fine clothes, magnificent jewels, and their daughters before one another. Maids vied for the attentions of young men. It was well known that any man, feeling amorous, had only to walk down the lane of pavilions to find his needs relieved. Many maids got husbands in this way, I am ashamed to say.

To my surprise, Elaine had still not married. She had been kept close, it is true, but not without opportunity to make contact with men. I was careful to stay out of the women's quarters for many hours each day, that she might gain some freedom. But when I questioned her guards, I found she had not stirred from her quarters the entire three weeks, and this amazed me. Apparently she preferred to go home in disgrace than to wed a man who was not High King. I could have told her that it might be worth the risk, that sometimes love came after, but she would not have listened to me, in any event.

I tried to pump Ailsa for news, since she knew Grannic well, but all she could discover was that Elaine sang to herself and stitched. That she sang boded ill; either she must be mad, or she had some scheme afoot. But why did she stitch? I had set her no tasks. I directed Ailsa to find out what it was she worked upon. But Grannic did not know. Whenever she was with Elaine, she stitched upon innocent things, cushions and such. But on the few occasions when Grannic surprised her, she was at work upon something quite different, which was always quickly hidden. Grannic knew nothing about it, save that it was blue.

I gave up trying to discover Elaine's plans and attended to my duties as hostess to all the folk who daily arrived in Camelot. Everyone had to be greeted and made to feel welcome, even though many came only to beg favors of the King. Arthur and I spent a good part of every day in audience with new guests. And most nights he spent in council with his Companions, since it was the only time he had for serious talk. This daily routine grew dull and difficult to bear, for I had to smile and curtsy and mouth courtesies and be stared at openly by strangers. But I bore it because Arthur stood beside me and bore it, as well. His recent victory over Melwas made him glamorous in everyone's eyes, and he was followed everywhere by admirers. We both began to look forward to the solstice as to the end of captivity.

Lancelot spent most of his time in the stables, overseeing the final training of the King's entries in the races. I went often to watch, or to visit Zephyr in her paddock. She was a valued broodmare now, having borne four foals to Nestor. The eldest was the fastest horse in the King's stables, and on him was Lancelot's full attention focused. But I liked to stand at the fence and watch Zephyr and the other mares graze in idle content, while this year's crop of foals romped and played about them. One mare, a chestnut, was barren. Usually such mares were kept apart, because they were nasty to the foals and bullied the other mares. But this mare had been accepted because she loved the foals and always watched after them, herding them away from danger, breaking up fights, leading them to their dams when they could not find their way. Whenever a mare was lost in labor, she was given the foal to raise. Her name was Netta. In the three years I had known her, I had never seen any sign of temper in her. She was loved by the broodmares and foals alike. I had brought Zephyr an apple from the orchards, but on second thought, I split it and offered half to Netta. She took it from me gently and nuzzled me in thanks. I laughed and pushed her away.

"You have a good time, don't you, my girl. Your days are busy and your work is important. You have kept your figure, too. You are content."

Lancelot came over while I was scratching her ears, and patted her kindly. "Good old Netta. I may have found a home for her at last. One of Gereint's sisters—"

"No!" I cried involuntarily. He looked at me strangely, and I blushed. "I beg your pardon. I did not mean to shout."

"What's the matter, Gwen?"

"Is there another mare that would do for Gereint's sister?"

"I suppose, but why? Netta is not needed here."

"But she is! Just because she cannot breed—have you noticed how she cares for the foals? How all the mares trust her? How they do not fight among themselves when she's about? She is the most valuable mare in the stable, if you but knew it. Don't think her worthless just because she cannot breed. I—I have taken a fancy to her, besides."

Very kindly he stepped closer and took my hands in his. There were tears in the corners of his eyes. "Then she shall stay. I had no idea."

"Do not pity me!" I hissed, my face hot. He took me in his arms, there in the open air, with the eyes of others upon us.

"Indeed I do not. But it breaks my heart."

I laid my head on his shoulder and wept. Why I could share my grief with Lancelot and worked hard to hide it from Arthur, I did not know. Except that my failure was not betrayal to Lancelot.

At length I stilled myself, and when I looked up all the grooms had vanished. Lancelot produced a clean cloth and wiped the tears from my face.

"Let time pass," he said gently. "All wounds heal with time."

"Thank you, Lancelot. I—I am not usually so close to tears. It must be the strain of preparations. Please do not tell Arthur. It would worry him."

"I do not talk to Arthur about you. You are the one subject we avoid. By mutual consent."

"May God forgive me. I never meant to come between you. I *must* not come between you. Don't let it happen, Lancelot, I pray you."

He kissed my forehead lightly. "It cannot be helped, Gwen. But the trust stands."

How recently had I heard those very words from Arthur's lips?

When finally the day arrived, it was glorious. The sun shone in a clear, deep sky and the breeze blew steady and cool. It was one of those days that June is famous for.

Arthur crept into my room at dawn, still dressed, and woke me up. "Good morning, Gwen. Day is dawning."

I yawned and stretched, and finally opened my eyes. "What, are you up already, my lord?"

"I have not yet been to bed. There was no time. I had a messenger late last night from Lothian."

I sat up. "Not Tydwyl? Surely he can handle the remnants of Aguisel's supporters?"

"Not Tydwyl," he said with a smile, and then changed the subject abruptly. "I have come about something else. Kay—"

"Is it so important it cannot wait?" I broke in, smiling, taking his hand and drawing it to my lips.

His face flushed, and he hesitated, then leaned down swiftly and kissed me. "I only wish it could. Ah, Gwen, how little time we've had!"

"It will be over shortly."

"Tonight," he said with fervor, and then straightened. "I was bidden to awaken you. Kay tells me Alyse and Pellinore are camped outside Glaston and are on their way here. What do you want to do about Elaine?"

It was the first time in three weeks he had mentioned her name. I met his eyes. "I will have to tell them. When do they arrive?"

"It shouldn't be much later than midday. You sent for them?"

"Indeed, no. I did not, at Elaine's request. They must be arriving in all innocence. Has Pellinore sent you no message?"

"Only one of greeting and congratulations in the ordinary way."

"Oh, dear. Well, it must be done. Have Kay send them to me when they arrive."

"Bravely done. I will." He paused, half turned to leave, and gave me a long, appraising look.

"The way you look now," he said roughly, "unbrushed and just awakened—five years seems a moment in time."

Then he turned on his heel and was gone.

I gathered up my courage and went to see Elaine. I had feared she would beg leave to be granted her freedom for the day, for her parents' sake, but to my surprise she flatly refused to see them.

"Tell them what you like," she said defiantly. "I will not see them. Say I am ill, or dead. It matters not to me."

"How not? You will go back with them tomorrow, alive and healthy."

Her lips drew back, but it was more a snarl than a smile. "We shall see."

I left her with foreboding in my heart, but even if I had had the time to think about it, I never would have guessed what she had planned.

The morning we spent in church, dressed in our finest clothes of white and gold, adorned with all the trimmings we possessed. Arthur wore his crown, and I wore mine. The bishop blessed us and led all the people in prayers for our happiness and increase. Arthur squeezed my hand, and it took some of the sting from the words. Then we filed out in great procession, with all the lords and ladies following, through the streets of Camelot to the field pavilion. There we sat all afternoon, watching the competitions. Kay had had the cooks busy for days roasting boar and deer in the fire pits, and stewing fowls in great cauldrons over open fires. All afternoon, as the games continued, servants passed meat and drink among the assembled throng, so that all partook of the King's meal. This was a special honor; for only a few hundred could be invited to the feast that night, and in this way Arthur made everyone part of his household. Kay had excelled himself. The food was excellent, the sauces rich. When he finally joined us midway through the afternoon, I complimented him well.

"And if you do not water the wine better," I told him, laughing, "there will not be a man left standing for the King's feast tonight."

He grinned. "Thank you, my lady. I will see to it. The lady Elaine has sent me to ask if she may be permitted to celebrate the day with a skin of wine. She also begs forgiveness for her rudeness of the morning." He said this without expression, for I knew his opinion of Elaine. He had offered for her once, long ago, and her rejection had not been polite.

"You may send it to her, Kay. Unwatered. Perhaps it is best. She leaves Camelot in the morning."

"It is arranged. King Pellinore and Queen Alyse have just arrived, my lady, and have set up their tent in the lane. The King told me I was to bring them to you. Will you see them here, or shall I conduct them to the meeting room?"

I glanced across at Arthur, who was intent upon the contest. "Bring them here, if you please. Let us hope the games engage them."

We made room upon the platform for two more, and when Alyse and Pellinore arrived I greeted them warmly. Pellinore gave me a bear hug, and Alyse a warm kiss of greeting. They were thrilled with the honor of sitting in the King's pavilion, and I did my best to make them comfortable with food and wine. Pellinore was instantly absorbed in the games; it was Alyse who asked after her daughter.

"Alas, madam, she is not feeling well. She begged to be excused from having visitors today. You may see her in the morning."

Alyse looked at me sharply but said nothing. She had known me from a child and could read my face, but if she scented a lie, she held her tongue. Grateful for her discretion, I turned the conversation to the state of things in Wales.

"I bring you grave tidings from Northgallis, Guinevere," Alyse said slowly. "Your brother King Gwarthgydd has lost his wife and daughters to a plague." She touched my hand lightly. "Do not grieve for him, my dear, for he does not grieve much himself. He is already betrothed to the King of Powys' daughter, a match he ought to have made in the first place, years ago."

"Indeed, I grieve for Gwillim, who has lost his mother and his sisters! This plague, Alyse, this is the first I've heard of it! Is it widespread?"

"No," she replied with a lift of her eyebrow. "'It has affected no one else, even in Northgallis. I have even heard that they died of a curse, and not a plague." Her eyes narrowed. "You know something of this?"

"No!" I said quickly, "indeed, I do not! And I do not believe people can die from curses!"

She smiled. "May you never cross a druid, and learn differently." Then, as if to atone for this remark, she crossed herself quickly and turned the subject herself. She had heard something of my abduction, and the King's fight with Melwas, and asked carefully about it. I told her what was already common knowledge, but made no mention of Elaine's part in it. I don't know why I put off telling her; cowardice, I suppose, for they would have to know by morning. But in my heart I still expected Elaine to do something to prevent the need of it. If Alyse noticed my uneasiness, she had the grace not to comment on it. Nor did she comment, as had many others, on my slim and youthful figure, cloaking condemnation in words of praise. For this I was doubly grateful and took trouble to answer her questions and talk with her awhile.

At length the horseracing began, and Alyse retired with most of the women, as the crowds grew rowdy. I was one of the few who stayed. There were seven heats, thrice around the field outside the flags, and then the final race between the seven winners. Zephyr's colt won going away, for he had foreign blood in him, but it was a good race, and well ridden. Lancelot was proud of the jockey, a lad of eleven he had personally trained, and of course he was proud of the colt, for whose bloodlines he was alone responsible. The King honored him before the throng, presenting him a new sword with jeweled hilt, made by the smith who made the King's weapons. Lancelot was speechless, and I smiled with joy to see the two men clasp each other so warmly, while the crowd of people shouted and cheered.

We walked back to the castle, the three of us together, arm in arm. It was one of the happiest moments of my life; I knew it then.

We had two hours to rest before the feast, and I bade Ailsa bathe me and comb out my hair. I heard the King in his room and hoped he might come in, but then I heard Lancelot's voice, as well, and knew they were in close conference. I took myself out to my terrace and sang softly while the light slowly faded from the sky, and Ailsa lovingly brushed my hair. At length, when I came in to take my rest, I heard no more voices and thought they were gone. But they had both been listening. For when I had lain quietly awhile, I heard them talking again, but softly, so as not to wake me. Two such noble men! Where else on earth could their like be found?

At the hour of lamp lighting Ailsa awakened me and shook out my new gown. This had been cut from a bolt of heavy silk Arthur had imported from the East as a Christmas gift. It was a bewitching color, a rich sapphire blue with crimson threads woven in, and in lamplight had a sheen the color of amethysts. I had cut the cloth myself and set my women to work upon it. The lines were simple and straight, with no fancy work or trimmings. I had stitched the bodice myself in purple thread, so the design of interlocking dragons was visible only in lamplight, and even then only at close range. For it was meant to compliment the giver. Arthur had never seen it. Tonight was to be the first time of wearing it.

Ailsa held it out before her and chuckled. "If I were half the size I am, my lady, I could not wear it. It's cut so slim it looks made for a boy."

"Ailsa, ever since I can remember, you have been saying that to me."

"Yes," she said, "and ever since I've known you it's been true. At least," she continued quickly, steering away from dangerous ground, "the bodice is cut low on this one. You're too often shy of that."

"The King will like it, I wager."

"Indeed he will!" she cackled. "Bless the man, the way he looks at you!"

"And," I continued firmly, "it is for evening wear. Such things are now accepted. I couldn't have worn this gown at seventeen, Ailsa. Admit it."

"I don't see why not. He'd have liked to see you in it. He's a full-blooded man, is our King, and always has been—may Bilis take me if I lie—like Uther his father. Now *there* was a man who loved women! Did I ever tell you—"

I sighed and smiled. She was off again on her favorite stories about Uther Pendragon's sexual prowess. There was nothing to be done; she always spoke so when she had had a little wine. I stood still while she dressed me and recited her lurid tales, and said silent thanks that Uther's son showed more restraint than his father. I began worrying about where Alyse and Pellinore would be seated at dinner. Ailsa sat me on a stool and began to dress my hair.

"You should see what the lady Alissa has done with the fabric you gave her," she said suddenly. "Very pretty, to my mind, it is, with trimming on the skirt and a ruffled neckline."

"Ailsa!" I shivered suddenly as a thought struck me. "Did Elaine get any of the leftover silk?"

"Why to be sure, my lady. You gave it to her with your own hands. The color does not suit her, really, her eyes are much too light."

"Do you suppose that is what she was sewing? The blue piece Grannic saw?"

"I wouldn't set much store by Grannic, my lady. She has always had trouble telling blue from green. It's my belief that Lady Elaine made a tunic from the fabric. I doubt there was enough for a gown."

"I wonder."

But I put the thought aside. What difference could it make? My distrust of Elaine had colored all my thoughts. I must forget it.

Ailsa dressed my hair without adornment, for Ygraine's crown was adornment enough. Instead of Arthur's great sapphire, I wore round my neck Ygraine's delicate choker of amethysts and river pearls. Wearing the stones brought out the dual colors in the gown, and the effect in my polished bronze delighted me.

"It's beautiful!" I cried in delight. "He will love it."

"*You* are beautiful," a voice said behind me. "And he loves it indeed."

I whirled around. "Arthur!" Ailsa dropped into a curtsy and backed out of the room.

The King stood smiling by the curtain, looking at me. "Are you flesh and blood? Or did you drop from Heaven? What magic is this!"

I colored. "My lord, this is the fabric you gave me at Christmas. I made the gown to please you. I am glad if I succeeded."

"It's not the gown," he said, coming over to me and running a gentle finger down my neck from ear to throat. "Simple silk cannot do such things to a man."

I lowered my eyes. Ailsa, had she been there, would have recognized her Uther in his son's face at that moment. But Arthur was not Uther. He kissed me softly on my neck and stepped back.

"Would I could stop time! I came to see if you were ready. We must go down."

Mischievously I smiled up at him. "I am ready, indeed, my lord."

He spun on his heel and walked away, then turned and grinned. "You are a witch! If you tease me so, Gwen, I shall not be able to help myself. Dinner will be late, and everyone waiting. We will disgrace ourselves."

I laughed. "The great Arthur, beyond control? Perhaps I should like to see it."

His eyes blazed. "By the Bull!" he breathed. "And so you shall!" He drew a long breath and managed a smile. "Later." He returned to me and offered me his arm. "What you will do to poor Lancelot when he sees you, I dare not think. It is cruelty, you know."

It amazed me that he spoke of it. I wondered, with joy and hope, if they had come to some new close fellowship, that they could bear me between them with better ease.

I placed my hand upon his arm. "I will behave myself. Let us go down."

The hall was full when we entered, and the assembled guests rose and cheered us to our seats. The King had placed Lancelot at his right hand, in the seat of honor, while I sat on his left. Alyse and Pellinore were some way down the table, out of speaking range, to my relief. Kay had managed things beautifully. Lancelot's eyes burned like hot flames, but he was too far removed for private speech. Next to me sat Bedwyr, who was my friend. But Arthur was right, Lancelot suffered.

There was something special about that night from the beginning. It wasn't the gown, or the occasion, or the full moon, or the soft June breezes. The very air was alive with promise. It was the smile of God before the bolt was thrown.

The feast was grand and lasted long. Arthur and I went round together to the tables, greeting guests and exchanging pleasantries. When I returned to my seat, Bedwyr sighed.

"You gild the lily with a vengeance, Gwen. Forgive me, but I wish you hadn't worn that gown."

"Not you too, Bedwyr. It's only cloth."

"It's devilment, by Mithra! There's not a man in the room who isn't bewitched."

"Poppycock." I grinned. "Water your wine better, you'll be all right." Then, seeing his face: "Is there truly something amiss? The King nearly told me not to wear it."

"For Lancelot's sake, no doubt."

"Don't, Bedwyr."

He lifted his chin, like a dog testing the air. "I don't know what it is, but there's something afoot tonight."

"You feel it, too?"

He shifted uneasily. "I wish Merlin were here."

I smiled. "There we part company. I am glad he is not. He disapproves of me, you know."

But Bedwyr looked grave. "Not of you, my lady, but of your fate. His only thought, waking or sleeping, is for the King."

I gaped at him, unable to believe my ears. He had deliberately touched upon my wound! My body began to tremble, and I could not still it. "How can I change my fate, sir? Tell me, and I will do it! I would gladly change places with the ugliest slut in Britain if it would bring the King a child!"

My words seemed to ring in the hall. Heads turned. Arthur and Lancelot whipped around.

"What's going on, Bedwyr?" Arthur demanded.

"One moment, my lord." Bedwyr turned to me with quiet gravity and took my hand. "Gwen, look at me." I raised my eyes and looked at him through tears. His face was full of love, and his voice, low and gentle, spoke softly. "You know, you must know by now that it cannot be." Arthur looked hastily away and began talking to Lancelot; others followed their example and once again the hall filled with noise. "Merlin has always known it. But know this, also, that it grieves you a thousand times more than ever it grieves the King. He has no time for children. Listen, Gwen, and I will tell you a secret. Merlin told me once that it is you who will ensure his glory. That your fate, which you curse as betrayal, will leave Arthur standing alone in glory, and because of *you*, his fame will be everlasting."

I stared, wide-eyed, as he told me these things.

He smiled gently. "So you see, even this dark cloud has a gilded lining. Enjoy the King as a man and forget the rest. It is with the gods. As for Merlin—I only wish he were here because I sense something in the air tonight, and I wish the reins were in his hands."

"Everlasting?" I whispered. "Bedwyr, is it possible?"

He shrugged, suddenly shy. "With true greatness it is possible."

I felt Arthur's hand on my arm. "Enough of this. Has he upset you, Gwen? What's this about?"

I turned to him, feeling suddenly light and free of a great burden. To think that I might serve him after all! I raised a hand to his cheek and smiled into his eyes. "Upset me? No, my lord. He has given me a great gift."

He looked amazed. "I can see that he has. May I know what it is?"

I shook my head. "I don't think I can tell you."

He clasped my hand, his dark eyes glowing. "Then I will not ask. It is enough to see you look the way you look!"

Lancelot rose and lifted his goblet. "To the Queen!" he shouted.

All the people rose and cried, "The Queen!" The men stomped and cheered and drank, and I saw tears in the eyes of those ladies nearest us. What, I wondered, had gotten into everybody?

Suddenly Grannic was there with goblets of neat wine, and the King and Lancelot drank my health with it, and then I drank to theirs. There was much cheering and shouting in the hall, and it was some while before the noise died down, and the bard came on. Only then did I think it strange to see Grannic in hall. I looked about and saw her standing by the wall with the other servants. I beckoned her over. She went white as a sheet.

"Why are you here tonight, Grannic? Why are you not with your mistress?"

She curtsied low. "The lady Elaine dismissed me from her service tonight, my lady. She said she had no more need of me. I—I thought it best to obey and to help out in hall." She trembled as she spoke, and two faint pink spots appeared on her withered cheeks. She looked terrified when she saw that I did not believe her, but just then the bard began to strum his harp, and I waved her away. There was plenty of time, I thought, to get the truth from her.

The bard, a master musician from Frankish lands, played fluidly and sang in a haunting voice, perfectly pitched. The wine was good, running through my limbs like gentle fire, and I sat back happily in my chair to enjoy the music. Gradually I sensed a change in atmosphere, as if one of those dry summer storms were approaching, that bring forked fire from the sky but no rain or wind. Colors grew sharper, the bard's balding head seemed haloed with light. I felt a tingling in my fingertips and toes, and a wave of excitement swept my body. I began to breathe in quicker breaths, yet had not moved. Nervously I glanced about, but no one else seemed so affected. I sat back and tried to attend the bard. But I could not keep my thoughts upon him. I kept thinking back to Melwas' cabin, when Lancelot held me in his arms and kissed me, and his hand had touched my breast— desperately I turned to the King, and he turned to me in the same moment. I saw instantly he felt the same, for his father's spirit blazed in his eyes, and his jaw was clenched with the effort of control.

"Sir," I whispered frantically, "I am ill, I think. I must retire."

"Stay a moment," he whispered back.

"But, Arthur—I think Elaine has poisoned the wine!"

His face lit with laughter, and he reached for his water goblet, to hide behind it. "It's but an aphrodisiac," he whispered. "And a powerful one. I can see you feel it. Have you never felt this way before?"

"Why, my lord, I—I—" I stammered. He waved me silent, and saved me from a lie. Beyond him, Lancelot sat with his arms on the table and his face buried in them, moaning softly. Clearly he had drunk the wine, as well. There had been three cups on Grannic's tray.

"If it is Elaine's doing, it gilds the lily," the King said softly, "for tonight we need it not. Wait till the bard is done, if you can. I promise I shall not be long behind you."

It was about the hardest thing I'd ever done, to sit quietly ladylike while my body burned and throbbed. I tried to think about Elaine, for I did not doubt this gift was hers, and why she had done it, but the drug robbed me of thought. I felt like gasping and could not. I felt like running and had to sit motionless. What exquisite torture we endured, to be so tossed by storms of desire and able to do nothing!

On the bard's last note I rose and curtsied low to the king. His was a demeanor long schooled in self-discipline; yet even he could barely drag his eyes from my bodice to my face.

"With your permission, lord, I will go."

He nodded. "Go," he said stiffly. Lancelot looked up once; my flesh felt scorched where his gaze touched it; he stifled a cry and buried his head again. I fled from the hall. Grudgingly the rest of the women followed. The bard was later well recompensed for the early departure of half his audience. He was assured the Queen had taken ill.

I ran to my rooms and cried to Ailsa for water, for my hair to be undone, for the fretful gown to be unlaced. Yet she did nothing fast enough for me. I paced, and mumbled, and fidgeted, and cursed Elaine, and cursed the King for his slowness. Ailsa said nothing, but I saw laughter in her eyes. I refused my bedgown, but wrapped myself in a robe and dismissed her.

"I will wait in the King's chamber," I announced with as much dignity as I could summon. It can't have been much, for she cackled heartily all the way down the stairs. I waited what felt like six days before I heard his footsteps. In the room below he dismissed Varric in clipped tones and bounded up the steps three at a time. At the door he threw off his tunic.

"Arthur!" I ran into his arms, driven, wild with waiting. He kissed me roughly and then suddenly drew back.

"Wait, Gwen."

"Wait!"

He grinned. "The drug takes hours to wear off, you know. Nothing we are about to do will change that."

"Please, Arthur—"

"Wait. I want to know if you truly meant what you said in hall to Bedwyr. Look into my eyes and say it to me."

I drew a long breath and looked into his beautiful eyes. "I would gladly trade places with the ugliest slut in Britain, if it would bring you a child."

His face softened, and he gently put his hands into my hair. "I would not make the exchange for any price," he whispered. I opened my mouth to speak, but met his lips, and the fire was upon us.

I awoke in the middle of the night with an idea. It came to me complete and in detail, and I am sure its coming was what awakened me. The room was still and dark. Beside me Arthur slept in peace. I slipped into my robe and crossed the room to the water carafe, for the wine had left me with a dreadful thirst. I poured water into the silver goblet and drank deeply. The aftereffects of the drug left me feeling light and drained. I poured a second goblet for the King, when he should awake, and brought it to his bedside. He stirred and opened his eyes.

"Here, my lord. For your thirst."

He grinned sleepily. "I pray you, no more. I feel like an old man."

I blushed at his jest. "It is only water."

"I know. Forgive me. Thank you for the thought." He drank thirstily and then sat back, looking refreshed. "Well, Gwen, what do you think of aphrodisiacs?"

I lowered my eyes. "I would rather do without," I told him, then looked up hastily, in case I had offended. "Not that I did not enjoy it, my lord—"

He laughed, and took my hand. "I remember your pleasure. Never mind. I know what you mean. I agree with you. It is better without, where there is no need."

I was glad he understood me. I hoped that he would still understand when he heard my idea. Now was the time, for he was relaxed, tired and content.

"Arthur."

"My lady?"

"I would ask a favor of you."

"It shall be granted. Name it."

"Make me no promise until you have heard what it is."

"My dear, if it is you who asks it, it cannot be base. I will do it."

"No, it is not base," I said slowly, "but as it concerns you more than me, you might not wish to grant it."

His attention focused on me sharply. "What is it Gwen?"

I stood on the edge of dangerous ground; suddenly nervousness consumed me, and I clasped my hands tightly together. There was no going back now.

"Arthur, is it true you have a son?"

He froze; not a muscle moved on his face. I stumbled on hurriedly.

"When I was a girl, even in Wales we heard rumors. Of a boy born to Queen Morgause, and hidden from King Lot. A boy conceived at Caer Eden on the night of the great battle that brought you into Kingship. Is it true? Is this your son?"

His eyes drilled me, and in spite of my resolve, I trembled. He had never spoken to me about it; it was his own, dark secret, and I had deliberately, and without his leave, flung it out into the light. I had no idea what he would do. He hardly breathed; but at length he dragged out the answer.

"Yes."

"And do you know where he is now?"

"Yes."

"Then," I said, drawing a shaking breath, "this is my request. Send for him. Bring him to Camelot. He belongs at your side. He must be now eleven or twelve—it is time for him to take his place here. Your Kingdom will accept him, and I—Arthur, I would welcome him as my own."

For a long moment he was deathly still. Then he slowly reached out and drew me to his breast, holding me tightly with his face pressed into my hair. I felt his lips move against my ear, but I heard no sound. He held me thus a long time, and when at last he relaxed his embrace, I saw his eyes were dry and his face alight with joy. It made me wonder if he had been praying.

"Guinevere," he said in a low voice, "you have touched my heart twice tonight, and robbed me of breath. Your generosity astounds me. How could you know how I have longed to ask this very favor of you, but feared to wound you?"

"I did not know it, my lord."

"I would do anything to spare you pain. How can you be sure you can bear this boy near you?"

"I know it, my lord. In my soul. I want him here, if he is yours."

"Oh, he is mine." He spoke with bitterness and avoided my eyes. "Do you know the true tale? Do you know his mother is—my sister?"

"Half-sister, my lord. Yes, I knew it. I asked Lancelot about it when he came to Wales."

His eyes widened at that. "Did you indeed? Before we met? When I was only an intimidating stranger to you? It gave you good grounds to reject me. As your heart lay elsewhere, why did you not do it?"

"He said you sinned in innocence, my lord. Everyone does that. How could I condemn you?"

"But such a sin!"

I shrugged. "Perhaps the magnitude of the sin reflects the magnitude of the man. You could not commit a mean sin, Arthur. It is not in you."

He looked away. "I do not deserve such mercy. Lust drove me that night. She was a stranger to me."

"You were barely fourteen. Forgive yourself."

His look lightened then, and he sighed. "Perhaps when I get to know the boy, that, too, will come."

"Then you will send for him?"

"I have thought of little else since the messenger rode in last night from Lothian. For years I have had a spy planted in his mother's household to search out the boy. But she has kept him well hidden. Last night I finally got word on his whereabouts."

So my thought indeed came straight from God! And I noted, as Lancelot had warned me, that he could not bring himself to speak her name.

"And what made you think of it, Gwen?" he asked. "Why should your thoughts run this way?"

"I don't know, my lord. Unless—unless it was my visit with Netta, and then what Bedwyr said."

"Ah, yes. Bedwyr. He has healed you, where I could not. What did he say?"

I looked down. There was no way to tell him. "He showed me that—that there might be a way I could serve you, other than bearing you sons."

"He spoke about the boy?"

"Oh, no, my lord, you mistake me. He spoke about the future. It—I—I really cannot—"

"Never mind. It is between you and Bedwyr. I care only that you are whole again."

"Have I been so single-minded? I was not aware of it."

He smiled kindly. "It was never far from your thoughts."

"I suppose not."

"Who is Netta?"

I grinned, blushing. "Don't ask me to explain, my lord. But Netta is a horse."

He laughed. "I might have known. Well, let be. I will not ask."

My thoughts returned to the boy, as his must have, also, for when I next spoke he followed my thought as if no other words had intervened.

"What is his name?"

"Mordred. It means, in the Orkney tongue, 'king from the sea.' "

I leaned forward and took his hand in mine. "Tell me what you know. What kind of boy is he?"

"By my spy's account, quiet. Reserved. Always watching. The odd man out among princes. The bastard."

"What princes? There are other sons?"

"Four by Lot. Gawaine is the eldest; he must be ten. I know nothing about them but that they are short, favoring Lot in stature, and red-headed, favoring their mother.

"And Mordred? What is he like?"

"He is tall," said the King, warming to it, "and dark. Nimble and swift-footed, with a clever wit and the patience of Job." He paused, his eyes seeing far into the distance. "A throwback, perhaps, to Ambrosius, or even Maximus, with his black eyes and Roman features." His voice died suddenly, and he breathed, "He gets it from both sides, you see."

"Mordred must stand out like a swan among geese," I hurried on. "What excuse is given for his presence? Does everyone know?"

"No one knows. Even Morgause"—and he spat out the name— "does not wish that shame remembered. She gives out that he was fathered by a fairy King, or a demon conjured by her magic, or an Elder Spirit, or a serpent from the sea. Her story changes as often as the tide. Certainly Mordred does not know. He knows nothing. He lives as a bastard half-brother to the princes of Orkney. A dogsbody, not a prince. It must hurt like hell." His thoughts were far away, his brow creased.

"You lived such a life once."

That brought him back, and he said brusquely, "Yes, but Ector is a good-hearted, selfless soul, and his wife a loving woman and a Christian. Morgause is a—" He paused, and changed the word. "—a witch."

"Then we must get him out of there."

He nodded slowly. "But it must be done carefully, without anyone's suspecting why. Think, Gwen! Think what I must tell him! How heavy a burden I must lay upon my son! If it is difficult for me to confess it, imagine how difficult it will be for him to hear it. I do not want him guessing before I make it known. There is risk here. God knows he has reason enough to hate me," he said slowly. "Who could blame him? I think I must bring his brothers with him and let them serve as a camouflage awhile."

"Can you do that, Arthur? Can you take her children from her?"

His face hardened suddenly, and his eyes went cold. "It would give me very great pleasure indeed."

Here was hatred, obstinate and possessive. Even the Saxons he did not so despise. Lightly I placed my hand upon his arm. "Arthur," I whispered, "did she do the murder at Dunpelder?"

His eyes slid to my face and then away, and I quailed at the look in them. "Yes." He shuddered and clutched at the bearskin, although the night was warm. "And that's not all." I waited, as he struggled to find the words. "She is killing Merlin, even as we speak. She once gave him a draft with poison in it, and although it did not kill him outright, it left the seeds of death inside his body. He is dying, and he knows it. He has gone back to his birthplace in the hills of Wales to find a cure."

I gasped. "It is true, then? Did Merlin confess it?"

Another sharp glance. "No. He admits nothing. But I know."

I watched his face a long time. It was true, I thought, that an evil deed leaves its mark upon the doer. Long ago, in his innocence, he had sinned a dreadful sin. Now it ate at him like a rotten canker and tainted all his thoughts. "He was an entire winter in the Caledonian Forest, with only a cave for comfort and skins for clothes. Surely that is why he lost his wits."

He would not look at me. "What sent him witless into the forest? He had seen the Witch three days before."

"Does Merlin confess this? Does he accuse her?"

"No. But I know it's true."

I took his hand between my own and kissed it. "And the massacre," I whispered. "Do you have proof she gave the order?"

"Of course not!" he responded angrily. "Lot gave the order. But once he wed her, Lot never did anything of his own will, except in battle. It's what made him so fierce." He shut his eyes suddenly and exhaled slowly. "I see the point of all your gentle questions, Guinevere. But do not bother to pity Morgause. I do not accuse her beyond her deserts. She is evil."

I dared push him no further. He sat still, his eyes far away. I put a hand to his cheek. "Forgive me, Arthur . . . Arthur?" He did not hear me; all the warmth of our loving night was lost in the cold horror of his own tormented hell. "Emreis," I whispered, and at once he turned, surprise and then feeling returning to his eyes. "It is God's will, my love, that Mordred be born to you. What will be, will be. Put it behind you."

He nearly smiled. "Now it is your turn to comfort me."

"I pray I can." I clasped his hand. "Can you bring him here, with all his brothers, without inviting suspicion? I am not the only one who has heard the rumors."

"You put it too lightly," he said with a twist of his lips. "I sometimes think there is no one who has not heard. I will think of some excuse to bring them here." Then he smiled and pulled me closer. "Bless you, Gwen, for charming me out of my ill humor. You have a gift for it." His lips found mine, and I yielded willingly to his embrace. His face had looked like death when he spoke of Queen Morgause; his heat was infinitely preferable to his cold.

Suddenly we heard heavy footsteps pounding through the King's apartments.

"My lord Arthur!" It was Kay's voice, in barely controlled panic. "Arthur!"

"Here, Kay! To me!"

The King leaped out of bed and grabbed his robe, as Kay raced up the stairs and fell to one knee at the door. I had not even stirred from the bed; there was not time.

"Oh, my lord, forgive me, but I bring bad news." In trembling fingers he held out a scroll.

"Tell me," Arthur said calmly, reaching for it.

"My lord, the courier—my dear lord, Merlin is dead."

Arthur gave no sign that he had heard. He took the scroll from Kay, broke the seal and read. When he looked up, his face a mask, only his eyes reflected his great grief.

"We leave for Wales. Now." He named the score of knights who would attend him. "Inform Lancelot."

Kay began to shake visibly. Arthur stood as still as stone. "My lord, we cannot find him."

"Look harder," Arthur snapped, with his first display of temper. "Now go. Send Varric to me."

Kay fled, and Arthur did not move. Slowly I arose and went to him. He shrugged off his robe and reached for his tunic in a daze. I recognized his state—I had felt the same just after Melwas left me. Varric arrived, hastily dressed and breathless, and gently took the tunic from his hand.

"No, my lord will want his traveling clothes, not the ceremonial finery. 'Twill be a dusty journey, I fear, at this time of year. A light cloak. Here we are." He talked steadily in a low, pleasant voice and glanced meaningfully first at me and then at the wineskin. Coming to my senses, I filled a goblet and touched it to Arthur's lips.

"Drink, my lord." But he did not hear me. I touched his shoulder, where the scar from Melwas' blade stood out red and ugly from his browned skin. "Please, Arthur, drink. It will help you."

Obediently he swallowed, then waved me away as Varric pulled the tunic over his head. In minutes Varric had him dressed and booted, and fastened his cloak at the shoulder with the gold enamel Dragon brooch. Arthur walked slowly to the door.

He stared vacantly in our direction, said, "Pray for me," and left.

Varric bowed low to me. "My lady."

"You will attend him, Varric?"

"Yes, my lady."

"Do not leave him alone."

"No, my lady. Don't worry. I will see to him." And he hurried down the stairs in the King's wake.

There had been many rumors of Merlin's death throughout the years. But this one Arthur believed. It did not seem possible it could be true—Merlin had guided Britain through her kings since before either of us was born! I glanced about for the scroll and found it on the floor where he had dropped it. It was a note only, short and to the point. It was from Niniane.

21 ♛ THE SEDUCTION AND THE SWORD

I woke to a scuffling noise and quick, urgent whispers. "My lady! My lady Queen Guinevere! Wake up, oh, please wake up!"

I opened my eyes and looked into Bran's worried face. With a start, I realized I was in the King's bed, and the morning sun streamed through the unglazed window. I gathered the bearskins tighter around me. The night's events came back to me slowly, but it all seemed dreamlike in its distance.

"Is the King gone, Bran, or did I dream it?"

His eyes were nailed to the floor. "He is gone to Wales, my lady."

"Where is Ailsa?"

"She has been looking for you, my lady. We all have been looking for you."

"I have been here all night."

Bran gulped. Sometimes he still looked fifteen. "No one thought—I mean, after the King left—"

I grinned. I had offended acceptable standards of propriety, I saw, but it did not concern me. "But his bed was warm, and mine was cold," I said, covering a yawn and stifling an urge to stretch. "It's been quite a night."

"My lady, shall I send Ailsa to you?"

"Please, Bran, unless you would care to attend me yourself?" He flushed scarlet to the roots of his hair and backed away. "I'm sorry." I laughed. "I'm feeling devilish this morning—I'm only teasing. I did not mean to be unkind. I would like to speak with the courier who rode in this morning. Tell Kay to send him to me when he is rested."

"My lady, please, they have been hunting the house down for you. Sir Lancelot wants to see you."

"Oh, good, they found him. Well, there is no rush about it. He is the Queen's Protector until the King returns, and he only wants to go over the day's schedule."

Bran shook his head.

"I don't think it's that, my lady. When I saw him, he looked ill. Sir Kay said something was amiss."

"Perhaps he only suffers from the wine we took last night. Send Ailsa to me now, and ask Sir Kay if he will see me in half an hour. Will that do?"

He managed a frightened smile. "I will go tell them you are found."

From his manner, I saw something was indeed amiss. And Ailsa, when she bustled in, confirmed it. She scolded me roundly for sleeping alone in the King's bed and hurriedly bathed and dressed me, chattering all the while about meaningless things.

"Ailsa," I said at last. "What is it you are trying so hard not to tell me? I've never heard you go on so."

Her hand shook as she pinned my hair in place, but she said nothing.

"What is it, in God's name? Has aught happened to the King?"

"No, no," she said quickly. "Not to the King. But Sir Lancelot must tell you, my lady. I cannot."

Then it was that I began to feel fear. But, since Arthur and Lancelot were unharmed, I could not imagine what catastrophe had befallen that everyone feared to tell me.

When Ailsa was finished, I went out to find Kay and met him in the corridor hurrying to my apartments. His tread was heavy and his face long.

"Queen Guinevere." He bowed.

"I know. Lancelot wishes an interview. Take me to him."

Kay hesitated. "He wishes a private interview, my lady. Indeed, I think it is best. I was reminded of your garden."

I stared at him in amazement and growing fear. Kay knew, clear enough, and even he was afraid to tell me.

"Then send him up."

He cleared his throat nervously. "Ah, my lady, I fear it would not look well if he, well, if he entered the King's apartments while the King was away."

Well, that was blunt enough. I had forgotten about the palace gossips. I reached into my pouch and drew out a key.

"Give him this. It is the key to my garden door. Let him go to the south tower, to the postern gate. He has only to get through a corner of the women's garden unseen. I will be waiting."

I set Ailsa and Alissa as guards upon my bedchamber stairs and went out on my terrace in a fever of anticipation. It was another glorious day, fair and warm and sweet-scented. How could anything bode ill on such a morning?

I sat myself on the stone bench behind the fountain, where I had a view of the entire length of the garden, and composed myself to wait.

He did not keep me waiting long. I saw him coming toward me with the reluctant tread of a guilty man approaching his executioner, and I began to fear in earnest. His face and hair were recently scrubbed, his tunic was fresh from the fuller's. Penitence flowed in every line of his body.

He fell to his knees before me and pressed my hand to his lips, kissing my fingers and then holding my palm to his face. Then he looked up. I gasped. He had tears in his eyes.

"What is it, Lancelot? What has happened! Oh, God, what catastrophe is this! Tell me!"

"Oh, Guinevere! I am a miserable sinner," he whispered. "An undeserving wretch. May God in His mercy forgive me. I don't think you will."

I sighed with exasperation. He was forever berating himself with sins.

"Dear God, Lancelot, you are frightening me to death! You are well and whole, are you not? Have you killed anyone? Is your life at stake? Are you in any danger? All right, then. So what have you done? It cannot be as bad as all that."

But he flushed hotly and looked away, holding tight to my hand. What could so deeply embarrass him? Suddenly I remembered his suffering in hall, and Kay's inability to find him in the early morning hours. I nearly laughed.

"I know what it is! You took a stroll down Maiden Lane last night and found someone willing. Am I right?"

His color only deepened. I put my hand on his head and ruffled his hair with affection. It felt like silk between my fingers. "Come, Lancelot, I am not a monster. I can forgive that. If she was willing, it was no sin. The drug was upon you—what else could you do?"

He shook his head sadly but did not speak. I touched his cheek, and he closed his eyes in pain.

"We will honor her," I whispered, "if that would please you, and send her home with gifts. Her father will think it a fair exchange for maidenhead. You need not be ashamed. Unless," I said with a touch of nervousness, "she is highborn." He flinched, and I swallowed hard. "Even so, it can be arranged to everyone's satisfaction. Leave it to me."

But every word I said was as a knife in his heart, and I did not know what to do. So I said nothing, but stroked his hair, and touched his face, and let him know that he could trust me with it, whatever it was, for I loved him. And all the while I wondered who she was, what she looked like, what she wore and how old she was, sure that however perfect she might be, she could not have appreciated him.

At length he drew on his courage and steadied himself.

"Guinevere," he began, meeting my eyes at last, and holding both my hands firmly to his breast, "you light my life. I will never love another. This you must know and believe before I tell you the rest. I will pay for last night's lust as long as I live, and it is right that I should, but she will never have my heart."

My heart beat painfully as I heard my guess confirmed. But Lancelot never forgave himself easily, and I feared for what punishment he might feel required to endure.

"Before I tell you how it happened, I must tell you—I must tell you, Gwen—I am betrothed."

"NO!" It burst from me in a hoarse cry; I stared in horror at his face. But he held my hands firmly, and I could not rise to flee. He absorbed my anger and held tight to me. "No, it isn't necessary! You go too far. What is a night only? You need not marry her."

"She is highborn," he said steadily, "and her father and mother were there when Kay found us this morning. I could do naught else. I could not dishonor her further."

I felt the tears slip down my face. "To lie with you is no dishonor," I whispered, and he took a quick breath, then let it out slowly. "Oh, Lancelot, do not leave me, I pray you. I love you so."

His control broke, and he buried his face in my lap with his arms around me. I bent over him and kissed his head. In my heart, I knew it was cruel. He was five and twenty. Most men his age had sons training to be warriors. He could not go unwed forever; to ask it of him was unfair. But the thought of losing him was more than I could bear. He was a man of honor, and he had promised. But it broke my heart.

For a long time we stayed thus, holding each other. With great effort I managed to speak the words I knew I had to say.

"What you must do, you must do. Have you given your word to her father?"

He raised his head and nodded.

"Then—then there is naught that I can say."

"I have not told you all."

"There is more?" I cried. "How can there be more? You are leaving me—tell me no more!"

He rose slowly and walked back and forth before the fountain. It was not fair to remind me of Arthur. I watched him pace and dared not think ahead. He was unhappy, that was clear enough, and determined, but he was also afraid. Was it possible he could hurt me more than this?

"When the King left the hall last night," he began, "I left soon after. With Bedwyr. He was tired and went off to bed, but I—I could not." I drew breath to tell him I understood it, but he raised a hand and stopped me. I saw he feared he could not say it, if he did not say it all at once. "I never intended to go looking for a maiden. I only meant to walk it off. The night was clear and cool, and I went first to the stables. But the colt was fine, and Lyonel was there. I decided to walk the perimeter of the wall. In fact, I ran." I bowed my head, remembering the frantic drive of the drug. While he had been running, I had been in the King's arms. It was not fair to judge him. "But I tired at last of running, and I had got no relief. I stopped to catch my breath and felt dizzy, and—lost my bearings. I did not know where I was. And so I left the wall and walked toward the lighted torches. I thought that if I got there, I could find my way. In my mind were pictures of my Breton homeland, and the streets of Benoic where I grew up. But when I got near the light, I recognized nothing. There were girls about. One, a brunette, came up and brushed my arm. I could not bear it; even the touch of her fingers set me aflame. How I wanted you, Guinevere! Your face was ever before me, as it had been all night. It seemed to me that you should want me, too, if you loved me, and find a way to escape the King and come to me." He stopped pacing and covered his face with his hands. "May God forgive me!" he whispered. "That I should ever wish to betray my lord!" Then he turned and continued, forcing it out. "I escaped her and went on, but I did not know where I was going. I was looking for you. I was—driven. To find you. And then I looked up and you were there."

I gasped, and he met my eyes.

"She spoke to me," he said, "in your voice. 'Lancelot,' she said, 'at last I have found you.' It was so very exactly what I wished to hear."

"She was fair?" I asked hoarsely.

"She was fair and lovely. She wore a blue scarf over her hair, which hid all but a little. But she was fair. And she spoke with your voice."

"And her gown?" I said, shaking, holding hard to the bench. He waited a long time before answering.

"It was your gown. The same I had seen you in an hour before. The gown that drove me mad. It was the same."

I simply stared at him in horror.

"She was standing in the doorway of a tent and beckoned me inside. Her gestures were yours. Inside the lamp was low. There was an inner chamber. She—said very little. But then, I did not give her much chance." He wiped his brow and drew a long, trembling breath. "I will say no more. When Kay woke me this morning, my eyes were clear, and I saw her face."

I put out a hand to stop him.

"Don't!" I jumped to my feet. "Don't, Lancelot!"

"Guinevere, I am betrothed to Elaine."

"Aaaaa!" I screamed, and swooned. He lifted me and held me. But the touch of his hands cleared my head, and I pushed him away.

"You will not do it!" I cried, shaking. "I forbid it! She has duped you, Lancelot, can you not see it? She has duped us all! Oh, God!" I whirled away, holding my aching head, wishing for death.

Now I saw, too clearly, all that Elaine had done. As far back as the Melwas affair she had planned this, when she lay on my floor and whimpered that I could not have them both, Lancelot and Arthur. How clever how she had been—making a gown of the same fabric as the one she knew I'd wear; the secret summons to her parents, who arrived in innocence because she had begged me not to send for them; and the drug, her stroke of genius, that would drive us half mad, ensuring that the King and I would leave hall early and spend the whole evening together, and leave Lancelot roaming free and vulnerable. What revenge was this! How she must hate me! But the worst of it was that she did not love Lancelot; she cared nothing for him; she did it only to take him from me. And yet she knew the man. She knew I could talk Pellinore out of holding him to his promise; she had not relied on her parents' presence for that. But she knew Lancelot's honor would bind him to her when he awoke and found himself in her father's house.

"I forbid it," I repeated coldly, turning back to him. "Do not be fooled by her. You consign yourself to a future of torment. A slut would better serve you and bring more honor to your house. There is not an ounce of goodness in her, Lancelot. I know her better than you. She planned to seduce you— she sent the wine— only because she hates me so. I will speak to Pellinore. You are released from your promise."

He looked pained. I knew what he was thinking—these words were not worthy of me, but he had come prepared to endure a woman's rage.

"Nevertheless," he said, "I must."

"You will not. The King will not allow it. You must have his permission."

"He will be back within a week. I will ask him then."

And suddenly I understood. Arthur would let him do it. Arthur would think of his home in Lanascol, held now in his name by his brother Galahantyn since their father died. Arthur would consider his future as an ally king, and what good could come of a strong arm in Less Britain. Arthur would look ahead to the training of Lancelot's sons as his own loyal knights—but at the thought of Elaine bearing Lancelot's sons, I cried aloud in anguish.

"NO! It will not be! I cannot live with this! You will kill me, Lancelot, as surely as you stand there! Oh, have pity on me, my love, and do not do this thing!"

He leaped forward and took me by the shoulders. There were tears in his eyes. "You don't understand! You were not there! I—I took her thrice, and she was virgin!"

"Lancelot!" I cried, clapping my hands over my ears. "Spare me the details! What do you want of me? I cannot bear it!"

"Understand me!" he cried hoarsely. "I am not a brutal man, but—but I caused her pain and suffering, through my impatience. I was no gentleman. I am responsible."

"She has her reward!"

"I owe her more than that."

"Not your life!"

"My name, at least. To save her from shame if she bears a child."

"Oh, God!" I closed my eyes on that, and fought back tears. "She would feel no shame. She has no sense of it."

"Gwen." His voice was very soft. "It is not like you to be cruel. I have hurt you very deeply. I am sorry."

I began to weep quietly, but his very tenderness made me angry.

"Don't pretend you love me!" I cried. "You knew it was not I who beckoned you. You knew I was with the King."

But it only hurt me more to wound him; he would not fight back, but only accepted shafts, one after the other, without complaint. "Yes," he said slowly, dropping his hands to his side, "I suppose that deep within me I did know it. I saw the way you looked at Arthur. That was why I left the hall when he did. I could not bear the thought—but let be. You have come to love him, and God knows that is as it should be. He has the gift of sowing love. And last night you wanted him. That is what made me so—fierce with Elaine. How I longed to hold you in my arms and lie with you! I confess it before God. So when I saw someone who resembled you, I shut my mind to the truth and believed the lie. I am responsible," he finished simply.

I fell to my knees and reached for his hand, splashing it with tears and pressing it to my breast. "Oh, noble Lancelot! Forgive me, I pray. I had no right to speak so!"

He lifted me in his arms and carried me to the bench. I wept on his shoulder, my arms about his neck. He held me on his lap and waited.

"She is not worthy of you," I whispered, "and you will regret it." But I knew he had made up his mind. When my sobs subsided, he spoke again.

"I will take her to Less Britain. I have been too long away. But she tells me you two have quarreled, and her movements are restricted. I must ask you, Gwen, to let her go."

I drew back and looked at his face. Then it was I realized he knew nothing of Elaine's part in the Melwas affair. And how could he know, unless the King had told him? For I had not, and he was on Ynys Witrin when her treachery was revealed. Here was a weapon to my hand, I saw it instantly. I could prevent his leaving if I told him what she had done. He would never marry a woman who had betrayed me into Melwas' hands. I opened my mouth to speak, when I saw the other side of that coin. And how would he feel, when he knew? He would feel as if he had lain with a snake, and the shame of it would eat at his very soul, as the shame of Morgause ate at Arthur. I knew then I could not do it. But the agony of wanting to brought back anger.

"Did she tell you why we quarreled?"

"She said you discovered her great love for the King and accused her of hubris, which she admits."

"Lancelot," I beseeched him, "does that sound like me? All the world loves Arthur. Would I lock one woman up on account of it?"

He looked puzzled, and then shrugged. "Before this interview, I would have said it was unlike you. But I—I confess I do not understand women well. If that was not the truth, then what was it?"

I was well revenged for wounding him. He cut me to my core. I had behaved abominably. And now, what could I say?

"It is partly true," I said at last. "But there is more to it than that. She— took advantage of her closeness to me to further her own ends and sought a private interview with the King. I don't know exactly what happened, but the King was angry and asked me to see to it that it did not happen again. It was more than foolishness, I fear, and I had intended to send her home to Wales. Today was to be the day of her departure."

"Then she is restrained on Arthur's orders?"

"She is not restrained enough!" I cried, then bowed my head. "No, the orders were mine. I—I felt personally betrayed. It is the kind of thing women do not forgive one another."

"Well," he said gently, "she has not your judgment, Gwen, or your control. But if the cause of this embarrassment is her love for the King, can you not forgive it? I will take her away, where she will never see him again. Then it is solved."

"She does not love you, my dearest, and she never will."

The ghost of a smiled crossed his lips. "And I will never love her." My heart ached for him; it was a future of dust and ashes. "Will you release her, Gwen? For my sake? Let her go to her parents until the wedding. You need not see her, if it pains you so."

The tears slipped out again, and I leaned against him, exhausted and relenting. "Yes," I whispered, "I will give the order."

He held me closer. "When Arthur gets home, I will ask formal permission. We will leave before the autumn winds close the seas." I shut my eyes. It was over and settled.

"Will I never see you again?"

"Of a certainty you will," he said, pulling away and drying my cheeks. "I will be back when the seas open, bringing Galahantyn with me. I will stay with you for three seasons out of four, while the King is about his business. He is my liege lord as well as my friend. I owe him service. And I desire his fellowship." He almost smiled and gently touched my hair. "But more even than Arthur, I need you. I will return."

At last he kissed me, and I clung to him, desperate with longing. His lips were warm and eager, and for a moment only I thought of nothing else. But it was only a sweet ending to the horrors we had suffered. It changed nothing.

By the time the King came home, the whole of Camelot was abuzz with rumors about Lancelot and Elaine. I had released her to the care of Alyse and Pellinore, who kept her close, sensing trouble. I could not see that Lancelot spent much time with her, a courtesy call in the evenings perhaps, for almost every minute he was with me. He certainly showed no inclination to return to her bed. But he had been to see the bishop, and so the rumors ran wild.

As for Arthur, here also rumors ran ahead of fact. Merlin was dead. The King had gone to the old enchanter's hilltop cave in South Wales, and found him lying cold and blue, as Niniane had said. The magic of the place had kept corruption from him, and Arthur spent three days and nights at his side in the hope that he still lived and might awaken. At length, facing facts, he filled the cave with treasures beyond counting; all round the countryside the folk brought gifts, and the King gave him everything he had at Caerleon, to send him to his gods. Then, to protect the grave from robbers, they levered the stones above the cave mouth and brought down an avalanche to cover the entrance and bury him deep in the hill. So it was done. And the King had not spoken a word to a soul after it was accomplished, but rode home in silence and would see no one.

It was the same when he rode into Camelot. Kay and the home guard awaited him on the steps. I watched from Alissa's window, which gave onto the forecourt. It reminded me of the first time I had ever seen him, except that now he moved like a man in sleep, and not like a leader of men. He spoke to no one, but dismounted, dropping the reins, and climbed the steps without seeing them. Kay gave him formal welcome; the King did not reply, but walked past him and into the castle without turning his head. The lady Niniane had ridden in behind him and sat her horse watching the king with a worried face. Even Pelleas, who rode beside her and would wed her within the month, could not turn her gaze from the King. The soldiers all looked puzzled, and Lancelot, standing beside Kay, glanced quickly toward my window and shook his head.

I retired to my chamber, to be there if the King felt need of me. Standing by the curtain, I heard his steps come up the stairs. His tread was slow and heavy. I heard Varric's voice and Bran's, and movement within the chamber, but the King did not speak. Then all was silent. I waited for a long time, hearing nothing. I was not sure he was even in there, except I had not heard him leave. I determined to go in, for had he not said himself that I was always welcome? Gently I pulled aside the corner of the curtain, but what I saw stopped me where I stood, and I went no further. He had stripped to the waist and knelt like a penitent next his bed. His back was to me, his head bowed against the coverlet, his long arms outstretched and his hands clasped. He was praying.

I went to Lancelot. The Companions had just broken up from council, and Lancelot briefed me on the news. While Wales was quiet enough, a courier from Rheged had come to the King at Caerleon while he collected treasure for Merlin's burial. The King had heard his news but had given no direction; indeed, Bedwyr said it was difficult to know whether or not he had understood a word the man said. King Urien sent to say that Caw of Strathclyde had died, leaving his kingdom in chaos. He had sired twelve sons and five daughters; the eldest boys were twins, thirty years old and wild. His sensible son was third born, one Hapgar, and the old king's favorite. But Caw had died quickly and had not had time to bequeath his kingdom into anyone's hands. Urien, whose lands lay next to Strathclyde, reported that the young men were fighting it out among themselves, and no one's life was safe out of doors. Urien's own sons by his first marriage were riding patrol upon their borders; his seven-year-old daughter Morgaine, Queen Morgan's child, had been kidnapped on a short journey near the border and held for a week by Heuil, the eldest twin, and raped repeatedly. He had her back now, but his wrath was high, and if the High King did not step in, there would be war.

This was black news indeed. But what was worse, Bedwyr despaired of the King's recovering from his grief in time.

"He was like this when Merlin disappeared, years ago, just before his first Queen died," Bedwyr said, twisting his hands together. "We thought the enchanter dead, and the King grieved deeply for months. We had the Saxons, then, and he came out of his fastness only to fight them. But this is worse, Lancelot. This is internal strife of a kind only the High King can settle. Caw had sworn allegiance, but none of his sons have bent a knee to Arthur. This is not a thing that you or I could settle in his place."

"Is there danger that the Saxons, sensing division within Britain, could test our strength again?" I asked him.

Bedwyr's frown deepened. "I had not thought of it," he confessed, "but knowing Saxons, it seems more than likely."

"Cerdic watches the borders closely," Lancelot remarked, "and I hear he has good spies. He knows already of this news, if it is five days old."

Bedwyr shrugged. "The King would not be hurried. He sent the old man off in proper style, I will grant him that, but it took ages. He could not leave him. For half a day he stood outside the rockslide, alone, as if he could not bring himself to say good-bye."

I touched Bedwyr's arm. "Remember," I told him, "that none of us has ever known life without Merlin, the King least of all. It must seem to him that he has lost a father, a friend, a trusted advisor, and more—a confidant of his heart. He is alone now, for the first time in his life, I think."

Lancelot straightened. "He is not alone."

I looked him in the face. "You are off to Lanascol, my lord, come fall. He has Bedwyr, Kay and Niniane, and me. And none of us is to him what Merlin was."

Lancelot took the slap without flinching. Bedwyr looked on with interest, but said nothing. No one but I knew Lancelot's plans, until he had confirmed them with the King. And that now seemed unlikely to happen soon.

Two weeks went by, and nothing happened. The messages from Urien grew more urgent. Border fighting had broken out; Urien kept his actions to defense, but his army cried out for blood to avenge the princess. The King hardly stirred from his room. He took his meals there and did not appear in hall, although Varric reported that he did not eat enough to keep a bird alive.

The rest of Camelot seemed to march in place, waiting. The people were afraid; the soldiers worried. Although relieved of his role as Queen's Protector now that the High King was home, Lancelot served as Arthur's proxy in Council and in hall when the King did not appear. I sat beside him in hall, but conversation was strained. Alyse and Pellinore attended every night, looking bewildered, and I could not bring myself to speak to them. Elaine kept away, not from shame, I was sure, but to avoid my fury. It was still in my power to foil her plans, and this she must have known.

I remember the morning when Ailsa told me, as she brushed my hair, that Elaine was deathly sick in the mornings. Grannic was full of the news, it seemed, and all the women were talking. I whirled on the stool, clutched her hand, and tore the brush from her grip.

"Leave me!" I shrieked. "Get out! How dare you bring such lies into my chamber! Go! I cannot bear the sight of you!"

But dear Ailsa merely cowered against the wall as I stormed about the room, cursing the cruel fates. At length my anger passed into despair, and I fell to the floor, where Ailsa held me and whispered sweet endearments while I wept most bitterly.

"It isn't fair! That she should—in one night—and I, Ailsa, *all these years!* I hate her, I hate her! Let me see her but once," I cried, "and I will kill her!"

"Now, now," Ailsa crooned, stroking my hair from my face, "would you, indeed, and bring dishonor on all the ones you love? That is not in you, my lady. Everyone looks to you for strength."

"To *me?*" I whispered. "Dear God, then we are lost, for I have none!"

"You are stronger than you know," she replied. "My little Gwen, in five years this will seem a small thing, looking back. Don't let it hurt you so."

"A small thing! Oh, Ailsa!" I sobbed, clutching her garments. "It can never be a small thing! She will have his child always by her—Lancelot's child!—and what will I have?"

"You are Queen, my lady. Oh, Gwen, my precious Gwen, even could you bear, you could not have his children. What are you asking of him? That he should stay unwed and childless for your sake?"

"No," I whispered. "Yes. No. Oh, Ailsa, I must be evil, for deep in my soul I do want that very thing—his heart is mine—I do not want to share him. There is no love between them, Ailsa—all this is wrong, so wrong!"

"Is it right that he should forgo his future and deny his kingdom heirs, to stay in Camelot and worship a woman he cannot have?"

I closed my eyes and pressed my face into her shoulder. "Stop, I pray you! I know I cannot ask it. I do love him, but this—this is so unfair!"

Gently she kissed my brow and hugged me. "If you truly love him, the way the King loves you, you will let him go and take what joy he can with her. You will always have his heart."

"I have not Arthur's forbearance," I cried, "nor his mercy. And he—he could not feel like this!"

"He keeps his pain inside, my lady. But it is there." She sounded very sure. It steadied me to think of Arthur, and made me feel ashamed. I had completely forgotten about the King, suffering in the next room. That he did not come in when I shrieked and wept was a telling sign of his illness. How could I have forgotten?

"But I am only a woman," I whispered, "and I have not his strength."

"You are his right hand," she asserted, "and you must control your tears for his sake. I will make you a posset that will let you sleep. We must have those tear-tracks gone before hall."

Ailsa performed what magic she could with potions and charms and hairbrush, but when Lancelot met me outside hall, he knew at once I had been weeping.

"Gwen, what's amiss?" he asked gently.

I shook my head and placed my hand on his arm. "I cannot tell you. It will pass. Let us go in."

But as we entered hall and everyone rose, I stopped, frozen in my tracks. Elaine stood between her parents, smiling and smug, her hands placed protectively upon her little belly, looking right into my eyes. She did not care that he loved me; she only wanted me to know she had conceived his child at his first bedding of her, and that however close I kept him to me, he was hers. I felt the blood drain from my face, and I gripped Lancelot's arm.

"What is it, Gwen?"

"You—you promised me, my lord," I whispered fiercely, trying desperately to keep my tears at bay, "you promised I should not have to see her again. Either take her away or lead me out. I cannot abide her in the room with me!"

He was shocked, but I would not move, and everyone was waiting.

"My God, Gwen, how can I? They are all assembled."

I raised my face to his and met his eyes. "Choose, Lancelot. Choose between us. One of us must go."

At length he nodded, and said wearily, "I will take her out. Let me seat you first."

He led me to my place, but I did not sit, and all the hall stayed standing. Bedwyr took my arm to still my shaking. I looked straight across the hall, out the windows, but from the corner of my eye I saw Lancelot go down the table to Elaine, speak softly to her and to Pellinore, and offer her his arm. Alyse was affronted, Pellinore bewildered. Elaine smiled triumphantly, made a pretty curtsy in my direction, and leaned upon his arm as he took her out. Utter stillness blanketed the hall. Bedwyr tugged gently at my arm, and at last I sat, and the meal was served.

Elaine kept out of my way after that, and everyone trod lightly around me. With Lancelot himself I was alternately furious and penitent, coldly indignant and self-indulgently forsaken, a ship without a rudder, while Arthur was not there. How Lancelot bore it, I do not know. That he did not despise me for my tormented behavior, nor chastise me for my cruel words, is a testament to the quality of the man and the deep love he bore me.

At last two couriers arrived with the news we dreaded. Urien's forces were shaping for attack; the King of Elmet and Tydwyl, Arthur's appointed governor of Lothian during Morgause's exile to Orkney, were being drawn into the dispute. It looked as if the whole north of Britain would be torn asunder within days. And Cerdic, King of the West Saxons, was quietly amassing a force near the border of his kingdom. So far they were patrolling only, but their numbers were growing. They waited, like wolves outside the boar's den, ready to pick apart the winner, weak from battle.

The Companions were beside themselves with frustration and worry. Niniane had tried to see the King, but he would not bear her name mentioned. Kay, Bedwyr, and Lancelot, who all had tried repeatedly to see him, and had all been turned away, drew me into conference. They begged me to go to the King and see what could be done to awaken him from his trance.

"But, my lords," I told them, "on the second day of his arrival he sent me word through Varric, ordering me to stay out of his chamber. It was not the request of my husband, but the command of my King."

Lancelot took my hands, his face white. "We are asking you, Gwen, to disobey him. For Britain's sake. He is so deep in his grief he knows not what he risks. He will thank you for it when his mind is healed."

They were so distressed, I agreed to try. Indeed, the state of the Kingdom was growing desperate. It was something Arthur could so easily have solved three weeks ago, simply by showing himself in Strathclyde. But now, who knew? It might already be too late.

"Get me his Sword," I said, thinking hard, "and his sword belt. Have Varric bring me his best cloak, with the Dragon brooch."

They glanced quickly at one another.

"What is your plan, my lady?" Bedwyr asked cautiously.

"I don't know yet, really. But I have an idea. I will not appeal to his heart, but to his honor. I will threaten to lead the troops myself."

"But you cannot! You are a woman! You may not touch the Sword!" Kay cried, distressed. "No one may draw it but the King himself!"

"Why is that?" I asked him. "Did Merlin put a curse upon it?"

"No, no," Bedwyr said quickly, "Merlin never dealt in curses. It is just tradition. The Sword was made for Arthur, a hundred years ago, and only he has ever touched it."

"Nonsense. It is the Sword of Maximus, who was my ancestor as well as his. Merlin has held it, and no doubt countless servants, as well . . . Well, I will risk it. Perhaps the sight of it in my hand will shock him as much as the very thought of it has shocked you."

Kay was calmer when he realized it was a ruse only, and that I did not really intend to lead the High King's troops to battle; Bedwyr and Lancelot thought it might work.

"Should it fail," Lancelot said, "and we should have to go north without him, we will take you with us. For I think your idea has more merit than even you believe."

Kay was aghast, but Lancelot turned the talk to the specifics of the plan. It was arranged that everything would be sent to my rooms during supper, when the Round Hall was empty and the Companions would not miss the Sword, which hung on the wall above the High King's chair. Then, in the evening at the time of my choosing, I should try to see the King.

They left me, then, alone with Lancelot. I was nervous about the plan and wished I had not thought of it, or they had not agreed. But I could see no other way. We talked for some time about what should happen if the plan failed. Lancelot was second in command, and to him would fall the leadership of the High King's troops. He would go north to Urien's aid. But the Saxon threat could not be discounted, and the King's fighting force must be divided, with a strong contingent left at Camelot under Bedwyr's command. They must make themselves visible along the Saxon border and discourage attack until Lancelot could return. It was risky. If Cerdic were clever, he would know what the display signaled, and he might attack.

We talked this way and that, and then at length prepared to go. At the door I stopped and turned to him. In three weeks we had said a good deal to one another, but Elaine's name had never been mentioned. I did not know if he had even seen her, except to remove her from hall.

"I must congratulate you, Sir Lancelot."

He looked blank and startled by the formal address. I saw he did not even know.

"On what?" he asked. "I have done nothing."

"Did you not know your betrothed carries your child?" I whispered.

He started as if struck and paled. I was both gladdened and saddened to see that it gave him no joy.

"How in God's name do you know?" he breathed. "They have said naught to me."

"I know. I would know even if I had not seen the triumph on her face. Ask her if it is not true."

He swallowed hard and shook his head. "No. If it is true, I will know soon enough. Let them keep it quiet until this fracas is behind us. Next to this it matters not."

I softened to him then and spoke gently. "I told you in case you wanted me to mention it to Arthur, if I can make him hear me. You have waited three weeks already to ask permission, and if we are to go to war—if you wait too much longer, all the world will be able to see why you are marrying her."

His eyes were shining, and he lifted my hand to his lips. "You are a noble woman, Guinevere. But I do not want you to plead my cause with the

King. Not in this. I will do it. If you can bring him round, I will speak to him. As for the rest, I do not care if all the world knows why I marry her."

I smiled at that, and we parted on good terms.

When I ascended to my chamber after supper, I found everything arranged. My best riding clothes were laid out upon the bed, along with the King's own cloak, and his gold and enamel brooch. I ran my finger over the smooth surface, the Red Dragon of Britain, from which he took his name. And it came to me again, that sense of shock, that this one man should be so important to the world. He was the center, and we all, like spokes, moved around him.

On the little needlepoint bench lay the great Sword. Up close, it looked huge. The scabbard was old leather, so old and well oiled it felt like silk to the touch. The thing lay balanced on the bench, dwarfing it, the great gem on the hilt winking in the lamplight. The jeweled belt it hung on lay carefully on the floor beside it. But the Sword itself must not touch the ground—that much I knew. I reached out a hand to touch it, but withdrew it. I dared not. It was a thing of magic and power, lying there so still in the dim light, shining with a glory of its own. It was not for me.

So I turned and thought again about my plan. Perhaps it was not wise to do this. I thought that I should first find out what the King had in his mind, and how he was. I would try womanly persuasion first and see what happened. With a sense of relief, I called for Ailsa to take down my hair and prepare it for night. I would go to him in the gown I had worn on our wedding night, the white one Elaine had sewn. Perhaps it would remind him of another time and distract him. At any rate, I knew what I was about in this and felt more comfortable. When I was prepared, and my hair was brushed and hanging down my back, the way he loved it, I bade Ailsa wait in my room. I went to the curtain. I heard nothing. Lifting it slowly aside, I took a deep breath, and went in.

I did not see him at first. The room felt empty. The fire was out in the grate, the wicks had not been trimmed, and the triple lamp burned smokily. Nothing moved. I was just about to turn back, disappointed, when I saw him standing at the far window, looking down. I nearly cried aloud. Was this the King, this pale shadow of a man? How could three weeks of fasting change a man so? He was still dressed as a penitent, in a loincloth only, and his flesh, once hard with muscle, now displayed his bones. His collarbones threw shadows on his shoulders; I could count his ribs.

"Arthur!" I said it on a sob, and he jerked toward me.

"Go away. I do not want you here."

"That's as may be," I whispered, "but I cannot obey you." Turning my eyes from him, I took flint and got the fire going. When the coals were burning, I put out the lamp, trimmed the wicks, and relit it. It shed a golden glow, and the room felt warmer. I fetched a wineskin from my own room, and I hung it to warm over the coals. The water carafe was empty, and I filled it from my own. Clearly he had not allowed Varric to attend him.

By this time Varric had arrived in the antechamber, and I whispered down to him to bring me a bowl of beef broth, a heel of soft bread, some cold chicken, cheese and fruit, and hot water, soap, and towels. He spread his hands out helplessly.

"My lady, I have tried. But he will not allow me in the room." He felt shame, I am sure, for the King's state.

"Never mind. Bring them to me, and I will see to it."

I swept the room and made up the bed with clean sheets that Ailsa brought me. I never looked at him. He would have to try a conversation if he wanted to speak to me. But he had turned back to the window and said nothing. Varric arrived with Kay, Bedwyr and Lancelot close behind. I would not let them mount the stairs, but went down myself into the King's antechamber and took from them the basin of hot water, which was heavy, and the towels and soap. I struggled up with them myself and set out the towels beside the low stool.

"Come, my lord," I said at last. "Sit here, if you will. It is time you had a bath."

Wearily he turned from the window. "Leave me, Guinevere."

"No, my lord. I cannot."

For the first time, I saw a spark of anger in his eyes. "Do you defy me? I said, leave me."

"Come sit here, my lord. You need a bath."

"And you are not a bath slave. Let it be."

"You will allow no one to attend you. Thus it must fall to me."

He looked at me sharply, and then came and sat. I suppose he thought I would not do it. But I bathed him, from his dirty hair to the soles of his unwashed feet. I toweled him dry, and rummaged in the trunk for his day robe.

"There," I said, when he stood clean and dressed. "That is closer to the lord I serve."

"You have shown me your devotion. Now go."

"No, my lord. I cannot." I carried the basin of dirty water to the landing, where Varric took it from me. The tray of food was waiting, covered by a clean cloth, and I brought it in and set it on his writing desk.

"I order you to go." His face was a study, angry and indignant, at the same time grief-stricken and powerless.

I took a deep breath. "Eat the meal I have brought you, my lord. Sit here, and I will serve you."

I lifted the clean cloth to let him glimpse the food.

"Guinevere! I am your King! Obey me!"

I lifted my chin and faced him. "You *were* my King. But you have not done much work in that line lately. You have put down the burden and left your friends to pick it up. I obey *their* orders now."

He looked startled, but then gave up the fight. I ached to see that submission. It was so unlike him.

"You do not understand."

"Sit and eat."

"I will not."

"Then I will not go."

We stood facing each other. I was reminded of childhood fights with Gwillim, which usually ended with some adult coming between us to settle things. But there was no one to settle things for us now.

He walked slowly to the table. "If I eat this, will you go?"

"Yes."

He sat down and began to consume the meal. At first he ate slowly, and I gave him only water, but then, as he felt better, and had more interest, I gave him watered wine, as well. At length he finished, and dipped his fingers in the waterbowl and dried them on a napkin. Then he looked up at me. There was nothing in his eyes but grief.

"Leave me now, Gwen."

I sat upon the edge of the table. "I have promised, and I will. But first tell me what it is I don't understand. Why are you doing this? It is not like you to stand idly by while Britain falls to ruin. The patient work of the last five years is about to go for naught. There must be a reason. What are you waiting for?"

To my amazement, he answered me.

"A sign," he said. "A sign from God. From any god."

"What—what kind of a sign?" He astonished me; then I remembered he had grown up under Merlin's cloak and must be familiar with wonders. "Is it an omen you seek?"

He shook his head. There was a haunted look about his eyes, a touch of fear. That was what made him look so different—I had never seen fear in him before.

"Why do you not ask Niniane about it? She has his power now."

He shot to his feet. "I forbid you to mention her name. She has betrayed him. At the last, she betrayed him."

I took a deep breath and spoke calmly. "How do you know this, my lord?"

With a heartfelt groan, he held his head in his hands and turned away. He sat heavily on the bed, bending forward, resting his elbows on his knees.

I followed him silently and stood beside him, grieving for the grief and pain he suffered.

"Merlin told me," he whispered finally. "He said it was his destiny, to die betrayed by a woman. He said it was his fate."

"And yet he went to it willingly, did he not?" I trembled at my own temerity, but he only shrugged. This was not what tortured him so. "What is it, Arthur?" I asked softly. "What else did Merlin foresee?"

It was a wild guess, but it hit its mark. He jumped up and strode back to the window. I thought for a moment he was going to order me out again, but all grief is easier to bear if shared, and after a struggle, he told me.

"He foresaw that he would go living to his grave," he said, the horror of it making him shudder. "It was the only thing I ever knew him to fear. And—and it was I who buried him. If—if I have buried him alive, the man I loved more dearly than a father—I waited three days, to be sure. He did not breathe, but neither did he rot. I knew not if it was magic, if the god he served protected his flesh, or if—if perhaps he truly lived but the life signs were hidden from me. But I could not keep the people waiting and had to come to some decision." He paused and swallowed. "I buried him so none could get at him, deep within the hill. But if he is alive—" He stopped. This was the fear that consumed him. "He will never get out."

"I see." Indeed, it was a horrible thought. And Merlin's foreknowledge, as everyone knew, had never been wrong. "And so you have asked God to send you a sign that he is truly dead?"

"God. Mithra. The Mother. The Elder Spirits. Any who will listen."

"What kind of sign will it be?"

"How do I know? But I will know it when it comes."

"Can you not—can you not accept, my lord, that Merlin knew what it was he went to, and that you could not prevent it? If he foresaw it, it had to happen. I see no blame here."

His smile was bitter. "Do you not? You had better go now. I wish to be alone."

I was near the curtain but did not turn to go. "My lord, the Kingdom is divided. Urien is at war. Leave this brooding and take up your arms. Britain needs you."

But he turned his back to me. "Britain will have to wait."

I gasped. But he had only shared his grief with me, not set it aside. I saw I would have to do more. I went back to my room and bade Ailsa help me change into my riding clothes and dress my hair for the road. She obeyed in silence. I had told her nothing of my plan, but although she saw the King's belongings in my room and must have been filled with curiosity, she said nothing. I think it was the Sword that kept her silent; indeed, its very presence filled the room with an awful majesty, and I did not say much either, and then only in a whisper.

When I was dressed, I donned the King's cloak. Ailsa's fingers shook as she fastened the Dragon brooch on my shoulder. The cloak was heavy, and so long that it dragged on the floor. I gathered the extra folds over my left arm. But we had trouble with the sword belt. It was too big and could not be made small enough to hang on my narrow hips. More than once the Sword itself nearly touched the floor.

"Never mind," I whispered at last. "I see no other way. I will have to draw it and carry it in my hand."

Ailsa clutched her amulets, her eyes wide, but said nothing.

I held the scabbard and put my hand to the hilt. It felt smooth and cold. Gently I drew the Sword, and we both gasped as the living blade caught the lamplight and threw it back, filling the room with a glorious light. It was heavy and trembled in my grip like a live thing, seeking action. Now was the time, or never, and I pushed the curtain aside and strode into the room.

"King Arthur!" I cried, and when he turned, I lifted the Sword to my forehead in salute, as I had seen his soldiers do.

He stared, dumbfounded.

"If you will not lead your troops to save Britain, I will do it in your place. I will not let her go down into the dark, even if I am only a woman. I can sacrifice my life as easily as you, and the men will follow me."

"Put down the Sword." He could not take his eyes from it, and the sight of it in my hand shook him to the core.

I held it aloft, where its weight was better balanced, and did not strain my arm so. "No, my lord. If I let it go, it will drop to the floor. Come and take it from me."

In four quick strides he was at my side and roughly took it from my hand. Then he went still. My arm felt dead, but his had come alive. It was as if the power from the blade ran up through the hilt and into his body, awakening the flame that had gone out. His face changed; the doleful marks of grief gave way to the eager quickness he was known for; his eyes lit with wonder. He looked down at the Sword and crossed himself. Tears of thanksgiving sprang to my eyes unbidden. He took it for the sign, as I hoped he would.

"What have I done?" he said suddenly.

Across the room, on the landing beyond the door, Bedwyr, Kay, and Lancelot kneeled and waited. He saw them and bowed low.

"My lords. If you can find it in your hearts to forgive me, I beg you will. I had no thoughts of abdication, but I see now it is what I have done. I was weak and allowed myself to be blinded. But this woman has opened my eyes."

He turned to me. He addressed me as he did them, man to man. "My thanks, Guinevere. We will speak of this after. And now, if I may take your cloak, which drags upon the ground?" His mouth twitched, and his eyes were smiling. I fairly tore the cloak off, as his knights ran into the room, all talking at once, and Varric threw open the trunk to find his traveling clothes.

The trumpets sounded as they left, and the signal fires were lighted to give warning of the High King's coming. He took Lancelot with him and sent Bedwyr to command the patrols along the Saxon Shore.

"This Queen," he had announced to all, "is her own protection."

22 ♛ THE FAREWELL

The High King arrived just in time. Urien was an experienced leader and knew the value of patience. He had waited as long as he could. When it became clear that Heuil intended to assume the kingship of Strathclyde and had got his twin's support, the other brothers came together and chose sides. Most joined Heuil, figuring once they had Urien off their backs, they could treat with Heuil for power. But Hapgar fled to Rheged with two younger brothers and allied himself with Urien, being disgusted with Heuil's rank injustice and his greed. The High King arrived on the eve of a pitched battle between the kingdoms. Hapgar knelt before him, swearing allegiance, and Arthur knighted him.

Against such war leaders as Urien, Lancelot, and Arthur, the Strathclyde forces had slim hope, and indeed, many of the soldiers fled as soon as they saw the Pendragon banner and realized who was there. Heuil and his brothers fought bravely, having the most to lose. The twins were killed in battle, and Hapgar was set upon the throne. All the brothers swore allegiance to the High King at day's end, and friendship with Rheged.

So those long weeks of worry ended swiftly. The Saxons, knowing their enemy well, did not attack, and Bedwyr was home before the King. All was quiet in Camelot. King Pelleas married Lady Niniane, but they stayed in Camelot, for she would not leave to the Lady's shrine on Ynys Witrin or to Pelleas' castle in the River Isles until she had seen the King. I spoke to her about it once, wondering how she felt about Merlin's going and whether she knew what the King thought of her.

"I know he prophesied betrayal at his end," she admitted in her quiet voice. "But Merlin gave me everything himself. Not his power only, but his memories. Everything that was in his mind is now in mine. I know the King thinks I betrayed him, but I do not know what he means by it. Whether it was the taking of the last thoughts, while he lay dying . . ." She paused, and

I shuddered. The image she conjured up was not a lovely one. "Or whether he means I took Pelleas to my bed while Merlin still lived. Both could be counted as betrayal. But truly, Guinevere, there was no harm in either. I have loved Merlin dearly, as father, counsellor, teacher, and man. I did what he bade me do. He wanted me to take it all from him, and time was short."

If she felt she had to justify herself to me, it seemed she was not free of guilt in this regard. I watched her closely.

"Then he is truly dead, and not sleeping?"

She turned to me, shocked. "Of course. How not?"

"You don't know the other prophecy, then? That he should go living to his grave?"

She took a quick breath and her eyes filled with tears.

"So," she said slowly. "That is what it was. I felt, at the very end, that he kept something from me. There was a wall. Even with his power, I could not reach beyond. The god stood there." She rose, trembling, visibly upset. "It cannot be. I felt his death come. May the Mother give me strength—Arthur will never forgive me and never trust me, if these things are true."

"Niniane, you are only human. Let me speak with the King when he returns, before you go to see him. I know your distress is real. Let me prepare the way for you. He will need you beside him in the future, and after all, that was Merlin's plan."

She nodded. "You have my thanks." Then she looked at me sideways and said hesitantly, "Do you know why the king has sent a ship to the Orkney kingdom?"

"Yes. To fetch his son."

She exhaled slowly and smiled at last. "I am glad you know."

"I asked him to do it."

"Indeed?" She raised an eyebrow. "That is generous of you. I wonder if you know what you are doing."

"If he is Arthur's, then I know I want him here."

She shrugged. "So be it. But don't start feeling sorry for his mother. Be sure he keeps the Queen Morgause in exile. To bring her into contact with her sons again would be disaster."

"Niniane, you are cruel! They are her children!"

She looked at me with cold, dark eyes. "She has no more mother love than an adder. The sooner she is dead, the better."

"She is of the King's blood. Can she be evil?"

Niniane's smile was bitter. "Yes," was all she said.

The King came home one hot morning past midsummer, and all the town turned out to greet him. He had a month of work to make up, a month's worth of petitions to hear, and reports to take from his commanders and knights errant. He was busy all the day.

The knights errant he heard first, always. These were those of his Companions whom he trusted most, and who understood his justice. They traveled across Britain for months at a time, visiting petty kings and lords, hearing their complaints and the petitions of the people, and dispensing the High King's justice throughout the land. They carried the King's seal and a writ of appointment for a term. But lest they should become corrupt with power, the writ was always dated, and any man who complained of their judgment was free to seek the High King's in Camelot. In this way, Arthur hoped to change the vagaries of laws, which had always varied from kingdom to kingdom, depending only upon the whim of the king, into something along the lines of Roman law, the same for all.

When a knight returned from his travels at the expiration of his writ, he gave a full report to the King in Council, so the King could judge how things stood. Then he received couriers, or sent them if need be, and then he heard petitions from all who came, high and low, to get justice.

All day Niniane and I waited to see him. But he worked steadily until midafternoon, then called the Companions to Council. This lasted until dinner.

When I met him outside the hall, I thought he looked a different man. He had put on flesh, though still was thin, but his love of life was back. He had come to terms with his fears, and looked serene.

"Welcome, my lord," I said, dropping into my curtsy. "We are glad to have you back!"

He smiled at me and slipped an arm about my waist and drew me near, although others were about. "How are you, Gwen? It's wonderful to see you. I would talk with you awhile, if you can await me, but it will be a late night, I'm afraid."

"I will await you, my lord."

"Have you forgotten my name?" he whispered, bending down to kiss me.

"I will await you, my lord Arthur," I replied, grinning.

Lancelot, behind us, coughed gently as the doors swung open. Arthur laughed and, releasing me, offered me his arm.

"I am reminded of my manners," he said with mock gravity, then beckoned Lancelot to come up on his other side, and threw an arm across his shoulders. "The King of Lanascol saved my life yet once again in Strathclyde," he said, looking at me. Then, turning to Lancelot: "My thanks again, friend."

So we three went into hall side by side. But my heart was heavy. By referring to Lancelot as the King of Lanascol, Arthur had let me know that Lancelot had made his request and that it had been granted. Although

I had fully expected it, I grieved to know it, and I could not share the King's joy.

After dinner, he sent for Niniane. He had stopped three days in Caerleon on his trip south from Strathclyde and had ridden over to Merlin's cave again. He had shouted, but heard only gentle echoes through the hills. All had been quiet, still and peaceful. It gave him ease of heart, and when he left, he was master of his grief. They were together a long time.

Afterward he called a meeting of the Companions, where Lancelot announced his news to all, and the date of his wedding was fixed.

During all this time I walked in my garden, for the night was hot, and a cool breeze eddied around the fountain. The moon in her first quarter rose late and yet sailed high in the night sky before the King came to me.

He walked along the path with an easy stride and, when I rose to greet him, took me in his arms and kissed me. "Hello, Gwen. Thank you for waiting."

"How did you deal with Niniane? She loved Merlin dearly and did not mean to betray him, if that is what she did. I spoke with her, my lord. She knew nothing of the prophecy you feared."

He led me to the bench, and we sat down together.

"I know. You need not champion her cause. I have apologized for my wrath. I've had time to think it through with a clearer head, and I see well she is the last person to wish Merlin ill. If she says she did not know, then she did not. Merlin must have wanted it that way. Anyway, that's not why I sent for her. I wanted to hear about his last hours . . . and get her advice on what to do about Morgaine."

"Yes?" I had been thinking the same thing myself. She was the King's niece, and there must be some way we could help the poor child.

"Urien had us to his castle after battle. He showed excellent sense in his handling of Caw's sons, and I did him all the honor I could. While I was there, he took me to his daughter." In the dim moonlight, his face was dark, but his voice was full of pain. "She is so afraid, poor child. She fears anything that moves. She fears her own shadow. She fears all men, even her father. He is afraid, and not without cause, that she will never recover her wits. I asked Niniane about the Lady's House of Healing, where Lancelot recovered from his grievous wound. I wanted to know if she thought the women there could help the girl."

"And what did she say? Surely they can do something?"

"She said it could be done, but it must wait. Time must pass. Certain things must happen."

He sounded uncomfortable, and I deduced that Niniane had had a vision in his presence. "What did she see?" I asked.

"Is my mind an open book to you, Gwen?"

I smiled. "I know you well."

"You do indeed. She bade me be patient. 'All things come to him who waits,' she told me. One of Merlin's favorite lines. I wonder if she knew she was stealing . . . well, I will wait and keep the child in mind. She is young to be taken from her mother, even though Morgan is more interested in witch-craft than in childcraft."

This was news to me. "Did you have speech with Queen Morgan, my lord?"

"No. I had no wish to. She has not made Urien's life a pleasure to him, and he is a good man. She has made him suffer for the honor of being my brother-in-law."

I realized there was no reason why Arthur should feel close to his sister. They had been raised apart and never met until he was made High King. Still, it made me shiver to hear him speak of her with coldness.

In the darkness, he was a shadow darker than the rest. I reached out, and held his hand. "Niniane told me you have sent for the Orkney princes."

"Yes." His voice went flat, and I felt his tension in his grip. "But their mother, I have ordered to stay in exile. She is a witch, Gwen, and her power over men must be seen to be believed. Even men with judgment, who know her to be evil, will do her bidding willingly, and not know why. I do not trust her here in Britain. If I brought her south, I might be forced to take steps I would regret."

"You would not kill her!"

"And bring a blood feud down upon my head? No, by God. I want Lot's sons to be my soldiers, to fight for me, not against me. I will give Lancelot the training of them. They will hold the north for me when they are grown. If they are Lot's sons, they will take to it like ducks to water. But I must get them young, or she will warp their minds against me. If she hasn't already."

"And Mordred? Will you single him out, or treat him like the others? What will be his status here?"

"Ah, I know not, till I have seen the boy. So much depends on him."

"When will they get here?"

"Give it two months at the outside. I wish—it is hard to wait, knowing they are coming. I feel the need to make up for the lost years."

"But you said yourself, you could not have had him by you," I whis-pered, hearing a father's love in his voice and feeling again the old, familiar pain. Arthur knew me. He sensed it instantly, and put his arms around me and drew me onto his lap.

"Gwen," he said softly, "he is your gift to me. Whatever happens be-tween us when he gets here, whether or not he can bear me as his father or his King, I will always love you dearly for this gift. Without you, I never would have known him."

"But for me, you might have known him sooner." I was trembling, thinking that had he not feared to wound me, had I not been so sensitive, he could have asked me years ago to welcome his son.

"Never think it. Had my wife borne children, I would never know him at all. He would be lost to me." His arms tightened about me, and I rested my head on his shoulder. Strength and peace flowed from him into me, and set my heart at rest. "Had you been other than you are, Gwen, everything would be so different. My Kingdom would not be whole. I have not yet thanked you for that."

"I am not alone responsible," I told him. "Everyone helped: Bedwyr, Kay, Niniane . . . Lancelot. We made a plan together."

"But you had more courage than all of them," he said quietly. "You disobeyed me to my face and gave me truth I could not swallow when you told me I was no longer your King. I cannot tell you what that did to me."

"It was not what turned you, my lord."

"No. But it planted the seed. And you alone had the courage to draw the Sword. No one else would have dared. My soldiers think you must have magic power, and I—I don't know quite what to think."

"I acted in ignorance, my lord. I did not know it was such an awful thing to touch the Sword. I merely wished to shock you."

I sensed him smiling. "You succeeded. But I was amazed you could hold it, that it stayed in your hand."

"It was heavy," I said, recalling the feel of it, "and hard to carry, for a woman. It trembled like a live thing and sought your grip."

He let out a long breath, I thought in satisfaction. "So, you felt its life. I wondered. All soldiers believe that good swords carry the breath of life in the blade. But that one—this is known—that Sword carries the spark of the god. It is no wonder my knights were afraid to touch it. I wonder they let you try."

"I put it off as long as I could. But something had to be done."

"Yes. God knows, that is true. I forced you to it."

He was quiet awhile, and I knew he felt more thanks than he could express. And then suddenly, softly, out of the dark it came.

"Guinevere, can you bear this—this parting from Lancelot?"

I froze. I wished heartily I were not sitting upon his lap, where he could feel my trembling and my every intake of breath.

"My lord," I whispered. "Don't."

"He told me what he told you. And I deduced that you had forborne to tell him the real reason Elaine was in disgrace." He waited, but I could not speak. "I gave him permission to wed her and take her away. But I grieved to do it. Not only for his sake, but for yours."

"My lord." I shook as the tears fell, and he hugged me gently.

"Why did you not tell him, Gwen? It would have kept him here. It would have foiled Elaine. It is a thing a man might wish to know about the woman he intended to marry."

I shook my head. "He—he had already lain with her. It was too late. If—if I told him, you know him, Arthur, where his honor is involved. He would never have forgiven himself. The shame would have eaten at him all his life."

"Ahhh. That is why I did not tell him myself." He held me tightly, and gave me a chance to control my tears. "Perhaps it is better this way," he said at last. "It may turn out well. He will be back . . . The wedding is fixed for next week. He asked me to tell you."

"Please," I whispered, touching his hand, "please, Arthur, don't make me go. I cannot—it is such a travesty—I cannot watch as he binds himself to Elaine."

"You are excused. I will be there. But I shall not enjoy it, either."

"Thank you . . . when does he intend to leave?"

"In a month. Perhaps sooner later. It depends upon Elaine. Do you know, after she schemed for this, she is surprised that he is taking her to Less Britain. Apparently she expected to stay here and be a thorn in your side for the rest of her days. Lancelot says she is angry at having to leave."

Had I not been so unhappy, I could have laughed.

"She counted on his honor to bind him to her. Now she must obey his honor's demands. All the sons of his house are born in Lanascol. She should have had longer sight. But that is Elaine."

He sighed. "So, you know. It was the last thing I had on my mind to tell you. I did not speak of it to Lancelot, but the news has been buzzing about my ears since I rode in. Bedwyr confirms it. She is with child."

I bit my lip hard. "I knew it before he did."

"Well, then. I see you understand." The tone of his voice changed, and I felt his lips against my hair. "All I ever wanted in a wife was someone pleasant, kind, and soft-voiced to come home to. When I saw you, I thanked the gods for the gift of beauty, as well. But such sense, such loyalty, and love, these I never counted on. These are your gifts to me."

"My lord," I breathed, blinking back tears, "they are easily given to such a man as you."

He pulled me closer and touched his lips to my face. "It is over a month since the solstice," he said softly. "So much time I have wasted!"

Lancelot and Elaine were married with Arthur in attendance. I gave out I was ill and stayed away. It fooled no one. From then on, Elaine sat on his right hand at table. It was her right, and I could not prevent it. She said very little to him, but I could say nothing at all. Alyse and Pellinore stayed in Camelot as the King's guests until the time of departure. This was put off until mid-October, when the winds were right, but it could not be put off forever, and at last the day arrived. The King had promised me an hour alone with Lancelot before he left, but in the bustle of preparations I feared there would not be time. And Elaine seemed determined to keep me from him; thrice in the last three days I tried to steal a moment of his time, and thrice she thwarted my desire. She followed him everywhere and hung on him shamelessly, looking helplessly up at him with her great blue eyes and never letting him forget his obligation.

I paced about my chamber in despair as the last morning dawned, my head so full of things to say I feared I should burst if I could not say them. At last a page arrived to say Lancelot awaited me in the King's library, and I raced from my apartments, eagerness overcoming sense, toward our tryst. When I reached the library I found it empty. But the garden door stood open, and I stepped out into the cool morning sun and called his name. Nearby, the gardeners worked preparing beds for winter; the chief gardener rose and ducked his head.

"I'm sorry, my lady, but Sir Lancelot is not here." He sounded apologetic and stared nervously at the ground. "We've all been here since sunup and have not seen him. I've heard tell he is with the King."

"And where, then, is the King?" I demanded crossly, wondering who had sent the page with such a message. He shrugged, and all the men looked sidelong at one another. Was it possible, I asked myself, she had duped me yet again?

"Never mind, good sir. I beg your pardon for my manners. Thank you kindly for your information; it is not your fault it is not what I would hear. I will find the King myself."

I hurried back to my chamber, this time more mindful of my dignity. I had not liked the knowing looks in the gardeners' eyes.

"Ailsa!" I called when I reached her doorway. But no one answered. Swiftly I mounted the steps to my chamber and stopped dead upon the threshold. On my terrace, wrapped in a traveling cloak and as cool as she could be, stood Elaine. Her back to me, she looked down upon my garden. I blinked twice and shook my head but she was not an apparition.

She turned as I entered, reached out a soft-gloved hand and pointed to the bed. "I came to return your gifts."

Every single thing I had ever made for her or bought for her or given her lay upon the coverlet. I walked closer, unbelieving. There lay the yellow gown—her favorite—which I had embroidered with stars eight, ten years ago? And the woolen sash I had made with her name stitched at the edges, to keep her warm in the long Welsh winters. The seashell I had found on the beach and polished for her, which spoke with the sea's voice when she held it to her ear, the leather pouch I dyed and sewed to hold her little treasures, the leggings, the pillow cover, the bracelets, pendants, and trinkets, the cushions and the slippers, all were there. I reached out a trembling hand and took up the comb of horn I had carved myself—how lovingly!—in Northgallis the winter my father had taken ill. I had made it to please my new cousin, whom he said I must befriend. My shaking finger touched the "E" carved at the crest; childish work, perhaps, but heartfelt, with love and hope in every stroke—yet even this she did not want.

Carefully I replaced the comb on the coverlet. "If you don't want them, I will keep them. They still mean something to me."

"I don't want them, obviously." She turned away with a careless shrug and looked once again down at the garden.

I walked out to her. "Did you send the page to draw me away?"

"Of course."

"Well. You have done what you came to do. Now get out. You are here without my leave."

"I care nothing for your leave. You are too full of yourself, Guinevere. I await my husband, who is with Arthur."

I followed her glance and saw, at the end of the garden, Lancelot and Arthur. Arthur's arm was slung around Lancelot's shoulders, and Lancelot held Arthur by the waist. They walked and talked together in close conference. I would have smiled to see them, if Elaine had not been there.

"Await him somewhere else."

"And let you have speech with him? Indeed, I will not."

"Why do you fear it? What are you afraid I will tell him?"

Slowly she turned and met my eyes. The autumn air, or perhaps her pregnancy, gave her pale skin a glow of health. With golden curls framing her aquiline features, she looked young and very pretty. But there was nothing soft and yielding in her face. Already one could see the woman she would become: hard, cool, and unforgiving.

"You care too much. You dare not tell him now. I keep him from you merely because you wish to see him."

I caught my breath and stepped back. "You never used to be so cruel!"

"I am as I have always been. It is you who have changed. You have forgotten your beginnings."

"And what is amiss with my beginnings?" I bristled.

She shrugged and smiled again that cold, unfeeling smile.

"Northgallis is a small, dark, and pagan kingdom. You came from thence into the light and power of Gwynedd, a Christian land. Had you not made that journey Arthur never would have noticed you. Yet you have never given us our due. Once here, you turned your back upon us and forgot our gifts to you."

"How can you think so! Why, Pellinore is—"

"I speak," she cut in coldly, "not of Pellinore, but of my mother and myself. You have turned the King against me to serve your selfish ends—"

"*I* turned the King?"

"—and your dreams of power. You would have served him better by stepping aside. You have consigned him to a future as barren as your own, and for what? So that you might be Queen!"

"That is not true! Ask Arthur yourself, if you dare! I—I—I cannot help my fate, but Arthur has chosen his of his own will!"

This time she smiled in pleasure and stepped closer to me, backing me against the balustrade. "Indeed he has. He has chosen more than he knows. Listen closely. I have something of importance to tell you before I leave. I have an informant on Ynys Witrin—this you knew—who serves the Lady's shrine when she is not in Melwas' bed. But for the gold I pay her, she would not stay to serve that insufferable Niniane. However, her information is beyond price. Have you ever heard of the Lady's Oracle?"

"Do you mean—in Northgallis we called it the Sacred Speaking, when—"

"—Every thrice three years when the full moon rises on the night of the equinox, the chief priestess climbs the Tor, sacrifices upon the Black Rock, and holds the sacred crystal to the moon's face. In it, if she is worthy, she sees a vision of the future."

"Yes. I know of it. So was Arthur's coming foretold."

"Well." She leaned closer until I felt her hot breath upon my cheek. "A month ago Niniane saw a future that she will not tell the King. The whole shrine is alive with whispers. Niniane secludes herself and speaks to no one."

I knew Elaine to be capable of every sort of falsehood; I knew her motives and the depth of her dislike; yet this revelation struck like a cold knife in my belly, and I shrank from her. Since the night of Arthur's return, no one had seen hide nor hair of Niniane.

Elaine's voice sank into a singsong whisper. "The wheel is turning and the world will change. Those who are weak shall grow in power, and the mighty shall be cut down. A dark prince from the Otherworld shall arise and slay the Dragon; a great serpent shall wade forth from the sea and swallow the Dragon's remains. The Dragon himself will be borne across water and buried in glass. Forever." I covered my ears with my hands to blot out her words. "And all this, Guinevere, is a result of the King's choice to keep you."

"No! No!"

"And a son of Lancelot," she hissed at me, opening her cloak and spreading her hands upon the hard mound of her belly, "shall, with a bloody sword and a righteous fury, renew the Light in Britain before she goes forever down into the dark. You will live to see it all. You will be spared nothing!"

I staggered back; my knees would not support me. "It cannot be! Dear God, it cannot be! You say it only to wound me—well, wound me, then, and have done. But Arthur—Arthur must be spared!"

She began to laugh softly. "This is not my vision, fool. Pleading with me changes nothing. I tell you so that you may know what fate you have brought upon him. You should have listened to me when you had the chance."

"I don't believe you! You want him still, and look only for a way to hurt me—why don't you go and let us all be?"

"When my husband calls me, then I will go. You will not have speech or comfort of him while I live. And once we are gone, Guinevere, you will never see him again."

A shadow darkened the doorway behind her. Arthur stepped ino the room, followed by Lancelot.

"What's this?" Arthur asked, glancing swiftly from my face to hers.

I could not speak, but Elaine turned to him with a guileless expression and made him a pretty curtsy.

"Cousin Guinevere regrets our departure, my lord. She would prefer us to stay." Lancelot frowned at her. Elaine smiled knowingly up at the King. "No. We all know the truth, don't we? She wishes my husband to stay." She stepped closer to the King and laid a small, gloved hand upon his arm. "It is an old story, my lord. Everyone knows it. She wants no one but herself to bear Lancelot's son."

Both men froze. But Elaine moved quickly. Before I could even draw breath to speak she pressed herself against Arthur, pulled his head down and fastened her mouth on his.

Lancelot cried out, "Elaine!" as Arthur recoiled and pushed her away.

She resisted, leaning close to him, her eyes intent upon his face. "You should have chosen *me*, my lord. All those years ago. I can give you what you want in a wife."

"Not," Arthur said darkly, turning his head to wipe his lips against his sleeve, "for the price of my soul."

Now Lancelot had her by the arm and pulled her roughly away. "Christ, Elaine! Arthur, forgive her if you can."

Arthur's eyes were on me. I did not know until that moment that my cheeks, my face, my gown were wet with tears.

"That is not so easily done," he said in a low voice. He turned to Elaine, who shrugged off Lancelot's arm with an imperious gesture. "I feel for your condition, Elaine, but not your fate. Don't pretend you are cruelly treated. You chose this with both eyes open. And it might so easily be worse." She heard the veiled threat and lowered her eyes. "Lancelot, keep her away from me. Take her to Lanascol and see that she stays there."

Elaine looked up and flashed him a look of open longing. "Arthur, let her go! She is your death! Ask Niniane!"

Lancelot gripped both her arms and turned her away from the King.

"Tell him, Gwen!" Elaine cried over her shoulder. "Tell him if you dare!"

They were at the door. In a moment they would be gone.

"Lancelot!" The words burst from me, sharp, shrill. "Is this farewell?"

Arthur's hand came down upon my shoulder. Lancelot paused, his heart in his eyes. Elaine laughed once, cruelly, and pulled him through the door and down the stair.

Arthur turned me to face him. "Dry your tears, Gwen. You will see him again. He'll be back come spring. I promise it."

I brought his hand to my lips and kissed his ring. "My lord, forgive me. I should never have brought her here!"

"It is not your fault, Gwen. I forgive her for it—poor girl, young and highborn as she is, she will find no happiness in life. She does not know how."

"I will *never* forgive her for it!"

"Yes, you will, in time. Let time pass."

I raised my head and looked into his dark eyes, warm and comforting. "Hold me, Arthur. Give me strength." He put his arms around me and held me gently.

"What is it," he said softly, "you must tell me?"

"Nothing! I don't know what you mean."

He laughed quietly. "What a terrible liar you are! Like it or not, you have the gift of truth, and I can read your face. Elaine told you something she wanted me to hear. Something you fear to tell me."

I looked up at him and wondered how he would feel when he knew. His arms tightened gently about me. "Tell me."

"Niniane is the one who should tell you."

"Ahhhh." Still his face was calm. "It is about the Speaking. I thought as much."

"Has she come to see you?"

"Not yet. But she will."

"Are you sure?"

"Very sure. Don't distress yourself, Guinevere, she has seen nothing Merlin did not see before her. Be brave and tell me."

"Did he see a great change coming? And a serpent from the sea? And a—" I gulped and clutched his tunic. "—a dark prince of demons who will—who will slay you?"

He caught his breath and let it out slowly. Still his face was calm, but his eyes looked far away. "Yes," he said at last, "all this he foresaw."

"And did he tell you—this was all because you chose to keep me? No wonder Merlin hated me all those years ago!"

"What nonsense is this? Merlin hate you? There was never hate in that man, even for my enemies. Is that what Elaine told you? Well, my dear, consider the source."

"Then—it is not true that you will die because of me?"

He laughed outright. "Certainly not. Quite the opposite. My fate, if Merlin is to be believed, was written in the stars before ever you were born."

"Then what does the Speaking mean, my lord?"

He smiled at that and shook his head. "This is a distant future, Gwen. Let it be."

"And—and Lancelot's son, did Merlin see that, too?"

He frowned and his focus sharpened. "What about Lancelot's son?"

"He will wield a bloody sword and bring the Light of righteousness to Britain—before she—no, that's all."

"To my knowledge, Merlin saw nothing regarding Lancelot. Are you sure this was part of the Speaking, or was it something Elaine perhaps invented?"

"For all I know, she invented everything."

He smiled and kissed me gently. "Britain will not go down into the dark. You need not fear to tell me what it is you fear the most."

"You *knew*?"

"I've heard whispers. But this, Guinevere, Merlin has seen, and often. It is a true Sight. Someday, when we are no more than memories in a bard's song, Britain will be the greatest land in all the world. And you and I, if we are constant, will have a hand in making it so."

I thought again of Bedwyr's words. "Everlasting?" I whispered.

His eyes were shining. "If you like. Long-lasting, at any rate. No King could ask for more. So you see why I do not worry about the future."

I looked up at him and smiled. "Even *you*, my lord, even you believe in visions when it suits you!"

He grinned. "Every king does. It's wise policy."

"Oh, Arthur, bring your son here quickly! If we are to build a lasting legacy for Britain, we must train him now!"

Something moved behind his eyes, and he drew me closer.

"He is coming." He paused. "Let us pray God he makes a King."

 BOOK II

THE HIGH QUEEN

23 ♛ ALL HALLOW'S EVE

Arthur and I sat silently in the hall after coming from mass. It was All Hallow's Eve. We had had frosts lately, and the night air carried a tang of sea salt. Down in the town and all over Britain, Samhain fires were burning, honoring the end of the old year after taking in the harvest, welcoming the new with prayers and incantations. On this night, Christian and pagan alike felt kinship with spirits, both blessed and fey.

I looked around the hall. Torches danced in the cool breeze; everyone was robed. Half the benches stood empty, so many were gone from us. The latest band of knights errant had left three days before: Lamorak, Bellangere, Dryaunt, Gillymer, Gauter, Gryfflet, and Agglavall, all good men and sorely missed. Thank goodness the King could not part with Bedwyr; with Lancelot gone, our fellowship was thinned beyond bearing.

The King picked at his food. Even silver-tongued Bedwyr ran out of patter and finally sat silent. We shared a heaviness of spirit that oppressed us like a fever in midwinter, with no escape but through suffering. The three weeks since Lancelot's departure had dragged by for both me and the King. Although this was an illness we shared, it was not one we could share together. Arthur filled his days with work as I filled mine with riding, and most nights we were too weary to say much more than good-night to one another.

Then, earlier today, a courier had come racing in from Ynys Witrin with the report that the High King's ship—there was no mistaking the Dragon sail—had been sighted in the estuary, and the long-awaited "shipment" from the Orkney Isles had at last arrived. Beside me, Arthur fidgeted. The knowledge that his son stood on ground that he commanded, so nearby but not yet within his gates, nearly drove him wild. And Arthur was the most patient man I knew.

We had no bard with us. The King called early for the wine to go around, and would, I knew, when the torture of dinner was over, stride off to his workroom to pace endlessly, hour upon hour, until the signal came. I prayed that the commander of the escort would have the sense to ride to Camelot tonight, and not wait on Ynys Witrin until daylight. For secrecy's sake, the King had sent no orders, and so must wait upon the commander's judgment.

"Gwen," he said suddenly, "I nearly forgot to tell you—we had a courier today while you were out riding. From Lancelot."

I caught my breath. "So soon? He is well?"

Arthur smiled and covered my hand with his own. "Very well. The crossing was a calm one, and they reached Benoic without trouble. His brother Galyn was there to greet him. They held a great feast in his honor."

"And to welcome his queen." I looked up into his warm brown eyes and somehow smiled. "Don't try to spare me, Arthur. I know full well the nature of the celebration. Lancelot is returned at last to take up the kingship of Lanascol, and he has brought home a bride already heavy with his heir. No doubt they are celebrating all over Less Britain. And so they should, to have such a king in their midst." The ache in my throat stopped my words.

Arthur lifted my fingers to his lips. "I cannot spare you when you face the truth so bravely. But that is behind you, Guinevere. Now look ahead."

I tried to smile. "As to that, now that the boy is almost here, I am scared to death to meet him!"

Arthur flashed a grin that lit his face. "And so am I!"

Suddenly we heard a commotion in the forecourt, raised voices and the clatter of hooves. I glanced quickly at Arthur; he had gone perfectly still. Minutes later, Kay entered the room, coughed politely, and went down on one knee beside the High King's chair.

"My lord, the Orkney party are without. Sir Lukan, the commander, wishes to know if you will receive them tonight or wait until the morning. They are"—he paused, and his stony face revealed a shade of consternation—"not quite presentable, my lord, and he knows the hour is late."

The hall went quiet. Slowly Arthur surveyed all the faces and then stood. Everyone rose. "Where are they, Kay?"

"In the courtyard, my lord. Dismounting. The wagons are just coming in King's Gate."

Arthur drew breath and squared his shoulders. "Take the boys to the barracks. Gereint will assign them sleeping places. He shall have their keeping, and Bedwyr their training. I will give them time to wash and rest. But I will see them all tonight. All five, Kay. Send Lukan to me in the library. Now."

"Yes, my lord."

Arthur turned and nodded to his Companions. "Bedwyr, Bors, Berys, Sagramor, you may attend me. Guinevere—" He looked down at me and held out a hand. "Will you come?"

"Of course, my lord. I wouldn't for the world miss meeting your nephews."

He laughed, half in pleasure, half in sheer excitement. "I don't expect much; they're clearly not up to Kay's standards. But I can't sleep until I know what they are made of. Let's hope, when the night is over, we have cause for celebration."

It was our custom to spend our evenings with the King in his pleasant workroom, where all the scrolls were kept. It gave onto the big garden, where we would stroll on summer evenings to take the air. In winter, we would sit around the log fire, discussing the day's events, or making plans for the spring, or honoring a guest. Sometimes I sang to them, sometimes we read aloud from the precious scrolls Arthur had got from overseas. Tonight, the King sat nervously behind his great marble table in the corner, fiddling with his winecup and talking to Bedwyr. The others stood by the fire, or sat on the cushioned benches, making small talk, wondering in lowered voices why a visit from his own nephews, boys not yet near manhood, should make the King so obviously uneasy.

The door swung open. Sir Lukan entered, face and hands wet from a hasty washing. Arthur rose.

"Welcome, Lukan. I'm glad to see you safely back."

Sir Lukan knelt at his feet and kissed the great Pendragon ruby on his hand. "My lord, I am glad to be back. It was not an easy journey, but we made it without losing a single man. As to your nephews, my lord, they were raised upon the sea and thrive in stormy weather!"

Arthur smiled and raised him. When he had thanked Lukan, served him wine, and sat him near the fire, he paused, his face solemn and intent.

"Tell me," he said simply.

"Well, my lord, we had good weather going and made Orkney at midsummer. The queen gave us a gracious welcome, and at first I thought it would be plain sailing with her as well. But—" He paused. Nothing moved in Arthur's face, but his eyes darkened. "She seemed to find a thousand excuses to prevent our leaving. First it was the preparations. Her boys had nothing fine enough to wear to greet the King."

Arthur snorted. I shot him a startled look, and Bedwyr hid a smile.

"Then it was a pox among the sailors, then the mast was damaged the night before our sailing, and we had to stay to build another." A thin, hard note of anger crept into his voice. "There is not a tree on Orkney, my lord King, that will make a decent mast. Our sailors had to row the queen's vessels clear to the mainland and float the lumber back. In midchannel a storm arose and nearly drowned us." He stopped and took a deep breath. "They do not call her a witch for nothing, begging your pardon, my lord. But we made it back alive."

"Do not beg my pardon, Lukan," Arthur replied coldly. "What she is, she has made herself. It is nothing to me."

I moved closer to his side and laid my hand upon his shoulder. He relaxed a little and beckoned Lukan to taste his wine, which the commander did with some relief. "She's a beauty, my lord," he said in a warmer voice. "I can't deny it, and there's not a man in Orkney who doesn't do her bidding. For all that, I believe she's false at heart."

Arthur smiled bitterly. "If you have just now learned it, Lukan, you come late to the lesson. How did she take my summons? Well or ill?"

Lukan put down his winecup with care. "Well enough, my lord, at first. She acted pleased her sons were called to Camelot to serve the King."

"Lukan." Arthur sat down opposite him and leaned forward, hands on knees. "Lukan, she is my half sister because my father's lusts got the better of his sense. Understand that she is nothing to me. I neither like her nor trust her; if you call her a venomous viper to my face, I will feel no insult. Now, man, tell me the truth. How did the witch take my summons?"

Lukan sat up straighter. "She was furious, my lord. Mad as a hellcat. Not that the boys were called to court, but that she was not. There was the devil to pay among her women. Half of them carried black eyes for weeks." Arthur grimaced. "For six weeks," Lukan continued, "she fought me. First, she threatened to disobey and bring her sons to you herself. She was certain I must have misunderstood the orders, but there it was, on parchment, for her scribe to read aloud. Then she refused to let them go. Beyond her protection, she said, they would fare ill at her tyrant brother's hands. Or—or—"

"Go on."

"Suffer poison, or castration, by his barren Queen."

Arthur's nostrils flared. "Did she say this in their hearing?"

"Indeed, my lord, these tirades were for their sake more than mine. But I think they knew it."

Arthur's expression hardened. "All right, Lukan. Go on."

"Then she tried fits of weeping, that we might pity her misfortune in losing all her sons at a single stroke, but she is not convincing in the pose of helplessness. Last she tried her witch's curses. She has cursed my line down to the sixteenth generation, my lord. They are all to be halfwit savages, every one."

Arthur managed a stiff smile. "I'd say you got off lightly. She has wished much worse on me. Good man, Lukan, to withstand her. She's known to be chancey to cross, but you have done it for me, and I thank you from my heart."

Lukan looked relieved. "At the end, my lord, she gave in with such grace and willingness, it quite surprised me. I was even on the lookout for some trick, but in the end, she let us go in peace, if you don't count the storms that assailed us as soon as we were through the straits."

"Well, she is nothing if not changeable."

Or perhaps, I thought, she had some new plan afoot; but I did not say it. They drank together in fellowship and talked about the weather. I watched Arthur's hands around the winecup, lean, strong hands, with nimble fingers, playing nervously with the beaten silver, turning and turning, as if he could not stop.

"And the princes?" he asked suddenly. "Fared they well upon the journey? No seasickness?"

Lukan laughed. "Those boys? Not a bit of it. Why, they were bred upon the sea and know her moods and tempers. They eat like young wolves and are never sated. You've no worry with your nephews my lord. A healthier, rowdier lot I've seen only in the kennels."

Arthur smiled and listened as Lukan recounted their shipboard antics, but I knew his mind was in the barracks. At last he rose, and Lukan stood. "I thank you for your service, Lukan. You've done splendidly, and I'll reward you. Go now to your well-earned rest. Tomorrow we'll speak again."

"Thank you, my lord. It is ever my pleasure to serve you."

When the door had closed behind him, Arthur whirled. "Bedwyr, send to Gereint. Say I wish to see my sister's sons as soon as they are ready."

But Bedwyr had not got halfway to the door before it flew open in his face. Tall and graceful, dark haired and pale complexioned, the Lady of the Lake herself strode in unannounced and stood before the King.

"Arthur!" she cried. "He is transformed! He is free! He is among us!"

Everyone stared. She was not wearing the white robe of the Goddess' servant, but her riding clothes—leggings, tunic, and mantle—and her hair had come loose from its braiding, falling in wild, ragged wisps about her face. Without a doubt, she had ridden straight from Avalon to see the King.

"Niniane!" He took her elbow and led her to the bench. "Be still a moment. My lords, I would speak with her alone." The men bowed and began to file out. I made Arthur a quick reverence and turned to follow, but he looked up swiftly. "No, Gwen, stay. And you, too, Bedwyr. Gwen, what have we to offer her to drink? She's had a vision of some sort—look at her eyes—and she's ridden instead of resting."

I passed him a winecup, and he lifted it to her lips. She drank without knowing it, her dark eyes wide and unfocused, her whole body trembling with some strong emotion.

"Arthur!"

"I am here, Niniane. Take a moment."

"I must speak to you alone!"

"Go ahead."

"Arthur, I have seen him! He is living!"

"Who, Niniane?"

"Merlin."

I gasped. The King went white. Slowly he slid to one knee and took both her hands. "Niniane. Calm yourself."

"Arthur, I have seen him! In the flesh!"

"How can that be? I buried him myself, there in the hill, and filled the cave mouth with stones not a company of my strongest men could move. He is dead, my dear, and beyond our call. You have said so yourself."

She met his eyes, and her breathing slowed a little. "Yes," she whispered, "I know it. When he lay dying, with his head in my arms, he told me to trust the Sight we shared. He—he must go to his grave, he said, and I must bear his mantle in the world of men. But—" She paused and looked at Arthur pleadingly. "I can't be sure. I thought I felt his death come. But as much as I took from him—I did as he bade me, Arthur, when I entered his mind. You must believe that! I did not steal his thoughts; he offered them to me—I did not take all. There was something else I could not reach; the god we serve forbade it. I don't know what it was."

Arthur held her hands firmly between his own and spoke kindly. "I know he wanted you to take his power. Don't torture yourself with the rest. But as you love him, Niniane, let him rest in peace."

"But Arthur! I saw him tonight. *Tonight!* He is alive!"

Bedwyr moved closer to me; the candles flickered in the draft. Arthur's voice came cool and calm and steady. "Tell me what you saw."

"In the workroom at Avalon, I sat before the peat fire, mixing herbs. Suddenly he was there with me. Not in the fire, Arthur. *In the room!* He spoke, and it wasn't a vision voice; it was his own. He bade me bring you to Caerleon and said he would see you there."

"Niniane—"

She fumbled with her pouch and drew forth an old copper ring. "He gave me this, as a token of the truth. He said you would have trouble believing me, else."

Arthur shot to his feet. "This was on his body, that we buried!"

"I know."

"But it cannot be!"

"It is."

In that moment his whole being changed. He lit from within. "Niniane, tell me only this—is it possible?"

"Not with ordinary men," she whispered, "but if he is, or was, or has become—a shapeshifter—then—"

Arthur tossed the ring in the air and let out a whoop of joy. "Bless you, Niniane! A thousand thanks! Bedwyr, stay here as Queen's Protector. Guinevere, I leave the boys to you." He strode for the door. "Geoff! My horse! My sword! Five minutes!" He turned. "I shall be back in ten days, or a fortnight, or whenever I can. Think of it! Merlin is alive!"

He was gone; the room still rang with his echoes.

Bedwyr whirled and whistled sharply. Men came running. "Sagramor! Tell Gereint to send an escort after the King! Quickly, man! Or he'll ride all the way to Caerleon alone!"

"Sir Bedwyr." Niniane spoke quietly. "Would you arrange an escort for me, as well?"

"Do you wish to accompany the King? If so, we must hurry—"

"No. Let them have their private meeting. As soon as you are able is soon enough for me."

"It will be done, my lady. I will see to it directly."

"Thank you."

Bedwyr turned to me and hastily bowed. "My lady, I will attend you in a moment; I want a word with Gereint before the escort leaves."

"Of course, Bedwyr. Go on."

The quiet castle came suddenly alive, with sentries running through the halls, pages fetching swords and cloaks, the calls of soldiers and the clatter of shod hooves on the courtyard stone. Niniane rose, looking more herself again, and thanked me formally for the wine and the escort.

"Anything we can do to please you, Niniane, is our pleasure to perform. You have brought the King great news."

She shrugged lightly. "Great news, indeed. But it is not without danger."

"What do you mean? Danger to whom?"

"A gift from the god is a double-edged sword. There is always another side. There is always a price to pay."

"Do you mean Merlin?"

She nodded slowly, her eyes, normal now, looked far away. "So long as Arthur walks on middle earth, the serpent shadows him that will one day strike at his heel. If my lord Merlin hopes to save him from it—if this is why he has returned—he risks disaster. He may not interfere. It is forbidden. He knows it well, but"— she sighed—"he loves the King."

I went up to her and took her arm. "Niniane, I understand your words but not their meaning. What is it you are telling me?"

She shrugged again and smiled. "Only that on occasion, love gets the better of sense. But this you know already, my lady Queen . . . I should be going."

"Will you tell me what a—a shapeshifter is?"

She laughed lightly. "What have you heard from bards' tales? An ancient spirit, neither god nor man nor beast, and yet all three. Never mind it; I don't even know if it is true. Perhaps, after all, he did not die. With Merlin, all things are possible."

With that, she left me, but I paced about in agitation. I never understood enchanters' talk, so garbled and so dire. Where lay the threat to

Arthur? Who was the snake? How everything had changed in the space of a lightning flash the instant she appeared! Here I was, alone in the library, when so short a time ago, Arthur and his Companions had sat here and interviewed Sir Lukan about the High King's nephews! Who would have believed that he would ride from Camelot without so much as speaking to them? To have his own son here at last, to be on the verge of meeting him face to face—and to leave everything, without a look back, just on the chance Merlin might still live! How he loved the man! How he trusted Niniane!

I sat in the King's favorite chair, near the fire. The King's hound Cabal raised himself from the hearth and shoved his wet nose under my hand.

"Well, Cabal," I said, scratching his ears, "here we are, we two, sitting in the corner, waiting upon events. How often, my old friend, has it been so? Men ride in, and men ride out, and we two are ever faithful, waiting. Always before when the King left, I had Lancelot for company. But I suppose I must count myself lucky, to be married five years to a traveling soldier and not find myself lonely until now."

Bedwyr returned within the hour. The escorts were gone, he reported, and the princes housed in the barracks, though not abed. They were far too excited for sleep.

"Well, I'm glad someone remembered them. But tell me, Bedwyr, what did Niniane mean? What is a shapeshifter? It is possible Merlin could endure death and return?"

He shuddered and covered it with a scowl. "Old wives' tales, if you ask me, my lady. I hope Arthur's not gone off on a goose chase. Haven't you ever heard the term before?"

"When I was a child my nurse told me tales at bedtime, about elves and witches and fairy people and such, who lived when the world was young. I think I remember a tale about a wolfboy who was a shapeshifter. But I thought these things were fantasy only and not something a grown man, or woman either, could seriously believe."

"Well, I suppose no one really knows. When our ancestors were children, when gods lived in every tree and rock and stream, people believed in spirits who had strange powers and who lived between the worlds of gods and men. They were real to touch and sight, and yet were creatures of the nether world, who came and went at their own bidding. In the songs I've heard, they were more evil than good. Nuisances, mostly. But really, Guinevere, it's been ages since anyone believed in them, much less saw one. I can't image what possessed Niniane to say that—perhaps it's true she stole Merlin's powers from him and is now pursued by guilt?"

I nearly laughed. "Not Niniane. I don't believe she betrayed him, but if she did, she'd never suffer a backward glance. No, I think she truly believes what she told Arthur. And how quickly Arthur accepted it!"

Bedwyr shrugged. "Well, he knows Merlin best. Perhaps it's possible. I've heard him say often enough, anything is possible with Merlin."

"Well. I suppose we will have to wait the arrival of a courier to know the truth. Now he has flown off without greeting his nephews, and it is left for me to do it. You must tell me what you know about them, Bedwyr. What are they like?"

With relief, he plunged into a subject much more to his liking. "They are a wild lot, which is not surprising, since they've grown up far from civilization and worship outland gods."

"What do you mean, 'outland gods'? You are a pagan yourself."

He grinned. "Mithra is a soldier and a gentleman. But in Orkney their gods are animals, as well. I have seen the Mother represented as a pregnant fish!"

"Not so strange," I murmured. "In Wales, I have seen her likened to a pregnant boar. But I mean, what do the princes look like? How did they fare on the journey? Did you speak with them?"

"Oh, yes. I felt it was my duty to get them settled, since Gereint and Kay had so much else to do. They are strong boys all, and none of them the worse for the journey. But then, as Lukan said, they have all but grown up on the sea. Fight like dogs they do, the redheads. Gawaine is first among them, although he is not firstborn. The eldest is a bastard. Half-prince, they tease him. They are all five safely stowed away."

I was nervous and pressed my hands together to keep them still. "What did they look like?"

Bedwyr's eyes narrowed. "Short and thickly built, my lady, red-headed with high color and short tempers. Except for the youngest, Gareth, who is a pleasant, cheerful child, and the bastard, who is of a different breed."

"Oh?" I failed in my attempt to sound casual. "And what is he like, this strange one?"

Bedwyr's gaze sharpened. "Altogether different. Tall and dark. Restrained. Thoughtful. A boy who keeps to himself. A comely lad, too, by the look of him, but not of warrior stock."

"You forget yourself!" I cried indignantly, and then flushed, biting my tongue too late. Bedwyr's eyes were alive with excitement. I rose and turned away from him, fighting to calm myself. Bedwyr waited, silent, until I came back and sat beside him.

"Another cup of wine, my lord?"

Gently he laid a hand upon my arm. "Guinevere, if I am to protect the Orkney princes, don't you think you had better tell me what you know about them?"

"I know nothing about them."

Bedwyr smiled. "Who is this dark lad you're so sure is made of warrior stock?"

I bit my lip and lowered my eyes. "Please, Bedwyr, do not ask me. I cannot tell you. I have sworn it."

"To whom?"

I shook my head.

"It is true, then," he said softly, unable to hide his elation. "So, it is true! I have often wondered. There was talk about them at Caer Eden, I remember. Ector's fosterling and Uther's daughter. But he was so young, and she already a woman. Few believed it. Anyway, it was long ago and nothing came of it, I thought, so I forgot it."

I raised my eyes to him. "It is better so," I said softly.

"He does not know who his father is," he said, smiling. "They tease him about it." I said nothing. "I will not press you for the truth, for clearly you have promised not to tell. But I have seen the boy. And I think I know why Arthur sent for him."

"Bedwyr." I looked into his eyes. "Whatever conclusions you come to, will you keep them to yourself?"

"Of course I will." His voice was gentle. "I swear by the Light of Mithra, all of the King's secrets are safe with me."

24 ♛ THE DARK PRINCE

I rose early the next morning and went to the stables. I was far too excited to sit and do nothing; I did not want to ride out and perhaps miss a glimpse of the boys. So I went to Lyonel, Lancelot's apprentice and now Master of the Horse in his absence, and bade him make ready the young bay stallion Rajid.

Lancelot had three years hence begun to train the war stallions along the lines set down in an old book the King had procured for him. It was a short scroll written by a Greek, one Xenophon. This man knew horses, and gave instructions for gentling them and training them for war. Lancelot had begun to follow his methods, and Arthur was well pleased with the result. Now he had developed a system of training that began when they were colts in the field, just weaned from the mares, and continued until their full maturity at the age of five. Lancelot and two others, Lyonel and a lowborn stable boy named Griff, were the only riders good enough to do this training. But Lancelot had desperately needed another pair of hands and, over time, had persuaded the High King to let me try. For two years now, I had helped them, and indeed, although it was ring work, I loved it nearly as much as a fast gallop over the downs.

What the soldiers thought of a woman riding a war stallion, I did not know. But ever since I had lifted the High King's Sword and lived, they had been more accepting of the strange things I did. They saw I was not like other women: I rode astride without a saddle, and hawked, and raced, and bore no children. They shrugged, and muttered to one another that it was Arthur's problem, thank God, and not theirs.

The young horse was put through a series of simple exercises to supple and strengthen him, and increase his willingness to obey. There were bending exercises, changes of gait, and turns and sprints and calm halts. Like dancing, it required control and was hard for young stallions whose instincts were for running, fighting, and breeding mares. It always took all my concentration, and it was for this reason that I went to the stable that morning. I could not bear the thought of Arthur's son so near—I, unable to go to him, and he, not knowing who he was.

By the time the rest of the palace was up and about, Rajid and I were hard at work in the big paddock. He moved like a dream, easy and fluid, and when he outgrew his fits of temper, would make one of the best fighting stallions in the High King's stable. We were doing changes of pace at the canter, and he sweated freely, lathering the oiled reins and chewing the bit as he worked. Suddenly a group of rowdy grooms burst from the stable door, shouting and pushing; the horse took fright, reared, spun, landed and bucked twice, and tried to bolt. By the time I had him in hand again and made him stand, trembling and blowing with fear, the shouting match had progressed to a fistfight. I turned, furious, to give the grooms a tongue lashing—anyone who worked around horses should know better than that!

But I saw instantly, in a single glance, who it was. Three red-headed boys in outlandish clothes wrestled in the dust of the stableyard, cursing each other in barely intelligible speech, scratching and kicking, fighting by no rules at all that I could see. At the fence, staring open-mouthed, stood a slim, dark-haired boy holding the hand of a small, red-headed imp, who looked up at me with wide green eyes and grinned delightedly.

"Dred," he said, tugging at the other's hand. "Dred, it's a girl."

I stared back at Mordred, Arthur's son. His father's face was so clearly stamped upon him, I did not see how anyone could doubt his birth who had ever seen the King. The wide brow, the straight planes of the face, the strong chin, generous mouth—these were Arthur's. Even his hands, well shaped and strong, were not his own. But his eyes were black; his hair, cut roughly by someone unskilled, was blue-black; his body slender without the promise of breadth—these belonged to him alone. He looked so like Arthur that I expected to feel the familiar warmth flow from him, of greeting, of recognition, or just of joy of living. But the eyes were fathomless and gave nothing back. He had run up with the child when the stallion was misbehaving, but now he just stood and watched me, whether in admiration or disapproval it was impossible to tell.

I saluted him gravely. "My lord," I said slowly, in case he had trouble understanding cultured speech, "can you not exert some control over yonder unruly brood? This is a stableyard, not a battlefield. They are frightening the horse."

His eyes widened. I could see he was pleased to be taken for the eldest, the man in charge.

"My lady," he began bravely, and then faltered. His voice was just changing; it had that tentative quality, as if he never could be certain when he opened his mouth which voice would emerge, the man's or the boy's. Suddenly he squared his shoulders in a gesture so like Arthur's, it brought a blush to my cheek. "My lady, please forgive them. They—we—are from a foreign land, where customs differ. Besides"—and suddenly the boy was back—"they cannot keep from fighting five minutes out of six."

"Hey, Gawaine!" cried the little imp, leaving Mordred's side to run toward the tussling boys. "Gawaine! Look at the lady on the horse! She rides just like a man! And better than you!"

At this the fight stopped, and the three boys all turned toward me. Two were identical: red-headed, green-eyed, and freckled, with the type of short, blunt nose that begs for a blow. Gawaine, a little taller and stronger featured, but no less unkempt, had at least some shred of dignity about him. As I was to learn, he always knew what was due him and saw that he got it.

He gaped at me and approached the fence.

"What's this?" he cried. "Since when do maidens ride the High King's horses? And without a saddle, no less! This is a bit high-handed—whose woman are you? Who's your lord? Why don't you answer? Do you think you can insult my uncle, the High King, without redress?"

"Shut up, Gawaine! Can't you see she's—" Mordred whispered, and was cuffed for his pains. I nearly cried out in indignation, but stopped myself in time. Mordred was used to such treatment, it seemed, and took it with even temper.

But Gawaine saw my anger and smiled. "There's more where that came from. Now give me an answer or get off the horse."

In a flash I understood why they did not know me. I had bound up my hair and covered it with a scarf, to keep it secure during the workout. And it was by the freakish color of my hair that strangers knew me. Only children had hair of such pale gold it was nearly white, but at twenty, I had yet to outgrow this color.

Sir Ferron had come into the yard behind the boys. He had obviously been looking for them and was out of patience. When he saw me he saluted; the greeting was upon his lips when I shook my head, and he went silent.

"Sir?" I said to Gawaine. "Who is it who speaks to me so rudely? Before I answer your accusations, give me your name and family."

Gawaine threw his chest out and shouldered Mordred aside. His speech was British, but with a thick, guttural accent and hard to follow.

"I am Gawaine, Prince of Orkney. Firstborn of King Lot and his queen Morgause. The High King is my uncle. And what business is it of yours, I should like to know?"

Ferron gasped, but saw my signal and was still. Beneath me the stallion, grown bored, began to paw the ground. I corrected him gently and he stood quiet.

"Is this the way you are taught to greet strangers, my lord? Here in Camelot, we are polite to those we do not know."

Mordred nudged him ever so slightly. "It's a stallion, Gawaine. Use your head."

But the hint was lost on Gawaine.

"I respect my betters, wench, and when you are one, you shall have it."

"That's enough!" Ferron cried, unable to bear silence any longer. He grabbed Gawaine by the collar and shook him, lifting the boy completely from the ground. "You'll be whipped for this, my lad! King's nephew or no! No one speaks to the—"

"Ferron!" I cut him off in time. "Spare him this once. For me. I should have told him. But I wanted to see his nature first."

"Well, my lady, you have seen it," he said angrily. Gawaine stared at me in bewilderment, and then at Mordred, who had already bent his knee to the ground. I beckoned to the twins; they came forward, surly and uncertain.

"Are you princes of Orkney, as well?"

One of them nodded, glancing quickly at Ferron. "Agravaine, my lady, and this is Gaheris."

"Have you no manners?" Ferron growled. "Has no one taught you how to bow?"

I slid off Rajid's back and beckoned to a groom to come and take the reins. Gawaine's eyes widened as I approached him. He came no higher than my shoulder. I knelt down to look the youngest in the face.

"And who are you, my wise little man?" He went suddenly shy and reached for Mordred's hand.

"His name is Gareth, my lady," Mordred answered quietly.

I stood. The top of Mordred's head came to eye level. I looked gently into the face of Arthur's son. "And you, sir? You are the eldest, surely?"

It was as good as asking him his parentage, but he did not blush or hesitate. "My name is Mordred, lady," he replied. "I am half brother to the princes, a bastard of the queen Morgause." He paused. I was not going to press him further, but he gave me the rest without my asking, baring his shame without a tremor. "I do not know my father's name."

I could not read his expression; he was so self-contained. I could see nothing there but bright intelligence, the flash of a mind working.

"Your father's name is none of my concern." I looked at them all. "You are nephews to the High King Arthur. On his behalf, I welcome you to Camelot."

I made them a reverence, and Ferron made them kneel. I walked past them and unfastened the scarf, letting my hair fall down my back. Gawaine and his brothers made the sign against bewitchment.

"Tell them, Ferron, after I am gone."

I left through the archway that led back to the palace. But before I had slipped into its shadows, I heard Ferron's angry hiss: "Now you've done it, you pagan scoundrels! Cooked your goose your first day here! Can't you tell breeding when you see it? That was the Queen!"

I had no sleep that night. My restless pacing awakened Ailsa, and she came into my chamber with a sleeping draught. But I refused it. "Thank you for the thought, dear Ailsa. I'm sorry that I woke you. Return to your rest, and I will walk in the garden."

"At this time of year, my lady? You'll catch your death of cold! I will not hear of it! Come to me, child, and tell me what disturbs you so." She sat me on the bed and held me, as she had done ever since I could remember. "Now, what is it, Gwen? Share it, make it easier to bear."

"It is Mordred," I whispered.

"Prince Mordred?" She looked puzzled. "He is the eldest of that wild bunch from Orkney, is he not? Why ever do you bother your pretty head about him?"

My hands twisted together in my lap, and I looked away. "He is more than that, Ailsa. He is Arthur's son."

She gasped and clutched her amulets, mumbling her ancient protections.

"I bind you to secrecy, Ailsa. You must not tell a soul. No one may know, until the King makes himself known to the boy."

She nodded, her eyes wide. "I swear by the ancient oak of Bilis, and by the black stone of Eroth, and by Shaitan, the beheader."

I smiled faintly. "It's not as dark a secret as all that. Be easy."

She glanced swiftly toward the King's empty chamber. "I am surprised, my lady, that he would bring him here without your consent," she said nervously. "Is all not well between you?"

I took her hand, amused, for it was she who had come to comfort me.

"All is very well between us. Arthur would never have done that. I asked him to send for the boy. Only—now I am beginning to have second thoughts."

"You *knew* he had a child?" She gasped. "Who told you?"

I shook my head. "I have known for years," I said slowly. "I heard it from a soldier."

"Eavesdropping!" Ailsa cried. "Listening at doors with Elaine! I knew it would land you in hot water one day!"

I nearly laughed and was surprised to feel tears spring to my eyes. "I hope I am not in hot water now," I cried, rising. "It's just that—he is so like his father!" I took a turn around the room, brushing the tears away.

"You have seen him, then," she said firmly, "and he upset you."

"No," I whispered, clasping my hands tight together, "he was perfectly behaved. He—it is the *fact* of him that upsets me. That he exists."

Ailsa knew me and said nothing, waiting.

"Knowing that he existed was one thing—and hard to bear— when he was in Orkney. But now that he is here—Oh, Ailsa! How I wish he had never been born! No, no, I don't mean that—I want nothing more than for Arthur to have an heir of his body— but I cannot look at Mordred and not resent it! It is unfair to him, and to Arthur, I know, but—but there he stands, flesh of Arthur's flesh, with the face to prove it, and I cannot—it fills me with jealousy and—and loathing for my rage—but I cannot stand the thought of it!"

Even to my own ears, my words sounded like ravings. I took a deep breath.

"Is is not jealousy of Arthur, exactly," I said slowly. "The King has a right to share his bed with anyone he chooses. Although," I added with some spirit, "I do not like it, and I think it is unfair that I am not allowed the same—and I have told him so."

"Gwen!" Ailsa cried, scandalized. "You never did!"

"I did. What's more, he agrees with me." I managed a small smile. "So you see, Ailsa, not even Arthur is perfect."

"May the saints preserve you! You always were a headstrong child! To say such a thing to the King!"

I sighed and drew aside the long curtain that covered the terrace doors. But the night was black with clouds; not even the stars were out. "He was not angry," I said, half to myself, "or even annoyed. He saw the justice of my complaint. But he said men were creatures less perfect than women; they were given greater strength, but less control."

"What a tongue he has in his head!" Ailsa laughed, relieved.

"Yes. That is what I said, too." I pulled the curtain shut and closed my eyes. "Oh, how I wish he was here! I need his strength now."

"Have you talked to the King about the boy, my lady?"

"Of course," I replied. "How not? And he is always careful of his speech, not wanting to hurt me." I turned to her then, as the tears splashed down. "But, Ailsa, how it *does* hurt! To see the boy here, to know he is Arthur's and not mine—it is a knife in my heart, truly it is!"

I fell at her feet, buried my face in her skirts, and wept. She stroked my hair and crooned in her gravelly voice, but the wound was deep and I had not yet shared it all.

"I am jealous of his mother," I went on, between sobs, "not of who she is, or of her night with the King, but—but simply that she bore him to Arthur. That is all. Only that. She bore him a son, and I did not!" I wept bitterly. Ailsa said nothing. When I looked up at last, I saw tear tracks on her face, and her sturdy body shook. It was easier for me then, and I kissed her rough hands in gratitude.

"Tell me, Gwen," she said at last, "why did you ask the King to send for the boy? What made you do it?"

I shrugged. "I don't know, really. It came suddenly, one night. I thought it came straight from God. But I did not know, then, how hard it would be." I relaxed against her and closed my eyes as she stroked my hair. "It was the night of the solstice—you remember, don't you? There was something special in the very air. Arthur was so loving, and he—we both—" I sighed, and started over. "He gave me great pleasure that night, and I wished to please him in return."

"Ahhhh," Ailsa said softly. "I remember. I remember his face when he saw you in that gown. Stirred his soul, you did."

"I remember you compared him to King Uther, your girlhood hero."

"Aye. And with reason. They say King Uther had the gift of giving women pleasure. Wherever he went, young girls would flock to his tent. He was known for it. Why, there was a maid in Northgallis, when I was your age, spent a night with him as he passed through Wales. And when she married, her husband prized her for the joy she took in the marriage bed. Like you."

"Ailsa! How you talk!"

"Would you care to hear the story?"

"Certainly not!"

Ailsa chuckled. "Very well, my lady, but Uther was as skilled in love as in war, they used to say."

I grinned at her. "Like father, like son."

"Well, then, Gwen," she breathed, "you are a lucky woman indeed."

I patted her hand. "How you have diverted my thoughts! Now you have made me lonely. I shall make you stay with me the night and keep me company."

"That I will do with pleasure, my lady. And I will tell you a true tale, by your leave, of something that happened in my village when I was a girl."

"Does King Uther come into it?"

"Not once," she said, smiling. "Not King Uther, but the Saxons. They burned our village when I was small, and we all took to the hills. One woman lost her husband and all her children. Another family was murdered as they sat eating round the fire, all but the baby in the cradle. The woman was wild with grief, I can tell you. She tore her hair and blackened her face with soot until you would have taken her for a hill witch. The orphaned babe was taken in by a family with seven children, and wailed all day, never getting the attention he deserved. One day a Druid priest came by. Everyone in the village came out to do him reverence, for it is as much as your life is worth to pass a Druid by. He took this woman by the hand, gave the babe into her arms, and bade her raise and tend it. He sang an incantation and blessed her, and her grief was healed. It is a fact that she raised that boy to manhood, and all his life he honored her and called her 'Mother' and cared for her in her old age, and buried her with tears when she died."

I took her hand and kissed it. "I don't believe a single word—Saxons in Northgallis! But I take your point."

"Take him under your wing," she whispered. "No one else will have time for him. Make him your own, Gwen. It will bring you joy."

25 ♛ THE WITCH'S SONS

The King did not return within the fortnight, but sent a courier to say he would stay at Caerleon with Merlin and we should join him there for Christmas. It really was Merlin the Enchanter, the courier said, returned in solid flesh, with nothing much worse to show for suffering entombment than a haunted look about his eyes. This news caused great rejoicing throughout the city. The people were proud of their Enchanter and revered his powers; over the bishop's objections we gave public thanks for his escape from death.

As for the Orkney boys, they were chagrined to miss the King, but the soldier's life at Camelot was exactly what they had always wanted. Indeed, their response to kind, even-handed treatment led me to believe they had not seen much of it before. They were given good horses to ride, only to discover that they could not ride them. They must have had only ponies on their island home, for handling a horse was beyond them. Lyonel himself took them in charge, but it was slow work, except for Mordred. The others had got into the habit of hauling their mounts around by the mouth; but the King's horses had never been handled so, and when the boys tried it they usually ended on their backsides in the dust. Only Mordred watched quietly and learned new ways. He even practiced his speaking and so slowly lost his accent. He was determined, he let fall to Ferron in a rare confidence, never to go back. All his life he had dreamed of the mainland and now he was here, he meant to stay.

They came to me in the King's library every day for lessons. The King had sent instructions only for Gareth, on account of his age. But I had them all brought, the first day, and questioned them on what they knew. None of them could write or read or figure; yet Gawaine hoped to be King of Lothian one day, and the others were not without ambition. Bedwyr was there, and a Roman scholar named Valerius who had gone adventuring in his middle years, ended up in Britain, and had recognized in Arthur the sort of man he said had vanished now from Rome. He shook his head in distress at such lack of refinement and learning in kings' sons.

Of them all, only Mordred noticed he was lacking something others around him possessed. He asked if he might have lessons with Gareth and learn to read and write and sum. This pleased Valerius, and it pleased me. Bedwyr, when he could take his eyes from the boy's face, noted my pleasure and marked it. The other boys sniggered at Mordred. They called him "baby-tender" and "nursemaid," and I guessed that he and Gareth stuck together, either from liking or for the child's protection.

"Prince Gawaine," I said firmly, and saw his chin go up. "Let us say you are a grown man of twenty, and King of Lothian." His eyes glowed, and he smiled contentedly. "You are out hunting with a troop of thirty men. You have made your kill and set up camp. Suddenly you find you are surrounded by your enemy, one hundred twenty strong. By how much are you outnumbered?"

Gawaine's mouth dropped open. Mordred grinned. It lit his face, and he looked so exactly like his father that I drew in my breath sharply. Bedwyr glanced sideways at me, smiling.

"However many they were, I should attack!" Gawaine exclaimed, embarrassed and therefore angry. "I would beat them back!"

"Hmmm." I did not laugh at him, but answered gravely. "When you learn the art of war from Sir Lancelot, or from my lord Bedwyr, you will learn what are the odds on winning such an attack, if it is two to one, or three to one, or four to one. You will learn what strategies are best employed. But how can you know what to do, if you cannot tell by how many you are outnumbered?"

I turned next to his brother. "Prince Agravaine, tell me, if your ship is charged fifteen silver pieces in harbor dues, and you pay the customs collector three gold coins, how much should you receive in return?"

He colored deeply, resenting it. "I don't know . . . my lady." This last after a sharp look from Bedwyr.

"Then you cannot know if you are cheated or dealt with fairly. For your sake, I hope the King employs honest men as tax collectors."

I looked at Gaheris, who was already blushing, and decided enough was enough.

"It is not my wish to advise you," I said calmly, watching them bridle at the very thought, "and your uncle the High King has left no orders regarding your instruction, although I am sure he assumed these were things you knew already . . . Be that as it may, you are free to attend lessons with Valerius. Prince Gareth and Prince Mordred and I will be here every afternoon after the midday meal. You are welcome to join us."

Valerius bowed low, and the boys shifted from foot to foot.

"When does war training begin?" Gawaine wanted to know.

"In the spring," Bedwyr said. "And with any luck, Sir Lancelot will be here to teach you. There is no one better."

"Where is he when he's wanted, and why did he go away?" Gawaine was petulant. Bedwyr sprang forward and cuffed him on the side of the head. The boy whirled and his hand flew to his dagger, but recognizing Bedwyr as his superior in rank as well as age and strength, he gave way.

"You will address the Queen as 'my lady' in every sentence you utter," muttered Bedwyr in a flat voice, "or I myself will send you back to Orkney and answer to the King for it. See you behave yourself."

To save Gawaine embarrassment, I answered quickly. "He is gone to take charge of his lands across the Narrow Sea. He is newly married and is settling his wife there. When the seas open, we hope he will return to us, and then your training will begin in earnest. Meanwhile, learn to ride and not abuse his horses, for he loves them dearly, and if he sees you haul at their mouths he will mount you on something that can take such abuse."

When they were gone, I turned to Bedwyr. "Well, Bedwyr, your conclusions must be drawn. The evidence is clear enough, I think."

He smiled. "Wonderfully clear, my lady."

"Have you ever seen such a likeness? It is disconcerting. On the surface, he is so like."

"But underneath, different, I think." His voice was thoughtful.

"What is it? What do you see?"

"Don't misunderstand me. I like the boy. He's quick, and respectful. I don't think he carries hate in him. He's just not . . . open."

"Would you be, I wonder, in his boots?"

"Probably not," he said, musing. "But Arthur would. In that they are different."

"Well, it is a beginning."

Until the court moved to Caerleon for Christmas, all five boys came every day. Between the three of us we taught them their letters, their numbers, and some elementary history of Britain. It was amazing how ignorant they were. They seemed to have learned nothing on Orkney but fighting, court gossip, curses, and the ways of the sea. They knew who Maximus was only because their mother descended from him. They were amazed to learn I descended from him, as well. After that, Gawaine forgot to say "my lady" less often. I thought Valerius would faint when he found they did not know where Rome was. To them, the civilized world ended at Britain's border.

But it was Bedwyr who truly astounded them. One day, he brought out his lap harp, tuned it, and gave them the Lay of Arthur in his clear tenor voice. They had never heard the whole of Arthur's story, which was known to every British child, and yes, Saxon, too, in those days, but that was not the only source of their astonishment. They simply could not believe that a grown man, a king, no less, would take up a harp and sing of his own will. This was bard's work and not the proper pastime for a soldier. But Bedwyr only smiled and sang with pride.

They sat with their mouths open when it was over, and then Bedwyr informed them he would give it to them again and expected them to have it by heart by week's end, certainly before they left to see the King. They stared aghast. Only Mordred listened with shining eyes and a stillness that went to his very soul.

On most days, I enjoyed these sessions and enjoyed watching Mordred, who learned quickly and took great pleasure in it. But oftentimes, in the evening, I would find myself in unexpected tears and weep against my will. I argued with myself and told myself I was behaving like a foolish, weak-willed woman, but this great grief, like love, seemed beyond my control. Sometimes the light would catch his cheek just so, and I would see Arthur, as he sat upon his horse in a sunlit clearing. Or suddenly, by the movement of a hand, I would see Arthur as he sat at table, toasting his Companions. It was a torture to me, to see the King reflected in this child; and yet it gave me joy, as well. Only when I looked into his eyes, black and secret, did I see the boy himself, and not the King. Thus I took to sitting near him, where I could see those eyes, and gradually, as time passed, was better able to bear his presence. He was not a shy child, but very reserved, and seldom spoke to me on his own. But he seemed to like it when I sat near, and slowly we grew easier with one another.

One day, I was in the library alone when the princes arrived. Bedwyr was at council in the Round Hall, and Valerius lay abed with a cold. I knelt in a recess by the window, looking in the chest for a scroll, and they did not see me. After the first words, I was afraid to show myself.

Gawaine went over to the fire and pushed Cabal out of his way, not gently. "Well, it looks like the bitch has forgotten us. The cat's away, let's have some fun."

"Hold your tongue, Gawaine! Are you mad?" It was Mordred, quickly.

Gawaine laughed. "Why should it offend you, bastard brother? You're no kin of hers. Come on, let's see who's strongest. Give me your hand, Gaheris."

"I know why," Agravaine crowed. "He's fallen in love, has Mordred. Can't you see it when he looks at her? Always fawning and bending his knee. Not content with a kitchen maid, he must have the High King's wife!"

The hackles rose on the back of my neck, as if some phantom breathed upon it. I would not have moved for the world.

"Ha-ha!" Gaheris taunted. "Lord Mordred, is that what you're after? King Mordred perhaps?"

There came a strangled cry from Mordred. "Shut up, all of you! I don't care what you say of me! But leave the Queen alone! Call me what you like. Call me landless bastard, that's your favorite. It's true enough. Well, I pity you heartily. Here you are at last on the mainland, in a civilized country, in the very heart of Arthur's Kingdom, where you have wanted to be since you first drew breath, and all you can do is moan about how hard it is to be a good knight, and make fun of his Queen because she cares about you. And I don't for the life of me understand why she bothers! Our upbringing is no concern of hers. As you so rightly pointed out, we are not her kin. Yet here she is, every afternoon, trying to make us fit to meet the King. Why can't you see that you are being done honor?"

There was a general grumbling. None of them had Mordred's power of fluid speaking. But Gawaine finally voiced his predictable objection. "I'm the boss here, Mordred. Just because Bedwyr treats you specially. That's because you like his music. He's just the Queen's fancy boy, anyone can see it."

"Gawaine." Mordred's voice was exasperated and tightly controlled. "She is grooming us. Patiently. Carefully. Think of what that means. In two weeks we go to Caerleon. Why is such care being taken over us? Can't you understand? Can't you tell how different we are? Everyone else you have met since you came to Camelot speaks politely, wears plain clothes and keeps them clean, eats a meal without spraying it over his neighbor, washes his hands and face daily and cleans his fingers after eating, goes about his work without complaint, and is never rude to a woman. Is it any wonder we stand out? If the Queen works hard at refining our behavior, have you

wondered why? Could it possibly be"—he paused, having their attention—
"could it possibly be because the King will not receive us else?"

There was a stunned silence as the boys watched their futures go up in
smoke.

"He's our uncle!" Agravaine cried. "He may not receive *you*, Mordred,
you fatherless bastard. Why, you could be the son of a wandering harper,
for all we know. But we're the sons of a king. He brought us here. He'll receive us."

"Are you so certain? Where is our mother, then? His own sister?"
Silence followed. "If he so valued bonds of kinship, he'd have sent for her,
as well. Yet you heard the orders. She stays in exile. And we don't even
know why."

"She's a witch!" Gaheris stated proudly. "He fears her power!"

"Are you jesting? Why should King Arthur fear a witch, when he's
been a friend of Merlin the Enchanter all his life? She's no threat to him."

"She is, though," Agravaine asserted. "She hates him. Doesn't she,
Gawaine? We've all heard her say so, often enough."

"Bah!" Gawaine said gruffly. "She'll say anything in a temper. She's
jealous of his power, is all. Even she is afraid of it."

"She is not!" Gaheris screamed on a rising note.

"Then why isn't she here, of her own will?" Mordred's quiet voice cut
through the panic. "She feared even the King's commander, who led our
escort. And what she fears, she hates."

"Let her come," Gawaine declared, "if she dares. I, for one, would welcome her, but as a King's man, not as a witch's son."

"She *will* come!" bleated Gaheris. "You wait and see! She *will*!"

"She'd better not," Mordred warned.

"Arthur will not harm her if she does," Agravaine replied with defiance. "After all, she is his blood kin, the daughter of his father. And he
would not dare, with us here—"

"Would not dare?" Mordred cried, aghast. "Would not dare *what*? Do
you imagine Arthur fears you? Listen to yourselves! What are you, Agravaine, and you, Gaheris, against even one of the High King's knights? They
are trained men, with real swords, and fine horses. My lord Bedwyr, whom
you dare to call a fancy boy, has killed more men in battle than you have
even *seen*! Don't make me laugh. What possible threat could you pose? You
have not even reached manhood."

There was much shouting and some fisticuffs, but they recognized the
truth of Mordred's argument and changed the subject. But I, huddled in my
corner, wished Arthur had heard it; if there was ever a boy ready and eager
and worthy of the challenge before him, it was Mordred.

They talked about Morgause awhile, and what she was doing all alone on Orkney, and whether they could ever persuade their uncle to ask her south.

"At least she acts like a queen," Gaheris said finally. "Not like this Queen of Arthur's, who looks like a woman but acts like a man."

"Just because she can ride as well as you can walk!" Mordred returned hotly.

"See! I told you he is soft on her!" crowed Agravaine.

"I like her," Gareth piped up. "She smells good. Not like Mother."

Here they all laughed, and I hoped they would let it rest. The Queen of Orkney was known for her use of perfumes and aging creams.

"Don't forget what Mother warned us about her—"

"Do you mean about poison and—"

"Perhaps she *is* evil, in spite of the way she looks—"

"Evil!" Mordred cried, beside himself. "How can you think it? There is not a wicked hair on her head! What has she done to you but paid you honor? And this is how you speak of her behind her back?"

"He has a point," Gawaine granted. "Mother might have been jealous and told us that to make us keep our distance. I don't think the High Queen means us ill. But even so, Gaheris is right, she is too—straightforward."

"Too bold," Gaheris said.

"Too forthcoming," Agravaine said.

"By the Light!" swore Mordred, and I smiled, hearing by the way he said it that the oath was new to him, something recently picked up from the soldiers' barracks. "Is it not refreshing to deal straight with a woman, and not always be wondering what she really meant, where things are as they are, and have no double meaning? Speak for yourselves, of course, but it's a relief to me."

"But she orders Bedwyr around," Gawaine complained, coming to the rub. "He's the Queen's Protector. He's in command here. But she leads in everything and he follows."

"She doesn't lead the soldiers," Mordred said patiently.

"But I heard that she drew the High King's Sword Excalibur!" Agravaine hissed. "And the High King nearly slew her for it!"

"I heard he kissed her for it!" laughed Gareth. I put my hand over my mouth to cover a giggle.

"And guess what else I heard?" Gaheris whispered. "You know this Lancelot they keep telling us all about? They say he is her lover." He paused, having their attention. "And King Melwas, too, who took her and kept her on his island!"

"Well, and what of that?" countered Agravaine. "Mother's had plenty of lovers, and some of them kings."

"Shut up!" Gaheris cried, weeping. "She has not!"

"She has so! How do you think Mordred got here?"

"You fools!" Gawaine spoke with contempt. "A queen without a husband has a right to take a man to her bed. But if Queen Guinevere takes a man to her bed, it is betrayal to the High King. He would kill her."

At last Mordred spoke. "I think you had better not repeat palace gossip until you know more about it. Do you think the High King would have spared Melwas' life if he'd lain with the Queen? These are rumors. How do we know there is truth in them? Men will say anything that sounds interesting in their cups. Wait until you have seen the King and Queen together, and until you have met Sir Lancelot, before repeating such gossip. You might regret it."

"Very wise words," came a cold voice from the doorway. It was Bedwyr, come at last from council. I turned my head a little. The boys all faced him, their backs to me.

"My lord Bedwyr," Gawaine said boldly, "is this Sir Lancelot everyone talks about the High Queen's lover? Has she betrayed our uncle behind his back?"

Then I rose, and then Bedwyr saw me. He never blinked an eye.

"Why don't you ask her yourself, if you dare?" And he bowed low in my direction.

They turned and gasped, all except little Gareth, who ran to me and hugged my skirts.

I looked at them, huddling together in fear, Mordred alone blushing for the shame of his brothers. He went down on one knee, bowing his head, and after a moment, the others followed.

"I am ashamed of you," I whispered.

The slither of metal lifted their heads. Bedwyr had drawn his sword and held it level with their throats.

"King's nephews or not," he said evenly, "I will slay the first man that so much as whispers aught against the Queen. I am the Queen's Protector. Never did I think to have to protect her honor from the likes of you! Uncouth outlanders all! Be gone! Out of my sight before I lose my temper!"

They went white and edged toward the door. Gaheris grabbed Gareth's hand and dragged him away.

"Prince Mordred," I said quickly, "stay a moment. I want a word with you."

Relieved, the others gladly left Mordred to his fate.

Mordred fell to his knees. "Please forgive us, my lady! I know it was unforgivable to say such things in the King's house. It is barracks talk only. We—we are not ready yet to live among you here. I—"

"Prince Mordred." I extended a hand and raised him. He stood facing me, shaking. "I wish to thank you. Not only for your defense of me, but more, for your defense of the High King and the way he has ordered life here. I know it must seem strange to you and your brothers, and it is hard to learn new ways, but your efforts will be rewarded. The King shall receive you. You will have a place here."

His eyes were shining with hope and excitement. "If that could only be possible, my lady—it is what I have wished for! Will we really get to see the King?"

"Yes. At Christmas. In Caerleon."

"And is he really—what they say of him?"

I smiled, looking into the image of Arthur's face, eager and bright and quick. "He is all that. And more. You will see."

He touched my hand very lightly to his lips. "Thank you, my lady."

They all gave me a good apology the next day, with downcast eyes and bent knees and humble demeanors, even little Gareth, who did not know what it was all about. After that, we were easier with one another, but it was never a pleasure to me to be with Gawaine, Agravaine, and Gaheris. The words they had said could not be unspoken. I knew, of course, as Arthur did, that rumors about Lancelot were as plentiful as daisies in summer, but no one had ever voiced them in my hearing.

And what was worse, I knew the three middle boys believed them, for I would catch them staring at me furtively from time to time, whenever Lancelot's name was mentioned, as if hoping to catch me out in a blush or a fever, like some village maiden with a crush upon her lord. It angered me, but there was naught that I could do. They had no sense bred in them. They were hot for one idea at a time, and that idea changed as quickly as the wind. Only Mordred was steady and cool.

As time for our departure neared I found myself growing anxious, and I did not know why. Bedwyr asked me thrice what ailed me, and I could not tell him. I would have shared it with him if I had known myself. I needed Mordred's company; I would seek him out and then when I was with him, I wished myself away. I did not know what drove me. As always, I sought solace riding and spent more and more of my days galloping over the downs at breakneck speeds. One day, I was out so long I made my escort late for the soldiers' mess; my apology made little difference; they would have to get what they could from the kitchens. Myself, I was not hungry, but stayed in the stable to tend my horse and be alone with my tormented thoughts.

Bedwyr found me in Pallas' stall, weeping mindlessly. He put a hand on my arm. "Better my shoulder, sweet, than the horse's mane." He held me in silence until at last the storm abated, and I could draw breath without sobbing.

"Forgive me, Bedwyr."

"My dear Guinevere, what is there to forgive? Tell me only why you weep, that I may know how I can help."

I shook my head.

"It is Mordred, is it not?" I made no answer, and he laid a hand against my cheek. "I know it's Mordred. I've seen the way you look at him. Tell me, Gwen, what it is that hurts you so."

"Don't mistake me, I—I love the boy, Bedwyr."

"Yes," he said. "I know."

"If only—if only he did not look so like Arthur!"

"He is very like. Even Kay is beginning to wonder."

"I don't want Arthur to see me like this."

"He would understand it."

"But he would take it upon himself. And it is not his doing, it is mine."

"Yours?" He sounded surprised. "How so?"

I drew a long breath and steadied my shaking voice. "In a moment of . . . tenderness, I asked him to send for the boy. I wanted—I wanted to give him a son. It was the only way I could."

"Ahhhhh." His face warmed, and he lifted my hand to his lips. "What a gift, Gwen! I did not know it."

I shrugged. "So you see, I brought it upon myself. But now I find—and it is too late. We cannot send him back!"

"Is that what you would like to do, if you could?"

"No," I whispered, "no. He will bring Arthur such joy. And—and I do not wish to part with him myself, now that I have got to know him. But I weep at nights. It comes upon me of a sudden, like a fainting fit. I don't know why."

"I know why." Gently Bedwyr took my arm and drew me out of the stall. We walked in silence to the small room where the saddles were kept, and there he sat me on a bench. I had not realized, until I sat, how weak my knees were. Bedwyr closed the door behind us and lit the lamp. He sat beside me and took my hands in his. "My wife's sister cannot bear, so I know the signs of that grief. She grieves because she thinks she cannot be a woman without children," he said softly. I gasped; the blow hit me squarely and took my breath. "She is not a fool," he went on, "but she is wrong."

"She is right!" I cried, trembling. "All the world thinks so! If you do not believe it, you have not seen their faces or heard their whispers! Ask Kay! Ask anyone!"

"Ask Lancelot," he responded. "Ask Arthur. Ask me."

"No, you are kind and wish to ease my pain. But truly, Bedwyr. Why did the High King marry a second time? He did not wish to. He married to get himself an heir. Do not deny it."

"I do not deny it. It is true."

"That is a woman's duty. We do not fight battles, or rule kingdoms. Do not say I am his companion, for he does not take me with him, and he is gone more than he is here. What purpose do I serve? Out of kindness—all right, love—he keeps me. But there is not another like him in the world. I am not whole, Bedwyr— can you not see it? I am but half a woman, and to hear others talk, half a man. I ride, I hawk, I jest with his Companions, I dared to lift the Sword—what am I fit for? Truly, I do wonder: Why am I here?"

Bedwyr had bowed his head, but now he lifted his face to me, and I caught my breath at the glow of love and compassion I saw there. He rose and looked down upon me.

"Guinevere," he said, "I can hardly believe my ears." He took a turn around the room and returning, knelt before me. "Listen to me a moment. I am going to talk to you about Arthur."

Surprised, for I had expected him to try and appease me with the usual compliments, I nodded.

"I have known him a long time, and I know him well. We were boys together. He was always a leader; I know that is not hard to imagine. He was always the best at games, the swiftest runner, the most daring rider, had the truest aim and the quickest arm. He led and I followed. His bravery astonished me. His compassion won my love. But even at ten I knew he was not whole." He paused. "There is that in Arthur which drives him to—reach out, to share, to draw in others to him. He has always been seeking something. Back then, though we thought him the bastard of one of Ector's petty nobles, in my eyes he was a king. He was so able, so confident, so sure."

"Yes," I said quickly. "I know what you mean."

"But in his soul, Gwen, he was lonely. He had no one to match him. For a time, Merlin filled that space. Those early years, just after his crowning, they were good ones. Good fellowship with soldiers, planning battles, knowing Merlin was behind him—he was almost at peace. Then, as he grew, Lancelot and I were dearer to him, almost dear enough. But his is a great heart, and a great need. Together, we could not fill it. When he married the Cornish princess, we had hopes—she was bright and gay and made him laugh. But, for whatever reason, he did not love her, and until her dreadful death, she touched him not."

"Bedwyr, you are very kind, but—"

"Hear me out. This is important. I cannot begin to tell you what you mean to him. But I can tell you that what he always sought, he has found in you. Now he is the man it was always in him to be. Now he is whole. Shall I tell you what he was like when you lay on Ynys Witrin, a prisoner of Melwas? Do you think you have seen anger? Or agony? Or cold fury? You have not, if you did not see the King. Do you want to know what he was like when he learned of your abduction? I am a strong man, yet I wept for him. Ask Bishop Landrum if any other of his congregation has knelt two days before the altar, praying, taking no food or rest."

I stared. "Arthur did that?"

"And more. It is not so much a passion of the heart, Gwen, as a need in his very soul. I cannot explain it. But it is real. From the first moment he saw you he has needed you. I pray you will consider this carefully. I am talking about much more than carnal love. You are his rest when he is weary; his joy when he is low; his quiet song when his ears are filled with human pleas and blandishments. What purpose do you serve? You give the King life. Without you, he would not be who he is."

"What a gift you have, dear Bedwyr! I see you feel the truth of what you say, and I thank you from my heart. No praise has ever touched me so. But—"

He gripped my wrist suddenly. "Gwen! Why can't you see that he would not love you if you were like other women? If you were coy or flirtatious or secretive or light-headed, if you filled your talk with gossip or your days with household chores and cares about children—you know the man! *Then* would you be like other wives, and *then* would your barrenness be a curse to him. But you are a woman a man can speak to! Why, even I—" He blushed suddenly and grinned. "Even I cannot speak to my dear wife as I speak to you. This is a gift, Gwen. Do not mistake it for manliness. That you, of all people, could ever think yourself unwomanly!"

I pressed a finger against his lips to stop him. "Oh, Bedwyr, I do thank you. I take your meaning. You are telling me that the things I do not value in myself are the very things the King values in me. If it is true—"

"Yes!" he cried.

"Then I do Arthur a disservice to have such doubts. Then I have done the right thing, after all, in bringing his son to Camelot."

"Yes!"

"Then I can serve him just by—just by being?"

"Yes, Gwen. Just by being yourself."

"Well, then," I whispered, looking past the window to the young stars, "perhaps the future will be possible to bear. I know his need of me—I have felt it often, although I have never understood it. And if it truly means what you tell me, then—why then, I am able to give to Arthur the gift he gives to me."

Bedwyr smiled and uttered a quiet prayer to Mithra. "Blessed are the givers, for they are the bearers of Light."

26 ♛ THE MEETING

We rode into Caerleon on the twelfth day of December. It had snowed hard all day, and the going was slow. To prevent our freezing, Bedwyr rode ahead with those of us on horseback and half a troop of mounted soldiers, leaving Kay and the wagons, litters, and rest of the force behind. I rode beside Bedwyr near the front, and the boys rode behind us. They had a hard time of it. I enjoyed talking with Mordred and often beckoned him to come up between us; but I had to be sure and pay Gawaine his due and spend as much time with him, even though he bounced so much in the saddle he could barely talk. Little Gareth had refused to ride in a litter with the women when we separated from those who moved more slowly, and he clung happily to Ferron's saddlehorn, held by a strong arm, never complaining. The Orkney boys were more used to snow than we were and had names in their own language for all its textures and forms. Of course they argued among themselves which name best applied. It kept them occupied.

We reached the garrison before dusk. Bedwyr halted at the King's house and lifted me down from my horse. He brushed the snow from my hood and cloak and offered me his arm. The sentries saluted as we walked to the door.

"Ailsa and the litters will be hours yet, I fear," Bedwyr said. "I will send another troop out to escort them, and see the boys safely housed in the barracks. You will be all right?"

"The King is here?"

"I understand he is expected. He might be here."

"No matter. I will be attended. Join us later, if you can, Bedwyr. He will have lots of questions."

"Does he know I know?"

I smiled. "No, but it will only need a look at your face. Go now. They are waiting. And thank you for all your kindnesses."

The house was warm, the tiled floors heated from below by the old Roman hypocaust system of heating water to boiling point in the cellar pit and sending steam through pipes laid under the floors. It was the one advantage the King's house at Caerleon had over the castle at Camelot, and it was why we always spent the cold months there. The women's quarters were deserted, for I was the first one there, all but young Hanna and Mary having chosen the litters. I had a hot bath, and Hanna washed my hair. She was shy and said little, but I was tired from the journey and the cold and enjoyed the peace.

I sat before the grate in my sitting room, while Hanna brushed out and braided my hair, and Mary brewed a hot posset over the fire. I must have dozed off, for I woke to their voices, whispering in the corner.

"Did you see him?"

"I saw him well. He rode beside me part of the way."

"So? What did he say?"

"Practically nothing. He is very shy."

"He has eyes only for the Queen."

"Not in that way, surely. She is old enough to be his—"

"Hush, she will hear you. She is not. Only eight or nine years between them. Less than between Queen Morgan and King Urien."

"Well, and what are you suggesting? That he is six weeks at court and plans to usurp the King?"

"Oh, hush, that is treason! I meant no such thing! Only that he admires the Queen and that he is old enough to."

"Perhaps. I say, Mary, do you know whom he resembles? I saw it suddenly, when we rode along. It came to me out of the blue—he looks like the—"

I coughed gently and sat up. At once they came to attend me, but they saw from my face I had overheard them. They were young, Hanna fifteen and Mary a year younger; even so, I had thought them old for Mordred. I made them sit before me, and I took both their hands.

"Listen to me, for this is serious. Young maids will talk and may be overheard sometimes and perhaps misunderstood. You would not willingly do the High King a disservice by your careless prattle, would you?"

"Oh, no, my lady," they said together, eyes wide.

"Well, then, keep a guard upon your tongues, especially where it concerns the princes of Orkney. They are his kin, and it would not do to start rumors you cannot put fact to."

"We spoke only of Mordred the bastard, madam."

"Treat Mordred no differently. He, too, is the High King's nephew."

Hanna nodded, but Mary was braver. "We have heard rumors, madam, about a different parentage for Mordred."

I looked her full in the face, and she lowered her eyes. "I have heard those rumors, too. Do you find me sharing them with others? Do you know if the rumors are true? Well, then, do not repeat them. They are told by people as ignorant of the facts as yourselves. Let be, child, and keep your own counsel. And never let Mordred get wind of this. That would be cruelty indeed."

They were sober after that, and I did not think they would talk. If they did, it would mean an end to gentle service in the Queen's household and back to their parents in disgrace, and they knew it. But I was unhappy to know that so many others besides myself could read Mordred's lineage in his face. It would force Arthur's hand, if he was not ready soon.

At last came the summons I awaited. The King was home and begged me to sup with him in his rooms. I went gladly, as eager to hear of his doings as I was to tell of my own. He must have just returned, for as I entered the antechamber and curtsied, his chamberlain Varric was hurrying away with his soaking cloak and boots, and a score of knights were leaving, laughing loudly and slapping each other on the back. Lamorak I saw, back from his travels, and Bellangere the Brave.

"Gwen!" Arthur took me in his arms and kissed me warmly, and the knights smiled at us as they went out.

"You need shaving," I told him, rubbing my cheeks where his bristles had poked me. "But even so, I am glad to have you back. You left in such a hurry! Although we heard what happened, tell me the tale yourself. And where is Merlin now? Is he still here?"

He grinned and called to Varric to bring a bath. "All is well, you will hear soon enough. But first, I must know—how is the boy? What is he like? Will it work?"

I laughed at his impatience, which was so unlike him. "I have no doubt of it, my lord. Yes, he is worthy. He is good and kind and bright. You need have no fear there. But this I must tell you, Arthur. He has your face. It is stamped upon him as clear as on any coin. I am not the only one to notice it."

"Ah. Well, then, matters must be settled soon, I think."

He was sitting on the settle, pulling off his wet leggings, when he stopped and looked at up me quickly. "You do not mind?"

"If you bathe, my lord? No, why should I? I am your wife."

"God bless you, that is not what I meant. But if you thought it was, then you are healed at last."

As always, Arthur knew my wounds and wished to spare me.

I went and sat beside him, and placed my hand on his arm. The tunic was icy cold, but his hand was warm. "No, Arthur, I do not mind Mordred's coming. I am glad of it. If you can deal with him, we will have a family. He and I, already, are on the way to it."

He smiled and kissed me again, with love. "I doubt not you have charmed the poor boy right out of his skin. He comes from a wild land where life is simple. He has never seen anyone like you."

I blushed. "From what I understand, my lord, he appreciates straight dealing, not having had much of it from Morgause."

"Then he and I shall appreciate one another."

Varric and two slaves came in with his bath, and as they bathed him, I sat before the fire and heard all about his wild ride north on All Hallow's Eve. He had ridden all night and had time to reconsider the likelihood of Niniane's story. It seemed to him, in the cold gray light of winter's dawn, that hers had been a vision born of longing, or regret, or even guilt. But by then he was halfway there; it was as quick to continue and verify the tale as to turn back.

When he got to Caerleon Sir Caradoc, the commander, was amazed to see him, having had no warning of the King's approach. Arthur asked him straight out if Merlin was in the fortress. Caradoc's jaw dropped, and he made the sign against enchantment behind his back. Swearing under his breath, half ashamed for being so easily duped, Arthur had allowed himself to be escorted to his rooms, and there he ate a good meal and went to bed.

"Then Niniane's tale was false!" I exclaimed. "Yet why would she lie? And she had the nerve to follow you here!"

Arthur smiled, soap suds in his hair. "Stay a moment. You go too fast. Have patience, Guinevere, and let me tell the tale."

In the early morning, Arthur had awakened to the quiet calling of his name. When he opened his eyes, there at the foot of his bed stood Merlin, white bearded, white haired, dressed in his familiar dark robe without so much as a fringe of ornament, and with the same black, unreadable eyes.

"I spoke to him, and he answered me, in his own voice. He came around where I could reach him and gave his hand to me, that I might feel his flesh and know him to be real, and not a phantom."

Behind him, the bath slaves paused in their work and exchanged nervous glances. A sharp word from Varric set them rubbing the King's body with their sponges, but even from where I sat I could see them trembling.

"Were you not frightened, my lord, to see him?"

"No. Not frightened. Not of Merlin. He is a father to me, and I am as dear to him as a son. But I was nearly speechless with amazement." He paused and turned to look at the slaves. "No one who loves me, or Britain, need fear Merlin. Akhet, Menor, do you hear? Whatever he is, man or spirit, he is our protection against the evil men do. Think of him as a lucky talisman and rejoice when he is near."

"Yes, my lord," the slaves mumbled, eyes averted. But I noticed that they stopped shaking and sponged the King with care.

"What on earth did he tell you, Arthur? How did he escape from the burial chamber?"

"Ahhhhh, my dear, that he will not say. I, too, wanted practical answers, but he gave me none. He said only that the walls that can hold him have yet to be built. King or no, I could not keep him where he did not wish to be."

"Then he was not dead? Oh, my dear Arthur! Did you bury him alive?"

Arthur shook his head. "He tells me he was living, but not in the world of men. He speaks with a tongue I can scarcely understand sometimes. He says he was with his god, who commands him still."

"Then—then he is not a man?"

"Not as we think of men." Arthur's voice was quiet, and his gaze slipped off into the distance. "I don't know, Gwen, if I can find the words to tell it. When Niniane called him 'shapeshifter' she used the ancient term we use for children's tales—but it will do as well as any other. He is able to assume the shape we knew him by—he can take on flesh and bone and blood, at least for a space of time. But he can also walk among the spirits, pass through time, he says, and sail across the Light. He can do what he wills."

"Did he die, then? Or not?"

"Ah, Gwen, your mind runs like mine. I asked him the same. He told me not to think of death that way. He gave me an answer that is not an answer: He walks a middle road between the Light and Darkness. How did Merlin put it? The god permits, for a while, his flesh to visit where his spirit will always be."

"I don't understand you, my lord. Is he flesh or phantom? Is he not returned forever, and if not, how long may he stay?"

Arthur shook his head, sending water flying. Akhet knelt hastily to wipe the floor; not stealthily enough—Arthur turned and begged his pardon.

"I cannot answer you, Guinevere. He is what he wills to be. In Merlin's words, his body failed him before his work was done; the god has granted him a gift and has let him return to see it completed. His magic and his Sight he has bequeathed to Niniane. He needs them not. Merlin the Enchanter is dead, indeed. But his power will reach out to us in our time of need: When we need to see him, he will take shape for us; when we need his counsel, his voice will speak into our ears. And when at length we need him no longer, he will vanish." He paused. "Does that help?"

"I hardly know. Where is he, when he has no shape and yet he speaks?"

Arthur shrugged. "In the gloaming. Between the stars. I am giving you Merlin's words, my dear, don't be impatient. I cannot enlighten you more. I don't understand it myself. It is enough for me that he is here." As he spoke, his voice tightened, and I heard in it the love and pain he felt for the man who had been by his side so long.

While Varric shaved him, I asked him if it might not be true, after all, that Niniane bewitched him and took his strength, so that he passed for dead but yet was living. Perhaps Merlin's pride might not allow him to admit this, even to the King. He took a long time to reply, but at last, while Varric packed away his razor, he sighed and shook his head.

"No. I put this to him, in a fashion, and he denied it. I know Bedwyr thinks it, and Kay, and others; I have wondered once or twice myself—"

"Do you suspect her, then?"

"I cannot suspect her and keep her as my counselor. The powers he had on earth she now possesses, but he gave them to her freely. I must take Merlin at his word." He frowned. His eyes were far away. "There are dangers ahead. For you and me." He looked at me quickly. "If we doubt him, he cannot help us. And when Niniane arrived at midday, he embraced her with fondness. Had she betrayed him, it could not have been so."

"Can you really not suspect her? She has his Sight, yet she told you he was dead. Either she has not dealt straight with you, my lord, or she is not the enchanter Merlin was, even with his power."

He stood dripping on the heated tiles, while the bath slaves toweled him dry. "You are quick to condemn her, Guinevere."

"Am I? She was quick to condemn me once."

"Ahhh." I did not have to tell him. He knew. Once she had accused me of betraying the King with Lancelot. "Well, it is true she is not the enchanter Merlin was. But had she been guilty of what you accuse her, would she have come to me the instant he appeared to her? And yet she flew straight as an arrow to Camelot, to tell me. You were there. You saw it."

"Yes. I did. Well, I am glad she is innocent of that. But, Arthur, why did Merlin not come to you himself in Camelot if he can go anywhere he wills? Why here?"

Arthur looked away suddenly, and I knew when he spoke he was keeping something back. "There were so many people at court, and he was always shy of crowds. He prefers private meetings."

I did not press him for what he did not say—who was it Merlin did not wish to see?—perhaps it was a secret held close between them, or perhaps the answer would cause me pain.

"Where is he now, Arthur? I must not wait to pay him my respects."

"My dear, you cannot. He is gone. No, not between the stars; rest easy. He's gone south with Niniane to stay with her and Pelleas awhile. I rode with them the first part of the way and was late getting back, or I'd have been here to greet you."

"But why ever did he leave? Everyone wants to see him and do him homage!"

Again, a shadow darkened Arthur's face. "He would not stay. He did not want to see . . . all the people."

"Well," I teased, to lighten his spirit, "if he can come and go as he pleases through the very air, why on earth did he go on horseback, through snow and ice, with Niniane?"

Arthur grinned. "Are you still asking me for explanations? He does as he pleases. In other words, I don't know."

Varric dressed him in a brown woolen robe, trimmed with rabbit, and a plain belt. Then they hurried away with the bath water and towels, and the King and I were at last alone.

He came forward and took me in his arms. "And now, enough of my tale. I am all ears to hear yours."

"Oh, Arthur, mine is nowhere so exciting."

"Nonsense. Yours is the more important, for the future. Tell me about the boy."

"Which one, my lord?" I countered, smiling, laying a hand against his smooth cheek. "If you mean Gawaine, he is red-headed and hot-tempered, with more arrogance about him than you ever in your life possessed."

He grinned and bent to touch his lips to my neck. "You would torture me with waiting?" Another kiss. "When I have been six weeks away, you would stall me longer?" A third kiss, hot against my flesh. "You wish to deny me, to prove your power?"

"My lord," I breathed, slipping my arms around him, "you need only ask."

The entrance of the chamberlains with trays of steaming food interrupted us. I had not realized until the meal was before me how hungry I was. Arthur, too, after riding most of the day in the snow, was ravenous and fell to eating with gusto. Suddenly I began to laugh.

"What's so funny?"

"Oh, my lord, you have some surprises in store for you! Wait until you see your nephews at table—even by the standards of the soldiers' mess they are uncouth. Kay was shocked."

"No manners?"

"None. Could they see you eat, they would mock you for prissy ways and call you my fancy boy, like as not."

His face darkened. "They would not dare insult you."

"My lord, they are boys and have been raised without restraint. All this is new to them."

"They have done it, then? Is that what you are telling me? And who have they called your 'fancy boy'?"

"Bedwyr and Lancelot both."

"Lancelot! Why, they have not even met him!"

"His reputation runs before him. Remember, they have been living in the barracks."

But this was no solace to him, for they were his soldiers. "Was this insolence punished?"

"Indeed. Bedwyr made them fear for their lives at swordpoint. And they all apologized the next day, on their knees."

But Arthur was distressed. "This is not the beginning I had hoped for. I thought you told me you and Mordred had reached an understanding."

"I was referring to your nephews, my lord, not your son. Mordred is altogether different. He has kept his mouth closed, and observed, and is learning our ways as quickly as he can. He even trains his speech to sound like ours. He says little and hears everything. But when Gawaine attacked me—" I blushed. I had not meant to give out the name. "When those things were said, it was Mordred who defended me to them. And not only me, Arthur, but our whole way of life. I wish you could have heard him. You would have swelled with pride. He told them they ought to appreciate civilization, that they should know when they were being honored and not bite the hand that feeds them. He is so happy to be free of Orkney, Arthur. Camelot is a wonderland to him. It is his dream. He is full of impressions and hope. Now is the time to speak to him."

The servants returned and cleared the trays and left wine warming by the fire. In the next room, they turned down the purple coverlet on the King's bed and, bowing, left us.

Arthur poured spiced wine for both of us and stood beside the fire. He looked pensive. "Were you there when all this was said, Gwen? Did they dare insult you to your face?"

"Not exactly, my lord." And I told him about the scene in the library. He was angry, but when I repeated Mordred's words, he softened. And when I came to Bedwyr's part, he smiled.

"Thank God for Bedwyr's sense! I hope he scared them well."

"Well enough. When will you see them, my lord? They have lived for this meeting."

"It was my intention to receive them formally tomorrow. And to confirm Gawaine as Prince of Orkney and, if he earns it, heir to Lothian, as well."

"That will please him and perhaps make things easier. My lord, if I may suggest—"

"Yes? Come, Gwen, you know them. What is it?"

"Wear your finery, my lord. And your crown. Nothing impresses them so much as display."

"Is that true of Mordred, also?"

"Perhaps not so much. But they are used to it, you see. Why, they won't stir from their rooms, even for wrestling, without all their copper armbands and silver buckles. And it would not hurt Mordred to see you in your splendor as High King."

He drained his winecup and held out an arm to me. I went to him, and he held me close.

"All right. If you advise it. But you must dress too."

"If the wagons get here," I whispered, smiling. But he was looking ahead, and frowned.

"Now that I am faced with it, I dread it," he said slowly. "I don't know how to tell him. I must know him first, at least a little. Is he so like? Do I not have time?"

"Bedwyr took one look at his face and knew."

"Did he?" He paused. "And where is Bedwyr now? I have not yet taken his report."

"He was worried about the wagons, my lord. I asked him to join us, but he probably went back with the escort to help them through the snow."

Arthur shrugged and, with a smile, began unbraiding my hair.

"More like, he chose to give us privacy." He kissed me again slowly and sighed. "This," he said, "is happiness. After a hard ride, to come home to a beautiful woman. I believe it's a cure for all ills."

There was a large hall in the King's house, and here it was that Arthur held court, met in Council, heard petitions, and gave judgments. It was not as big as any of the halls in Camelot but was a handsome, well-proportioned room with columns holding up a carved ceiling and mosaics of Roman gods upon the floor. Bright tapestries hung against the walls to keep the wind out, for the house was a hundred years old, and the plaster walls had cracks.

Kay had seen to it, long ago, that a dais was built at one end of the hall, with two gilded chairs upon it. The large one with a Dragon carved upon the back was the King's; mine was smaller, and bore the white stag of Northgallis. Arthur preferred to stand among his knights, or sit at table with them, and not sit perched above them in his high chair, but this formal setting was useful for granting judgments and for impressing newcomers, so he kept the dais.

That morning, all who had come to Caerleon gathered in the hall to see the boys presented to the King. They came for many reasons, but the rumors had been flying, and I am sure most men were there to see what happened when Mordred faced the King. The wagons had arrived past midnight, and poor Ailsa had been half the night unpacking and shaking out the clothes. When I found her in the morning she was cross and grumbling discontentedly. I did not blame her; while she worked, I had been peacefully asleep in the King's arms. I kissed her warmly and obeyed her meekly, and she had me ready in time.

When I saw Arthur, just outside the hall, we grinned at one another. We were dressed in white and gold, with ermine trimmings and jewels everywhere. A great golden torque encircled his neck, etched with dragons and set with gems. And he wore his crown: a simple crested band of beaten gold. Against his dark hair it shone like a diadem. He did not wear it often; for that reason, we all went silent when we saw it, reminded of his authority.

I sank into my curtsy. "My lord Arthur."

He raised me and searched my face. "What is it, Guinevere?"

He did not know he had a majesty about him, a glory of his own that lit him from within and inspired reverence. But all the others saw it and bent their knees. Arthur stood silent. Then he took my hand, squared his shoulders, and led me into the hall.

The first business, as always, was hearing reports from the knights errant. Gereint stepped forward and gave news from the northern lands and the fort at Olicana where the Tribuit runs. The fort there had been enlarged and the pass widened. Now the road needed renovations. But the country was quiet enough.

Bellangere stepped forward and told of his adventures along the Saxon borderlands, of intermarriages and new towns sprung up, where Briton and Saxon lived in wary peace, of children being born dark-eyed and tow-headed. I felt my interest awaken and glanced swiftly at Arthur to see how he took it. He was frowning. Several more were heard from, and then Arthur drew them all together, thanking them well and giving each a gold coin for his service. Then he signaled Bedwyr.

"Bring them in," he said.

There was a scuffle outside the doors, and then all was quiet, and they opened. Gereint led the princes in, Gawaine first, Mordred second, the rest following in order of age. Someone had gone to great lengths to groom them and dress them for the occasion. Their hair was cut, and they wore new clothes of good, soft wool in muted colors—no more necklaces and ornaments of shell, and crude emblems of purple and crimson. Their belts were plain leather, and their boots new. But their copper armbands, crudely etched, they would not part with.

They had been washed well and instructed how to behave. Gereint led them to the foot of the dais and bent his knee. They followed his example, one by one. I looked around for Bedwyr and saw him leaning against the double doors, looking exhausted. So I knew whose work this was. Arthur rose and went down to meet them.

First he raised Gereint, and thanked him for his care of the boys and promoted him on the spot. The boys, still kneeling, were having a hard time keeping their eyes down. Finally Arthur addressed them.

"You may rise."

They looked small next to the King's height, and I saw that even Gawaine had lost his bluster, awed by the splendor around him. The boys stared in wonder at the King's garments, at his torque, at his crown, and especially at his wonderful Sword. For once, they were speechless. I looked at them all, but my attention was on Mordred. Half a head taller, slender where they were thick; dark where they were fair; clear-headed where they were bewildered—he looked Pendragon from head to toe in his plain garments. I was amazed that everyone did not see it. Mordred threw me a quick look; his eyes were shining. The others had eyes only for the High King.

Arthur looked them over well before he spoke.

"You are the sons of Morgause, my sister," he said, loud enough for all to hear. "Kings' sons all." The boys glanced quickly at one another, startled. Arthur was making a confession to the hall, and only they did not know it. "Be welcome, nephews. Now, tell me your names."

Gawaine bowed, trying to be correct. "I am Gawaine, my lord. First-born of King Lot and Queen Morgause."

Arthur inclined his head gravely. "Gawaine, Prince of Orkney, I confirm you as your father's heir. Orkney will be yours. If you earn it, you shall inherit Lothian, as well. Until then, Tydwyl holds it for me."

Gawaine's mouth dropped open, and he fairly fell to one knee.

"Thank you, my lord." A word from Arthur had made him a king and Arthur's servant forever.

Then Arthur stepped in front of Mordred, and the whole room seemed to hold its breath. The King searched his face. I knew what that penetrating gaze was like and wondered that the boy stood it without trembling. He looked up at the King and seemed to lighten and grow taller. At last Arthur spoke.

"And you are Prince Mordred," he said gently.

"Yes, my lord," Mordred whispered. "Only—only I am not a King's son. I am a bastard, sir, half brother to the princes. I do not know my father's name."

Arthur inclined his head. "That is not a misfortune, Mordred, unless you make it so."

Mordred flushed gratefully and sank to his knee. Arthur passed on to Agravaine and Gaheris. They introduced themselves in turn and made no mistake, to Gereint's evident relief. Even little Gareth the King treated with grave courtesy, asking his name, and how he had fared on the journey, and what he liked best about Camelot so far.

"The horses and the Queen!" was Gareth's excited reply, and Arthur laughed. It was a full-bodied laugh of great joy, and others near us joined in. The hall seemed to exhale in relief.

"I must introduce you to Lancelot," he said. "He is a man of your taste." He winked at me, and I grinned. The boys, even Mordred, were staring at him in shock. They were so young, their world was still simple. But they covered their surprise when the King faced the gathering.

"My lords and ladies, I present to you my nephews, the princes of Orkney, and Mordred, their half brother. For my sake, make them welcome here. From the look of them, they will make Companions one day."

Then he signaled to Gereint to take them off. But to this, it seemed Gawaine and Mordred objected. I heard Gereint say, "There is nothing but business left. You would not enjoy it." He glanced quickly up at Arthur, who was tempted to keep them near him, but shook his head.

"Next time, perhaps," the King said kindly, and the boys were led out.

Arthur sank gratefully into his chair, and I leaned over to whisper in his ear. "Well, my lord? What do you think? He is Pendragon all over."

He passed a hand across his brow. "I am shaking, Guinevere."

"Is he not like you?"

"No," Arthur said slowly, collecting himself. "I confess I cannot see it. He reminds me of Queen Ygraine, my mother. Quiet power. Ambition. Quick pride held in with hard control. He has already learned how to endure."

"Well," I replied, smiling, "then we are both right, for all that is true of you."

Then the first petitioner came forward, and he gave his mind to the business of ruling.

27 👑 THE BOAR HUNT

As the great feast day neared, celebrating both Christmas and the King's birthday, the palace was busy with planning and preparations. Arthur saw to it that the boys followed a strict regimen of exercise and study. He provided them all with short swords and spears, except Gareth, and had Perseus, his master-at-arms, begin a rigorous training schedule. Every morning they practiced in the great yard within the fortress walls, and the trained troops who drilled there watched them with smiles. Their idea of a sword fight was to run the blade straight in; they had no idea of strategy. And every afternoon they would gather in the King's library, where Arthur's hound Cabal lay before the fire, and take instruction from Valerius, Bedwyr, or me. I was usually there.

Several times Arthur himself came in to see how they were getting on. At such times they fell silent and began to concentrate. Gawaine, Agravaine, and Gaheris remained astonished at all they had to learn and that the High King himself thought it important that they learn it. One day while the King was there, Gareth begged Bedwyr to bring out his harp and give them the Lay of Arthur. Bedwyr glanced at the King, who shrugged. While Bedwyr sang, recounting the events of Arthur's life, the boys surreptitiously watched the King. He had fallen into a study, his gaze far away. Every now and then a smile would cross his lips. After the last chord had faded into silence, Mordred spoke.

"My lord King, is it true?"

Arthur turned to him a face so full of feeling, I caught my breath.

"Yes," he said simply. "It is a true tale."

From the surprise on their faces, I saw the boys had thought it a myth, like the story of Pegasus, which was also a favorite of Gareth's.

"The Sword of Maximus," Mordred continued, his eyes fastened on Arthur's face, "is that the very Sword you wore when you received us, my lord?"

"Yes." Arthur looked at Mordred, and I knew that for him, no one else was in the room.

"Would you—my lord, would you tell us about the raising of the Sword yourself?" Mordred scarcely breathed; he looked as if the words had come out without his willing, and frightened him.

"I will do better than that," the King said, and had a word with Bedwyr, who went out and returned with the Sword itself, carrying the old scabbard flat across his palms. He knelt before the King and offered up the Sword with reverence. Arthur drew the Sword in silence, his right hand grasping the familiar grip without thought. The boys gathered slowly around, their eyes shining. They stared at it in wonder, but no one lifted a hand to touch it.

"I will give you its story," the King said quietly, "as Merlin gave it to me, and as I saw it myself."

As he spoke, his voice low-pitched and commanding, I watched Mordred's face. The princes were completely absorbed in the King's tale. Mordred never took his eyes from the Sword. When the King came to the raising of the Sword from the stone, and the cold fire that burned in the hilt when he drew it forth in the presence of all the lords and knights, the room went suddenly still. Something holy was there with us, and we all felt it.

King Lot, Arthur told them, had been the first to kneel, he who had been Pendragon's enemy but hours before. Thus all the kings of Britain had united behind him, which enabled him to push the Saxons back from their lands.

"And the Sword?" Mordred whispered. "Will it protect Britain always?"

Arthur's brow furrowed.

"I don't know," he answered slowly. "I have always been told it is my

Sword." He looked directly at Mordred then, and I saw he was embarrassed, but no one else noticed it.

He sent the Sword back with Bedwyr, but stayed and answered other questions about the Lay. Agravaine wanted to know how many Saxons he had killed himself, and Gaheris wanted to know whether his mother, too, was a witch.

"No, indeed." The King laughed. "Queen Ygraine was a Cornish princess, and a lovely one, they say. If she bewitched men, it was by her beauty."

"That's how all the trouble came about," Gawaine added, showing off. "She was the Duke of Cornwall's wife when King Uther—" He stopped suddenly, realizing he had gone too far.

Arthur frowned. "I see your mother has taught you well what she wished you to know." But as he could never be less than himself, he admitted the truth. "It is true your grandfather, the High King Uther, lusted after another man's wife. Duke Gorlois attacked the King's troops, which is treason, and died while Uther lay with the young Ygraine."

Agravaine laughed nervously. "It seems that lust runs in the family."

To the surprise of all, color flooded the King's face, and he turned and walked away from them. Of course, the boy was referring to his mother and her train of lovers, but he had hit the King on his open wound, unknowing.

"It seems to me," Bedwyr said easily, stepping into the breach, "that my young lords would do better to keep their own counsel regarding things that do not concern them. Uther Pendragon was a good king, whatever his faults. He held Britain for fifteen years. His son has beaten the Saxons back and holds us in his hand, in peace. For the first time in five generations, Britons may go about their business without the daily fear of war. Be thankful for it. Now go."

They filed out in silence, bewildered and afraid. Not one of them had any idea what they had done to offend the King.

When they were gone, Arthur gripped Bedwyr's arm in the soldiers' embrace. His face was still flushed. "My thanks, Bedwyr."

Bedwyr shrugged. "It was a small service, my lord. He referred to Morgause."

Arthur grimaced. "I know it now." He glanced swiftly at me, still embarrassed. "But there was truth in what he said, and we all know it."

Since the King had confirmed him the heir of Orkney and Lothian, Gawaine had been friendlier to Mordred. Secure in his superior position to the older boy, he now treated him with an easy condescension. Mordred bore it without change of demeanor; he took it as Gawaine's due and did not resent it. But I resented it on his behalf and wished Arthur could bring himself to talk to his son. He was not without deep pride, but he had no place in the world, and felt it. He had told me so himself.

Sometimes, after lessons were over, he would stay after everyone was gone and talk to me. For some reason, he had come to trust me and knew I would not babble to others the things he said.

"Queen Guinevere," he had said with wide, dark eyes. "What will be my place here? Not that I expect anything—indeed, the High King has been more than generous to me, seeing I am only his sister's bastard. And I do not think he loves me for her sake," he observed acutely, "for he can barely tolerate the mention of her name. But how can I serve him? Has he plans for me?"

I reached out and took his hand. "Yes, Mordred. He has plans for all of you. Why do you think we take such trouble to instruct you? You and your half brothers will be his Companions one day."

"I—I heard him say so, my lady. But I can scarcely credit it. My brothers, yes. They are princes. But I—I have no standing here. Not really. No claim upon him at all."

I knew this must be something the others pointed out to him daily, and I grieved for him. "What do you desire from life, Mordred? What is it you would be?"

He lifted his head and his face came alive. "I want to make a difference," he said eagerly, and I was startled to hear Arthur's very words resounding from the past. "I thought I should die on that godforsaken island, and then there came the summons from the King. And now that I am here, I know that I am where I belong. In the center of things. I feel it. I wish—I wish to do something great, that will be talked about with wonder in a hundred years." He stopped suddenly and withdrew into himself, afraid he had said too much. But the air around us rang with echoes of his words.

"You shall make a difference, Mordred," I said softly. "It will happen as you wish."

He lifted my hand to his lips and kissed it. And ran from the room.

There were hunting parties out every day, and after the boys had gained a little expertise with spears, they were allowed to accompany the men once or twice. On the day before Christmas, Bedwyr organized a boar hunt, for large tracks had been found in the deep woods, and boar would be a great boon to the King's birthday feast. Gareth was kept behind, but the others went. They were gone all day and well into the night. Finally we heard the clatter of hooves in the courtyard and the soldiers' songs ringing in the frosty air. From a window I saw the huge carcass dragged in, saw the cooks' delight as they ran out to greet the hunters, and watched as the men dis-mounted and dispersed toward the barracks and a well-earned meal. I looked about for Arthur and the boys. At first I did not see them; torches waved and flickered, sending shadows dancing everywhere. Then I caught sight of Gawaine, surrounded by soldiers who slapped him on the back and jested with him. Behind him strode Agravaine, angry, if I read his step aright. Nearby a crowd of men moved forward slowly. Could that be Arthur, walking at such a pace? I gripped Ailsa's arm as she knelt beside me.

"Ailsa! Has aught happened to the King? Can you see?"

"Surely there would have been a courier, my lady."

"No, there he is! With Bedwyr. Thank God, he looks all right! But who is that he carries in his arms?"

Two men came running from the house with a litter; the crowd parted for a moment. I gasped. "It is Mordred! Oh, Ailsa! He must be wounded!"

Carefully, and yet with speed, the boy was laid upon the litter. Arthur, with Bedwyr and the rest of his Companions, followed him inside with a solemn step.

I found myself shaking and could barely control my voice. "Ailsa! Send to Bedwyr and bid him come to me at once, if the King can spare him."

I paced my chamber, back and forth and back again, in a fever to know what had passed. How on earth could such a thing happen, with so many people about? How dare Gawaine be so unconcerned? Why was Agravaine so angry? Why had the soldiers treated Gawaine with honor? How could the boys themselves ignore their brother's condition? Surely he could not be mortally wounded—there had been no sense of panic in that yard, but per-haps they had concealed it. I clasped my hands together and spun on my heel. I was not his mother, I could not go to him unbidden. Arthur would send for me as soon as he was able, but how long would that be? What would the physicians allow? They were proud folk, physicians, always sure no one but they could understand their art, always eager to prove their im-portance by making people wait. When they made kings wait, they were important indeed!

But Bedwyr was a true friend and would bring me news. On the thought, I heard a step in the corridor and heard his voice answer Ailsa's at the door.

"Bedwyr!" I threw open the door, took his hands, and drew him into the chamber. "Bedwyr, what news? Is Mordred wounded? Will he live?"

"Indeed!" He laughed. "Be easy, Gwen, it's a cloud with a silver lining. He was gored, but not badly. He'll be on his feet as soon as they have leeched and bound him."

"Gored?" I cried. "By the boar? Was no one with him? How did such a thing happen?"

Ailsa plucked at my elbow to remind me of my manners. I begged

Bedwyr to sit with us by the hearth and sent Hanna for some wine. Ailsa brought him warmed water to wash his hands in, for he had come straight from the hunt, and his tunic bore witness to the slaughter of the great beast.

"Never mind," I told him when he begged pardon for his condition. "I don't mind the smell of boar's blood. But tell me how such a thing could happen, with so many people about to watch over the princes? Was everyone looking the other way?"

"Nay, my lady, pray do not accuse us of negligence. It's not easy to ride keeper on those boys, but because the King was with us, they were well enough behaved. It was just an accident, the kind that may befall anyone, any day."

"Tell me!"

"It was past nightfall when we cornered her, near her lair. I won't name all the knights who killed her—Arthur's was the first spear she felt, and mine the second, but I reckon she didn't begin to lose her fight until she carried fifty. During the chase, the charges, and the battle, be sure the boys were kept away and safe. Indeed, I don't think Gaheris had much stomach for it, but Gawaine was keen enough. At last, when she was on her knees and dying, the King allowed Gawaine to take his shot. It was a good throw, caught her in the throat, and she bellowed mightily. Then Agravaine, impatient for glory, and seeing Arthur signal for the kill, quickly threw his spear—too quickly; his horse shied, unseated him, and dumped him in the snow. The boar turned suddenly and heaved herself up for one last charge. No one expected it—she was all but dead, but boars are unpredictable, that's why protocol must be observed. She whirled and came at him, head down. Agravaine screamed, which only spurred her on. The fool tried to stand and flee, but he'd caught his foot in a buried branch and his horse had run beyond his reach. Mordred, who was nearest, threw himself on top of Agravaine and kept them both down, deep in the snow and as still as he could. Her tusks had been broken in the fight and were sharp as razors. Mordred was lucky she was spent. She gave him a thrust in the side and then died at his very feet."

"Where was Arthur? Did he see it?"

"Indeed, my lady. We all saw it. But it happened too fast to prevent. He was at the boy's side in an instant, with a complexion paler than the snow. But it's a shallow wound, and bled well. That's a good sign. He'll recover."

"Bleeding is a good sign?"

"Indeed. It's always so. A good bleeding prevents festering."

I shuddered, and Bedwyr smiled. "This is something every soldier knows. But you need not know it, my lady."

"On the contrary. I am a soldier's wife." Hanna arrived with the wine, and while she served Bedwyr I rose and walked about. "Bedwyr, you must be leaving something out. I see now why the men congratulated Gawaine. I grew up with five brothers; I know it's good luck to land a spear on your first boar hunt. But why is Agravaine angry? And why, if the wound is a small one, did Arthur carry the boy himself, and why does he tend him still?"

"Ahhhh," Bedwyr said, setting down his winecup. I was bewildered by the satisfaction on his face. "I told you it was a cloud with a silver lining. Hear the rest. Once they saw Mordred was not mortally wounded, those ill-bred outlanders turned on him quicker than a whiplash. Gawaine was annoyed that Mordred stole his thunder and had all the King's attention. He felt he deserved praise for his stroke, but because of what followed, he never got it. Agravaine was furious all around. Of course it was his own fault, but he would not admit it. He resented Mordred's protection, he was embarrassed the soldiers were blaming his hot-headedness for the whole mishap, and he took a tongue-lashing from Gawaine, as well, in front of everyone. Gaheris, the coward, stayed well out of it. The minute blood is spilled, he heads for the women's skirts."

"Easy, Bedwyr. He's little more than a child. Give him time."

"Time, my lady, will not change him."

"Was there a fight, then, between the boys?"

"Oh no, with the King there, it never came to blows. When they turned on Mordred they contented themselves with calling names."

"In front of Arthur?"

"It all took place in front of Arthur." Bedwyr shrugged. "And why not? None of them knew they had any reason to fear the King. They are true-born princes. Who is Mordred but Morgause's by-blow? No, it never occurred to them to temper their tongues."

"At last!" I cried. "At last he sees what his silence forces Mordred to endure!"

"Normally, those boys stand together, but let anyone do Mordred honor, or even look at him twice, and that is a distinction they are over-quick to make. They were all ashamed they had not done what Mordred did."

"And so they should be. They taunted him, then, in front of the King? What did they say?"

"I can't repeat all of it, Gwen, but most of it had to do with his parentage. How dare he try to save Agravaine, a king's son, when Mordred was, as everyone knew, the bastard seed of a witch and her lovesick fancy boy."

"Oh, Bedwyr!"

"That's a mild sample. They let Mordred know in no uncertain terms that he'd taken a liberty he had no right to take. He'd gone above his station, presumed a privilege he had no prayer of ever earning, his pretensions to rank insulted them all, and more of the same."

"I see. And everything they said wounded Arthur to the core. At last he understands Mordred needs the protection only he can give him. But how did Mordred take this?"

"Usually he takes it without the flicker of an eyelash. But tonight he was in pain and frightened and had no defense against such insults. He said nothing to them, but his eyes were wet, and when they had finally stopped and turned away, he swore viciously in the Orkney tongue. And then, in a low voice he thought no one else could hear, he cursed his father, whoever he might be, for begetting him and disappearing, leaving him no word, no legacy, no name, no armor against such insults. He was already, he avowed, a better man than his father would ever be."

I began to smile. "And did Arthur hear this?"

Bedwyr smiled back. "Indeed, my lady. We were both right beside him. The King spoke not a word, but carried the boy in his own arms back to the fortress."

"At last! He will tell him now, to give him back his pride. He wouldn't be Arthur, else."

Bedwyr filled a winecup and handed it to me. "If I am not mistaken, he's telling him right now. I came to you when Arthur cleared the room. Let the last physician depart, and he will speak. I am sure of it. He could not take his eyes off the boy." He raised his winecup to mine. "A toast," he said, "to the successful conclusion of a boar hunt."

It was two long hours before word came. Bedwyr was gone about his duties; around me, the daily routine of the fortress went on undisturbed; the watch changed, the guards patrolled the gates, the barrack lights were snuffed, and Caerleon slept under a light fall of snow.

At first I paced my chamber in a fever and spoke sharply to Hanna when she would have brought me wine. Then I fell on my knees and prayed God might be merciful to both father and son. For Arthur must do what he most dreaded doing: lay open his secret shame to his own son and endure his judgment. And Mordred, who in a moment's rage had cursed his fate, would be faced with another he had not dreamed of, but only at a cost. Too high a cost? Would he be able to forgive his father? Could Mordred, young and pagan as he was, find such mercy in his heart? If he could not, how ever would Arthur bear it?

I was so long on my knees I could hardly rise when Ailsa came to me at last with a hot posset. She wiped my face of tears and redressed my hair, clucking softly and calling me endearments.

"Sir Bedwyr is without," she said, giving my hair a last pat. "There. Now you're fit to see him."

"What?" I cried. "You have made him wait while you dress my hair? Ailsa! How could you?"

"You were not ready to be seen, my lady. Drink that up, there's medicine in it."

It was useless to argue with her in her motherly mood. I downed the posset and hurried out to Bedwyr. "What news, good Bedwyr? Where is Arthur?"

"In the library. Alone."

"And?"

Bedwyr shook his head. "I don't know, my lady. He said nothing. He wants you first."

I fairly ran through the corridors, not caring who saw me. I knocked, but hearing no response, gently opened the door, and slipped inside. Arthur stood alone at the window with his back to me. His hands were clasped behind him, and he looked for all the world like a man admiring the beauty of the midnight snowfall.

I took a breath and gathered my courage. "Arthur?"

He turned and smiled.

"Thank God!" I cried. There was a host of emotions on his face, but the uppermost was joy. I ran into his arms and he held me tightly.

"It is done," he said at last, "and all is well."

"Oh, tell me what happened, Arthur! Bedwyr told me about his wounding and about the things he said."

He led me to a cushioned bench near the fire. We sat together, and he took my hand between his own. The firelight played upon his face and threw shadows along his cheekbones. There was an awe, an excitement, a contained exhilaration behind the gravity of his features. Something long held in had found release.

"First, know that he is not badly hurt. A scratch, really, but it was his first, and frightened him. He is up and about now, and has eaten. He—"

"Up and about? My lord, surely he should rest!"

Arthur smiled. "And will, no doubt, in a little while. At the moment, he is too excited to stay abed."

"How did you tell him, Arthur? I have been on fire to know!"

"His anguish forced me to it, else I might have put it off for the thousandth time. But when he cursed his father, he said nothing that was not true, or well deserved. It was as if he saw into my very soul and aimed his arrows well."

"He did not know it was you he hit."

"Had I told him before, anytime before, these last twelve years, I could have saved him that!" He took a breath and released it slowly. "When the physicians left him and I stayed, he was discomfitted. He felt I must be angry at his outburst—"

"*His* outburst!"

"Just so. Compared to his brothers, it was a whisper. But for Mordred, it was an outburst indeed. He thought, as the princes' uncle, I stayed to chastise him. He assumed I was angry, too, at his presumption. He apologized to me for his rude words."

"Oh, Arthur!"

He passed a hand across his face. "I couldn't bear to have *him* apologize to *me*. The words I've thought so often how to say— they came quickly after that, and of their own accord. I told him I was not angry, but ashamed. His words were not rude, they were no more than truth. He had a right to demand just treatment from the man who begot him. He had a right to be angry for those long years of neglect. I told him that the object of his scorn stood before him and begged his pardon with an abject heart."

"Oh, well done," I whispered, holding tight to his hands.

"He was astounded. He stared at me as if I were a demon from the Otherworld. I lost my composure before those eyes and had to look away." He paused. " 'You are my father?' he asked me outright. 'You? The High King of all Britain? Who is my mother, then?' " Arthur cleared his throat. "And I told him he had lived with her all his life. My own sister. Morgause." He looked quickly away as he said her name, and I lifted his hands to my lips. "I held my breath, waiting for the first sign of disgust or horror, waiting for those vile Orkney curses to strike again. But he said nothing. He shrugged once. That was all."

"He is pagan, Arthur. It makes a difference."

He raised his eyes. "I know. It was not that he forgave me. It was as if there were nothing to forgive. But it is an ancient sin, and was so before Christ walked the earth." He rose suddenly and paced the chamber with swift, long strides. "Remember Oedipus."

I stood. "That was different. Mother and son. The oldest prohibition. And he was a god-cursed king. You are blessed."

Arthur shuddered. "He sinned in ignorance, and yet his fate came upon him all the same." He paused in midstride, and his face went white, as if a shadow fell upon him and drowned his spirit. With a visible shrug, he shook it off. "Mordred was not ashamed. He told me it happens everywhere in the islands—there are so few people, they are all inbred." He stopped and faced me. "Gwen, he told me this to ease my distress." He came back to me and took me in his arms. His whole body trembled. "His first thought was not of himself and the future he had just discovered; it was of me. His first act, given the gift of power, was to offer solace to a penitent. Guinevere, he will make a King."

"I know it," I whispered. "I know it is in him. He is Pendragon."

"I—I took a chair at his bedside while he came to terms with it. With all his ambition, he had never dreamed to reach so high. He hardly dared believe it—I had to tell him the story of how it happened, the part that Bedwyr left out of the Lay."

"You never dreamed it, either, at his age. Yet you knew it was your destiny, when you drew the Sword from the stone."

"Tonight I gave him the same future and lived again that revelation, reflected in his face. I wish you had seen it, Gwen. He was reborn."

I drew his face down to mine and kissed him. "It was well done, Arthur."

"He is young for it, but more than willing. We spoke long about the past. I see now what my silence cost him. As you can guess, it has not been easy growing up as Morgause's sideslip. He has seen his father in every handsome face who's crossed her threshold. To his own half brothers he's as much servant as kin. Yet he has always known he was meant for something better than life in Orkney. He's always been quicker, cleverer, and cooler than other boys. He can see three steps ahead, where they see one. He understood it, suddenly, tonight. I have told him I will keep him at court, with his half brothers, until he is grown enough to travel with me."

"Will you acknowledge him, my lord?"

"I have done so to him. But to the people, no. Not yet. It may be a small sin to Mordred, but for an anointed Christian King to announce such a thing, and expect reverence, smacks of hubris. We will give him his due, and let people draw their own conclusions. There is risk here, Guinevere. I intend no deception. But neither do I desire publication of the evil I have done."

"Arthur, if I can forgive you, and Mordred himself does not blame you, why can you not forgive yourself?"

He smiled sadly. "Mordred ought to blame me. It was my doing. But he has not been raised to know sin. As for you, my dearest, you are far too merciful."

He kissed me lovingly, and I held his body close. But tonight there was no urgency behind his tenderness. The boar hunt and the interview with Mordred had taken their toll. I loosed myself from his embrace and made my reverence.

"God has given you a great birthday gift, my lord. You will want some time alone to sort out your thoughts. If you like, I will retire."

"Thank you, Gwen. You know me too well. By the way, Mordred has asked to see you. He is far too excited to sleep and awaits you in the garden. Go to him before you turn in. He will get no rest else."

"It would be my pleasure."

He was watching me with laughter in his eyes. "Do you know the boy is in love with you?"

"What?" I blushed to the roots of my hair. "You are jesting."

"I am not. He is about the right age for first love, and you have captured his heart. So tread softly."

"My lord! This was not intended."

"Will you attempt to tell me you have never inflamed a man's love without intention? Be easy, Gwen. You cannot help it. Beauty, charm, and sweet temper will sway any man. And as you said, he is Pendragon, and thus your slave."

"Now who is sweet-tempered? You will charm me out of countenance, my lord, and I shall not be able to face him. And you know well he only wants to tell me all about you."

He kissed me good night then and let me go.

The garden terrace had recently been swept of snow. Mordred paced back and forth across it, his cloak swirling behind him. It was not cold, but hushed and still. I pulled my hood forward and stepped out from the colonnade to greet him.

"My lord Mordred. You wished to see me." I made him a deep reverence, and he hurried to raise me.

"Oh, no, my lady, you mustn't. Not to me. You are Queen, and I am still only a bastard."

His face in the torchlight was light and shadow; it was Arthur's face, as I had seen it by firelight, with shadows beneath the cheekbones, the face of a King.

"You are his son. It is enough for me."

"You knew all along, didn't you? I—I always had the feeling when I was with you that I was someone special. But until tonight—" He stopped and shivered. I took his arm, and we walked to and fro, to keep warm and to ease his tension. "I cannot believe it yet. It feels so right somehow, but I cannot believe it is me he spoke about. What a King he is!" Even in the dark, his eyes were bright.

I laughed. "He is indeed. Mordred, you have given him great joy."

"Not half so much as he has given me," he said fervently. "To learn I am Pendragon . . . it is beyond my wildest hope. It is true that I have wanted a place to rule—but Britain!"

"It will not come to you unless you earn it," I said cautiously, not having discussed this with Arthur. "He has publicly declared the Dukes of Cornwall to be his heirs."

He nodded. "I had heard that. I will try to be worthy in every way I can. All I want is a place of my own. I don't mind if it is small."

He had grown up in a queen's house with four legitimate princes already in place. He had never had much that was his own.

"Be patient, Mordred, as the King is. Who knows what is ahead?"

We walked in silence awhile. He moved stiffly, but seemed to suffer little pain. When I looked at him, I saw he was frowning.

"He is ashamed of my begetting," he said in his quiet voice.

"He is Christian, Mordred. For us, it is perhaps a greater sin than for others. All sins of the flesh are so."

"I am afraid, my lady, that every time he looks at me he will be reminded of this shame. I would do anything to ease the pain of that memory for him."

I squeezed his arm. "And so would I. But that is between him and God. Do not worry about it. When he looks at you, he is not thinking of Morgause."

"Are you sure of this, my lady?"

"Oh, yes. Very sure."

He was easier then, but still, something bothered him. "He told me that you think I resemble him, and that others have noted it. Is this so? I do not see it."

"You have his face, Mordred, but for the eyes. Brow, cheek, and jaw. And his mouth." He looked uncomfortable, and I remembered Arthur's words to me. "But you are like him in other ways, as well," I went on quickly. "You are cool and reserve judgment."

"I wish that were so," he said unhappily. "But tonight I swore like a fishwife at my own father."

"You had cause. The King knows this. And you did not know your father heard you."

But this was not what worried him; he shifted a shoulder and looked down. He was coming to it.

"The King told me—he was talking about the day when he first knew he wanted to have a son, to pass things on to. He was standing on a hilltop, surveying the lands about him, with Merlin, the great enchanter . . ."

"Yes? Go on."

"He was speaking casually about it, watching me and smiling, but—but when he spoke Merlin's name aloud—something happened." He went still, and I tried to read his features, but we were facing away from the torches and he was in shadow.

"What was it, Mordred? Tell me."

"It was as if a cloud covered the sun. One moment he was filled with pleasure, and then, when he thought of Merlin, he grew cold, like stone, and looked into the distance. I felt invisible. I felt he was afraid." He paused, and a trickle of fear ran up my spine. I, too, had seen a shadow strike Arthur but a little while before, as he talked of fate. "I know Merlin has power, I know he is long-sighted. Even my mother fears him. His visions, they say, are always true."

"Yes."

"Merlin has made many prophecies," he hurried on, trying to get it out before his courage failed him. "From something my mother let drop once— about my future—and from the King's face when he spoke of Merlin, I wondered, I wondered if Merlin had made some prophecy concerning me."

"If he has, I do not know of it," I said, surprised. "Why did you not ask the King yourself?"

Mordred shuddered. "I could not. He went so still. The light in him went out. It felt like death."

I shuddered myself. "Think no more of it, Mordred. If it means something, you will know in time. Merlin still lives. Perhaps you can ask him yourself."

"Truly? Where is he, then? I thought he was here in Caerleon, but the soldiers say he is gone."

"That is so. He, um, he comes and goes as he wills, with little notice to anyone. It is the way of enchanters."

"When he returns, would you take me to see him?"

I smiled. "Oh, no. You would do better to go alone. Merlin doesn't like me. We do better away from each other."

"How could anyone dislike you? How could there be anything in you that gives offense? You are—you are—" He gulped, and I laid a hand on his arm to stop him.

"It is not personal, Mordred. But to him, I am only Arthur's wife. And I have failed to bear him children. It may be my fate, and Arthur's, but Merlin grieves for it."

He straightened suddenly, as if I had struck him. "I—I am sorry, my lady."

"For what, Mordred? It is no doing of yours."

"That is why he sought me out at last, is it not? Because he has no other sons?" He whirled away from me and strode to the end of the terrace. I stood amazed at his anger. What was in his heart, to make him feel so? When he returned, he held himself stiffly and spoke with constraint. "I see it now. But I will not stay here on those terms. Even more than being the King's son, I want to be—" He stopped, flustered, and then rushed on, "I won't stay here and be a thorn in your side! How can you be so kind to me? Does it not gall you to look at me? How could he bring me here, and insult you so? I will *not* be the instrument of your pain! I would sooner go back to Orkney!"

He moved me to my soul, with his new pride and his sweet infatuation and his generous heart. That in this greatest moment of his young life, he should think of how I felt! Arthur was right; he would make a King. All the bitter heartache of the past weeks lost its biting edge when Mordred spoke those words to me.

"Mordred," I said softly. "Be easy. You are young and you reckon without love. Because he loves me, the King would not have sent for you unless I wished it. And because I love him, I asked him to bring you here, when I knew I could not bear, that he and I might have a son to raise."

He gaped at me and then flung himself to his knees.

"My lady!" he cried. "Then it was you!"

"Come, Mordred." I raised him and hugged him like a son. "Calm yourself. You must stay with us in Camelot. It is where you belong."

He kissed my hand. "I should have known," he breathed in a voice so soft I had to strain to hear it. "I should have known a gift this wonderful could only have come from you!"

And while I stood blushing at his fervor, Mordred bowed low, turned on his heel, and left.

28 ♛ THE RETURN

The court moved back to Camelot at the equinox, while the ground was still hard before the spring rains. Then for weeks we suffered through cold, cloudy weather, downpours, storms, and chills. By the end of April the land was green; trees brought forth new leaves, wildflowers filled the meadows, and the horses bucked for joy to be free in their pastures again.

Arthur had been gone eight weeks to visit Cornwall, to pay homage to his mother's deathplace and lay flowers on her grave. And also to meet with Duke Constantine, Cador's son, his official heir. Everyone with a head could guess what he meant to talk about, but nothing was publicly announced.

Once the weather turned fair, I hardly saw the boys. They were all day with the soldiers learning the skills of war. As they improved, they grew more disciplined and began to take pride in their accomplishments, and to see themselves as King's men. This was a relief to me. Arthur had not left it too late, after all. By treating them with honor and courtesy, he had engendered their affection and respect.

Gawaine, especially, had grown more civilized. Part of this was due, I think, to his feeling at last secure in his status as King Lot's heir. Orkney was his, and Lothian if he earned the right to hold it; this was his pride, and it meant so much to him that he held it in, manlike, and did not boast. Part was due to his recognition of Mordred's status. For the King had told him the truth about Mordred. He believed Gawaine had the right to know. Just what Arthur said to him to make him hold his tongue, I do not know, but he kept silent. He and Mordred had a cautious respect for one another and acted more like brothers than ever they had before.

Once spring came, only Mordred and Gareth came to lessons, and not always Mordred. He was quick and learned everything fast. The only place I found him lacking was in his reverence for gods. All the boys took instruction from Bishop Landrum; Gareth was easily converted, Gawaine and the twins preferred the worship of the Goddess they had grown up with; Mordred remained his own man. He was respectful and willing to bow his head to whatever god was sacred in a place, but never gave his heart. Indeed, the only worship he gave, he gave to Arthur. I did not press him; the King himself paid public homage to whatever deity served his purpose. He told me once he believed all gods were one God in the end. Perhaps, I thought, Mordred would come to this in time. One had to make allowances for the lonely life he had led and the things that had been done to him.

Of Merlin we saw nothing. Niniane returned to Camelot with the court, but when Arthur left for Cornwall, she took herself off to Ynys Witrin and to her role as Lady of the Lake. She had kept away from me of late. At first I put it down to being newly wed; her husband Pelleas was a handsome king in Arthur's service, level-headed and strong-willed, as a man must be to marry an enchantress. Then I wondered if perhaps she knew of my doubts of her I had expressed to Arthur. But Mordred told me it was because I spent so much time with him, and that Niniane could not bear the sight of him.

"Whatever do you mean?" I asked him.

"Just that, my lady. She will not meet my eyes, but whenever she comes across me, looks the other way. A great cold comes from her; it makes me shiver."

"Well," I said to comfort him, "she never used to like me, either, before we got to know one another. I used to think her hostile. She is a powerful magician and not like other women. It is just her way."

He accepted this and said no more, but I saw he did not believe that was all there was to it. When she left Camelot, Mordred breathed easier.

On the first of May Bedwyr and Ferron came to me, wearing secret smiles, and bade me come on a birthday outing. The boys, even Gareth, were all out on a two-day deer hunt with the soldiers, and Ferron was enjoying a respite from their care. The High King, they told me, had left three gifts for me. If I would dress for riding, they would show me the first. When we arrived at our destination, they would show me the second. And later that night, they would show me the third.

Delighted, I did as they bade me, and went with them to the stables. The grooms had their war stallions ready, bridled in gold, and next to them held Rajid, his blood-bay coat shining in the sun, his mane and tail braided with ribbons threaded with silver.

"What's this?" I said, turning to Bedwyr. "Does Lyonel want Rajid galloped over the downs?"

Bedwyr grinned. "He is not Lyonel's charge anymore, my lady. He is yours."

I gasped, staring. A war stallion! For me?

"Does Arthur know of this?" I cried. Both of them laughed.

"It is his gift," Bedwyr said. How far he had come since that first day we went hawking, when he was loath even to let me ride without a saddle!

The stallion whinnied as I approached him and nuzzled me with affection, blowing his warm breath onto my cheek. It was unheard of, for a woman to ride a war stallion. I had never taken him beyond the ring; now we were riding down the streets of Camelot, in public view. It was Arthur's declaration, as clear as any trumpet, that his Queen was due a warrior's respect. Neither Bedwyr nor Ferron was offended; they seemed pleased, and I was grateful to them.

We rode out King's Gate and along the causeway that crossed the rolling downs toward Ynys Witrin. The stallion was fresh, and his spirits high. I had my hands full for the first hour. The pace was easy; the two knights seemed to have no purpose in mind other than exercise in the soft, clear air. We passed the road that led to Melwas' castle and continued on toward the estuary. The sun was high overhead when they called to me to turn off toward the northern hills.

"We will be met there for a picnic," Bedwyr explained. "That is the second part of your gift."

Indeed, as we neared the wooded hills, I saw the tracks of many horses in the dust. The trail wound up the hill, and we slowed, riding single file. Rajid was winded now, having spent the winter in the stable, and easy as a lamb to handle. Near the summit we came upon a group of horsemen in a clearing, dismounted, and gathered around a fire. Cloths were spread and baskets of food set out; clearly they had been waiting for us. But they were not King's men. They wore no badges. I did not know a single face. But they, apparently, knew me. All of them went down on one knee and made me reverence.

Their leader came forward as we dismounted. He was a young man, about my age, and he moved with grace. I caught my breath as I looked into his face; a handsomer man I had never seen. He was tall, and lithe, and black-haired, with downy brows and clear, long-lashed gray eyes. I felt my chest tighten so I could barely breathe. He was the image of Lancelot, except his nose was straight.

He knelt and kissed my hand. "My honored lady, Queen Guinevere of Britain, I am your servant. We come from Less Britain to take service with your lord, the High King Arthur."

I raised him, trembling, and gripped his hand so he could not withdraw it.

"Your name, sir?" It came out in a whisper. I thought he almost smiled.

"Galahantyn of Lanascol, my lady."

I held myself still somehow, remembering the eyes upon us.

"Where is he?"

Then he did smile. "On the hilltop. Take the trail to the left. He is waiting."

Bedwyr was grinning, and Lancelot's men were smiling. They had planned this all, I saw, for my pleasure. I tried to school my pace, but five steps up the path I was running, and when I reached the knoll at the top I fell breathless into Lancelot's waiting arms. He swung me around, laughing.

"Oh, Lancelot! Lancelot! You are back!"

"Happy birthday, my sweet," he said, and kissed me eagerly. I held him close and returned his caresses with passion. When I drew away, I thought I caught movement out of the corner of my eye and, turning, saw Galahantyn coming up the path. He had stopped, startled, and looked embarrassed. Lancelot, an arm around my waist, laughed and beckoned him closer.

"You have met my brother, Gwen? Is he not everything I told you?"

"He is beautiful, Lancelot. But we have put him out of countenance."

He put an arm across his brother's shoulders and kissed me again.

"All the world knows I love you," he said simply. Then turning to his brother, who stood with eyes downcast, he said, "Is she not everything I told you, Galyn? Have you ever seen such a woman?"

"Lancelot, that is not fair," I protested earnestly. "What do you expect him to answer, without insult to me?"

At this Galahantyn raised his head and met my eyes. "An honest answer is an easy one. I do not wonder at my brother's adoration. When I saw you on your warhorse, you reminded me of the tales the Saxons tell of goddess-warriors, and you could have been such a one, with white fire for hair."

The color rose to my face, and I made him a deep reverence.

"My lord speaks with a poet's tongue," I replied. "I thank you for the compliments. I must introduce you to Sir Bedwyr, who shares your gift."

"Has Bedwyr been paying you compliments, then, all winter, in my stead?" Lancelot asked with mock jealousy. His face was near; I could not help it; I kissed him again.

"He is the Queen's Protector now."

"And what is this I hear about a warhorse? You are not riding Pallas?"

"Rajid, my lord. Arthur's birthday gift."

"Rajid!" he exclaimed, distressed. "What did they geld him for? He was the best of that year!"

"He is whole, never fear, yet he is mine."

Lancelot whistled softly. "It is because you drew the Sword!" he said reverently. Galahantyn crossed himself.

"What do you mean? There is no mystery here. The King gave me the stallion I have been working with six months. Don't look at me like that!"

I reached an arm to him, and he embraced me. We both forgot that Galahantyn was there. With his arms around me, he whispered, "Don't you see it is the King's message to his troops? To put superstitious fear at rest, he must make you worthy in a soldier's eyes. He gives you a stallion not two of his best knights can sit and proclaims you royal. Pendragon. It is a sign."

"You and your signs." I sighed, kissing his lips softly. "Oh, Lancelot, I have missed you so!" For minutes then we two were alone beneath the pale sky, alone in the world, heedless of everything but our great love and our joy at his return. When he broke away from me at last, Galahantyn was gone.

"Ah," sighed Lancelot, "I see I will have some explaining to do. Come, let us go down to the others and ease my poor brother's fear for my soul. Let me have the news. What have I missed?"

"More than I can tell you in a day. And some of it is for your ears only. But we cannot be private here. Tonight in the library, with Bedwyr, you shall hear it all."

"I have heard rumors about the Orkney boys," he said, following me down the path. "Has he brought them here?"

"Yes."

"And Morgause?"

"Still in exile."

"Ahh. I'll bet she wears that like a nettle shirt. And Mordred?"

"You have come to the heart of what I want to tell you. He knows."

Lancelot stopped dead, and I turned. There was fear on his face. "He has been acknowledged?"

"Privately, yes. Publicly, no." The fear faded.

"Ah. Well, then. The King is now in Cornwall, I understand?"

"Yes—have you been in touch with Camelot, then? And I did not know it?"

He grinned. "I sent a courier when we landed. Bedwyr thought it would please you to have a birthday surprise, so he sent a message to me secretly, and thus it was arranged. What is the King doing in Cornwall?"

I watched his face closely. "The reason given was to visit Ygraine's grave and pay his respects to Duke Constantine."

"And the real reason?"

"He did not tell me otherwise, Lancelot. But I imagine, as Constantine is his declared heir, he has gone to talk to him about his son."

Again I saw the flicker of fear on Lancelot's face, but I did not understand it.

"When does he return?"

"I don't know. We have had no courier. He is expected any time . . . Lancelot." He would have moved on, but I stopped him. "You had better know that Mordred—that Mordred is dear to me. And to the King."

He smiled gently. "I am glad, Gwen. Glad for your sake, and for Arthur's."

I saw he was sincere and it confused me. "Then why are you afraid?"

He paused. "I am afraid Arthur may love him too dearly. He cannot be King, Gwen. You must see that he cannot rule Britain."

All of my defenses went up at once.

"Why not, if he proves worthy? There is no other child of the King's body who is fit. Mordred is twice Pendragon."

I stopped. Lancelot nodded. "Yes," he said, very softly, "that is the reason. He is a child of incest. You know this. No bishop will anoint him."

Stricken, I turned away from him. "In Wales, when you came on Arthur's behalf to take me from my home, you said yourself—you asked me to forgive the King this sin. I thought you had forgiven him, as well."

"Indeed, I have," Lancelot said gravely. "He sinned in innocence. I hold nothing against Arthur."

"Then how on earth can you hold it against Mordred?" I cried. "He is the one who was wronged! He is the most innocent of all!" I was near tears. I already knew what he would say. But at least he said it sadly.

"Mordred, by virtue of incest, was not born innocent. He will carry the stigma of his birth all his life. He cannot be anointed. Arthur knows this."

I wept then for Mordred, and he took me in his arms and held me. He tried to bring me comfort. "If the King has taken him into his household and acknowledged him as his son, it is an act of great kindness and mercy. Especially as the boy is dangerous." He gasped then, and swore under his breath.

"What do you mean, dangerous?"

"I—I should not have spoken. Guinevere, forgive me."

I dried my eyes and pulled away, to better see his face. "What do you mean?"

"Please, Gwen, do not ask me. I cannot tell you."

Unreasonably, I grew angry. "I command you to tell me!"

He took no offense, but looked unhappy. "My dear, if it were my secret, I would obey you. But it is by the King's order I am silent."

"Did Arthur tell you this? Directly? Or did you guess it?"

"It slipped out once, accidentally, when he was thinking aloud. There was no one else present. He bound me with an oath."

"Well, you have not broken it. I have heard something, a whisper only, that led me to wonder if Merlin had ever prophesied to the King about the boy."

I saw by the way he schooled his face to stillness that I had guessed aright. It filled me with foreboding; how dare the old enchanter cast such shadows across our lives! And where had he gone, that I could not reach him?

"There is nothing to be done," I said at last. "He is our son now and is accepted as such by almost all the court. Arthur may be an anointed Christian King, but Mordred is pagan to the core. If kingship is his destiny, he will not need anointing." I smiled at Lancelot's horror. "Never mind. What will be, will be, to steal from Merlin. Let us go down."

He followed me in silence. But when we reached the bottom of the path, before the last turn that would reveal us to the soldiers, I summoned up my courage and turned back to him.

"Lancelot. I have not asked for your news. Your—queen must have been delivered of the child. Is all well? Are you a father now?"

His smile was one of joy and pride. "She bore me a son at the equinox. His name is Galahad."

I curtsied low. "Congratulations, my lord. May he thrive and grow strong."

He raised me and held my hand, searching my face. "You are not bitter? I did not speak before, not wanting to bring you grief."

"Thank you, my dear. But you know I always wished you well. I pray he will grow to be a joy to you."

"Why, Gwen," he said softly, coming closer, "what has happened, to heal your heart?"

I met his eyes defiantly. "Mordred," I said, and turning, led him into camp.

In hall that night we celebrated Lancelot's return. His brother and all his train were made welcome. Now they wore openly the badge of Lanascol they had hid from me before, the screaming hawk with outstretched wings. All the company were glad to see them, and Lancelot was warmly greeted. It was like old times with him sitting beside me, but better, because Elaine was not there. When the wine went round, Bedwyr rose and presented me with the King's third and formal birthday gift. Everyone waited expectantly while I opened the linen wrappings and the inner wrap of soft black cloth. Within was a necklace of brilliant gems, as clear as crystal but so bright they hurt the eyes to look at, strung on a thread of gold. I lifted them for all to see, and the others were as amazed as I was.

"What are they, Bedwyr?" I whispered, awed at the splendor of their reflected light.

"Diamonds, my lady. They come from a distant land, far to the south. Beyond the Inland Sea."

"How beautiful!" I exclaimed, turning them this way and that so they glittered in the torchlight and even the knights at the far table could admire their sparkle.

"Allow me, my lady," Lancelot said, and taking them from my hand, he laid them around my throat and fastened them behind my neck. The touch of his hands made my breath come faster, and I kept my eyes in my lap. It had always been so; it was beyond my power to control. Then he raised me and walked me about the room so that everyone might admire the High King's gift.

After hall, Bedwyr, Lancelot and I gathered in the library for talk. The men stood near the hearth, and I sat on the settle, between them. Bedwyr told Lancelot of all that had passed, of Merlin's return to life, of the boys' arrival, and what they were like. They were due to come back the next day, and Lancelot was to be put in charge of their sword training, so Bedwyr gave him a full report. He told him everything, even of their poor horsemanship and did not dwell on Mordred more than on the rest.

"Well," Lancelot said, "if they are Lot's sons, they will make warriors eventually. As for Mordred—" He met Bedwyr's eyes and read respect there. "He could come of no finer stuff. It will be my pleasure to teach him his trade."

"You will do him honor, Lancelot, in time. You will see. Whatever you teach him, he will learn it."

A smile touched Lancelot's lips. "Pendragon ambition. It's in the blood."

"And how have you kept yourself, my lord?" I said quickly. "Who keeps your lands for you and your infant heir?"

This was the first Bedwyr had heard of Galahad, and he slapped Lancelot warmly on the back and congratulated him. Lancelot glanced sidelong at me and grimaced.

"It is good to be back. The winter was a long one. Truth to tell, I am not fond of women in pregnancy."

I smiled, to show I did not mind it. "That is a problem easily solved, my lord."

Both Bedwyr and Lancelot laughed heartily and sat down one on either side of me.

"How refreshing it is to speak straight with a woman!" Lancelot said with fervor, holding my hand. "You deal honestly and set no traps for my tongue."

I did not tell him I had warned him; I did not tell him he had chosen it; all this he knew. "Deal honestly with us, then, King of Lanascol. Who guards your coasts? What is happening in Less Britain?"

He stretched, and sighed. "My cousin Bors is regent. I hope to bring him over next spring. But here is something of importance: I paid a visit to my neighbor King Hoel, Arthur's cousin, King of Brittany. Things are happening beyond our borders that may demand Arthur's attention. I have come to call him to a conference in Less Britain at summer's end. Clodomir, King of the East Franks, is getting restless. He covets the Burgundian territories that lie on his border."

"He is the eldest son of the great Clovis, is he not?" I looked up at Bedwyr for confirmation.

Lancelot looked surprised. "He is indeed. I did not know you knew Frankish history, Gwen."

"I only learned it lately. Valerius has been teaching the boys. He was dismayed at their ignorance—they did not know Cornwall was a part of Britain, or that Less Britain lay across the sea—you should have seen his face when he realized they had never heard of Rome! He has taught me much that I did not know myself. Before he came to us, he traveled through Frankish lands and spent a month with Clodomir, and afterward with Childebert, his brother."

"King Childebert's all right," Lancelot affirmed. "He is King of the West Franks, and his lands border mine. So far he has been content with what he has. Perhaps it is because we have Arthur behind us. That is one reason I'd like Arthur to visit us in state. If formal ties of friendship are renewed, Childebert will think twice before attacking."

"Is he himself in danger from his brother, Clodomir?" Bedwyr asked, frowning.

"No, but Clodomir underestimates Burgundian power. If it should come to war, I fear he may lose it. If Clodomir falls, Childebert will move eastward, I am sure of it. And the Burgundians will most certainly move north. Then either we shall have the Burgundians at our border, or if Childebert defeats them, a very powerful Childebert with an empire at his back. I like neither. I want Arthur's advice on it."

I was staring into the fire, thinking about the Franks. Where the words came from that I spoke, I do not know. "The Saxons lie between us for most of the length of Britain—between Arthur's Kingdom and the Franks. They might turn like a sword in the hand, if trouble arose. Or we could deal with them and become an empire ourselves."

"Deal with Saxons!" Lancelot gasped. "Are you out of your mind?"

I turned to him, startled by my own words. "Am I? How so?"

"I beg your pardon," he whispered, coloring deeply and lifting my hand to his lips. "I apologize abjectly. It is a shock to me to hear—from Arthur's wife—we have only just driven them from the land—"

I glanced at Bedwyr, who was silent and frowning.

"Do I speak so out of turn, my lord?" He shrugged. I turned back to Lancelot. "But we have not driven them from the land. The King has drawn a boundary, yes, which they respect. But twenty thousand of them live on Britain's shores. They cannot be discounted. Would they not be better allies than foes?"

Lancelot shot to his feet, distressed, and paced the room. "You cannot know what you are saying! Saxons as allies! It is a contradiction. They are uncivilized Northmen. They love nothing more than killing, not even honor. Show me a Saxon, I'll show you a murderous dog, by God—"

"Lancelot!" I slid off the settle to kneel before him. "I beg your pardon if I have offended you. I spoke out of turn—I forgot how you have risked your life in battle against them, many times, for all our sakes."

The anger went out of him then, and he raised me quickly.

"I have no right to be angry with you," he said gently. "It is my fault. I am an old dog who likes to lick his wounds and prefers not to learn new ways."

His face was near mine; he held it so, and then stepped away. I sank onto the bench and looked up at Bedwyr, who was watching the fire with no expression at all on his face.

To save us further trouble, he pulled out his harp and gave us some songs about the Saxon wars and the valorous doings of Arthur's knights. What with the wine and warm fire and the fresh air and excitement of the day, I am afraid that I fell asleep as Bedwyr sang, with my head on Lancelot's shoulder and his arm about my waist.

I awoke to the warm clasp of hands and the gentle touch of lips upon my own. I knew without opening my eyes who it was, by the touch of his hand, by the feel of his mouth, by the very scent of the man.

"Arthur!" I cried, throwing my arms around his neck as he lifted me from Lancelot's arms. "Oh, my lord! Thank you for such a wonderful day! Thank you for coming home!" He hugged me tightly, lifting my feet from the ground without effort, and then kissed me.

"I wouldn't miss your birthday if I could help it," he said softly into my hair. "We had a full moon, so we pushed on. How are you, Gwen?"

I pulled away to see his face. "I have never been so happy, my lord."

He smiled. "Then you are easy to please—a good horse, a pretty necklace—"

I laughed up at him. "And Lancelot is back and you are home. We are complete."

Behind me, Lancelot rose, and Arthur turned to greet him. They gripped each other hard and then embraced.

"Welcome back, Lancelot. We have sorely missed you."

Lancelot laughed to cover his emotion. "I have missed events of great moment, I hear from the Queen. Merlin lives? And you have thwarted Morgause and called your nephews into your service."

Arthur glanced swiftly about him. The only people in the room with us were Bedwyr, Kay, and Galahantyn, who had come in with the King.

"My nephews," he said firmly, "and my son."

Lancelot grasped him by the arm and held him. "I congratulate you, my lord, on your mercy. You confer great honor upon him. I look forward to meeting him."

Arthur's eyes were dark, unreadable. "And I congratulate you on the birth of your son. Your lady queen fares well? And you have brought me this fine knight, your brother, for which I am already grateful. See how we increase in fellowship."

I made a low reverence, standing between them. "With your permission, my lords, I will retire. You have much to discuss. Arthur"—I met his eyes—"I will await you."

He nodded, and I left them. Bedwyr ushered the rest out, and I waited down the hall for Galahantyn.

He saluted me, and I fell in step beside him. He had been right at the King's side when he awakened me and took me from Lancelot's embrace; he heard the words we spoke; he had seen my face and could judge, if he had sense, the truth and depth of my reactions. But his face was carefully void of all expression, and I could not tell what he thought.

"Good Galahantyn," I said slowly, "your brother is the finest man I know, next to the King. Have no fear for his honor. I would never shame him. All is well in Camelot."

He looked up swiftly, surprised. "My lady Queen! Forgive me, if I gave you cause to doubt me! It is true that earlier today, I was—disconcerted. But I have seen with my own eyes the worship the King pays you, and you him. Britain's honor is not tarnished, even round the edges, but shines as a bright beacon for others to follow."

I smiled. "Thank you for your forbearance."

"Not at all. It was very good of you and Arthur to receive us this evening, especially as I understand you have visitors of state."

I turned to him, bewildered. "Visitors, my lord? Only you and Lancelot."

He frowned. "But surely—I understood—I know I heard them say the queen had at last arrived."

I stopped and he stopped with me. "What queen? My lord, what did you hear? Who said this?"

He shrugged. "Some soldiers. Young men. Outside the barracks as the High King's troop dismounted. I was flattered the King greeted me so warmly, since the voice I overheard had said the queen would not presume to make her entrance tonight."

"Entrance! Whatever did they mean, I wonder?"

"I beg your pardon if I distress you, my lady. I did ask Sir Bedwyr, but he did not know. He said perhaps you would."

"Indeed, my lord, I do not. Do you remember the exact words you heard?"

"Let me see. One voice said, 'Listen, brother, the queen has returned. She is here in the city, even as we speak.' The second voice replied that she would do well to stay away. The first voice then said, 'Do not worry. She will not make her entrance tonight.' That was all. It made me wonder if my brother and I had come at an inopportune time."

I smiled. "You and your brother are always welcome here, my lord. Any time at all you choose to come. I speak for Arthur as well as for myself."

He bowed. "You do us both great honor."

"I don't know who it is who has come among us and is staying away, but I'm sure it will come to light in time."

Then I left him to await Arthur in my chamber and did not give another thought to the words I had so casually spoken.

29 ♛ THE SLANDER

The summer sped by. Lancelot proved to be by far the hardest taskmaster the boys had yet known. Until he came, they had been growing proud of their prowess with their new swords and often fought mock battles in the practice yard with the soldiers watching. As they were the High King's nephews, the soldiers gave them respect on this account; but Gawaine and his brothers took it for respect for their skill with swords. Not for long. Lancelot was aghast at their clumsiness, and only his great love for Arthur saved them from disgrace.

As I expected, Mordred and Gareth alone paid him the respect he was due. He gave Gareth his first sword and thereby earned the boy's undying love. This was a special devotion, one that took Lancelot by surprise. The youngster worshipped him. Mordred was Gareth's friend, but Lancelot was his idol. By summer's end, Lancelot loved him as a son.

Once Gawaine challenged Lancelot's harsh tutelage, demanding to know by what right he could treat the High King's nephews with such contempt.

Lancelot laughed aloud. "By what right? Why, the right to save your skin! I would do my lord small service if I allowed you out in the real world with such skill as you have now! Would you like to see real swordplay?" He had seen the King crossing a nearby courtyard, and sent a page to beg his attention for a moment. When Arthur came, Lancelot tossed him a practice sword.

"I am a Saxon prince, my lord," he called out, grinning, touching the sword to his forehead, "and you are a Celtic dog, bred of the Spaniard's seed, Uther's bastard whelp, Dragon's spawn." The boys gasped in horror. These epithets were well-known Saxon curses, all names for Arthur. Everyone knew them, but no one dared speak them aloud. The King caught the sword in the air, delighted, returned the salute, and advanced, calling "Come, then, prince of godless savages, king of the dung hill, emperor of breeding maggots! Come to me!"

The swordfight that followed left all the boys amazed; for a tall man, the King moved like a boy, quick, eager, and graceful, but Lancelot was swifter, if not as strong, and parried him stroke for stroke. After the first twenty minutes, when all the strokes the boys had learned were displayed, from every angle, with every dodge and feint, and with every defense, the two men began in earnest to best each other. By this time, soldiers had begun to gather, and then courtiers, and then townspeople. The sun rose high, and they grew damp with sweat, but fought on without stopping, inventing as they went. Lancelot turned and leaped like a dancer. His sword moved faster than the eye could follow, a bright blur in the noonday sun. But Arthur was Pendragon, and driven to be the best; he persisted, cool and furious, giving way when he had to, but always pushing on. They fought beyond fatigue, each determined to outlast the other. At last, close to exhaustion, Lancelot flung his sword to the earth and bent his knee.

"I yield, my lord." He gasped, smiling up at Arthur, who stood staggering above him, the sweat dripping from his chin. "No Saxon power can withstand you. You have improved—that quick thrust up from below on my shield side, that's a new trick. I'm in your debt. You're the better man today."

Arthur grunted and took his hand to raise him. "Today and always. Fatherhood has made you lazy, Lancelot. We have been at it but two hours!" And they fell into an embrace, slapping each other's backs and throwing punches at each other's shoulders. The boys, who had cheered at Lancelot's submission, took it all in and learned a lesson in manners as well as swordplay.

The King traveled that summer, north to Rheged for counsel with King Urien, then to Galava to see his old friend Count Ector, Kay's father, thence east to York, and on to Dunpelder to visit Tydwyl. He came home along the eastern borders, skirting the Anglish and Saxon lands. He took Bellangere with him, who knew this area and could speak some Saxon, and he saw for himself what the six years of Arthur's Peace had accomplished. Arthur's justice ran the length and breadth of Britain; hill bandits and marauders had been systematically pursued and wiped out. The people of Britain could go in peace about their daily business, could till the land without keeping a sword at their side, and could count on redress for their wrongs. All this pleased him.

But when he came to the Saxon borderlands and saw the easy communication across the boundaries, the intermarriages, the blood ties that had developed, yes, and alliances, too, he liked it not. A new language was growing there, a broken British-Saxon, that in several valleys threatened to replace pure British speech altogether. He came home thoughtful. I knew from Bedwyr that Lancelot had told him of the words I had spoken in the library, seditious words to Lancelot's mind, but the King never faced me with this.

All he talked to me about that summer was Mordred. The boy was ever foremost in his thoughts. He had grown a head in height and now was taller than I was. If he kept it up, in a year or two he would reach the King's height. His voice had settled in its lower range, and his beard was starting. He soaked up knowledge like a sponge, could ride well, could throw a spear with accuracy if not force, and had grown as skilled with his sword as the least skilled of Arthur's soldiers. He had grown comely, as well, and I noted my maidens' eyes followed him everywhere. But in this it seemed he was less Pendragon than his brothers, who lusted openly after every woman they saw. Mordred kept himself to himself, in mind and body, and devoted himself to learning the craft of kingship.

I had hoped that Lancelot and Mordred would come to friendship and respect. All the princes respected Lancelot for his skill; but except for Gareth, none of them grew to love him. Mordred was always courteous to him, indeed at times he was overly so. I got the impression he respected Lancelot more for his being beloved by King and Queen than for the sake of the man himself. And Lancelot himself would say very little about Mordred. It made me wonder sometimes if he even liked the boy.

Lancelot was with me all summer as Queen's Protector. Bedwyr went north with the King and spent two months in Brydwell with his wife, whom he liked well and seldom got to see. We were busy enough in Camelot; Arthur had called a convocation of all his nobles for the second week in September to discuss events in Less Britain and plan the journey; we were all summer getting in supplies. Carpenters built pavilions to house those of the guests who could not be accommodated within the palace; the stables were extended; the smith were busy at their forges, anticipating new demands for horseshoes and weapons. And in the Severn estuary, the King's ships were gathered and refitted for the hundreds of soldiers and horses and servants they would have to carry across the Narrow Sea.

One day near midsummer, when the King had been gone a month, Lancelot came to me in the small park Arthur had built between the western tower and the fortress wall. There was an orchard here, which in autumn gave us apples and sweet pears, and a lovely walk between rose beds with benches set in the shade of the trees. Hanna was attending me, but as Lancelot came up, she withdrew to a far corner to give us privacy.

He had just received a courier from Less Britain, who brought news from King Hoel and from his cousin Bors. The news from Hoel was all about the preparations for receiving the High King, and Lancelot reported all he had said. Then he fell silent.

"And the news from Bors?" I prodded gently, seeing reluctance in his face. "Is all well at home? Surely nothing has happened to your son."

"No, Gwen, all is well. Except—I dislike to tell you this, but you will hear it from others if I do not tell you myself."

I smiled, although I was uneasy, and held his hand. "Courage, Lancelot. Surely you are not short of that, who called the High King 'Dragon's spawn' to his face!"

He smiled. "That was jesting. This is not. Well, you must know it. I have had word that Elaine is with child again."

I stared. "She would not dare!"

Lancelot shook his head, looking a little embarrassed. "You misunderstand me. It is mine."

I had no right to feel so, and I knew it, but I shook with helpless rage.

"So!" I cried, tears springing to my eyes. "What a master of control you are, King of Lanascol! So eager were you to come to see me, you could not keep from her bed—she whom you claim you cannot love, and who was just delivered of your child!" I tried to rise, but he held tightly to my hands and kept me there. He looked ashamed. "Oh, Lancelot!" I whispered. "Forgive me! I have no right, and she is your wife." I pressed his hands to my lips. "Do not be ashamed, my love."

His head went up suddenly, and he pulled away from me. Mordred stood at the end of the walk, observing us. He came forward with a steady stride and bowed stiffly. Lancelot rose. Mordred's eyes were on the tear tracks on my face.

"What right have you to treat the Queen so?" he demanded, in his man's voice. "Your place here, sir, depends upon her husband's love." He bowed to me, and his voice was suddenly soft. "Are you all right, my lady? Is there aught that I can do?"

Lancelot stood straight as a sword, his face a mask. No one, not even Arthur, had ever rebuked him so. From anyone else he would not have taken it. But for Arthur's sake he kept still.

"Prince Mordred!" I said sharply, and then paused, lowering my voice.

"I do not need protection from my Protector. I thank you kindly for your concern, but I assure you Sir Lancelot has treated me with honor and dealt gently with me in bringing me bad news. There is nothing more to it."

"There are tears upon your face, my lady Queen." He was adamant.

"Women do weep, my lord, for foolish things," I replied, trying to smile. Mordred stood his ground. He had poise, had Arthur's son. "You, my lady, are not foolish."

"Well, Mordred," I said gently, reaching out to place my hand on his arm, "I am a woman and can grieve for things a man thinks nothing of. Sir Lancelot would never willingly distress me. I do assure you of it."

I could read nothing in his eyes, and he had learned to school his face like any courtier. But his body twitched as if I had slapped him.

"You would do well to believe the Queen," Lancelot said evenly.

Mordred looked from one of us to the other and bowed deeply. "My lady, my lord, I apologize. I will honor and obey you, for my father's sake." With that, he turned coolly on his heel and withdrew.

"How dare he!" Lancelot muttered, furious. "The nerve to throw Arthur in my face! I tell you, Gwen, he is ambitious—" He stopped, seeing my distress. "I'm sorry," he said quickly, sitting down beside me again. "I know he is young, but—what is it?"

I shook my head. To my own surprise, I was shaking from head to foot.

"He knows now that you love me," I whispered.

"All the world knows that."

"In a general way, perhaps. But Mordred saw it here, between us. And he saw that I love you."

"Will he misunderstand it? Galyn did not."

I spread my hands helplessly. "I do not know what he will think. It is not a secret, God knows. I don't know why he did not believe it before."

"Ahhh," said Lancelot, "I know that."

"You do?"

"Gwen." He took my hands again and held me firmly until I was still. "The boy is head over heels in love with you. You must know that."

I cleared my throat. "So Arthur told me. I—I had hoped he would outgrow it. He is my son."

"He has grown into it, more like. He would protect you from me, if he could. Now he will add jealousy to his dislike of me. It matters not."

"But it may matter, Lancelot. He does take things to heart. As for jealousy, it is ridiculous!"

But Lancelot was sober. "He is jealous for the King's honor, and for your own. And he does not look at you with a boy's eyes for his mother, but with the eyes of a man for a woman. Let him go to the King with it. Arthur will set him straight."

334 • QUEEN OF CAMELOT

"He will not take it to Arthur." I spoke with certainty. "I know him. He will hold it inside his soul, closely guarded, and someday it will out. That is my fear. I think I must speak with him."

Lancelot shrugged. "You know him best. But go carefully, Gwen."

When Lancelot left me, I sent for Mordred. He came, all stiff and proper and formal. Little Hanna began blushing and batting her eyelids. I sent her from the garden; Mordred hardly noticed her. He began again to apologize to me, but I stopped him, taking his hands in mine, as he had seen me holding Lancelot's.

"Mordred. Do you know I love you?"

Color flooded his face, and his composure broke. "What?" he whispered.

"This is a thing I want you to know, to be sure of, to seal in your heart. You are my son, as well as Arthur's."

He looked down, away. "Thank you, my lady."

"I do not say this lightly, Mordred. For love is bound to honor. I could not love a man, and not honor him, as well."

His head came up then, and his black eyes met mine. He began to understand what I was saying.

"The King your father I honor above all men living. He is my husband and my lord. More than that, he is Pendragon, Savior of Britain. There is no more worshipful man in all the world."

He nodded reverently but said nothing.

"Sir Lancelot is his closest friend and most trusted knight. He and the King owe their lives to each other, many times over. This man I also love and honor. As you will learn to do, as well, and as your father does."

He swallowed. There was something he would say but could not.

"You have been hearing barracks gossip; Camelot abounds with courtiers whose purpose would be served by weakening the King's bond with Lancelot. If you are going to listen to them, use your head, and judge them carefully. Remember this: I am your Queen, and Arthur's wife and servant. Do you understand me?"

"Yes, my lady," he whispered. But in his eyes I saw pain, and adoration, and the agony of unrequited love.

"You are young yet," I said gently, to ease his suffering, "and life is complicated. You will understand in time how it is. Be assured, Mordred, that we have no secrets from the King. His honor is sacred to us both."

Mordred slipped gracefully from the bench to the hard ground and bowed his head.

"You are the soul of kindness and goodness and mercy, my lady," he said quietly. "And I honor you above all." Then he rose and walked quickly away. I was left, bewildered, wondering how it was so clear a message could have so unintended an effect.

Nearly every day I rode out on the downs, in fair weather or poor, with an escort of picked men. Ever since my abduction Arthur had been loath even to let me out King's Gate, but I would go mad if forced to stay within the fortress walls, so he contented himself with sending a small army of soldiers with me. One hot day that summer I rode out when the heat of the day was past, to spare the horses, and came back toward evening, while light still filled the sky. Ferron was the leader of my escort, and rode beside me. We pulled up near the foot of Caer Camel, where a stream ran through the woods on its way to join the river. We dismounted to let the horses drink, and I knelt on the mossy bank to splash my face with cool, clear water. From the corner of my eye I caught movement and looked up. Some ways away an old woman stooped to gather herbs and cresses. Women from the town often came down to the stream for the purpose, and sometimes brought their children here to bathe, but they seldom came alone. I did not think I had seen this woman before; something about her carriage, or the rags she wore, or the way she moved, struck me as odd. I bade Ferron wait for me, and I approached her to ask her if she wanted escort home.

"Mother," I began. She turned quickly, and I stopped in midsentence, startled. Her face was not old, after all, despite her posture, but in the middle of her cheek was a large, black mole, and from it grew a single long, dark hair, so long it bent under its own weight and curved down her face. It moved and trembled as she spoke, so ugly, so fascinating, I could hardly take my eyes from it, although I tried to, for courtesy's sake. Her hair was wrapped tightly in a shawl; earrings of bone, crudely etched, dangled from her ears. Her skin was clear and unwrinkled, with fine lines at the edges of her lovely eyes, green and slanted like a cat's. While I stood there tongue-tied, she curtsied awkwardly, her bent, clawlike fingers pulling at her coarsely woven skirt.

"My lady Queen."

"You know me, mother? I don't remember seeing you before."

"I'm new in the district. But everyone knows Queen Guinevere—by her child's hair." She spoke with a heavy lisp, in a hoarse voice that did not suit her age. Although her words were rude, she inclined her head politely. She seemed to be comprised of contradictions; confused, I struggled to keep my thoughts straight.

"Would you like an escort home? The day is going, and I would be happy to lend you the protection of the High King's soldiers."

She smiled, showing blackened teeth. I shivered. "What need have I of men's protection?" she lisped, and pointed with a crooked finger to the basket beside her, full of lichens, herbs, and moss. "I've powers of my own, my dear. It's men who would do well to fear *me*." The noise that issued from her throat was nearer cackling than laughter. The mole hair danced against her cheek.

"I'm sure, mother, you could frighten anyone you wish."

"I'll do more than frighten, indeed I will." She glanced swiftly at the soldiers behind me, and her voice fell to a hiss. "I'm out to geld the randy stallion who's been making rough sport with the girls in town." She nudged me with her elbow and leered. "You understand."

"I have no interest in such matters," I returned quickly. "Take your salacious tales to someone else."

"Stay, lady," she whispered, as I turned to go. "This is a serious matter. He is a King's man."

"All men suffer that distemper," I said sharply. "Keep your daughters indoors, and you've nothing to fear."

"Oh, aye, wise words from a Queen abducted against her will! Or was it by your leave, after all?" She leered.

"How dare you!"

"It's known all over Britain, lady. What did you do, when the lecher accosted you?"

"I refused him, of course. What do you think?"

"And how much use was that?"

I found myself trembling beyond control. "What are you saying, mother?"

Her lips twisted in an ugly smile; the mole hair twitched against her cheek. "It does my girls no good, either. The ones the lecher cannot seduce, he forces. Three are with child of him now, against their wills. Four babies born last winter, with his stamp upon them. He is a villain if there ever was one."

I shuddered. "A King's man, you say? Mother, bring this matter to the High King himself. Arthur honors women. He will see the man makes reparation."

She held up a fist of greenstuff, with moist, dark roots. "I have a better way, and one more certain of results. See this? This will castrate the rutting stag. A powder of these roots slipped into his wine, and he will never lift his spear again to any woman, even his wife!" She chuckled heartily, the mole hair shivered, and the hackles rose on the back of my neck.

"Surely you would do better to bring this to the King. He will take care of it."

She looked up with narrowed eyes. "In this case, even if he were here, he would do nothing."

"You do not know Arthur."

She shook the herbs in my face. "This is what the girls have asked of Sybil. And this is what Sybil will do."

She glared at me fiercely, and I stepped back a pace. "Sybil, you cannot poison a man so. I tell you, Arthur will see justice done, even to one of his own men."

"Ahhh, but he is more than a King's man. He is the King's dearest friend. So we cannot expect justice from the King." She leaned closer and hissed in my ear. "Not against Lancelot!"

"You lie!" I cried. "It is not Lancelot! It cannot be!"

Her sly smile again. "Indeed? You do not believe me, lady, you of all people? Then do not wonder longer why we cannot tell the King."

"But it's a lie! And you do ill, Sybil, to spread such slanders! Lancelot's honor is stainless! Debauchery is beneath him!"

"As well as you know him, Queen Guinevere, you know him not at all. He has a past that dogs him, like a black shadow, every step he takes. He may spend hours on his knees praying to the Christian God, denying his carnal nature, but when he rises, there is his shadow, back again."

"You lie. He does not yield to such temptation. I know this."

Her green eyes slid sideways, and she lowered her voice. "He does not yield to *you*, my lady. 'Twould mean his life if he did. No, indeed. But when his fire burns, he comes to town and takes out on our young innocents the pent passion of his dark desires."

"No! I do not believe you! How dare you suggest it! It discredits you even to think the thought!" Furious, I wiped away a tear. "I bid you stay out of this business, Sybil. If you poison him with your evil herbs, you will face more than the High King's justice! You will face my vengeance, sure and swift!"

She began to laugh, a low, ugly sound. I turned my back on her when she reached out and touched my arm—a light touch and oddly compelling. "Think, my lady, not of the man, but of the children. Think of the precious innocents he has fathered and the miserable lives they lead. They live in hovels; their mothers are barely out of childhood and cannot feed them. Does he send a coin? Or a loaf of bread? He sends nothing to sustain them, and they are starving." She dropped the horrid plants in her basket and faced me directly. "To you he is a friend. But he shows you only what he wishes you to see."

I drew myself up to my full height, fighting the ache in my throat. "I do not believe you. There aren't any children."

"No? Would you believe Lancelot, if he told you so himself? Ask him, then, ask him about Black Lake in Benoic. Ask him about Vivienne, the Lady of the Lake, and how he used to spend his time with her. Ask him if his Christian father did not beat him for his stolen visits."

I covered my ears with my hands, but still I heard her.

"Ask Lancelot if Vivienne did not prophesy for him:

'You will seek love;
You will find honor,
Glory shall be your reward,
And the sins of the flesh your undoing.'

"Ask him if he did not love her more than life and seduce her from the Goddess. Go on. Ask him, if you dare." She moved closer, and I shrank back. "And I have proof, if you are shy of asking or the coward will not admit it."

"He is not a coward! You have no proof!"

"I will send you one of the maidens he debauched. I will have her bring the child she bore him. Poor girl, she will never get a husband now. Is it any wonder she begs my help against him? And yet she does not ask for death, which I could give him as easily; she begs only for castration. And I will do it."

"No! No, I mean, let me see the girl first. I must hear it from her own lips before I will believe it!"

"Very well. I will send her to the kitchens with a gift of cabbages for the King. Be there tomorrow, at noon, and you may have speech with her. Her name is Grethe." She paused and looked at me thoughtfully. "Her hair is near the color of yours. Perhaps that's what inflamed him."

She turned away, without waiting for my leave, and vanished among the dappled shadows. I watched, rooted to the ground, held powerless by fear.

In hall that night I sat beside Lancelot, but could not bring myself to speak. I had no stomach for small talk. He asked me if I was ill, and did not believe me when I told him nothing was the matter.

I could not get Sybil's words out of my mind; witch, wise woman, sorceress, whatever she was, she haunted my dreams that night and stole my sleep. I was up before Ailsa, well before the dawn, and paced half the morning in my garden, up and down the garden paths, around the little fountain where the water played in the morning sun, trying without success to convince myself my worries were for nothing. Yes, Lancelot was a passionate man, and as a good Christian he fought against his passions. It was true he loved women and had a weakness for beauty, but what man did not? His seduction by Elaine was an aberration; she had drugged his wine; he was not himself when she led him to her bed. More, she had disguised herself to look like me. Even drugged, he had not gone looking for her.

But what was all this talk about a shadow in his past? A sorceress? A lake near his home in Benoic? A prophecy? Surely that ugly woman was telling lies to frighten me. But to what purpose? For the thousandth time I strove to put these thoughts behind me. I could do nothing until I had met with his accuser. If she came.

At noon I was standing by the back door of the kitchens, looking out on the kitchen gardens. The cooks glanced nervously at one another, and the servants hurried about with lowered eyes. I had no wish to disrupt their business, but I dared not leave. I waited until the sundial marked well past noon. Just as I drew breath in relief, I saw a young girl come in by the outer gate. Dressed in sacking, barefoot, she held a toddler by the hand and carried a basket under her arm. She looked carefully about. Her dark kerchief covered a head of bright, golden hair.

With sinking heart I stepped out of the shadow and beckoned her forward. "Pray, what is your name?"

She dropped me a deep curtsy and made her little boy bend his knee. "Grethe, my lady. I bring cabbages for the King." The boy unsettled me. With black hair and gray eyes, he bore no resemblance to his mother. Indeed, as Sybil warned me, she was barely out of girlhood herself; her face had not yet lost the round contours of her early years, yet the child with her could not be less than two. As I looked at those two innocents, hand in hand, eyes lowered, my throat closed and I could hardly breathe.

"Keep the cabbages," I whispered. "Grethe, come with me." I led her to a shaded place in the corner of the building, where steps that led down to the cellars had been built into the earth. I bade her sit, but she would not, while I stood.

"Sybil told me, Grethe, how you got your son. But I should like—I mean, I need to hear the tale from your own lips."

But she only shook her head and would not meet my eyes. I strove to keep my voice calm and kind. "My dear, I would help you, if you will let me. If I ask you questions you may answer with a word or a nod, will you do it?"

She nodded.

"Very well. Sybil told me that you are not wed. Is that right?"

Another nod.

"And that the man who begot your son on you took you by force? Against your will?"

Two quick nods and a turn of the head away.

"Also, that you know the man's name."

After a long pause, another nod.

"Grethe, I must ask you for his name. I will not supply this for you. If you wish justice done you and reparation made, you must accuse him yourself."

The girl trembled but did not speak.

"Grethe, who is his father?"

The toddler looked anxiously up into his mother's face and began to whimper. She leaned down and picked him up and wiped dust off his leggings. Then she looked up at me. There were tears in her eyes.

"Sir Lancelot," she whispered, biting her lip and crossing herself quickly.

My knees were jelly. I put out a hand against the wall to steady myself. She watched me anxiously, as the tears made muddy tracks on her dusty face. "I'm sorry, my lady. Truly sorry. But I had to say it."

I nodded, groping for courage. "When did this happen, Grethe?"

"Three springtimes ago, my lady."

"How old were you then?"

She thought hard, counting back. "Thirteen." I shut my eyes. It was not possible he could have done it. Not the man I knew. And yet she named him.

"Has he—have there been—any others?"

She nodded, adjusting the weight of the child on her hip. "Vorn was the first. But there are others."

"You must—it is only fair that he face his accuser. Can you bide here a bit with the child?"

She looked bewildered. "What for, my lady?"

"I will go and get Lancelot—"

"Oh, no!" she cried, gripping the child and swiftly backing away. "No, never!" I reached out and caught her just as she turned to run.

"Grethe! Here—I will not make you face him—take this coin as my thanks for your courage in even coming." She threw the coin down, not pausing to see if it was gold or copper, and gathering the child in her arms, she fled from me as fast as she could.

I collapsed against the cool stonework, shaking, my ears throbbing with the violence of unvoiced sobs. The terror on her face could not have been contrived. I had felt the same when Melwas—when Melwas—Arthur! I cried silently, shutting my eyes against the welling tears. Don't come home, my Arthur! Gone is your fellowship forever! There is nothing here but dust and ashes! Don't come home!

30 ♕ THE HONOR OF LANCELOT

For three days I kept to my quarters. Every day, every hour, Lancelot sent to ask if I was ill, if I was better, did I wish to see a physician? He came himself and spoke to Ailsa, but she would not let him up the stairs to my chamber. And while I lay abed and fretted, or paced my garden and fretted, all I could think of was the black-haired child, and the others like him, scrubbing for bread in the village while coins clinked in Lancelot's purse and silver armbands gleamed upon his wrists. He could not know! I cried over and over. He could not possibly know those children existed! And yet it was his duty to find out.

In the end, it was those fatherless children who drove me from my bed. I arose, donned a fine gown, and bade Ailsa dress my hair. "Light the torch in my garden," I told her, "and await me here. I shall be back within the hour."

Hall was just ending. I waited until the Companions were gathered in the library, and I went straight in. They had not yet lit the candles; the long summer twilight lingered still. Lancelot stood in the corner by Arthur's table, half turned from me, a frown upon his face. Nearby, Lamorak rose from his seat upon a bench.

"My lady Guinevere! How glad we are to see you!"

Lancelot whirled, his face lighting. "Gwen!"

"Thank you, Lamorak. I am over the worst of it, I think."

He withdrew as Lancelot came up. "My sweet, how are you feeling? I've been worried sick about you. You are pale yet, I see, but you've got your spirit back."

"Indeed, I have." It was all I could do to look up into his eager face. "Lancelot, a matter has arisen that concerns us both. I must see you privately."

The smile died. "Shall I bid the men leave? Shall we go into the garden?"

"More privately than in this public setting. We must not, on any account, be interrupted."

He frowned, searching my face. "Name the place, Gwen. I shall be there."

"My own garden. In an hour. Tell no one."

He stifled a gasp. "My dear, do you really think it wise?"

"Of course it is not wise. But we must do it. Ailsa will attend us. No one else. You—you still have the key to my garden gate?"

He nodded, a trifle furtively. "But, Guinevere—"

"Make certain no one sees you." The light in his eyes aroused my temper. "This is not a tryst, Lancelot. Nor a game."

He stiffened and squared his shoulders. "My lady Queen, I am your servant." He bowed formally. I turned on my heel and left.

He came on time. I sat on the stone bench that hugged the garden wall, with the torch behind me, so my face would be in shadow and his in light. He bowed and sat beside me, more puzzled than worried.

"All right, Gwen, what's this about? It must be desperately important, to risk all this."

"What would you say, Lancelot, if I told you Arthur had seduced—no, I mean debauched, a girl barely past childhood, a girl of thirteen. Against her will."

Lancelot gaped. "I would not believe you. He would not do it. What are you doing, Gwen? Is this a test of loyalty you have devised?"

"And that he had got her with child and knew it not."

"Nonsense. You know Arthur better than that. Who has been telling you lies?"

"More, that he never sent her so much as a loaf of bread, though the child was starving."

"Stop this. It isn't funny."

"More, that she lives here in Camelot, not half a league from his home."

Lancelot rose quickly. "Enough! *No one* has ever said that about Arthur!"

I rose slowly and faced him. "No. You are right. But they have said it about you."

He stared at me, uncomprehending, in perfect silence. *"What?"*

"A wise woman told me. It is known throughout the town. And this girl is not the only one. There are others."

The disbelief, the hurt on Lancelot's face was a knife in my heart, but I steeled myself against it.

"And you believed her?" he croaked.

"I have seen the girl. And the child. She named you as his father. To my face."

His jaw dropped. "What?" I stood and watched him as he paled, sank to the bench, and buried his face in his hands. "Oh, God," he choked, "what have I done to you, Guinevere? You cannot forgive me for Elaine, is that it? You will believe any calumny against me, just because I lay with her?"

"No," I retorted. "Of course I did not believe it. Not at first. God knows—God knows I do not want to believe it now. But I saw the girl, Lancelot."

"Christ!" He looked up. "She was lying!"

"Why?"

"How can I know that? No doubt for money."

"Not for money. Poor as she is, she threw away the gold coin I pressed into her hand."

He stared in exasperation. "Then for love, or hate, or jealousy, or fear—how can I tell? I've never seen her—for pity's sake, Gwen, how can I prove I did not do it?" He rose and gripped my shoulders. "Listen. Put aside your anger for just a moment. Remember who I am, what I have done, what we have been to one another." His fingers dug into my flesh; I welcomed the pain; it kept my tears at bay. "I have never forced a woman—I would not do it—it is an evil; it is sin. You know—who better—how circumspect I've been. The only woman I got with child I married, though I cared nothing for her, so the child might have a name. I have always put honor first, *always*"—his voice shook—"even when it killed me to do it, even when I thought I could not survive it, even when it meant giving you up to Arthur. Ahhhhh, God, Guinevere!" He shook me gently, his hands sliding down my arms and across my back in a long caress. "How could you think I would behave so? I would do nothing to hurt you, or shame you, or cause you a moment's grief. How could you think it? What has happened to you?"

Through tears I looked up into his face. "Lancelot," I whispered, "I know you did not do it! My dearest love, can you forgive me? I—I—I am acting just like a jealous woman!"

He bent and kissed me and held me in his arms. "Guinevere, when you lose faith in me, then am I lost forever."

"I am a fool." I hugged him tightly. "But you have an enemy, Lancelot, who has taken pains to construct a slander. It can't be that poor girl. Who can it be?"

I pulled away; he dropped his arms, and we stood watching one another. Together we sat carefully on the bench, well apart, not even our fingers touching.

"That is the question I must answer. Tell me from the beginning how you heard this."

I told him the whole story, leaving nothing out. When I came to the shadow in his past Sybil had recounted, he rose, frowning, and began to walk about. When I described Grethe and her son, he stopped and passed a hand across his face.

"Poor girl. Grethe is her name? I will find her and—"

"No, Lancelot! She is terrified of you! That's why she ran away, she thought I would make her face you. That is when—when I saw her face—I believed—I recognized that terror, you see."

His face hardened. He, who had rescued me from Melwas, had seen the terror firsthand. "It is not me she's frightened of, Gwen," he said very gently. "But whatever it is, she must be freed of that fear. No doubt someone has threatened her. Someone powerful." He straightened. "This Sybil seems to know a good bit about me. You say she's new here? I wonder who she is, who she's working for."

I watched him standing in the torchlight, thinking hard, a tall, slender knight with a supple body, a man in his prime of life. I looked quickly away and fought to slow my breathing; perhaps it had been a mistake to bring only Ailsa. He, too, moved back a pace.

"Well, Guinevere." He drew a long breath. "I suppose you will want to know about Vivienne."

I nodded. "If you will tell me."

"It's not all that important. Really."

"Mmmmm. Is that why no mention, no hint of her has ever passed your lips?"

He smiled bleakly. "If I do not tell you, you will imagine her the focus of my life."

I did not reply to that, but watched him twist his fingers in a nearby vine.

"In Lanascol, deep in the Wild Forest about a league from Benoic, there is a lake. Black Lake. In the middle stands an island. On the island, when I was a boy, lived the priestess Vivienne, Lady of the Lake."

"A pagan priestess?"

He nodded. "A servant of the Goddess, like Niniane."

"An old hag, perhaps?"

He shook his head. "Not quite."

"Loosen your tongue, Lancelot. Tell me, and have it over."

He sighed and sat on the arm of the bench, a good three feet away. "We were forbidden to go there, Galyn and I. My father was a Christian, and a hard one. He feared the Lady. But the villagers loved her dearly; she blessed their births and deaths, treated their sick, danced with them at Beltane, and led their dark rites before the Samhain fires. We were always curious about her." He stopped.

"Go on. Is this so hard to tell? It's clear you loved her, Lancelot. But everyone has a first love. What is it you dread to say?"

If I was not mistaken, he colored. "It was more than love," he said quietly. "It was obsession. A thirst I could not slake. I put it down to sorcery, until I met you. Then I knew, as Sybil does, the fault lies in myself."

I twisted my hands together in my lap and kept silent. Suddenly I did not want him to go on.

"I was twelve when I met her. After a fight with my father I rode straight out to Black Lake and swam across to the island. To prove I could do it, to defy him. She was waiting for me and called me by my name. 'Lancelot, Prince of Lanascol, you have come to me at last. Don't be afraid, my lord. You are a better man than your father and will outshine him in glory, could he live a thousand years.' I smiled at that. She always knew how to bring me happiness." He cleared his throat and did not go on.

"What was she like?" I prompted. "Dark or fair? Short or tall? How was she featured?"

He waited a long time, and when he spoke his voice was soft and far away. "Dark. Dark hair, as dark as night. Dark eyes, dark skin, as smooth and soft as silk. A voice like honey. A touch like fire."

"So that is why the men call you Lancelot of the Lake. I have often wondered. Does everyone but me know this story?"

The color rushed to his face. "No. It is not much of a story. But those soldiers from Less Britain have heard the name and—well, you know how soldiers like to jest. It is little more than barracks teasing."

"I see. Go on . . . You had just washed up on shore."

"I visited her often. Whenever I could. I had to sneak out, of course. When I was fourteen, she made me a prophecy, the night before my father took me to Britain to fight for Uther at Caer Eden."

"Where he died, and where Arthur was made King."

"My father was wounded there and came home. But when I met Arthur, I found the service I had dreamed of all my boyhood; I found the cause, the glory, and the King. I gave no thought to returning." He smiled briefly. "I was young. But Arthur knew better. For a month each summer, he sent me home to see my father. Of course, I went straight to Vivienne."

"Of course."

"She was proud of me. She called me a man. And she taught me many things my father's priest knew nothing of. About women. About the art of love."

In the flickering light, his eyes met mine and held them. My heart began to pound, and I pressed my palms into the cool stone of the bench, to anchor me there. I could not look away.

"I burned for her," he whispered, clenching his fist. "With pain so fierce I wept. And she always, always quenched the fire and gave me peace and brought me back to laughter." Beads of sweat stood out on his brow, reflecting the torchlight. "It was a sickness of the flesh, a desire so deep I had no respite from it. I thought it was a spell she put upon me. I did not know, then, it was my nature. When I was here with Arthur, it was better; she was far away, and we had the Saxon wars to fight. But let me set foot on a ship for home—I was half mad until I was back in her arms again." He drew a long, trembling breath and slowly rose. "When I was eighteen my father died. I went home to see him buried. Something in me changed when I wore the crown of Lanascol. I knew it was time to say farewell, but when I went to see her, she was not there. Had not been there for months. The village people said she had left them in the spring, when my father first took ill." He held his hands out helplessly. "I never saw her again."

"That's all there was to it? Where is the harm in that? This cannot be the shadow that dogs you, Lancelot. She loved you, and you her."

"She is not the shadow." He thumped his fist against his chest. "The shadow is in *me*. It is the fire in my blood. The fever that burns my soul. It is not the curse of a sorceress, but a flaw in my very being. I will never be free of it."

"Lancelot." I reached out a hand to him, and he held my fingers tightly. "This is a plague all men suffer from. Even Arthur."

"Oh, God! That I could have Arthur's strength! Against my will I love you, Guinevere. I cannot help it."

"I cannot help it, either."

"Vivienne was nothing to me, beside you." He trembled violently; I saw he truly suffered, and I saw, too, how cruel I was to bring him here alone. "There are times when I am not master of myself. Believe the truth of that. Else Elaine would not be pregnant."

"Lancelot, you judge yourself too harshly. This is a common foible, not a curse upon your soul."

"*The sins of the flesh*," he whispered, "*will be my undoing*."

"Perhaps. But with love, and honor and glory, it is hubris to ask for more."

He managed a smile. "Bless you."

We stood and looked at each other. Our joined hands were one hand, indivisible, a sweet secret of the dark. Behind my back I signaled Ailsa, and saw Lancelot's relief when he heard her steps approach.

I raised my chin. "It's time we parted. Everyone will wonder where you are."

He went down on one knee and kissed my fingers. I saw him smile. "There is no one in Camelot," he said, "who does not know where I am."

"You are playing with fire, my lady," Ailsa said primly as she pulled the pins from my hair.

"I know, I know!" I cried, slumping on my stool. "But I had to see him alone!" Through the open terrace doorway we heard the soft thud of the garden door closing and the clink of the key as it turned in the lock.

"Why do you treat him so? What has he done, after all, that other men have not?"

"Nothing," I whispered miserably. "Nothing. But he is Lancelot."

"And what do you want of him? That because he cannot have you, he should forsake all women and deny himself the pleasures of manhood? You are selfish to ask that."

I shook my head angrily, scattering pins all over the floor. "Pleasures of manhood, indeed! What right have men to demand such self-indulgence, when women are denied it, from cook to queen! I tell you, Ailsa, in spite of what I said to Lancelot about a foible, sometimes I think it is merely a convenient lie they tell us, to keep us chaste while they make what sport they please!" I turned on the stool and grabbed her hands, holding hard. "I *hate* it when I know Arthur has lain with some other woman! Even if he confesses it to me himself and begs my pardon—it is a weakness in him and he knows it. *I* do not permit myself such freedoms! And yet, and yet," I breathed, meeting her eyes, "I burn, I ache, just as he does, Ailsa, all the while he is away—and—and for Lancelot, always, always! Since first I saw him—it is a passion I can scarce control! Yet I must bear it without complaint. Oh, God, it isn't fair!"

Ailsa flushed to the roots of her graying hair. "My dear child," she said quickly, "calm yourself!" She hurried to the terrace and drew the curtain, as if by so doing she could protect me. "You will drive each other mad, if you make this known to him. Do not see him alone again, Guinevere, I beg you."

Half laughing, I wiped away the tears that ran down my cheeks. "Dear Ailsa! How can you think he does not know? He has known for years. And Arthur—Arthur has known since before he wed me."

Ailsa stared at me in horror; I slipped to the floor, covered my face, and wept.

A week went by with no word from Lancelot. From Lamorak I learned he attended Council meetings and did not neglect his routine duties in Arthur's absence, but I saw nothing of him. Sir Villers he left in charge of drilling the troops, and Lyonel in charge of the stables. He did not come to dinner and never joined us in the library after hall.

But Lancelot was not the only one I missed. More than once I sent to the barracks for Mordred, only to learn that he and his brothers had all but disappeared. They attended drills every morning and showed up for the soldiers' mess every evening, but between those times no one could find them. I asked around quietly; people shrugged; no one had seen them, and no one missed them much. Mordred's absence bothered me more than Lancelot's. At least I could guess what Lancelot was about.

One morning a page came to me as I sat in the High King's workroom reading from a scroll.

"My lady Guinevere, Prince Mordred begs your attention for a moment."

I rose quickly. "Prince Mordred? Where is he?" Behind the page I saw Mordred in the shadow of the doorway. "Mordred! At last! Come in, come in."

Mordred came and made his reverence. He was very pale.

"Mordred!" I raised him and hugged him. "Wherever have you been? I've sent everywhere to find you!"

He flushed and replied quickly, "I've had matters to attend to in the town, my lady."

"In the town!" I scanned his face and noted his uneasiness. "And your brothers, who have been as hard to find? Were they also in the town?"

He nodded shortly and kept his eyes on the floor. "My lady, I bring you a message from Sir Lancelot."

I stared. Lancelot send Mordred with a message? "Why, where is he that he could not come himself?"

Mordred flushed again and lowered his eyes. "Please, my lady, do not ask me. I mean no disrespect, but I cannot answer."

His discomfort confused me. I watched his face, half man, half boy, and covered a sigh. If he did not honor me with his confidence, I could not force it from him. "All right, Mordred. I yield. What is the message?"

"My lady, it is more like a riddle. He said that if you were to retrace your steps to the kitchen gardens, you should find there the answer that you seek. But I do not know what the question is." He watched me with curiosity.

I gripped his arm. "When, Mordred? When am I to go?"

"Why, at once, my lady."

My mouth went dry, and I held hard to his arm. "Will you escort me?"

"Of course. With pleasure." But as we walked, his curiosity got the better of his courtier's manners. "What's in the kitchen gardens, my lady? Sir Lancelot insisted I come to you at once with the message. He seemed to think it would not wait another hour."

"Indeed, Mordred, perhaps it will not wait." We went through the corridors as fast as I dared without giving the impression of haste. "I only hope it is not too late! Unless I am mistaken, I have waited a week for this."

"Waited a week? What is it, my lady? It can't be something amiss with the cooks; there would be no mystery in that."

Suddenly I stopped and turned to him. "Mordred, I will make you a fair exchange. You wish to know what awaits in the kitchen gardens, which is a secret I share only with Lancelot, and I wish to know what you have been doing in the town, and how Lancelot came to choose you as the bearer of his message. I will tell you the one, if you will tell me the other. What say you to that?"

He considered this indelicate proposal with a thoughtful face, chewing his lip, and at last he nodded. "It is more than fair, my lady, as I have no right to know your business. But where it concerns Lancelot, for my father's sake I wish to know it."

"Mordred." I spoke gently, but in my heart I cursed the palace gossips. "There is nothing about Lancelot that your father does not already know."

He lifted his chin. "I do not trust him, my lady."

"You do me insult, Mordred, to think so little of him."

"Oh, no, my lady! That is not what I meant! I—"

"And that is why I am willing to share this secret with you. To show you the kind of man he really is."

"Very well, my lady. If I am wrong, I will admit it."

At last I could smile. "Thank you, Mordred. Now tell me"—as we started down the corridor again—"where is Lancelot now?"

"In the town, my lady."

"Pray, where in the town, and doing what?"

"He is—he is—dealing with a witch, my lady."

"A witch? You mean the woman Sybil?"

He looked up quickly but took time to frame a reply. "Yes. That is the name she goes by. He is turning her out of Camelot. With soldiers."

A tinge of anger crept into his voice, but I could not imagine why.

"Well, Mordred, he would not do it without cause. She must have breeched the law in some respect. Pray God she did not poison anyone!"

"She did *not* poison anyone!" he cried.

"Why, Mordred, do you know aught about her?"

A quick look away and a light frown. "Enough, my lady, to know she is a difficult woman and a proud one. But she has done nothing to warrant being thrown out of Camelot by the High King's troops!"

He ended on a note of vehemence, but his lowered eyes and compressed lips signaled a reluctance to say more. There was more here than he would tell me willingly, and I decided not to press him.

"And how did Lancelot choose you as his messenger?"

"My lady, I went to the house of the witch and—"

"Why did you go there?"

"To—to find Gaheris, my lady. I heard—I knew he was there. I met Lancelot coming out the door. He commanded me bring this message to you, without delay."

We descended the broad steps to the kitchens. "So you did not find your brother?"

"No, my lady, not exactly. But he was there. I heard his voice."

I greeted the cooks and scullery maids, who made us reverences as we crossed to the garden door. In the cool, shadowed passage I pulled Mordred aside.

"You have kept your part of our bargain, Mordred, and now I will keep mine. I am going to meet a girl who a week ago accused Lancelot of fathering her child." His eyes widened, and I hurried on. "She has come this time, I hope, to tell me the truth. But she may be shy of you, so I beg you, stay well away."

"My lady," Mordred breathed, "how do you know she was not telling you the truth before?"

I met his eyes squarely. "Lancelot denies it, and I believe him." He said nothing, but politely lowered his eyes.

Drawing a deep breath, I pushed open the heavy door and stepped out into the brilliant sunlight of the garden. At first I did not see her and feared I had come too late, but she was waiting in the shadows on the cellar steps. I came up to her; Mordred waited in the doorway.

"Hello, Grethe. Thank you for coming."

She curstied low. Her face was very pale, and her hands trembled. This time she had come without her son. "My lady Queen."

"I have had a message from Sir Lancelot saying you wished to see me."

"Yes, my lady."

"Well?" But she was shaking with fear and could not look me in the eye. Struggling to keep myself calm, I sat on the steps and bade her sit beside me.

"Grethe, nothing good can come of holding back the truth. I will not punish you if you have told me lies; I know you did it to protect your son."

She looked up at that. "You *do* understand, my lady? You really do? I thought, since you had no children of your own, you would only think me weak and foolish."

I winced at the blow—as if childlessness affected the working of one's wits! "Indeed, I understand you better than you know. Anything you do to keep your child from harm will be forgiven. There is no excuse for cruelty to children. That is the one sin I could not forgive. And that is the sin you laid at Lancelot's door, last time we met."

She lowered her eyes. "I know."

"Is it true?"

"No," she whispered, a small tear forming in her eye, to be hastily brushed away.

"Tell me, Grethe."

She shrugged. "Madam, until he came to me this week past, I had never seen Sir Lancelot before." I let out a long breath in relief. "When he came to my father's house, I did not even know who he was."

"Ah, thank God, thank God."

"I thought he was supposed to be a handsome man," she said in her child's voice, "but he had a broken nose. I didn't believe him when he told me who he was, not at first. Why, that boy in the doorway is better looking."

"Judge a man by his actions, Grethe, and not his face. To those who know him, he is handsome enough, indeed."

"Yes, madam."

"Why did you lie to me?"

But she turned her head away and began to tremble. I kept my voice as gentle as I could. "Come, Grethe, surely this is a question you expected. If you did not know what Lancelot looked like, you could not have known that your son resembled him. But someone else did. Who told you to name him to me as the boy's father? . . . Was it Sybil?"

She bit off a cry of terror and stared at me in wonder. "Yes, madam," she breathed. "How did you know?"

"And Sybil sent you to me?"

She nodded quickly. She was shaking from head to foot.

"But it cannot have been for gold. You did not take the coin I gave you."

She said nothing, but simply stared at me in dumb fear, like an animal caged and expecting death.

"What did Sybil expect to gain from such a lie? Do you know?"

She shook her head.

"What threat did she use against your son to force your compliance? How did you fall into her power?"

Here was the heart of her terror. She shoved her fist against her teeth and whimpered.

"Be easy, Grethe, the witch is no longer in the town. Lancelot himself has thrown her out King's Gate and seen her on her way. She cannot hurt you."

Her eyes widened. Suddenly she bent her head and began to weep. "Oh, my lady! She is a sorceress! She told me it did not matter where she was, she would haunt me if I betrayed her! She said she would turn herself into an eagle and carry Vorn away if ever I told the truth! She said she would know every word that passed my lips! We are doomed, we are doomed!"

I put an arm about her shoulders and held her close. "Nonsense, Grethe." I hugged her shaking body. "She said that to frighten you into silence. She cannot change herself into an eagle any more than I can. Once she is gone, you will be safe from her."

She sobbed wretchedly. I waited until the force of her weeping diminished. "Where is your son now, Grethe?"

"At home. With Mother."

"Why don't you go get him and bring him here? You can have a room within the castle, and I'm sure Ailsa can find you some employment. You can keep your son by you in the King's own house. Would you feel safe then?"

She looked up at me in astonishment. I wiped the tears from her dirty cheeks and dried her eyes. "There. That's much better. For your son's sake, Grethe, you must be strong. What do you say? Will you bring him to live here?"

She grabbed my hand and kissed it. "Oh, my lady!"

"Good. Go home and pack your belongings and bring them to the south gate. Ask for Ailsa, the Queen's woman. She will be expecting you."

She thanked me again and curtsied and kissed my hand and blessed me a thousand times and promised good service and undying devotion; when she left the garden in the sunlight, she was smiling.

"That was well done, my lady," Mordred said softly. "You are very kind."

"She was very frightened. And I wish to know why. Eventually I will know it."

He walked me back through the kitchens and up the stairs toward my rooms. "How much did you hear, Mordred?"

"Nearly all, I think, my lady."

"Then you see what Lancelot has done. He did not content himself with denying wrongdoing; he sought out the cause of the accusation and seeks to put it right."

"That is one way of looking at it," he said stiffly.

"Why, and what other is there?"

"You will not want to hear it."

"Tell me anyway."

"My lady, the girl is weak. She acts from fear. Someone frightened her into accusing Lancelot, and now he has frightened her into changing her story. It can't have been hard to do."

"You do not know him," I said sharply. "He would not do it. And you heard her say herself that the witch frightened her into making the accusation."

"I heard *you* say it, my lady. You supplied the name, not her. Please, my lady, do not be angry. I do not know the truth of it. And you were generous indeed to offer her a place in the High King's household. But—"

"Go on."

"I do not believe the witch put her up to it."

We had reached the door to the library, and I stopped and bade Mordred follow me inside. I sent a page with the message for Ailsa; I had intended to take it myself, but then I had not dreamed that Mordred, sensible, thoughtful Mordred, could be so blind.

When we were alone, I sat him down on one of the cushioned benches, and I sat opposite him, where I could see his face. He was pale and uncomfortable, but he held himself straight and did not avoid my eyes.

"Now, Mordred, tell me what this witch is to you. You have defended her at every turn, as if you are loath to think ill of her. Does she have you, too, under her spell?"

"No, my lady."

"But you know her. You have spent time with her. You went to her house."

"Yes, my lady."

"Why?"

He did not answer. He was not afraid or ashamed or guilty, but I saw by his face that I trod on private ground. This time I did not let him evade me. "You must see, Mordred, the importance of this matter. The High King's nephews, and the High King's son, have kept company with a witch who has conspired to defile the good name of the High King's chief lieutenant, his second-in-command, his closest friend. Lancelot has exiled her from the city. If you persist in keeping silent about your part in this, what choice do you leave me but to place the matter in the High King's hands? He will be here in another week. Are you and your half brothers ready to answer the questions he will have?"

"No, my lady." Mordred trembled, but did not give ground. "If I could tell you, my lady Queen, please believe me, I would. I would not have you distrust me for anything in the world! But I have promised the witch I would keep her secrets."

"A foolish promise, Mordred."

"Probably. But she made us all swear by the very things we hold most sacred that we would reveal nothing about her. And I must keep that promise."

"Even before the King, your father?"

Mordred looked up desperately, beseechingly. "Even before the King. Oh, my lady Guinevere, do you have to tell him? Is it so important? You don't know for certain that she forced the girl to lie, and anyway, Lancelot has got rid of her by now, so couldn't you, couldn't you just let it rest?"

"No," a stern voice said behind me, "she could not."

We both jumped up. Mordred stood at attention; I turned to find Lancelot in the doorway. His appearance astonished me. He looked pale and shaken and very, very angry.

"Lancelot, I am glad to see you. Perhaps, between us, we can come to the truth of this matter."

He bent his knee and kissed my hand, but he did it without thought. His eyes were cold; all his concentration was on Mordred.

"I have come to make my report," he said woodenly. "In private."

"May not Mordred stay? I would like him to hear, firsthand, what you have discovered."

"No need, my lady," Mordred said quickly. "I should be going."

"No." Lancelot spoke with the voice of command, and Mordred froze. "Perhaps you are right, Guinevere. Perhaps he should hear it. But first, I want to know"—he stood before Mordred and frowned down at him—"who is that woman?"

"My lord, to tell you would require me to break an oath I swore."

"Swore to whom? Not to that hag?"

Mordred bristled. "Yes, my lord. To the woman Sybil."

"King's son or no, you are a fool."

"Lancelot!"

He turned to me a face white and drawn with anger and fatigue. "I'm sorry, Gwen. But when you hear—it is no more than truth, though for Arthur's sake, I should forbear to say it. I beg your pardon, Mordred. Your youth, perhaps, forgives you something."

There followed an awkward silence. No one moved. Finally I seated myself on the bench. "I have seen Grethe, Lancelot. Thank you for sending her to me."

"Was she coherent? She's done nothing but weep for three days past. She's been badly frightened."

"She told me you were not the father of her child. She told me she had never seen you before, and when I suggested that Sybil had somehow forced her to the lie, she assented."

Lancelot grunted. "The witch threatened the girl with public exposure and shame. If Grethe hadn't lied, *she'd* be the one tossed out of Camelot instead of Sybil."

Mordred stiffened; Lancelot turned toward him. "It might interest you to know, she confessed it to me. Bold as brass, and as shameless. Your precious witch has kept her ear close to the ground since she's been among us." He turned back to me and passed a hand through his hair. "You see, Gwen, she found out what the girl has tried so hard to keep a secret. She discovered who the boy's father really was. If that were known, why, the girl and her child would have to leave the city. They would have to be discredited. Poor souls, they would be allowed no choice."

"But why?" I whispered. "Who is the father?"

"It does not leave this room." A direct look at Mordred. "After Arthur, the most powerful man in Britain. Bishop Landrum."

"Oh, no!" I crossed myself quickly. But it did not surprise me. "He—he seduced her?"

"A child of thirteen?" Lancelot's voice was bitter. "No. He took her by force. That part of the tale was true. All of it was true, except the name. He *is* the scourge of Camelot. She is not the only one."

"Oh, my God."

"His victims dare not speak. But Grethe told her mother, and the witch found it out."

"But, Lancelot, what did she have to gain by forcing the girl to lie? Why accuse *you?*"

Lancelot's lips twisted into a bitter smile. "In the witch's own words, for her amusement. She wanted to cause us pain. You. And me. And Arthur."

I glanced at Mordred. He stood straight and pale, his face unreadable. Lancelot sat heavily on the bench. He looked suddenly ill. "Ahhhh, Gwen, that's not even the worst of it."

"There's more?" I whispered. "What more could there be?"

"After I sent Grethe here, when I went to the witch's house to face her with it, I found—" He glanced swiftly at Mordred, who kept his eyes fastened on the wall, "I found Gaheris there."

"Yes, Mordred told me—"

"In her arms."

"Wh-What?"

"In her embrace. In her bedchamber. Half dressed."

Mordred gasped. We both turned. The boy was livid, his hand clapped against his mouth, staring at Lancelot.

"He is eleven years old!" I cried.

Lancelot nodded wearily. "Yes."

"No!" The word burst from Mordred, beyond his control. "I do not believe you!" he shouted. "I *will* not believe you! You are only trying to blacken her name because she accused you!" His hands bunched into fists, and he raced from the room.

"Lancelot!" I cried, "Forgive him! He is young himself to know about such things!"

Lancelot shrugged. "He fears more for her reputation than for his brother's safety. I will never understand those Orkney brats. Well, whatever spell she wove is broken now. If he had not believed it, he'd not have run away. And she is gone. The soldiers have orders to escort her as far as Aquae Sulis and send her north. She enters Camelot again on pain of death. Once I charge her in Council with such a crime, her life is forfeit."

"And yet," I breathed, "she has done no more than the bishop himself has done. Arthur must know this."

"You will set the place by the ears, if you tell him. No one will confess it. And in truth, his sin is the more understandable. You yourself believed it possible of me."

"Ahhhh, my dear, can you ever forgive me for that?"

He smiled briefly. "I forgive you anything."

I clasped his hand, and we sat silent for a while.

"I have given the girl a place in my household. She will bring her son to live with us."

He squeezed my hand. "I thought you might. I'm glad you did. She will feel safer here, although she must still see the bishop twice a week. But he will know she has the Queen's protection. For her, at least, that should be the end of it."

"Arthur should know about Bishop Landrum."

He sighed. "Tell him, if you must. He can do little about it unless the man's victims accuse him."

"He knows I have always loathed the bishop, since I first came to Caer Camel. But he has never understood why."

Lancelot rose and raised me. "And I must tell him about the threat to his nephew. I wish I knew who that woman was. Of a certainty, she is evil."

"Perhaps I should ask Niniane about her."

"Or Merlin."

I shuddered. "I don't know how to summon Merlin. He appears to Arthur now and again, but never when I am there. Have you seen him, Lancelot?"

Lancelot crossed himself. "Once. Away from court. I've no doubt Merlin could put an end to that witch. She thinks he is dead, you know. She boasted to me I could not touch her, for since Merlin's death she was the most powerful sorceress in Britain. I did not enlighten her."

"But Niniane has Merlin's power. She is not afraid of Niniane?"

"No. She is not afraid of any woman. And I fear, Guinevere, she will come back."

"But if she does, you will accuse her!"

"She might wait until I'm gone. She boasted that King's Gate could not keep her from the King."

"She is after Arthur? To do what? If it is Arthur she threatens, then her cause is lost, for Merlin will protect him."

He nodded, thinking hard. "Yes, but she does not know that. And it was not only Arthur that she threatened."

I gripped his arm. "Did she threaten you?"

"Oh, yes. And you."

"Me!"

Lancelot looked away and a flush rose to his cheek. "She said the time would come—despite our vows, despite our wills—she said she had seen it in the crystal—she said you and I will lie together, and so betray the King."

I slid to my knees and held tightly to his hands. "How did she dare! It cannot happen without our will!"

Then he looked at me with hot gray eyes and his strong hands lifted me to his lap. "No," he whispered, his lips against mine, "it will not happen without our will."

I laid my head against upon his shoulder. Arthur! I cried inside my soul, Arthur! Come home now!

31 👑 THE WITCH OF ORKNEY

The King came home the first week in September. The kings of Britain followed within a fortnight, all gathering for a great Council to discuss policy toward Childebert and the Franks. With so many preparations, and so many guests to greet, the events of summer faded in importance. Lancelot told Arthur about the attempted seduction of his nephew, but as he had predicted, Arthur could do little about it; the witch was gone, and Gaheris and his brothers were under a stricter regimen now that the King was back. I told him about the girl Grethe and her lie about Lancelot, and how I had believed it, and why, and what the truth was. He saddened when he heard it and ran a gentle finger down my cheek.

"Lancelot would never hurt you by intention," he said gravely. "And if by accident, he would confess it. This you know. Had it not been for Melwas, you'd not have given such a lie a second thought."

"Perhaps not, my lord."

"As for the bishop, he is a man of many sins, but he is still a man of God. I will let him know, in a roundabout way, I will not tolerate such profligate behavior and will give shelter to his victims if they ask it. I will let him know I am considering sending a courier to Rome. I wager he will take the hint."

We had little time for private talk, with so many people arriving and so much public ceremony. Niniane arrived with King Pelleas, her husband, and King Urien of Rheged brought his wife, Morgan, Arthur's full sister. She lodged with her husband in the palace, and I heard from those who saw her rooms that she kept far grander state than I did. Haughty and cold featured, she could scarcely bring herself to speak to anyone lower ranked than Arthur himself. This was fine with me; I did not enjoy her conversation.

The Orkney princes were excited at the gathering of all the men they had learned so much about in Valerius' lessons; most of these had fought beside Arthur in the Saxon wars. But as the boys were too young to be knighted and made Companions, they could not attend the Council meetings and were usually sent out hunting with whatever King's men were going that day. So large a host required a constant resupply of game. Duke Constantine was among the guests; he looked to be a proud man, who would not be easily displaced. Perhaps the King sent the boys hunting to keep Mordred out of his way.

The Council of kings lasted a week. It was resolved that the High King should go to Brittany with Lancelot, to meet with King Hoel and send a message of formal greeting to King Childebert. To represent a united front, many of Britain's lords went with him: Urien of Rheged, Ector of Galava, Hapgar of Strathclyde, Constantine of Cornwall, Drustan of Elmet, and Pelleas, to name a few. My dear uncle King Pellinore of Gwynedd went, also, more to visit his daughter Elaine and see his new grandson than to parley. They were seven hundred men in all, and four hundred horses. The thought of what might happen should storms assail the seas was enough to stop the heart.

Bedwyr stayed as regent and Queen's Protector. As King of Brydwell he deserved a place among this distinguished train, and I asked him if he did not regret having to stay at home and make sure I behaved myself.

He laughed. "The King does me far greater honor by entrusting you to my keeping. Why is Lancelot always appointed the Queen's Protector when he is here? Not for the reason you think, perhaps, although Arthur is an understanding man. It is because Lancelot is most trusted and most able. In all the Kingdom, there is no higher honor." It was a gallant reply, and I thanked him for it; but had I been he, I would have wanted to be traveling.

Parting with Arthur had become easier with so much practice, but parting from Lancelot was difficult indeed. It was mid-October when they set out for the estuary. He would be gone until mid-March, at least. Half the year seemed a lifetime. And since Camelot was full of strangers, we had no privacy for our farewell. Arthur talked long with me the nights of the last week, but Lancelot I bid adieu in the forecourt of the castle, in the public eye.

"Take good care of my lord the King," I told him, doing him deep reverence, "and God speed your way there and back again. We are not the same in Camelot without you, good Lancelot. And as you are a merciful man, give your lady wife a rest from her labors."

His mouth twitched, suppressing a smile. "Gentle Queen," he murmured, "I give her no more labor than she can bear."

"For my sake," I countered, "let her lie idle the long winter, that she may labor and bear no more." Arthur's eyebrow lifted in warning; I gave Lancelot my hand and let him go.

They rode out King's Gate and down the broad causeway to the shore road, and left Camelot behind, ringing with emptiness.

Things were not dull for long. No sooner was Arthur gone than his sister Morgan began to seek out my company. I often went riding with Bedwyr or Ferron, and sometimes Morgan and her courtier Accolon, who dogged her like a shadow, accompanied us. She alone had remained after the host had left; the King had made her welcome, having no other choice, and she had chosen to stay until her husband returned. Arthur was not happy about it, but I told him I did not mind. Until he left, she kept to herself. Accolon never left her side, even at night, said the palace gossip. He was younger than she was, well made and strikingly handsome, with light hair, dark eyes, and a fine complexion. That he was her devoted slave was clear; his adoring eyes followed her everywhere. Her husband King Urien was a graybeard, old enough to be her father.

Morgan was Urien's second wife. His first wife had been dear to him, by all accounts, and had given him four sons, Coel, Uwain, Lyle, and Drian, now grown men who served the King. If he had married Morgan to replace what he had lost, he soon knew of his mistake. She had borne him a daughter, Morgaine, and if rumors could be trusted, had hardly spoken to him since. Her compassion as a mother seemed no greater than her compassion as a wife. Only sixteen months before, at the age of seven, Morgaine had been kidnapped and savagely raped by the villain Heuil, leader of the Strathclyde clan, during a border dispute with Rheged. Morgan's response to her daughter's ordeal was to shut her away and treat her like something soiled.

After one of our outings I asked Morgan how the child fared, to see what she would say. She replied, with coldness, that she grew and thrived and had been revenged for her attack. I shuddered at the thought of what she had been through and expressed my deep sympathy to Morgan.

"Well," she said icily, "you should know." And turned away.

I stared after her, astonished. No one had heard her remark but I; I let it pass. I realized then that sharp tongues had been at work, and that at least some in Britain chose to believe Melwas had been successful. If any believed it, it only reflected better on Arthur's mercy, so I said nothing.

When Arthur left, Niniane returned to Avalon. But before she left, she gave the King two words of advice: first, that he should lock King's Gate against all comers, and second, that he should lock up his Sword. Arthur objected to locking the fortress gates. It was his policy, he said, to make Camelot and the justice dispensed in the Round Hall open to anyone in the kingdoms. To lock the gates would be to cut off Britain from her vital center, and he would not do it. But he did lock up his Sword. He was not taking Excalibur to Brittany, for this was a mission of peace and friendship, not of war. So a guard was posted, day and night, outside the door of the Round Hall, where the great Sword hung in its hanger above the High King's chair. No one went in or out without Bedwyr in attendance.

One night when the King had been gone a fortnight, Bedwyr and I were sitting before a good log fire in the library, reading from the scrolls of Xenophon. The wind had risen and promised storm the next day. Drafts whistled through the corridors, around the edges of the tapestries, and made the fire welcome. We had fallen to talking about Lancelot when the door burst open, and Kay ran in.

"Bedwyr! Fire! The stables are afire! Call the sentries—in this wind, it will take every man to save the horses!"

I leaped to my feet, but Bedwyr was already at the door. He turned. "If I cannot be with you, Gwen, get to your rooms. Don't be alone."

I nodded, and he flew away. Now I wished I were a man and not a woman! To have to hide in my quarters with my women, while my precious horses were at risk! Would they have enough men to man the buckets, build a firebrake, and lead the horses out? Would they have time, with this wind? We were so short-handed, with so many troops gone with the King! But I could do little to help. It was man's work, and I had orders to obey.

I went silently along the corridors. It was strange to see no sentries line the walls. As I passed the hallway that led to the Round Hall, I caught movement from the corner of my eye. I turned to look. The torch near the Council chamber had gone out. Why had the guard not relit it? I went to see. When I came to the door, I understood. The guard was not there. Remembering Niniane's warning, I determined to check on the Sword. On tiptoe I grasped the nearest lighted torch and lifted it from the sconce. It was not heavy, but my hand shook, and the door seemed to tremble and sway. I pushed it open slowly, but could hear no sound at all. The chamber was in darkness. Outside the glazed windows I heard dimly the shouts of men, but here was only stillness and peace. I made my way to the great round table and looked up. There it was, still in its hanger, cold and forbidding in the torchlight. I sighed in relief. I did not stop to wonder why the great emerald lay quiet, when usually even the smallest flame set light flashing from its facets; I was so pleased to see the Sword, sheathed in its old scabbard as the King had left it, that I chided myself for my foolish fears and closed the door.

I myself stood guard on it. I disliked to disobey Bedwyr, but the King's orders came first. The Sword must be guarded. Before long, I heard running feet and panting, and a young sentry came racing toward me.

"Who's there, in the King's name!" When he got close enough to recognize me, he cried out and fell on one knee. "My lady Queen Guinevere! What—what's amiss?"

"Nothing. The Sword is there. But when I came by I found the door unguarded, and so took up the post."

He kissed my hand with fervor. "My lady Queen, you have saved me from disgrace! Sir Bedwyr was so furious—I was wrong to leave the post, even for fire, but I thought—no matter. You have saved me. I am forever in your debt."

"What is your name, gentle knight?" I asked kindly, for I saw he was young and frightened.

"Hugh, my lady—and I am not yet knighted."

"Arise, Hugh, and take this torch from me, if you will. It grows heavy with holding."

He had it from me in an instant and, relighting the one that had gone out, returned it to its sconce.

"One good turn deserves another," I said, noting the smudges of soot on his face.

"Anything, my lady! Ask it!"

"Tell me about the fire. What is going on?"

Thus far, he said, the fire was contained in the new additions that now stood empty. It had started in the hay, no one knew how. But the King's stables, built of stone, were not yet threatened, and already the horses were being taken to the pastures. People from the town had come to help, seeing the smoke, and it was likely that disaster would be avoided.

"Thank God!" I sighed. "This is good news indeed. Now it will be possible to wait for Bedwyr's report. I thank you, Hugh."

He was profuse in his thanks to me, but I felt sorrow in my heart for him. He would never make one of the King's Companions, for he had no sense. And after this, even though no harm had come of it, Bedwyr would never trust him.

Bedwyr came to me after midnight to make his report. He was tired and out of temper, but pleased with the results. He had washed his face and hands and scrubbed his hair, but his clothes were stained with soot and burned with embers. It had been a near thing, because of the wind.

"If we ever find who set it, I shall take his life with pleasure," he growled.

"Who *set* it?"

"It was no accident, my lady. The hay was newly harvested but well dried. I checked it myself. And we found the ashes of hot coals. That's how it was started. If the Sword had been touched, I would have suspected a diversion, but as it is—" He passed his hand wearily across his brow. "I know not what to think. But someone has done evil, and I will find him."

The next morning, although it had begun to rain, Queen Morgan announced that she and all her train were leaving.

"Perhaps it was unwise to stay and await my lord," she told Bedwyr in my hearing. "My brother should have left his fortress in more capable hands. After last night, I cannot be sure that we will have mounts left when we wish to go." Bedwyr took it without flinching, but his eyes flashed. I flew to his defense.

"Sir Bedwyr is among the finest men in Britain. Although," I added thoughtfully, "I see where you might find his manner of administration somewhat foreign. He metes out punishment only where it is well deserved, and does not blame children for the sins of their elders. As to horses, my husband's sister is always welcome to animals from his own stables"—I made her a reverence—"that is, if you can ride them."

Morgan stiffened; Bedwyr covered a smile. Even Accolon looked at me with admiration. I began to feel sorry for Urien.

"Thank you, Queen Guinevere," she snapped, "for your gentle offer. As you no doubt rule in Camelot, your advice about governing is clearly worth having. I would beg you remember I am a lady and do not ride stallions. That is for men, and for ill-bred maidens who wish they were."

I heard Bedwyr's indrawn breath and saw the stony faces of the men behind him. When she called me maiden she insulted even Arthur.

"Even were I maiden," I said slowly, letting the words fall singly into the icy silence, "I would have the mother love to seek healing for a child so abused as little Morgaine and not leave her to suffer nightmares and terrors of the dark all on her own. It has been over a year," I finished softly.

In fury she turned to Accolon. "We will go," she commanded. "I will not stay to be instructed by Arthur's barren wife on child rearing!" With that, she flounced out, Accolon following, and left us in peace. The men in the room were afraid to move. Even Bedwyr glanced at me nervously.

I smiled and took his arm. "Do not fear, Bedwyr. She has not the power to hurt me. If those are her sharpest barbs, I am in no danger. Elaine gave me a tougher hide than that."

Bedwyr exhaled in relief and returned the smile. "She is known for her sharp tongue and the joy she takes in making people cower. But my lady bested her this day."

I shook my head. "To be queen of shrews is no honor. I should not have spoken so to Arthur's sister. I only demeaned myself. Pray, let's hope she keeps her word and leaves."

Morgan was gone by nightfall, and Bedwyr and I looked forward to a calmer stretch of time. There was much to do before we moved to Caerleon at Christmas; the harvest must be brought in, beasts slaughtered and their flesh smoked and dried for soldiers' rations, wool and flax and dyes prepared for winter's weaving, the festivals celebrated and thanks given before the new year at the Samhain fires. Everyone was busy. At this time of year, there was scarcely a village in Britain that could not have used an extra pair of hands. Each morning we rose early, and often by hall we were so exhausted we bid each other good night as we rose from table and went straight to bed.

On one such night a courier arrived just as the wine went round. An Orkneyman by dress, the message he delivered announced the arrival of Queen Morgause.

I looked toward Bedwyr in surprise. He stared, stunned, at the kneeling courier.

"The Queen of Orkney is *here?*"

The man nodded. "She is without, my lord. Awaiting entrance."

My head ached with fatigue, and I grumbled to Bedwyr, "Arthur has too many sisters. What does this one want, I wonder?"

"Not much," came a smooth voice from the doorway, "beyond a courteous greeting from his Queen."

I blushed to the roots of my hair. Queen Morgause stood watching, her escort behind her, as Bedwyr rose and went forward to welcome her to Camelot on the King's behalf.

Never had I seen a woman so lavishly dressed; even her cloak was trimmed with golden beading. Her hair, once red-gold like Uther's, had darkened to dull russet, but she wore it bound in golden mesh; where it framed her face it accented the creamy pallor of her skin. Hands, wrists, neck, and ears were hung with gold and rich enamels, all worked intricately in the way of the northern Celts. Her face had Arthur's bones, but not his features. She had a small mouth and nose and narrow forehead, and lashes too black to be unpainted. Beauty, yes—by anyone's standards she was beautiful, and yet there was something spoiled about it, something slack, stale, beyond its best. But then, she was past thirty.

She acknowledged Bedwyr and made her reverence, a dip of the knee, no more. Cat eyes, long, narrow, slightly slanted, glinted green. I went to Bedwyr's side. She was not as tall as I was, but her shape, even after bearing five sons, would have outdone any maiden half her age.

"Welcome, Queen Morgause." I did not apologize for my rudeness; had she obeyed Arthur's orders and stayed in exile, she would not have heard it. "We have lately had a visit from Queen Morgan. How sorry I am you did not come a month ago, when both your brother and your sister were in Camelot."

She regarded me a moment in silence, and my flesh crept on my bones. The dread I felt seemed so familiar! The eyes narrowed suddenly; sweat broke upon my brow. She turned to Bedwyr. "It is unlikely that either my brother or my sister will regret missing my visit. I came to see my sons, but I do not see them in hall. Are they not here?"

"No, madam, they eat in the soldiers' mess. Let me arrange rooms for you and get you settled, and I will have them sent to you." He did not tell her that the reason they ate with the soldiers was because, even after a year, they had not acquired the manners to eat in hall—except for Mordred, whom the King did not wish to single out.

She looked slowly around the gathering and slowly smiled. "Very well. Show me to my rooms."

Kay bowed low at her side. "My lady, I will escort you."

She turned away, ignoring the arm he proffered. "I will have meat and broth brought to me, and unwatered wine, as well. See to it."

She swept out, followed by her attendants, and Bedwyr and I looked at one another. We had thought Morgan a handful!

"It is no accident she comes when the King's in Brittany," he said with feeling. "She has disobeyed his direct order. But how can I imprison the High King's sister, when he is gone and her sons are here?"

"What do you suppose she wants, Bedwyr?"

He shrugged. "Nothing good, you may wager what you like on that."

"I fear you are right." I did not tell him my deepest fear: that she had come, somehow, to reclaim Mordred.

She swiftly became a general nuisance and as great a thorn in my side as Elaine had been at her worst. She disliked me; not, I discovered, on account of my unthinking rudeness, but merely because I was dear to Arthur. Kay and Bedwyr she treated as her servants and bade them have things brought, replaced when they did not suit her, and taken away when she was weary of them. For Arthur's sake, they held hard to their patience and did her bidding.

Most days, she held court in the High King's library. There she would send for whom she wished to see. Instead of going to the practice field to see her sons' progress, she would send for them and engage them in reminiscences about their Orkney homeland. Gawaine and Agravaine chafed under such treatment; they wanted to show off their prowess with spear and sword. Mordred bore it with grim patience; Gareth frankly fell asleep after a while. Only Gaheris truly enjoyed every minute in his mother's presence. Indeed, I was amazed at the change in his demeanor. I had thought him a sour, whining child, but now he positively glowed with joy and pride. It was a pleasure, I told myself when I was wont to anger at her presumption, to see the boy so changed. Everyone else was ready for her departure when she had been a week in Camelot, but Gaheris at least had come into some sort of bloom.

She stayed past the harvest, past the fall of the first snow, and the longer she stayed, the more fractious we became. Everything she did rubbed someone the wrong way. And Morgause herself not only enjoyed the disruption of our peace, she went out of her way to make trouble. Once she sent a maid of mine to her chamber, to fetch an amber bracelet from her jewel chest. The girl asked Hadarta, Morgause's chief attendant, to fetch it for her. But Hadarta could not find the chest. She searched everywhere, and flew into a panic, crying out that Camelot was full of thieves, and Morgause would have her life if it could not be found. Little Anis helped her search the queen's rooms; they spent half a day looking for it and weeping. Finally Anis came to me in tears with this silly story and asked me what to do. Neither of them dared tell Morgause the jewel chest was missing; indeed, Hadarta was packing her belongings into a sack, preparing to leave Camelot altogether. Slightly annoyed, I followed Anis to Morgause's chamber and searched the place myself. There were plenty of furs and cushions flung about, and a fine linen tunic too small for a man to wear lying on the floor near the bed—could she be mending it for one of her sons?—but the chest was not there.

"It is a small box," Hadarta wailed, "but very precious! The cover is embroidered with crimson threads and sea pearls! Oh, oh! She will be in one of her horrid wraths, she will have my eyes out!"

"Not in my domain, she won't," I said firmly. "Come, Hadarta. There is nothing to do but face it. Delaying telling her the news will not make it any easier. Come with me, both of you, and we will tell her together."

Morgause lounged in the library before the fire, admiring the rings on her fingers. Anis fell into a curtsy; Hadarta hung shaking at the door.

Morgause listened calmly to my explanation and, with a light little laugh, waved us all away. "Oh! I had quite forgotten! I have the chest with me. And here is the bracelet on my wrist—I found it just after the child went after it."

And that was it: no apology, no regret, no expression of gratitude for half a day wasted by two women on her behalf. Anis and Hadarta were happy enough to escape without punishment, but I could barely control my anger. Watching me, Morgause's long green eyes began to narrow and her lips slowly twisted in a smile. I turned on my heel and walked out.

Not even Arthur's hound was left in peace. Morgause had brought with her a white-haired cat, which she often kept upon her lap and stroked. Whenever she brought it into the King's library, she had Cabal kicked out from his place on the warm hearth, although he cared nothing for cats, so that her darling might not be affrighted and scratch her with his claws. Cabal was stiff with age and winter cold; I let him sleep near my grate, but it was not the same as a good log fire.

Poor Bedwyr had the worst of it. I, at least, could escape on horseback, for riding was beneath Morgause. She traveled only in a cushioned litter, lined with velvet. But as regent, Bedwyr could not escape. The only place he was free from her was in the Council chamber. The guards had orders to physically restrain her if she tried to enter, but wisely, she did not. Councils grew longer and longer, and I had wine sent in to the men, which Arthur never allowed, to help them prolong their session and to signal that I understood.

Dinner became something to be endured. The springs of conversation dried under Morgause's scorching wit; no one cared to venture an opinion and then be made to look a fool. How I wished we had a bard, that we might listen to the sweet sounds of music! Hearing this, Bedwyr offered to fetch his harp and give me a song or two. I was delighted and begged him to do it. Morgause wondered, with a lift of her lip, how the Kingdom had come to such a pass, that the Regent of Britain should stoop to harping for himself. Did he garden, too, she wondered, and spin his cloaks himself? I had opened my mouth to snap back an answer, when I caught Bedwyr's eye and was silent. He gave us the song that Merlin wrote for Arthur, about how Britain waited in darkness for a thousand years until the King should be born that would bring her into light and glory, an everlasting glory that men would forever honor. As he sang about Arthur, the soldiers in the hall grew solemn and the women misty-eyed. Only Morgause looked on in half-concealed contempt. When the last note had faded to a sweet vibration, more felt than heard, Morgause rose and faced me.

"In my life, I have never heard the truth stretched so. One might almost believe Arthur had written it himself. As for the singer, be sure to reward him, my lady Queen, as I hear only you can do, who are so liberal with your favors, for the honor he has done us all." She made me a low curtsy, and swept out.

Every man in the room was on his feet, crying out in protest.

I stared after her, aghast. "Bedwyr, why does she hate me so?"

He gripped my shoulder firmly. "Pay her no mind, my lady. To show anger is to play into her hands. She's a different breed from Arthur."

"Indeed!" I breathed. "Niniane warned me, but I did not believe her. She is a devil."

I fought to keep my temper, but I could not bear the way she treated Arthur's friends as her servants. The final straw came late one afternoon when I had returned from a ride upon the downs and sat in my chamber while Ailsa combed my hair. A page scratched at the door, sent by Morgause.

"The Queen of Orkney is in the library and commands the Queen's attendance," he quavered, knee to the floor.

Ailsa stiffened. " 'Commands' her attendance? Surely not. 'Begs' you mean, Brynn."

"No, madam," the page whispered, trembling. "She said 'command.' "

"Repeat the message," I ordered.

" 'You there, go to the High Queen and command her to attend me. I have heard she has a lovely voice. I wish to hear her sing. Have her come and sing me a song.' "

Ailsa gasped. "How dare she! How dare she send such a message!"

The poor page shook so badly he could hardly speak. "Madam, I told her I could not take the Queen such a message, but, but—she said she'd have me whipped if I did not!"

I went to the child and raised him. "She cannot touch you, Brynn. You serve the King, not Queen Morgause. These are idle threats. Unless you believe them, they have no power. Where is Sir Bedwyr?"

"In Council, my lady."

I hid a smile. "Very well. Take him a message from me. You are to attend him in Council and see the men have wine and mead enough. Do not return to Morgause."

"She bade me return at once with your consent."

"You cannot do that, because you do not have it. Forget her. I myself will give her the reply she deserves."

When he was gone, I returned to the stool and bade Ailsa resume her combing.

"What will you do, my lady?" she asked nervously.

"What I have learned from Bedwyr is best to do," I replied. "Nothing."

I took my time and let Ailsa dress my hair with ribbons and donned Arthur's favorite gown of sapphire blue. It was dark when I went down at last, and the lamps had all been lighted. Anis, Hanna, and Mary attended me. We walked slowly through the corridors, talking and laughing, and as I expected, the library door opened as we neared it, and Morgause came out.

"Ah, there you are at last. I must say, Guinevere, you have kept me waiting long enough."

The sentries near enough to hear her drew breath together; my girls froze. I did not pause, but kept walking.

"What, would you snub the High King's sister?" Morgause hissed.

I turned slowly. "I beg your pardon. Were you addressing me?"

"Is your name not Guinevere?"

"Queen Guinevere to you, Morgause."

To my surprise, she smiled. "Surely, sister, we may use first names between us. My father was High King of Britain when yours was fighting hillmen for his tiny patch in Wales. Do not imagine you outrank me."

I clutched my gown and stilled myself and answered quietly. "Have you anything else to say?"

"Come sing for me, Gwen. I should like to hear your voice."

I have never done anything so hard, but I turned away without speaking and, reaching out a hand to my shaking maids, continued down the hall. From a distance, we could hear the witch's laughter.

That night, Mordred came to me. I saw him in my antechamber with Ailsa in attendance. He went on his knees, his features solemn, and his voice tight with control. "My lady Queen, you must make her leave. You must find some excuse and make her leave."

"Mordred, is this your mother you speak of? You wish me to send her away?"

"Yes!" he cried. "You must! She means nothing but mischief."

"Mischief can be endured. How would your brothers feel about it?"

"Gawaine and Agravaine would not much care. They were pleased at first to see her. As I was. But now, but now she is a nuisance. They want to be soldiering, not waiting on her hand and foot. They are tired of it. We all are."

"Gaheris, too?"

He looked quickly away. "Gaheris—would be better off without her. It is partly for his sake that I have come. Can't you send her back to Orkney? Didn't the High King send her into exile? Hasn't she disobeyed him in coming here?"

"Yes and no. When Lot died, Arthur gave the governing of Lothian to Sir Tydwyl, as regent for Gawaine. That left Orkney for Morgause. Orkney or another husband. She chose Orkney. It wasn't exactly exile, and yet it was. You know better than I how far away Orkney is."

"But when the High King sent for us, he did not send for her. Sir Lukan read the orders aloud. She was commanded to stay in Orkney. So hasn't she disobeyed by coming here?"

"Yes, Mordred. She has disobeyed."

"Then can't you have Bedwyr send her away?"

"As she is the King's sister, we are loath to do it. It is, well, a personal matter between them. Until she gives us good reason to do otherwise, we must treat her with the respect she is due. As Uther's daughter and as Arthur's sister."

His face shuttered. "The matter between them is my begetting." He spoke with no emotion. At thirteen, he already had Arthur's hard control. "He will never forgive her that, and she will use his shame against him, while she feels none. It is clear to me now."

"What is clear, Mordred?"

He looked up at me. "She intends to stay. Here in Camelot. Forever. She intends to take it over, as you have seen. She won't let Arthur stop her; she has a weapon against him. The life you have led this month past, she intends you will lead forever."

I gasped, as much at the pain of hearing him speak so of his parents as at the horror of the future he described. "How do you know this, Mordred?"

He shrugged. "I have heard the way she speaks of my father. I have heard the way she speaks of you. You are—so easy to make angry. Forgive me, my lady, but it gives her such delight."

"When Arthur returns, he will deal with her."

"What will he do? If he sends her back to Orkney, he must have a reason why. That means he himself must publicize his shame. I don't think he will do that."

He was right. Unless Morgause publicly transgressed, or breeched the law, what reason could he give for treating his sister so? He, who was revered as the just King, the wise King, who treated others fairly, no matter what their station—his hands would be tied. I saw why Mordred had come to me. I was not so bound. I could do whatever I willed and answer for it to Arthur, who would be relieved not to have to deal with it himself.

"But even I, Mordred, must have some good excuse. Else it will look like spite and still reflect upon Arthur. She came and made a nuisance of herself and teased the Queen, who could not take a jest and sent the King's sister away. You see?"

"Yes."

"Thus far, she has done nothing but disobey Arthur's wishes."

"I could tell you something she has done," Mordred said slowly, his eyes on the ground. I said nothing but watched his face. Not an eyelash moved. "But—I want there to be another way."

"Perhaps I should speak with Bedwyr."

"Or Merlin." He looked up suddenly. "She would fear Merlin. She has heard rumors of his return, but does not believe them. Can you not ask him what to do?"

"You and Lancelot give me the same advice," I said softly, and watched color flood into his face. "But I do not know how to summon him, even if I were willing. Merlin and I do not, well, see eye to eye."

He drew a long breath. "I see." He paused. "Does the King love Lamorak?" The question came out of nowhere and took me by surprise.

"Of course. He's one of the Companions."

"He's in danger."

"What kind of danger?"

But he rose quickly and bowed. "Perhaps I've said too much."

"All right. I will keep my eyes open. I appreciate your coming, Mordred."

He hesitated, chewing his lip. "Why don't you come to the library one morning, when we are there with Mother? I—I may have something to show you then."

I rose. "If you advise it, I will."

"Perhaps," he breathed, "there will be no need for Merlin."

Several days later I did as Mordred bade me and joined Morgause in the library as she sat with her boys. Gareth was asleep on the hearth in Cabal's place; Gawaine and Agravaine played a covert tug-of-war with their little fingers, and Gaheris curled at her feet, his head resting against her knee. Mordred sat nearby, rolling a chunk of coal between his fingers, working the coal dust into his flesh. He did not look up when I entered, but they all, well trained by Lancelot and Bedwyr, jumped to their feet.

"Good morning, Queen Morgause," I said pleasantly. "You look well rested. I am glad to see it. You may be seated, boys."

Morgause shrugged gracelessly as I sat and took up a piece of needlework.

"We were talking," she snapped, "about private matters."

"The boys are late for sword practice. Perhaps you should let them go and save the private matters until they are at leisure."

Hope lit Gawaine's face, and his mother saw it.

"First I will tell you of the time your father King Lot defeated Caelric, the Saxon king, single-handed."

"Oh, Mother," Agravaine groaned. "We have heard this tale twenty times before. Mayn't we go to the practice field? We'll be in trouble with Sir Berys and Sir Lamorak if we miss more training."

"Don't you worry about Lamorak." Morgause smiled coyly. "He will do as I tell him. As for Berys, he will follow Lamorak's lead. Now, attend me." Mordred shot me a swift glance, and I understood at once the kind of danger Lamorak was in.

She continued with her story, dressing it up with details that reflected on Lot's glory but that could not possibly be true, when suddenly Mordred rose, white-faced and determined.

"Excuse me, Mother."

Morgause looked up. "What is it, Mordred?"

He bent down to her ear and put a hand up to cover his mouth. He whispered something and as he drew away, his dirty fingers touched her cheek. She turned toward me. I gasped. He had left a dark blot on her cheek, and suddenly I knew that face! The long, green eyes, the clear skin, the dark, ugly mole: Sybil!

Shaking, I rose to my feet, staring. She lifted a hand to her face, realization dawning. At her feet Gaheris turned to look up at her. Gaheris! Gaheris and Sybil! I screamed and covered my mouth with my hand. My stomach heaved; on the verge of sickness, I put out a hand to steady myself and found it grasped by Mordred.

"Mordred!" It was more a curse than a cry. He would not look at her, but led me out, calling to the guard.

"Take the Queen to her quarters. She is ill. I will inform Sir Bedwyr."

"Mordred!" I looked back at him through tears. "Oh, Mordred!"

32 ♛ THE ACCUSATION

When Bedwyr came to see me he found me pacing around my chamber, cloaked and shivering with cold. He stood awkwardly by the door while Ailsa fussed about with possets and hot cloths.

"Mordred sent for me, my lady. He said you were taken ill, and indeed, you look so. What has happened? What's amiss? Was there a courier while we were in Council?"

I shook my head and beckoned him farther into the room. Behind me the thick leather flap hung across the entrance to the High King's bedchamber; I lifted it and checked to make sure no chamberlain was listening.

Bedwyr approached nervously. "What is it, Gwen? It is the King?"

"No." I sat him upon my stool and paced back and forth before him. "Oh, Bedwyr, I do not know how to tell you. I am afraid you will not believe me. We must imprison Morgause. Now. She has committed a grave sin. For the—for the second time. And she is endangering a child."

"Guinevere, be still a moment. If you accuse her, I will imprison her. But first I must know what she has done."

My hands twisted together as I fought for calm. "She has—she is—she has seduced Gaheris."

His dark eyes slowly widened. "Incest?" he whispered, making the sign against evil as I nodded. "Are you sure?"

"I am not the only one who knows it. Let me tell you what happened while you were gone with the King this summer." I told him the whole tale, from meeting the witch in the forest to recognizing her that morning. I told him all about Grethe and her accusation, and about what Lancelot found when he went to Sybil's house to try to clear his name. I left out only my private interview with Lancelot, as it was nobody's business but mine; no doubt he heard about that already; no doubt it was already stale barracks gossip.

When I finished, he pursed his lips and nodded thoughtfully. "So it was Lancelot who found them together."

"He told Arthur about it, but of course we did not know she was his mother! As Lancelot had expelled her from the city, he thought the problem solved. Had Arthur known—oh, Bedwyr! When Arthur knows this, he will kill her! And then, think of the stain upon his soul! We must prevent it, at all cost!"

Bedwyr took a cup of warmed wine from Ailsa and bade me sit and drink it. I sat on the edge of my bed, with Ailsa's arm about my shoulders, and tried to calm myself. All I could think of was Arthur's face when he learned the truth.

"Guinevere, attend me. I cannot arrest Morgause."

"What?" I cried. "Why not?"

"You cannot accuse her. You have seen nothing. Lancelot is the only one who has seen them together, and he is not here."

"My God, Bedwyr, do you think Lancelot was lying?"

"No, of course not. But I must be fair. She has the right to face her accuser."

"Would you be fair to a demon? To a witch?"

"Yes," Bedwyr replied sensibly, "even to a witch. And so would you. It is Arthur's way. Think, Gwen, if you have seen anything at all."

"I saw—I saw the boy's tunic on the floor by her bed!"

He shook his head. "Even if you *knew* it to be Gaheris' tunic, and I can see by your face that you do not, it proves nothing. There are a hundred other reasons why it might be there."

"But, Bedwyr, this is true! She is corrupting her own son! We must do whatever we can to spare him! If you don't believe me, ask Mordred—Mordred has known it for a long time. Only, only don't ask him to accuse his mother. He was brave enough to betray her to me, but it was stealthily done. If his brothers find out—you know how they are—his very life could be at risk! We must keep Mordred out of it, but send Morgause away, permanently away, from Camelot!"

We argued about it a long time. I wept and pleaded and demanded, but Bedwyr was adamant. He could take no action until she was formally accused, and the only ones who could accuse her were Lancelot and Mordred. Mordred had already risked a great deal in revealing to me what he had kept from Lancelot; I refused to ask him to do more. When Bedwyr had gone, I stood alone in my room and cried Merlin's name aloud.

"If you hear me, King's Enchanter, take shape and come to me! The Kingdom needs you. *I* need you!"

Merlin might not care much about Gaheris' soul, but he would want to keep Arthur's honor clean. And even though I dreaded meeting the enchanter face to face, I would do anything to free Gaheris from the witch's curse.

Days passed; nothing happened. Merlin did not come, and Morgause's behavior did not change. Mordred's brothers, it seemed, had noticed nothing. I avoided Morgause as much as I could. She was cold to Mordred but when she looked at me she seemed always amused. Finally, I could stand it no longer. I rose early one morning after a sleepless night, determined to face the witch myself and demand to know the truth. I had appealed for help and gotten none. I would see what I could do myself, woman against woman.

Wrapping my cloak about me, I hurried through the cold corridors. We'd had a biting frost the night before, and my angry breaths hung in clouds in the freezing air. I climbed the stairs to her apartments and tapped upon the door. No one answered. Annoyed, I pushed it open; Hadarta slept in the antechamber hard by the grate, snoring loudly, an overturned wine-cup near her pallet. As I stood there, gathering my courage, the inner door opened, and a shirtless boy backed slowly out.

"Before moonrise," he called softly. "I will come again, Mother. I will bring you a present. Wait until you see." In his hand he held the tunic I had seen on the floor. As he slipped it on he turned and saw me. Gaheris froze. And then, as if in imitation of the witch herself, his green eyes narrowed and his lips slid into a sly smile. He said nothing, but passed by me and went silently out the door.

"Come in, Guinevere," Morgause called, stifling a yawn. "I've been ex-pecting you for days."

She sat amid her rumpled sheets, sleepy and unbrushed. The harsh morning light displayed a thousand lines around her eyes, mouth, and neck; her chin sagged, her full breasts flattened in her shapeless shift, the slack flesh on her inner arms shone sickly white, like a frog's belly. And still she smiled at me.

"Does Arthur know you spy upon his guests? That you are a snoop as well as a coward?" The long eyes narrowed and the hairs stood up upon my arms.

"Leave him alone!" It burst out of me before I knew it. "Leave the child alone! You are corrupt and filthy! As you value your life, Morgause, let him be!"

"But, my pretty pet, he enjoys it so." I gasped. She did not bother to deny it! "There is something about a young boy, so new to love, that I find appealing. And there is nothing a boy will not do to please his mother." She was watching me, and as my disgust progressed to horror, so her amusement grew to contemptuous satisfaction. "He's no Arthur, of course."

"Oh, God!" I cried, flinging my hands to my ears. "Stop it! Have you no compassion in you at all?"

"I show you as much as my dear brother has shown me!" She flung aside the covers and sprang out of bed, pulling on a silken robe of dark green. She glanced in her polished bronze at her reflection, then whipped around and faced me. "You bitch. You have no right to outshine me. I will be revenged on you for that. I will tell you what it was like with Arthur."

"You will not! I will call the guard and have you taken to the tower!"

"On what grounds?"

"You—you have lain with your son!"

"And with my brother. But if you accuse me, I will deny it."

"I saw it!"

"No. You saw a boy leaving his mother's room. What harm is there in that?"

"Oh, God! You cannot, you *will* not go free!"

"No?" She smiled again and took a comb to her hair. "I will do just exactly as I please. If you accuse me, I will tell them what a little whore you are. I will name names."

"That is a lie!"

"So? Lies have ruined reputations before now. And they are hard to disprove. There will always be doubts. And be sure I will bring Arthur's shame to light. What a fine, strong youth he was! So eager and so proud. I was his first woman, did he tell you?"

"Of course not! He hates the very—"

"Fresh from his first victory he came to me, all fire and hot breath. He knew nothing."

"My God, have you no shame?"

"None." She picked up a jar of scented balm and began to rub the cream into her skin. Magically, the lines began to disappear. "He was a pleasure to teach, I will say that for him. And he learned well, did he not? Does he please you with those beautiful hands of his?"

"Don't, I pray you! How can you?"

She leaned closer and whispered. "Every time he touches you, my pet, think of me."

"No! Oh, no!" I found myself sobbing into my hands, I, who had come so bravely to her door not half an hour before! Was it witchcraft, or had I just been naive about the depth of cruelty a woman's heart could hold? I wiped away my tears and faced her. "You do not deny, then, Gaheris has shared your bed?"

"Not to you. It amuses me to confess it."

"For this you deserve death."

She shrugged. "In your narrow Christian eyes, perhaps. But none of you can kill me. I do not fear you."

"I will have you imprisoned."

"You can try. Come, Guinevere, I am tiring of this game. You have voiced your outrage. Now go back to bed."

"I will not! Guards! Guards!"

Morgause began to laugh. "You will not even awaken Hadarta, much less rouse a guard."

"What have you done to her? Drugged her wine, I suppose?"

"Clever girl."

"That is enough, Morgause. You are evil, and I will see you put away."

"Will you, indeed? We shall soon see, my sweet, which of us is more powerful. It's been clear for more than a month now, there is room for only one Queen in Camelot."

I gasped at her audacity. "How dare you! And *you* call *me* a bitch! I'll see you flogged!"

"You shallow, empty-headed fool! I'll make mincemeat of you, and *then* see how my brother likes you! I will serve him well for leaving me to rot on that sea-swept rock!"

"Ladies! Ladies!" cried a male voice from the doorway. "What's all this fuss?" Lamorak walked in, looking from one to the other of us in consternation. "My lady Queen, Sir Bedwyr is looking for you. Whatever are you doing here?"

"I have come to lay a charge against Queen Morgause. Take her in hand, Lamorak, and call the guards. I will not stir from this chamber until she is imprisoned."

"Why, what has she done?"

I hesitated to tell him, until I saw the smirk on Morgause's face.

"The charge is incest. Corrupting a child. One of her own sons."

"What!"

He turned to her, and the face she lifted to him was so totally changed, so full of charm and hurt innocence, I pinched myself to be sure I was not dreaming.

"Good Lamorak, I fear the Queen is ill. Her long barrenness has affected her wits at last." I gasped as I saw the line she meant to take. What a gift she had for finding the sorest spot and plunging the knife straight in! "She burst in upon me this morning, unannounced, and started raving at me. She has got this wild idea about my bedding a boy. No doubt these are her own secret dreams she turns upon me."

"How can you deny it?" I cried. "I saw him here with you!"

"Begging your pardon, my lady, but you did not. There was no one here for her to see, Lamorak. It is absurd and disgusting. What would a grown woman want with an untried boy? Men, experienced men, are much more to my taste."

She sidled up against him and looked up at him with sultry eyes. Lamorak's breathing quickened as he gazed down at her, and his hand slipped stealthily inside her robe. In another moment they would be asking me to leave. I groaned in exasperation. Was there no man in the castle proof against her? On the thought, Bedwyr came through the door.

"Queen Guinevere! There you are!"

"Bedwyr! Arrest her! I charge her now!"

He looked at Morgause and then at Lamorak, who stood beside her, hands at his side. "Well?"

"I deny it," Morgause said proudly. "It is ridiculous. It is beneath me."

Bedwyr grunted. "It was not beneath you once. Lamorak?"

"Uh, my lord, I was passing by and heard words between them, and so came in. I know nothing about it, really. Except I cannot believe—"

"What you believe does not matter. Go downstairs and tell Prince Mordred—"

"Mordred?" Morgause spoke sharply. For the first time I detected a hint of fear. "Where is he? I wish to speak with him."

"Tell Prince Mordred to await me in the Council chamber," Bedwyr finished. Lamorak saluted, bowed to us, and left.

"Where is he?" she repeated.

Bedwyr hesitated a moment before answering and noted the change in her composure. "He was belowstairs as I came by, looking for the Queen, and detained me when I tried to come up."

"If he is still there, bid him come and see me. I have something of importance to tell him."

Bedwyr looked at me.

"He was here when I came to the door, Bedwyr," I whispered. "He was in her chamber. Half dressed. She in a shift, and his smell upon her. At dawn. What more do you need?"

"I deny it!" Morgause spat, seeing Bedwyr's face.

"And sneaked away, no doubt, the coward. You should see him, Guinevere, when blood is spilled, the lily-livered—"

"Silence!" screamed Morgause. "He is not a coward!"

"Indeed?" Bedwyr retorted, his eyes lighting. "Why, he's worse than his twin, who cannot stomach—"

"I'll have you know that Agravaine has killed three men bare-handed!" She caught her breath, but too late. Bedwyr was smiling.

"So we are agreed," he said softly, "that we are speaking of Gaheris."

Trapped by her own tongue, Morgause went still. Bedwyr grasped her arm and turned to me. "Mordred did not know you were here, my lady. But he thought Gaheris was. That's why he tried to keep me away."

I exhaled in relief. "So. You believe."

Bedwyr's face went cold. He held Morgause well away from him, as though she were a viper. "Oh, yes," he said. "I believe."

Morgause stiffened. "You will regret the day you crossed me, both of you."

Bedwyr sighed from the depths of his soul. "I regret the day I ever laid eyes on you, Witch of Orkney."

Morgause lay that night in the tower cell and the next day was brought before the Council. I expected her sons to be outraged, but although they frowned and wore long faces, they said nothing. They knew, all of them, the charge was true, and they were torn between anger at their mother's imprisonment and shame for her behavior. Bedwyr had confronted Mordred, who told him the truth of what he knew. But Mordred did not want to speak publicly against his mother. Where he had grown up, the queen did as she pleased, no questions asked, and he did not see why we could not imprison or exile her if we willed. But Bedwyr was worried. It all depended, he said, on whether the Companions could be brought to believe the charges. Most of them thought well of women; none of them would want to believe such evil of Arthur's sister.

Morgause sat in the Chair of Complaint, composed and lovely. Lamorak was not her only admirer at the Round Table. As her chief accuser, I sat at Bedwyr's right hand. The High King's chair, below the Sword Excalibur in its embroidered hanger, remained empty.

Bedwyr got straight to the point. He laid the charge of incest against Morgause and named me as her accuser. The Companions stirred, shocked. Bedwyr then told them what Lancelot had witnessed that summer; had we known then Gaheris' seductress was his mother, she would have been brought before both Lancelot and Arthur and made to answer for it. At this, the Companions frowned and shifted in their seats. If Lancelot had seen it, it was true. There was much discussion between them. Finally, one of them asked who was present when Lancelot revealed what he had seen between the woman and Gaheris. After a quick glance at me, Bedwyr told them: the High Queen and Mordred. There was a small silence. Then Lamorak rose.

"I mean no offense to the High Queen, Sir Bedwyr, but may we not hear from Prince Mordred, as well? Where Lancelot is concerned, we feel, uh, his memory might be more dispassionate, and thus clearer."

I flushed, but held on to my temper. I would have liked to believe Morgause had put him up to that, but it was something any one of them might have said. What was between me and Lancelot had never been a secret. He had said it as delicately as he could, and God knows, there was truth in it.

Sir Bleoberys then stood. "May we not hear from Prince Gaheris, as well? He is accused, as well as his mother."

"He is a child!" I cried. "You cannot ask him to accuse his mother to her face!"

"But my lady Queen," Berys said politely, "are we not asking that of Prince Mordred?"

I shot Bedwyr a desperate glance. "We are only asking Mordred for confirmation of what Lancelot told me in his hearing, are we not?"

Bedwyr nodded and signaled the guard. "Send for Prince Mordred only."

He was not far away and came at once. Plainly dressed and holding himself straight and tall, he looked so much like his father, it was almost like having Arthur in the room. In answer to Bedwyr's question, he confirmed what Lancelot had said. He did not tell them he had refused to believe it. But when Bedwyr dismissed him, Queen Morgause rose.

"Please allow my son to stay." They were the first words she had spoken, and all heads turned toward her. "You have allowed him to hear the accusation against me. I demand he be allowed to hear my reply."

Bedwyr nodded and motioned Mordred to one of the empty chairs. "Very well. What do you say in your defense, Queen Morgause?"

She stood easily and surveyed the gathering with contempt. Richly dressed and hung with ornaments, the silver crown of Orkney with its milk-white stones upon her brow, she was higher born than any man in that room, and she wanted them all to know it.

"My lords. Queen Guinevere. I am wrongly accused of a foul act. I am as innocent as any one of you. Not only do I deny the charges, I am ashamed of you for bringing them against me. I am heartily ashamed. You demean yourselves to even think it. But, my lords, the cause is clear enough. This summer, I gave Sir Lancelot cause to hate me, and we all know, my lords, what that can lead to. No one has a stronger advocate anywhere on earth than Sir Lancelot has in Queen Guinevere." She curtsied prettily in my direction; heads turned; I held hard to the arms of my chair and returned her stony stare. "I pray you, my lords, never say a word against his stainless honor, else you find yourselves in my position."

"What did he do?" whispered one of the Companions.

Bedwyr frowned. "Silence. We are not gathered to accuse Lancelot. Answer the charge, Queen Morgause. The High Queen claims she found Gaheris in your bedroom, half dressed, at dawn. What say you to that?"

"She is lying." She met their eyes, one by one, except for Mordred. "I deny it absolutely. Gaheris is my son. What she suggests is disgusting."

The men nodded, frowned, and murmured.

"Nevertheless," I said firmly, "he was there. Pulling on the tunic he had left on the floor by your bed days before. Setting a tryst for moonrise, promising to bring you a gift. He was closer to me than you are now."

Morgause's lips slid into a smile. "You have been snooping in my chamber, my lady Queen? What is this obsession you have with children? Is it because you are unable to bear any of your own?"

I shut my eyes and drew a deep breath. At least I had seen it coming. She had given me fair warning the day before.

*

"My lords, have pity on the Queen. Think what she has suffered, unable to bear my brother the King a son. Imagine how it preys upon her mind, day and night, year in, year out, as all about her women conceive and bear. Yet she cannot grow the High King's seed." Against my will, tears crept from my eyes and slowly fell, in long, wet tracks, down my cheeks. Morgause lowered her voice. "Poor woman in a girl's body," she said sweetly, "her barrenness has turned her wits. All she thinks about is children. They must haunt her very dreams. I think, my lords, that this must be how it happened: Still dreamstruck, she came to me and accused me of something she had imagined while she slept. I can find no other explanation. But I forgive her; I would not trade places with her for all the world." She paused. I could not open my eyes. Did they all think me dreamstruck? Did they all think this an answer to the charge? "My lords, is the Queen the only accuser you can find?"

There was silence. Bedwyr cleared his throat. Suddenly a chair scraped against the flooring, and Mordred's voice rang out calm and clear. "No. I accuse you, also, Mother."

I looked up. Arthur's son stood straight, his fists upon the table, and faced the witch. She stared at him, open-mouthed.

"My mother has lain with my brother since before we left Orkney." The men gasped. "At first I only suspected some intrigue. And even when Gaheris hinted at it—"

"He never did!" she cried, trembling.

"—I thought it was a twisted kind of boasting. He has always needed her affection more than any of the rest of us." He looked around at the men, sad and determined. "But when Lancelot told me what he had seen, I knew it was the truth. All the things I had seen before finally made sense. I knew she would return as soon as the High King left with Lancelot. And when she returned, I kept a watch upon her."

"Dragon's spawn!" she hissed, leaning toward him.

"For Gaheris' sake, I have tried to keep him from discovery. I failed in that. But sooner or later it had to come to light." He looked directly at her. "You knew that, surely. You knew it, and you did not care. You don't much care what becomes of Gaheris."

Her eyes were slits; the look in them made me quail, but Mordred stood fast. "No, you bastard whelp, but I care what happens to you! And you will never escape me, Mordred. I have known your fate from the moment of your conception."

"I don't care."

"How like him you are, to turn against me! You will be revenged for that, I do assure you."

"I don't care."

"Brave words, from one who is powerless to prevent disaster! Be certain I will—"

"My lords!" I rose and found my voice. "You have heard the accusation. Will you come to a decision, or must we listen to more of this hateful woman's spite?"

Amid her ranting, the men decided on imprisonment, but away from Camelot, someplace where her sons could not see her except by the High King's leave. They settled on a stronghold in the south, not far from the Winchester garrison. Castle Daure, later known as Castle Dour on account of her temper, was a strong fortress near Saxon lands, held by one Arres, a graybeard king who owed to Arthur the keeping of his kingdom. Until the courier was sent and preparations made, she would be held in the tower.

I took Mordred aside and thanked him for my rescue. Pale and contained, he merely nodded and kissed my hand. Morgause screamed at the sight of it, and as the guards took hold of her, she flew into a rage.

"Bitch!" she snarled. "You two-faced bitch! You barren whore!" Conversation died; men turned; she flung off the grip of her captors. "Cowards! You are all cowards! I curse your children, and all the generations of your descent!"

"Guards!" Bedwyr said sharply. "Hold her. Bind her if you have to." One of them drew forth a length of rope.

Morgause stamped her foot and writhed and swore vengeance upon them all, but they ignored her and bound her fast.

Suddenly she grew calm. "Go ahead, brave men, and bind a woman's flesh. You think that gives you power over me. But you will do my bidding in the end. Guinevere!" She leaned toward me; against my will I shrank back. "Do not think you have beaten me. Do you imagine any fortress in Britain is strong enough to hold me?" She smiled; my innards turned to water. "And those boys of mine whose service Arthur covets, and whose minds you are trying to recast—remember this: They are *my* sons, all of them, and they will never be yours. Not one of them." Her eyes slid to Mordred; I seemed suddenly unable to breathe. "I have sown the seeds of my revenge in them, though they know it not. You cannot remake them. It is already too late." She began to laugh, an ugly sound, full of hate and satisfaction. "Arthur will live to rue the day he sent me into exile!"

"That's quite enough," Bedwyr commanded.

"Silence!" she cried, and froze him with a look. The men went still. The very air began to waver. The spell she wove ensnared the will of soldier, Queen, and prince alike.

"I will destroy my brother. Like Queen Medea, I have brought my enemy a gift that will be his death. He has accepted it; his fate is now out of his hands." I shuddered. I saw it pleased her. "But you, Guinevere, I have already destroyed. Attend and hear your fate. The Great Goddess, who gives life, who takes it and withholds it, listens to my entreaties. You are barren as a mule, and it is *my* doing, it has always been *my* doing! I have sacrificed to the dark moon, in the black pool, every month since you married my brother! It is a powerful enchantment. Because of me, little child queen, the only son you will ever give to Arthur is a son of mine!"

A scream pierced the air. High and wild, it shattered the light and plummeted into nightmare blackness. Pain struck my head; my throat rasped raw—it was my scream, my hate, my terror that lay stretched out on the cold stone floor.

Bedwyr's face swam above me; the witch's high-pitched laughter tore at my wits. "You fools who worship the ground Arthur walks on! He is not the saint you think him! The very crime you accuse me of—" Another scream, was it mine or hers? The door flew open, a great wind rushed in, the cold dark was upon us. Strong hands lifted me and set me in my chair. All the men huddled in the corner, Bedwyr included, hands before their faces, making the sign against enchantment. Across the Round Table, Morgause stood alone, eyes wide with terror, one fist pressed hard against her mouth, one hand held out to ward off a blow. Slowly the faintness passed, and I saw clearly.

Merlin stood before Arthur's chair, black-robed, white-bearded, his flesh seamed with a thousand wrinkles, his eyes as bright as black water. He stared at the witch, and she seemed to shrink even as we watched.

"You!" She gasped, fighting for breath. "You are dead!"

"Yes," he said.

She bit off a cry of terror and collapsed into her seat.

Merlin lifted a long finger and pointed it at her. "I seal your lips upon Arthur. You will say naught against him. Nor against the Queen."

Her eyes widened, but she did not open her mouth.

"The Goddess deserts you. From this moment on, the only power you command will be such as any woman of your age and birth commands." He glanced at the Companions and beckoned them forward. "Take her away and do not fear her any longer. Whatever prison you take her to, there will she stay. I myself will see to it."

Bedwyr bowed. Morgause whimpered. But she was not without courage. "Are you real, Merlin? Or a phantom? Come here and let me touch you."

Something moved behind his eyes. "As real as your shadow, Morgause, which you are never without."

"Except in darkness."

"And where is your shadow in darkness, but lying in wait for the light? It is there, though you cannot see it."

Morgause gasped. "I don't believe you can do it! Wh-What are you? A spirit or a man?"

He lifted his hands, and his black robe spread like wings. "I am Arthur's servant. And you are his enemy. Like Medea, you are cast out, and will not accept your fate. And like Medea, you will be taken away."

"I will tell—" she began, and then her lips froze, though she stamped her foot in anger. At last she spat at him. "Do your worst, then, King's enchanter. Given time, I shall find your weakness and make you pay!"

Merlin signaled to the guards. "Take her away. Go on. It is safe. Though you do not see me with you, I am there, and will protect you from her."

Morgause was led away without a word of complaint. The Companions, tongue-tied and staring, mumbled their thanks to Merlin and filed out. At last only Bedwyr and I remained.

Merlin turned to me. "You have acted bravely, Guinevere. You have no more need to fear her. Her power is gone."

But for the cold that encased him like a second skin, he seemed the same Merlin I had known, and feared, before.

"Thank you, my lord. I—I am grateful for your coming. I had no defense against her."

He smiled kindly. "You have more than you believe. No one here believed her words but you, my dear, not even Morgause. But for Arthur's sake, as well as yours, I could not let her continue."

"My lord—" I paused, trying to brave the question that had knocked against my lips since first he spoke. "My lord, if—if she has lost her power, does that mean, could that mean, I—I—I could bear to Arthur?"

He took both my hands in his. His grip was warm, real, and brought me comfort, but I knew by the gesture what he was about to say.

"She lied, my dear, when she claimed to have caused your fate. It was an empty, vicious boast. She is no more responsible for your barrenness than you are. Courage, Guinevere. We have spoken of this before."

"Yes, my lord. You told me it would grieve me more than it ever grieves the King. And so it does."

"There is a reason for it."

I looked up. "So Bedwyr told me. But—may I ask you? Is it true?"

Merlin nodded. The great cold that had come in with him seemed to warm as he spoke. "Arthur will live in glory everlasting, as long as men are alive to tell his tale. And that will be in no small part your doing, Guinevere, because he has no son to share it with."

"But, my lord," I said quickly, "he has Mordred."

Merlin froze. The room grew frigid; the air itself turned to ice; a dark cloud took shape around him and from its depths I heard his frosty whisper: "Mordred the Bastard! May his name be cursed forever!" With a sound like a whip-crack, the ice broke, the mist thinned, and he was gone!

I jumped and looked at Bedwyr. His face was white.

"Bedwyr! Am I dreaming?"

He shook his head. "If you are, then I am, too."

"Where did he go? What did I say? Why should the mention of Mordred send him away?"

Bedwyr's hand shook as he reached out to me. "Being merely a mortal man, I cannot say. Ask Mordred what there is between them. He ducked out the moment the enchanter swept into the room. Out that window." He pointed to a window behind the table that gave onto the courtyard.

"He has never seen Merlin before! Why was he afraid?"

Bedwyr shrugged. "I don't know. Why is anyone afraid? Ask Mordred. Come, Gwen, you are tired and in need of rest. And I am, too. In a week we go to Caerleon, and the witch to Castle Daure. There are a thousand preparations, and not much time."

33 ♛ THE PROPHECY

Three days before we left, Morgause sent to me begging an audience with Mordred. She did not ask to see any of her other sons. I called Mordred to me and asked him if he wished to see her.

He shrugged. "I suppose so, my lady. I know there is something she wants to tell me."

"It is probably something you do not wish to hear. She cannot be pleased with you, Mordred. She must look upon your words in Council as betrayal."

He lifted his eyes to mine and spoke like Arthur's son. "Nevertheless, I will hear her. She can say no word against the King, or against you, either. And as for me, well"—he shrugged again— "she is the one who forced me to choose between her and my father. Attacking Lancelot is one thing: He is a man and can defend himself against her, as he proved. But Gaheris—Gaheris is a child." He shifted uncomfortably. "She enjoys inflicting pain. This is not news. But if she expected loyalty, she should not have let me meet my father. Now I know, as I never knew before, what worship is."

"Ahhhh, Mordred." I reached out a hand to him.

"She cannot hurt me more, my lady. She knows I have cast my lot with Arthur. If she wants to scream at me, let her scream."

"You are a brave man." He smiled at the appellation. "Before I let you go, I will make one request."

"Anything, my lady. Ask it."

"If, in your judgment, what she tells you will affect the King, or the Kingdom, I would like to know of it."

"Of course, my lady. If it concerns the King, it is your right to know. And my lord Bedwyr."

"That depends on what it is. You must use your judgment."

"I will tell you everything, my lady Queen, I promise it."

I smiled at his ardor. "You have been so brave, Mordred, and I owe you so much. If you will take me into your confidence, I would be in your debt." He rose to go. "Mordred." The question came out without my willing. "Why did you run from Merlin?"

His eyes grew wide and he shivered. "My lady, I do not know."

He went to see Morgause and did not come back.

I paced about in a fever of impatience. Something must have happened. A fine, cold rain had soaked the ground and made it muddy. It was not a day for riding or walking out; I sat in my rooms and stitched with my women. It was never a thing that brought me comfort.

I expected Mordred to come to me after dinner, but he did not. When I sent for him, they told me he had gone to bed early. I sent for Berys, who commanded his barracks.

"Have you seen Mordred?" I asked him. "How does he?"

"Well enough, my lady. Only—"

"Yes?"

"He suffers from a heaviness of spirit. He went to bed early and asked not to be disturbed. He told me he would pay you his respects tomorrow."

With that, I had to be content. But on the morrow, he avoided the castle and kept to the barracks. Gareth came in at midday for his lessons, but Mordred was not with him. At last I sent for him, only to be told he had ridden out alone at midmorning for Avalon. Nervously I awaited his return. Niniane was at Avalon. So something *had* happened. Whatever it was, it had distressed him to the point of seeking advice from the enchantress he so disliked.

The day was cold and dark clouds hung heavy over Caer Camel. But it did not rain until we were in hall, and then the skies opened. We seemed a melancholy group at dinner. So many were gone from our company; the King's chair was empty. And Mordred kept away.

Finally, when Bedwyr, Kay, and I had gathered in the library, I could stand it no longer.

"My lord Kay," I said, making him a reverence, "the Queen's compliments to Prince Mordred. If he is in Camelot, I would like a word with him."

"Shall I bring him here, my lady?"

"At once."

When he was gone, Bedwyr went to stoke the fire. He set the wineskin near it and then turned. "There's something amiss, isn't there, Gwen? May I know what it is?"

"I don't know myself yet, Bedwyr. But I fear it."

"The boy has been unhappy, Berys tells me. He doesn't eat, and he doesn't sleep. He is afraid of something. Do you know what?"

"No. But I hope to find out."

"He rode out this morning for Avalon."

I shrugged. "He must be back by now. In this rotten weather, where else could he go? Besides, he has made me a promise, and I know Mordred. He will keep it."

On the thought, the door opened, and Mordred came in. His face was pale, but he held himself straight. There were shadows under his eyes. He bowed politely. "My lady Queen Guinevere. I am at your service."

"I expected you before this, Mordred."

His face was stone, but something moved in his dark eyes. "I beg your pardon, my lady. I had matters to attend to. I could not come."

I saw then that he would not speak except in private. I turned to Bedwyr and Kay. "My lords, I would have a word with him alone."

Kay did not like it, but could not say so, as Bedwyr moved at once to go. I motioned Mordred to a seat before the fire and poured him a goblet of warmed wine. As soon as we were alone, he started to shiver.

"Drink this," I said gently. "Say nothing yet." I could see that he was more than frightened; he was moved to his very soul by fear. He sipped the wine and stared moodily into the flames.

"I would rather not tell you, my lady," he said suddenly. "And you, you would rather not know."

"But you have promised, Mordred."

He nodded slowly. "All right. But I warn you, I have seen the lady Niniane. And I have spoken to Merlin. There is nothing to be done."

"You spoke to Merlin?"

I watched his hands grip the goblet, Arthur's hands, strong hands. They were shaking.

"My mother, the queen Morgause," he began, forcing himself to it, "told me she was pleased the King had taken me into his household, and confided in me, and trusted me. She was pleased, she said, to see you so attached to me, and the trust that had grown between us. That surprised me. Until she told me why." He paused and drained the winecup. He turned to face me, then, with that direct look of Arthur's that searched the heart. "It was her plan from the beginning. From before my birth she has raised me to be Arthur's undoing. She was pleased because in accepting me, he has donned a garment that will kill him. Those were her words."

I stared. The flames in the grate snapped loudly. Mordred hardly breathed.

"She told me she conceived me because she knew I would be his doom, and she has always hated him. She kept me carefully hidden, and tended, and when Lot died, brought to her, and then sent to Arthur, so that I could be the—the certain instrument of his death."

There were tears in his eyes, and in mine. "How?" I whispered. "Oh, Mordred, this cannot be true!"

"She told me she had seen it in the fire, in the stars, in the crystal. But she is nothing if not a liar. She told me also Merlin had seen it. That was why I went to Niniane."

I waited, holding my breath. The future trembled in the silence.

He looked away. "It is true, Guinevere. It is a thing known by those who have the gift of Sight. Arthur's bane, Niniane herself called me. Somehow, someday, whether I will or no, he shall die because of me."

I shot to my feet. "No! You would not kill him! These things cannot happen without men's wills!"

"I would not harm a hair on his head," Mordred whispered. "I demanded to see Merlin. Niniane told me how to find him. She sent me to a wood atop a hill in Avalon as the mists were rising. She gave me the words to say, that would call him forth." He grimaced suddenly. "I felt like a fishwife, spouting charms against the weather!" He ran a hand through his hair, then steadied himself. "You see, like you, I could not accept it. Somehow, I had to make the Seeing false. I was sure that if anyone could break the curse, it would be Merlin. Everyone knows, pagan and Christian alike, there is no one more powerful in all of Britain. So I called him forth out of the mists." He gulped suddenly, and I knew well what courage that had taken.

"He came at once," he said in a shaking voice. "In a spectral shape, shrouded in mist. I—I thought he was a haunting!" He shivered. "It was freezing all around him! And then, as he stepped forth out of the mist into solid flesh, the thunder cracked, and the sky grew dark all around. He was wrapped in a black cloak. All I could see of him were his ancient face and his eyes of ice. How he hates me, Guinevere! I have never met such hate, face to face. I shook so hard I could barely speak."

I took his hand and held his cold fingers tight between my own. And in my heart I cursed Merlin for deliberately frightening the boy. He was Arthur's son!

Mordred stared down at the floor and spoke woodenly, forcing it out. "I told him I loved my father, and on my life I would not harm him. But he said it mattered not what I did or felt. My existence was all that mattered.

On the day of my birth, Arthur's fate was sealed. Simply by living I am a danger to him."

I cried aloud, remembering Lancelot's words: The boy was dangerous! And Morgause's threat—here was Medea's gift! Mordred himself! I turned away from him, hugging my arms about me, holding on.

"He said there was a time for everything: good and ill, joy and sorrow, glory and shame, the doing of right and the doing of evil. As Arthur had been begotten in the Light, so I was begotten in the Dark. As Arthur was destined for glory and greatness, so I was destined to bring it to an end. Nothing lasts forever. If I was wise, he said, I would think no more of it than that."

"Oh, Mordred! How cruel! That cannot be all he said!"

"He looked at me as if he would like to watch me burn alive." Mordred slowly raised his eyes to me, black and full of grief. "I told him to kill me, I offered him my sword."

"Dear God!"

"He refused, saying he would not wound Arthur so. Neither would I, I cried. I was angry, angry at Merlin, and angry at the fates, which could treat a man so unfairly. What had I done? I asked him, to be so condemned before my birth?"

"What did he say?"

Mordred paused. "The lightning flashed as bright as daylight, and the thunder cracked so near, I jumped. For a moment I could not see him, and I thought he had disappeared. But he was standing looking up into the sky. He was silent a long time. Then he spread his arms, and the wind, which had been gusting, suddenly died. It was not my fault, he said. It had been written in the stars before ever I was born, that Arthur's bane should be the son he begot upon his sister." Mordred turned his head away, and I felt myself begin to burn with anger. He had never been ashamed of it before!

"He is only shifting blame from his own shoulders!" I cried. "It was *his* fault, if it was anyone's! Merlin, the all-powerful magician! He was nearby the night Arthur lay with her. Arthur did not know Morgause was his sister, but Merlin did! Ahhh, Mordred, it is not you he hates, but himself! This explains why he cannot abide you near him, even for Arthur's sake. He feels guilty—as well he should—but will not admit it!"

Mordred looked at me a long moment and then shrugged. "So you, too, my lady," he said softly, "agree I should never have been born." He half smiled as I gasped. "No matter. I think the same. I would rather not have been born at all than be born to kill such a man as Arthur."

"Oh, Mordred, that is not what I meant!" I knelt at his feet and clutched his hands. "You know I am a Christian and it is a grievous sin. But it is Arthur's sin, my dear, not yours."

He smiled sadly. "It is no one's fault. Perhaps Merlin was right. But it isn't fair. Even Merlin must see that it isn't fair. I begged him to release me from my fate. Surely, I said, if he loved Arthur, he would do it." His face grew grim. "If he would not, I threatened to slay myself, to save my father."

"Oh, Mordred, you would not! It would kill Arthur more surely than a swordstroke!"

Mordred shrugged. "He said he could not release me. It was not within his power. Arthur had committed a heinous sin and must pay the price. Nothing he could do, or I could do, would change that. Even my death would not change it now; it would only bring Arthur grief he might be spared."

"Had he—had he no solace to offer you at all?"

"He told me I would be King." I held my breath; Mordred's smile was bitter. "I replied I would sooner die at Arthur's death than succeed him. He smiled, then, and told me to be careful what I wished for." His hand formed a fist, and his jaw tightened. "I told him I hoped Lluden of the Underworld imprisoned him in chains forever! I told him I hoped he roasted long in Hell! Enchanters are nothing but meddlers!" With an effort, he calmed himself and drew a deep breath. "He said one thing more before he went back into the mist and the rains began. Guess what it was."

"I'm sure I cannot," I breathed.

" 'Take what comes and live without complaint. What will be, will be. Life is woman's gift; death is God's.' "

This timeworn commonplace was known as Merlin's litany, so often had it fallen from his lips. There was not a child in Britain who did not know it. And this was all the comfort Merlin could offer Arthur's son!

"Oh, my God, my God!" I bent my head, weeping. "How can it happen without your will?"

"I don't know. But it will. I will be the cause of it, somehow. I would never raise a hand against him, but just by having been born, I will be his death. Oh, the gods are unjust!" he cried suddenly, and buried his face in his hands.

I rose and sat beside him, and cradled his head in my arms. When we both were calmer, I said, "The King knows."

He nodded. "Yes. I know he knows. I remember now the times he has recalled it, when he was with me. I remember how the light left his face. And guess who told him! Merlin, of course." He clenched his fist. "He was only a little older than I when he learned it—that his own half sister carried his child, who would one day be his death! Can you imagine it? He should have killed her before she bore me! I should never have been born! How has he managed to be the man he is, knowing this?"

He rose suddenly and began to pace the room. I could not watch, he reminded me so of Arthur.

"The King knows, yet he took me in," he said fiercely. "Not only took me in, but searched for me. Educated me. Trained me. Trusted me. He has done me nothing but honor. And for what? That I should reward him by bringing him his death? *I will not do it!*"

He tore at his hair and then stopped, willing himself to stillness. "I have made a vow." His voice was quiet again, and grave. "I have vowed I will not outlive him. No one, *no one*, will be able to accuse me of that ambition."

I knew he referred to Lancelot. But before I drew breath to defend him, Mordred came and knelt before me. He looked suddenly young and lost.

"Why did he do it, my lady? Why did he take me in, knowing I am his fate? Can any man be that brave? Or is it that he would rather see his death approaching than wait, unknowing, for the blow?"

"I do not think it was bravery so much as love," I said gently, taking his hands. "He would do what is right by you, whatever the outcome."

He nodded, swallowing. "I will do the same by him. I will serve him with my life. If this—cruel injustice cannot be averted, at least I can show him that by my will I love and honor him."

I stroked his hair, and he laid his head in my lap. So Bedwyr found us when he came in later, in a pose of love, with tears on our faces.

Two days later the court moved to Caerleon for Christmas, and Queen Morgause left for Castle Daure. Arthur had wanted to be home by Christmas, but storms had closed the seas, and we had no word. We went about our business, Mordred and I, as if nothing were amiss. He was resolved upon his course of action, of loyal service until death, and in an odd way this had calmed him and matured him. I was the one who could not sleep at night, haunted by bad dreams and ghostly voices. Merlin was wise to stay clear of me, for I was eager to give him a piece of my mind. Rumors drifted in that he had been seen near his precious cave in South Wales. I determined to ride there and face him, but was prevented from going by a snowstorm. The storm became a blizzard and kept us penned within doors. I thought some days I should scream in frustration.

"Oh, Arthur!" I cried alone at night. "Come home and take this burden from me!"

Bedwyr was my only solace. If he knew of the dreadful prophecy, he did not show it. He was calm, and kind, and wise. If he was puzzled by my moodiness and outbursts of anger, he did not reproach me, but put it down to womanly weakness, or loneliness for the King.

Christmas, the King's birthday, the feast of Mithra, passed without word from the King. And then at last the weather broke, and we had two weeks of thaw. I rode out every day, on Pallas if I wanted a long gallop, on

Rajid if I needed a challenge to my skill. Bedwyr became worried and spoke to me thrice about not risking my neck while under his protection.

"I am pursued by enchanters!" I retorted. It was the only clue he had to what was wrong.

The day the King returned I was out riding. Berys was the leader of the escort, and although I had led him leagues from Caerleon, he followed meekly and let me have my way. I was well paid for such foolishness, for on the way home his horse threw a shoe, and we went at a walk all the way. It was well after dark when we reached the fortress. The sentries met us with evident relief.

"The King is back and wants to see the Queen!" they cried in greeting.

Berys swore under his breath. "Just my luck, by Mithra! Now I am for it!"

"The fault is mine," I told him. "Don't worry about the King. He knows me."

He grinned, and I realized suddenly it was the first time in a month I had made anyone smile.

I hurried to my quarters and found Ailsa ready with my bath. From her chatter I gathered that the King had returned at midday and had been clos-eted all afternoon with Bedwyr, Gawaine, and Mordred. Thank goodness he had learned from other lips of Morgause's crime and imprisonment, al-though with Gawaine there he would learn little enough of the details. How far away that trouble seemed to me now! How swiftly had my worry over the corruption of Gaheris been swallowed up by my fear for Mordred! How much had happened—and all of it dreadful!—since Arthur had left Britain!

The King took his dinner in his rooms, still in conference. Ailsa brought me some bread and soup, but I could eat none of it. I did not want to greet the King in public. I was not sure I could trust my tongue. So in spite of Arthur's orders that I was to be brought to him as soon as I was ready, I waited until the page reported that Mordred and Gawaine had gone.

He was in his sitting room with Bedwyr, standing before the fire. I avoided looking at his face and curtsied at his feet.

"Welcome home, my lord." I tried to hide my agitation, but of course he saw it. When he took my hands to raise me, his grip was firm. As always, I felt calm and warmth and strength flow from him, and I looked up in des-peration. "Oh, my lord!" He embraced me then and held me close while I struggled against tears.

"I know what it is, Gwen. Go ahead, let it out," he said softly, and at long last I let go and sobbed like a child in his arms.

"It is not fair!" I cried against his breast. "Oh, Arthur! God could not be so cruel!" He held me until my weeping subsided and pressed a cool cloth gently to my brow. Bedwyr handed him a cup of scented wine, which he put to my lips and bade me drink. I felt dizzy with so many tears and collapsed into the chair. Arthur sat across from me, holding my hands. Bedwyr stood gazing at the flames.

"Oh, my lord! This is a terrible thing! I shall go mad unless you help me! Has—has Mordred spoken with you? Does Bedwyr know?"

He answered me calmly. "Mordred has made his report, and Gawaine his. And Bedwyr has told me what they could not. I know all about Morgause and your bravery on behalf of Gaheris. Thank you, Gwen. No one else I know would willingly face my sister. Including me." He paused. "I have approved the Council's actions."

"My lord, I do not mean the trouble with Gaheris!"

"I know, my dear." He touched his lips to my hand. "About the prophecy that worries you—no, Mordred did not speak of it. And yes, Bedwyr knows. I have just now told him of it." He paused, frowning. "I wish you had shared it with him, Gwen, and saved yourself such suffering. You are naught but skin and bone and sorrow. He tells me you have had no rest for weeks. It is no wonder you are ill."

"It was not my secret to share," I whispered. "Oh, Arthur! Tell me it is not true! Niniane would not come to me, and I would have gone to Merlin, but—"

He smiled, a shadow of his grin. "There was a timely snowstorm. Yes. And now you see why Merlin has avoided Camelot and comes to me only in private. He cannot bear the sight of Mordred, although for my sake, he does not say so."

I shuddered. "If Merlin loved you, Arthur, he would never have told you this!"

He sighed. "I know this is hard, Gwen. It was hard for me once, too. That's why I never told you myself. But what is it, after all? Just an event foreseen. Knowing or not knowing will not change it; all it will do is bring joy or pain to those who know. I can see that my son has accepted this. It has made him a man. And it must have been more difficult for him than ever it was for me. You will have to accept it, too, my dear."

"I cannot!" I cried, and appealed to Bedwyr. "Bedwyr, make him see it must be somehow averted! His own son!"

Bedwyr's smile was sad, and his eyes were full of grief. But he only shrugged and said gently, "Listen to Arthur, Gwen. If he can bear it, then we all must, for his sake."

"Arthur! Speak with Merlin! Let it not fall to Mordred—what has he done to deserve it? He is innocent. Let him be free of this!"

"Yes, he is innocent," Arthur agreed. His warm brown eyes held my own, and I felt the soft, light touch of his will, soothing, calm, serene. "We must both do all we can to help him, to protect and honor him, to ensure that his fate will be undeserved."

I was held, helpless, in the web of his powerful love, and gradually felt my anger drawn from me, until I was left empty of grief. I slipped from the chair, sat at his feet, and kissed his hands.

"Leave us now, Bedwyr," I heard him say.

"My lord," Bedwyr said softly, and went out.

Arthur lifted me in his arms and carried me into his chamber. He undressed me quickly, wrapped me well in warm blankets, and put me in the bed. Then he stoked the fire and brought me watered wine and made me drink it. He called for the page and sent for hot broth. When it came, he took it and fed me himself. When I could take no more of it, he set it aside and, sitting down beside me, looked into my face.

"Why would you not let Bedwyr tend you?" he asked gently. "He is sick with worry about you. You do not eat or sleep. He feels he has failed me."

"I did not know he felt so, my lord. He has been so kind to me, and my thoughts were always elsewhere—I did not notice his distress. It was selfish of me. I will beg his forgiveness."

Then he smiled and gently touched my face. "That is more like the Guinevere I know. Let it be. I kept him here this evening to show him what it was that ailed you, so that he did not feel it was his fault. He knows it now."

"How did you know, my lord?"

"I looked at Mordred's face, and I knew the witch had told him."

"I made him tell me. He did not want to."

"He should have been stronger. But he loves you."

I closed my eyes on that, but two small tears slipped out. "Oh, Arthur," I whispered. "I do not want you to die."

"Ahhhhh." He breathed it out slowly and kissed the two tears. "Now we are coming to it. It is death you fear. You are young, and you have not felt its touch before."

How could he know? Did he know my every thought?

"I fear your death. I cannot envision life without you. And to die by his hand—"

His finger closed my lips. "Don't, Gwen. We don't know that. Not even Merlin knows how it will happen. Only that it will. And that is not such precious knowledge, for every man must die. I do not think about it. It is what we do in life that matters."

He was so calm, so strong, so sure, he gave me strength. I looked at him in wonder. "Is it because you are a soldier, you do not fear death?"

He smiled lightly. "Every soldier fears death, before every battle. But not during it; there is not time. And yes, it is easier, to have faced it and come away. Now listen, while I tell you another of Merlin's prophecies."

"No! Please, no more!"

"You will like this one," he said, coming closer, pulling the pins from my hair. "He promised me I should have time to accomplish what I most desired. Time and to spare, he said. So, you see? You need have no fear that this wicked day of destiny is near, for I have plenty of plans still to carry out. Many things remain to do. But I will need you beside me to do them."

He took my hair down and let it fall around my shoulders. What with the warmth of the fire and the wine and the hot broth, my shivering had gradually subsided, and I began to relax within my warm cocoon of blankets. When he was with me, death seemed infinitely remote.

"Arthur," I whispered.

"My love."

"You are—you are such a force for life."

He smiled and kissed me gently. "And you, my dearest, are more than life to me. I am nothing without you. Now sleep. I will sit here by the fire."

"But—"

"There will be plenty of time for love." He grinned. "This also Merlin told me."

I laughed. It seemed like the first time in years.

34 ♕ THE WITCH OF RHEGED

What on earth did you say to my sister?" the King asked with a smile, looking up from the papers at his desk.

"Your sister, my lord?" I waved away Hanna, who was fanning me, and turned in the chair to see him better. The library doors were open to the terrace, where Kay, Bors, Galahantyn, Bedwyr, Lancelot, and I sat languidly in the midday heat in the shade of the Camelot oak. Nearby, the new fountain, an alabaster dragon tipped with gold on claws and tail and fangs, spewed spring water in a refreshing tinkle of sound. It made us feel cooler just listening to it. We had barely moved the last hour. Only the King had energy enough to work. I peered into the cool dimness of the chamber. He had just broken the seal on a scroll, which he read with some astonishment.

"Yes," he said, beginning to frown. "My sister Morgan. Witch of Rheged, as she likes to style herself. Listen to this." He paused and, keeping his finger on the close and flowing penmanship of her scribe, began to read carefully in Latin. " 'And whereas your good lady Queen did insult me, in the company of sundry lords and princes, who will bear witness to this on their oaths as King's men, and as this took place in the royal city of Camelot, albeit while you yourself, my good lord King and brother, were abroad with my most reverend lord King of Rheged, I do beseech and require of you justice to the satisfaction of our honor, as we two Pendragon'—I can't make this out, I think she wants a hearing— 'and set aside the enmity between us of past years, by setting aside the very root and cause, which, however lovely, brings forth naught but a rank and barren blossom—well, I guess the gist is clear enough. Oh, yes, she goes on to wish me 'happiness and increase' and refers once again at the end to my youth and Urien's strength. He was fifty when he got Morgaine on her. I suppose she means to tell me it is never too late."

In spite of myself, the color rose to my face. I lowered my eyes. The bruise still gave pain, when tapped sharply.

"Oh, God." Lancelot groaned, watching me. "Not again. You settled all that years ago, Arthur. She can't be serious. She's just being nasty."

"But why?" asked the King, rising and coming out to join us. He sat on the plinth of the fountain pool, facing me. "She says here"—he tapped the letter—"that she's coming to Camelot to settle the matter. What matter? What happened while I was gone last year?"

I looked up from my lap and met his eyes. "I should have told you, my lord. But it seemed so small a thing at the time. The morning after the stable fire, when Queen Morgan left with her train, she said some very rude things to Bedwyr." The King glanced at Bedwyr, who nodded. "I only meant to defend him," I continued, "and return her remarks in kind . . . you know, my lord, the sort of things women will say to each other in a fit of temper, where a man would keep silent. It really was nothing at all."

Lancelot and Kay, who had heard nothing of it, sat up a little straighter.

"Did you insult her, Gwen?" Arthur asked calmly. "If you did, I am sure she deserved it. But I must know what you said."

Good Bedwyr jumped in to my rescue. "Your lady sister insulted you, as well, my lord, which was what upset the Queen."

"Oh?" He raised an eyebrow and turned to Bedwyr. "How so?"

"Ah, she implied your marriage to the Queen was, ah, unconsummated."

To my relief, Arthur laughed. "Oh, I see. A catfight. Say no more. I will disregard it. She also says here that she is bringing Morgaine, her daughter, and to be sure to let Guinevere know. Does this signify anything?"

I lifted my chin. "Yes, my lord. I had no right to do it, but I told her to her face she was an unloving mother to leave the child untended for so long. That is the insult. But see now, she will bring her, so perhaps it was all for the good."

"Perhaps. But I do not like the tone of this letter. She asks for a formal hearing. It sounds almost like a Plea of Complaint."

"Against the Queen?" Lancelot sat forward and would have risen but for the look on the King's face.

"I assure you, my lord, it was a small thing!" I cried. "When she was gone, I thought no more upon it!"

"Nor did I," Bedwyr said quietly.

"I—I suppose I should have remembered it, and told you, but so much else was happening—with Queen Morgause—and I forgot," I finished lamely.

The King's eyes were kind, but his face was grave. "Be easy, Guinevere. I do not blame you for this. As you said, it is a small thing indeed. What you said to her, if impolitic, was true. But it seems she would make something of it. I would like to know what."

He looked around at the company in expectation.

"It is clear," Lancelot said hotly, "that she wants the Queen put away." Bors and Galahantyn looked at him swiftly.

The King shook his head. "No. That is what she wants us to think. She was just indirect enough to hope we would think so. But I have publicly declared I will not do it. This is known throughout Britain."

"It is known in Less Britain, as well, my lord," Galahantyn offered.

"So. What is it she wants?"

But no one answered him. He rose and paced slowly back and forth before us. The very air shimmered as he passed.

"When is the lady Morgan arriving, my lord?" Kay asked. "And with how many?"

"In a week. With twenty men and the child."

"Not with King Urien?" I asked quickly.

The King stopped his pacing and looked sharply at me. "No. That is what makes this so interesting. Urien is in Cornwall to see his youngest son married to Constantine's sister. I will wager he knows nothing about this."

"Her husband's son wed to the sister of the High King's heir?" Lancelot asked. "And she the High King's sister? This smells of ambition."

"Oh, Lancelot," I said in irritation, "you smell ambition everywhere."

He flashed me a look, and Arthur saw it.

"I don't like it," Bedwyr muttered.

"Nor do I." Arthur sighed. "She is up to something. But I fear we will have to wait to see what it is."

A page appeared at the library doors and bowed from the waist. "My lord King! Sir Lamorak is returned from Castle Daure, my lord, and requests a word with you."

"Bring him here."

"Yes, my lord."

"What's this?" Kay asked. "You recalled Lamorak from the Winchester garrison?"

"Not exactly." The King smiled wryly. "I should have done last winter, but now it is too late. He is enamored of Morgause and no doubt comes to beg me for her freedom. For the third time."

Lancelot rose. "Shall we leave you, my lord?"

The King waved him back to his chair. "No, no. He knows what I will say. He will be glad to appeal to you. Watch him well. Do you remember Lamorak?"

"Of course, my lord. A good knight, bold and sensible. A good shot with a bow. A fine swordsman."

"With an eye for women," Bedwyr added.

The King rolled up Queen Morgan's letter and tucked it in his tunic. "You will find him changed," he said shortly.

Lamorak came in behind the page, knelt at Arthur's feet and kissed his ring.

"My lord King! My thanks for this audience. You do me great honor."

"You have given me good service, Lamorak. I will hear you," the King replied politely, raising him.

Lamorak was a well built man of middle height, about Arthur's age. He had never married; rumor had it he loved women too well and never could settle on a single one. His demeanor now was one of boyish eagerness; with shining eyes and flushed face and fluid tongue, he described Queen Morgause as a changed woman, a sorrowful and humble penitent who, under the encouragement of good King Arres, had given up her pagan ways and accepted the True Christ. She had confessed her sins, he said, and received absolution. She had forgiven them all, even Merlin. But now she spent the long winter nights weeping for loneliness and the hopelessness of her condition, doing Arthur worship always, and praying mightily for his soul. She would beg, and he begged for her, to spend her last days in freedom, living quietly in some distant corner of Britain, wherever the King might choose to send her.

At the end Lamorak lay on the paving stones and kissed the hem of the King's robe. Arthur said nothing, but glanced at his Companions with a meaning look. I saw Galahantyn was moved by the knight's desperate pleading, and Bors, too, had a face of sympathy. But those of Arthur's men who knew Morgause looked sickened.

"Good Lamorak," Lancelot said gently. "Beg not so piteously for the freeing of a witch. She is not some innocent, unjustly imprisoned. This abject pleading does you no honor."

Lamorak rose, and some dignity returned to him. "Sir Lancelot, she is a witch no longer. All her charms and magic she has renounced for the True Christ. She repents of her past deeds, sir, and lives now a Christian life."

"Then," Bedwyr said dryly, "she should beg permission to remove to a nunnery."

Lamorak flushed. "My lords have sport with me. No matter. This is a lady wronged, and I would see her righted."

"No." Arthur said it flatly, and the word hung heavy in the unmoving air. "Your intentions may be honorable, Lamorak, but you are led astray."

"But, my lord—"

"I have not wronged her," the King said quietly. "It is she who has wronged me. And my wife. And her sons. And more than once. She has no one to forgive. And she has not asked those she has injured for forgiveness. For the crimes she has committed, she deserves death. But I do not kill women. She will stay where she is."

Lamorak drew himself up and met the King bravely. "I am betrothed to her, my lord. With your permission."

Arthur stared at him, shocked beyond speech.

I rose. "Sir Lamorak." I dipped him a curtsy, and he bowed to me.

"My lady Guinevere."

I put a hand on his arm and felt how it trembled. "You are an honorable man, and lately of the King's fellowship of Companions. We have missed you since you have been stationed at the Winchester garrison."

"Why, thank you, my lady."

"Have you thought well, my lord, about this step you take? Does Gawaine know you would be his stepfather? What think the twins?"

He paled slightly. "I have said nothing yet, my lady. First I seek the King's permission."

"Ah. Let us give this some thought." I took his arm, and we strolled around the fountain. The splashing of cool water kept our words from other ears. "What is it a man seeks in marriage? A warm bed, a loving pair of arms to come home to, a ready smile, a forgiving heart? Yes, if he is lucky. But these any village maiden can provide. What does a man want who marries a queen?"

"It's not that!" Lamorak gasped. "Do not accuse me of hubris, my lady. This is not because she is the High King's sister! I love the lady!"

"You misunderstand me, sir. I meant, any queen. You must know she has held the reins of power in Orkney since her husband's death. She is a woman of strong will. Would you agree?"

He licked his lips nervously and nodded. "What of it?"

"What will you come home to, Lamorak? A woman who can listen to your cares and understand them? Who may speak her mind, but bow to your will in a dispute? Who will temper her judgment with soft words, when it disagrees with yours? Who will put anger aside for your sake? Will Queen Morgause put you, who have never ruled a kingdom, higher in her estimation than herself?" The longer I went on, the more uncertain he became. I spoke very kindly to him, and he had no resistance against kindness. "Happy is the man whose wife loves his honor more than he does. Will Queen Morgause put your honor before her own?"

I could see he knew her well enough, despite infatuation, to know the answers to these questions. He wavered. "Well . . ."

"We will grant you time to rethink it, dear Lamorak. In the meantime, stay with us awhile and renew your friendships here. If at month's end you still seek the King's permission, ask then. But do not ask today."

He knelt and kissed my hand and, bowing to the King and his Companions, left us hastily.

Arthur rose and came to me, taking my hands between his own. "Thank you, Gwen."

"I spoke the truth, my lord. And he heard it. He has not yet lost all his sense."

"He is besotted," Sir Bors muttered.

"Bewitched, more like." Bedwyr added. "If she is Christian, I am King of Rome."

Kay laughed. "They are lovers, surely. How else did he know she wept all night long?"

"He is her pass to freedom," Galahantyn observed acutely.

But Lancelot said nothing. He sat in quiet agony, his eyes aflame, watching and trying not to watch our hands clasped together. Arthur let go of me and turned. Lancelot looked away.

"Blessed is the man," the King said, "who does not have sisters!"

Queen Morgan came to Camelot in state, riding at the head of her company with Sir Accolon at her side. In a closed litter some way behind rode her daughter the princess Morgaine. It was said that since her terrible ordeal, the child had not uttered a single word; she could hum a melody but she could not speak, and she hated the sight of men. It was my dearest hope that Niniane would take charge of the girl and heal her.

The King stood on the castle steps with his company of knights, gave his sister the ritual kiss of greeting, and saw her installed in her rooms. Then he washed his hands of her and returned to his work. Two steps he took in precaution. He sent to Avalon for Niniane, and he sent a message to Urien in Cornwall, begging his attendance in Camelot as soon as the festivities were over.

I was kept out of Morgan's way, which suited me well. We had no relief from the heat, and I and my ladies sat all day by the fountain in their garden, or in mine, stitching and listening to birdsong. It was enough to drive one out of one's wits. Everyone's temper was frayed. When I saw the King in the evenings, it was all I could do to be civil to him.

"What has your precious sister come for?" I would accost him. "Make her speak—has she some complaint of me? I will see she regrets it! Oh, Arthur, do *something*! If I have to stitch another cushion I shall scream."

And he would laugh and give me cool fruit drinks, chilled with ice they kept in the cellars, packed in straw. He was almost too sweet-tempered to bear.

Finally, Queen Morgan went to see the King. He came to me shortly after, to tell me what she had said.

"I have called a Council meeting in the Round Hall, at her request, when the heat of the day is past. She wishes to make a formal Complaint, but will not tell me what it is. You must be there, Gwen."

"Whatever pleases you, my lord."

"It does *not* please me," he said, suddenly cross, staring at the dull white sky. "But you must do it. Christ! Why won't it rain?"

When the Council met two hours before dinner, the heat had grown worse instead of better. The sky was darkening, but the air was still and oppressive. It hung so heavy, it took effort to breathe. Arthur and his Companions gathered in the Round Hall, mopping their brows and looking damp and ragged. I sat on the King's left hand. Lancelot took his place on his right. Directly opposite the King was the Chair of Complaint, sometimes known as the Perilous Chair, on account of some judgments given against false accusers. Here sat Queen Morgan, robed in rich velvets and crowned with the crown of Rheged, cool and steady, looking not in the least uncomfortable. That was when I knew for certain she was a witch.

Behind her chair stood Accolon, handsome and proud, dressed lavishly to match her. He held himself still, but he had not her steadiness. His eyes darted here and there, watching the faces of the Companions, and more than once drifted to the High King's Sword and then quickly looked away. I shivered suddenly, though the heat was stifling.

When everyone was gathered, Queen Morgan rose. "My lord King, my brother, and all you gentle knights, I come to bring Complaint against the Queen."

There was muttering among the Companions, and Lancelot shifted in his chair. The King stared at her; waiting.

"When last I was here, as your guest, you, my brother, had no sooner taken ship for Less Britain when your lady Queen turned upon me and insulted me to my face. Sir Accolon will verify it; and if he tells the truth, Sir Bedwyr will, as well. I have no doubt," she continued as Bedwyr, on my left, stiffened with anger, "that it is difficult for a backwoods princess to be brought so high, by your favor and grace, my lord, and all in all, she has done well, and is beloved of your company. But without your strong hand to guide her, she is a ship cast off from moorings. And this time, my lord, she has foundered upon Pendragon rock."

If she thought the way to get at Arthur was through flattery, she was mistaken. He sat perfectly still, but his nostrils flared and his eyes looked right through her. Beside him, Lancelot barely controlled his fury; I could read his thought upon his face: backwoods princess indeed! It made me smile, and Queen Morgan, seeing it, began to lose her temper.

"I am the daughter of the High King Uther and his Queen Ygraine! I will not be insulted, my lord King, by anyone in the kingdoms, without redress. It is my due."

Arthur considered her long and then answered. "I know of what this 'insult' consisted. I know also of the words you spoke to Guinevere. This is not a matter for the Council, Morgan, but for you two women only. It seems to me that apologies are due on both sides. Let us dismiss this matter."

"No!" She was truly angry now, and her haughty features looked hard and cold. "I will have redress! You are famous for your justice, my brother— would you withhold it from your own kin? I will not have anyone speak to me so!"

The King sighed wearily. "What redress do you seek? The High Queen will apologize." I rose.

She paused and gathered everyone's attention. "She has dishonored you, my lord King. Put her away."

The Companions shouted in protest; the noise filled the hall. Arthur was surprised, and showed it. He could not believe she had come all the way from Rheged for this. He did nothing to stop the shouting, but waited until the noise of dissent abated. Gently he took my wrist and sat me in my chair. He felt my trembling and said softly, "Courage, Guinevere." Then he faced his sister. "No."

"Hear me out, my lord. You will see the words I speak are truth. You are enchanted by her beauty, as is every man in this room. How not? And if she had done Britain her duty in bearing sons, I should demand less. But in truth, my lord, she has failed you and betrayed Britain; she has ended the Pendragon line and put a final stop to what you and our father have accomplished. This is not news—this she can see herself. But Pendragon must be her enemy, else she would step down of her own accord, and do you the grace and favor you have done her. But she has not; she is content to do your line dishonor and bring it to a close. She is not Queen enough for you, my lord, however much you love her. Not Queen enough to put your honor before her own; not Queen enough to treat your sister with common kindness; never mind the loving favor she bestows upon your Companions." Here Bedwyr gripped my hand beneath the table and held on tightly. "And her favors, my lord"—her voice went smooth and silky— "are so generously bestowed! Can you not see with your own eyes, brother, how she treats Sir Lancelot, or Sir Bedwyr, or King Melwas?"

I gasped, and the Companions stared at her dumbfounded. The implication was perfectly clear. The deliberate mention of Melwas cast the same shadow over them all; she meant they were my lovers, and every man there knew it.

Arthur shot to his feet, white-faced. His right hand pushed hard on Lancelot's shoulder, keeping him in his seat.

"That is enough." His voice was flat, and when one saw his eyes, the room grew colder. "This is unpardonable."

I held tight to Bedwyr's hand and kept dry-eyed. Later he showed me where my nails had drawn his blood.

"You have had more redress than you deserve," the King said in a low voice. "I have allowed you to publicly insult my wife. I should have known you better."

Amazingly, Queen Morgan looked contented with this response and smiled a smug smile.

"There is no question here of betrayal, madam, except on your own part. All Britain knows I will not put the Queen away. Neither"—and he let his glance fall on the stunned faces of his Companions—"will I allow her to leave me, so long as I am King. That is an end to it."

"I insist that she go." Morgan's eyes were bright and eager; what did she hope from this defiance?

The King leaned forward, furious. "I refuse."

Queen Morgan shrugged and signaled Accolon. The young knight stepped forward and came to the edge of the table.

"King Arthur of Britain," he said formally, with barely a tremor in his voice, "my lady the Queen of Rheged is dishonored by the Council's refusal to give her redress for the wrongs done her." He had got it by rote; this was planned. He drew a glove from his belt and threw it on the table. "On behalf of my lady the Queen Morgan, I do challenge King Arthur to personal combat—with the Sword of Britain against the Sword of Rheged. I contest your right to rule."

Everyone gasped. Arthur looked bewildered behind his shock. Lancelot jumped up, shaking from head to foot.

"Traitor!" he cried. "You foul, murderous traitor! I will kill you myself before you lay a hand on the King! How dare you!"

"Lancelot!" Arthur held his arm but could not still him. The room was in an uproar. Everyone was shouting. Queen Morgan looked quietly pleased; Accolon stood white and determined beside her. My eyes went swiftly to the Sword, behind the King's chair. Something touched my neck like a cold draft, and I felt the hairs rise. When I looked away, I felt Morgan's icy gaze upon me and shivered.

Amid the hubbub, Arthur collected himself and grew thoughtful. He

could not fathom her intentions, but his immediate course was clear. "I accept the challenge, Sir Accolon. On the morrow we meet."

Again the knights protested, each one offering to fight for the King,
each one protesting that he should not risk his person for such a one as
Accolon.

Arthur raised a hand and silenced them. "I thank you, my lords, for the
offers. But he has challenged my right to rule. And she has challenged
the Queen's honor. I will meet him myself, and with pleasure. Kay, see to
the arrangements." He looked at Morgan. "Now get out."

She swept out with stately dignity, Accolon in her wake. The Companions crowded around Arthur.

I turned to Bedwyr. "Let me go! Let me go!" He released me, and I
sprang from my chair and flew to my rooms. Suffocated, oppressed with misery, I ran to my garden to find solace in private tears. I wept long and
heartily. No matter what I did, I brought grief to Arthur. Morgan was
right—I was not Queen enough for him. It had never occurred to me to
leave him, to withdraw, but had I been less a backwoods princess and more
a queen, I should have thought of it and done it. And now? Would it be too
late? He had declared he would not let me leave, but perhaps that was to defend my honor in that public place. Perhaps he would allow it, if I went quietly without his knowing. The old wound was reopened, and I felt I could
not bear it any longer. But to part from him now—I would be but half myself without him. Yet how could I stay, and subject him to insults for my
sake! He was forever defending my honor with the blood of his body!

I wept until my head felt like splitting, and still the tears flowed freely.
Suddenly I felt a cool touch upon my temples and a gentle hand stroke my
brow. I lifted my head to see a child, thin and dark and pretty, at my side.
Her face was narrow, her expression somber, but her warm brown eyes were
luminous and filled with love. She hummed a little tune, and as she touched
me, I felt my tears subside.

"Who are you?" I whispered, taking her little hand in mine. "Who are
you, who looks at me with Arthur's eyes? What is your name?"

She said nothing but kept humming, and then very gently kissed my
cheek. I reached for her and hugged her to my breast, this little angel with
the healing hands. She embraced me; her thin arms, delicate as a bird's
wings, went round me, and I was comforted. Without warning, she stiffened, then broke away and left me, quick as a wink. I looked round for her,
but she had vanished. I did not believe in fairies; I thought I must have
dreamed it.

Then I saw Arthur coming down the path to me. He knelt beside
me on the flagstones and took me in his arms. "Dear Gwen! How she has
hurt you!"

"My dear Arthur," I cried, laying my head on his shoulder. "Why is it I am such a heavy stone around your neck? I cannot bear that I should be the one to put you in jeopardy! Your sister was right in that—until you are free of me, you will forever be defending my honor against slanders that are nothing but truth!"

"I knew it!" he whispered fiercely. "I knew you would take it so. For this, and not for Accolon, I will be revenged upon her!" He pressed me close and held me while I wept in his arms. "Listen to me, Guinevere, for I do not say this lightly. You are the joy in my life. Have you ever thought what it is to be a King? Daily am I besieged by other men's problems, pressed upon by a crowd of personalities around me, always easing the friction, finding the smooth path, making the way straight, always giving, giving, giving. I cannot tell you what pleasure it is to come at last to you. There I can be free of obligation. I can say anything to you. This is a rare thing in a woman; so for this I treasure you and would have none other."

I listened to him and was struck with wonder. These were Bedwyr's words from Arthur's lips.

"My—my lord, I thank you. But I wish you would not take up arms for me." Because the day was hot, the breast of his tunic lay open, and I ran my fingers over the scar on his shoulder. "The Saxons never harmed you in all the years you fought them," I whispered. "The only mark you bear, you got for me, by Melwas' blade. I am ashamed of it, Arthur. It should not be thus."

He tried to smile. "What, would you have me covered with scars, like old Caius Lucius?"

"Please, Arthur," I begged, the tears returning, "please let some other fight in your stead. I could not bear it if you suffered injury on my account."

"My dear wife," he breathed. We stayed thus, silent, arms clasped about one another, struggling for command of our emotion.

I felt a light touch and looked up. The sweet child stood behind us, one hand on Arthur's head, one hand on mine. My tears dried, and I breathed more easily. Arthur looked up and saw her. She did not move, but looked straight into his eyes, so like her own, then gently touched his face with her small hand. He dared not even breathe, lest he break the spell. The child stepped closer and took his head in her frail arms, cradling him against her slim body. The King closed his eyes. Two small tears welled up and spilled down her rounded cheeks. Lightly she touched his head above his ear and caressed the spot as if it pained him. From nowhere came a low voice, ghostly, that echoed around us.

"Thus shall it be on the last day, the wicked day, when the King sends his spirit home. He shall lay his head down in her gentle lap, and lay down his burden at last . . ." The voice trailed off into silence. Even the birds were still.

Then Niniane stepped out from the shadows, holding her head in pain; the King opened his eyes and sat up; the child ran to Niniane and hugged her skirts. Niniane sank down on the stone bench, head bowed. The child touched her temples and began to hum.

The King gripped my arms, breathing fast. "Stay with me, Guinevere, I pray you. Don't leave me."

"My lord!" I whispered, meeting his eyes. The moment passed. He steadied himself and drew a long breath.

"Is there aught I can get for you, Niniane? I know Merlin used to take a potion after visions, but I know not how it was made."

She looked startled. "Did I prophesy for you, my lord? My head feels like it, but I can remember nothing, except darkness and flame. Yes, I can see by your faces I said something of importance. Let this child finish . . . thank you, Morgaine, that is better." The little girl sat down on the bench beside her and waited quietly, swinging her thin legs back and forth. Niniane smiled lightly; the harsh lines from brow to hairline told of her headache, but her eyes and voice were back to normal. "This is Morgaine, Queen Morgan's daughter. She has the gift of healing and of Sight. She is especially sensitive to pain in others. That must be what drew her here, for I was on my way to the Round Hall to see you when she disappeared from my side. She is now in my care." She raised her chin. "She will be Lady of the Lake after me."

"Thank you, Morgaine, for comforting the Queen," Arthur said gravely to the child. She kept her eyes down and would not look at him.

"She does not speak," Niniane went on. "But she has the gift of thinking in pictures, which can be seen and understood by an adept. In this way, she has told me something of importance, my lord, which you should know."

"Tell me."

"The sword hanging in the Round Hall is not Excalibur."

I gasped, and the King started. "Are you certain of this?"

"She knows where the true Sword is. In a dark place, underground. Safe. Somewhere in Rheged. After I have taken Morgaine to Ynys Witrin and dedicated her to the Lady's service, I shall go to Rheged and find it for you."

Arthur nodded. "Now I understand my sister's plan," he said slowly. "She never expected me to put you away, Gwen. In fact, she chose as her demand the one thing she knew I would not do. All she wanted was a confrontation, so her poor dupe Accolon could issue his challenge."

"So now that you know the sword is a fraud, you will not fight him? This duplicity can be revealed, and all will be well."

But the King shook his head. "No. I will meet him. His honor demands it. Let him have the chance to change his mind."

"But you will not fight with the weapon they have substituted? Surely they have designed it to shatter in your hand."

He was adamant. "There are more ways to kill a man than by running him through with a sword. If Accolon does not yield to me, he will die tomorrow."

"He will die tomorrow," Niniane repeated absently, but the words on her lips sounded final. She rose to go, and we both rose with her.

"I have frightened you, Guinevere," she said with concern. "Your hands are like ice. I beg your pardon for it. What did I prophesy?"

"Only my death," Arthur said with a light smile, and a gentle kiss to my forehead. "But I promise, I shall not fall to Accolon."

In fact, the contest with Accolon was barely a contest at all. Accolon came magnificently dressed; the King wore his plain fighting garb. I watched Queen Morgan's face as the men approached one another. When the King put his hand on the hilt of the sword and accepted it without thought, her face lit and her eyes grew eager. I felt sickened; he was her own brother, yet she wished him dead. If Lancelot looked for Pendragon ambition, he need look no further than Ygraine's daughter Morgan.

Accolon, knowing the weakness of the King's sword and wishing to put a quick end to the contest, lifted his weapon and swung with all his might. The King blocked the blow; his sword shattered in his hand.

"An omen!" Queen Morgan cried. "See how the sword fails him!"

But before the words were out of her mouth, Arthur drove the jagged remnant of the blade into Accolon's face, then reached for his dagger and stabbed him to the heart, all before the poor knight could lift his sword a second time.

The King knelt down at Accolon's side and spoke to him and took his hand. When he died, the King saluted him and turned away. Not a single tear graced Morgan's eye; she was angry and kept declaring that God had sent an omen to Britain, that Arthur was no longer worthy of the Sword.

Lancelot laughed. "The Sword of Britain, madam? Or that piece of glass? So this is why you came to Camelot!"

At a sign from the King, a guard formed around her, and she was taken prisoner. That night Urien arrived and learned all that had happened. He was closeted with the King for hours, and when they parted, both men looked at ease with one another.

"He has put her away," Arthur told me later. "He has given her into my keeping and is content to leave Morgaine with Niniane. I will send Morgan to Castle Daure to join her sister. The garrison at Winchester can be fortified to supply the troops. Let the two of them match their wits and magic against one another. As long as they are out of my hair!"

"What did she hope to gain?" I asked him. "Did she think to replace you herself? Surely she knew the men would not follow her or Accolon."

"I think she intended to present Urien with an accomplished fact and persuade him to take over the Kingdom himself. I tell you, Gwen, he is glad to be rid of her and would have put her by long ago, but for fear of offending me."

He stood behind me, brushing my hair. With the coming of dark the heat had given way before a light sea breeze. I had bathed, although the entire castle thought me strange to want hot water in summer. But it refreshed me more than chilled wine, and for the first time that day I felt at ease. The danger to the King was past, and he had suffered no hurt for me.

"Will you be in any danger without your Sword, my lord?" I asked him.

"No, Gwen. It is a symbol now, more than a weapon. It has been years since I lifted it in battle."

"Then all is well," I said with relief. "Niniane told me once that you were destined to be the victor in every field you took—I should have remembered that."

"It was Merlin's prophecy," he said in a tight voice, "before it was hers."

I turned on the stool and clutched his wrist. With great care, he set down the brush. "Like that of today?" I said hoarsely. "Had you heard that before?"

He shook his head. He was not afraid now. He had already accepted it. "No. The vision came to her there in the garden. It was new to me."

"What does it mean, my lord? That—that you will be slain? That cannot be, if Merlin's vision is true, and you are always victorious."

He looked puzzled. "I don't know what it means. But what is this? Do you try to argue with visions?"

I stood and slipped my arms around his body. "I mean only that perhaps Niniane is not the seer Merlin was; perhaps it was not a true vision."

"She has Merlin's power," he said gently. "Don't distress yourself, Gwen. Put it behind you."

"Do you believe these things she sees must happen? Don't you believe that men's wills count? Are we God's puppets, or do we earn His love by making choices for good or evil?"

He stepped back from me and looked into my face. "We are responsible for our actions," said the King.

I swallowed. "Then perhaps these dark fates may be avoided, if we will. I have thought long about this, Arthur. Perhaps these are warnings only, of what will come if we stray from the right path. If we make our own futures, who is to say what they will contain?"

He frowned and took a turn about the room. What love he bore for Merlin, never to question him! I felt suddenly guilty that, like Eve, I offered him uncertainty, where before he had made his peace.

"What are you telling me?" he said. "Today, in Morgaine's embrace, I felt my death blow." He raised his hand and touched the side of his head. "Do you mean that what I felt was only possibility? One among many?"

I began to tremble. "I—I think—oh, Arthur! Remember what else Merlin told you! That it should be Mordred's doing!" The sudden pain on his face brought tears to my eyes. I ran and knelt at his feet. "Forgive me, my lord."

He raised me and said slowly, "I had not forgotten."

"But he will not do it!" I cried, and then everything I wanted to say came rushing out in a tumble of words. "This was my first thought, when Niniane spoke today, that it could not be true, not that vision and the one of Mordred both, because he will not raise a hand against you. This I know, he has sworn it to me! Morgause terrified him—how evil, to tell her own son he would be the death of his father! But he thought, as Niniane told him, it might be something indirect, like, like falling from a horse on your way to see him, or some such thing. This would be beyond his power to prevent. But this horror of today—this he can and will prevent! For Mordred loves you, Arthur. I know Lancelot thinks him ambitious, but he will not know the boy. He would not harm you if his life depended on it. He has suffered so from this foul prophecy! But if you are to die in battle—and how can that be, if you are always victor?—then by his will, Mordred can be free of this thing! He has sworn not to outlive you." I gasped. I had gone too far; I had not meant to tell him that.

He looked at me a long while in silence. "A boy's oath, that the man must break. He will be my heir." His voice was flat. I dared not move.

Rarely was he out of temper and rarely had his wrath touched me. But this time I had offended him deeply. The skin around his nose and mouth looked pinched and white, his eyes cold and black. Slowly he turned his back to me and walked out on the terrace. Only then I felt my knees shake and clutched the bedpost for support.

"Arthur!" I whispered. Would I never learn to guard my tongue? But for me, he would have peace of mind. I was forcibly reminded of my words to Lamorak—how pompous they sounded now! The King came to me for comfort after the day's ordeal, and I wounded his heart.

He stood stiffly by the parapet, staring out at the dark garden below. I knew by the way he held himself that he fought his own fury. I sank to my knees and whispered a quick prayer, for Arthur's sake. He must get past this anger, and understand that what drove both me and Mordred was nothing but fear for him. He could command fear; could he admit, and forgive, that we could not? I trembled again at the thought of what I had done. If he could not get past it, what then? Surely our close fellowship was ended, and he would trust me no longer. I bowed my head as tears slipped out—how was the Witch of Rheged proved right about me, after all!

After a long while, I heard his step and felt him touch my hand. "Arise, Guinevere. I would talk with you a moment."

I looked up quickly; he was calm, the black anger gone. "My dear lord, please forgive me. Lately I am but a thorn in your side."

His features warmed; he almost smiled. "Hardly that." He led me past the leather curtain and into his own chamber. He sat upon the great bed and beckoned me to sit beside him. "I cannot long be angry with you, Gwen. But I must know this about Mordred."

Haltingly I told him about Mordred's distress when Morgause had told him of Merlin's prophecy and about the solemn vow he had made.

"Lancelot," Arthur said evenly.

"Yes, my lord," I said sadly, looking away. "I fear that was the reason. Mordred suffered great anguish, Arthur, and I believe he still means to keep his vow."

"He is young yet." Then a whiplash of anger cut across his voice. "Between you, you have robbed me of my future!" Stilling himself, he took my hair in his hands and slowly let it fall through his fingers. "'Gwen. You must make an effort, for my sake, to ignore these prophecies. They are nothing, really. They do not affect us. They are simply things seen by those who have Sight to see them. If they are true, they are true, and if false, false. Live as though you had not heard them. My sweet wife, it is the only way. Give up trying to decipher them and reconcile them; you have not that gift, thank God. Forget them."

He leaned slowly forward to kiss my cheek and neck and throat. With a sigh, I let go of my fear and my worry—he took them all upon himself.

"Thank you, Arthur," I whispered, and found his lips on mine.

Gently he pressed me back against the bearskin coverlet and leaned over me, filling my vision. "I am a King, and I do what I must. When he is King, he will do the same. Understand this, Gwen."

"Yes, Arthur," I breathed, "you are right."

He smiled slowly. "And now, is your fear gone?"

"Yes, my lord," I said, reaching for him.

But he resisted, holding himself away, looking down at me. "Are you sure? A moment ago it consumed you, body and soul."

I lifted a hand to his face. "You have the power to dispel it, my lord," I said softly. "You have always had this power. Since the first day I met you, Arthur."

Gently he caressed my cheek with his finger and then ran his hand slowly down my shoulder and over the soft fabric of my gown.

"Do you remember how frightened of me you were then?" he asked with amusement, watching my face. "You put me in mind of a wild filly; you wanted to run."

"I remember it well. You gentled me like a master."

He laughed lightly. "No, hardly that. Does it not seem odd to think we were strangers once?"

I caught his roving hand and pressed it to my lips. "Come, Arthur. I have not your patience."

"And now," he continued, smiling, "you are like dry tinder awaiting the spark. See what comes of overcoming fear?"

I took his face between my hands and drew him down to me. "If you possess the spark, my lord, bear in mind that too much wind may blow it out."

He laughed, bent down, and kissed me.

35 👑 THE HOMECOMING

"Well, Gwen," Arthur said, smiling, "who do you think is coming to see us?"

Council had just broken up, and the Companions lounged leisurely near the windows in the Round Hall, passing the wineskin and enjoying the breezes of early summer. Lancelot and Bedwyr stood near Arthur. They had been arguing as I entered the chamber, but broke off, and turned to me with lightened looks. I knew a courier had come that day from Wales, and I knew that several of the knights errant had returned to report on their travels, but I could not guess what it was that so pleased Arthur.

"Who, my lord?" I asked, as he raised me. "An old friend from Wales, perhaps?"

"Close to the mark," he replied. "An old friend, indeed, and one you have not seen since well before you came to Camelot. But not from Wales."

"Not from Wales? But before I came here I did not know anyone who was not from Wales! Unless you count my tutor Iakos?" I glanced up and saw his eyes were dancing.

"Someone you liked better than Iakos, I imagine. Someone tall and fair and handsome, to use your words. A king's son when you knew him. Now a king."

"Not Fion!" I cried. "Oh, Arthur! Is it really Fion? Is he coming to Camelot at last?"

"Not to Camelot. We go to meet him in Gwynedd." He turned to Bedwyr. "Do you remember him? The Prince of Ireland? He came to meet us along the Glevum road when his countrymen had ransomed him from Pellinore. He'd led a raid on Pellinore's coast and been caught. Gwen was the one who found him half dead on the beach and wrapped him in her cloak, though it was midwinter, and saved his life, thereby enslaving his affection."

Lancelot was watching me, and I protested.

"It was nothing so dramatic. He would have lived in any event. It would take more than a winter's night on a Welsh beach to silence Fion. Where have you heard these fantastic tales?"

Arthur laughed. "Why, he told me so himself. He talked about you a good deal, as I remember." I looked away, but could not keep from smiling in delight. I had not seen Fion in ten years, since I was fourteen and had stumbled upon him, a wounded pirate with golden hair and eyes of unbelievable green. He was the first man who ever spoke poetry to me, or sang to me, or tried to win me. This was at an age when a grown man's admiration means more than life to a lass. I would have married him, had he asked me.

"It was Fion who proposed her for Queen, was it not?" Bedwyr asked.

"No, no," I said quickly, feeling Lancelot's eyes still on my face. "That was my cousin Gwillim. At least, that was what Pellinore told me."

"True enough," Arthur said easily. "But it was Fion's praise of you that decided me. I knew him to be an honest man."

"Just how well did you know him?" Lancelot blurted. "I thought he was Pellinore's hostage."

I grinned at Arthur, delight getting the better of sense. "He was the handsomest man I've ever seen! Oh, it will be so wonderful to see him again!"

Arthur laughed outright as Lancelot colored. "You see, Lancelot, we are but second best. In her heart there is another who comes first."

To hide my face I made a deep reverence between them. "Not so, my lords." The jest had gone far enough, and Arthur knew it. He slung an arm about Lancelot's shoulders.

"Things are as stormy in Ireland as they ever were, with six cousins after his throne. Even his marriage to a northern girl did not stay the plotting against his life. So he has sent a message seeking counsel."

"But I thought he was not coming to Camelot."

"Indeed," Arthur said, lowering his voice, "he is not. He is setting his enemies a trap. He has given out that he comes to Camelot to consult with me. That is a month's journey by sea and land and back again. Plenty of time for the pretenders to foment a riot. But he will do no more than touch land in Gwynedd, pay us his best wishes, and return to catch them red-handed. If he is successful, he might be able to unite his realm."

It sounded like Fion. He was a better poet than a leader of men; quick and clever, he could charm his way out of anything. Except, perhaps, the ambitions of his relations.

"Oh, Arthur! Won't you take me with you? Please, my Lord, just this once!" Ever since King Melwas had abducted me, Arthur barely let me ride three leagues from home without the entire army at my back. To go home again, actually to go home and see the Western Sea and the wooded mountains of my girlhood! My thoughts must have shown upon my face, for Arthur slipped an arm about my waist.

"Yes, you are coming. But it will not all be pleasure. I have need of your diplomatic skills. Besides—" He hesitated, and smiled again. "I doubt either you or Fion would forgive me if I went alone."

"You are right about that! When do we leave? And with how many?"

"In two weeks. With half the army."

"So many? To greet Fion? Ahhhh. I see there is more to it. Do you expect war, then? What is amiss?"

"No," Arthur said quickly, "or you should not come. Not war. But the situation is difficult."

"What situation?" Their faces grew grave, and Lancelot and Bedwyr avoided looking at one another. I felt a sudden foreboding. "What has Maelgon done?"

I knew, of course, that Elaine's brother Maelgon was king now in Gwynedd, poor Pellinore having broken his neck in a hunt the previous autumn. My cousin Maelgon was but a younger, stronger version of the hot-headed Elaine, and was capable of almost anything. He was certainly capable of picking a fight with any one of his neighbors, but the King had said he did not expect war. On the other hand, with half the army along he was clearly ready for it. I thought of the Welsh lords I knew, of my brother Gwarthgydd the King of Northgallis, and the kings of Powys and Dyfed and Guent. They had all liked Pellinore well enough and were loyal to Arthur. I did not think it likely Maelgon could stir them up against Gwynedd in so short a time. But whom else might Maelgon have offended?

Arthur glanced at me and shook his head. "I told you both," he said to Lancelot and Bedwyr, "she knows the man."

"I do indeed. You frighten me by your silence. What has he done?"

Arthur sighed wearily and began to pace back and forth. The men near the windows stopped their idle chatter and stood quietly, listening. At length the King turned and faced me. "Maelgon has taken it into his head to purify Gwynedd. To wipe out the Druids."

My hand closed automatically over the crucifix at my throat. This was a thing Arthur had feared for years. Christian power was growing in Britain, and he knew there would be those who tried to win a name for themselves by championing the Christian cause and justifying slaughter in the name of righteousness. And this, Arthur abhorred.

I looked at Lancelot, but his face told me nothing. He stood stiffly, waiting, looking nowhere. With every passing year Lancelot grew more devout, as if by prayer and fasting and strict adherence to his faith he could purge from his soul our long, deep-rooted passion. But Arthur, an anointed Christian King, respected the old ways and was well known to honor the gods sacred to any place. He had worshipped at the Mithraeum in York; he had honored the Great Goddess; he was known to stop at wayside shrines and leave offerings to the Elder Spirits; he had been formally blessed by both the Archdruid Salowen and the Lady of the Lake. His broadmindedness had been marked and appreciated by his people. Only a small group of fanatics dared to criticize his fairness. But Bishop Landrum was among them and had preached more than once against such tolerance. And the bishop's power was growing.

Salowen the Druid! I thought suddenly. The Isle of Mona, the Druids' Isle, lay but a league off Gwynedd's shores. Even in Pellinore's day they had caused trouble with the Christian community, always competing with Father Martin for recruits, their schools and music outshining anything the Christian brothers could produce. Mona was an ancient seat of learning, and her sacred grove of Nemet one of the holiest places in all Britain.

"Arthur," I whispered, "do not tell me he has done insult to the Druids on Mona's Isle."

"He has done worse than insult," came the cruel reply. "He has done murder. Not directly, but through another."

"In a good cause," Lancelot murmured, and I stared at him, astounded.

Arthur frowned, but checked his anger. "A man should not be murdered for calling his God by a different name," he said firmly, looking around the room and catching everyone's eye. "I will not have that said of me, nor of any who serve me." He did not look directly at Lancelot, but the point went home.

"Amen," I said quickly, praying Lancelot would take the hint and be still. "How did it happen?"

Arthur resumed his slow pacing, his hands behind his back. There was utter silence in the room. The gathered Companions stood in two groups, Kay, Gereint, Gryfflet, Sagramor, and the other Christians by the open window, behind Lancelot, and Villers, Dryaunt, Bleoberys, and Bellangere with the other pagans nearer Bedwyr. Already was Arthur's council divided.

At last, Arthur spoke. "Did you know a youth named Balyn in Gwynedd? I believe he was the son of one of Pellinore's nobles."

"Yes, I think so. There are two of them, are there not? Twins? Balyn and Balan. Rambunctious boys, as I remember, the type to find trouble everywhere. And not very clever."

"Your memory serves you well. Not clever enough by half. They were very close as children, as twins are, but when they came of age they fought over a maiden. It grew into a feud, they say, until their father split them up in order to protect them from each other. He himself owed a favor to Salowen, so he offered him Balan's services for a term of years in repayment of the debt. Balyn he sent into Pellinore's service. Pellinore made him a Christian."

"Ah, yes," I said, recalling to mind the rather thick-featured boy with badly cut hair who always said his prayers aloud, at twice of the volume of anyone else. "He was very enthusiastic about whatever he undertook; but he seldom looked ahead toward consequences."

Grysﬂet moaned under his breath. "Aye, my lady, you know the lad all right, may God rest his soul and the Good Goddess preserve his spirit from harm." Grysﬂet, at least, was making an attempt to straddle the fence.

I turned to him. "He is dead? Do you mean he was Maelgon's agent?"

"He led the raid on Mona's Isle at Maelgon's command," Arthur said shortly. "Nine Druids were slaughtered, including his brother Balan, whom he slew himself, not knowing who he was."

"Dear God!"

"The priestess Viviane was beheaded," Villers growled.

"Three Christian lives were lost." This from Gereint.

"And Balyn himself was slain by Balan, who, at Salowen's command, had sworn peace with his brother a year hence," Bedwyr finished sadly. "But he knew him not."

My hands twisted together as I looked at all their faces. "This is terrible! Is there now a holy war between Druid and Christian in Gwynedd?"

"Not yet," Arthur said, watching Lancelot from the corner of his eye. "That is what we go to prevent. I will talk sense into Maelgon or remove him from his throne." Now I saw Arthur's need of me; Pellinore's widow Alyse must be kept from interfering in such treatment of her son; she was not a weak-willed woman, and she had been powerful once.

"You had better talk to Salowen, as well," I said nervously, and was gratified to see Lancelot's expression soften. "He will want revenge."

Arthur came to a stop. "I have sent to see him. If I can get him and Maelgon into the same room and talking, there is a chance we can settle this. But if we cannot"— his voice sounded hollow, and his gaze looked far beyond the chamber wall—"then all I have done has been for naught. Once Briton is pitted against Briton, the Saxons need not even lift an ax to conquer us."

At the mention of Saxons, the two groups of knights drew closer together; Lancelot met Bedwyr's eyes.

"Arthur," I said firmly, taking his arm and bringing his thoughts back to the present, "it will not happen. You will see when we get to Wales. I am sure I can make Alyse see sense, and I'll wager any amount you like Maelgon still fears her. And don't forget Fion. The tongue he carries in his head can charm anyone with ears. All will be well. I am sure of it."

We left as soon as the solstice celebrations were ended. Mordred, who had just turned fifteen and been inducted into the army, was coming with us. Being only a new recruit he could not ride with the King, but was stuck at the back of his company where he swallowed dust the whole way. Even so, he was thrilled to be coming, especially as Gawaine, at fourteen, could not.

The journey to Wales was easy and swift; we had glorious weather, the roads were dry and we made excellent time. There was only one incident along the way to mar my joy at setting out for home. I rode the first part of the way with Niniane. She was on her way to the Lady's shrine at Avalon, and we provided her escort as far as the causeway across the marsh. But she was not good company. She was distracted, barely listening to my attempts at conversation, wincing at the bright sun as if it hurt her eyes. As we left the rolling downs and came to a flat plain by the river Camel, she shuddered and moaned aloud.

"Niniane!" I whispered, putting out a hand to her. "What is it? What is amiss?"

She shook her head impatiently and waved away my questions. "I don't know. It is nothing. Let me be, I pray you. This—this place stinks of death."

I looked about, but could see no carcass anywhere, nor any cause for her complaint. "The plain of Camlann?" I wondered aloud. "Why, it is wonderful country for galloping. And the air is sweet."

But her breath was coming fast and labored, and she cried out angrily, "It is a battlefield, I tell you! There are dead men all about! And so near Avalon . . ." I was frightened, then, lest she be having a vision of some horrible misfortune, and I called to Arthur to attend us. He rode over immediately and spoke to her. But as soon as she heard his voice, her irritation left her, and she faced him calmly. "Beware of false messengers!" she cried, and the voice that came from her lips was not her own, but the hollow, ringing voice of the god. I crossed myself quickly, and Arthur took her arm to steady her.

"What messengers, Niniane?" he asked softly. "Welsh messengers? From Gwynedd?" But she only shook her head, unable to speak, and slumped in the saddle. Arthur made her drink from his flask and soon brought her round. But she remembered nothing she had said, either about messengers or battlefields. I was distressed, but Arthur shot me a warning glance, reminding me not to worry about her Seeings. This was not unusual behavior from Niniane, who carried Merlin's power within her, so we let her be. At least she no longer felt a horror of the beautiful country we rode through. And I strove to follow Arthur's advice and put her words behind me, since I could make no sense of them, and I owed him obedience to my promise.

We rode into the forecourt of Pellinore's castle one fine summer afternoon. Everything was much the same as I remembered, only smaller. The stables, I saw, had been well maintained, and the outbuildings looked all in good order. I wondered, with a secret smile, if Maelgon had discovered and repaired the crack in the wall where Elaine and I had eavesdropped on so many of Pellinore's councils. Maelgon himself greeted us at the threshold. He was a well-built young man, strong and able, with Pellinore's stern visage and bushy brown beard, but not, underneath it, his endearing warmth. And though it was a hot day, he was dressed in every piece of finery he owned, from the heavy crown of Gwynedd to embroidered cape, jeweled belt, and gold wristbands encrusted with gems. Arthur, bareheaded and dressed in simple traveling clothes, was much the finer figure as he stood before Maelgon and accepted his homage.

Vainly I looked about for Alyse; by all rights she should have been there, but she was not. Instead, a timid wisp of a girl with thin dark hair and overlarge dark eyes stood trembling at Maelgon's elbow, overdressed as he was, looking like a child in her mother's clothes. I covered my shock as Maelgon introduced us to his bride Anet. She was the youngest child of old Caw of Strathclyde, whose sons had given Arthur such trouble after his death. Her brother King Hapgar had ruled there since Heuil's defeat, and although he himself had sworn allegiance to Arthur, he was powerless to keep his quarrelsome siblings in line. The worst behaved was Gildas, Heuil's pet and now a Christian priest. This arrogant philanderer had studied once in Ireland and now fancied himself a second Plato, a modern Pliny, a poet and a recorder of events, well above the rank of common men. He was more dangerous to cross than a viper; he could, and would, for spite or a piece of gold, ruin a man's reputation with a single stroke of his pen.

I regarded little Anet with sympathy. What an upbringing she must have had! With twelve wild brothers for companions in childhood, perhaps she knew no other response to life than seeking shelter. Arthur greeted her gently, and she almost smiled at him as she knelt to kiss his ring. But me she could only stare at, trembling, as if I were some demon come straight from Hell to fetch her. Though I spoke softly and chose my words to please her, she could not utter a sound, but licked her dry lips and shrank from my touch.

We were given the finest rooms in the castle, outside of Maelgon's own. Ailsa and I found ourselves standing in the very chamber Elaine and I had slept in as girls. The bed was the same, and the pearwood chest at its foot, but there were new pieces, as well, all worked in the old Celtic patterns they still cherished in the north.

"I will wager you, Ailsa, that this is little Anet's room, and Maelgon has turned her out of it on my account. No wonder she hates me!"

"Hates you, my lady? Certainly not."

"You did not see the way she greeted me. She could not bring herself to look me in the face."

Ailsa chuckled as she began her unpacking. "Not from hate, you may be sure. I saw her when your back was turned. She could not take her eyes from you. It is not hate, Guinevere, but envy. A little slip of a lass like that would give anything she possessed to be as strong and as beautiful and as sure of herself as you."

I turned from her, finding the room suddenly oppressive. "No doubt that will end as soon as she finds herself with child," I said bitterly, and left before she could try to offer comfort.

I went up to the tower to see the sea. None of the sentries were men I knew, but they all knew me and let me pass. How wonderful to look again upon the Western Sea, stretching endlessly blue and beckoning beneath the summer sky! For the first time in many years I longed for Elaine's company; I could almost hear her eager, conspiratorial whispers in my ear. Her spirit seemed to hover in the salt breeze. I had noted well how much more warmly Maelgon greeted Lancelot, his brother-in-law, than Arthur, his King. I would have to remember that Lancelot had special standing here, on Elaine's account; he would have to remember it, too. Why, I wondered suddenly, had I come? This was not the homecoming I wanted—Pellinore gone, Alyse in seclusion, every childhood memory of Elaine saddled with the cruel acknowledgment that she was Lancelot's wife. How could I have thought this would be bearable?

I heard a step behind me and turned. "Arthur!"

Beyond him, the sentries had snapped to attention and stood staring at the sky beyond the parapet with concentrated effort.

"Well, I have found you at last. These are not tears of joy at homecoming, I think," he said gently, brushing my cheek with his finger. "It's not quite what you expected, is it?"

I shook my head, and he took me in his arms. At length, when I was calm, he loosed me and leaned upon the parapet, looking out toward the sea.

"This is the view you have always wanted to see from Camelot," he said with a smile. "I can see why." He hesitated. "We can always go to Caer Narfon, Gwen. The soldiers would prefer it; there are better barracks. And the King's house is not bad. It's been rebuilt since you last saw it."

"No," I said firmly. "Not even for you would I give Maelgon such pleasure."

He grinned. "Good. Then we will stay and make him behave himself." His gaze traveled slowly over the castle grounds, the paddocks, the meadows, the wooded hills within his view. "So this is where you lived. I wish the Saxons had not landed in the north that spring. I should have liked to come and take you out of Wales myself." I looked away. And if he had come? Then Lancelot would not have come in his stead. Arthur shifted. "Lancelot suffers more than you do. As kin to Maelgon, he must listen to his bragging and laugh at his jests." I felt a blush creep into my cheeks, but I had ceased to be amazed that Arthur read my thoughts. "Tell me more about Maelgon. What do you suppose made him choose such a child for a wife? She cannot be much of a helpmate."

"Maelgon would sneer at the very idea of a helpmate. He is a bully, Arthur, pure and simple. And she, poor girl, must have been bullied her entire life. They are probably well suited . . . But what her life must be like!"

"She is in awe of you, you know," he said quietly. "Like Mordred. Like me."

"Flatterer. You are only trying to cheer me up. But how is Mordred?"

He straightened and laughed. "Last I saw him he was covered with dust and sore from the saddle and trying in spite of it all to be dignified." He paused and lowered his voice. "I have asked him to be my eyes and ears among the men, and in the village. As he is pagan himself, he can go where the Christians will not. And in the tavern, men take little notice of a youth his age and in their cups may let something slip."

I moved closer to him and watched his face. "And what is it you seek to know, my lord?"

His lips thinned. "I want to know where Salowen is. He has sent no message."

"And what do you want of me?"

As he turned toward me his features softened. "I leave the women to you. I want Maelgon weakened, even a little. There is no check to his power, I find. No one will oppose him."

"No doubt he has banished all those who ever offered him advice he did not like."

"Awe is a powerful weapon, Gwen," Arthur said slowly. "Use it." He smiled suddenly, took my hand, and slid it through his arm. "Give Maelgon a wife like mine, and I can leave him with an easy heart . . . Come, come, don't blush so. This is not flattery, but truth. And now you must come with me, for I am bidden to bring you to Alyse. She has been asking for you, and I offered to act as page."

That, at last, made me smile. "Well, you haven't the least idea how to go about it. You must bow your head and lower your eyes. You cannot look me in the face; you cannot touch me."

With a bark of laughter, he bent and kissed me, then lifted me in his arms and carried me past the sentries and down the tower stairs.

I hardly recognized Alyse. She sat in her rocker wrapped in shawls, small and thin and faded. She who had been a powerful queen and Pellinore's right hand, the leading force in my childhood, she was an old woman. Leonora and Cissa, who still attended her, did not look half so changed.

She was pathetically happy to see me and rose to kiss my hand, embracing me with tears of joy. "Ah, Gwen, how good of you to come with the King! You grow more beautiful with every passing year! How I wish dear Elen could see you now!"

Startled at the reference to my mother, whom she never mentioned in my hearing, I mumbled some reply, and Leonora hastened to make tea at the grate.

"I looked for you in the forecourt when we rode in, Aunt Alyse."

"I could not be there," she said with a spark of her well-remembered anger. "I am not on speaking terms with Maelgon."

"No?" I was amazed. Of her three children, he had always been her pride. I waited, but she was not ready to talk about Maelgon.

"Let me look at you, my dear. How you delight me! You bring the sweet air of summer in with you—I could almost feel young again." Her grip on my arm was strong and steady. I sat across from her and observed her closely. She wandered on, remembering the old days, but remembering them quite differently than I had known them. "I always knew you were destined for greatness, Guinevere. Everyone could see it." This, though she had schemed and fought to get me married early and out of the way so Elaine could pursue Arthur! I glanced quickly at Leonora and caught her hiding a smile.

I handed Alyse her tea. "I am sorry to learn of Pellinore's death. He was almost as dear to me as Father."

"Thank you, Gwen. They say he never felt the blow that killed him. That's a mercy. He never bore pain well. Always demanding to be cosseted and nursed for the smallest scratch." I nearly smiled, unable to envision the brawny Pellinore acting like a child.

"And how do you get along with your new daughter-in-law, Anet?"

Alyse snorted unkindly, and the years seemed to drop from her. "Just the type to suit Maelgon. A convent flower, not hardy enough to last a year on this rocky soil, I warrant. Do you know, Guinevere, that since that old devil Caw put her in the convent at the age of five, she had never seen the outside of it until Hapgar gave her to Maelgon?"

"Not even to go home? Do you mean she spent her whole life there?"

"I do, indeed. And by all accounts, it's no more than a jumble of rubble with thatch for a roof, hidden in some godforsaken valley in the wild mountains of Strathclyde. Her Latin is atrocious, and her speech is thick with old Celtic expressions our grandfathers had forgotten!"

I laughed at her indignation. She was faded and wrinkled, yes, but not old; it was her will that commanded her flesh, and if that could be revived, Alyse could yet become a forceful ally.

"Why did Maelgon choose her, then?"

She looked at me slyly. "Why do you think? Not for her beauty, poor thing. Maelgon's ambition extends beyond Gwynedd, even beyond Wales. No daughter of Powys or Dyfed was good enough for him. Alliance with Rheged would have suited him best, but of course Urien has no daughters to speak of." Thus did she dismiss little Morgaine. Alyse was returning to form, and Cissa and Leonora were smiling. "So he looked to Strathclyde. Hapgar's daughters are eight and ten, but Maelgon had not the patience for a long betrothal. So he took Anet. She is twenty, if you can believe it."

"Twenty! I did not think her above fifteen!"

Alyse laughed unkindly. "And even after he saw her the young fool would not be dissuaded." She closed her eyes and sank back into her chair. "Such willfulness. It reminded me of my sister Elen. Everyone advised her against Leodegrance. Northgallis was too small; he was nearly old enough to be her father, with grown sons already from a former marriage; she was so beautiful she could do so much better! But she would hear none of it. She loved Leo and would have him or none other." She sighed deeply as my face flamed. How did she dare speak so about my father to my face? But I held my tongue and reminded myself sternly what I was about.

"It is possible, you know, Alyse, that the little convent flower is only waiting for the gardener's hand to bloom into something lovely. Who has her trust?"

Alyse shrugged. "God knows. I do not. And I care not, Guinevere. That is behind me now."

I took her hand and held it in my own. "And if Pellinore were to walk in that door right now, what would he say to hear you say such things? He would scold you for faintheartedness and bid you train the girl to her task. She will never be a queen without you."

She opened her eyes and smiled slowly. "Pellinore never scolded me in his life, and you know it well. He did not dare." The smile faded. "And I do not wish to hear it from you. It matters not to me if Maelgon has a queen or a doormat for a wife. He chose her. Like Elaine, he has made his bed and now must lie in it."

I left her soon after for she was tiring, and I had no wish to discuss Elaine's marriage. She begged me to come see her daily, and I agreed. Already she looked better than she had when I arrived, and her interest in affairs was reviving. Before I left I drew from her a promise that she would attend dinner with us every night of our visit. Whatever there was between her and Maelgon, I felt sure neither of them would voice it in Arthur's presence.

In this I was right. They never so much as looked at one another. But this only served to make conversation at dinner more difficult. Maelgon our host did not want us there; we were interfering in his affairs, but he was obliged to make us welcome. Arthur did not want Maelgon to know his real purpose in coming to Gwynedd, which Maelgon was trying hard to learn, but he wanted to know what the current situation was, which Maelgon was trying hard to hide. Anet kept her eyes in her lap and spoke to no one. Alyse plied Lancelot with questions about Elaine, her daughter, which he strove to answer in a low voice so that I would not hear. What with that, and the necessity to chuckle at Maelgon's jests and nod at his asides, poor Lancelot looked as comfortable as a cat on hot bricks. The awkwardness of the situation grew amusing, and when Arthur, catching my eye, winked at me, I nearly laughed aloud and disgraced myself. I looked forward to less formal talk after dinner, when the mead was passed around and the men talked more freely about affairs of state.

I should have remembered we were not in Camelot. Too soon for me, little Anet rose and led the women out. Alyse retired immediately to her chamber, but I was obliged to follow Anet to the meeting room and engage in pointless chatter while we waited for the men. After a time, it became clear that the men were not coming. Perhaps I should have expected it, knowing how different Maelgon was from Arthur, but it was a blow. I sat on the long bench by the unglazed windows, looking out on the paved forecourt, the grassy embankment, and beyond to the woods, longing for the freedom to escape to the stables. If this was to be nightly repeated, I should go mad. The men were discussing events of importance, while we idled talking about the weather. My gaze alighted upon a woven hanging that was new to me, and I sat up a little straighter. It was skillfully worked and designed by someone with a sense of color and style. It depicted an ancient Celtic king being feasted by his companions after a successful cattle raid. The firelight threw half his face in shadow, and his eyes seemed to burn through the very fabric. I rose, shocking the women into silence, and went over to get a closer look. The source of these wondrous effects then lay revealed; here were threads of many colors I had never seen before, shades and gradations of common colors, and hues completely unknown in nature.

"Whose doing is this?" I asked, turning back to the women.

To my amazement, little Anet rose, trembling, and made me a reverence. "It is mine, my lady."

"This is wonderful work, Anet. Did you design it? Where did you get the dyes to make such colors?"

Her face flushed crimson with my praise, but some of her shyness left her as she approached. "Thank you, my lady. Yes, I designed it. It is taken from a woodcut of King Cunedda I had in childhood. But I added the firelight. It was done at the convent, for there all the women are skilled in weaving. And Sister Boudice showed me how to make many of the dyes, but some of them I discovered for myself."

Her eyes glowed as she spoke, and all hesitation disappeared from her speech. In my heart I thanked God for revealing to me her gift.

"Do you mean you invented these dyes? Why, they are wonderful. I wish you would show me your workroom, that I may see how it is done."

She curtsied, flushing with pleasure. "Nothing would please me more, my lady. Would—would you care to see it now?" She looked so hopeful that I assented at once. Not all the women followed us; probably they saw enough of the weaving room during the day. There were three looms, one of ancient make, twice the size of the others. The room itself had been extended, at the expense of Alyse's garden, and contained great vats for dyeing, benches and tools for the preparation of the dyes, twenty or so spindles, quantities of raw wool and tubs for washing and bleaching. Once started on her topic, nothing would stop Anet's tongue, and during the next hour I learned more than I had ever wanted to know about the preparation of plants, lichens, roots, barks, and earth to get the dyes she used. She was an accomplished spinster and could spin the finest thread I ever saw. She showed me sketches she had made on parchment for a large hanging for the dining hall. Maelgon stood at the center, surrounded by his ancestors, with his precious hunting dogs at his feet. I thought this in questionable taste, seeing how Pellinore had met his death, but of course the pose was Maelgon's idea. I praised her work, and she blossomed under the praise. Anet was a skilled craftsman whose lot it was to be a queen. And while her nature might be unsuited to her role, she had pride. She could do this one thing very well, and she knew it. It was a beginning.

I bade her sit with me upon the bench while I fingered a skein of woolen thread. She had lost some of her awe and spoke readily about the quality of thread, which wool suited her best, how the blue-fleeced sheep of Rheged grew the finest wool for cloth.

Slowly I turned the skein in my hand. "Ask Maelgon to procure you some," I suggested. "He is on good terms with Urien. You could keep your own flock."

She gasped. "Oh, I do not dare! Ask him for something for myself?"

"Why not? It would be to his benefit, as well. It costs him little, and gives you great pleasure. Surely he would like to add to his livestock. Why not try it?" She trembled and grew shy again.

"I lack the courage," she whispered. "He does not listen when I speak to him."

I took her hand and leaned close to her, lowering my voice. "Ask him in bed. There even a king is defenseless against a woman." Her little face grew red, and she giggled, covering her mouth. I laughed with her, but in truth I pitied her heartily. I could not imagine that Maelgon had much tenderness in him.

"Do you—with the High King?" She managed, her eyes wide.

"If it is important enough. He is a man, after all."

"Everyone knows you share the High King's counsels."

"If I have his ear, it is because he has learned to trust me. But that takes time, Anet. It did not start out so. And you have been married, what? Less than a year? It is time to make a small beginning. You are not asking for a sword. This is a woman's concern, and Maelgon should not object. You have your sphere of influence here in the castle. Make it your realm, as Alyse did."

She looked lost and frightened. "But—I am only—what if no one does my bidding?"

"You are queen," I said firmly. "They will do it. They expect to. Have you never given anyone an order?"

She gulped and looked nervously about the room. "Only my women. Only in here. Here—it is safe."

"Who enlarged this room? Who dared to sacrifice Alyse's garden?"

"Maelgon," she whispered, looking hastily away. "He asked if I needed more room for the looms. He was glad to do it."

So he had deliberately provoked Alyse. He had made it clear to her he was king, and she had no power over him. This steadied my resolve.

"Did it please you to lose the garden?"

"It pleased me to enlarge the room. But I was sorry to lose the garden, and Queen Alyse was so angry."

"Well, then, why not enlarge the garden? At this time of year the gardeners will have time to do it. I know which blooms Alyse likes best. What say you? We will go together in the morning, and you will give the order for it."

She had been ready to object until I offered to come with her. But she finally agreed and thanked me profusely for the trouble I took.

"No thanks are due me, Anet. It behooves us all to please Alyse. Gwynedd, Wales, even Britain will be the stronger for it. I only wish I knew why she has quarreled with Maelgon."

"Oh, I can tell you that!" Anet exclaimed. She blushed faintly, but her joy in our newfound sisterhood had loosened her tongue and she told me the truth without prompting. It seemed that when Pellinore died he had been buried without proper Christian ritual. Father Martin had succumbed to illness the previous summer, and although the bishop in Caerleon had promised to send a new priest to Gwynedd, none had arrived when Pellinore had his accident. Alyse had wished to wait, even months, to see him properly buried, but Maelgon had refused and finally had performed the rites himself. It was his right, as king, but Alyse was furious, resenting his kingship as much as his use of power. Afterward, when the promised priest finally arrived, Maelgon publicly rejected Alyse's demand to have Pellinore disinterred so his body could be properly blessed. Instead, he bade the priest say the blessings above the gravesite. For, he said, what difference could a few feet of earth make to the Almighty Creator?

"Queen Alyse was very angry," Anet whispered, shifting uncomfortably. "Maelgon was not very polite."

"That I can well believe," I agreed dryly. "Politeness does not run in this family."

"She said in front of everyone that she would never speak to Maelgon again until he had apologized for his rudeness."

"Then she played into his hands."

"Yes, my lady. It seems so. I know that he laughed."

I turned to look at her. She had fine, dark eyes and a straight nose. If her hair were better dressed and her gowns more carefully chosen, she might yet make a presentable queen. "Anet," I said suddenly, "would you rather be Queen of Gwynedd or a princess of Strathclyde?"

Her jaw dropped. "What do you mean?"

"Listen carefully. Your future is in your hands. If you care for Maelgon, or for your place here in Gwynedd, attend me well. Maelgon must change his ways or yield his throne."

"Yield his throne?" she whispered, shaking.

"Why do you think Arthur is here?"

Her hand flew to her mouth, and she covered a shriek. Clearly, she had no desire to return to Hapgar's court and be pawned off to one of his petty lords.

I slipped an arm about her waist and hugged her gently. "Do not be afraid. That is the last resort. And you can do much to prevent it."

"I?" There were tears in her eyes.

"Yes. You. You share Maelgon's bed. You have the opportunity to sway him. He must learn that the greatest Christian virtue is that of love."

424 • QUEEN OF CAMELOT

"You—is this about—the Druids?"

"Yes."

"Oh, my lady Guinevere! I told him—everyone told him—it was wrong! It was cruel! But he has a hate within his soul he cannot control! I knew he would bring suffering upon us all! I knew it!"

I cradled her against me, rocking her as she wept. "He is a man now, and a king. He *must* control it. Without control, how can he rule? Discipline can be taught, Anet. He can learn it."

"But—but how?"

"Little by little. We will start with small steps. First we will give the order to enlarge the garden."

Late that night when Arthur came to me, I told him all that had passed. He was pleased. It had been harder going with Maelgon. Most of the men were still drinking and looked to be at it till dawn. Maelgon would not let Lancelot go, no doubt hoping that in time the drink would loosen his tongue.

"All I have been able to learn," Arthur said wearily, "is that he has scouts posted throughout the forests, watching all the approaches to Gwynedd. If he does not expect an attack from Salowen, he is giving a good imitation of it."

I shivered. I would not want to be in Maelgon's boots, with a Druid's curse upon my head, never knowing from which direction violent death would come.

"Surely Salowen must know you are here."

Arthur shrugged. "Even the Saxons know I am here. Let us hope he can get a messenger safely past the scouts."

"And Fion? When does he arrive? Will Maelgon make him welcome? How long will he visit?"

At last Arthur smiled. "I should have known who was foremost in your thoughts all this while. Thanks to you, he is on excellent terms with Gwynedd. We have had no message from him, either, but we should see him soon."

"You know very well, my lord, that he is not foremost in my thoughts."

"Do I?" he whispered, coming closer and putting his hands into my hair. "Then you must prove it to me. This may be a homecoming for you, my lovely wife, but to me it is like stepping into a strange sea. I cannot get my bearings."

36 ♛ THE MESSENGERS

By the end of our first week in Gwynedd Alyse was walking with me about the castle, gaining strength daily, and beginning to look forward to seeing Fion again. In her eyes he would always be Pellinore's ransomed hostage, but I did not think that would bother Fion. To get her out in the sun again, I asked her to take me to Pellinore's grave, that I might pay him my respects and place flowers upon his resting place. This she did with great dignity, saying little, and keeping her eyes dry. On the way back I took her past the garden. In a week the gardeners had almost doubled its size and had built a little bower where she could sit and doze out of the bright sun. When she saw it, she stopped as if struck, and I felt her hand tremble on my arm.

"Did Maelgon do this?" she whispered.

"No, madam. Anet gave the order for it."

"Anet?" She turned slowly toward me, and I saw tears in her eyes. "This is your doing, Guinevere, may God bless you. Anet never gave an order in her life."

"I do assure you, she did. She told me herself she felt responsible, since it was on account of her looms that you lost it."

She shook her head. "Maelgon was responsible. Yet he permits this? Has he seen it?"

"Oh, yes. He has seen it. But he is too busy worrying about Arthur to worry about gardens."

A small smile twitched at the corners of her mouth. "And well he should worry," she said under her breath.

Just then Anet looked out from the weaving room and waved to me. "My lady Guinevere! I want your advice!" She lifted her skirts and came hurrying breathlessly up the path. "The cooks are angry because we have taken the carrot bed and the vines—I have an idea for expanding the kitchen garden, as well! Oh!" She stared in disbelief at Alyse, who stared in wonder at her.

"My lady Queen Alyse!" She fell into a curtsy. "Please forgive me—I did not know it was you!"

Slowly Alyse put out a thin hand and raised her. "Anet. My daughter." They looked at one another in silence for a moment. Then Alyse released her hand and slowly smiled. "Guinevere tells me I have you to thank for re-placing what my son had taken away."

I shot Anet a warning glance, and she read my thought. Gulping, she nodded shyly. "Does it—I hope it pleases you, my lady? If there is aught you do not like, or would rather rearrange, you have only to say so."

"And you will see that it is done? Thank you, Anet. That is a generous offer."

"Oh, Queen Alyse, I would do anything to please you!" The truth of this heartfelt avowal was so clearly written on the girl's plain face that even Alyse was moved.

She patted Anet's hand as we walked together through the garden. "Perhaps you would care to take some refreshment with me this afternoon, when the heat of the day is past? Guinevere has been coming daily to see me, but we are tired of reliving old times and could do with some new conversation."

Anet was nearly struck speechless by the honor being done her, but commanded her fear enough to accept politely. When she had excused herself and returned to her weaving, I bent and kissed Alyse's soft cheek.

"That was graciously done, my lady queen. You will not regret it."

Alyse chuckled. "Well, it was what you wanted, was it not? I am not blind, Guinevere. I see what you are after. And I owe it to you. For the garden."

It was never easy to fool Alyse.

One night at dinner, when the heat of the hall was oppressive, the air unmoving, the torches smoking and everyone's temper was frayed, a sentry came to Maelgon's elbow and announced the arrival of a messenger for the High King.

"Who sent him?" Maelgon asked gruffly.

"He will not say who sent him, my lord, but he says to tell you he bears a message from Salowen to the High King Arthur."

Maelgon's eyes blazed. "Throw him in the dungeons and let him cool his heels! I will not have the filthy vermin in my hall!"

Arthur's body went taut, and his eyes grew cold. But he waited.

The sentry licked his lips and shuffled his feet, but made no move to obey. "My lord—"

"Well?" Maelgon cried, slamming his tankard on the table.

"My lord, I cannot. He is a King's man." The sentry looked nervously at Arthur, and Maelgon glared at him, but at length, having no choice, waved his hand in assent.

Into the room walked a slim youth in a plain tunic, bearing himself like a soldier, and showing neither fear nor awe. When he approached Arthur I gasped aloud. It was Mordred! Arthur rose, and Mordred bent his knee.

"My lord King."

"Arise, Mordred. You have a message for me?"

"Yes, my lord."

"Is it a private message?"

"No, my lord. It may be publicly given."

"Who sent you?"

"I don't know the man's name, my lord. But I know that he is a Druid from Mona's Isle, and the message is from the Archdruid Salowen."

"And how did you come to be the bearer of this message?"

"I was in the town with some soldiers when a boy approached me and took me to this man who had the message." Then he lifted his face to Arthur and flashed him a quick look full of pride and love, before dropping his gaze to the floor once more. "I put myself in the way of it," he murmured.

Arthur did not move, but I sensed his pleasure and approval as surely as if I had seen him embrace the boy. "Give me the message."

Mordred stood very straight and closed his eyes to get it word for word. "Salowen, leader of the Sacred Order, who serves the Goddess in Nemet and walks between the standing stones, sends greetings to Arthur, High King of Britain. Hear this, King of men. The Great Goddess has been raped by heathen murderers and cries aloud for vengeance. Before the new moon falls from the sky, death will fall upon Gwynedd." Here the men stirred, and Maelgon would have spoken, but Arthur lifted a hand, keeping his eyes on Mordred's face, and they were still. "Because the High King has shown himself to be a just man, Salowen will speak with him, if he wills. But not so long as he lives beneath the roof of Maelgon the Murderer, or eats his food or drinks his wine. Let the High King remove to Caer Narfon with no protection but his own troops, and Salowen shall meet him at his pleasure."

Mordred opened his eyes and looked up at Arthur. "That is the message, my lord. But the man told me that every night and every day until the new moon, Mona shall be invisible to men, that none may find it." All around the table men crossed themselves, but Arthur looked with pride upon Mordred. It took courage to recite that message before Maelgon himself, and I could see the boy's legs were shaking. Arthur thanked him gravely and sent him back to the barracks with an escort.

As soon as the door shut behind Mordred, Maelgon spoke. "If the Druid approached him, my lord, the boy must be a pagan himself."

Arthur, still standing, turned. "Yes."

"Did you know this? Why did you bring him here? Only Christians are welcome in Gwynedd."

A hush fell over the company. More than one of Arthur's men knew that Mordred was his son. For a long moment Arthur said nothing. When he spoke at last, the very gentleness of his voice revealed the depth of his anger. "I choose my soldiers, Maelgon, for the strength of their sword arms, not for the names they call their gods. If you wish to contest this, say so. We can settle this tonight. Sword against sword."

Maelgon blanched. He knew now that the High King was willing to wage war over the Druids. He glanced hopefully at Lancelot, but Lancelot's eyes were on Arthur, awaiting a signal.

"Of—of course my lord is welcome to choose his soldiers by any standard he deems fitting," Maelgon stammered hastily. "But in Gwynedd we are all Christian."

"I am glad to know it," Arthur replied evenly. "Let every Christian keep the commandment to love his neighbor as himself, and we need worry no longer about who is pagan and who is not."

Maelgon opened his mouth to object, but found everyone staring at him and thought better of it. Swiftly Arthur leaned across the table until he breathed into Maelgon's face.

"If aught happens to that boy while we are in Gwynedd, you shall answer to me with your life. I promise it."

Maelgon drew away and Arthur straightened. The moment passed before anyone knew what had happened, yet fear swept the room. Alyse and Anet huddled together. The sweat stood out on Lancelot's brow.

Someone broke the silence with a nervous cough, and Maelgon bowed his head. "As you wish, my lord King."

Appeased, Arthur took his seat and signaled the wine bearer. Relief loosened everyone's tongue and soon the hall was noisy with conversation.

"What did he mean about the isle becoming invisible?"

"It is an old Druid trick. But half their power is in the minds of their believers."

"What do you mean? What trick?"

"The calling of the mists. Old Salowen's a master at it. He doesn't mean the isle will disappear, just that he will shroud it in mist so you can't see it from shore. That's all."

"It's true! I was fishing out past the point in the coracle at dusk and saw a great mist creep off the sea in the west!"

"Well, don't excite yourself. The isle is still there. You have only to go through the mist to find it."

"Go through a Druid's mist? Who would dare?"

"My lord Arthur," Maelgon said loudly, stilling the other voices. "Do you intend to leave for Caer Narfon to meet with Salowen? I assure you, I will not stand in your way."

Lancelot lifted his goblet to hide a smile. Arthur, straight-faced, answered politely. "Thank you, King Maelgon, but I will see Salowen at my leisure. And it would be a shame to leave so soon, after the hospitality you and your good queen have provided us. We will stay until we have feasted our honored guest. We await Fion."

Maelgon shrugged rudely and left it there, but it was obvious to anyone with eyes that he was furious. It was a relief to me when Anet rose to lead us out. I only hoped that she had sense enough to know better than to ask Maelgon for her blue-fleeced sheep tonight.

Three days later we had another messenger. Arthur, Maelgon, and most of the men were out hunting when Maelgon's scouts brought in a young man in ragged clothing, bound at the wrists and beaten to senselessness. They threw him in the dungeon to await Maelgon's return. I learned of this through Ailsa, who had been dozing near a window when he was brought in. I went at once to Anet and let her know if it. She stared at me blankly.

"Surely, my lady, we can wait to know who he is until Maelgon returns."

I sent her women from the room and sat her down. "This is an opportunity for you to do great good, Anet. And to increase your power. At Camelot, I visit the dungeons almost daily to speak with the men there. Not to console them, but simply to be kind. I do not need to see that they are not mistreated. Arthur is a fair man. But he wishes those he must imprison to learn from their mistakes and not to leave with a grudge against his judgment. I simply go to see them, and be seen by them, and listen to their complaints. We do not have many who return, once they are freed."

"You want me to go see this man?" She began to tremble, and I held her hand firmly.

"I will go with you. If he is a messenger, which is what Ailsa thinks, it is wrong to imprison him."

"You want me to free him?" Anet whimpered. "Oh, no!"

"No, you cannot free him. But at least you can see that he is not cruelly treated. You have the right. This is your domain." I sat beside her and spoke more gently. "They have taken his weapons, if he had any, Anet. You cannot come to harm. Maelgon's sentries will obey you. Why not? It will be like the gardeners, you will see. Come, let us go now."

Anet went unwillingly, only because she could not deny me. The sentries looked astonished to see her, but to a man they bent their knees and let us pass. We found the prisoner senseless on the dirt floor, his hands still bound, a filthy gag in his mouth. He was a mere youth with his beard just beginning. In the corner of his tiny cell two rats sat boldly watching him. To my surprise, Anet hardly noticed the vermin. It told me something about the convent.

At her order, given in a shaking voice, the guards unbound the boy, removed the gag, and washed his face. It was all we could do for him, and it was little enough. But the change it wrought in Anet was wonderful. She grew excited at her power to ministrate to the needy, and boldly asked the guard to send to her the scouts who had brought him in. Astonished, the guard demurred, until I murmured sweetly that King Arthur was expecting a messenger, and we hoped with all our hearts that this was not the man. The guard broke into a sweat and said at once he would send for the scouts.

When we were back in the fresh air of the garden, I hugged Anet and kissed her for joy. "Well done! Well done, Queen Anet! I could not have done it better myself!"

She colored and then said eagerly, "It was so easy! That poor youth! He is hardly more than a boy, and they beat him so!"

"They probably think he is pagan. Perhaps he is. Here in Gwynedd, that seems to be enough."

"Do you think Maelgon will be offended, when he hears?"

"That you had his face washed? Can he be that petty?" Then, because I knew the answer to that, I hurried on. "You know, Anet, that every queen has the power to give protection to those who ask it of her. In old Celtic law, not even your husband could violate that protection. Because it is a powerful weapon, you must use it wisely and sparingly. But if you do not use it, you give up the right."

"But this man has not asked it of me."

"No, I am not thinking of this man. But in the future, there may come a time . . . In order to grant protection, you must have the power to enforce it. Give Maelgon's sentries time to get used to obeying your commands. Then one day they will do it without thought."

"I shall go into the dungeons every day!"

When Maelgon returned, he had the scouts brought before him, and learned, as we had already done, that they had stopped the youth upon the road into Gwynedd. That he was pagan was clear enough; he wore the symbol of the Mother on a thong about his neck. They did not even have to put him to the test of the Lord's Prayer. He had confessed quite openly he was not Christian, and they had not waited to hear more, but had taken him prisoner.

Arthur was furious. He openly demanded to know why his laws were not obeyed in Gwynedd, and when Maelgon stood up to him and claimed the right to govern his own kingdom as he saw fit, Arthur, with his hand on Excalibur's hilt, and every eye in the room upon his hand, asked if that meant he could do insult to anyone he pleased without redress. There was silence. Were those laws? Arthur demanded. Was that justice? Had not the High King sworn to protect the rights of his people, down the the lowliest peasant? Did not Maelgon agree that this man had been unjustly treated? They did not even know yet what his crime was.

Grudgingly Maelgon backed down, and everyone exhaled. The prisoner, now awake, was brought before them. He fell on both knees in front of
Arthur and kissed his boots. His name, he said, was Nuathe. His mother
served the Lady's shrine at Avalon. He bore a message for Arthur from
Niniane, the Lady of the Lake.

"Give me the message," Arthur said.

"Do not go to Rheged, my lord!" Arthur looked startled and waited for
the rest, but nothing more came.

"That is the message, Nuathe? Nothing else?"

"That is the message, my lord. The lady Niniane gave it me herself. She
bade me hurry. I was chosen as the messenger because I ride fast."

Arthur frowned, and Maelgon, seeing his chance, began to grumble.
"What sort of a message is that? Are you telling us the truth, boy?"

"It is the sort of message Niniane might send," the King cut in. "And in
any event," he added lightly, "he was speaking to me."

Arthur thanked the youth for bringing him the message, and for endur-
ing such hardships along the way—this with a pointed look—and begged
him to rest well before his return journey. Maelgon took the hint, and
housed the boy with honor until he left, escorted by Maelgon's troops, two
days later. After all, it was known throughout Britain that to harm a King's
messenger was to insult the King and was asking for bloodshed. Before he
left, Nuathe publicly thanked Anet for her treatment of him while he lay in
the dungeons and praised her for her Christian charity. All of Arthur's train
did Anet honor, and Maelgon could do no less than join them.

Three days later we had a third messenger. This one, although a pagan,
came dressed as a soldier and carried a messenger's pouch; Maelgon's scouts
let him pass. He arrived at sunset, as we all gathered before going into dinner. He bowed politely to Maelgon, to me, Alyse, and Anet, then went on
one knee before Arthur. He came, he said, from Rheged.

Arthur took the scroll from his hand, examined the seal, broke it, and
beckoning the torchbearer nearer, slowly read the message. His face grew
grave, and he read a second time. Then he tucked the scroll in his tunic and
faced the messenger. "Your name?"

"Cathbad, my lord."

"Whom do you serve?"

"Sir Uwain, my lord. King Urien's son."

"Are you a Christian, Cathbad?"

The man's eyes flashed, and he hesitated just a moment. "No, my lord. I
am not. I serve the Mother."

"Do you know what this message says?"

"No, my lord. It was sealed before it was given to me."

"Tell me what you know of events in Rheged."

I watched Arthur anxiously, wondering why he was treading so carefully, wondering what the scroll said. Lancelot watched him, too, frowning. Maelgon looked at Cathbad in disgust.

"King Urien has been summoned to the defense of Strathclyde. King Hapgar sent a message begging his help a week hence. The Picts have broken their borders and attacked in great numbers." Anet sought my hand. "King Urien thought that many lives might be saved if you could but show your face in Strathclyde, my lord. Since you are by chance halfway there already, and the Picts know it not." He paused. "They would not stand against you."

Arthur's frown deepened. "Is Urien going?"

"Indeed, my lord. We are bound by treaty to do so. Preparations were well under way when I left."

"Does Uwain go with him? Who stays as regent?"

"Coel stays, my lord. The eldest son. All the rest go with him. This is a major attack."

Arthur drew a deep breath and bade the man rise. "Thank you, Cathbad, for bringing the message. Get you a night's sleep. In the morning we will take up our arms and accompany you back to Rheged."

This set the castle buzzing. Maelgon was of course delighted to be rid of Arthur and was consequently ebullient and condescending throughout dinner. Arthur himself was silent, and though the conversation among the men centered on the savage Picts and the glory of war, he would not speak about it.

I excused myself early from the women and went up to the tower to think. It was a fine, warm night and the stars were out. In the northwest the mist still lay upon the sea. Salowen's mist, they were calling it already. We had been in Gwynedd a fortnight and nothing had been done about the Druids. In five days the new moon would rise, and Arthur would be in Rheged. Without him behind me, would I have the courage to defy Maelgon should the need arise? Why was Fion not here? I felt now as Arthur felt. I could not get my bearings.

Arthur came to me before midnight. I heard his voice bidding the sentries keep watch upon the stairs and leave the parapet to us. When I turned to greet him, he took me in his arms and kissed me hungrily, unbraiding my hair and letting his lips slide down my throat.

"Arthur! What is the matter?"

He laughed hoarsely and pulled me closer, kissing my lips. "I do not want to go, Gwen. This is the false messenger. I am sure of it."

"Then do not go, my lord! Niniane has warned you twice about it!"

Abruptly he loosed me and began to pace back and forth along the parapet. "I must go. Urien is a major king and ally. If he calls me, I cannot delay."

"But if the messenger is false, then he does not call you."

"Yes, but I cannot really know that until I get there, Gwen. Suppose Nuathe was the false messenger? Have you ever seen him before, among any of Niniane's attendants?"

"No, my lord. But it is his mother who attends her. Not Nuathe."

"Still. It is just possible his message was a lie."

"Sent by whom?" He shrugged. I thought carefully back. "He came in on a red roan, lop-eared. I've never seen that horse before."

"Probably borrowed from the garrison at Caerleon, or hired from some inn. Surely he didn't ride it all the way from Ynys Witrin. Not if he was in a hurry."

"Then perhaps it was Mordred's message that was the lie."

His head came up, and he stopped his pacing. "I've thought of that. Mordred cannot identify the man who gave it to him. He was robed and his face hooded. If it was indeed Salowen who sent it, it could easily be a lie. Truth and untruth are much the same to the Sacred Order. But in that case, I must still go to Rheged. And the moon is waning fast."

"But you suspect Cathbad. I saw it in your face."

He smiled bleakly. "Let us hope no one else is so observant. Yes, I suspect him. For one thing, he told me exactly what was in the scroll. No more, no less. As if it were rehearsed. He admitted he could read. Does he imagine all couriers are so educated? And the scroll itself. It is Urien's seal, right enough, but the Latin is not quite right. It has an odd flavor, like those old scrolls found at York years ago, which Valerius swears are verbatim translations from the Celtic tongue. And I know Urien's scribe. His name is Junius. He was trained by his father, who was a Roman." He turned away and began to pace once more. "Cathbad was dressed like a soldier, but he did not carry himself like one. Did you see his eyes when I asked him if he served Christ? It was as if I had offered him poison. If he is not a Druid himself, I am a Saxon." He paused. "And the timing is so perfect. Something is about to happen here in Gwynedd. But the King's presence is a problem. How to remove the King? Send him a plea for help he cannot refuse. It is just too obvious."

"Then don't go."

He whirled and faced me. "I must. Even though I know it to be false. I must go. Men are not given perfect knowledge. I cannot be sure. I cannot risk offending Urien if I am wrong. It would cost too many lives."

"What would you like me to do? How can I help you?"

He sighed and stared up at the night sky. "Wait here for Fion and watch Maelgon every second. I am leaving Lancelot in command of half my troops. He is the obvious choice; he has Maelgon's ear, much joy it brings him. Talk to him about Maelgon. Learn as much as you can. And take him out riding now and again. He will lose his wits if he has no release."

I went up to Arthur and took him in my arms. I could feel the tension in his body. He was strung as taut as a bowstring before the arrow flies.

"Arthur," I whispered. "All will be well. God has not brought you here to stab you in the back. Go, do what you must do, and come back quickly. We will be here, awaiting your return. Have faith in us."

"Ah, Gwen," he breathed, bending down to me. "How I rely on you!"

37 ♛ THE ISLE OF MONA

With Arthur gone, Maelgon grew light-hearted and everyone around him breathed more easily. Anet received his promise for her sheep. Maelgon publicly complimented her upon the new garden, and even went so far as to apologize to Alyse for his high-handed treatment of her. Happiness, it seemed, had been restored.

But Lancelot was uneasy. Maelgon could not be trusted out of sight, he grumbled. He did not fear Arthur enough. Following Arthur's instructions, I took Lancelot away for a while each day. Sometimes we rode, sometimes we walked, and we kept our talk to political events: Maelgon, Arthur, the Druids, and the future of Gwynedd. Lancelot firmly believed that the Druids, with their mists and magics, were dying in Britain and that our future belonged in Christian hands. But while he approved of Maelgon's wish to have a Christian kingdom, he did not believe that Maelgon had a right to persecute men simply for being pagan. Maelgon's treatment of Nuathe had shocked him, as it had many of Arthur's men. Maelgon, he admitted solemnly to me, as if it were news, had not the temperament for kingship.

Spending less time with Maelgon, Lancelot began to relax a little and smile more. He was kind to Anet, whom he called my pupil, and complimented her upon the new way she wore her hair. And he found time to spend with Alyse. I tried to anticipate their meetings and leave them alone, but I was not always successful. Alyse could not imagine why it distressed me to hear Lancelot speak of Elaine and Galahad.

We had no more messengers. It was too soon to hear from Arthur, he had barely reached Rheged. He had taken Mordred with him, since the boy was safer fighting the Picts than staying with us in Gwynedd.

On the night of no moon a deathly hush descended upon Gwynedd. The sea mist seemed to hover just yards offshore. Few soldiers slept that night, and in the morning everyone was grumpy. Whatever was coming was coming soon; the new moon rose at midnight.

About midday, tired of the edginess that enveloped the castle, I coaxed

Lancelot out for a ride. Maelgon had bragged he would go hunting and then called it off at the last minute. His scouts had formed a tight ring around the castle, and he had archers posted at every window. In disgust at such cowardice, Lancelot rode out openly with me and a small escort. We rode up into the hills I had known so well as a girl. The air was sweet with pine scent and the woods alive with birdsong. It reminded me of that day, long ago, when we had met.

"Lancelot! Do you know where we are?"

He grinned. "I was thinking the same. The clearing is up ahead on this path, is it not?"

I nodded. He gave the signal to dismount and handed the reins to the captain of the escort. "Take the horses down to the stream to drink, then post a guard and rest awhile. There is a small clearing around the bend in the path. I will be there with the Queen."

"Yes, my lord."

The clearing was smaller than I remembered, crowded with scree around the edges, the grass grown long. Near the center, where Lancelot had stood when I first saw him, grew a young laurel. I plucked a leaf from it and crushed it between my fingers, releasing its sweet scent.

"This is the place," I said softly, half to myself. "I could never forget it."

Lancelot took my hand. "Yonder is where I first saw you. Sitting on your white mare with your mantle thrown back and your hair loose around your face. Never in my life had I seen such a beautiful woman." Gently he pushed a few stray strands from my brow. "Never in my life will I see such another." He stepped closer, and trembling, I turned away from him. A great oak stood at the edge of the clearing, must have stood there for generations, and I leaned against it, grateful for support. Slowly Lancelot walked toward me. I was no more capable of telling him no than of growing wings for flight. When he put his hand upon my waist I leaned into him. When he touched his lips to my face and whispered to me, all I could say was "Lancelot. Lancelot." And when he began to kiss me, first softly and then with sweet demand, I held his body close and clung to him, wishing with all my heart this would never end.

Suddenly he was gone. Rough hands grabbed me and something foul was thrust into my mouth. My hands were bound behind me. Gasping for breath, I saw Lancelot on the ground, kicking and writhing while seven men in ill-dressed skins gagged and bound him and took his sword. One he kicked in the groin, another in the knee. The leader lifted a club and smashed his head. I drew breath to scream, but choked on the gag. With a grunt, Lancelot lay still. It had all happened in a moment, and in absolute silence. The birds still sang undisturbed in the treetops.

There were twelve men altogether. They bound Lancelot and tied his senseless body to the oak. A thin stream of blood seeped from his ear. Then two of them lifted me as easily as they might carry a brace of quail and headed down an animal track toward the shore. Since I could do nothing against them, I lay still, but I could not keep the tears from my eyes. Had they killed him? Would his own soldiers find him there at length? If he lived, he would wish himself dead before he faced Arthur's men bound and gagged, the Queen taken and his sword gone. Oh, my Lancelot! How cruelly the fates were wont to treat us!

The men carried me a long way, without speaking so much as a whisper. I knew we were getting near the sea; I smelled it. Near the water's edge, they dumped me rudely on the sand, stripped off their skins, and buried them under a rock. From the same hiding place they drew forth robes, roughly sewn of coarse gray cloth, and donned them. For belts they had only simple twine. Two by two they ran into the brush and pulled out little lightweight coracles made of bone and wood and tanned skins, well waxed.

"Gorn, you and Llyd take her. Yours is the biggest."

"She will sink it. Let Bilin have her. His is strongest."

"If she comes with me there will be no room for Nidd. I cannot paddle her alone."

"Do as I say, Gorn. The soldiers will find him soon. So what if she is taller than we thought? Try it. If she struggles, strike her."

Hands grabbed me and hauled me into the tiny craft. I could not believe they were going to trust these primitive constructions to the sea. They rocked and swayed and spun about, dangerously deep in the water. I shut my eyes and in my heart said every prayer of penitence I knew.

Time crawled by in silence. The only sounds were sea sounds, the chuckle of water as the waves lifted and dropped us, the soft kiss of the paddles, the muffled cry of seabirds. I felt unaccountably sleepy and struggled to open my eyes. We were enveloped in gray mist so thick the robed men seemed to disappear before my eyes, although they were certainly there, pressed hard against me, swaying with the effort of keeping the horrible little craft afloat. I felt a sob well up within me and gulped to keep it down. I knew now who these creatures were. They were Druids, and we were going to Mona's Isle.

To me it seemed like years before we reached the shore. Even then the men were quiet, talking to each other in low voices, two of them carrying me as they had before, the others carrying the little boats and hiding them in the bushes. Then they marched single file through the pine woods that grew close to the water's edge, and up a small rise and out of the cold mist, into brilliant sunshine. I looked about as best I could. We were in a sheep meadow, where sheep and goats grazed with a shepherd boy and his dog in close attendance. It looked for all the world like any peaceful meadow in Britain.

Suddenly I heard chanting. It began as a low hum, steady and throbbing, but as we approached its source I could distinguish the words, ritual and meaningless, chanted to a pounding rhythm that beat heavily, insistently like a hammer at the smith's forge. The men's gait changed; now they marched to the chant, swinging left and right. I felt the steady pounding in my belly, and thought I would be sick. Above us on both sides rose dark standing stones, breathing cold upon my neck, pricking my flesh like eyes on one's back. At the end of the avenue the men stopped. I tilted my head back and saw a tall man in a white robe standing before a wide door carved into the hillside behind him. His hood hid his face. He raised his hands in a solemn blessing and then said curtly, "Take her below. The cell is prepared. Well done."

As the men began to move, he came around to get a better look at me, and I saw, tucked in his embroidered belt, the long crescent knife of sacrifice. The white hood bent lower, and within its shadow gleamed a row of sharp, even teeth. He was smiling. I fainted.

When I awoke I lay upon a narrow pallet in a small cell. The floor was dirt, beaten hard and swept clean. Walls of undressed rock sweated moisture. Through a crevice crept a draft of sweet air. There were no windows, and only one door, low and curved and ill-fitting. Beside the pallet was a stool of carved wood, and on it, a horn cup and a candle. I sat up as memory flooded back and groaned. They had wrenched my shoulder when they dropped me on the beach. I moved my arm tentatively; stiffness, no more. Where the cruel rope had torn my wrists, and the gag cut my mouth, someone had applied a soothing balm. The smell was familiar—oil of spikenard? I shook my head to clear it and, bracing my hands against the rock, I managed to stand, although my head was spinning. I gasped, looking down at myself. I was dressed in a white Druid's robe and nothing else! I was naked beneath it. They had taken my tunic, my leggings, even my undergarments and my boots. My bare feet were clean, my hair was clean—they had stripped me and bathed me and even scented my hair! Surely they must have drugged me to do so much without my waking! I began to shake, and sat down quickly upon the pallet. That I was being carefully readied for something was certain, but for what?

Someone scratched upon the door and then slowly pushed it open. A young man's face looked in, and he smiled when he saw me awake. Nodding politely, he came in holding a wooden pitcher.

"Good evening, my lady. You must be thirsty. Would you like some more water? Why, you haven't touched your water yet."

"I don't know what's in it."

He grinned. "You think it might be poisoned? Poison is a dirty tool. Servants of Christ may stoop to poison. We do not. See? I will drink some myself." This he did, with no ill effects. When he refilled the cup and passed it to me, I drank gratefully.

"Thank you. What is your name? May I know it?"

"Kevin, my lady."

"Thank you, Kevin. I am in your debt."

He set the pitcher upon the little stool and bowed to me.

"Who are you, Kevin? Why are you kind to me, when the others were not? What are you doing here? May I ask these things?"

"Well, you may ask them," Kevin said easily. I judged him to be about nineteen, but it was hard to tell. "The ones who brought you here are servants, really. I am a graduate of the School. I am an acolyte. Soon I will be an initiate."

I attempted a smile, but my mouth was stiff from the gag. "Congratulations."

"Can you stand, my lady? Would you like a hand?" He extended his hand, strong and warm, and I took it. I was taller than he was by a head. He took a step back and surveyed me slowly from head to toe.

"You are a beautiful woman," he said bluntly. "It was a pleasure to prepare you."

I blushed, affronted at such directness. "What did you do to me? Prepare me for what?"

Kevin smiled. His teeth looked very white in his short black beard. "Do not be afraid. We who serve the Goddess take vows of chastity from full moon to new. But tomorrow, when you are made one of us, if you are willing . . ."

"Made one of you? Is that what I am prepared for?"

"It is a lesson to Maelgon. You will be offered to the Goddess. If She claims you, one of Maelgon's own family shall be numbered among us. A just retribution, don't you think?"

"How am I to be offered? How will She claim me?"

"Ahhh." Kevin sighed. "Now you are asking questions I may not answer. You must wait for dawn, when the new moon stands above Nemet."

I shivered and clutched the robe about me.

Kevin smiled and backed toward the door. "Do not be afraid, beautiful one. Salowen himself has consecrated you to the Goddess. You have been done great honor."

"Salowen! Was he here?"

"Indeed. He oversaw the preparations."

My hand went to the crucifix at my throat, but of course it was not there. Kevin observed the gesture and smiled again.

"We are not savages," he said gently, "no matter what they teach you about us. You will live to see your husband and children again. Good evening." And he closed the door behind him.

"Children!" I cried. "I have no children! Kevin! Kevin! Come back! Who do you think I am?"

But the door was locked, and no one answered my pounding. I threw myself on the pallet and wept until I was beyond feeling. Hours passed. I tossed fitfully, unable to sleep. I did not know what awaited me. The Goddess I had worshipped as a child, the Goddess Niniane served, was the Good Goddess, the Mother of men, whose gifts were life and health and fertility. To Her belonged the spring blooming, the full, rich living of high summer, the planting and harvesting of all good things, the yearly renewal of life. But here on Mona Salowen worshipped the Dark Goddess, the Great Goddess, who lived in Nemet and exacted retribution for one's sins. Her gifts were justice, victory, vengeance, and death. And yet they were one Mother. Like the gold coin of Britain, with Arthur's image stamped on one side and his deadly Sword Excalibur on the other, so did the Goddess have different faces She turned to men.

"O Holy Mother," I whispered, kneeling on the dirt floor and clasping my hands tight. "Blessed Mary, Bearer of Light, Giver of Death, whatever name it pleases You to take, Mother, hear my plea. Spare Lancelot's life and deliver me from the trial that awaits me. Send me Arthur! Send me Merlin! If escape be possible, oh please, please rescue me. If not—if not, give me strength to endure what is ahead. Let me not shame Arthur, whatever happens, more than I have done already. O Mother, Mother, give me strength!"

After this, I was able to sleep. But I woke as soon as the door opened. It was Kevin, bearing a new candle.

"Kevin!" I leaped up and went to his side. "Oh, Kevin, what hour is it now?"

"The new moon has risen. I have just come from the ceremony." Indeed, there was a milky calm about him, and his voice was thick with sleep. I wondered if it were true, that the Druids drugged themselves for worship, and if so, why?

"Kevin, tarry a moment, I pray you." I placed a hand upon his arm, and he turned swiftly to me, a light in his eyes. Only then did I remember that his vows of chastity no longer bound him, and I stepped back a pace, holding hard to my courage. "You told me before, I should live to see my children again. Kevin, I have no children. Do you not know me? I am Guinevere, Queen of Britain. King Arthur's wife."

He went pale and stared at me unmoving.

"I must see Salowen the Archdruid. If he is able, after the ceremony—

send him to me at once. I must see him before the dawn. His very life, the future of the isle itself, is at stake."

Slowly, with great care, Kevin turned away from me and lit the candle with a steady hand. Then he went to the door and stopped. "If he will see me, I will tell him what you have said."

"Make him see you!" I cried. "Surely there must be one among your number who knows me by sight! Bring him here." But the door was closed, and Kevin was already gone.

I waited a long time. I sat on the pallet and dozed, hearing the Druids' chanting in my dreams, but waking afterward to deathly stillness. Suddenly, when I had nearly given up hope, a robed figure slipped silently into my cell. I blinked to make sure he was not a vision. His hood was thrown back, revealing a thin face with narrow eyes, a long, hooked nose, and thin, cruel mouth. His white hair was cropped close to his head; I could see the bones of his skull. Around his neck he wore a thick collar, beautifully patterned. His hands, long and thin and sensual, made a quick sign over my head, and then disappeared into the folds of his robe.

"I am Salowen," he said. His voice, deep and rich and vibrant, was that of a man half his age and twice his size.

I struggled to my feet and made him a reverence. "You do me honor, Salowen, to see me. I asked you to come because I fear you have made a mistake."

"I do not make mistakes."

"If you think taking me will anger Maelgon, you are in error."

"You are his sister."

I gasped. To be taken for Elaine! What cruel irony was this?

"I am not his sister! Elaine is in Less Britain with her sons. She has never left since she went there as a bride. Surely you must know this!"

He nodded calmly. "As I know that you have befriended your brother's wife, the new queen, and have reconciled her to your mother."

He had spies in Maelgon's very household! "My mother is dead. I grew up in Gwynedd as Pellinore's ward. Queen Alyse is my aunt, although she has been as a mother to me."

"And Maelgon a brother."

"No. I never liked Maelgon, and he never liked me. He always was a bully. That is why Arthur came to Wales, to bring peace between you or remove him from his throne."

"Ha!" He laughed harshly, and the patterned collar around his neck began to move. My hand flew to my mouth to cover a scream. The collar slowly unwound itself into a great snake, sliding down his arm toward me, its eager tongue flicking in and out.

"Do not move," Salowen commanded. His long hands stroked the slithering flesh as the snake descended, sliding smoothly across the floor, brushing my feet. Gracefully the snake lifted its head, wrapped itself around my legs, and began to climb. I shut my eyes and held myself still. I was terrified that I might faint. I heard a low-pitched whistle, and at once the snake retreated, uncoiling gracefully from about my ankles and returning to Salowen's outstretched hand. When he had settled it again about his neck, and I had begun to breathe, he smiled, showing his little cat's teeth.

"That is a point in your favor. It is well known that the lady Elaine cannot abide serpents."

"It is well known that Elaine has never left Lanascol!" I retorted angrily.

Something flashed in his eyes, and I shivered. "It is well known," he hissed softly, "that Guinevere has never left Camelot."

"How can I prove who I am? Is there no one here who knows me?"

"There is Cathbad. If he returns in time."

"Cathbad! Then—then it was you who tricked Arthur into leaving Gwynedd?"

Again he smiled, and again a frisson of horror slipped up my spine.

"Tell me this," he said softly, leaning closer, "if you are not Maelgon's sister, what were you doing in the forest, alone with her husband?"

I flushed scarlet, avoiding his eyes. There was no reply to that. Pleased, Salowen stroked the snake and regarded me dispassionately. "If you are Guinevere, then are you Maelgon's cousin. And if you are dear to Maelgon's sister's husband, so much the better. You are a woman like any other. The Goddess herself shall judge you."

"I will not become one of your cult!"

His smile grew broader, and his voice grew softer. "Indeed, you will not. Is that what Kevin told you? Kevin is an acolyte. He knows little. But he will know the truth before dawn."

He turned away from me.

"What will you do? Be sure you will answer to Arthur for it! Have you not the courage to tell me?"

He whipped around. His eyes were burning slits in his face. "You wish to talk about courage? You will need it. At dawn you will be offered to the Goddess. If She accepts you, She will spare your life and you will owe it to Her always. If not, you will die."

"It is three hundred years since the kind of sacrifice you speak of was banned in Britain!" I cried, fighting back a sob.

"And it is a thousand years since a priestess of the Goddess was beheaded at her prayers," he spat.

"I am not responsible for that."

"And I am not responsible for the Goddess' judgment."

"How—how will I be judged?" I whispered helplessly.

"By fire."

In the still predawn Kevin returned. He carried a tray of food, which he placed carefully on the floor by my pallet. I sat watching him. His hand shook, and he did not want to meet my eyes.

On the tray was a slice of new bread, a comb of honey, and a cup of goat's milk, warm and fragrant. It was the ritual meal of sacrifice, as I had heard it told in stories when I was small. In the old days, before the Romans came to Britain, the Druids sacrificed once a month to their bloodthirsty Goddess. In the old days.

"I'm sorry, my lady," Kevin said in a low voice. "I did not know."

"You are forgiven."

"I wish there were something I could do."

"Get word to Arthur. Afterward—somehow, get word to him, and see he learns the truth."

Kevin bowed his head. Surely what I was asking was forbidden by his vows. "I will do it."

"Thank you. God bless you."

"I will pray the Goddess to spare you." He gestured toward the tray. "Please, my lady, drink the milk."

"I cannot touch it. I will be sick."

He looked up briefly, pleadingly. "I have put something in it to help you. That is all. To help you." Then he rose and left.

God had answered my prayer. I was not to be rescued, but here was something to enable me to endure. Even so, I had not the courage to take it until I heard them coming for me. Then I downed it all in one swallow.

The procession moved slowly. They formed two lines, gray-robed and softly chanting, with me between them and Salowen at the head. The chanting was tuneless, more a gentle rhythm than a song, and they shuffled to its beat, left, right, left, right, through tunnels lit with smoking torches, left, right, up shallow steps, left, right, and out into the damp dark thick gray mist. I hardly felt my feet touch the ground. The beat was in my blood, bearing me onward. My gray-robed companions vanished in the mist; I followed Salowen, the white-robed, who led me into the dark grove where a mystery awaited. The path narrowed, the chanting quickened, trees leaned down to caress my face with their light fingers as I passed. Ahead stood a great circle of standing stones in a wide clearing. The mist gathered strength and swirled around the clearing, bearing me up and up onto a platform in the center. A thick rope was placed around my waist and tied to a pole behind me, pinning my arms to my sides. Before me stood Salowen at an altar. On the altar lay a black stone, hollowed out, and beside it the gleaming knife of sacrifice. So this was Nemet, I thought calmly. In the old days, this is where the victims met their end. I gazed about the clearing. Gray-robed figures huddled at the feet of the standing stones, swaying to their chanting, filing in to take their places. All of them were hooded.

Suddenly Salowen raised a great staff above his head and the chanting stopped. In the guttural language of Druids, he cried out some ritual words, looking to the heavens, and the Druids replied. This he did thrice; then the staff descended and the chanting began again; this time the cadence changed. It was deep, vibrant, dolorous, and slow. Salowen began to speak above the chanting, reciting the wrongs done the Druids over the centuries and justifying the vengeance he was about to take. I did not attend him. I leaned against the pole and watched the thin, bright crescent of the new moon creep above the treetops. How lovely she was, how pure and innocent—how far from earth! Everyone who had ever been dear to me I then remembered, my father Leodegrance, Gwillim, Gwarth, everyone who had been so kind to me in Gwynedd when I was an orphaned stranger; everyone who had welcomed me to Camelot, all Arthur's Companions, his commanders, and his soldiers. Good Bedwyr, my friend, who now held Camelot in the King's absence, and Kay, Gereint, Ferron, and a hundred others. But to Lancelot and Arthur, I could not bring myself to say farewell. Heaven held no joy for me without them.

Salowen raised the staff again, and the chanting grew quick and restless. Men began to shuffle about in small knots, circling slowly around me. Three of them held torches. Faster, faster, eagerly the chant beat against my ears, closer, closer came the fire, stinking of resin, stinging my eyes with smoke. The brushwood under my platform must have been damp with Druid's mist; it took them a long time to light it, but at last, it caught. Through a wall of shimmering heat I watched them slowly back away, hoods falling askew, mouths slung open in excitement, devouring me with feral eyes. They had all gone mad.

A wild yell rent the morning; a black horse broke through the trees bearing a knight with a slashing sword, singing a victory paean. Other voices took up the cry—from the woods came a phalanx of foot soldiers with shields and swords, scattering the Druids, cutting them down. The stallion screamed as he neared the flames, but for Lancelot, he bore them. Down came the deadly sword, the rope fell from me, and I swooned in his arms as he lifted me and carried me away.

I dreamed that I was home at last, or in Heaven; I was somewhere I had always longed to be.

Slowly I opened my eyes, but could see nothing. As my senses returned to me, I heard sound—no more than a whisper, near my ear. Someone was praying. I lay protected, enveloped by strong arms, wrapped in a cloak, gently held, gently kissed.

I slid an arm around his waist and pulled him closer, until the length of his body pressed against mine.

"Oh, Lancelot," I whispered.

"Guinevere. Thank God."

"Is this a dream? Do I live?"

In the dark he found my lips and kissed them. It was the only answer I wanted. Tears welled up and spilled freely forth. He held me while I wept and whispered sweet endearments to me, words that I remember to this day. At length, when I was quiet, he arose. I saw then that we were in a large cave with smoothly rounded walls—man's work. Lancelot went to the cave mouth and spoke to a soldier there. It was dark beyond. I lay on a mat of leaves and bracken covered by a soldier's cloak. Lancelot's own cloak was wrapped about me, and underneath, I still wore the white robe of sacrifice. Where were we? And what had happened to the day? The men spoke softly and dared no light. We could not yet be in Gwynedd.

Lancelot returned with a skin of weak wine, and bade me drink.

"We are still on Mona's Isle?"

He nodded but said nothing.

"This wine is bitter. Have you any water?"

He shook his head. "We could not find a spring, although there must be one about. This place is clearly used regularly. It was perfectly clean."

"What day is it? Have I slept long?"

He smiled, and I lifted a hand to his face, that face which I had thought I should never see again!

He caught my hand and held it against his breast. "You have slept since you fainted. You were probably drugged."

"Yes. Kevin did that for me. I took it willingly."

"The murdering bastards. There are not so many of them left now."

"Did you find Salowen? The leader in the white robe?"

"I saw no one in a white robe. Was he there himself?"

"Yes. Lancelot, I told him who I was. He was going to sacrifice me anyway. Arthur must know this."

"He will know it," he said shortly.

"He took me because he thought I was Elaine."

He bit off a cry and bowed his head. "It is my fault he took you for Elaine."

I kissed his hand and stroked his hair. "You did nothing without my consent. I am to blame, as well. Tell me what happened, from the beginning. Have we time? The last I saw you, they clubbed you and left you for dead."

"We cannot leave before daylight. There is plenty of time." He made light of the beating they had given him, but in fact he still suffered from dizzy spells and sometimes saw things double. The troopers had found him and brought him round. They had tracked the Druids as far as the beach, where they found Lancelot's sword buried with their skins under the rock. Lancelot was all for dashing across the channel at once, but could barely sit on his horse. The troopers sensibly made him return to the castle, where Alyse took charge of his care and would not allow him to rise or speak.

"She probably saved your life."

"Perhaps. But, Guinevere, I did not want to live. To hand you to Maelgon's enemies through my weakness—"

"Stop." I placed my hand over his mouth and leaned into his embrace. "Do not dwell on it. We were both at fault. But God is moving. Can you not feel it? We are part of a pattern. And we are not yet come to the end of the skein. Go on with your tale."

Gereint had been his lieutenant. Through Gereint, he commandeered what fishing craft could be found in the village; Maelgon's ships lay at anchor in Caer Narfon, half a day's ride away. Gereint had canvassed Arthur's men for volunteers. And even though it meant going through the Druid's mist on the night of the new moon, every man of them had volunteered. There was only room for thirty in the boats, and Gereint picked men who could swim or row. While everyone was at dinner, Lancelot escaped Alyse's vigilance and made his way to the stables. He wanted cavalry, but it was a long swim. Five men brought their horses; only his own stallion Nestor survived. While the men took turns at the oars and fought the current, Lancelot spoke to the horse, cajoling and encouraging him across by the sheer strength of his will. Every time they tired and feared they could not go on, they seemed to hear Merlin's voice in their ears, ringing from the sea, the air, the sky, compelling them to greater effort.

"Merlin?" I whispered, awed. "Did you see him?"

Lancelot shook his head. "No, but he was there, more a shadow than a shape. A voice. A presence. But he gave us the strength to get across."

An hour before moonrise they struck rocks on the eastern shore. They managed to get everyone safely landed, but lost the boats and nearly lost Nestor on the beach. If they had not stumbled across a stream within a hundred yards of shore, two men might have died, and the horse certainly would. Fresh water and rest revived them; they posted a guard and slept as best they could. Lancelot, who could not sleep, roused them well before dawn, and they scouted the shore for, as he put it, the Druids' lair. Nestor, stiff and exhausted, hobbled along behind him.

They found the Druids by their chanting. They formed a phalanx, but when Lancelot smelled the smoke, he did not wait to make a battle plan, but spurred Nestor to action and burst in among them. When he had me, he had not dared to return to the clearing to his men for fear of putting me at risk. For although they do not carry swords, Druids are deadly fighters. Their knives fly silently through air, wood, or stone, men claim, and never miss their mark. Indeed, when he met Gereint at the appointed meeting place and gathered the men, he was astonished at their losses. The Druids had scattered immediately upon the attack, offering no resistance, but melting into the misty woods. In vain did Gereint's men search for them, daring them to step forth. And one by one, as the soldiers hunted them in the brush, they were cut down by swift-flying knives without ever seeing the hands that threw them.

When they regrouped, Lancelot had but twelve men left of the thirty who had come. And although many Druids had died that morning, we were still outnumbered many times. They had taken to the hills to look for a defensible spot where they could tend me. The cave gave onto a ledge of rock that overlooked a small valley. It was easy to defend, if your enemy had swords. Gereint stood guard at the cave mouth; the men and horse rested in a grove below the ledge. They had no fresh water. At dawn, they must scout for a spring or a stream and try to snare a rabbit. The rations they brought with them were all but gone; they had to plan an attack on the Druid's storehouses if we were to survive until Maelgon or Arthur could mount a rescue. He spoke with confidence, but I knew it was for my sake. Our chances did not look good. Although he did not say it, I knew he was afraid for Nestor, as well. After the swim and the day's trek into the hills, it would be a miracle if the horse survived.

I told him then about the coracles that lay beached somewhere along the shore and about the sheep meadow and the goats. He dismissed the coracles—he would not trust me to one, he said, and would not ask Nestor to make that effort twice. But the sheep and goats were a boon, indeed, and I heard the relief in his voice. I told him about my conversation with Salowen, and about who Cathbad was, and everything that had happened to me. It all came tumbling out, as I sat in his arms and we waited for dawn.

"Did you arrange with Maelgon to come rescue us if we did not return?"

"The coward says he cannot come himself; he must wait upon Fion. But he sent two couriers after Arthur."

The shadow at the cave mouth moved, and Gereint approached softly. He bowed to me, smiling kindly. "My lady Queen Guinevere. I am glad to see you awake."

"Thank you, Gereint. I am glad to be awake."

"My lord, we think we hear the sound of chanting, far off down the slope. Gryfflet has volunteered to scout them and see what they are up to."

Lancelot did not move, but his arms about me tightened, pulling me closer. "Is he strong enough?"

"He is the fittest among us."

"Let him stay out of knife range, then. I cannot spare him."

"Very good, my lord. I will tell him."

"Gereint!" Gereint turned back and I felt Lancelot tremble, and still it. "Is Nestor standing?"

"Yes, my lord."

"Send young Sagramor into the hills above this cave to seek a spring. There must be one about. Guinevere tells me she has seen a meadow where they tend sheep and goats."

"That is good news."

"Indeed. It is our best hope."

Gereint returned to his post, and Lancelot and I sat silent, holding each other in peace, waiting. Before long we, too, could hear the chanting. No more than a murmur at first, it stirred the air and grew into a low hum that snaked around the cavern walls and set my heart racing. Lancelot rose and went out to Gereint. They left the ledge, and when he returned, Lancelot was alone.

"Tell me," I said, sensing he was braced to give me bad news.

"Gwen." He sat down beside me and took both my hands. "We are surrounded. They are coming up the valley, shoulder to shoulder through the trees, in a tight ring. They know we are here."

"Can we defend against them?" When he did not answer, I brought his hand to my lips and kissed it. "Come. Tell me. I can face death if I am with you."

"Ahhhh, my beautiful Gwen, you are braver than I," he whispered, pulling me to his breast. "The men are hidden among the rocks. Nestor is set free in the forest. It is all I can do. If only I had brought an archer!"

I took his face in my hands and kissed his lips. "Lancelot. It is not your fault."

"We have an hour, perhaps. No more."

He drew me down onto the makeshift pallet and held me, whispering to me between kisses. "We have always known—since first we met—that this was a love sent to us from Heaven— Guinevere—I cannot bear to part this life—without having held you in my arms thus, at least once—at least once—permit me, my dearest love, to lie with you."

His seeking hands slid under the Druid's robe and found my flesh.

"Lancelot," I breathed, joy and terror battling in my soul, "I cannot deny you." And I gave myself up to his ardor.

He was so unlike Arthur, whose delight in touching and native gift of patience gave him the power to shape a woman's desire as skillfully as ever a potter shaped his clay. He could start with nothing and build to pleasure by slow degrees, with joy and care and laughter, until the heart cried out for its sweet release; or, himself ablaze, could fire the body in a flash to meet his need. Lancelot's passion was a conflagration, burning and unmanageable. I gave myself to his flame, feeling nothing but heat and wild excitement, fed by his eager fury. I had no will but his will, no future beyond this moment; without a look back I surrendered to his engulfing holocaust. His body crushed me; I could not breathe; cold terror gripped my soul; suddenly I saw clearly into the heart of this consuming blaze: It was ash. Cold. Dead. Forgotten. Crying out, I hammered at his shoulders in panic.

"NO! Lancelot! I cannot! I cannot do it!"

He backed away at once, gasping for breath, with glazed eyes that knew me not.

"Oh, Lancelot, Lancelot, forgive me if you ever can. But I cannot do it. It is death."

"Gwen!" he whispered, surfacing. "My God!"

We stared at one another, and I fumbled to sit up and straighten my robe.

He sat beside me and passed a hand across his brow. "Dear Christ, am I possessed? This is madness. It will be the end of us, forever."

"Yes."

I saw he was shaking as badly as I. I could not voice the terror in my soul. Twice in one day I had stared into the abyss, black and beckoning, from which there was no return. The approaching Druids frightened me no longer. The steady thrum of their chanting anchored me firmly to the dark, cool earth, and I welcomed it.

"I love you, Lancelot," I whispered sadly, touching his hand, "but there is no hope for it."

"Guinevere, forgive me."

"My dear, you are forgiven without asking." I drew a ring from my finger and placed it in his hand. It was the love knot cast in gold that my father had given my mother during their courting. "Take this, Lancelot, and keep it by you. I love it dearly. Take it in exchange, if you will, for what I cannot give you."

He pulled the leather lacing from his tunic and, threading it through the ring, tied it about his neck. "If it is the last thing I ever do, Guinevere, I will protect your honor."

A strange calm came over him. He rose and handed me up. With great dignity, he walked me halfway to the entrance to the cave. Beyond, the sky was lightening. Treetops swayed gray-green in the early breeze and the valley erupted in birdsong; it would be a beautiful day.

"Guinevere, if it should come to death, we will not wait here like trapped rats. We will climb up the hillside and find a cliff that reaches out over the sea below. If there is no help for it, we will choose death together, you and I. Are you with me?"

I smiled at him and took him in my arms once more. "I am always with you, Lancelot."

With great tenderness, he bent his head and kissed me farewell.

"For shame!" a voice cried out in anger. "Unhand the Queen, you blackguard! For shame! My God—it's Lancelot!"

There in the cave mouth stood two men with drawn swords. Foremost was Maelgon, staring open-mouthed at Lancelot. Behind him, with eyes only for me, stood Fion.

38 👑 THE PRISONER

Lancelot's sword leaped to his hand, but Maelgon did not advance. Confused, he wavered and lowered the weapon. I could see his thought upon his face. His exalted standing among the kings of Britain lay in his being my cousin and Lancelot's brother-in-law. As outraged as he felt he ought to be, it availed him nothing to be outraged at us.

But as Maelgon lowered his sword, Fion stepped forward and crossed Lancelot's blade.

"In the name of Arthur of Britain, yield or die." There was iron in that lilting Gaelic voice, and I saw Lancelot go stiff with anger.

"Lancelot!" I flung myself to my knees between them as they each moved forward. "Do not harm him, I pray you! This is Fion!"

But even as I spoke, Lancelot lowered his sword. He knew he had no right to defend me against anyone who spoke in Arthur's name. Fion's swordpoint touched his breast. With his sword at his side, Lancelot took one step forward into the blade, drawing blood as Fion hastened to withdraw. Acknowledging the gesture, Fion inclined his head, sheathed his weapon, then extended his hand.

"Yield your sword, sir, in the King's name."

Lancelot hesitated, then bent his knee to the ground and offered up the sword in the ritual gesture of surrender, with the blade held flat across his palms. Fion took it. Lancelot was now his prisoner.

"Fion." I rose shakily and looked at my old friend. The morning sun behind him threw his face half into shadow but lit the bright gold of his hair and glittered off the great jewels at shoulder, wrist, and waist. His face had grown rugged with the cares of kingship, and he now carried himself like a warrior, but his eyes, brilliant green and smiling, were unchanged. He was still the handsomest man I had ever seen.

"My lord King Fion," I said with firmness, making him a deep reverence. He let his eyes travel slowly from my hair, loose and unbraided, to my bare feet.

"My lady Queen Guinevere." He bowed gracefully from the waist and, with laughing eyes, said gravely, "How the fashions have changed in Britain since I left!"

It broke the tension, and everyone relaxed a little.

"I do assure you, my lord, I would I were better gowned to greet you. But the Druids dressed me." I became suddenly aware that the chanting had stopped. In the valley now we heard only the voices of soldiers, calling out to one another and singing victory paeans. "Have you subdued them? Have you found Salowen?"

"Subdued them?" Maelgon broke in. "Aye, you could say so! We have sent them all to meet their precious Goddess face to face!"

"Do not kill them all, for my sake!" I cried, ignoring Maelgon and speaking only to Fion. "There is at least one among them I would save. Not everyone took part—spare the innocent, I pray you!"

Maelgon snorted, and Fion glanced at him swiftly.

"We have disarmed every man we could find. Those who offered fight are dead. When we find their headquarters, we shall gather them for your inspection, and you may decide who lives and dies, if you wish."

I shuddered, and Fion reached out to take my arm. Lancelot moved instinctively to protest, then stopped himself in time.

"You, Lancelot. I remember you now. When I knew you last, you were Arthur's closest friend and ally." His voice was cold. Lancelot flushed, but held himself still and said nothing. My heart sank. I could see he was prepared to accept all the blame for everything that had happened; he had already convinced himself he deserved it. "You will come with me, sir. I will take you to Arthur."

"Now, now," Maelgon grumbled uneasily, clearing his throat. "I will take charge of him, my lord Fion, if you like. He is my sister's husband."

At this Fion turned to him and stared. "Elaine's husband? Then I had better keep him close for his own protection. Between you and Arthur, he can be judged."

Maelgon, who never could see beyond the end of his nose, was at a loss for a reply.

I gripped Fion's arm and looked up into his face. "I pray you, my lord Fion, before you judge what your eyes have seen, listen to me. I will tell you truth."

He drew closer, and the smile returned to his eyes. "Fair enough, fair Queen."

"Above all men on this earth, Arthur loves and honors Lancelot. And I do promise you that Lancelot loves and honors Arthur. He would die for Arthur gladly, no questions asked. You do him an injustice to think him traitor. He saved my life this day past, and not for the first time. Why do you think the Druids came after us? Yesterday at dawning the Archdruid Salowen tied me to a stake and offered me to the Goddess." Fion's eyes widened, and he glanced quickly at Lancelot. But Lancelot was stone. "He did not merely threaten, he bade them light the fire."

"Fire?" Fion whispered, incredulous. "They gave you to the fire? That is the fate reserved for—"

"Traitors and whores. Yes. I know it. And they lit the fire. If it were not for Lancelot, I would not now be with you. Lancelot and his companions rowed across in the night, braving the Druid's mist on the night of the new moon, losing boats and horses, and rescued me at the very moment I succumbed to the smoke. They have tended me all night, going without water or food. When we found ourselves discovered and surrounded by the Druids before dawn, we prepared to die." I looked up into his brilliant eyes, so near my face, and hoped he remembered the day he bid me farewell in Gwynedd. "What you saw, Fion, was our farewell."

He did remember it. I saw his features soften, and he straightened. "Well, Lancelot. If I have misjudged you, I beg forgiveness. You have saved the Queen from a cruel fate, and all Britain is in your debt. I, too, thank you from my heart." He held out Lancelot's sword for him to take.

But he did not take it. Bowing stiffly, Lancelot said in a tight voice, "You are merciful, my lord. But my gracious Queen does tell but half the truth."

"Lancelot!"

"It is my fault she was abducted by the Druids. If I am the villain who put her at such risk, surely it is no more than my duty to save her from it. This justice demands. I have wronged Queen Guinevere, and I have wronged King Arthur. I cannot take the sword back. Give it to Arthur. I am in his hands."

"Lancelot, I forbid you to do this! Are you mad? But an hour ago you swore me protection!"

He looked at me then. I could not bear to see such pain in his eyes. "I swore," he said gently, "to protect your honor."

"This is not the way! Think, Lancelot, how you would hurt him!"

"He will know it, Gwen. There is no help for that. All it takes is one look at your face."

"Or yours!" I retorted angrily. I hated the martyr in him. Why could he not forgive himself? "Do not sacrifice Arthur on the altar of your guilt!" He turned away, but there were tears in his eyes. Fion looked slowly from one of us to the other.

"This sounds," he said coolly, "like a lovers' quarrel."

"No, no," Maelgon cut in hastily, "I'm sure it is not. The Queen my cousin spoke truth. They said farewell. Nothing more. She would not dare. It would be her death."

Fion cast him a look of mild contempt. "You do not know Arthur." He looked sadly at Lancelot and at me. "You must both return to Gwynedd with me. Whether you go to Arthur as prisoner or free man, as Queen or penitent, I leave to you. But to Arthur you must go. There is more here than I have time to unravel. Or"—with a long look at me—"than I desire to know."

He moved back and gestured for us both to walk before him. But as we stepped onto the ledge and into the bright morning sun, we heard scuffling above us, and a shower of pebbles and dust fell over the lip of the cave at our feet.

"Who's there!" Maelgon cried, drawing his sword. Down the rockface slithered a young knight in a torn tunic, with a wineskin slung around his shoulders and a rope in his hand. At the other end of the rope staggered a tall thin man in a filthy white robe. The young man gave the rope a forceful tug, and Salowen fell in an ungainly huddle at his feet.

"Sagramor!" Lancelot cried. "Well done! Is that the archdruid?"

"So he claims," Sagramor replied with a grin. "He's cursed me and all my descendants about a hundred times. What a tongue he has!"

Salowen struggled to stand. His wrists were bound and bleeding, and his face cut and bruised where Sagramor must have struck him. But he pulled himself up to his full height, looking upon us all with grand contempt. He still had his dignity, and he said nothing.

"He tried to kill me at the spring," Sagramor continued lightly, coiling the rope. "But his aim wasn't very good. I didn't think those knives ever missed. But he was out of sorts because I killed his snake." Salowen's eyes slid to him for a moment, full of hate.

"*This* is the man who put you to the fire?" Maelgon cried excitedly. "Cousin, speak! Is it he?"

"Yes."

"King Maelgon—" Fion reached out to stay his arm, but too late. With a mighty thrust, Maelgon's blade split the Druid's body from throat to groin. Without a sound, he staggered and collapsed into a pool of his blood and innards. Gagging, I hid my face on Lancelot's shoulder, and his arm came around me.

"Sagramor!" he called. "Is that water you carry? Bring me some for the Queen!"

The water revived me; sweet and cool, it eased my sickness. I made Lancelot drink of it, also. Fion stood between us and the slaughtered Druid, to screen me from the sight. Maelgon delighted in hurling the bloody remains off the ledge and stomping upon the dark-stained earth.

"Food for kites," I whispered. "That is all he is become. And by his own lights, he was a religious man."

"I will build him a cairn, to mark his deathplace," Fion promised. And he did. Before we left the Isle of Mona two days later, he built the cairn with his own hands.

Fion's ship lay at anchor in a sheltered bay, and it was there they took me. At first I was dizzy and light-headed, but when Fion brought me broth and bread, I felt better. I had not eaten, I realized, since before I took Lancelot riding in the woods. Was it only two days hence? It seemed to me I had been on Mona for half a lifetime. I saw to it that my brave rescuers were fed, as well. For two days Maelgon's men scoured the island for stragglers, buried the dead, tended the wounded, and questioned the Druids they found. I refused, to Maelgon's disgust, to identify my tormenters. How could I be sure? They had been robed and hooded; I had been drugged. And I did not want any more to die because I named them. Salowen was enough. Their power was broken. Nestor they found grazing placidly in the sheep meadow, fully recovered from his ordeal. But however hard the soldiers searched for the sacred grove itself, or for the avenue of standing stones that led to it, they could not find it. Nemet had disappeared.

They did not find Kevin. I grieved to think him dead on my account. Maelgon and Fion, and even Lancelot, could not understand my tears. They put it down to the terror I had undergone. But Arthur would have understood it.

Maelgon at length decided to sever his ties with Lancelot and treat him as a traitor. In a tight place, he probably reckoned, blood ties to the Queen outranked ties by marriage to the King's dearest Companion. He insisted Lancelot be confined to the ship and allowed no contact with anyone, save the servants who brought him food. Fion objected, on the grounds that what Lancelot had done to save the Queen was known and attested to, but what he had done to disgrace me or the High King was unknown. Nevertheless, Lancelot assented to imprisonment with a willingness that surprised everyone, except me. If he had shouted from the hilltop, he could not have proclaimed his guilt more clearly.

Leaderless, the Druids who wished to remain on Mona's Isle to tend their sheep and live quietly were permitted to stay. Their knives were taken from them.

We were a solemn procession, coming home to Gwynedd. I was given immediately into the care of Alyse and Anet, who seemed to have come to friendship in my absence. They were wild to know what had happened, and how and why, but I feigned exhaustion, kept to my rooms, and held my tongue. Maelgon had not the nerve to throw Lancelot into the dungeons, much as I knew Lancelot himself wished to go. Instead, he confined him to his quarters to await the arrival of the King. On the third day a royal courier arrived. The hoax about the Picts had been discovered as soon as they reached Rheged, and Arthur was on his way back as fast as he could ride.

When I heard this from Anet, I rose from bed and bade Ailsa bathe and dress me. I chose a deep-blue gown to wear with the sapphire earrings Fion had given me as a wedding gift. My hair Ailsa dressed with sapphire netting and strings of river pearls, scenting the long coils with rosewater imported from Gaul. She shook her head, mumbling under her breath about duplicity and wickedness and the snare of beauty.

"Ailsa," I said firmly, "when a woman wages battle, she is entitled to any weapon she can lay her hand to. Hush your chatter, and send to beg an audience of King Fion."

Most of Fion's train were still housed in his ship, Maelgon having few rooms to spare. But Fion was given a chamber of his own, and this is where he saw me. He sat near the window with two of his companions; when I entered, they leaped to their feet, eyes wide and mouths agape. Fion, too, I noted with satisfaction, was struck dumb by the change the gown had wrought. I made him a deep reverence. "My lord King Fion."

He cleared his throat. "Queen Guinevere. Be welcome."

"Thank you, my lord. I have come to beg a favor of you. But I would prefer to speak privately."

With a wave of his hand he dismissed his companions. Fion came forward and took both my hands. "I have been hoping for this, Guinevere. Are you quite recovered? I heard you lay abed, ill from your long ordeal."

"Oh, yes, my lord, I am recovered. But my ordeal is far from over."

"Ah." He leaned down and softly kissed my cheek. "Don't be so formal with me, lass. I'm still the man you knew as Pellinore's hostage."

I smiled up at him and saw his eyes grow luminous. "Indeed? Then I am still the orphaned princess, standing in the shadow of Pellinore's daughter."

At this he laughed and handed me into a chair by the window. "By all the saints in Christendom, you never stood in anyone's shadow! Did I not tell you, when last I saw you, that a great future lay before you?"

"You did indeed. But how could you have known?"

"By my eyes!" he exclaimed. "God does not bestow such uncommon beauty on a maid to have it hidden in a corner of the kingdom. It is a gift with a purpose. Only from the heart of Britain could your light blaze forth to bathe this embattled land in its resplendent glow—"

"What a tongue you have, Fion!"

"There was only one man for you, Guinevere."

"He is the finest man, the strongest, truest, bravest, and most beloved in all the world."

"Ahhhhh." He exhaled with what seemed to be relief and kissed my fingers. "I am glad to hear you say that."

"I know you doubted me. And after what has happened, who will not?" I looked unhappily out the window, where the wooded hills lay still and shimmering in the heat of high summer. "And because it is Lancelot," I said slowly, "I fear that Arthur, too, might doubt."

Fion hesitated. "Surely, if anyone can relieve him of that doubt, you are the one."

"I pray so. But—but because it is Lancelot—"

I fell silent and felt Fion's eyes on my face. At length he spoke. "As the Greek poets tell us, the gods do not give lightly of their gifts. If they shower a man with virtues, they will see he suffers for it, or endures a cruel fate, or is born with some fatal flaw, to insure against hubris."

I turned to him, my eyes filled with tears. "Yes," I whispered.

He took my hands, and held them. "And yours is Lancelot."

I nodded.

He leaned very close and lowered his voice. "Tell me truth. Are you lovers?"

"No." I returned the pressure of his grip and faced him directly. "No. Never. But who will believe it now?"

Joy returned to his features, and he sat back, relieved. "Who needs to believe it, besides the King?"

"How can you ask that, and you a king yourself? You would be thought a fool by all your people."

He laughed lightly. "I am already. But I take your point . . . How did he ever become husband to Elaine? It is easy to see where his heart lies."

"She seduced him," I said shortly. "By a cruel trick designed to hurt me. But she has hurt everyone by it, not least of all herself. Now she is in Less Britain. It is Lancelot's home. She will never see Wales again."

"Ahhhh." He smiled lightly. "It seems she and Maelgon have that in common; they act before thinking and take one step farther than their eyes can see."

"Indeed."

"Well, my lass, if you wish to convince me of your innocence, you have only to declare it. I do believe you. But with Maelgon's men and Arthur's, it is another matter."

"I know."

"Lancelot is not helping matters."

I rose in agitation and paced the room, twisting my hands. Fion rose and stood, watching.

"He believes he is protecting my honor by taking all the blame upon himself. He does not see that all he is doing is proclaiming his guilt—and mine—far and wide. Sometimes I wish—sometimes I wish he had but the smallest splinter of Arthur's sense!"

"Or yours."

"He cannot be allowed to speak with Arthur. Not alone, and certainly not in public." I turned toward him and knelt upon the floor. "This is the favor I come to beg of you, Fion. He is your prisoner. You have his sword. Do not allow him speech with the King. For all our sakes."

Gravely he came and raised me and held me gently in his arms. "My sweet lass, I do not see how I can prevent it. Maelgon has imprisoned him, not I. To my way of thinking, saving you from the flames forgives him all his other sins. I'd honor him myself, but he refuses to be honored."

"But you have his sword. By formal right, he is yours. Speak to Arthur yourself. He knows Lancelot well. He will know what to do. Just don't let Lancelot open his mouth."

"And what," he said slowly, "would he say? What's at the bottom of this, Gwen? How did you come to be abducted in the first place?"

I held him firmly in my arms and looked into his handsome face. "We visited the clearing in yonder woods where we first met. We were alone, but the escort was within call. He held me in his arms, as you are holding me now, and kissed me. That is all. We were attacked by twelve men and subdued before he could draw his sword."

"He must," whispered Fion, "have been besotted." He bent and kissed me himself, a warm kiss with passion behind it. I pushed him away lightly and saw him smile. "Ahhh, gone are the days when a Celtic king had to share his queen with his allies! Now I am as guilty as Lancelot."

"More so," I returned, "for we were in the open woods, not unattended in his chamber."

He loosed me and grinned. "Cleverly managed, my lass. If Arthur can get the better of you, I salute him."

I smiled back. "He is not easily deceived. Indeed, few have had the courage to try. He must know the truth, Fion, but not the whole truth. For his own sake, and for Lancelot's, and for mine. It will hurt him so!"

"Certainly it will. But are you going to tell me that after all these years with you and Lancelot living daily at his side, he could not bear that hurt? Come, Guinevere. You have sense. He will know it all. Lancelot was right, you know. All it takes is one look at your face." I covered my face with my hands. "What would you have me do?" he went on gently. "I cannot prevent the High King from talking with his lieutenant when and where he wills.

This business of the sword is formality only. The only power I have over Lancelot is what power he grants me. You know this. We are in Maelgon's house, on Maelgon's lands. I am Maelgon's guest. If Maelgon wants to call a formal council and lodge a formal charge and demand the King's Judgment, I cannot prevent him."

"Council!" I cried. "Charge! What charge? He would not dare! Oh, the scoundrel! He thinks he sees a chance to climb to power over Lancelot's body! The braggart! The bully! The swine!"

"Surely," Fion said calmly, "he is not the first."

"Oh, Fion, Fion! You must prevent this! Do not let him take charge of the proceedings. He is a coward at heart, I know him. Face him, and he will back down."

Fion sat me down and gave me water from the carafe. When I was calmer, he spoke in a friendly, sensible tone. "I've enough on my hands at home, lass. I'll not risk war with Gwynedd, even for you. And for what? To spare Arthur pain he cannot be spared? You say he knows Lancelot well. Then he will know what drives the man and what to do to save him. He is not High King for nothing. I should imagine he could handle Maelgon with one arm tied behind his back. It seems to me the only tough problem Arthur has is you." I stared at him. Fion looked at me with great kindness. "There is something you are keeping from me. You, who were put to the fire and escaped death by minutes, you have not once mentioned the Druids. All your thoughts are upon something else. I do not ask to know it. But what is a kiss in the woods? You would not be so afraid, for so small a transgression. Will you fear Arthur might discover I kissed you here? No, I thought not. If I can see this, do you really believe Arthur will not?"

He offered me his kerchief, and I wiped the tears from my cheeks.

"You are right," I whispered at length. "I can keep nothing from Arthur. And it is from me he must know it. Oh, Fion, this will be the hardest thing I have ever done."

"Harder than facing the fire?"

"A thousand times harder."

He smiled and clasped my hand. "I am glad to hear it. You do love him."

I shrugged, unable to see past my tears. "I love them both."

Late that night Ailsa scratched at my bedchamber door, to say that Queen Anet was without and wished to see me. I was not yet abed, being too restless for sleep.

"Let her come in to me, Ailsa. At this time of night, it must be some secret thing, or something urgent. Stay within call."

To my surprise, Anet was dressed and cloaked, and so alive with excitement that I hardly knew her.

"Why, Anet! What means this?"

"Oh, my lady Queen Guinevere!" She sank to her knees and clasped her thin hands together. "Oh, my lady, I must tell you what I've done— what has happened—I pray you will forgive me—but I was following your advice, and Queen Alyse agreed— she has helped me, indeed—I wouldn't have known what to do but for her, and for you. Oh, say you will not be angry with me!"

I suppressed a grin. "I will try not to be angry, Anet, but first you must tell me what it is. How alive you look! You are quite changed."

She nodded eagerly. "Indeed, I am! Maelgon says he hardly knows me! Oh, but he does not know what I have done! And he will be so furious with me when he discovers it! Tell me what to do!"

I drew her up onto the bed beside me and calmed her as best I could. "First tell me what you have done."

"I have given sanctuary—protection—to a Druid!" she whispered.

"Oh, Anet! Under Maelgon's very roof?" She nodded, her eyes huge. "Where is he, then? He is not in the chapel!"

"No, no, he stays in Alyse's rooms during the day, and at night he sleeps in the garden bower. It is not patrolled. I take him out every evening through the weaving room when Maelgon has retired."

"How did this happen? What does he want?"

"He wants to speak to the High King. He came ashore the morning Maelgon and King Fion left for Mona's Isle. King Fion's ship had landed at nightfall, and Maelgon met him on the beach with the news of your abduction and Lancelot's attempt at rescue. They made ready to sail again as soon as they could, but the wind died. Just before dawn they departed, and before the sun was at half height, this Druid came ashore in the smallest boat I've ever seen. He came to *me*, Guinevere, to me!"

"Well, you are queen, Anet. It is right that he should."

"He—he threw himself on my mercy, with tears in his eyes, and said he had dolorous news for King Arthur and must speak with him in person. He had vowed he would do it. So I had no choice, had I? Did I do the right thing in taking him in?"

I gripped her arm suddenly. "Vowed to whom? Anet, what does he look like! Describe him!"

"W-Well," she stammered, taken aback at my eagerness, "he is about Maelgon's height, and young, with a black beard and white teeth."

"His name! Do you know his name?

"It is Kevin."

"Oh!" I cried, "Thank God! He lives! Yes, my dear Anet, you did the right thing! Oh, I bless you for it!" And I kissed her and hugged her and wept upon her shoulder.

Startled and delighted, she embraced me. "He wanted to see you, my lady, as soon as you were better. He was so happy when you were rescued. And he has been so worried about your illness. But we heard today that you were up and about, so he begged me to ask if you would see him."

"News travels fast. I only went to see Fion."

She looked at me sideways and dropped her gaze. "If you are not yet well enough, of course, the visit can be postponed." She had not been spending time with Alyse for nothing, I noted with amusement.

"I daresay I could manage it, this once," I replied.

With Ailsa clucking in distress behind me, I threw on a cloak and followed Anet silently down the back stairs, through the weaving room and out into the moonlit garden. We were not in much danger of observation; the garden stood at the back of the castle and only the women's rooms looked out upon it. Nevertheless, we strolled slowly arm in arm, feigning leisure, until we reached the bower. It was dark within, but I saw Kevin by the whiteness of his smile.

"My lady Guinevere! The Goddess spared you! How glad I am to see you safe in Gwynedd!"

I smiled and clasped his hands. "She sent me Lancelot. And not a moment too soon. Without your help, good Kevin, I should not have withstood the trial that awaited me in Nemet."

Anet crossed herself quickly, and Kevin made the sign of peace between us. He begged me to relate what had happened, so I told the story. Anet grew still as I told it, and Kevin bowed his head.

"So," he said slowly, when I finished. "Salowen is dead. It is a sad ending for a great man. Of course he was wrong to abduct you, even if you had been Maelgon's sister, but he was possessed by hate after Maelgon's attack. The priestess Viviane—you heard what Balyn did to her?"

"Indeed we did, may God rest her soul."

"She was a great and powerful woman. And beautiful, they say, in her youth. They were lovers, when Salowen was young, and she was the Guardian of Nemet. You would find it hard to believe now, but he used to be a man of peace, with great charity toward others, even Christians. That is why I did not believe—even when they told me—what he meant to do to you."

"It's all right, Kevin."

"No, my lady, it is not. By his act, Salowen has put our very future in jeopardy. What will the High King do, when he learns of it? We shall be lucky if he does not burn the island from end to end."

"That is not Arthur's way."

"No? It is Maelgon's. And he is our neighbor. Are there any left living on Mona?"

"Some. But many died, Kevin. I feared you were among them."

"I could not take part in the ceremony. But neither could I prevent it. I did what I could. I spent the hours before dawn seeing to it that the brushwood was well watered. It was odd." He hesitated. "There was a spirit there, black-robed, with an ancient staff and an icy breath. He was new to me, but he was powerful. While he was by me, I worked with the strength of ten and did not tire. At dawn, when we heard them coming, he bade me take a coracle and come across to find King Arthur."

"Oh, Kevin! I owe you my life, indeed! You and Merlin! It was your doing the fire would not take! Bless you both! A matter of minutes was all that lay between me and next world, I assure you."

"Ah, my lady Queen," he breathed, and held me in strong hands and kissed me firmly on the lips, while Anet frowned. He released me and fell to one knee. "I beg you will let the High King know I am here and that I wish to plead with him for mercy toward the Druids. We are in his power now, all of us. And Maelgon would destroy us. I place myself under your protection, if you will."

"No," I said slowly, "I think the protection of Queen Anet will suffice. This is her house, not mine. But I will undertake to speak with Arthur, if— if he will hear me."

"Thank you. I could not ask for more."

When we were back in the weaving room, Anet finally found her tongue.

"Did they really tie you to a stake and set it afire?" she quavered. "Oh, I did not believe it when Maelgon told us! Queen Alyse said they would never dare!"

"They did dare."

"But Kevin tried to foil their plans? Then he has betrayed them. What will happen to him now? Can we make him a Christian, do you think?"

"On the contrary. I was thinking he might make a good leader for those who remain. In his heart he worships the Light. With Kevin in charge, perhaps Nemet would not be such a fearful place."

"He was bold to kiss you, my lady! Why did you allow it?"

I sighed and drew her arm through mine. "Druids have not changed in a thousand years, Anet. In the old days, before the Romans came to Britain, customs differed. A Celtic king, like the King Cunedda in your tapestry, took a beautiful woman to wife for a purpose. Her sovereignty was something shared by all his people. If a lord, a priest, or an ally, or even someone lowborn performed a great service to the king, the king was honor bound to grant the man a favor. Nine times out of ten, it was the queen."

"No! I never heard such a thing!"

I smiled down at her. "You were raised in a convent, my dear. I grew up on these tales. Let us thank God we are living in more civilized times."

"Is that—is that why you and Lancelot—" She stopped as I froze. "I mean—I didn't mean to—oh, Guinevere! Forgive me!"

"Finish your question."

"No! I dare not!"

"Finish."

"I have made you angry now, and I never intended to! It's just that I did not believe it when they said that you—you and Lancelot were—were— lovers in the woods when you were taken." She gulped and covered her mouth with her hand, shaking.

"Who told you this?"

"No one. Everyone." It was a whisper.

I turned away, surprised to find myself trembling as violently as Anet. "Arthur is not Cunedda. Arthur is as Roman as he is Celt. You presume too much!"

"Oh!" She gasped, sinking to the floor. "Please, please forgive me! I am ashamed I spoke!"

I sighed wearily. I had no cause for anger at poor Anet. And if I could find no answer for her, how on earth would I ever answer Arthur? I raised her from the floor and made her face me.

"There is both truth and untruth to what you have heard. To understand, you must be willing to set aside your judgment."

"You—you would not betray the King!" Anet breathed in terror.

I held her firmly by the shoulders. "I would not, and I have not." She nearly swooned in relief, but I shook her and bade her attend me. "Think of Arthur as a great tree, the tree of Britain. I am the flower, the froth, the transient bloom upon the bough. Lancelot is the strong branch that supports me; yet he is nothing without the tree itself, and neither am I. Without Arthur, we die; and without us, he is made less than he is." I looked into her face, and saw by her sadness that she began to understand. "We try, all of us, to walk the straight path. But we are none of us without flaw." She began to cry, and I let her go.

In the dark, still room I sat in the shadow of the ancient loom and gazed out at the midnight garden. We were all held powerless in a sticky web of intrigue, secrets, fears and desires, plotting at cross purposes, caught up in our own petty plans, accomplishing nothing. We awaited Arthur's coming like the onset of the winter gale: destroying summer's leavings, sweeping the past away. Only Arthur could do it.

39 ♛ THE JUDGMENT

"Guinevere," Alyse said firmly, "I must speak with you." Coming down the length of the garden in the midday sun, she seemed once again the queen of my childhood, a powerful tyrant who brooked no opposition. I was annoyed to find myself trembling and made an effort to stand straight and still as she approached. Behind me in the weaving room Anet watched from the window. I had spent the morning there, trying without success to occupy my mind with threads and patterns. But the constant clacking of the looms gave me a headache, and in irritation I quitted her company to seek peace in the garden. There was no peace to be found. Alyse took my arm and guided me toward the bower. If she could not say what she had to say in public, I did not want to hear it. But lacking the courage to tell her this, I was bound to listen. She came straight to the point.

"We must do something about Maelgon. He is on the verge of doing Gwynedd irreparable harm."

"How so?"

She shifted uncomfortably. "Have you not heard, then? I thought Anet must have told you. He has concocted some wild story about you and Lancelot together in the woods—I am ashamed of it, Gwen, and pray you will forgive him for it. He does not care that he disgraces his poor sister, and thereby his mother, with the tale. He gives out the man attacked you—forgive me, my dear, but it is best that you know this beforehand. He wants to call a Council and bring a formal charge against Lancelot—Lancelot, of all people!—thinking, the half-wit, that this will somehow please the High King and gain him a place at his side! I told him he had been out in the sun too long. There is no one closer to Arthur than Lancelot, and if he thinks to please the King by telling him this sordid tale, then he deserves what Arthur will do to him! But *I* do not deserve it, Guinevere, I do not! The King is expected at sundown. Somehow we must keep Maelgon silent. Clearly, you owe him nothing. In your place, I would probably let Arthur destroy him. But he is my son, and Pellinore's, and Elaine's brother—if you ever loved us, Guinevere, will you not help us now? Speak to Maelgon! Warn him of his danger."

I believe I stared at her. I know that I was speechless.

"What a fool he will look when Lancelot denies it! There is no point to it! He is embarked upon a course that can only bring him ruin! He thinks, because he has destroyed the Druids, he is a great power in Britain that Arthur must reckon with! The pig-headed child!" She paused, plucking at her skirts in anger, and I cleared my throat and found my voice.

"What if Lancelot does not deny it?"

"What do you mean? Why shouldn't he?"

"He was responsible for me, when the Druids took me."

"You were set upon by twelve men! What kind of odds are those?"

"But it was his doing that the odds were twelve to one. Besides, he has done something—else that Arthur would not like and is feeling guilty about it now. You know his sense of honor, Alyse. If he feels he deserves chastisement, he will take it in any form it is offered."

She looked at me sharply. "What do you mean by that? That he would accept punishment for an offense he had not committed?"

"That is exactly what I mean. He has done it before."

She snorted in disgust. "Well, Elaine told me he could be insufferable. Don't misunderstand me"—this as I flushed scarlet and moved to protest—"I am not unhappy with the match. He is a good husband to her; he has given her a kingdom and sons every year. Two healthy boys she has now, and another on the way. She has no cause for complaint. If there is no love between them, well, God knows that is common enough. And she only has to tolerate him in the winters. That is little enough to bear, it seems to me . . . Guinevere, you are shaking. Have a seat, my child. What is amiss? Are you ill?" She drew me down onto the bench beside her and pressed a hand to my brow. "Surely, this is nonsense about desiring punishment for anything because one is guilty of something. It is foolishness, pure and simple. You are an old friend of Lancelot's. Can you not make him see sense?"

I wanted to laugh, but my throat was so tight I could make no sound at all.

"I bade Anet speak to you about it, because we agree that Maelgon is cutting his own throat, but she told me today to let sleeping dogs lie. So I came myself."

"It was good advice, Aunt Alyse."

"Maelgon is my son. I cannot sit idle and watch him destroy his future—" She broke off and rose unsteadily. A great silence filled the garden. The looms had stopped. Alyse bent her stiff knees in a curtsy, and I looked up. A tall man stood at the end of the path in the shadow of the gate. Around us the world held its breath.

"Arthur," I whispered, rising slowly as Alyse sank to the ground and bowed her head. In a dozen long strides he was with me, had his arms around me, held me so tightly I could barely breathe, and hid his face in my hair. And I did not know until he embraced me how I had longed for his embrace! His strength and his joy gave me the peace I had been seeking; he was my rock, my rest, my certainty.

"Arthur!" My tears flowed freely down my cheeks and soaked his tunic. I hardly knew if they were tears of joy or pain. "Oh, Arthur, Arthur, at last!"

"You are alive!" he breathed. "Alive! Nothing matters beside that!"

He kissed my tears and kissed my lips with a desperate joy that stirred me to my soul. Nothing mattered, nothing mattered beside this.

He held me a long time. Alyse had gone, the weaving room was empty—the day stood still and time silent, all for us.

"When I heard—what Cathbad told me—Guinevere, the light went dark."

"Yes," I whispered, remembering the approach of the abyss. "The light went dark."

"What a fool I was to go! When Niniane twice warned me—"

"Don't," I begged, putting a finger to his lips to stop him. "Don't, Arthur. You, of all people, are not to blame."

"I left you."

"But for foolishness, I would have been safe enough. When did you hear of it?"

"Cathbad told me of the sacrifice. Not willingly, you may be sure. We caught him trying to escape one night in Rheged; I suspected him and had him watched. In fear of his life, he told me their plans." He stopped. "I nearly killed him. Had Ferron and Bellangere not dragged me off him, I would have. I lost my wits, I think." He pulled my head to his breast and kissed my hair. "I put all my faith in Lancelot."

"He saved me, Arthur, at the last moment. But he was not alone. Merlin was there. And one of the Druids helped me. They—they thought I was Elaine."

"Salowen may have thought so. But Cathbad knew the truth. And he let the plans go forward." I shivered at the cold in his voice.

"Salowen is dead."

"Yes."

"You knew?"

"Fion met me on the road two hours hence with a small party. He said they had been out hunting and seen our dust."

"Did he? Bless the man! He is a true friend."

He pulled away and looked down into my face. "Did he come to me at your request?"

"Yes, Arthur."

"Ahhhh. To blunt the force of Maelgon's accusation, no doubt."

"You have spoken to Maelgon?"

"He met us at the outer gate. He would not stand aside until he had voiced his grievance. I had to command him to move out of the way, so I could come to you." He kissed me again, slowly and with love. In his arms, I found the courage to face my fears.

"Arthur, have you spoken to Lancelot?"

"Not yet."

"He has taken it all upon himself."

"Well," he said slowly, "he is responsible."

"Not alone. I—I share the blame, Arthur."

He took the blow with barely a tremor; still, his eyes were kind. "He saved you from the flame. For that, I will forgive him anything."

"Don't let Maelgon bring a formal charge. Please."

"I cannot prevent that, Gwen. He has done so already. We meet tonight."

"*Tonight?*"

"It is his right. I must hear him. But I will make short work of it, I promise you. It is easy to see what he is after. I want the women there—will you be ready? Are you recovered enough?"

With a lie I could postpone it, but I could not lie to Arthur. "Yes."

"Don't distress yourself so. You can't believe I would bring judgment against Lancelot."

I held him tight and fought back tears. "You have not seen him yet."

With a firm hand he lifted my chin and looked long and searchingly into my eyes. What he saw there brought him pain and bitter joy. At length he dropped his hand and said sadly, "What you have done has scarred your soul. That is punishment enough, I think."

"Lancelot will die if you forgive him."

He shrugged. "I can deal with Lancelot. It is you, Guinevere, whom I must heal."

I stared, stunned to hear Fion's words so soon repeated. Arthur turned. Maelgon and Anet, Fion and his companions, Ferron, Gereint, and Bellangere awaited us at the gate.

"Duty beckons," Arthur said gently, offering me his arm. "You who faced the Druids with such courage, you must be brave yet awhile longer."

Maelgon called the Council an hour past dinner. Ailsa laid my gown out on the bed while I paced the room in distraction. How had things come to such a pass? Why could not this embarrassment be avoided? Why, oh why, should everything I did reflect shame upon Arthur? That I was the root of all this sorrow was plain enough. The King had spent all afternoon with Lancelot and afterward had paced the garden alone, his hands clasped behind his back, looking solemn. I had seen him from my window, when I could bear to look.

"Come, my lady, it is time to prepare."

She had laid out my finest gown, my best jewels, and had the sapphire netting ready for my hair.

"Oh, Ailsa. Put them away. I cannot wear them."

"But—my lady—"

"I will not go dressed for a celebration, when I am the source of such distress! Dear Lord, save me from hubris! Find me something plain. Dull. Ugly."

"But where—"

"Send to Cissa. There is an old trunk in Alyse's room, I think. I remember a gray gown. If they have not given it away, I will wear it."

"But, Gwen! You cannot—"

"Very well, I will go myself!" I cried impatiently.

Scowling, Ailsa dipped me a curtsy and hurried to the door. But there she turned. "If I were you, I should worry about pleasing the King."

"Oh, God!" I wailed. "If only that were all that mattered!"

She returned some time later with a dove-gray gown. I made her remove the lace trimming from bodice and sleeves and declined the jeweled belt Cissa had sent.

"One would almost think," Ailsa said sourly as she bent over her task, "that you wish to be a prisoner yourself."

I stopped pacing to face her. "That is precisely what I wish! Maelgon may treat me as a victim, but I am one with the accused. And I want Maelgon to know it. It is the only thing I can do to help save Lancelot."

Her eyebrows lifted. "Lancelot! You cannot think he is in real danger, my lady. The High King would never condemn his closest friend."

"Oh, Ailsa, it is not that simple. In council friendship cannot be considered. Arthur must pass a Judgment the council will accept. Maelgon counts on Alyse and Anet to side with him. And they might, to protect the honor of Gwynedd. I have done my best with Anet, but he is her husband, after all. That leaves me, Fion, Lancelot, and Arthur. Fion will be diplomatic of necessity, and I know already what Lancelot will say. What can Arthur do? If he gives a Judgment that contradicts the council, Maelgon will contest it, and we shall have war. That is what Arthur came here to prevent. His very fairness will tie his hands. I must do whatever I can to make Maelgon think twice." I lifted the soft, dull fabric in my hand. "Arthur will not like this, but I think he will forgive me the gesture."

The gown fit snugly and without its laces was plain and self-effacing. I wore no jewels, no earrings, no adornments of any kind. At my command and against her will, Ailsa pulled my hair back from my face and bound it with a thong. If I did not look like a prisoner myself, at least I looked like a penitent. Not even Maelgon could mistake the signal.

The page arrived to fetch me, and I turned to Ailsa. "Well? What do you think? Am I plain enough?"

She smiled in her motherly way and made me a reverence. "You have done your best, my lady, and a valiant effort it is. But the effect would surprise you."

"Whatever do you mean?"

"The color of the gown sets off the perfection of your skin. You have a matchless neck and shoulders. I do not worry any longer about the King."

"Ailsa!" I cried in panic. "What are you saying? You think to humor me, that is all!"

She smiled again. "Of course, of course. The page is waiting, my lady. You must go." And she pushed me out the door.

When I entered the council chamber everyone but Arthur was already there. Thank God it was a small council, with only the six of us and no advisors, no lieutenants, no servants. Only four men guarded the door, two of Arthur's and two of Maelgon's. I recognized Gereint and Bellangere, trusted friends both and men who could keep their mouths closed. Predictably, Maelgon wore all his finery, even his crown. Anet was in her new gown, and her hair was dressed in the way Ailsa had taught her servant. She looked almost pretty, but the change in her went deeper. She was calm and self-possessed, even though she was excited. She was a woman who had found a joy in power. I did not think she could go back now to what she had been before.

Alyse, stiff and formal, sat beside her. She looked at me with dismay and disapproval, but said nothing. By her words that afternoon she had placed herself in my debt, and she dared not speak against me now. Fion, on the other hand, was astonished. When he rose to hand me to my seat I saw the question in his eyes.

"What can I do to serve you?" he whispered as he bent over my hand.

"Defend Lancelot," I murmured.

"Aye, that I could guess myself. But how far?"

I looked up into his brilliant eyes. "Keep this foremost in your thoughts: Where would I be now without him?" He squeezed my hand in answer.

Lancelot himself I could barely look at. He was dressed as plainly as I and sat straight in the chair opposite Arthur's empty seat. Around his neck he wore a leather thong, half hidden by the tunic. I knew with certainty that it held my ring, and wondered what on earth had possessed him to wear it here. He was furious with me, as well. His black brows came down over his eyes when he saw me, and he scowled at me across the table. At least, I thought in grim amusement, we did not look like lovers.

The night was warm and damp, with sea fog cloaking the shore and clinging to valleys. A thick mist crept in through the narrow windows and haloed the torches with light. There we sat, we six, watching one another in silence and waiting for Arthur. Time passed. Maelgon began to frown, and sent a page to discover if aught was amiss with the High King. It was unlike Arthur to keep anyone waiting. The page reported that the King was coming. But still we waited. Lancelot began to worry; Alyse looked pointedly at me; I shrugged. Anet cast a nervous glance at Maelgon, who was slowly growing angry. And Fion, his eyes dancing, looked amused.

At last we heard his steps. The soldiers snapped to attention. The High King paused in the doorway, gathering everyone's eye, and entered. It was worth the wait. He was plainly dressed in white, cool and majestic, the crown of Britain shining in the torchlight against his dark hair. Around his waist he wore his jeweled swordbelt, and at his side hung wonderful Excalibur, the great emerald blazing from the hilt. He shed light all about him, and as he moved the mist seemed visibly to part and let him through. We all rose. Maelgon, already sweating in his heavy, colored velvets, bowed as he passed. I made my reverence to the floor. After a long hesitation, Arthur raised me. His eyes ran over the gown and met mine. I could not read his face. There was a gravity about him that I feared.

He signaled the guards to close the door, then stood and looked slowly around the council table, searching every face. The air was so still I could hear voices far off in the outer courtyard, but in that chamber I did not hear so much as a breath. At last the King spoke.

"Let God be my witness, I will have the truth spoken. King Maelgon of Gwynedd, bring your complaint."

Maelgon rose, looking hot and uncomfortable, knowing he had not Arthur's air of command, and resenting it.

"My lord King Arthur," he began. "We of Gwynedd beg your Judgment upon Lancelot. As king, I am responsible for all that happens on our soil, but a tragedy has occurred, my lord, for which I will not accept the blame. A grave injustice has been done to your lady wife, my cousin Queen Guinevere, while you were in Rheged. As my lord knows, she was abducted by Druids and taken against her will to Mona's Isle. This travesty took place on my lands, and I will not bear that shame without redress. My lord, it was not through my doing she was taken. She was in the company of Lancelot, and of no other." He licked his lips. "He may be a loyal and faithful knight, he may be first among the King's Companions, but he has failed you, my lord, in his protection of the Queen." He stopped and looked nervously about. No doubt the humility he saw on Lancelot's face gave him courage, for he straightened and drew breath. "I formally charge Lancelot with negligence in his care of the Queen." Maelgon's eyes flitted to each face around the table. No one moved. "Indeed, my lord, I charge him with more than that.

When my lord Fion and I came to his rescue, we found him alone with the Queen. We found them—" He hesitated and dropped his gaze, unable to withstand Arthur's steady glare. "We found them in an embrace. My lord, I believe he was alone with her all night."

Silence fell on the small company. My eyes were in my lap. I could not look up. When Arthur spoke, his voice was ice. "Which of them do you accuse? What is the charge?"

"Oh, no," Maelgon sputtered, hastily retreating, "my lord mistakes me. I lay no charge against the Queen, my cousin. After her ordeal, no one could blame her for clinging to any one of my lord's soldiers for support. It is Lancelot who is guilty of taking advantage of her state, of seeking that from the Queen which he had no right to ask. I accuse him of—of—of," Maelgon stammered, seeing Arthur's face, seeing his future go up in smoke before him, "of conspiring to betray the King," he finished, sweating.

"I have heard you. Sit down," Arthur commanded, his face pinched with anger. Maelgon sat.

Arthur looked toward Lancelot and bade him rise. "Lancelot, I have heard your account of these events today from your own lips. I do not ask to hear it repeated now. But I charge you to answer three questions, upon your oath and before God. Have you ever conspired to dishonor me or my wife, Guinevere?"

Lancelot faced his friend and met his eyes. "No, my lord."

"Have you been negligent in your care of my Queen?"

"Yes, my lord."

"Last," Arthur said, a trace of warmth creeping back into his voice, "did you risk your life, and that of your companions, to save Guinevere from the Druids' fire?"

"Yes, my lord," Lancelot replied woodenly, staring hard at Arthur. Clearly, they had come to some agreement—how Arthur had managed it I could not guess—but Lancelot said nothing beyond the barest truth; in exchange for what? What was Arthur's part in the bargain, that would restore Lancelot's honor in his own eyes?

"Sit down," Arthur commanded. Lancelot obeyed. "My lord Fion, you accompanied King Maelgon to Mona's Isle. Tell me how you found my lady Queen. Of the charge of negligence you can tell us nothing, but address, if you will, the charge of betrayal."

Fion rose, standing at ease, and spoke in a conversational manner. His beautiful voice, melodic as a bard's, captured every ear. "Well, my lord, we found your Companions trapped at the head of a tiny valley. The Druids were approaching with drawn knives, knowing they had no escape. The Queen had been taken to a cave to give her rest and revive her. She had been drugged, as I understand it, to enable her to undergo the burning without shame." At this Anet clapped a hand to her mouth, and Alyse began to mumble under her breath about reaping what one sows, looking straight at Maelgon. Arthur's face was stone. Fion went on as easily as if he had been talking about the weather. "She spent the night in a drugged sleep, guarded by both Lancelot and Gereint, and awoke to hear the Druids chanting. There was no need for silence, my lord. They chanted to let Lancelot know his fate approached him."

I looked up and met Lancelot's eyes. In that moment we both relived the terror of that dark morning. I began to tremble. Beneath the table, Arthur took my hand.

"When my lord King Maelgon and I fought our way through them and reached the cave, we found Lancelot and the Queen together, as Maelgon says, in an embrace. But they were at the cave mouth, my lord, not hidden in the dark recesses. The Queen tells me they were saying farewell, knowing death to be but a knife throw away. I believed her then, and I can see no reason to doubt her now. Lancelot, when challenged, surrendered his sword to me as a token of his faith." Fion reached behind him and brought forth the sword, placing it on the table in front of the King. It lay sheathed in its old, plain leather scabbard, the cross of rubies on the hilt winking balefully in the mist. "Indeed," Fion continued, "he stepped unarmed into my sword-point, drawing blood, to signal his innocence."

Maelgon snorted rudely but Arthur's eyes were warm as he thanked Fion and bade him take his seat.

But Fion hesitated. "My lord King, as we speak I am fighting for my kingdom's life at home. I have left my wife in the care of trusted lieutenants. It is easy enough for me to imagine myself in your place, and I would tell you this: If ever my wife were made to face the trial your Queen has faced, I would bestow my everlasting blessings upon the man who saved her from it. It would not matter to me what else he had done."

A smile touched the corners of Arthur's mouth. "Thank you, Fion." Lancelot looked away in despair. Gently Arthur loosed my hand and bade me rise. "Guinevere, you have heard the charges made against Lancelot. What answer do you make?"

I faced him. "My dear lord, the charge of betrayal is false. No man loves you more than Lancelot. And as for negligence—" I lowered my eyes and took a deep breath. "My lord, there is no one at this table who does not love you, or who would knowingly do you a disservice. I am sure"—and I raised my head to look at Maelgon—"that if we had it to do again, each one of us would act differently. I, for one, would not ask Lancelot to ride out with me when vengeance of some kind was expected from the Druids. And Lancelot would not dismiss the escort, that we might have private conversation. And I feel certain, my lord, that Maelgon would not call in all his scouts from the forest to ring the castle so tightly, thus leaving the beaches unpatrolled. And even you, my lord," I said quickly, as Maelgon drew breath in anger, "you would not go to Rheged. You probably would not allow me beyond King's Gate."

Arthur listened unmoving, watching Maelgon.

"What happened was an accident of fate. We were all at fault. We were none of us at fault." I turned directly toward Lancelot. "But since my friend Lancelot stands accused, let me remind everyone of this. It was Lancelot and no other who cut me from the Druid's stake when they had already lit the fire. I owe him my life. Should you find him deserving of punishment, I beg you will allow me to share it with him, in repayment of the debt." Lancelot leaned forward and buried his head in his arms to hide his face. As he moved, the ring fell free from his tunic and swung forward on its thong into the light. Arthur stared at it, speechless. "And—and if it were not for the quick action and bravery of King Maelgon and King Fion—Oh, my lord," I pleaded, laying a hand on Arthur's arm, seeing the grief on his face, "do not be deceived by appearances. All is not as it seems. These are Lancelot's kin, his wife's family. He honors Gwynedd, he would not bring shame upon it."

"I quite agree." Alyse spoke firmly, rising. "My son is new to kingship, my lord Arthur, and has not yet attained Pellinore's wisdom. There is truly no cause for discord between him and Lancelot. They are brothers. Listen to your lady Queen, my lord. I know her words to be truth."

Maelgon sat open-mouthed in anger, then leaped to his feet. "What nonsense is this? My lord, my mother has retired from life these nine months past. Disregard this unseemly advice—"

"Unseemly advice?" Arthur cut in coldly. "She told me to listen to my wife, your cousin."

"I will not bear any part of this shame!" Maelgon cried, his face red. "Your lady wife was abducted, and it is Lancelot's fault! I demand your Judgment upon him!"

Arthur rose and drew himself to his full height, facing Maelgon.

"My Judgment he shall have," the King said slowly. Maelgon exhaled, appeased, and sat down. "But I have not yet heard from Queen Anet. I would like to know her counsel."

Maelgon stared, and Anet flushed.

"My lord," she quavered, rising to face him. "I am the last person to wish shame upon Gwynedd, or blame upon one of your Companions. My lord Maelgon may be new to kingship, but he is wise and able, and cares as deeply about the honor of Gwynedd and the glory of Britain as my lady Queen Alyse or his father the great King Pellinore." She stopped uncertainly; both Maelgon and Alyse were staring at her in amazement.

"I am sure you are right," Arthur said kindly. "Have you any counsel to give me about the charges?"

She clasped her hands together tightly and did not take her eyes from his face, drawing strength from his very presence. "I know nothing about them, my lord. But I cannot imagine that any insult was intended, to you, to Gwynedd or to Britain. As to what the Queen has endured, I did not know a woman could possess such courage. To my mind, honor is due not only to the Queen, but to Lancelot and Maelgon and Fion for saving her life, which was twice in jeopardy. I wish—my lord, I wish we could celebrate her safe return and disregard how she came to be taken from us!"

Arthur smiled. "That is my wish, as well, Lady Anet. Maelgon is lucky to have such an intelligent woman at his side." Maelgon, who had jumped up to protest, stood sputtering aimlessly at this compliment, proud that his wife should receive such commendation from the High King, at the same time angry that she dared to voice an opinion different from his own.

While these three were standing the doors flew open and a group of soldiers pushed into the room, shouting and cursing, calling for Maelgon's attention. Lancelot shot to his feet, and Fion beside him. Between them the soldiers hauled forward a man in a Druid's robe, with blood streaming from his nose and one eye swollen shut in a bruised and battered face, and a slim youth with black hair, bound by the wrists. The mist seemed to thicken with their entrance, and I leaned forward to see them better.

"Arthur!" I whispered, clutching at his sleeve. "Oh, stop them! It's Mordred!" He drew breath in slowly and went still, watching Maelgon.

"My lord Maelgon!" the soldiers cried. "We found them in the Queen's garden, my lord! This is a Druid from Mona's Isle, he confesses it!"

Maelgon stepped forward, and Anet behind him.

"Arthur!" I whispered. "Do something! They have bound him!"

"Be still a moment," he said softly. "He is not hurt. Let me see what Maelgon does."

"You again!" Maelgon sneered at Mordred. "You cannot stay away from the vermin, can you? Want to be one yourself someday, is that it? You filthy pagan, stand aside." He turned his back on Mordred, leaving him bound, and turned to Kevin. "What are you doing in my precincts? How dare you set foot in Gwynedd without my leave! I will have you horsewhipped, you pagan snake!" And he raised his fist to strike that beaten face yet once again.

"No." The word fell into the pause like a rock into a still pool. Anet, trembling visibly, stepped forward. "No," she repeated. "Do not strike him. He is here with my permission, Maelgon. He has my protection."

Every eye in the room turned full upon her. Maelgon's fist was still raised, arrested, above his head. The color drained from his face. *"What?"* he whispered, incredulous. *"What* did you say?"

"He is here with my permission," Anet repeated, her small voice gaining strength. "He came ashore the morning of the sacrifice, having done what he could to save the Queen on Mona, and begged for my protection. He wants to speak to the High King."

As she spoke, Maelgon regained his color and, with it, his temper. "Protection be damned!" he shouted. "You have no right to disobey me! I am king!" He shook his fist wildly in the air, grinding his teeth, his spittle frothing upon his lips. Anet, shaking, stood her ground.

"Nonsense," Alyse said coolly, rising. "Every queen has the right to grant protection. It does not depend upon the king's desire. To deny her this right is to dishonor Gwynedd, and Strathclyde, as well. You have given no order, Maelgon. She has not disobeyed you. She has shown sense and calm and tolerance. She is to be commended."

Maelgon slammed his fist down on the table. "Tolerance!" he shouted. "Not to Druids! This is a Christian land!"

"I hope," Alyse retorted, "you are not going to question her devotion to her faith."

Maelgon looked at his convent wife and scowled. "No, no, of course not. That is not what I meant. But—"

"This man performed a service to the High Queen, and thereby to the High King. He has been granted protection in order that he might speak with Arthur. I suggest you let him do that, if your men have not already beaten him beyond the power of speech."

"I will hear him myself first!" Maelgon snarled, trapped between his women. "I wish to know what he was doing with this, this unholy miscreant in the garden."

I gasped at his reference to Mordred, but Arthur stilled me with a touch upon my hand.

"You. Druid. Attend me."

"His name," ventured Anet, "is Kevin."

Maelgon ignored her. "Druid. What were you doing in my garden?"

Kevin, stiff with pain, looked him squarely in the face and said nothing. He had about him something of the milky calm I had seen in him before, when he had just come from a ceremony in Nemet. Slowly he turned toward Anet and, raising his bound hands, made a sign before her face.

"What is he doing?" Maelgon cried. "Stop him! Guard!"

The soldiers grabbed his shoulders, but Kevin offered no resistance and stood quietly.

"My lady Queen," he said thickly, through swollen lips, "the Great Goddess has blessed you with child. You have done me a service and in return I give you this knowledge. At the spring equinox you will be safely delivered of twin children, one male and one female. The son you bear will add his light to the greater glory of Britain, and your daughter shall be beloved of the finest warrior in the realm." He stopped suddenly and shook himself awake to find the entire company staring at him.

"My lord Maelgon," he said in surprise. "I was coming to see you. I must speak in private with the High King Arthur."

Maelgon was caught completely off guard. His anger was swallowed up in his confusion. Anet, trembling and blushing, was led away by Alyse to take her seat. Maelgon had been honored, and he knew it. But he could not bring himself to thank the Druid. "What were you doing in my garden?" he repeated dumbly. "Why were you there?"

Kevin frowned, as if trying to remember. "I was waiting to see the King, my lord, and then he came himself into the garden to speak with me."

"You lie," Maelgon returned. "He has been in this chamber all this while."

Kevin looked about, bewildered, and then saw Mordred.

"Here he is. Ask him yourself." Then to Mordred: "Tell them, my lord, that you came to me while I waited for you, and that I asked for your mercy toward my people."

"What impudence is this?" Maelgon cried. "*This* is the lad you took for the King?"

Kevin looked blankly at Maelgon. "Yes, my lord. The High King of Britain."

Mordred, his dark eyes wide with terror, looked helplessly toward Arthur. And at last, Arthur stepped forward.

"Maelgon. Stand back." Through the misty lamplight they made a path for him, and he stood before Kevin, tall and glowing, making the Druid look small and dark. "Untie his hands. And the boy's."

"But—"

"Untie them!" Arthur snapped, and the guards obeyed. "They are not armed," Arthur said evenly to Maelgon. "Your men have seen to that." Maelgon grunted and Arthur addressed Kevin. "I am Arthur, High King of Britain. It is I you seek. Kevin, leader of Druids, do you know me?"

Slowly Kevin's eyes traveled upward from his glittering sword to his face and rested there. A look of puzzlement swept his features.

"King Arthur. Yes, my lord. I know you. Then who is—" He turned swiftly to Mordred and passed a hand across his eyes. "But I saw the crown. I saw it. The very one you wear, my lord, I saw it upon his head."

There was a deathly silence in the hall.

"Treason!" Maelgon croaked, but he trembled. Mordred froze, his eyes on Arthur's face.

"Kevin," Arthur said slowly, "have you never had the Sight before?"

Kevin stared in surprise. "The Sight, my lord? Why, no, only Salowen has—had—" He faltered. Arthur took his arm to steady him.

"It has passed to you," he said gently. "And his power, as well, if I judge aright. You came to ask my mercy for your people, and your Goddess herself has given your people into your hands. You lead them now, Kevin. From this moment forward."

"But I am unready!" Kevin whispered, astounded. "The initiation! The ceremony!"

"Come south with us when we leave Gwynedd. Niniane, Lady of the Lake, can perform the initiation. You would do well to learn from her. When you return to Mona you will be Archdruid in Salowen's place."

Kevin knelt at his feet and kissed his ring. "You are more than merciful, my lord King. And I am undeserving."

"No," Arthur replied, "for your aid to Guinevere you deserve whatever is in my power to give."

Kevin's glance slid swiftly to Mordred, still standing rooted at his side. "And this youth, my lord? What does this Seeing mean? Will he be of service to you?"

"Indeed, that is my hope," the King replied with a quick smile. "He is my nephew, my sister's son. He serves me now, and may come to kingship in time, if God is willing."

Maelgon stared at Mordred in wonder and at Arthur with growing consternation.

"Mordred," Arthur said gently, "what were you doing in the king's house tonight? Did you come to see this Druid?"

"Oh, no, my lord," Mordred replied, licking his dry lips. "I did not know he was there. I came—my lord, I came to see the Queen." Arthur lifted an eyebrow but did not interrupt him. "All the men were talking about her abduction, my lord, and her terrible ordeal. They wondered if she could withstand it. They thought she might lie gravely ill and the news be kept close. No one had seen her, my lord, and everyone knew you had been all afternoon pacing in a brown study." A wry smile touched the King's lips; Lancelot saw it, Mordred did not. "So the captain of my company bade me see what I could discover about the Queen. I came to the garden, my lord, because the Queen is known to walk it of an evening. I did not know she was in Council. The only one there was Kevin, and he addressed me strangely." Mordred gulped. "He talked about a crown and such. I was about to leave when the soldiers grabbed us."

"You see the Queen before you now," Arthur said. "Does she look ill?"

Mordred glanced at me shyly and lowered his eyes. "No, my lord. Sad, perhaps, but not ill. And very beautiful."

I felt heat slowly rise to my face as Arthur smiled. "She is indeed. Thank you, Mordred. You may take this report back to your captain."

Mordred knelt and kissed his ring. Maelgon's soldiers stood aside to let him leave, but closed again around Kevin. Clearly Maelgon, who was losing his case against Lancelot, was not about to let Kevin escape his grasp. But before he could open his mouth to speak, Arthur turned and faced him.

"Maelgon, I am ready to give my Judgment, upon Kevin and upon Lancelot."

As this was what Maelgon had called him there to do, he dared not object, but he grumbled as he nodded, and signaled his men to keep hold of the Druid. We returned to our places around the council table. Everyone sat but Arthur. In the misty light everything around him looked dim and dark, but Arthur himself shone forth like a beacon, in his white raiment and his bright jewels.

"When I came to Gwynedd, I found this land at war, Christian against Druid." He slowly looked at the faces turned to him around the table. "This is the cause of all our distress. This is why the Queen was taken. If harmony is not restored there will be worse to come. I will root out the source of discord," Arthur said firmly, looking at Maelgon, "wherever it lies. Anyone who serves me serves my cause." He turned to Kevin. "Loose him," the King commanded and the soldiers obeyed. "Kevin, step forward. For the wrongs done your people, for the murder of the priestess and the massacre of worshippers, I grant you Mona's Isle in perpetuity. And I forgive you the abduction of my Queen." Kevin sank to his knees as everyone gasped. "Your people shall have my protection for as long as I hold Britain. But because none but you lifted a finger to prevent the sacrifice of what is dearest to me, I will require that your worship be restricted to Mona. Your people are free to come and go in Britain, but not to worship here, not to recruit, proselytize, pray, teach, practice magic, heal, curse, or even sing. Do not thank me. This is a death sentence I pass upon you. But you will have peace." His hand moved to Excalibur's hilt. "If you are threatened again, send for me. I will destroy your enemies."

Maelgon was livid, but held his tongue. Anet's hand touched his sleeve, begging restraint. The Druid had changed her life with his words, and she sought to remind her husband of it. Arthur must have read my thoughts; he leaned his hands on the table and said quietly to Maelgon, "This man has given you a great gift, if you but knew it. If you have sense, you will thank him for it."

Maelgon scowled but seeing Anet's face, relented, and signaled his guards to leave the room.

Kevin bowed to Arthur. "I am unworthy of the honor you do me, my lord. I have not Salowen's power, but I will serve you any way I can. You have but to command me."

"Druid! Disperse this mist!" Arthur commanded.

Startled, Kevin raised a hand, and a breeze sprang up from nowhere, thinning the mist and blowing the clouds from the stars. Kevin himself gaped in surprise, but Arthur smiled.

"You will serve me well," he said.

Speechless, Kevin withdrew, and the soldiers at the door, all Christians, crossed themselves as he passed by. Then, as silence settled upon us, all eyes turned to Lancelot.

"Rise, Lancelot, and hear my Judgment."

Lancelot stood stiffly, and I found my hands twisting together in my lap. If Arthur forgave him, Lancelot would labor all his life under the burden of that obligation, and Maelgon would not be able to bear the slight. Yet everyone had voiced a plea for mercy, and Arthur had moments before publicly forgiven the Druids. How could he now hold Lancelot to blame?

The two men faced each other in the clear light.

"Of the charge of betrayal which Maelgon brings against you," Arthur said slowly, "you deny it, and there is no other witness but the Queen. I free you of this charge." I whispered a small prayer of thanksgiving. Lancelot stared steadily at Arthur.

"But I find you negligent in your care of my Queen," Arthur said heavily. "In all the years I have known you, this is the only time you have failed me. Because it was you alone who saved her from a fate not even a dog should undergo, I do forgive you as her husband. But as King I cannot forgive it; through your action was her life put in jeopardy; I require of you penance before I see your face again." He stopped, and Lancelot began to breathe. Life returned to his features, and he knelt gracefully before Arthur.

"My gracious lord, name what penance you desire. I shall faithfully perform it."

"Of that," Arthur said, warmth returning to his voice, "I have no doubt. You will accompany King Fion back to Ireland with a troop of men of your choosing. Place yourself under his command. You may not return to Britain until his country is at peace and his rule no longer threatened. However long that takes, so long shall you be parted from us."

Lancelot looked at Arthur with worship on his face. "My lord," he said fervently, "it shall be done."

"This is your doing, Guinevere," Maelgon growled. "I will not forget it!"

"And when you return," Arthur continued, "you will stop a month in Gwynedd and rebuild on Mona's Isle all that has been so recently destroyed by Christian troops. And I make you, Lancelot, a Christian king, responsible for keeping the peace between Mona and Gwynedd. You will come yearly to Gwynedd to visit with Kevin and with Maelgon. I am sure that, as you are his sister's husband and kin to him, King Maelgon will not object."

Maelgon, who had half risen in protest, sat down again and fidgeted uncomfortably.

Arthur straightened and looked about him. "What say you to this, Fion?"

Fion flashed him a smile. "I bless the day I came to Britain," he replied. "Everyone honors me here."

"Queen Alyse?"

"Very satisfactory, my lord. Honor is conferred all around."

"Queen Anet?"

"Thank you, my lord, for your mercy."

"Guinevere?"

"My lord has pulled a swan's egg from a wasp's nest. It is well done."

"King Maelgon? You have heard my Judgment. Do you accept it?"

Maelgon hesitated, frowning as he worked it out. He had wished to be rid of the Druids. And Arthur had banned them from Britain. But Kevin had been honored, and he dare not attack Mona again. He wished to lay blame upon Lancelot, and Lancelot was being blamed. But Lancelot was being honored, also, and was no less powerful than before. On the other hand, Lancelot's ties of kinship would be renewed perforce, and Maelgon's ties to power could only be strengthened thereby. He did not like it; this was not how he would have done it; but he could find no flaw in Arthur's Judgment.

"Very well, my lord," he assented at last. "I will accept it."

Gravely Arthur turned to Lancelot and took up his sword from the table.

"Arise, Lancelot. Take back your sword and commend yourself into Fion's service. Go now and return to us swiftly. The Queen and I will pray for your safety every day you are gone from us."

Lancelot took the sword from his hands and flashed me a look of joy.

"For the glory of Britain will I go." And he kissed the King's ring.

Arthur walked with me back to my chamber. He dismissed Ailsa and closed the door behind us. He took off his swordbelt and carefully laid the Sword upon the chest in the corner. His crown he removed with his own hands and placed upon the Sword. Then he stood and looked at me. "You are the bravest woman I know."

"How did you do it, Arthur? How did you find the right path? You have given him back his dignity, and your friendship is undamaged. I did not think it possible."

He came toward me and took my hands. Lightly he rubbed his thumb against my finger where my mother's ring had always been. "Well," he said very gently, "there has been damage, but not beyond repair."

"Arthur," I whispered, meeting his eyes and feeling again the tremendous power of his affection, "do not misunderstand it."

"I hope I do not."

"It was in exchange for what I could not give him. He had done so much for me."

"I know."

"And—it was a lesson to us both, not to be forgotten."

"And what did you learn?"

I raised both his hands and kissed them, then looked up into his face. "You are the end and the beginning. I love you, Arthur, more than life."

He drew a long breath and let it out slowly. "Then I am glad it happened. And I forgive you for it. Now, Guinevere, can you forgive yourself?"

I stared at him, and suddenly, amazed, I understood. What I had so clearly seen in Lancelot—the guilt, the remorse, the self-recrimination—both Fion and Arthur had seen in me.

"I—I don't know. Sometimes it seems that everything I do does you harm."

"I am unharmed." Again he touched the place the ring had been. "Even so, I am unharmed."

"Oh, Arthur, I never meant to hurt you!" I looked quickly away and stilled my trembling. "I thought I should never see you again, and I owed him my life."

His hands slid slowly up my arms and cupped my shoulders. His touch was comforting; he steadied me.

"Gwen, I understand it. Let it go." I looked up. His warm brown eyes held me, offering solace. "He is my friend, too."

I saw he meant it; he *was* unharmed; in some incomprehensible way we three were closer now than before, and would always be so, bound forever by our love, whose boundaries we had so recently discerned. To me, it was the lifting of a great burden, and for the first time since we came to Gwynedd, I felt lighthearted.

"Thank you, Arthur. Then I am not afraid any longer."

He smiled in relief. "How many times must I tell you, you need never be afraid of me?" He stepped closer. "Indeed, you are the one men would do well to fear. Who brought Alyse back to life? Who put spine into Anet? It is your doing Maelgon was soft clay in my hands, as it will be largely your doing if there is peace in Gwynedd. He is a new man with those two women at his side. I could not have done it, Gwen, without you."

I flushed with pleasure at his praise and ruffled his hair. "What a tongue you have in your head, my lord King! I suppose you did nothing at all!"

He laughed, freeing my hair from the thong and running caressing hands along my shoulders to my neck. "The next time you try to look plain," he said lightly, "do not choose a simple gown. It only proclaims to all the world that your beauty lies in your bones and your skin, and not in your ornaments. I have wanted nothing the last hour but this." He bent his lips to my neck and kissed me.

The summer Mordred turned seventeen, Arthur knighted him. Both he and Gawaine had become members of the King's army on their fifteenth birthdays and had enjoyed the honor of entering into official manhood. They had traveled with the King on his journeys around the Kingdom, had sat at the back of many meeting halls, and at the farthest table in even more dining halls. The glamour had rapidly worn off. Mordred was content to watch, and wait, and listen to the councils of his elders, but Gawaine chafed at inactivity. He was forever longing for a good fight.

Seventeen was young for knighthood, but all the Companions knew Mordred deserved it, rumors about his parentage aside. He was an able fighter and a good swordsman; only Lancelot, Galahantyn, Bedwyr, and the King could best him. But more than that, he had a cool head in a crisis and could always look three steps ahead and judge consequences. He had the makings of a statesman. The only thing he lacked, it seemed, was Arthur's ability to lead men by inspiring their love. Lancelot said he had no endearing warmth, no inner light, no central reservoir of strength and serenity for men to draw on. He was young for that, I retorted. Arthur had had it in abundance at fourteen, was his reply.

The second reason Arthur knighted Mordred was to elevate his status, while not yet acknowledging him openly. He no longer had to sleep in the barracks, but was given rooms in the castle. He was one of the High King's Companions and sat in the Round Hall with the other knights at Council.

The uneasy tension between Mordred and Gawaine was strained by this elevation, but not to breaking point. Gawaine knew Mordred was the King's son. But he also knew he would soon be a king in his own right, well before Mordred could ever hope to rule. And he knew the King was not ready to declare Mordred openly his heir.

It seemed that Lancelot's judgment had been acute. Christian power had grown in Britain during Arthur's long reign. Most of the kingdoms were Christian, as were most of the knights who now served him. The only man Bishop Landrum would bend a knee to was the High King himself. On Ynys Witrin, the monastery of Christian monks grew as powerful as the Lady's shrine. Only the hill folk, and men from the outland kingdoms of Orkney, Lothian, and parts of western Wales, still worshipped old gods. And Mithra, the soldiers' god, even Mithra was remembered only on his great feast days.

This was a problem for Arthur, for as Lancelot had predicted, there seemed to be no question of Mordred ever becoming an anointed King. Duke Constantine of Cornwall, who had grown more manifestly devout as Mordred grew in favor, was fond of reminding all who would listen that Britain must have a Christian King. But until Arthur acknowledged to the people of Britain that Mordred was his son, such talk as Constantine's could be scoffed at, and forgotten. So Arthur kept quiet, and kept the peace, and gave Mordred honor and status in other ways.

That same summer Agravaine and Gaheris turned fifteen and joined the company of men. They celebrated by getting drunk and tearing up the town in their revels, picking fights with soldiers and accosting every woman they saw. The King made good their damage with gold to all who asked for it and chastised the twins for this behavior. But his words were remembered only until the next chance for rowdiness came along. Gawaine was of their temperament, but his future as heir to Orkney meant much to him. Neither Agravaine nor Gaheris had aught to look forward to but what honor they could gain by killing the King's enemies—and the country was at peace.

I stood in the library garden three weeks after the solstice, directing my women as they pruned the roses. Fion had sent me some lovely glass bowls for my anniversary, which he never forgot. These were of many shapes, some deep and some shallow, all etched in the pretty way the Irish have. The bowls turned the light and set it shimmering in the very air. I poured clean water into them and, filling them with roses, set them in the King's room, in his library, and in Mordred's room and my own, to please the eye and scent the air. I was teaching the art of pruning to my two newest girls, Claire and Linet, when Claire clumsily dropped her knife and, blushing, tucked a stray wisp of hair into her net. As I opened my mouth to chide her, I saw Mordred coming down the walk toward us, and I smiled.

He was as tall as Arthur now, although he would never have his father's shoulders. But he had his face and was a handsome youth, admired by all the girls in Camelot.

"Queen Guinevere." He bowed politely.

"Why, Sir Mordred, how glad I am to see you. I miss the days when we were daily together."

"As I do," he said fervently. "I thank you, my lady."

I saw he would talk with me, so I gave some last instructions to the girls, which I doubt they even heard, and led him off deeper into the bower.

He adjusted his pace to suit mine and kept his voice too low for overhearing. As a courtier, he was skilled. "My lady, I have just come from the

King. I was with him when a courier came, and I asked if I might bring you the message. As I see you so seldom nowadays," he finished, smiling shyly.

"I am glad of it. Tell me."

"The message came from Castle Daure. From King Arres."

I glanced at him quickly, but his face was carefully neutral and his eyes were on the ground. "From King Arres?"

"He begs the King to allow the Queen of Orkney a last visit with her sons."

I stopped, and Mordred stopped with me but did not look up.

"A *last* visit? Is she ill?"

"No" came the quiet answer, "but she is on the verge of taking orders and will remove to a nunnery next autumn where men are not admitted."

I stared at Mordred. Was it possible Lamorak had told us all the truth? "I was not aware the King had given her leave to go."

Mordred looked up at last, his dark eyes unreadable. "Indeed, my lady, he has not. She has not asked him. This is the first he has heard of her plans."

"So she has got King Arres to do her bidding? If she is truly Christian, no doubt Arthur will let her go."

"I advised him against it." Mordred drew a deep breath. "Every word from her lips is a lie," he whispered. "This is some trick she has devised to regain her freedom or renew her hold over Gaheris—I don't know what she is planning, but I know, I *know* she lies. She is no more Christian than I am. Arthur should disregard Arres' request."

"He cannot. On the chance it might be true. He must at least make an effort to find out."

He nodded. "I know. But I don't like it. He tells me that some years ago she enslaved Sir Lamorak, who even bid for her hand in marriage. And that you talked him out of it."

I smiled. "He is flattering me, Mordred. Arthur sent him to Brittany to serve King Hoel, to cool his ardor and hope that he would wed a Breton lass. I have not heard what became of him."

Mordred looked grim. "I will tell you. He is back now in the King's service. Sir Gereint passed through Winchester last spring and says that Lamorak is stationed there at the garrison, second-in-command. He still sees her."

"Well, he has not renewed his request for her hand in marriage," I said with a frown.

Mordred looked uneasy, then shrugged. "He claims he is still betrothed to her and, from what Gereint told me, enjoys all the privileges thereof."

I glanced up to see his face and caught a quick blush on his cheek. If Mordred, her cool-headed bastard, felt shame for her behavior, what would her hot-blooded sons think if they knew?

"This is rumor, surely. If she is preparing to live a life where men are not admitted—"

"Exactly, my lady! It is all a lie! Not about Lamorak—I've no doubt he is her lover. She has never denied herself the indulgence of even her smallest desires. When I was a child"—his voice shook—"I remember a constant stream of men going in and out of her apartments. I used to see my father's face in every one of them." He looked away and squared his shoulders. "In any event, Arthur has decided to grant Arres' request and send us. But he is uneasy about it. He will send Sir Sagramor to the nunnery to find out if she really plans to retire there. And he has decided to ride south and inspect some fortifications not far from Giants' Dance; it is an excuse to accompany us the first part of the way."

I smiled. "That sounds like Arthur."

"Where is Merlin?" Mordred asked softly. "Why can't he do this, instead of Arthur? The King risks himself to come within a hundred leagues of her!"

These were his parents he spoke about, and it grieved my heart to hear it. "For years Merlin has been no more than a shadow and a voice. Now Arthur believes Merlin is gone. He says he has gone to his gods in that cold Welsh cave of his. The King even pays a servant to tend the place, that it may retain its holiness, and so honor Merlin." To my surprise, Mordred looked stricken. "Don't be distressed. Arthur told me it was a sign we needed to worry about Morgause no longer."

Mordred grunted. "He is worried enough about her now."

"When do you leave, and who attends him?"

"Within the fortnight. Gawaine is at Caerleon and must be sent for. Bedwyr, Gereint, Villers, Galahantyn, and Bellangere attend him." He paused and lowered his eyes. "Lancelot stays as Protector."

I grieved to see he still could not accept it. "And Gaheris? Does he know?"

"Yes. He and Agravaine followed the courier in, to hear his news."

"How did he take it? Is he eager, or afraid?"

He hesitated. "He is beside himself with joy."

"He must be guarded! Oh, Mordred, do not let her see him alone!"

He shivered. "Believe me, my lady, the troops who escort us have orders to attend us every minute. Orders given in the presence of Gaheris. The King takes no chances."

We walked on in silence. I was as worried for Mordred as for Gaheris. His brothers never knew the part he had played in the accusation of Morgause. They blamed Lancelot, who was not then even in Britain, and they blamed me. I feared Morgause might take joy in telling them the truth and setting brother against brother for her amusement.

"He will take me with him when he goes to talk treaty with the Saxons," Mordred said suddenly, brightening.

"Will he? I am so glad, Mordred. You are ready for it."

"Readier than most, my lady," he said, warming to it, "for I have learned some Saxon on the sly."

"Really? From whom? Have we Saxons in Camelot?"

"Two of them are grooms in the stable—Saxons are magicians with horses—Lancelot employs them all unknowing! They told him they were Irish, and he put down their straw-colored hair and strange accents to that. I have taken the trouble to make their acquaintance and learn what I can of their tongue. If they speak slowly enough, I can understand them."

I watched him thoughtfully as he spoke. Lancelot was right about him; he saw opportunity everywhere. As he would need to, to be a King.

"Are you sure they are not spies?"

"Oh, no, my lady. They are not. Each carries a blood price on his head and left the territories to save his skin. All they want is to work with good horses and be left in peace. They curse their former king and have sworn allegiance to Arthur. And anyway," he finished, "I tell them nothing of what passes. I go to them only to learn."

"This is excellent, Mordred. You may perhaps do the King your father a special service, if you understand their speech, and they know it not. You can attest to the truth of the translations. More than that, you can listen to what the soldiers mutter to one another and see how the land truly lies."

He nodded eagerly. "That has been my thought, my lady. Their nobles, their 'thegns,' I must have speech with, to find out whether it is only King Cerdic who desires to deal with us, or if his men are behind him."

"And our men?" I asked with hesitation. "Are they behind the King? Or is there grumbling and superstition? Do they think it reasonable we talk with Saxons, or do they think the King is growing soft?"

I saw by his disconcerted look that I had hit a bruise. He wished desperately that I had not asked him. Arthur had evaded the question with assurances, but Mordred answered me.

"Opinion is divided, my lady. Among the young men—" He gulped hastily, seeing my face, and changed his wording. "I mean, among the youths of my age, some would follow the King even into the gates of Hell, but some prefer to hate the Saxons, mostly because they want war. These would fight their own kin for a rag of glory, if they thought they could get away with it."

"You might be describing your own brothers," I teased him, to lighten the tone.

He did not smile. "I am. All but Gareth, who, like me, takes no joy in killing. My brothers are among this group, and some black Celts from

Wales. Most of the Christians are behind Arthur. As for the older—er, the proven warriors, who fought with the King in the Saxon wars, they are divided, also. Some cannot let go of their hatred and look beyond it. The others will do whatever the King commands, because he is who he is and has done what he has done."

"Amen," I whispered.

"The foremost of those opposed," he said slowly, "is Lancelot."

I touched his hand and smiled at him. "Do not worry about Lancelot. He is opposed with his lips and his head, but his heart and his sword are with the King. He would follow him anywhere, even beyond the gates of Hell. Do not for a minute doubt him."

"If you say so, my lady." But he did doubt; I could see it in his face.

I shook my head. "Ah, Mordred. It is my fondest dream that you and Lancelot should grow in trust and friendship. You both are men of honor, and you love the King. But neither of you will know the other. There is some great reluctance between you."

Mordred took my hand and bent his knee to the ground. "You are so full of gentleness, my lady, you would have everyone you love, love each other. And when I am with you, it seems almost possible. But, dear Guinevere, beyond the sphere of your influence, beyond these castle walls, lies a world of slanders, lies, fierce competition, and mean acts. To be in your company, yours and the King's, it is like coming up from the depths to breathe pure air."

I took his head in my hands. "Is life so difficult for you, Mordred? Are you still badgered about your birth? If the King's silence makes it troublesome, tell him."

He shook his head quickly. "No, no. Let that be. I understand the silence. It must be so. Only—" He paused and swallowed audibly. "Only I sometimes wonder what the future holds for me. He has never told me what he intends."

I touched his cheek. "If he has not told you, I cannot," I whispered. "But you know him, Mordred. He is your father, and he loves you. What would you do if you were he?"

He looked at me with his black eyes, wise and deep and tragic. "But I am not enough like him," he said so softly, the words hovered on the edge of sound. I felt a thrill go through me like an arrow of truth.

"No two are the same. But there is much of him in you. If you cannot see it, I can. And knowing Arthur, what do you think he will do?"

He kissed my hand with fervor, and I raised him.

"Go with God," I told him, and sent him back to Arthur.

Lancelot and I strolled in the garden after hall. The night was warm and scented and dark with a new moon. Some light spilled from the open library doors, where a single cresset burned, but the depths of the garden were deep in shadow. Claire and young Linet attended me, but they sat discreetly by the fountain in the light, comparing the valor of the young knights they worshipped and, out of custom, paying us little attention.

In darkness, Lancelot clasped my hand and held it close against his breast. We walked thus, silent, taking pleasure in the still beauty of the night and in the touch of our flesh.

"I wish, Gwen, I could bring Galahad to meet you. I worry sometimes that he is kept too close at home."

"I would be honored, Lancelot," I replied, "to meet your son. What do you mean, 'kept too close'?"

"Oh," he said lightly, lifting my hand to his lips, "he is too fond of his mother."

"That is normal for a boy his age, I think. Soon his heroes will be men."

He shrugged. "I am not there enough. And she sets his mind against me, young as he is. He would be better off living here. Like Mordred. Like Gareth." It was the nearest he had ever come to telling me about his life with Elaine. I could see well it was death to him.

"Then leave the other two with her and bring him. You are his father."

He shuddered and then looked quickly away. My heart filled with rage against Elaine—that he should dread that confrontation so! Lancelot, bravest of men!

"I would like him to grow up like Gareth," he said quickly. "He left his mother early enough, it seems. He is full of gentleness and honor and the love of doing right. Galahad strives for high ideals, but knows only those his mother feeds him. He should be at Arthur's court."

"Then bring him," I said warmly, slipping my arm through his and entwining my fingers in his own. "Shall Arthur send for him?"

He looked down at me, and a stray wisp of light caught his smile. "No, my lady Queen. This I can do myself."

"Brave Lancelot!"

He laughed and drew me close. "This is a great myth you women raise us to believe: that you are powerless and we must risk life to protect you. I have yet to know a woman who does not rule her husband in anything she wills." He kissed me softly, letting his lips linger on mine.

"You know *me*."

"You pretend you do not rule Arthur? Why, three years ago he felt about Saxons as I do. You would no more have caught him treating with their leader than—than bathing in boiling oil. And now he proposes to parley with Cerdic himself, and talk new treaties, as if the thieving dog were his equal!" With an effort, he calmed himself and lowered his voice. "I know who has his ear, Gwen. Don't think I cannot guess whose idea this is."

We walked on a little farther, and I gave him time to settle his emotions. Like Gawaine, he was quick to anger, but unlike him, he was just as quick to cool.

"Is Cerdic a thieving dog," I asked gently, "or a ruler beset by greedy lords at his back and a growing population on his shores? In all these years he has kept his word to Arthur and not strayed across the border anywhere. And yet, you know, his chieftains must be hollering for more land every year and spreading rumors about his growing age and unfitness for his crown. In his place, my dear Lancelot, what would you do?"

"I would keep my word," he said with some defiance.

"And so he has. The King asked for this parley, only to set the stage for the future. If they meet in friendship now, perhaps his chieftains will wait to see what comes of it; and in the meantime, they will be our buffer against the Franks."

"Yes, yes, I know the reasons," he said impatiently. "But even now that Clodomir is dead, we are not threatened. Childebert has treaties with me and with Hoel. So why do we need a buffer? And what makes him think the Saxons will listen, or abide by what is agreed?"

"They will listen, because he is Arthur of Britain. And Cerdic has shown that he can keep his word. We have nothing to lose, Lancelot, and much to gain, perhaps, in the future."

He sighed. "I know your dream of a united Britain. But there might be a lot to lose. Many are against it."

We had reached the stone bench that hugged the wall at the end of the garden. I could see nothing here, it was so black. I put out my hands and laid them against his chest. His own came up and covered them.

"And you, Lancelot? I know you disagree with Arthur, but will you follow him?"

"Unto death," he whispered, and kissed me. For a moment, I allowed myself to respond to him, giving in to the demanding fires that burned in me whenever he was near. But at last, trembling, we broke apart and sat together on the bench, remembering who we were.

"You are right, Lancelot. He does this because of me, and because of Mordred, who has caught fire with this idea. But although Arthur sees the sense in it, he is not eager to pursue it far. He says it is not his destiny."

"That's Merlin talking."

"I know. But he believes Merlin. He has always believed everything the old enchanter said."

"He wasn't always old, you know, Gwen." I heard the smile in his voice. "Bedwyr knew him when he was not much older than Arthur is now. In his prime. And when I met him, at Caer Eden, where he stood beside Arthur in front of all those gathered lords, he was magnificent! With Uther dead, and the Saxons camped across the river, there wasn't a man on the battlefield who'd have risen for the boy Arthur if Merlin hadn't been there. His very presence was more powerful than the entire host of war leaders. You should have heard my Christian father mumbling all the ancient protections! He sounded like a Druid!" He laughed lightly. "He was a strong enough man then. Terrifying, at times."

"Don't I know it! Lancelot, did you know that Merlin is dead?"

"What, again?"

"No, I mean it. Last spring, before we left Caerleon, he came to Arthur in his sleep and said good-bye. 'I am gone to my fathers; I will be with your children; you shall live forever in glory, the once and future King.' It is odd, is it not? But Arthur understood it, it seems. He awoke in tears, and yet he did not grieve. But he said that Merlin was truly gone, taken into the hill by the god who dwells there. Now the place is holy and tended as a shrine."

Lancelot grunted but said nothing.

"I wonder if it is because Arthur believes Merlin dead that he holds himself to this destiny of his—to hold Britain safe from the Saxons. I keep thinking, how much safer would we be, if they were part of it!"

"They tried to be part of it once," Lancelot protested, "in Vortigern's day, and nearly destroyed us. Perhaps in time they might become civilized, but really, Gwen, they are primitive savages."

"Well," I said, "let be. You know them, and I do not. Niniane does not see any harm in the trip for Arthur, so I hope I shall not have cause to regret his going."

Just then we heard voices, and a light came bobbing uncertainly down the path. Lancelot dropped my hand and rose. It was a page, and behind him, a courier.

"My lord Lancelot, Queen Guinevere," he said hastily, "an urgent message for you, my lord. Will you receive it here?"

Lancelot drew the man ten paces away and heard him. By the lantern light I saw him take bad news and grow solemn. He thanked the man and gave him a coin and sent him off to his meal and bath. Then he came back to me.

"What is it, my dear? Nothing's amiss with the King?"

In the new darkness I could not see him, but heard his voice, full of contrition. "There is no word from Arthur, or from Arres. This was from my home, Guinevere. Alas, my wife is dead."

"What? Elaine dead? Oh, Lancelot, how can this be? She is younger than I am!"

He felt for my hands and held them tightly. "She was delivered early of a stillborn daughter. They could not stop the bleeding."

"Oh, Lancelot, how terrible!" It was how Arthur lost his first wife, and I knew the horror it brought a man, to be the cause of a woman's death. "May God give rest to her unhappy soul," I whispered. I felt him come closer in the darkness.

"Pray with me, Gwen. I should feel more grief than I do. I did not love her, and she hated me, but she bore me three sons, and she was my wife. Help me mourn her."

So we sank to the ground and knelt side by side, hands clasped in prayer upon the bench, and together we prayed for the salvation of Elaine's departed soul. Lancelot was deeply moved, not by grief, but by self-recriminations. All that he had ever said or done, or not said or not done, on account of Elaine, he now remembered. He took her death upon him, and felt he owed God for it. It was his way—I could not change him.

And I, I remembered our childhood days together in Gwynedd. Bright, happy, full of life, she had welcomed me into her home with open arms, never once pitying her orphaned cousin; she had made me feel at home from my first day. How I had loved her for it! She led everywhere, and I followed. I remembered our gallops along the stony beach upon our fat ponies, and the time she tried to teach me Irish braiding—it took Ailsa three hours to get the knots out of my hair! And how we eavesdropped on her father's councils, and stole cream from the kitchens, and plied our tutor with mead to escape our lessons . . . and how, when I had stumbled upon a half-dead Irish pirate early one frozen winter morning, Elaine, her cheeks flushed with excitement, had brought me the news that he was a real Irish prince and worth ransom! Thus Fion had entered our lives, and so began, in all innocence, a competition between us for the notice of men. Poor Elaine! How sad that only at her death should my anger toward her finally slacken! Now that she had suffered a heavier punishment than any I would have laid upon her, I pitied her from the bottom of my heart. From childhood she had worshipped Arthur, as prince, as King, as man, only to see her rival wed him. And although she had hated the man she married, she had done her duty and had borne him sons. What had I wanted from her, but love for Lancelot? She was no more capable of that than I was of love for Melwas— dear Elaine!—if only she could forgive me! If only it were not too late!

Eventually, when the night was well spent, we heard whispers behind us in the dark. I finished my prayer, crossed myself, and turned. Linet and Claire stood there with a candle, their eyes wide in wonder. They dipped quick curtsies, and the light trembled, casting shadows.

"What is the matter?" I asked softly. "Why have you come?"

"My—my lady," Claire whispered, shaking, "it grows late and we were worried. We did not hear your voices. And—and we felt we neglected our duty. As your chaperones . . ." Her voice trailed off. Lancelot knelt, head bowed, his back to them.

I rose, wiped the tears from my cheeks and guided them slowly away. "We have come to no harm, as you see. Sir Lancelot has had bad news. Now wait for us by the fountain. I will be with you in a moment." They went obediently, and I watched them thoughtfully. I wondered if they had been sent.

When I returned to Lancelot, I found his thoughts running the same way.

"Spying on us, were they?" he asked, rising. "Who sent them?"

"I don't know. Let's not jump to that conclusion."

He sighed with a great weariness. "There is a faction of young men who have taken against me. You had better know this, Gwen, especially as Arthur will not hear it spoken of. They are young yet, but their power is growing. All the Orkney boys are in it, except Gareth."

My heart beat suddenly fast, and I felt my anger rising. "Do you include Mordred in this group?"

His voice was very gentle. "Oh, yes. By some he is thought the leader. He and Agravaine. They would catch us in some amour, if they could. They think I lie with you and so betray the King."

"They do not dare! Tell me this is not true!"

He slipped my arm through his and started back down the walk. "But it is true and cannot be discounted. And in my heart," he breathed, so low I could barely hear, "in my heart I am guilty. Whenever I lay with Elaine, in my heart it was you I held. This is a sin."

"Dreams are phantoms!" I protested. "We are all fools in our dreams! You cannot be guilty, Lancelot, of sins your flesh has not committed. I will hear no more of this. This is folly."

He squeezed my arm. "That is just what Arthur says."

"Well, Arthur knows the truth. You are the last man on this earth who would betray him."

At last I heard the smile back in his voice. "Thank you for that. I only spoke to warn you. Sometimes the appearance of a thing is all that is re-quired to produce conviction. You know the saying: Where there is smoke, there is fire."

"Only fools think so." We approached the light, and he gently dropped my arm, so that we walked without touching.

"There are plenty of fools about," he said lightly. "We should, perhaps, be more careful of the smoke."

41 ♔ THE MURDER

Arthur returned a day or two later, having seen the boys halfway to Castle Daure. He had waited near the Great Plain to hear if there were trouble, but all had apparently gone well. Morgause received her sons without incident, and they would stay a fortnight in her company before Mordred and Arthur left to meet the Saxons. Relieved, Arthur threw himself into the daily routine of ruling, joining me and Lancelot on occasion for a day hawking or a good gallop over the downs.

One evening, after a hard ride, a hot bath, and a good meal, we sat late in the library, playing chess. The doors stood open to the garden and the sweet scents of summer, of roses, honeysuckle, and new-cut grasses, drifted in on the soft night breeze. With us, stretched on the benches asleep or recounting the day's events over a cup of neat wine, were the best loved of the Companions: Lancelot, Bedwyr, Gereint, Ferron, Lyonel, Bleoberys, and a few others. In the corner, a trio of my maids sat and stitched.

With a deep sigh of contentment, I gave my mind to the game. Arthur and I were usually well matched, but that night he was not at his best. His beloved hound Cabal had died that morning while we were out hunting. The news had met us upon our return, and he had grieved to hear it. Within the hour the houndsman had brought some young dogs to the King, and he had chosen a new Cabal, white-coated and dark-eyed, with paws and ears too big to suit his size, and a mischievous eagerness that made the High King laugh. As he sat before the chessboard, Arthur held young Cabal in his lap, and twice put his bishop in jeopardy while he played with the pup's floppy ears. At length the dog, eager to regain Arthur's attention, shoved his nose under the King's arm and pushed hard. Pieces flew off the table and Arthur bit off a cry of disappointment.

"Just when I was about to trap your knight!"

"My lord is dreaming!" I laughed, leaning down to pick up an errant pawn. "You were four moves from checkmate, maybe less."

He grinned. "Nonsense! I had you right where I wanted you."

"Indeed? What kind of strategy is that, to lose two pawns to every one of mine?"

"Why, a ploy to disarm you through overconfidence."

"What a clever strategy! Is this how you won Britain, my lord King? No wonder the Saxons could never get your measure!"

Two or three of the men looked our way, smiling.

Arthur shook his head. "When you are too sure of yourself, my dear, you make mistakes."

"Do I, indeed? Would you care to name them?"

He laughed outright and set the dog upon the floor. "No, I would not. I am not such a fool as all that. I grant you the game, Guinevere. Does that content you?"

"To be given as a gift something I had earned already?" I retorted, smiling up at him as he rose to stretch. "Nothing will content me but to hear your admission that I bested you tonight."

He took my hand and raised it to his lips. His eyes met mine, and heat rose to my face. "Ask it of me again when the night is over." I heard chuckles from the men and felt Lancelot's eyes upon me clear across the room. The dog, impatient of attention, leaped up on Arthur's chair and thence to the table, scattering the pieces wildly all over the room. With loud cries of laughter, the men chased the dog and scrambled for the pieces on all fours, while the pup ran circles all about them, yapping in glee.

In the middle of this mayhem, a knock came at the door. Arthur was beside me, on his knees, whistling for the dog, and I saw his face as he glanced up. He went suddenly pale, and slowly rose, the black queen falling unnoticed from his fingers.

Kay stepped in, grim-faced, and bowed. "My lord. A courier. From Castle Daure." Behind him, white as a nether spirit and still dusty from the road, stood Gareth. Alone.

"Bring him in."

In the corner, little Linet, a pretty dark-haired child with eyes bright as a bird's, looked up and smiled shyly at Gareth. She was only thirteen, but already had lost her heart. Gareth fell to his knees at Arthur's feet, so consumed by some strong emotion he neither saw nor heard anyone else in the room.

"Uncle," he whispered. "Uncle."

At Arthur's signal, the maids gathered up their work and departed, the Companions rose, bowed, and filed out in silence. Someone grabbed the dog. Lancelot awaited me at the door; I made Arthur a reverence.

"No, Gwen. Stay. You, too, Lancelot. The boy will need your aid."

I looked down at Gareth's bowed head. I knew my thoughts were one with Arthur's: Something had happened to Mordred.

"Arise, Gareth," the King said quietly. "Gwen, a winecup. Drink this, son, and sit down. Collect yourself. Whatever it is you have ridden so far so fast to tell us will still be true five minutes hence."

Gareth obeyed. At fourteen, he was a well-grown youth, as strong and thickly built as his brothers, but of a kinder nature. His gentleness and good humor lent his plain face an honesty that the others' lacked. He trained daily with Lancelot and had grown to love honor. The wild streak so apparent in his brothers was tamed in him, and civilized.

Arthur stood before him. "All right, Gareth. What has happened?"

The boy looked up with eyes dulled from suffering. "My mother—Queen Morgause—is dead."

I gasped. "Dead! How?"

"She was murdered." He spoke lifelessly. Arthur reached out a hand to his chin and raised his face. Through the dust on his cheeks were trails of former tears; he met Arthur's eyes directly; he was telling the truth.

"How?" Arthur asked sharply. "Who?"

Gareth turned his face away and dropped his eyes. "My lord, Gaheris killed her."

"Gaheris!" I cried, sitting hard on the bench beside him."Oh, no!"

"I think," Arthur said slowly, "you had better take your time and tell us the whole story. Lancelot, set a guard upon the door and see we are not disturbed."

With an effort, Gareth stilled his trembling and, drawing a deep breath, began to speak. "At first, everything went smoothly. Mother greeted us all with the show of loving warmth she always puts on for strangers." I bowed my head to hear him speak so; even Gareth! "Sir Lamorak took charge of our escort and saw that we were well attended. We got to see her in the evenings, in the common room, either in the company of Sir Bellok, the garrison commander, or of Sir Lamorak, or of King Arres himself, who did us the honor to come and greet us. We were never alone with her. Gaheris—Gaheris began to chafe under such surveillance. And Mordred took to staying awake nights, just to be sure he slept. My lord, I think he kept watch over Gaheris, covertly, all the while."

"Bless him," I breathed.

"But then—" He shivered suddenly. Lancelot's hand came down upon his shoulder, and his voice steadied. "If only Mordred had enlisted my aid, we could have watched in shifts! One night he dozed off and woke well past midnight to find Gaheris gone. Although it was so late, he made his way to her rooms without difficulty. No one even asked his business. No one, he told me later, appeared to think twice about a youth making his way to her apartments after dark."

"Oh, Gareth!" I clasped his cold hand.

"They were only surprised that he did not know the way. When he came to her chamber, he found Gaheris weeping at the door. They heard voices within, and laughter, and sounds enough for Mordred to know—and, and Gaheris, too, may God forgive him—how she was engaged. Mordred sought to draw him away, but Gaheris refused to leave. Finally, Mordred took him by the shoulder and shook him, pointing out that such obsession was a sickness, and when Mother was alone they could come back. At this Gaheris apparently went wild, drew his sword, and kicked open the door."

He stopped and drained the winecup. "I will give it to you, my lord, as I heard it from Mordred's lips that very night. I cannot ever, ever forget his words. His voice was so cold." He wiped sweat from his brow and Lancelot tightened his grip on the boy's shoulder. "They found her in bed with Lamorak, coupled, and so absorbed in each other they were slow to react. Mordred grabbed his arm, as Gaheris began shouting obscenities—this probably saved Lamorak's life. He leaped out of bed and made for the chair where he had left his sword. Mordred of course assumed Gaheris would try to slay Lamorak, so he was completely unprepared for what actually happened." His voice grew tight, but he kept on. "Gaheris turned to Mother, lying naked on the covers and, with a cry of such anguish that it froze them to where they stood, brought down his sword across her neck."

"Dear God!" I stared up in horror at Arthur's face. "Oh, Arthur!"

He passed a hand across his brow and crossed himself.

Gareth plowed on in a lifeless voice. "Gaheris fell to weeping and flung his sword away and began embracing her body amid the bloody sheets. Then Mordred urged Lamorak to dress and get going, to put as much distance as he could between himself and Gawaine before the news was out. He got Lamorak away and bid him hie back to Brittainy until the storm blew over. Then he locked the doors behind him, gave Gaheris into Agravaine's care, and came and told me about it. He bade me take horse at once and come to you. He said I was the one courier you would believe. But I think, my lord, I think he wanted to get me out of that awful place!" His voice finally broke, and he covered his face with his hands. Lancelot sat beside him and with an arm about his shoulder, hugged him to his breast.

After a moment, Arthur spoke. "How did Gawaine react? Do you know?"

Gareth struggled for composure. "Yes, my lord. I—I was there when Mordred told him." His smile was bitter. "You know Gawaine. Nothing will serve but he must kill Lamorak. Not even Mordred could make him see reason. Mordred told him Lamorak was her betrothed—that this was known by five or six of your Companions—and that it gave him a right to her bed. But Gawaine will have it that Mother was dishonored."

"Is he mad?" I cried. "His mother is dead by his brother's hand!"

"He has no love for Gaheris. And he knows it was no rape. But her death is a small thing, beside her honor."

"Her honor!" But I said no more; Gareth was her son, as well.

"And Agravaine, too, is breathing revenge." The boy faltered. "He considers it all Lamorak's doing and wants an eye for an eye. I know he always protects Gaheris, but—and now Gawaine is the leader of our clan. We are headed for disaster! It is too soon, too soon. I can't believe she is gone."

"Come, Gareth." Lancelot spoke in a low voice full of tenderness. "Come with me to the chapel. Together we will pray for the salvation of her soul. There is great comfort, I have found, in heartfelt prayer."

Gareth's eyes widened. "Oh, my lord! I had forgotten! Kay told me about your wife and daughter! To lose two of your kin in one stroke—and here I am grieving for a mother I did not love in life."

Lancelot glanced at me swiftly, then raised the boy. "Whatever turmoil lies within your heart, prayer will ease it and give you the peace to sleep."

Gareth nodded. I could see he was close to exhaustion. "Very good, my lord, I thank you. I would like to go."

I glanced at Arthur but he shook his head, and Lancelot and Gareth went out together. When the door had closed, Arthur turned to me. "Let them be. He is better alone with Lancelot, and Lancelot alone with him." He took my hand and held it between his own. "Gwen, the hour is late, our fellowship is broken. Would you take it amiss if I asked you to retire? I have to fetch the scribe, have orders written out, and there are couriers to send. I will be late, I fear."

There were new lines in his face and a drawn, weary look around his eyes. I thought suddenly, and for the first time, *He is no longer young.*

"My lord, may I await you?"

He half smiled and brushed his lips against my hand. "I would like that very much."

He was very late, but at last he came. I had wine ready, and cool fruit drinks, and cold water, and had filled the bowl on his nightstand with fresh roses. I waited in my own room until Varric left him, and then I went in.

"My lord Arthur." I walked into his embrace, and he kissed me fondly.

He was not too tired to smile. "Ah, Gwen. Bless you for waiting. I am so weary of it all. Let us have peace a moment."

We went out onto the terrace to enjoy the coolness of the night. He sat in the chair, and I stood behind and rubbed his shoulders. At first it was like pressing fingers into bronze, but with time, his flesh grew more human to the touch. At length he sighed and thanked me, and I came around and sat at his feet, my head resting on his knees.

"By her death, Morgause has sown the seed of blood feud into my company of knights," the King said flatly. "Even now, I am not free of her curse! Gawaine has sworn to avenge himself on Lamorak. Should he succeed, Lamorak's cousin, Drustan, King of Elmet, will be avenged upon

Gawaine. We shall have the kingdoms at war with one another at a time we can least afford it."

I took his hand and held it hard. "What steps have you taken?"

He sighed again. "I'm going to have a devil of a time convincing Arres that I will not hold my sister's death against him. But I have sent him a message explaining things as best I can. I have banished Gaheris. If, as I believe, he has lost his wits, he will come somewhere to the fate he deserves. I cannot kill him; that would divide the Kingdom right down the middle. Thanks to Mordred's quick thinking, Lamorak has vanished. If he has sense, he will not go to Drustan, which is where Gawaine will look for him. He has a distant relation in Cornwall and friends in Brittany. Either place would serve him well. When and if this blows over, I will welcome him back into the Companions. He has done nothing amiss. I am the last man on earth who could condemn him."

"Stop it, Arthur. That is behind you."

He shrugged. "For the present, I will keep Gawaine and Agravaine close by me. I have ordered them home at once. Time may temper their hatred. I have no doubt that Gaheris will get word to Agravaine, and I hope that Mordred, through him, will be able to keep me informed as to what happens. I can do no more than this, but wait."

I kissed his hand, and he gently stroked my hair.

"Lancelot feels more sadness at the passing of a wife he did not love than those wild boys do for their own mother," he said softly, in sorrow. "Even Gareth is more shocked than sorry."

"That is the difference in the man."

A smile touched his lips. "Yes. It will be good to have him back with us again the year round." He stopped there, but looked down into my upturned face. I reached up and put my arms about his neck, drew his face down and kissed him. It awoke the flame in him, and he responded, drawing me up onto his lap.

"My lord," I breathed, "in time, all will be well. And see, Merlin was right. There was no more need to fear Morgause."

He sighed. "When I am with you, Gwen, I can believe it. I can believe almost anything, even that Gawaine will grow into sense in time."

"He may, with age. He is but sixteen." I paused. "My lord, is it true that some of the young men have taken against Lancelot?"

He went still a moment, then nodded. "Yes. From envy. They see he has the trust and favor of both King and Queen. This is a natural thing. They are a small group, boys without power and small hope of gaining it. Pay it no mind."

"But, my lord, is Mordred one of them?"

He looked at me sharply. "No. Who has said so?"

"Lancelot himself thinks so. I did not believe it."

"Agravaine is the leader. A fifteen-year-old hothead whom Lancelot could slay with one arm tied behind him! It is ridiculous to pay them heed. Mordred bears Agravaine little love, but recognizes the blood tie and would keep him from harm if he could. That is why he goes to their meetings, and drinks and dices with them, to protect me and Agravaine. If Lancelot has seen them together, he has drawn the wrong conclusion."

I exhaled in relief. "I am so glad, my lord. I was afraid—I wish them to be friends, and not enemies."

"As do I. Sometimes," he said heavily, "I wish we could escape court and all its intrigues, and take up arms in the open field against a worthy foe—good, clean fighting is preferable to this!"

I ruffled his hair. "To a man, perhaps. But most certainly not to me, who must wait here until the battle's end for news. It is like sitting upon hot coals."

But he did not smile. His gaze was distant and pensive.

"A coin for your thoughts, my lord."

With an effort, he smiled. "Oh, I am feeling my age, is all. My days of leading armies into battle are behind me."

"I pray to God they are," I said with fervor, "but that has nothing to do with age, but with the success of your leadership as King. Why, you are but one and thirty! Ambrosius was your age when he took Britain!"

He grinned and suddenly looked twenty again. "What a honeyed tongue you have, my child queen."

"Child, my lord?" I put a hand to his cheek. "You do not treat me so."

He kissed my neck, my throat, my shoulder, and his fingers sought the fastenings of my gown. "I know your body better than my own," he whispered. "You have not changed a whit, in all the years I've known you, except to grow more precious to me."

My breath caught as I felt his hands against my flesh, and I began to tremble. "We will stay young together, then," I breathed. His hands moved; his warm eyes grew fierce.

"We are as we do," he growled, and lifted me and carried me indoors.

That night was unlike any in my memory; the heartache and emotion of the past hours found vent in a wild, desperate loving that gripped us both and then, talons in, would not release us. We slept, and woke, and slept again, exhausted. At dawn the King awakened me with kisses and made sweet love while the birds sang to us beyond our window. When he finally arose from bed, his step was that of a young man and not another word dropped from his lips about the complaints of age.

On a beautiful day a week later, Arthur and his host left for the Saxon territories. Lancelot and I bid them farewell on the castle steps. It was a formal
leave-taking; the men who went had to know this was an embassy of state.
They were not a large army, for Arthur did not wish to threaten Cerdic,
but they were all mounted, for the Saxons feared the power of Arthur's cavalry. The King invested Lancelot as regent and Protector of the Queen. I
scanned the faces of the troops and could detect no raised eyebrows or sidelong glances. Bedwyr was going, and Galahantyn, Bors, Ferron, Villers, Bellangere, and Gawaine. Mordred, too, of course. In the three days they had
been home, he and Gawaine had hardly spoken, but in the army they would
be required to be civil to one another. Agravaine was left behind; his out-
spoken hatred of all things Saxon made him a dangerous companion behind
Saxon lines. And gentle Gareth, who would have been welcomed by the
King, was only fourteen and still in training.

I kissed Mordred on both cheeks and handed him a packet wrapped in
soft linen.

"This," I told him, "is for Cerdic's lady or, if he has none, for the leading woman of his house. Tell her it is from me."

Mordred looked surprised. "What is in it, my lady?"

"A small necklace of silver, of Celtic design. And a net of little sapphires and river pearls for her hair."

He looked disconcerted and glanced swiftly at Arthur. "But, my lady,
their—I hear their women wear their hair as maids do, in plaits, always
down."

I smiled. "Give it to her anyway. You don't know women, Mordred. If
she likes it, she will find a way to wear it."

Arthur grinned and took my hands. "He has time to learn it. Well,
good-bye, Gwen. Keep the Kingdom for me, and take good care of
Lancelot."

I kissed him on both cheeks, and then, remembering Lancelot's words
about smoke and fire, I kissed him full on the lips. "I keep everything
of yours near my heart, my lord," I said, just loud enough for the closest men
to hear.

His eyes were laughing at me, but he gravely inclined his head. "I rely
upon you."

Turning, he gave the order to mount and go. We watched them out
King's Gate.

"Lancelot," I said softly, as the last horse trotted out of view, "did you
know you are employing Saxons in your stables?"

His eyebrows lifted, and he offered me his arm. "I did. They are born
horsemen. But I didn't know you knew. Who told you?"

"Mordred. He has been learning their language from them. He thinks
you believe them to be Irish."

He laughed. "There is a lot about me Mordred doesn't know." We passed through the door as he spoke, and I saw Agravaine just entering the hall. At Lancelot's laughter he stopped dead and glared at us both, before turning on his heel and going back swiftly the way he had come. "They give out that they are Irish to avoid the ire of the people. They are common men, not warriors. Do they worry you?"

"Oh, no. I just found it hard to believe you couldn't tell a Saxon from a Gael. Mordred should have known better."

"Indeed." He said no more, but walked on with a set face.

"Lancelot."

"My lady?"

"When do you take the troops out for drill?"

"Arthur said to give him a couple of days. First we will drill in the downs, then farther east. By the time he meets with Cerdic, we should be within shouting distance of the border."

"Take Agravaine with you."

He stopped, startled. "Why Agravaine? He makes nothing but trouble. No commander wants him in the company. Giving him an order is like swimming upstream, much effort is expended for little result."

I met his eyes. "Nevertheless, take him. He is trouble looking for a place to alight. Give him work, the hope of a fight, anything but the inertia of castle guard duty. He will be a danger if he stays here."

He thought on it and finally nodded. "There is sense in that. And his horsemanship could do with work. I will give him to Gereint; he will stand no nonsense." He smiled. "But Gereint will make me pay for it, someday. Still, perhaps it will take the boy's mind off his brother. Have you heard what they are calling him?"

I nodded. "Yes. Gaheris Yellowbelly, killer of women. For his own sake, I pray he stays away from court forever."

We had reached the parting of our ways, and he bent over my hand. "Britain is too small a place to hide such a one forever. We will see him again."

42 ♛ THE BEATING

M y lady! My lady! Oh, please wake up! Please come!"
I opened my eyes. A candle wavered inches from my face, and a small white hand plucked urgently at the bedcovers.

"Who is that? What's amiss?" The candle fell back, and slowly Linet's frightened face came into view. Her robe was hastily tied about her bed-gown, and her dark hair, braided for the night, was disarranged.

"Linet! What has happened?" I slipped out of bed and made her sit down upon it. She was shaking. I took the candle from her and set it on my nightstand.

"It's Claire," she whispered. "I came for Ailsa first. When she saw her, she sent me to awaken you."

"Don't worry about that," I said, chafing her hands. Her fingers were ice cold, although the night was warm. "Tell me quickly, child. What has happened to Claire?"

Her teeth chattered, but she struggled valiantly to speak. "He has beaten her!" she cried, gulping. "There is blood, and—and her face is askew—and I don't know why she ever allowed him—I am afraid she will die!"

"Die?" I threw my robe about my shoulders. "Beaten? Who has done this? What are you talking about it? Who has been with her?"

I clutched her shoulders and held her still, holding her eyes. "Tell me, Linet."

"It was—it was Agravaine," she whispered, tears spilling from her eyes. I said nothing, but took the candle and bade her follow me.

The girl lay on a pallet in her room. Ailsa bent over her, pressing cool cloths to her head, a bowl of bloodied water on the floor beside her.

"My lady!" she cried. "Oh, see poor little Claire. She cannot speak, poor child. I think the beast has broken her jaw." I came up beside her and looked down at the beaten girl. Her face was bruised and already swollen to twice its normal size. Her lips were thick and broken, her nose awry and crusted with drying blood, her eyes swollen half shut. A thin stream of blood had trickled from her ear and now lay drying on the pillow. And her jaw was crooked. I knelt at her head.

"Claire. Can you hear me? This is Guinevere." But she could not speak, and I could see it would pain her to nod. I took her hand in mine. "Two fingers for yes," I said quickly, "and one for no. Can you hear my voice and understand me?"

Yes.

"Can you speak?"

No.

I turned to Ailsa. "Send the page for the King's physician. Quickly!" She rose and left. Then to Claire: "Did Agravaine do this?"

Yes.

"Do you know why?"

Yes.

"Does Linet know why?"

Yes.

"You are a brave girl, Claire. I will see justice done. Be patient awhile longer, and we will ease your pain. May I ask Linet to tell me why?"

A long hesitation, and then, slowly, yes.

I looked up at Linet, who stood trembling by the bed. "Tell me, Linet." Her eyes widened in fear. "Oh, no, my lady. I cannot! Indeed, I cannot!"

I pulled her down to kneel with me at Claire's side, where she had a very clear view of the poor girl's face. Anyone could see that she would be deformed forever.

"Do you wish this crime to go unpunished?"

"Oh, no, my lady!"

"But it will, unless you speak. Claire herself would tell me, but as you see, she cannot. Answer my questions, then, Linet, if you cannot speak out. Take her hand. She will signal to you when you go wrong. Am I right in surmising that this was not the first time Agravaine was in these chambers?" As Linet's room was next door, this was something she would know on her own.

"Yes, my lady."

"He is her lover?"

"She is—sort of promised to him, my lady. I mean, they are betrothed, only it is unofficial."

"Of course," I said bitterly. "It is always unofficial. He would have to have the King's permission. And mine." I stopped and looked at Claire. "Do you still have affection for him, Claire? Do you wish to be his wife?" Despite the pain, she shook her head. I was relieved to see it. If I knew the type of man at all, Agravaine cared nothing for her and would never take her now. He had used her and for what? For the satisfaction of his lusts? Any girl would do for that. But only a Queen's maid could give information about the Queen. I drew a deep breath. "What did he want of her, Linet? Did he ever ask questions about me? Or the King? Or Lancelot?"

Linet shrank back, unwilling. Claire looked pleadingly at her and moved her fingers. Linet was clearly terrified. Her very fear told me what I wished to know.

"Linet. I will not be angry with you, no matter what you have to tell me. Take courage and speak. Agravaine is the High King's nephew, and what he does has implications for many futures. The truth here is important. Do you wish Gareth to be dishonored?"

Her eyes flew up to mine then, and she stared. "Oh, no!"

"Then tell me, for God's sake, before the physician comes! What did he want of her?"

"He—he set us to spy on you and—and Sir Lancelot, my lady," she blurted, looking away.

"Ahhhhh. I thought as much." I knelt down at Linet's feet and gently took her hands. "My dear Linet, do not fear to tell me. I know well what is in Agravaine's mind. He wishes to have proof that Lancelot and I are lovers. Is that not so?"

She nodded, staring at me in horror.

"He cannot come by such proof, for we are not. I do not fear him. So why, I wish to know, do you?"

She looked wildly at Claire, whose eyes were on my face. She looked surprised.

"Answer me."

"I—we—the—we—oh, my lady, please forgive us! But we thought it might be true! Agravaine said we must unite to save the King's honor!"

I held tightly to her hands, for she shrank from me. "Why did you think it might be true?"

She shook from head to foot and would not meet my eyes.

"We saw you together often. Sometimes—in the garden, holding hands. And—and once Claire saw him kiss you. In the way of love, not of friendship."

I smiled at her and lifted her chin so she could see I was not embarrassed.

"Yes," I said gently, "these things are true. I do confess them. They are evidence of love. And I love Sir Lancelot. All the world knows this. The King himself knows it. But you must be careful what conclusions you draw from this."

They were both staring at me now, but their fear was leaving them. I rose and stood before them. "The King knows my heart. He would not leave me in Lancelot's care if there were not trust between us. Do you understand this? That there can be love without surrender or betrayal? I would not expect Agravaine to understand it, but you are my women. You know me better."

"Oh, my lady!" Linet cried, in tears. "I told him it was impossible! For Ailsa guards your door. And I have seen the tenderness between you and the King. I told him it could not be so! But— but—" she gulped, and stopped.

"He probably told you," I said slowly, "that where there is smoke, there is fire."

She nodded eagerly. "His very words! And when he came tonight, we told him we would not spy upon you longer, for we were convinced he was wrong. We told him of the dark night of no moon, when we crept up upon you in the garden when we had not heard your voices, for thus he had instructed us, and—and we found you praying."

"Is this what inspired his rage?"

"Yes, my lady. He called us fools and cowards. He would not believe it, but would have that we were lying on your behalf. He said he knew that Sir Lancelot had the—the key to your garden gate upon a thread around his neck. He had seen it. He lost his temper, and—and struck Claire. Again and again and again!" She covered her face with her hands and wept.

A slow anger began to burn within my breast. Ailsa arrived with the physician, and I went out to find the page.

"Send Lancelot to me. Here, in the girl's room." I pulled a ring off my little finger. "Give this token to him and say I request his presence urgently. A matter has arisen that must be settled now. Be sure and tell him," I added bitterly, "that I am well attended."

He was longer than I expected. The physician had completed his ministrations and was shaking his head sadly over the beaten girl. He had given her a sleeping potion, so she was beyond her pain. When Lancelot entered, I understood his delay. He was carefully and completely dressed, down to his sword and his boots. His own chamberlain accompanied him, and stood outside the door. Ailsa and Linet clutched at their bedgowns and lowered their eyes. I myself had been careful to fasten my robe up to my throat and down to my ankles, although the night was warm. When he knelt before me and placed the token in my hand, he did not meet my eyes.

"My lady Queen Guinevere. I am at your service."

"See, Sir Lancelot, what has been done to my poor maid!"

He went to Claire and spoke with the physician. She would heal, the man said, except for the jaw. She would live, if she could eat soft foods, but she would probably never speak again. Poor Claire. If she was ashamed to go home, then her future lay in God's service, in some convent where vows of silence were respected.

When Lancelot turned from her bedside I could see he was angry.

"Is it known who did this thing?" he asked me.

"Yes, my lord. It was the High King's nephew, Agravaine."

He drew breath slowly and met my eyes. The message passed. He understood it all. "I see."

"I will have justice done, my lord. He shall not go free of this."

"Indeed he shall not. But justice might be better served by awaiting the High King's return," Lancelot said carefully.

"But he might be weeks! This must be dealt with now. I will not have the women under my protection made sport of by King's men."

He nodded slowly. He saw I understood the gravity of the situation. It fell to Lancelot to punish Agravaine and make his hot-headed opponent his deadly enemy for life. But it was a matter of honor, and Lancelot understood it well.

"Do you wish to be present when I confront him?"

"I most certainly do."

"Think carefully on this, my lady. He has little control of his tongue."

"There is no other choice. He violated my protection. I must be there."

Lancelot glanced sadly toward the sleeping girl. "What is the maid's wish? Does she wish to wed him?"

"No. Yesterday, perhaps it was her ambition. But now she would not take him as a gift."

His eyebrows lifted. He inclined his head. "I shall send for him first thing in the morning."

"Lock him up tonight. Now. Put him in the tower under guard. He does not deserve a moment's freedom while she endures this pain."

Everyone was staring. Lancelot met my eyes and waited. He commanded Camelot. This was in his purview, not in mine. But I was his Queen, and he had sworn to obey me. Yet I knew, even as I glared at him, that I could no more try to command him than I could try to command Arthur. With as much grace as I could summon, I made him a low reverence.

"Forgive me, my lord. I am in an intolerable position."

He moved instinctively toward me, but stopped himself at once. Before others, he would not even touch me. "I understand your anger, Guinevere. The man who did this will be punished. But I cannot imprison Agravaine until I have confronted him and heard his defense. You know this well. It is not Arthur's way."

"But in the meantime, she suffers. It is not fair."

"No," he agreed in a gentle voice, "it is not fair. But I will not make two injustices where before there was only one."

"As you will, my lord."

"Thank you, my lady." Then he guarded his face and said carefully, "I think you might investigate the manner of the man's entry into these apartments."

I was startled. Since Agravaine had been her lover, I had assumed Claire had let him in. "What does my lord mean? Linet, did she not give him entrance herself?" The frightened girl shook her head and cowered in Ailsa's arms. "Then how did he come to be here?" But she could not speak, before all these people, and merely shook with fright. Somewhat impatiently, I turned to Lancelot. "If you know aught of this, sir, please tell me."

He cleared his throat, frowning. "There is a way in, through the postern gate, into the ladies' garden. It is known in the barracks as the Gate of Heaven."

"Who dares to call it so!" I cried indignantly. Of course I knew of the gate; Lancelot himself had come that way once. On the thought, I felt my face flush with color, then grew angry at my own reaction. I was innocent; he had come to me for private talk, not for love. I lifted my chin and faced him. "I take responsibility for that. Henceforward the gate shall be sealed. And while we are speaking of garden gates, does my lord still have the key to the gate of my private garden, which Sir Kay gave you many years ago? If so, I should be glad to have it returned." I held out my upturned palm.

Linet and Ailsa gasped aloud; but Lancelot's composure never wavered. I saw from the flicker in his eyes that he guessed at Agravaine's accusation.

"It is in my possession, my lady, but not upon my person. I will have my chamberlain bring it to you, immediately I return to my apartments. I beg your pardon for keeping it so long; it had slipped my mind I had it."

I nodded. He had said before witnesses what I had given him the opportunity to say.

"I accept your apology. Until this matter arose, I had forgotten, also. Clearly, I must guard my women more closely than before. I am beholden to you for your advice."

He bowed, and after promising to call me in the morning before Agravaine was brought before the Council, he left. The physician left close on his heels, and we women were alone.

I turned to Linet. "Is this true, what Sir Lancelot tells me? Have many men gained entrance by the postern gate? Speak, Linet, and do not fear me. But I must know the truth."

"Since I have been here, my lady, Agravaine and Gaheris are the only ones I know of. But it is rumored that over the years—" She stopped, seeing my face. I had been a fool not to suspect it, as several of the maids who served me had got pregnant first and husbands later.

"Has Gareth been here? Or Mordred?"

"No, no!" Linet cried, weeping. "Oh, no! Don't think it! Gareth would not, my lady! And Sir Mordred—what would he want with your waiting women?" She clapped her hand over her mouth and turned away, sobbing. I gave it up. There was nothing to be done now but deal with Agravaine. But my heart was heavy that night, for I felt myself partly to blame, through negligence, of what had happened to poor little Claire.

Had the full Court been assembled, Agravaine would have been called to the Round Hall to be accused before his fellow knights. But most of the Companions had gone with the King; others were traveling the Kingdom as knights errant. Only a few remained in Camelot. These, Lancelot assembled in the King's library, before he had Agravaine brought in. I sat on his right hand, as Agravaine's accuser in Claire's place.

Gareth came with him. It was clear from his bewilderment that he had not spoken to Linet and did not know why his brother was summoned before the Council. But I saw that Agravaine knew. He stood somewhat defiantly before the assembled knights, and his smile, when he bowed to me, was nothing short of insolent.

"Agravaine of Orkney, son of Lot," Lancelot began, "there is a formal charge laid against you which I call you to defend."

"Who brings this charge?" he asked boldly, looking about him at the gathered warriors.

"I bring it," I said slowly. "I bring it on behalf of a maiden in my service, whom you have beaten and maimed."

I saw Gareth pale and look swiftly at his brother. It was a mean offense and beneath him, but he saw the truth of it in his brother's face, and it sickened him.

"Last night," Lancelot continued, "you secretly entered the apartments of the Queen's ladies and beat a girl named Claire of Swiftwater, whose father serves King Pelleas. There is a witness to the beating; one Linet, daughter of Lucius of York." Here Gareth flushed and then began to anger. At least, I thought irrelevantly, her affection for him was returned. But Agravaine seemed unaffected. He just stood there and looked at Lancelot with hate.

"I witnessed the harm you did the girl, as did the King's physician and the Queen. She will never speak again, nor chew. Her jaw is broken." The knights looked astonished and murmured among themselves. They were gentlemen all, and such behavior had been beneath them, even as boys. "What have you to say in your defense?" Lancelot asked.

Agravaine sneered. "Since when is it a crime to strike a woman? The wench contradicted me. She deserved it."

I shot to my feet, trembling in fury, so angry I could find no words to speak. He did not even bother to deny it! Lancelot took me gently by the wrist and held tight. Gareth pulled futilely at Agravaine's elbow. Lancelot rose and forced me slowly back into my chair.

"It has been a crime in Britain," he said to Agravaine in cold rage, "since the day that Arthur wed Guinevere. This is not Orkney; this is a civilized land. The King respects women, and so do all those who enjoy his favor. You are a coward, boy, to raise your hand to one who has no defense against you. I am ashamed of you; so is your own brother. Where is your honor?"

"You dare to call me coward! If you think," Agravaine sputtered furiously, "that I am going to stand here and listen to *you* speak of honor! You, of all men! You, you snake in the grass! We all know what goes on whenever the King's back is turned! Your lust is infamous! We know you lie with the—"

"Agravaine!" Gareth cried in horror. "Be still, I pray you! If you force his hand, and he calls you out, you are a dead man. Think twice, I beg you! For our dead mother's sake; for the sake of our exiled brother; Gaheris needs you living. Curb your tongue!"

The anguished words got through to him, and Agravaine stood silent, flushed with anger. Lancelot himself was barely in control of his temper. But he did not want to have to kill Arthur's nephew and begin a blood feud. If he killed one of them, he would have to kill them all.

Into the strained silence, I spoke. "The girl has been permanently maimed. She will never be able to speak; she will never marry. You have robbed her of her future. Unless you make her restoration, her father will be after your head."

But Agravaine was not ready to admit defeat. "I demand a hearing of the full court. I will not be judged by this—this conspiracy of intimates. I will go to my uncle the High King—"

"Yes," I cut in softly, "why don't you do that? Go tell Arthur how you violated my protection, how you insulted the Queen's privacy and tarnished her name." Agravaine went white. He knew well that Arthur had, more than once, risked personal combat against better men then Agravaine, to save my name. "You dare not do it. It is as much as your life is worth." He swallowed, and Gareth took him aside, speaking to him softly and furiously. They argued for several minutes, while Lancelot canvassed the other knights and found, as he expected, that they were unanimous in their condemnation of his act.

At last Agravaine shrugged Gareth off and turned back to Lancelot, looking sullen.

"If I am in the wrong, I beg your pardon," he said gruffly. "I lost my temper with the girl. I did not mean to harm her."

"That's as it may be," Lancelot said flatly, "but harm you have done. And restoration you shall make, as much as is in your power. Her future is in her own hands. If she chooses to retire to a religious house, you will pay her upkeep, you and your heirs, for her lifetime. If she chooses to return to her father, you will pay what ransom he deems fit."

Agravaine was aghast. "And if I cannot pay it?"

"What you cannot pay in coin, you must pay with service, by the sweat of your brow. The Earl of Swiftwater will have work that needs doing. Every religious house has the need of strong man's labor. One way or the other, you are responsible for her."

Agravaine shifted from one foot to the other, while Gareth continued to urge him to accept this judgment. I could see that he was debating whether he might not do better if he brought the case to Arthur, but he did not wish to risk the power of my pleading with the King. At last he gave way and shrugged gracelessly. "As my lord wills."

Lancelot inclined his head. "So is this judgment given and accepted. Take care, Agravaine, that you do it. I myself shall hold you to it."

Unbelievably, Agravaine smiled slowly. "As long as you have power, you can try." Gareth grabbed his arm and, bowing quickly to me and to Lancelot, dragged him away, still whispering furiously.

The nearest of the Companions turned to Lancelot. "My lord, you have made an enemy this day."

Lancelot sighed wearily. "I have indeed. But I saw no way around it."

"There was no other way," I assured him. "You have done the right thing; if he despises you, it is to your credit. Think no more upon him."

"On the contrary," Lancelot said. "When we go on maneuvers, I shall keep him in my own company, where I can keep an eye on him. I want no foment at home while the King is on such a delicate mission."

"Can you not take Gareth, as a page? He seems able to influence him for the good."

Lancelot's expression softened, and he looked at me gratefully. "An excellent idea. Gareth will be a comfort to us both. I thank you, my gracious Queen, for the suggestion."

"Anything," I replied lightly, meeting his eyes, "to bring you ease."

Lancelot took the army out the next morning, and they stayed on maneuvers within half a day's ride of Cerdic's stronghold until Arthur and his cavalry left the Saxon Shore and rode into their camp to join them. They all returned to Camelot together on a hot, dusty day in August. I stood on the castle steps with Kay and Ailsa and several other of my women who had husbands among the returning knights. They were a weary group when they arrived, hot and covered with grime. By my order, Varric had prepared the King a hot bath, and I sent him to it as soon as the greetings were over. He looked tired, but not unhappy, so although he said nothing of what had passed, I knew the meetings had gone well.

Mordred and Lancelot came up the steps together behind the King, followed by Bedwyr and Gawaine. Their faces were set, and except when they greeted me, none of them smiled. This, I thought, was Morgause's legacy: The seed of discord was sown in Arthur's Court and had taken root. Agravaine himself I did not see. He must have kept well out of sight among the soldiers.

I went in to wait in the library garden. When he had washed the dust of travel off and changed his clothes, Mordred came to me there. We sat by the fountain, where the splash of water cooled the air and hid the sound of our words from other ears. He was eager to tell me all about the journey and about the strange sights he had seen. They had been well treated, he assured me, royally so. Cerdic himself was an old man now, and attended by his son Cynewulf, who was just short of Arthur's age. This man had the look of a warrior, fierce and stern, but Cerdic was still the leader. He was a legend among his own people. It seemed, Mordred said, that each village had its own king, and until Cerdic had united the West Saxons, one village had had little in common with its neighbor. Even now, the West Saxons felt themselves a people apart from the East Saxons and South Saxons. They spoke of these tribes as if they were separate peoples, and not all from the same homeland.

"It sounds like Britain, before Arthur," I said.

Mordred nodded. "Cerdic is no Arthur, though. He has united the West Saxons, but so far as I could tell, looks no further. But as reverently as Cerdic was treated, it was nothing to how they treated Arthur. They never stopped staring at him. He was a legend come to life. The servants shook as they served him, afraid to touch even his cloak. He was served first, even before Cerdic, and given the best of everything. Nothing was too good for him."

I smiled. "And rightly so. They can never defeat him."

"Well," Mordred said, "Cerdic at least knows that. I don't know about Cynewulf. And truly, my lady, I doubt it would be possible to push them into the sea. They are too many, and have been there too long. Cerdic himself was born there, and his father before him."

"Yes. Which is why we must deal with them. Tell me how it was and what agreement you came to."

Mordred hesitated, then chose his words with care. "I think perhaps it will take more time than I had envisioned, my lady. You see, they are not, well, not really civilized, at least by our standards." I could see he was disappointed, but did not want to disappoint me. "They govern by council. All the thegns have a voice; Cerdic is war leader, that is the role of the king."

"And when there is not war?" I asked him.

"Then his role is diminished. In Cerdic's case, his reputation as leader is well established, and no one questions his authority, but this is unusual. When Cynewulf becomes leader, he will have to prove himself. This much I gathered from Cynewulf himself, for we had some time for private speech. He of course talked about wars with the South Saxons, but that was probably no more than a diplomatic choice. They very clearly want more land and are looking westward."

"So you think we will have peace only until Cerdic dies?"

Mordred shrugged, looking down. "That is what the King thinks."

"And you, Mordred? What is your assessment?"

He looked up, and the eagerness was back in his face. "I think we have no time to waste. If there is war ahead, we will be ready to fight it. But if we can establish trade links with the West Saxons, then they might have something to lose by attacking us; at the same time, if we send them goods from a civilized culture, dressed stone, bricks, iron plows, wool garments, imported silks and tapestries, jewelry—why, everything that we can do that they cannot, then perhaps we may raise the level of their living and make them more like us."

"What, have they not these things now?"

"Well, they have jewelry. It is of beaten gold or copper, all in the shapes of animals. The workmanship is skilled, but the design is primitive. Why, when the queen saw what you had sent her, the whole tribe was amazed. They could not believe that human hands had made that sapphire net or worked that necklace. They thought it was from our gods." He grinned. "And you were right, my lady. When Cerdic's queen was told the net was for her hair, she had it redressed on the spot and wore it."

I laughed. "All women are alike in their vanity."

"You have her thanks." His black eyes twinkled. "They have heard of you there, of your great beauty, your white-gold hair and your dark-blue eyes and your ageless skin. They have a song about you, which they sang for us on our first night there." I blushed to hear this and lowered my eyes, but Mordred continued. "They picture you as a warrior queen, riding a war stallion and holding aloft a jeweled sword." I gasped in dismay, and Mordred laughed. "Don't worry, I think the image is patterned after one of their warrior goddesses. It is a great mark of respect."

I rose and paced before the fountain, wringing my hands. "You don't know how much I regret ever having touched the Sword! I wish I had not done it!"

Mordred rose and stood awkwardly. "Be easy, my lady. The King does not regret it, this I know. So why should you? He says you saved the Kingdom that day. He recalls it with fondness."

I stilled myself and smiled at him. "He is a good man, and generous with his praise. But I was wrong to do it, and this every one of his soldiers knows. But about the Saxons, Mordred, I am amazed at what you have told me. What do you mean they have no bricks or stone? Can this be true?"

"Oh, yes. They build entirely with wood. None of the buildings is very big, and the roofs are all of thatch. The walls of most are only sticks and branches, bound together and cemented with wattle. They dig pits, and have their floors below the level of the earth, to keep out drafts. In the larger dwellings, these are boarded over and serve as storage places beneath the floor. The only dwelling we saw that looked like it took more than a day to construct was Cerdic's own meeting hall. A single room only, but very long, with a hole in the middle of the roof, above the hearth, for the firesmoke. This is where all of Arthur's party slept, and where we met and dined, for it was the only place big enough to hold us all. I tell you, my lady, such a place as this"—and he spread his arms wide to indicate the whole of the castle—"this would surpass Cerdic's power of imagination. They would not believe it unless they saw it." He smiled again. "I know, because I tried to describe it, but Cynewulf thought I was boasting."

I stood amazed. How could such primitive peoples wield such power? How could they ever have threatened to destroy us?

"What are their horses like?" I asked, knowing they had them, although they did not use them for war.

Mordred grinned again and shook his head. "You would laugh to see them. They are more like ponies than horses, thick-bodied and short-legged, dun-colored, with stripes down their backs. And small eyes."

I thought of the animals in Lancelot's care, those tall, fleet, graceful steeds with large, dark eyes that spoke of their foreign blood. No wonder neither Lancelot nor Mordred doubted the Saxon grooms!

"Do they use iron at all?" I wondered.

"Yes," Mordred replied. "In their weapons. I make no disparaging comparisons there. They don't use swords much—I saw some, but I did wonder if they were taken from our dead in battle. But their spears are full seven feet long and tipped with cold iron. And their two-headed axes." He shuddered. "They tie feathers to them for each man the ax eats—they think of them as live things, needing sacrifice. I saw many of them. Cerdic's own was so covered with feathers it could be taken for a bird. And each one stood for the life of a Briton." His voice went cold and low and deadly; I stared openly at him. I had never seen this hard anger in him until now. But he was Pendragon, and speaking of Saxons. Perhaps it ran in the blood.

"And did you, Mordred, have a sense of whether the thegns are more interested in war than peace?"

He shrugged. "They want more land. They live by farming. The soil thereabout is rich and fertile but their numbers press upon them. They are excellent boatmen; their craft are shallow and they prefer to navigate waterways and settle by them. They don't build roads. They want territory inland from Rutupiae, on the river Thames. They would prefer not to fight for it, if they can bargain for it instead. This is what Arthur holds out to them, to bind them as a buffer state between the Alemans, the Burgundians, the Franks, and us. At the moment, they are pleased at the prospect of more talk. I do not think they will try war. At least"— and here he gulped—"not while Arthur lives."

He said no more. I wondered if he was thinking of his oath not to outlive the King, the oath that had made Arthur so angry.

"Well, then, it sounds like a successful journey, taken all in all," I said. "Be not disheartened. It is a small step, but a step nevertheless. And if you had not been here to champion this cause, dear Mordred, I know well the High King would never have gone." I paused, but he said nothing. Clearly, there was something on his mind. "And now, to more immediate matters. I assume Lancelot has told the King what passed with Agravaine." His eyes flew to my face, but their expression was carefully guarded. "How does this place you, Mordred? You may not love him, but he is your half brother."

He shifted uncomfortably and struggled with himself awhile. "Why do you always ask me such pointed questions?" he said at last. "Most women would skirt such unpleasant issues, but you always face them head-on. It's as hard as answering the King."

I put a hand on his arm and felt him tremble. "It is my way," I replied gently. "I am unwomanly, perhaps, but then, I am Queen. How can I aid and advise my lord if know nothing of these things? I am chained to his castle, Mordred. I cannot go where you go; the King does not take me on his travels. When once he did—well, you know what happened. I am a danger to him outside these walls. So I have no way of knowing what passes within Britain, if the men I love will not speak to me."

He slid to the flagstones at my feet and kissed my hand. "Oh, dearest Guinevere! I meant no disrespect, you must believe me! Unwomanly! How could you think it? I meant only—"

"Hush, Mordred," I said, smiling and ruffling his hair. "I know what you meant. Do not be afraid to speak your mind. You are my son. I will keep your counsel."

He collected himself then and met my eyes. "Well," he said at last, "I condemn Agravaine, of course, for his base action. And I cannot deny that Sir Lancelot's judgment was fair. But—"

"But?"

"But it would have been more politic to wait for the King's return," he said carefully. "There are those who object to the judgment because it was Lancelot who gave it. Had he waited for Arthur—"

"Ahhhh. He wished to. But I would not let him, for the maid's sake. He knew well it would make him an enemy, but for my sake he went ahead. You cannot deny his courage, Mordred."

"No, madam, I do not. But he has made more enemies than only Agravaine. There is a faction of young men growing . . . Agravaine has sway with them. Most of them think it no great crime to strike a woman. They think Lancelot a proud man who reaches too high. They also think—" He stopped and lowered his eyes.

"Yes," I said sadly, "I know what they think." Mordred still looked away, and I turned to face him. "And you, Mordred? What do you think?" He looked up then, and again I could not read his thoughts.

"I believe what you tell me, my lady," he said quietly. "You have told me the rumors are not true. But that does not mean Lancelot has nothing to fear."

"So he told me himself."

Mordred's eyes widened. "I am glad he knows it. There are those who would dislodge him from his place near the King. Please, my lady, guard yourself when you are with him, for the very walls have eyes." He stood abruptly and bowed. "Forgive me if I have said too much."

"No, Mordred, you have told me nothing I did not already know. Are there any—any men of Arthur's age who feel the same?"

"Not to my knowledge," he replied. "These are all young hotheads eager for action. This long peace does not suit them. And since they dare not speak against the King, they plot against his second-in-command."

"And you?" I said softly. "You play a double role here, do you not? They think you are one of them. Is this hard for you?"

A bitter smile touched his lips. "Oh, I am used to that, my lady. I have played a double role for most of my life, it seems. They trust me because they know I have no love for Lancelot."

He straightened suddenly and squared his shoulders. I turned to follow his gaze and saw the King coming out from the library.

"Say nothing to the King about Lancelot!" Mordred warned. "He will not hear it talked of!"

Mordred bowed to his father. I went to greet him, and as always, he took me in his arms and kissed me warmly.

I smiled up into his face. "Welcome home, my lord."

"Thank you, Gwen. I am sorry you and Lancelot had trouble while I was gone."

I glanced swiftly at Mordred, but his eyes were politely on the ground. "I am sorry, too, my lord. The timing was poor; but we did not choose it."

He sighed and handed me back to my seat. He sat beside me, where Mordred had been, and Mordred moved back far enough to give us private speech.

"I have spoken with Agravaine," he said, coming directly to the point. "I have told him that had I been here, his punishment would have been harsher, for the King cannot ever give the appearance of favoring his relations and still be considered just. I would have had him dismissed from my service, as well. There is no honor in hating women."

"How did he take this?"

"Oh," Arthur said, his mouth twisting in a grim smile, "he did not like it. But there was nothing he could say. I wanted to make him feel he had got off lightly, but he is determined to carry a grievance against Lancelot." He paused. "Is the maid still here? I would have a word with her."

I took his hand and kissed it fervently. "Oh, my lord, I bless you for this. Yes, she is here. As soon as the swelling has subsided, she will send for her father and go home. The physicians say she may not travel yet."

"The poor girl," he said sadly. "I will send her with a royal escort when the time comes. I will do her all the honor I can, seeing he is my nephew, and my responsibility."

"Thank you, my gracious lord. It will mean much to her. It means much to me."

He slid an arm about my waist, pulling me closer. "I know not what it is in their blood, that makes them treat women so. Perhaps they always hated Morgause and did not know it. I am thankful that Lancelot dealt with Agravaine so fairly. Even so . . ." He let it drift.

"Mordred and I have been talking about the Saxons," I said, to change the direction of his thoughts. "Are you pleased with the mission, or do you think it was a mistake to go?"

"Oh, I am well satisfied. They fear us still; they know our power. My demands are reasonable. They will not break the peace." He turned and beckoned Mordred forward to join us. "It will take time, but we will get their cooperation in a defense treaty."

He talked for some while about the journey, including Mordred in the conversation, but it became slowly clear to me that he was keeping something back; that he was speaking optimistically for his son's sake, or for mine, but hiding something dark behind his words. When at last Mordred begged to be excused, Arthur embraced him and let him go. I watched him out of earshot and turned immediately to the King.

"And now, my lord," I said, laying a hand on him arm to prevent his going, "what is amiss? Tell me your true thoughts. Is there war ahead?"

He looked startled and then chagrined. "You would make life easier for me, Gwen, if you did not know me so well."

But I would not be diverted. "Tell me, Arthur. I can see in your face, you do not believe we can ever deal with Saxons."

He frowned and began his steady pacing, hands clasped behind his back. "All right, then. You are right. I do not trust them. As long as I live, they will be our buffer. They have no choice in that. But what you and Mordred dream of, that they should become part of us one day, whether through trade or any other means—no, this I do not believe will happen."

"Why not?"

"They are savages," he said shortly. "Cerdic is a gentleman by their standards, yet you would certainly call him a savage. The differences between us are too great. What you dream of will take more time than we have." He spoke fiercely and with conviction. "Cerdic talked of tribes in the far eastern lands, more primitive and savage than even the Saxons. They are on the move. They are leaving their grasslands and crossing the mountains in the hope of plunder. They destroy everything in their path. These are the people who are pushing the Saxons out of their homeland, who are pushing the Burgundians westward and northward, who are pushing the

Franks. Eventually, we, too, will be pushed. While I live, if Merlin is to be believed, we can hold them." He stopped suddenly and turned to me. His eyes were dark. "But after I am gone, will we be strong enough to stop them? They will come across the border like the storm tide over a sea wall."

"Then you must live, my lord! Live until we have civilized the Saxons!"

He laughed, but there was no mirth in it. "Then must I live five hundred years!" He shook his head. "No, Guinevere. They will never be like us. We are so far beyond them, you would find it difficult to imagine. When they come across the border, they will kill everyone in their path. They know not mercy, nor honor, as we see it. They will kill for the sheer joy of taking life. Their axes thirst for blood. It will not be like the Romans. The Saxons will destroy us, or drive us into the hills and starve us. Either way, we will be gone. They are our fate."

"My lord Arthur!" I cried, falling to the ground in tears, wringing my hands. "Oh, no! God would not allow such things to happen! All this that you have built cannot go for naught! You have made Britain! We were tribes ourselves, and now we are a nation! Please do not think we ever could go back! What has happened to you to drive you to such black thoughts?"

He came to me, raised me gently, and held me close. "I'm so sorry, Guinevere. Do forgive me. It was thoughtless of me to distress you so."

"No, my lord, I asked for your true thoughts. If these are they—I brought them upon myself, and I thank you for your honesty. But do you really think these things?"

He shrugged and kissed the tears from my face. "Sometimes. I had bad dreams there. Perhaps it was the unaccustomed food."

"Can we speak with Niniane? Could she not dispel these fears?"

"I have asked her this before. She sees no further than my death." I shuddered, and he pressed me closer. "Let it be, Gwen. If it comes, it comes. In the meantime, we will do what we can to avert it. That is why I went, after all. In case there is some possibility of preventing annihilation."

"Is that why you went, my lord? I cannot believe that such a primitive people could destroy a civilized land. If we are so far advanced, how can they conquer us?"

"The example lies everywhere before us," he replied. "Even Rome herself is not immune, if some of the strange tales that have reached this shore are true. When men rise above the level of killing for joy, like Bedwyr, Lancelot, myself—we leave ourselves vulnerable to those who still have savage instincts, like Agravaine, Gaheris, Gawaine."

"You must be stronger than they."

"Yes. As long as we are stronger, we shall hold them." He said no more, and my thoughts cowered before the vision of Britain without Arthur. But he was in his prime—surely, we could look ahead to thirty or more years of peace! And who knew what the Saxons would be like in thirty years?

"Tell me of Gawaine," I said, to change the subject. "Does he back a treaty with the Saxons? Does he feel his brother unjustly punished?"

Arthur sighed and, taking my arm, began walking. "For once, Gawaine is holding his own counsel. I have told him clearly what I expect from him. I fear he thinks Agravaine's punishment too severe—if he is willing to forgive Gaheris the killing of their mother, he is not likely to see a mere beating as much of a crime, although it was base. But I have told him I abhor it and, as his King and uncle, will hold Agravaine to Lancelot's judgment. If Gawaine wants to rule in Orkney, he will see things my way or keep quiet. It is as much as his future is worth to oppose Lancelot. In anything." His voice was cold.

"It seems," I said slowly, "that Gawaine is learning some hard lessons rather fast."

"Let us hope it makes a man of him." He came to a halt and, drawing a deep breath, took both my hands and faced me. "Oh, yes, and Gwen"—he hesitated for a fraction—"I am to let you know that Lancelot leaves for Lanascol tomorrow."

This was news to me, and I am afraid my face gave that away. "But why, my lord? He is not in danger?"

Arthur smiled. "When did he ever turn his face from danger? No, he asked permission to go home to see his wife's grave. He will be back before winter and will bring his eldest son with him." The laughter lines deepened at the corners of his eyes. "And you will have another boy to raise."

"Oh, Arthur, that would be wonderful, if Lancelot is willing." But I was thinking, Why had he not told me this himself? Why send Arthur? Then Arthur lifted my hand to his lips and kissed it, and held it against his smooth, shaved cheek. His eyes were deep with some great grief.

"What is it, Arthur?" I whispered. "Does he not have your blessing?"

He started three times to speak, but could not bring himself to it. I began to fear he had some dreadful news to tell me.

"Arthur, what is it? Will aught happen to him while he is away? Has Niniane seen anything?"

"No," he said gently, "not that. Be easy, Gwen."

"What then?"

He drew a deep breath and spoke. "You both have heard the rumors. I want you to know that it is my wish that he bring his son to Camelot, and that you and Lancelot raise him together. It would give you both great joy to be as parents to the boy. I would like to see it. He has had so little joy in his life."

I dared not breathe. He had himself broached the forbidden subject! While he struggled to find the words, I held hard to his hand.

"What joy he has found, Gwen, he has found with you. I bless you for that."

"Arthur!"

"I know it cannot be helped. But it grieves me that I should be the cause of his suffering. His is such a noble heart!"

"My dearest lord!" I cried, blinking back tears and taking him in my arms. "It is not your fault! He loves you better than his own self, and his joy is to serve you!" I felt how he trembled, and I laid my head against his chest.

"There is nothing to be done. I will not give you up," he said.

"I would not go."

"It is God's will, I suppose. But it is cruel. I would ease his pain by any means in my power. But you are the means, Gwen."

I raised my face to his. "My sweet lord, I will with pleasure raise his son, if he wills. But it is because of you that he brings him here. You are the lodestone that draws us all to your side. Arthur, do not pretend it is me! We are none of us anything without you."

He kissed me with sudden feeling, right there in the garden, and I heard the quick, soft steps and gentle rustling of courtiers, knights, and servants fading swiftly into the castle depths, leaving the King alone.

43 👑 THE HEIR

From the first, Galahad foiled the King's plans. Although the boy was an eager student of Bedwyr and Valerius, he would learn nothing from me. He was always polite, at times overly so, but his heart was closed to me. He was only five years old when he first came to Camelot, yet already Elaine had trained his thoughts against me. And against Lancelot. I was shocked to find that so young a lad disliked his father. His boyhood hero had been his uncle Galahantyn, whom he worshipped. As time went by, and Galahantyn spent more time in Lanascol, holding Lancelot's lands and caring for his younger sons, this worship Galahad transferred to Arthur. Bedwyr encouraged this, hoping that as he grew older, and saw how Arthur loved Lancelot, he might in time be softened toward him. But this did not happen.

Galahad was a strange boy. Like Mordred, he was quiet and held his tongue. One never caught him in a hasty speech or careless act. Even at five, he was serious and thoughtful. But while Mordred loved life and could laugh at himself, Galahad rarely smiled and had no sense of humor. When he was not at lessons, or learning riding or swordplay, he was in the chapel praying. He thirsted for a glory unattainable even in Arthur's Kingdom.

He had a great disdain for beauty, whether in man or woman; he thought it a temptation to do evil. This was odd, for he himself promised to outdo both his father and uncle in physical beauty. He preferred plain clothing, wore no decoration, and shunned all forms of ceremonial trappings. Had he been ugly, it would have pleased him better. He sought holiness in squalor, Lancelot said. It was the only unkind thing I ever heard him say of his son. But it was true. I sometimes wondered if his young life was a burden to him, the way he bore it so solemnly.

As time went by, I saw clearly that his dislike of me and his disapproval of his father were grounded in our love for one another. This was perfectly understandable. If the boy had loved his mother dearly, he must have seen that his father did not. And when he came to Camelot, he must have discovered, as everyone else had, it was I who had Lancelot's heart. Naturally, then, he despised me. I tried every way I could think of to reach him and make him think better of me, but to no avail. Lancelot and I both grieved for him. Had he been blessed with a more loving, open nature, he might have given us such joy. But he was not that kind of child.

His censure of us hurt his father deeply and put a strain upon the affection between us. Lancelot was careful never to be with me alone, and when we were with others he forebore to touch me. Even the ceremonial kiss of greeting he denied himself, when his son was watching. Since we were no longer easy with one another, we began to long for each other more and miss the companionship we had shared for so many years. Some nights I could not sleep, wishing only for the touch of his hand in mine. Thus, on the rare occasions when circumstance threw us together unobserved, and this long smoldering passion found vent, we were driven close to the edges of control and left quaking with fear at the strength of our feelings. I began to see how wise Arthur had been to let us be; with freedom, this other long love had not endangered that I felt for the King. But now, this maddening pattern of long restraint and brief, fierce release looked to drive us both toward some disastrous conclusion.

Lancelot could not ignore his son's censure. "He is my conscience speaking," he would say to me. "He knows that in my heart, I sin against God, for I covet what is Arthur's. I am not able to ignore him." Pleading with him did no good. He felt he deserved the torture the boy put him through. But I did not feel I deserved it, and there was no one I could confide in. I certainly could not talk to Arthur about it. He would let no one bring the subject up in his presence; and even when we were alone together, he would steer around it. Since the day he had opened his heart to me about Lancelot, he had grown so sensitive, it was as if he protected a tender wound. My love for Lancelot he had accepted long ago, but he did not want to be reminded. On occasion I would find him looking at us both with help-less compassion, but truly, there was nothing he could do.

Galahad's closest friend at court was young Gareth. Although the Orkney prince was nine years his senior, Galahad was always ahead of his age in everything. Gareth treated him as a beloved younger brother and took him on outings and taught him tricks with bow, sword, and spear. He had the boy's confidence, if anyone had. And yet, although Gareth loved and honored Lancelot above all men, he was never able to sway Galahad toward a more lenient regard for his father.

When Gareth entered Arthur's service at fifteen, he and Linet became formally betrothed. Being a gentleman, he promised her he would not come to her bed until they were married. Before that, he wished to have the ap-proval of her father, who lived in York. So one fine spring day in Gareth's sixteenth year, Arthur sent Gareth and Gawaine on a mission to Festus, governor of York. He had appealed to Arthur for settlement of a minor dis-pute among the bishops there, which touched not on religion but on their property. Gawaine was now a man of eighteen, newly knighted, and one of the King's Companions. This was the first time he had been the leader of a diplomatic mission, and he carried himself with great pride. He did not know that Arthur was relying on Gareth's presence to ensure that proper judgment was rendered.

Linet's father Lucius was a prominent man in York, a landowner and a knight in good standing with Festus and with Drustan, King of Elmet, whose stronghold at Caer Mord lay but a day's ride beyond. Linet's grand-father was old Caius Lucius, who had served with both Ambrosius and Uther in Britain's wars and had gained for himself the honorable reputation of being the most battle-scarred man in the Kingdom. He was himself de-scended from a Roman governor in the time of Maximus. Linet could hardly come of higher lineage, and the match pleased both Arthur and Lucius.

Festus held a great feast upon their arrival, and unbeknownst to them, he had invited Drustan himself to the celebration. Drustan was a big man, a graybeard by this time, but hard as iron and with a reputation of a tough and deadly fighter. He was a proud man and had only been slowly won to Arthur's service. But the Angles lived close along his southern borders, and he saw the sense in uniting against the barbarian foe. He was an honest sol-dier and a just man, and since he gave thought to what he did, he had small patience for quick tempers or hotheadedness. Thus he was not well pleased to find Gawaine sitting near his elbow at dinner, for Lamorak, whom Gawaine had sworn to kill, was his nephew by marriage. Being Drustan, he took this bull by the horns and asked Gawaine outright how the matter now stood with him.

"Are you my sworn enemy, Sir Gawaine?" was how he put it. "Or, have you grown into sense since you swore vengeance upon my nephew Lamorak?"

He had a booming voice, and everyone near him heard this: Gareth, Festus, Lucius, and a score of other men. Gawaine had to think quickly, which was never his strength. He and Gareth were surrounded by Elmet's friends, and many of Drustan's own soldiers sat in the hall. And even Gareth might not defend him, for he abhorred blood feuds. To declare himself Drustan's enemy would be the height of folly. So he denied it.

"My lord," Gawaine said stiffly, "I bear no one in your house ill will. Once I was Lamorak's enemy, for I felt he shamed our mother. But it is true that our mother was herself as guilty as he."

"Then you forgive Lamorak," Drustan pressed, "and withdraw your challenge to him?"

Gawaine swallowed hard. "Yes, my lord. As far as I am concerned, he is one of the High King's Companions, as I am, and I would greet him as such."

Drustan slapped him hard upon the back. "I am glad you have come to your senses, lad!" he cried. "For I have called Lamorak out of his Breton fastness and bid him stay the summer with me. I intend to apply to King Arthur to have him accepted as one of your number in Camelot. It is appropriate he should have your backing. Thank you, boy. You may tell the King, when you return, that Lamorak should be here by the solstice."

Gawaine was silent and continued so for the rest of his visit in York. This was unlike him, as everyone knew, but no one could fathom the cause. The judgment he gave in the bishops' case was a fair one, being a compromise, and everyone praised his sense. When he left, he left with everyone's thanks and best wishes. Gareth stayed on at Caer Mord at Drustan's invitation; Gawaine returned to us alone.

He never gave Arthur Drustan's message. Instead, he gave it to Agravaine, who was in secret communication with Gaheris. In doing so, he considered he had kept his bargain; for he did not come against Lamorak himself, and he had not promised Drustan, or so he thought, that he would send no other. In this and in other things, his mind worked like a child's. Although even children knew that truth must be told from the heart, and not from the lips only.

One day not long after, Agravaine disappeared. Mordred came to Arthur as he walked with me, to tell him this, and to discover whether the High King had perhaps sent him on a mission. On learning Arthur had done no such thing, Mordred told us he was sure Agravaine was on his way to meet Gaheris.

Arthur frowned. "Where is the boy hiding, Mordred? Do you know?"

"My lord, I know nothing with certainty, but I believe he is somewhere in the hill country west of York."

"And what do you think this disappearance signifies?"

"My lord, I know not, but they rarely dare a meeting. Something important must be going on. And it cannot bode well."

Arthur looked at his son a moment and then nodded. "Well, then, I will send you to York with greetings to Festus and a message to Lucius. Keep your eyes open, Mordred, and see if you can find them or discover what they may be up to. It is time I spoke with those boys. If you can get word to them, say that I have charged you with a message for Gaheris; that if he publicly repents his crime and swears to accept such penance as I shall give him, he may be received again at court."

Mordred bowed. "You are merciful, my lord, to treat the ruffian so. Truly, it is more than he deserves."

Arthur sighed. "Men like Gaheris have a way of getting what they deserve. Yet he is my nephew; I must do what I can for him. Gareth is staying the summer with Drustan; perhaps he can help make Gaheris see sense."

So Mordred departed and Lancelot breathed easier at court. Mordred traveled north into wild and hilly lands. There were still outlaws in the deep forests there, and travel could be chancey, but he was a King's man, well trained and young, and he reached York without trouble. Festus received him with delight.

"You're just in time, my lord," he cried, "to celebrate Lamorak's return from Brittany! He's here now, a guest in my house, and tonight we will feast him long and well!"

Mordred knew at once why Agravaine had come. He asked quietly after the twins; no one knew anything about them. But York was a big place, nearly a city, with a thousand places to hide.

Lamorak was guest of honor at the feast. He looked fit and healthy, and younger, Mordred thought, now that he was free of the witch's curse. The feast lasted late into the night, with an excellent bard and excellent wine, Lamorak's gift from the vineyards of Gaul. Before they broke for bed, Mordred pulled Lamorak aside and bade him take an escort on his journey to Elmet, and told him why. But Lamorak, full of wine and confidence, scoffed at the idea that two such ruffians could harm him.

"Then let me ride with you, Lamorak. If we are together, they will not chance a meeting, and I have messages to give you from the King."

Lamorak grinned drunkenly. "You carry messages from the King? A fine thing—I'd rather go alone than with a bastard of that witch. Oh, all right, Mordred. I owe you my life, after all. If it's so important . . . Be ready at noon, I'll meet you at the town gates."

But when Mordred arrived at the gates near midmorning, he found Lamorak already gone. He had left after breakfast, the sentries told Mordred, he had ridden out alone, chuckling to himself.

Grimly Mordred set his spurs to his horse. After a half-day's hard gallop on the dusty road, he had given up all hope of preventing disaster when he heard shouting beyond the next bend. Summoning one last burst of energy from his exhausted horse, he galloped forward.

He was almost in time. Even as he watched, Lamorak, whose sword was engaged with Agravaine's, was felled from behind by Gaheris in a coward's killing. He toppled from his horse, pulling Gaheris' sword from his hand. Gaheris leaped down and, whipping out his dagger, cut Lamorak's throat. At this Mordred shouted, and his shout was echoed by another farther up the road. Drustan himself had come to greet his nephew and rode forward at the head of a small party of knights. Foremost among them was Gareth, who galloped forward, screaming.

"Agravaine! Gaheris! Touch him not! Oh, oh, what have you done?" He went white when he saw Lamorak was beyond help.

Gaheris retrieved his sword and wiped it on Lamorak's clothing. "Fear not, little brother. I have revenged our mother's honor."

"Honor!" Gareth cried in horror. Then, seeing Mordred: "Dred, are you in this?"

"Certainly not," replied Mordred coolly. "I came to stop them, but I was too slow."

As the High King's deputy, it was his duty to arrest the twins, but already Drustan's troops surrounded the four Orkney boys with drawn swords.

"So," Drustan said, hard and furious, "this is how Sir Gawaine repays my trust! I will see you both hanged."

"You dare not!" Agravaine shouted. "Our uncle the High King will destroy you!"

Gaheris, looking spent now that his goal had been accomplished, remounted sluggishly and swung his horse to Agravaine's side. "We have no quarrel with you, sir. You would be wise to let us go."

"My lord," Gareth quavered, seeing Drustan losing control of his rage, "let me speak with them a moment." Drustan glared at him, then finally nodded and drew his knights away.

Gareth faced the twins, with Mordred behind him. "Please my brothers, be reasonable. You cannot expect him to let you go, when you have killed his nephew in cold blood. You have broken the High King's laws."

"It was a fair fight," Agravaine insisted. "We challenged him outright with his crime."

"Two against one is not fair," protested Gareth.

"I saw the killing," Mordred said quietly, and Gaheris stiffened. "Gaheris took him from behind. That's not in any of the rules of combat I know."

Gareth looked sickened. "You dishonor us all, Gaheris. Drustan is a fair man, and his anger is righteous. Let yourselves be taken captive; behave and beg his pardon. I can probably get you off with your lives."

"The High King—" Agravaine began, but Mordred cut him short.

"I would not wave the High King's name about, as if it were a banner of protection. You know well whose side he will take in this affair. You have shamed Gareth, you have shamed me, and you have shamed Arthur by this deed."

"Then," Gaheris said boldly, "do not tell him of it! You always were a snake in the grass, you bastard brat!"

Mordred stared him down and then turned away to fall back with Drustan's men. But Gaheris, suddenly enraged, raised his sword and attacked. Gareth blocked his way and parried his sword thrust, crying a warning to Mordred. Many things then happened at once: Mordred whirled, Drustan's knights spurred forward, Gaheris attacked Gareth, screaming in fury. Gareth, Lancelot's star pupil, fought his brother off and pierced his sword arm to make him drop the weapon. But one of Drustan's knights, eager for vengeance, threw a spear. It struck Gaheris' chest and came out his back. He screamed and fell from the saddle. Agravaine lifted his sword, to find it taken from his hand by Mordred.

"Don't be a fool," Mordred growled. "That way lies death."

Gareth, in tears, knelt in the dust by his brother, and with Drustan's help cut the spear shaft so he could lie easily on the ground. He was senseless, but did not die. They fashioned a body sling, and several of the knights carried him on foot back to Caer Mord. Lamorak's body was slung over an empty saddle. Gareth rode back beside Agravaine and argued with him all the way. Mordred, feeling both helpless and responsible, rode at Drustan's side. At last Drustan turned to him and spoke.

"I have heard about you, Sir Mordred. You are Arthur's son, are you not? By the witch-queen, mother of these boys?"

Mordred froze. In all his life, he had never been asked this question outright, had never even discussed it except with Arthur and with me. He had grown used to the fact it was a subject everyone avoided. And as the King had not publicly acknowledged him, he was at a loss for a reply. But he felt, after what had just passed, that he owed this man the truth.

"My lord king," he said at last, "I am."

"And why are you here, then? In the cause of your brothers? Or in your father's cause, if the two are different?"

"My lord Drustan, the causes are indeed different. I came north at King Arthur's request to find out how things stood with Gaheris. We suspected Agravaine would get in touch with him, and I had instructions from the King to find them both and discover what they were up to. But I was too late. As for Lamorak, my lord, he was well loved by my father and would have been welcomed back at court. I believe the High King was trying to clear the way to bring him back, when he sent me to seek Gaheris."

"Ah, then Agravaine's boast is a vain one."

"Indeed it is!" Mordred cried. "I have made it clear to him, as well. You need not fear Arthur's vengeance, my lord. His anger will be all on your side. He will never hold Gaheris' death against you."

"And you yourself, Sir Mordred?"

Mordred looked away. "Like Gareth, I am ashamed to be their kin. Gareth is an honorable man. But I have had a bellyful of the others."

Drustan laughed shortly. "It was Gawaine who set this up, for besides Gareth, he alone knew Lamorak was coming. Let King Arthur know this, Mordred, when you return. I have no wish to pit kingdom against kingdom in a blood feud, when we have enemies enough beyond our borders. But let him know that when I next come to Camelot, I would speak with Sir Gawaine. Alone."

Mordred nodded, heartsick and weary. What Arthur had most wished to avoid had come to pass. Morgause's curse lay upon his Kingdom still. With Gaheris dead, and Gawaine's future so threatened, what would Arthur do?

But as it turned out, he did not need to do anything, for Gaheris did not die. He was a year recuperating in Drustan's castle, under guard, but he lived. Mordred and Gareth stayed at Caer Mord a full month, doing Drustan service, and they kept Agravaine with them. Finally, after Agravaine had begged Drustan's pardon most abjectly, Drustan formally forgave him and allowed him to go. For Agravaine had at least engaged Lamorak face to face.

These three returned to Camelot one hot day in July, and that was the first any of us heard about this terrible affair. They came to the King in the library, where he sat working with his scribe, while Bedwyr, Lancelot, and I waited upon his pleasure in the garden. Thus we all heard this tale together. Bedwyr was stricken with sadness; Lancelot alternated between fury at the insult done the King and pride in Gareth's noble behavior. I watched Mordred's face throughout, and saw his grief and his anger at his inability to prevent this tragedy. How he longs for power! I thought to myself. Arthur alone was still.

When they had told everything, all eyes turned to the King. He rose and walked out into the garden, staring at the sky. When he returned, his expression was grim.

"Agravaine." The youth paled and went down on one knee.

"My lord."

"When you took service with me, you took an oath not to lift a sword against any man, save only the King's enemies. Lamorak was not my enemy. He was a trusted knight and still served me. Your oath is broken. You are dismissed from my service." Agravaine gaped, and Gareth closed his eyes in sorrow.

"But, my lord—" Agravaine whispered, unable to believe it.

"Go," Arthur said flatly. "Get your belongings from the barracks. You can find a room in town, if you want to stay. Gawaine will give you protection, no doubt, since I judge you did his bidding." Dumbfounded, Agravaine opened his mouth to protest yet again, but Arthur cut him off, showing temper.

"Be gone before I call the guard!" Agravaine fled.

Arthur paced back and forth, scowling. Lancelot and Bedwyr stood at attention. Mordred and Gareth were on their knees. At last the King sighed deeply and put his anger behind him. He stood before Mordred and Gareth and addressed them solemnly.

"I thank you both for your noble efforts on my behalf. If Drustan remains my ally, you have done me a great service. Gareth, I will honor you publicly in Council; you have shown calm and sense and honor in a matter that must have touched your heart nearly. For this, I am grateful."

"Thank you, my gracious King," Gareth murmured. Arthur raised him, clasped him, and kissed him. "Go to your brother Gawaine and tell him I will see him here in an hour. Try, if you can, to make him see the gravity of this affair."

Gareth promised and withdrew. The King turned back to Mordred, whose dark head was bowed in anguish.

"My lord," he cried, "please forgive my failure! I should have prevented this and could have, if I'd had my wits about me!"

A smile touched Arthur's lips, but Mordred did not see it. "Rise, Mordred, my son. You are not to blame for this."

Mordred's eyes flew to the King's face. Arthur grasped his arms and embraced him. "Even had you ridden at their side, even had you cried a warning to Lamorak, you could not have prevented his slaughter. They would have killed you first, to get to him. And I need you living."

Mordred drew a trembling breath, and color flooded his face. For a moment they stood thus, father and son, holding each other. Bedwyr and Lancelot stood flattened against the walls, staring straight ahead, unseeing—the sentry's stance. Arthur was the first to turn away, deeply moved. "I thank God you and Gareth were there," he said slowly. "As it is, we shall have peace awhile longer, if I can deal with Gawaine. Tell me how Drustan stands in this."

Mordred swallowed, stilled himself, and gave the King his report. Arthur seemed satisfied and nodded.

"There is hope," he said.

"But, sir, there is one thing more. You should know," Mordred said with a tremor in his voice, "you should know that Drustan asked me straight out if I were your son. It was just after the killing, we were bearing Gaheris and

Lamorak back to Caer Mord and he needed to know where I stood. But he asked me, instead, who I was." He hesitated, and the King met his eyes.

"I hope," Arthur said carefully, "that you told him the truth."

"Yes, my lord," Mordred said, relieved. "I could do naught else. So—so now he knows."

From where I stood I could see him shaking, and my heart went out to him. Tell him, Arthur! I cried in my thoughts, it is time to let him know your intentions! But Bedwyr and Lancelot were there, and I did not think he would. Arthur stood looking gravely at his son.

"It is well he knows," he said slowly, "so he will accept you one day as his King, should he outlive me."

Mordred went white; his eyes widened in amazement; my own filled with tears. Lancelot and Bedwyr were staring at the King, Bedwyr with warm approval, Lancelot with frank dismay.

"My lord," Mordred whispered.

Arthur smiled. "You did not think I would leave Britain in Constantine's hands, while my son is living and able? You are my heir, Mordred, none other. Give me another year, and I shall publicly declare it."

"My lord," Mordred breathed again, at a loss for words.

"You have things to learn yet," Arthur said gently. "But you are worthy." Then he grinned. "If you don't believe me, ask the Queen."

When Mordred looked to me, my kerchief was over my face, and I began to weep. This broke the tension, and all the men laughed. I drew Lancelot and Bedwyr out into the garden and left Arthur some time to be alone with his son. At length, we all left him, for Gawaine was due, and he wished to speak with him alone.

While the King met with Gawaine, Mordred sought me out. I had gone to the stables to visit Rajid, and he found me leading the stallion out to graze. When I saw by his face he wanted private speech, I beckoned him to walk with me, and we went down the path to the meadows beyond King's Gate. As we passed the outer ramparts, Mordred lifted a hand, and four sentries fell in smartly behind us. I smiled to myself. Clearly Arthur's soldiers recognized Mordred's authority.

When the stallion had settled down to peaceful grazing, and the sentries stood some fifty paces off, Mordred seemed unable to begin. He fidgeted and looked away, clearly moved by strong emotion.

"Well, Mordred," I said gently. "He has told you now what all Camelot has known for years. And Duke Constantine, as well, unless I miss my guess. You are his heir."

Mordred straightened and met my eyes. "I can hardly believe it. I have both wanted this and feared it."

"Feared it, Mordred? You? Fear power?"

He looked away quickly. "Guinevere, do not forget my oath."

This was the rub. I had half expected it. I reached for his hand and held it tightly in my own. "When you made the oath, Mordred, what was in your mind? Remember back to that day."

"I did not want Lancelot to accuse me of ambition," he admitted.

"Yes. But you are Pendragon. Ambition, the drive to be the best—it is in your blood. Lancelot knows this. And now he knows, as he did not know then, that you love and honor the King."

"And," he continued, as if I had not spoken, "I wanted to thwart the prophecy. I still want this. If I die with him, how can I be his death? I want to deny this curse more than I want anything else, even"—he swallowed—"even being High King." He shook his head slowly. "He has done me such great honor. I will give up anything, even the future he offers, to be free of this prophecy. But Niniane says this is beyond my power. Oh, Guinevere," he cried, "what am I to do?"

Arthur's words had lit a fire in him; he glowed with pride, with confidence, with the knowledge that he had at last received the call to his destiny. He had been born to kingship—looking at him now, no one could doubt it. And yet he was ready to renounce it, to accept death instead of glory, and all for Arthur's sake.

My eyes were on the ground. Near my foot Rajid's lips gripped the meadow grasses, his strong teeth softly tore the shafts, which sprang back into place at half their height. As time passed they would grow tall again, as if the horse had never been there, for although the shaft was gone, the root still lived.

"Take your mind off Arthur and Merlin's prophecy," I said suddenly, looking up into his black eyes. "Think of Britain. Think of the people all over Britain who live in peace. All Merlin ever said or did, he did for Britain, and Arthur after him. We are bound into a nation now. Keep our welfare always before your eyes, and God will guide your steps."

He slowly sank to one knee, pressing to his lips the hand that still held his. "My dearest Guinevere. You are a Queen, indeed!"

I raised him quickly. "Come, Mordred. I have said nothing you do not know already, in your heart. Had you asked the King, he would have told you the same."

He looked solemnly at the ground and moved the toe of his boot over the short blades of grass cropped by the horse's teeth. "Let me tell you my dream," he said in a low voice. "It is a dream that consumes me. . . . All men may be warlike, but everyone in his heart values peace. I dream that someday—beyond our lifetimes, surely—but someday, all the civilized world may be one nation! Britons and Saxons, Franks and Bretons, Romans, Egyptians, and men of other nations we know nothing of—they will all sit down together and talk of peace. Yes, I know it sounds impossible. But look at Arthur. Not so long ago men would have said it was impossible for Britain. But he has shown us how it may be done. Men serve gladly if they are well led."

This was a speech for Mordred; his eyes were shining and his face was alight. Then did I see his father's spirit in him, and I made him a low reverence.

"My lord," I whispered, "what a King you will make!"

He smiled shyly. "I have said too much. But I wanted you to know what is in my heart . . . However, these are dreams, and there are practical matters to be faced. How will he get the Christian lords to accept me? Even to Lancelot I am an unholy abomination."

"It is not as bad as all that. I am Christian, and I accept and love you. Do not worry about Arthur. If wisdom and patience can accomplish it, it will be done."

"Wisdom and patience," he said slowly, "and the love of the people."

I took his hand and held it hard. "When they know you, Mordred, as I do, they will love you."

He met my eyes and lifted my fingers to his lips; together, hand in hand, we turned back toward Camelot.

What Arthur said to Gawaine, I do not know, except that it was harsh. I am sure that he forbade him to seek revenge against Drustan, even if Gaheris died. Whatever chastisement he administered, Gawaine took it and kept silent. He took charge of Agravaine, paid for his lodgings in the town, and saw that he went to his yearly service for the Earl of Swiftwater. But he was no longer as friendly with Gareth, and Mordred he avoided altogether. To ease matters, Arthur kept him moving. When he traveled, he took Gawaine with him, leaving Mordred co-regent with Lancelot. When he was home, he sent him to Caerleon, or Cornwall, or Rheged, or Lothian. Thus was Gawaine's deadly energy put to use and friction prevented.

In this way, Gawaine became known as the High King's right hand, a forceful knight who shared the King's counsels and knew his mind. His quick temper was put down to his youth. Men respected him.

Meanwhile, Mordred and Lancelot came to an understanding. Thrown together as they were by Arthur's orders, each knowing the other bore a special place in the King's heart, they learned to work together. Gradually, Lancelot passed more and more of the daily work to Mordred, allowed him more freedom to make decisions, and finding him a sober, careful, hardworking man, let him take the reins of power into his own hands. Lancelot was still the Queen's Protector, but as time went by he allowed Mordred to assume most of the work as regent. In return, Mordred treated Lancelot with new respect and seemed to like him better.

"I may have been wrong about him, Gwen," Lancelot said to me once. "He is a good man and will make a good King. He understands men. His judgment is never colored by his feelings. This used to make me think him cold, but he is not. I used to think the army would not follow him. But now most of the soldiers are his age or younger, and have known since their first day here who he is. Perhaps, after all, Arthur is doing the right thing."

"That you should doubt him!" I cried, delighting in his words. "And when has Arthur ever done a wrong thing?"

"Not," Lancelot said very gently, "since he begat him."

One day late in summer I went riding on Rajid. The King was in Rheged, and Gawaine with him. Mordred sat in the workroom, reading petitions. Lancelot was out on the downs, drilling new recruits. I came in from my ride, dismissed my escort, and told Lyonel I would tend the horse myself, for I enjoyed it. I rubbed him down and brushed him, and put him in his big box, which looked out on the paddocks. He was tired, and stood quietly dozing. Grateful for a moment of solitude, I sat cross-legged in the clean straw in a corner and pulled an apple from my pouch. I was suddenly reminded of my girlhood in Gwynedd, when I used to hide in my horse's stall and overhear the grooms spreading palace gossip. Twenty years dropped from me as I sat there, for once again I heard voices coming down the aisle.

"I just don't understand it," a boy's voice said. "A good knight slain, your brother mortally wounded, and all for a woman? Why do men do it?"

"You will understand the attraction of women someday!" the other voice laughed. "Even when they are not witches, they weave a powerful spell."

"There are no witches," the young voice said firmly. "That is superstition."

"You may think so," the other replied indulgently, "but I know better. My mother was one. She had power."

"Then it was God's power, or Satan's. There is no other." This dogmatic assertion I recognized as Galahad's. The other voice, the gentle one, was Gareth's. They had pulled a horse out of his stall and, by the sound of it, were grooming him.

"Well, have it your way, then," Gareth said. "She had the devil in her, I will not argue that. But women can be angels, too. Linet is such a one. And the Queen is another."

"You know," Galahad said stiffly, "how I feel about the Queen."

"Yes, but you are awfully quick to judge her, for one so young. Can she help it if she is beautiful? It is a gift from God."

"But my father loves her!" the boy cried in anguish.

"And if he does?" Gareth's voice was gentle. "What of it? So does my lord Bedwyr. So does Galahantyn, Bors, Lyonel, Mordred, Ferron, and a hundred others I could name. So do I. Would you condemn us all?"

"Yes."

Gareth laughed. "What a young wolf you are! Time will teach you tolerance, I wager. The Queen has always treated me with kindness and forbearance. She is good, and gentle and charming, as well as lovely. It would be base of me indeed not to return her affection and respect."

"That is not what I mean," Galahad objected. "You know my father loves her in a different way."

But Gareth skirted the question. "What has she done, little prince, to hurt you so? Why do you hate her?"

"She was cruel to my mother!" He was near tears and struggling to control them. How my arms longed to reach out to him in comfort! "She hated my mother and banished her from court!"

"Now, now," Gareth said soothingly, "who has been telling these tales? All the world knows your mother was the Queen's best friend in childhood. They grew up together. Why, the Queen brought your mother to court when she married the King, and kept her near. Are these the marks of hatred, or of love?"

"My mother told me it herself," Galahad declared. "They were friends until she married my father. Then the Queen turned against her and sent her away. The Queen loves my father, Gareth. And he loves her, as he never loved my mother. He loves her not in the way that you do, or Sir Bedwyr. He loves her in the same way that the King does. As a wife. I know this to be true."

"Hssst! Hush, young tyrant! This is treason you accuse your father of! Now tell me truly, Galahad, were you there when the Queen broke with your mother? Do you know both sides of this quarrel? Then you do not know the truth of it, but only your mother's version. Let it be. It does not concern you. Why, if I had believed every tale my mother told me, where should I be now? As for Lancelot, he is a man of honor. If he were not, neither King nor Queen would love him. He has not betrayed the King, nor the King's bed, and he never will."

"He has broken God's commandment in his heart," came the implacable reply. "In God's eyes, he has lain with her a hundred times!"

My face was wet with tears, and I pinched myself hard, to keep from sobbing. My poor, dear Lancelot!

Gareth sighed heavily. "Oh, let it be. You cannot know that. If God so condemns every man who ever lusted after Guinevere, then in God's eyes Arthur is a thousand times cuckolded! Such things are fancies only. Forgive him, Galahad. We cannot help whom we love."

"I will not forgive him."

Gareth grunted. "Well, well, perhaps in time you will come to see the honor in him. No one is without sin, Galahad. Not even the High King. You must learn to forgive it."

"Mordred is an abomination." I gasped aloud, but they did not hear me, for the horse moved at that moment and scraped his hoof against the stone flooring.

"Watch your tongue!" Gareth cried. "He is my brother!"

"Yes," Galahad replied calmly. "He is your brother and your cousin both. He is abomination."

There was a long silence. At last, Gareth spoke gravely. "If you wish to live, little prince, you will learn to keep your thoughts to yourself. Mordred may well be your King someday."

"If he attempts it," Galahad said slowly and clearly, "I shall slay him."

"Oh, God!" I whispered, covering my face with my hands. "Oh, God! Oh, God help us all!"

Gareth hushed him and took him outside with the horse. I sat in Rajid's stall for over an hour, weeping. Galahad was then seven and a half years old.

44 ♛ THE SLAUGHTER

It was a black night. Thick clouds raced across the moon's face, and the trees in my garden bent double in the wind. I knelt at my bedside and prayed for the King's safety. What must the sea be like on such a night? The heavy leather flap between our chambers lifted in the gust, then fell to with a loud slap. Varric had not shuttered the unglazed windows in the King's room, for the night was not cold. But I had a good log fire in my own grate.

Even after prayers I felt restless and could not sleep. The castle was quiet, but I could not shake the feeling that something was amiss. The pretty songbird in his willow cage was fast asleep, head tucked under his yellow wing. From the antechamber I heard Ailsa's snores. I wondered if the noise kept Linet awake. We had had six new girls come to us that summer, and good Linet had given up her room and moved in with Ailsa, as her wedding was nigh anyway. I should miss her company terribly! Four years she had been with me, and a sweeter, kinder maiden I had never known. Now at seventeen she was a real beauty and hopelessly in love with Gareth. How lucky they were to marry for love! They waited only for the King's return to accomplish it. Gareth was now eighteen and knighted, a treasured Companion of the King. Lancelot loved him more dearly than his own son; he was incapable of meanness or dishonesty and could always be counted on to defend a just cause. I smiled to myself. It seemed like only yesterday Gareth had come to Camelot, a little boy holding tight to Mordred's hand. Now here he was grown and about to be married. Well, I told myself, at least Camelot was his home, and although Linet would exchange my service for his, she would live here and I should see her.

A stray draft set the flames dancing in the grate, and I shivered. What was this strange foreboding? Surely it could not concern the King, for Niniane had sent no warning. The country was still at peace. Mordred's dream of a trading treaty with the West Saxons looked possible now that the Council had ratified Arthur and Cerdic's defense treaty. Only the situation with the Franks was unstable—but Arthur himself had gone to lend strength to Hoel. This was not a real threat to our peace, not yet. To honor Lancelot, Arthur had taken Galahad as his personal page, and also Gawaine, who now led a troop of cavalry under the King's command. Mordred was regent, and Lancelot Protector, as had been so twenty times before. Nothing was amiss or out of place. Then why could I not sleep?

I went to the glazed doors that gave onto my terrace and watched the angry wind beat down my garden plants. I knew what I should find in the morning—apples and pears all over the paving stones, split and bruised, a feast for the late bees. And leaves everywhere, and broken branches—oh, God! What was this heartache? I clasped my hands together at my breast and felt the pounding of my heart within. Something was amiss. I thought suddenly of Agravaine. He was just back from his yearly duty at Swiftwater, and Mordred had informed me that there was a meeting tonight in the room Agravaine and Gaheris shared in the town. I thought the King had been lenient with Agravaine; after dismissing him from service, he had commuted the sentence and agreed to let him return after three years, if he behaved. Such mercy angered me, but Arthur told me the boy had to have a future he valued, or nothing could temper his rashness. He had only one year to wait now, and although he had not killed anyone, which was all Arthur expected by good behavior, he remained an active thorn in Lancelot's side and a lodestone for every dissatisfied young hothead in the army. Because we had peace, kings and dukes lived to be old men, and their ambitious sons grew restive and eager to snatch power. These were the kind of men Agravaine gathered around him. Gaheris, healed of his dreadful wounds and bearing horrible scars, lived with him, forever banned from the King's presence and having nothing in his heart but hate. Mordred they no longer trusted, since he had begun to assume power in the King's absence and had come to better terms with Lancelot. But Mordred was clever and kept a close watch on their movements and their meetings. Gareth was never of their party, for he loved Lancelot more than any man but Arthur, finding in him the father he had never had. Thus far, Mordred assured me, their meetings did no more than give vent to their feelings; they drank and diced and whored and slept it off. But I did not like having such ruffians so close. Was it this that made me nervous? Mordred knew of the meeting; surely his spies would watch the house. All the castle guards were loyal to the King. Lancelot, Mordred, and Gareth were the three best swordsmen in Britain, after the King, so what was to fear?

I shrugged and drew the soft curtain across the terrace doors. The truth was, I thought with a grim smile, I missed Arthur. I missed his company and the peace of mind his presence brought. And I missed him for another reason. When he was gone, Lancelot and I could not so much as look at one another. But when Arthur was there, when he was with us, we could touch and gaze and find some little relief. How cruel, I often thought, that it should be so. No one, not even Galahad, dared speak about us to the King. Thus did he grant us his protection.

Suddenly I heard footsteps and whispered voices below my stairs. Trembling, I stood by the fire and tried to compose myself. In a moment, Linet came up and peeked hesitantly into the room.

"My lady Queen! You are up! A courier has just ridden in, with a message from the King."

"Let him come up then." She beckoned behind her, and a young man, still breathing hard from his exertions, stepped into the room and knelt at my feet. In his hand was a scroll with the High King's seal.

"I come from the coast my lady," he recited quickly. "The King put ashore today at Potter's Bay. He pushes on with the cavalry without delay; he may be no more than an hour or two behind me. He gave this to me himself and bade me deliver it into no hands but your own." He ducked his head, his message complete, and withdrew hastily.

"Stay, Linet," I bade her, "until I have read this, to see if there is some reply."

I broke the seal and saw the neat Latin hand of Arthur's scribe. It was a short note only, to inform me of his early return and imminent arrival. But the language was urgent and hidden in it was a warning. "Send for Lancelot and Mordred," it said, "and tell them this news, but do it secretly, that no others may know of my coming, or even guess at it." After that, it was signed with his love. I looked up at Linet.

"Three things, Linet. First, see that the courier is housed apart and is allowed to speak with no man until morning. Impress upon him that his mission is secret. No one is to know he comes from the King."

"Yes, my lady. He is very full of this knowledge already, my lady. He would not tell us from whom he came, but I would not let him see you without knowing the source of the message."

"Who among my women knows his errand?"

"Only myself and Ailsa."

"Good. Next, send a page to Sir Mordred to beg him come to me at once. Do not tell him why, only that it is an emergency. Tell him the Queen commands his presence."

"Commands?" Linet asked, startled.

"Third. Send to Sir Lancelot with the same message. Command him to attend me here. At once."

Her eyes widened, and she curtsied low. "Yes, my lady."

"Oh, and one thing more. Perhaps most important of all. See that I am well attended. I want six or seven maids below, fully dressed, and you and Ailsa in this chamber. You have ten minutes."

She flew downstairs, and I went back to the fire to scan the letter. What was it Arthur feared, that he could not say straight out? Some treachery at home? From whom did he wish to keep his coming secret? I tucked the letter in my pocket and pulled my little stool to the hearth. There was another chair in the corner, which I dragged over, and then I got a third one from the King's chamber. When all was ready, I inspected myself in the polished bronze. My robe was of cream-colored velvet, with long, close-fitting sleeves and a high throat. Only the toes of my slippers showed beneath it. It was the chastest garment in the entire castle. My hair was braided for the night and held in a net. Satisfied that no one could take me for a siren, I sat on my stool, closed my eyes, and waited.

Within minutes I heard Lancelot's voice belowstairs, urging Ailsa to hurry and refusing to ascend before her. Linet came in first, then Ailsa, gray-haired and bent with the pains of age. They took their places at the doorway and curtsied as Lancelot entered. He was fully dressed, but shod in slippers and had come, this time, without his sword.

"Guinevere! What is it?" he cried, taking my hand and pressing it to his lips. Our eyes met and locked; then carefully, he lowered his and bowed.

"I have had a message from the King," I told him. "Let us wait for Mordred."

He looked up in surprise. "Did you send for Mordred? He's not in the castle. I know this, because a half hour since I tried to find him myself and bade his chamberlain send to me when he returned. I have heard nothing yet."

My breath caught. "My lord, you came to me alone?"

Anger and bitterness flashed across his face, instantly suppressed. "No. I am not a fool. Three men attend me beyond the outer door. One of them is Gareth. He was up, unable to sleep. So I brought him."

At that moment, one of my maids appeared at the doorway, breathless, to say that Sir Mordred could not be found.

I nodded. "Very well, Lise, tell them to keep looking. See that he comes to me the instant he is found." She scurried back down the stairs to her post below, and I bade Lancelot take a chair.

As he read the King's letter, I held my hands to the fire to warm them. They trembled uncontrollably. At last, after scanning it a third time, he put the scroll down.

"Well?" I asked. "What does it mean, my lord?"

He shook his head. "I do not know. He has had some information is my guess." He glanced swiftly at Ailsa and Linet. Ailsa had been with me since Northgallis, and Linet was Gareth's betrothed. He could trust them. "It seems he fears some treachery, but in truth, Gwen, I do not know what it is."

"Well," I whispered, "so long as you and Mordred are free of suspicion, I can bear the waiting. The courier said he might be here within two hours."

"Good." He shut his lips tight on the word, then looked into my eyes with longing. I had to look away to keep from blushing.

All of a sudden we heard raised voices and the heavy tread of boots. Then a hoarse shout, from the King's room! Lancelot leaped to his feet and faced the curtain. I screamed as a sword thrust through—suddenly the room was full of men, armed and stinking of stale mead—one Liander was foremost, a Welshman. He was drunk. His sword waved before Lancelot's face. Mellyot from Gwynedd was behind him, and then Agravaine, Gaheris, Collgren, Mador, Lovell, and last, behind them in Arthur's chamber, I saw Mordred running up. Everything that happened, happened at once, and yet I saw it—I see it still—as if it happened in a different time, slowly unfolding like the petals of a flower.

"Put up your swords!" Lancelot shouted. "I am naked!" It went against all the rules of knighthood to attack an unarmed man, but their intent was clear from their faces. All their swords were drawn.

"You are ever naked when you lie with the Queen!" Gaheris screamed, pushing Liander forward. Lancelot ducked the raised sword, grabbed my little stool, and brought it up against Liander's sword arm, at the same time landing a hard blow across his wrist. The man bellowed in pain as the bone snapped, but in the next instant he lay dead at Mellyot's feet, run through by his own weapon, which Lancelot now held before him.

"Cowards!" he cried, enraged. "Swine! Get out!"

"Traitor!" Gaheris and Agravaine howled together, surging forward. Then the room was alive with clashing swords, and blood sprayed everywhere.

"Gare-e-e-th!" Linet screamed, backing toward the landing, clutching Ailsa. "Gare-e-eth!"

I pressed flat against the wall, unable to breathe, watching Lancelot defend himself against them all. His rage was an unholy thing, wild and possessive. He was blind to all else but the pressing blades. He did not see Gareth come bounding up the steps to his aid; he did not hear Mordred shouting to them to stop, in the King's name. He slew Agravaine with no more thought than he'd waste on a Saxon, he slew Mellyot, and Lovell behind him. Gareth came forward, sword raised in his defense; Lancelot saw the weapon only and ran his blade through Gareth's breast. He turned to the next foe, while Linet fell screaming over Gareth's body. When Agravaine fell, Gaheris had turned to me, blood lust in his eyes.

"Bitch!" he shrieked. "Whore! This is your death day!" I gasped as he leveled his sword and came at me. But Mordred got between us and engaged him. Lancelot whirled and took him in the throat. Gaheris, killer of women, died at my very feet, and his blood soaked my slippers. Mordred looked up to find Lancelot's sword pointed at his breast. Contempt swept Lancelot's features; he lunged, and Mordred blocked the blow. I cried out, but he never heard me. Linet was wailing, the women were all screaming, and the King's guards were thundering up the King's stairs. Everyone else was dead.

Mordred was skilled, but no one could match Lancelot man to man; yet Lancelot did not kill him. He had opportunity, more than once, and I saw that even in his fury, for Arthur's sake, he would preserve his son's life. Finally, with the guards at the curtain, Lancelot locked his blade and tripped him, wrenching the sword from his hand. Mordred staggered.

"Coward!" Mordred gasped, reaching for his dagger. In exasperation more than anger, Lancelot ran his sword through Mordred's shoulder. The dagger dropped; Mordred lunged, slipped, knocked his head against my bedpost, and fell senseless to the floor. Lancelot stood alone in the slaughter, covered in the blood of his attackers, breathing heavily. Slowly his vision cleared, and he saw me.

"Gwen!" he gasped. "Is that blood yours? Are you hurt?"

Dazed, I looked down at my spattered robe and stepped out of the pool of Gaheris' blood. I could not speak, but shook my head. He came to me and took me in his arms, pressing me close. His whole body shuddered violently, and I felt him sob. I was numbed. I felt nothing. I saw, without interest, that even the bed hangings were spattered with blood; my mother's little stool was broken, the fine needlework slashed beyond repair, the birdcage lay trampled on the bloody carpet, the bird gone. Eight men lay dead, and the King's son wounded, and all by his hand.

The guards at the curtain didn't know what to do. They looked anxiously at me for some sign. Linet wept uncontrollably over Gareth, and Ailsa with her. Finally, Lancelot seemed to notice them. He looked up and shook his head, as if to clear it.

"What is that? Who has fallen?"

Then, slowly, feeling flooded back, and with it, terror. I gripped his arms, to keep him by me.

"It is Gareth."

"GARETH?" he cried. In anguish, he tried to free himself from my grip. "Dear God! Gareth! Let me go, Gwen, I must see to him!"

"No, my lord. Don't add to her pain. I saw the stroke. He is dead."

"I will be revenged for it!" he cried, on a sob. "Who slew him?"

I did not answer, and Linet looked up then. He saw his answer written on her face. He went still, grew pale and began to tremble.

"No! No!" he whispered frantically. "No, tell me it was not I! Please, Gwen, if you love me!"

I wished I could weep, but the tears would not come. My throat ached so that I could hardly speak.

"You were not yourself, Lancelot," I whispered hoarsely, "when you killed him."

"Ahhhhh!" he cried, and covering his face, sank against the wall.

Then I beckoned to the captain of the guard. "Take Sir Lancelot to his chambers and guard them well. Let no one in or out save the King's physician." To everyone there, it sounded as if I was putting him under house arrest, and they were all amazed. But I was thinking of Arthur, who was due in soon, with Gawaine at his side. The guards were for Lancelot's protection.

"Take Sir Mordred to the physicians first and have them see to his wound. He is not mortally hurt, I think, but we must be sure. And after that, clear the bodies from my room." I shuddered. "Alone of them all, take Sir Gareth to the chapel. His will be a burial with honor. The others—I will instruct you later what to do with them."

The captain bowed low, relieved to have definite orders. "It will be done, my lady."

"After that, have this room cleaned. Take everything out. I—I cannot bear it!"

"Yes, my lady," he said swiftly, afraid of tears. I turned and helped Ailsa pull Linet from Gareth's body. She was faint with weeping and as limp as a rag. We got her downstairs and put her to bed with hot bricks in her blankets and a cold cloth on her brow. Poor Ailsa was not much better. I made her take some brandy and put her to bed, as well. The six maids who had been below during the slaughter stood huddled by the door. They were frightened out of their wits but could not leave until dismissed. When Ailsa was settled, I dismissed them, all except one, whom I bade stay and keep watch upon the others. Then I went out and stood in my sitting room, alone and dazed. I did not know what to do. Bedwyr! I thought. I must find dear Bedwyr! I rummaged through Ailsa's trunks until I found a cloak. It hid most of the bloodstains. With this wrapped around me, I hurried through the corridors to the King's library. The sentries stared at me as I went by, against regulations. As I reached the library door, Kay came around the corner and saw me. His jaw dropped.

"Queen Guinevere!"

He ran up and took my arm. I had not realized I was shaking so, until I felt his firm support. "Come, my lady, come in here. I will light the fire."

"Bedwyr!" I whispered.

"Yes, I'll send for Bedwyr." He snapped an order over his shoulder to the nearest sentry and gently led me into the room. It was cold and dark, and the fire had long gone out. I was astounded at this; in my mind's eye I had seen it as I always saw it, warm and bright and comforting. I could not be thinking clearly. Perhaps Kay was right when he put me in the King's big chair and covered me with blankets.

He lit the fire himself, good man, and tended me like a servant until the page brought Bedwyr. He was quickly dressed, and still tousled from sleep.

"What's up, Kay?" he said, covering a yawn. "The sentries look as if they've seen a ghost."

"They've seen the Queen, which is near enough. Here, boy!" he called out to the page. "We'll need some warm spiced wine and some hot bricks. Be quick about it, there's a lad."

"What's amiss with the Queen?" Bedwyr asked sharply, and then coming to where Kay stood, he saw me in the chair.

"Gwen!" He took my hand. "She's cold as ice! What in the name of Mithra has happened? There's blood in her hair!"

"Aye." Kay kept his voice low, although no one else was in the room. "There have been doings aplenty this night. I've just come from Sir Mordred and the physicians—he's been in a swordfight."

"Does he live?" Bedwyr cried, paling.

"Aye, he's very lucky. Got his shoulder sliced is all. It's clean. He was awake. He would not say how he got it. He bade me go and rescue the Queen."

"Rescue?" Bedwyr whispered, staring at me. "From what?"

"Krinian made only a brief report. I will tell you what I know. There are eight men dead in the Queen's bedchamber, and she has locked Lancelot in his room and put guards at his door."

Bedwyr whistled slowly and dropped to his knees, holding my hands and looking worriedly into my face. "Is this true?" he asked softly. "Gwen, can you tell us?"

My teeth began to chatter, and I clenched my jaw to keep them still. Bedwyr rubbed my hands between his own. Arthur's hound Cabal came up and pushed his head in between us, sniffing, nosing under the blankets. Bedwyr shoved him aside.

"When the physicians are free, send them here," Bedwyr said. Kay rose as the door opened, and the wine and warming bricks came in. He arranged silver goblets on a tray nearby and set the wineskin to warm above a flame. Then he went to a shelf behind the King's work table and took down a silver brandy flask. He poured a little in a cup and held it to my lips.

"Drink this, my lady. Just a sip will do." But it smelled foul, and I turned my face away. Bedwyr's grip on my hands tightened, and he pleaded gently with me.

"Please, Gwen. Please take some, for my sake. Arthur trusts us to take care of you, and we would not betray that trust." And because once before I had ignored his ministrations and suffered by it, I obeyed him and swallowed the fiery liquid. It left me gasping, and my eyes grew wet, but still tears would not come. I shivered as the fire burned in my belly, then slowly spread its gentle warmth throughout my body. I felt better, and Bedwyr saw it.

"By all the gods that are," he breathed, "I bless your courage! Say nothing yet—I see you cannot do it. Let me slip these bricks under your feet." He lifted the blankets and cried out in horror.

"Kay! See this! Her shoes are soaked in blood! And the hem of her robe—no wonder the dog was interested. By the Bull, there has been a battle!"

Kay came over, frowning, and sent for a bath slave, for towels and hot water. "Bring her women here!" he commanded, and I struggled to arise.

"No!" I cried, my voice a shadow of itself. "No, they cannot come! They cannot—they saw it—they are abed—they cannot—do not ask it of them!" Bedwyr gently pushed me down into the chair. I could not believe how little strength I had.

Kay turned toward me and spoke kindly. "They saw this bloodletting? Then we will leave them and tend to you ourselves. Dear God, I wish the King were here!"

I suddenly remembered his letter. He was almost here! He was coming! But it was a secret, and I could not tell them! I looked wildly from Kay to Bedwyr.

"Gawaine!" I cried, and my voice flew free, echoing off the walls. They jumped. "Oh, find him, Kay! Take Gawaine and lock him in a safe place and let him speak to no one—*to no one*—until the King has heard it. As you value your life, do this!"

Kay looked bewildered. "But Sir Gawaine is in Brittany, my lady, with the King."

I groaned, hugging myself, and rocked slowly forward and back. "Gawaine will be here. He will be here within the hour. Do not let him speak to anyone. Not anyone. It is as much as his life is worth. If he dies, I shall die with him."

Kay stared, astonished, but Bedwyr's eyes narrowed. He caught the change of reference; he knew I spoke of Lancelot at the last. In an instant, he saw a glimmer of what had happened, and rose, taking command.

"Do as she says, Kay. Set extra guards at the entrance, in case he rides in. Stop him at King's Gate and have him escorted. Be sure to treat him with honor, but seal him off from rumor. There is more here than we yet know. Trust the Queen."

Kay obeyed and left us. Bedwyr knelt at my feet.

"What is it, Gwen? Here, take this wine and sip it slowly. It will calm you. Trust me. It is Lancelot you fear for, is it not?"

I took the wine and nodded, shivering and rocking, my eyes upon the fire.

"After this night's work, Gawaine will want to kill him?"

I nodded again and drank thirstily, emptying the cup.

He took it from me. "Then Lancelot has slain one of his brothers?" I met his eyes and groaned.

He gripped me hard, to stop my rocking. "Which one? Agravaine? Gaheris?"

From deep within me I felt the pain beginning, and my breath came in quick gasps, as it fought its way up and out.

Bedwyr began to shake me and call my name. "Guinevere! Stop! Oh, Gwen! Please don't!"

But it could not be stopped. I heard wild laughing and then an unearthly shriek; it was my voice; it came from me, my body ripped by searing pain, and I bent double, falling into Bedwyr's arms.

"Ahhhhhhhh! All! All! He has killed them all! Oh, Bedwyr, what will Arthur do!" I was sick, I think; I lost my senses for a while, but I remember the sweet, sickly smell of it through the fog of feeling, as he held me tightly across both his arms and sat with me close to the fire to warm me. He wept himself; I remember his tears falling on my cheek. He wept for Gareth; he wept for Lancelot; he wept for Arthur and the good fellowship of his Companions, now forever broken. I pressed my face into his shoulder and gave myself to weeping. I lay racked with sobs, I don't know how long, until I was exhausted and could no longer cry, but only twitched helplessly with grief. I believed myself close to death; I even wished for it.

Bedwyr groaned and kissed my face.

"We must believe, my dear Gwen," he whispered. "It is the will of the gods. We must believe."

At last the door flew open, and I heard Arthur's voice.

"Bedwyr! Where is the Queen?"

Bedwyr straightened quickly. "Here, my lord!"

In four strides he was with me, and I looked up into his face. He paled, and his eyes grew dark.

"Guinevere!"

"My lord," I whispered, but no sound came out. He pulled aside the cloak and looked at my bloodstained robe.

Gently he took me from Bedwyr and placed me in the chair. Behind him stood Kay, and the bath slave, and a host of dusty soldiers.

"Get out! Close the door!" he barked. "Kay, do I not still employ physicians?"

"Yes, my lord," replied Kay, who was not used to rebukes from the King. "But at present they are with Mordred."

Arthur hesitated a fraction, then said shortly, "Is he mortally wounded?"

"No, my lord."

"Then surely he can spare one of them to tend the Queen. Get him!"

Kay withdrew. Arthur glared at the bath slave, who deposited his burdens at the King's feet and dashed out. Gently Arthur removed the sodden slippers and washed my cold, stained feet himself. He would not let Bedwyr assist him, and Bedwyr, remembering a time long past when I had bathed the King, did not insist. He dried my feet and wrapped them in the warm towels the bricks had come in, then placed them on the bricks.

"Why is she not attended?" he snapped at Bedwyr.

"She would not let us send for her women—she said they saw what happened—I gathered they were in the same state."

Arthur's face looked pinched. "But she is the Queen," he said evenly, "and they her servants. Go yourself and bring one of them here with a robe. This thing reeks—I will have it off her. Go."

It was odd, how I could see him and hear him so clearly, and feel the touch of his hands, but I could not speak, or move, or do anything of my own will. I was empty, drained of strength, and was content to give myself into his care. Slowly, awkwardly, he got the filthy robe off me and rubbed my poor body with the blankets, and wrapped me tightly in them. Bedwyr was back soon after, dragging poor Lise in her nightdress, carrying a blue robe. The child had been weeping, for her face was swollen, and she was frightened to death to find herself face to face with the King. But he had no time for courtesies.

"Stand at the door, let no one enter," he commanded Bedwyr. Then he directed the poor child to help him dress me. She blushed a thousand shades of pink at my nakedness, but Arthur was gruff with her and bore no hesitations. Try as I might to help them, my limbs would not obey me. Between them, they got me dressed at last. Arthur tucked the blankets in around me, thanked the girl, and dismissed her, and then called Bedwyr in. Kay and the physician were close behind. God bless Arthur, he would not let the man leech me; he knew I had a horror of it. So the physician contented himself with mixing me a posset and advising more heat to my feet.

"She's had a shock," he told the King. Arthur kicked him out. He stood Kay and Bedwyr before him.

"Tell me what you know."

While they spoke, I began to feel a lazy warmth seep into my limbs, and gradually, as I relaxed, I drifted into sleep. When I awoke, Cabal had his head in my lap, and the King stood before the fire, alone, watching me. I tried my limbs gingerly and found they obeyed me. I pushed myself up straighter. I felt lightheaded, but myself again. Cabal's tail beat eagerly against the floor. Arthur came and knelt at my feet, taking my hands. His face was grave, the lines of care carved deep from nose to mouth. His warm, loving eyes were desperately worried. I tried a smile, and found that my lips moved at least a little.

"Oh, Arthur!" It came out in a whisper. "I am glad you are home!"

He kissed my hand and laid his head in my lap, whispering a prayer of thanksgiving. He did not care that I heard it. I stroked his hair gently. The dog's big tongue licked my hand in joy.

"You will want to know what happened."

He lifted his head. "There is no need. I have seen Mordred."

I shook my head. "He did not see it all. I saw it all, Arthur. I saw it all."

He closed his eyes and bowed his head. "So you did. All right. Tell me."

I told him all of it, without a tremor; it was like taking a great burden, which I could hardly bear, and placing it on his strong shoulders. He bore it for me, and I could breathe again.

When I finished, he sighed deeply, and a smile touched his lips. "And after that, you had sense to give clear orders to the guards and to tend Linet and Ailsa. I tell you, Gwen, you have more courage than many of my soldiers. If you could learn to wield a sword, I would make you a captain of my horse." Then he rose and paced once about the room.

"Where is Gawaine?" I asked him suddenly.

"With Ferron. In the Round Hall. We were met by your orders at King's Gate. I saw them obeyed. I knew there was a reason."

"Have you—have you spoken with him yet?" And he knew by my voice that I did not mean Gawaine.

"No," he said wearily. "Not yet. You came first."

"He was naked, and they attacked him."

"I know, Gwen."

"He did not even know Gareth was in the room, until after."

"I know."

"And Mordred—he thought he was one of them—it was an easy mis-take to make, he followed them in. And he had three chances to run him through and let them pass. He only wounded him to disarm him."

"So Mordred told me."

I stopped, my lips dry. Arthur handed me a winecup, and I took it. My hand was trembling. "What will you do?"

He looked at me with compassion and then sighed. "I don't know. But after this, Britain will be too small to hold them both."

I·met his eyes. "Yes. I see that."

He shrugged. "Then they have taken it out of my hands."

I said nothing. He was right.

He could not keep Gawaine waiting much longer, so at last he sent for Lancelot. He bade me keep my chair and himself stood near me, so that we received him together. Lancelot came, scrubbed clean and ready for the road. Grief for Gareth had already etched new lines in his face. He saluted Arthur and kissed his ring. When he rose, he stood with a soldier's straight-ness and waited for his commander's judgment. But Arthur, who loved him, embraced him.

"Lancelot!" he cried in a low voice. "Was there no other way?"

Lancelot shrugged, but his eyes were wet. "I am your servant, Arthur. Do with me what you must."

Arthur spread his hands out helplessly. "What can I do? I must send you home. You cannot stay in Britain. And keep a guard around you, all the days of your life."

Lancelot nodded. "You are merciful, my lord. It is more than I deserve."

Arthur swung an arm around him and gripped him by the shoulders. "You are my right hand. My shield. My other, better self. A warrior with stainless honor. A man without compromise. You deserve better of me than banishment. I only do it to save your life."

Lancelot cleared his throat. "And Galahad. Will you keep him with you? He is better here than in Lanascol. With me."

"Whatever you will."

"That's all I ask. Except—" He paused, and with an effort kept his voice steady. "Except to beg your pardon for wounding your son. I saw his raised sword in front of the Queen—I wanted only to disarm him, but he is too good a swordsman."

"Thanks to your teaching," Arthur said, his voice gone suddenly rough. "Lancelot, I know well all you did was in defense of the Queen. You saved

her life tonight. You know what that means to me. It is not a gift I can repay. Were it not for Gareth, I could square things with Gawaine and keep
you here. Everyone else deserved to die."

Lancelot nodded but could not speak. He would never forgive himself.

Arthur embraced him again and kissed him on both cheeks. "I will
have Ferron arrange an escort. You'd best be gone tonight. The ship we took
still lies at Potter's Bay. I'll send a courier to the captain." He looked at us
both with sadness. "I give you an hour to take your leave of the Queen. Be
gone when I return." Tears crept from Lancelot's eyes as Arthur left, setting
a guard upon the door.

Lancelot sank to the floor at my feet, and I cradled his head in my lap.
There was nothing to say. Arthur might sail to Lanascol, but unless
Gawaine should die, I would never see Lancelot again.

"Guinevere," he said at last. "Do you remember when I came to take
you out of Wales, long ago, and you did not believe me when I told you the
kind of man King Arthur was?"

"Yes, my dear, I remember it well."

"Now you see the truth. There is not another like him in the world."

I smiled. "Sweet Lancelot, this is not news."

He looked up and held my gaze. "When I am gone, do not grieve for me
and pine for what might have been. Give him the love you would have
spent on me. He is worthier by far."

"Lancelot," I slid down and sat beside him, and embraced him. "Dearest Lancelot. I would do it if I could. But you know well what is between us
is beyond my power. From the moment of our meeting, I have loved you. I
will love you always, past parting, past death."

He kissed me and held me close. "If I had life to live again," he said, "I
would change nothing."

He held me thus and kissed me, and we talked of times long past, of
Wales and of Camelot when the Kingdom was young. We even came to
laughter once or twice. We had not shared such closeness since I tended
him on Ynys Witrin, ten years before. And we kept coming back to Arthur.

"He has done it," Lancelot marveled. "He has fulfilled our dreams.
Where he has fallen short, it is because other men failed him."

So in Arthur we found solace for our souls; and when at last he took his
leave of me, our eyes were dry. We shared a pride that Arthur's honor was
untarnished. When he had gone, I wept most bitterly awhile, but these were
tears of self-pity, and I soon stopped them.

I sat by the fire and stroked Cabal, afraid to look into the future, afraid
to recall the past. When Arthur returned, he found me thus, and joined me
on the hearth.

"Well, I have done what I could, Gwen."

"Was Gawaine wild when you told him?"

"Indeed. But there is only one door to the Round Hall, and I stood before it. Had I not been High King, I think he might have run me through, to get to Lancelot."

"He is safely away?"

"Yes. With Ferron and an escort. I made it quite clear to Gawaine I want no more killing here. He understands the twins behaved as traitors and, had they lived, must have suffered death. Their lives were forfeit the moment they entered your chamber. But Gareth—" He paused and shrugged. "Gareth's death is cause for vengeance. Not even Lancelot denies it. I had to allow the justice of his complaint."

"Of course, my lord. Where is he now?"

"I sent him to see Mordred. He wanted a firsthand account; he wants to vent his anger and say his piece. Mordred will listen. I am tired of it."

His face, turned to the fire, looked carved in stone; a noble face, but lined with care and weary of the burdens a King carries. Mordred is twenty-one, I thought suddenly. I am glad of it. But will he ever be as strong as this King?

"I have given Gawaine Orkney. After we bury Gareth with full honor, I will invest Gawaine with kingship. Then he will travel north to take up his rule."

I let out a long breath in relief. "How wise you are, my lord! Sending Gawaine north and Lancelot south."

He shrugged. "Temporarily expedient. Orkney is a small place for a man of Gawaine's energy. He will be back."

"He cannot go to Brittany without your leave?"

"He is a king now. He can do what he wants. He can risk my displeasure and the consequences it brings."

"But he will swear allegiance to you when you invest him?"

"Oh, yes. But then, he made an oath to Drustan once."

I clasped his hand tightly and, once again, drew strength from him. "Oh, Arthur, how I grieve for your good fellowship of knights, now torn asunder! It is not right that you should have to give your time to these feuds and rivalries, when there is so much else to do."

He smiled briefly and lifted his shoulders. "If Kingship were only battles, it would be easy," he said. "This may turn out well, Gwen. Who knows? They may both live to serve me; the group of rebels is disbanded; our treaties are not affected. And Lancelot in Lanascol makes Less Britain stronger, and that is where trouble will next arise."

With a gasp I recalled his letter. "Arthur! Why did you send the letter? What treachery did you fear? Was it this?"

He laughed bitterly and shook his head. "No, indeed! I wish now I had never sent it! If Lancelot had not been followed to your chamber—"

"Never mind that," I broke in hastily. "Why did you send it?"

"I had word through a traveling merchant that Constantine was on the move, and with troops. To me, that meant only one thing: an attempt on Camelot, and Mordred. But I did not like to say so, in case he had an informer here."

"Do you suspect that, my lord?"

He sighed and passed a hand across his brow. "With Gawaine beside me, I suspect everyone. He sees phantoms everywhere. No one is safe from his suspicion. Not even Mordred."

"Why Mordred? He knows your plans for Mordred."

"Yes, but he does not like them. Remember, as a child, he was used to thinking Mordred a fatherless bastard, and beneath him."

"But now he knows he is your son!"

"Yes," Arthur said wearily, "but he suspects him of the same ambition all Agravaine's friends suffer from—of wishing to supplant their fathers upon the throne."

"You know this is not true of Mordred."

"Yes." Arthur spoke gently. "I know it. I did not say Gawaine was wise or knew men. Just that he is eager to see slights everywhere. It is my blessed sister's legacy to me, this bloodbath, this disruption of my peace."

I grieved to hear him speak so gloomily and longed to bring the light back to his face.

"Tell me about Mordred, my lord. I meant to ask after him before. How fares he? Is he in pain?"

Arthur grimaced. "Pain enough. Lancelot knew well what he was about and missed the bone. The physicians have stitched it, as Merlin taught them, and with luck he will keep the use of his arm. But it is his first real battle wound," Arthur said, sounding a little amazed, "and he is a grown man."

"That is a testament to your Kingship. Tell me what he said about the attack on Lancelot. And where was he when we could not find him?"

"Ah, yes," Arthur said, brightening. "He was in the town, spying on Agravaine and his friends. They were drunk and tending to violence, and he wished to keep them from causing trouble. Someone came running from the castle to say Lancelot had gone secretly to the Queen's room, alone."

"This, though he brought three attendants and came at my summons!" I cried, aghast.

"I know, Gwen. This news roused them. They thought they saw their chance and took up their swords and broke into my apartments. Mordred followed them, and when he saw what they meant to do, he tried to stop them. But they were too many and pushed him aside. He sent for the house guard and ran after them to my room."

"Just in time to stop Gaheris and save my life!" I shuddered.

"Did he really threaten you?"

"Indeed, my lord. He called me names and leveled his sword at my heart."

"Mordred told me what he said," he said shortly. Then his voice softened. "Yet he was loath to name Lancelot as his attacker. He kept silent before Kay and Bedwyr. He only told me because I commanded him, straight out. He assured me that Lancelot mistook him for one of the conspiracy."

"Yes," I said sadly. "Lancelot always mistook him."

Arthur rose and helped me up. "Well, it is over. I pray God for a space of peace, to bury the dead and regroup. Can you sleep, Gwen? Or would you like a potion?"

"Oh, Arthur!" I cried, shivering. "Do not send me back to my quarters! It will take a week to clean away the blood!"

He gently put his arms about me. "That is not what I meant. Of course you shall not go back. Stay with me until you are ready to brave your chamber again. But can you rest, or should I send for a sleeping draught?"

Relieved and comforted, I slipped my arms around him. "Such rest as I can find in your arms, my dear Arthur, is all the rest I desire."

At last, at long last, his face lit with joy, and he smiled.

45 ♛ THE THREAT

I was out riding when the courier came from Brittany. It was a cold March day with a fitful wind and small, fierce showers of rain. Not a day for sailing, but ships could always get across if the message was dire enough. I rode with Bedwyr and Ferron and three others, far across the downs to the eastern woodlands, just for the pleasure of exercise and riding free in the wind. Ferron teased me that I enjoyed riding in bad weather, but Bedwyr seemed to understand my restlessness. I believe he felt it, too.

Truth was, the King was aging. He was but forty, with a third of life ahead, and yet he laughed less often, brooded more, and seemed sometimes to long for times gone by. Ever since Lancelot's banishment five years before, grief had grown upon him and slowly encircled him, until even his closest friends longed for the daring warrior they had once known. Bedwyr was near his age and was not so changed. I did not understand this deep sorrow. Sometimes the King was more my father than my husband, though only five years older; when he called me his child queen, it made me want to scream. He knew he was changing, and he knew I was not.

When he sent Lancelot away, it took something out of him that could not be replaced. Only a few of us could make him smile: Bedwyr, Mordred, and especially Gawaine. Gawaine was the high-spirited Companion whose jests and boasts and antics could bring light into the King's face. And for this I honored him. He loved Arthur deeply and would have done anything he asked, excepting only forgive Gareth's murder.

So we galloped over the downs that day and missed the courier. We little thought the future was so close upon us. I raced Ferron, and won; raced Bedwyr, and lost by a nose; for my new stallion was only four and, although faster than Bedwyr's gray, could not go ten strides without bucking. At last, tired and laughing, we turned for home. Halfway back, we were met by horsemen bearing the High King's banner. The messenger's face was grave. Sir Bedwyr and Sir Ferron were summoned at once to Council in the Round Hall. They saluted me and left. The remaining guard formed close around me, and we followed hard upon their heels.

In the stable Lyonel and two grooms were gathered around a tired black gelding whose head hung low. They had covered him with blankets; his coat was drenched, his neck steaming. The grooms sponged his legs with cold water.

I beckoned Lyonel closer. "When did the courier ride in, Lyonel?"

"About an hour hence, my lady."

"And where from?"

He cleared his throat. "From Less Britain, my lady."

I met his eyes. "From whom?" But he shook his head. He would have loved to tell me the man came from Lancelot, but he did not know. I thanked him and went back to tend the stallion myself. While I worked, my thoughts drifted to my old friend, so long gone from me. Arthur had been twice to see him and had told me he looked well. He and Galahantyn had formed a strong alliance with old Hoel, their neighbor, and had treaties with King Childebert of the Franks. Galahantyn had married a Breton girl, who adored him, and she was raising Lancelot's younger sons along with her own. He seemed, said Arthur, to have found a sort of peace in this close family and to have grown into a king.

I looked up as a groom led another horse in. This one I recognized: a chestnut mare with a white star and a white stocking on her near hind. She belonged to Niniane, and she was sweating. I went immediately to find Lyonel.

"Did a messenger leave Camelot for Avalon after the courier arrived?"

"Why, no, my lady. What's amiss?" he replied, seeing my distress.

I shrugged. "I don't know that anything is amiss. But Niniane is here. Send a groom to see to my stallion. I must find her."

All I could think of, as I hurried to my quarters to bathe and change, was that Niniane had come unbidden. That meant she had known through her Sight that she was needed. Something of great importance had happened, or was about to happen, and it concerned Arthur.

My girls dressed me quickly, and before the hour was out I was waiting nervously in the King's library for the Council to be over. If only I were allowed in Council! As the High King's advisor, Niniane, alone of all women, could attend. To exclude me was mere foolishness; the King shared all his thoughts with me, and took my advice and valued my opinion enough to argue with me when we differed—what more did his Companions do? Some of them, like Gawaine, did not even do that, but simply shouted out their feelings and gave no thought at all to what they said. Simply because I could not lift a sword—I laughed to myself and quit this foolish thinking. I had no desire to be numbered among the men; rarely did I wish for the honor of sitting through the drudgery of Council meetings. I was merely impatient for news!

I strode across the room and back again, Cabal following at my heels. I tried to imagine what the news could be. Had Hoel died? He had been ailing for years. But he had grown sons who had sworn allegiance to Arthur and who were friends of Lancelot. Hoel's dying could not be a disaster, however unexpected. And if Niniane was here, the news must be dire. Could aught have befallen Lancelot? But Galahantyn was there, and loyal. All Less Britain was bound with treaties. Perhaps Childebert had died, or been supplanted. That might require Arthur's presence across the Narrow Sea. But would it bring Niniane out of her fastness? I shivered. Niniane's presence frightened me. I feared that whatever news had come cast some shadow across Arthur's destiny. But that meant Saxons. Arthur and Mordred had only last autumn sealed the trading treaty that was so dear to Mordred's heart. It was the first step toward friendship between the mainland kingdoms; it acknowledged the West Saxons' right to the territory they already had occupied for sixty years, from Seal's Bay to Rutupiae. Even if Cerdic should die, his son would be a fool not to honor a treaty that acknowledged their place on British soil. Where, I thought desperately, where could the threat be?

The country was quiet. Gawaine, King of Lothian and Orkney, held the north. Hapgar held Strathclyde, and Coel, Urien's eldest, ruled in Rheged. Drustan and his sons held the northeast solidly for the High King, and between my brother Gwarthgydd in Northgallis and Maelgon, who had sway over the lords of Powys and Dyfed, Wales was secure. Cornwall, I thought suddenly, only Cornwall might betray him. On Mordred's twenty-fifth birthday not quite a year ago, Arthur had at last declared his son to be his heir. To his own surprise, the country did not rise up in protest, or bring up the ancient scandal, or deny Mordred's right to kingship. The sin that ate at Arthur through his life and made him sensitive to every touch upon it was forgotten by most other men. It was old news; everyone knew Mordred was the High King's son. Only Duke Constantine nursed a grievance. He proclaimed it loudly to any who would listen, but since even a fool could see his motives, men smiled and shrugged and drank to Mordred's health.

I did not think Constantine could command much of a following, certainly not against Arthur. Nor could he foment trouble in Less Britain, not with Lancelot there. Arthur's wise rule, Arthur's treaties, Arthur's friendships—these things held Britain strong and safe. Where lay the threat? I could not see it.

"Well, Cabal," I said, patting him kindly, "we will just have to wait."

They were in Council four hours. When they broke, I heard shouts of joy and laughter in the halls, and someone sounded a horn, a call to arms. The door flew open; I jumped up; the King entered, smiling, his arm around Mordred's shoulder. The years had fallen from him in a single day! He was alight and happy. I knew what it meant. He was going to war.

Behind him came in Bedwyr, Gereint, Bellangere, Agglaval, Dryaunt, Villers, and Bors, all jesting with each other. I had seen to it that the wine-skins were full of warm, spiced wine, and pitchers of mead stood on a low table. Men found counseling thirsty work.

"My lord Arthur," I greeted him, dipping him a curtsy.

He swung his free arm around me and, lifting me off the floor, kissed my lips. "I have stirring news, Gwen. We are raising an army."

"I guessed that much, my lord. Who is our enemy?"

He grinned and turned to Mordred. "I told you, she is the only one who does not like to hear it."

He had walked us to his writing table. Now he stopped and looked back at the gathering of knights around the fire across the room. They filled their cups and raised a toast to him.

"Arthur of Britain!" Bors cried. "Victory and long life to the King!"

"Long live Arthur!" the knights chorused. Arthur inclined his head. When he turned to me, he spoke gently.

"We are not yet directly threatened, Gwen, but if we do not go now, with a show of strength, war will be inevitable."

"But who, my lord? Who is our enemy?"

The smile left Arthur's eyes. He told me straight out. "Rome."

Rome. Was it possible? Arthur grasped my elbow and sat me down in his own chair.

"Arthur!" Bors called. "Do you believe Gawaine can raise a thousand? When Tydwyl never mustered above five hundred men?"

Arthur glanced swiftly at Mordred. "Stay with her and answer her questions, if you will. She will have many. I will join you when I can."

Mordred sat on the edge of the table. His eyes were shining.

"Rome?" I whispered. "This is folly, Mordred. Would Rome threaten us again?" But before he could answer, a shout of joy went up from the knights. I saw them gathered around Arthur, pounding him on the back, prophesying slaughter and boasting already about great feats of bravery. I stood.

"I must get out in the air," I said quickly. "Have you a cloak?" He brought me Arthur's, heavy and warm and lined with fox pelts. I wrapped it around my arms to keep it off the floor, and Mordred followed me out to the garden. It was misting, but the air was sharp and clean. I breathed in deeply and walked along the damp paths among the sleeping plants. Mordred followed patiently.

"All right," I said at last. "Tell me about it."

It appeared there was a new Emperor in Rome, one Justinian, who hoped to return the Empire to her former glory. He had sent one of his generals, Lucius Quintilianus, also called Hiberius the Spaniard, to demand tribute of King Childebert and King Hoel in return for "protection."

I stared aghast at Mordred. "Protection! From whom? Do they think to invade us again, as in the days of the Emperor Claudius?"

"The King thinks they look for an excuse for it," Mordred admitted. "The tribute demanded is more than Hoel could ever pay, and Hiberius knows it. The Romans claim that they will keep the Burgundians from our borders, if we pay the tribute."

"The Burgundians!" I cried. "But the Franks have held them off for years! What nonsense is this?"

"Yes, my lady. But Rome has stirred them up."

I stared at him. "I see the game. Did you say, Mordred, that we are being blackmailed? Has the demand for tribute come to us?"

"No, my lady. Not yet. But the King knows that if Hoel and Childebert have been approached, sooner or later it will be asked of him. The threat will not be reduced by waiting. The time to act is now."

I nodded. "Clearly. What will he do?"

"Hoel and Lancelot and Childebert have gathered at Kerrec for council. They believe their only hope is in a joint defense, and a strong one. No one knows the strength of Hiberius' army, or even of the Burgundians. But a strong front now, with Arthur of Britain behind them, might give the Romans pause. They know well he has never been beaten."

I managed a smile. "The Unconquered King. I hope they know it. How many men will he take?"

"Ten thousand, if he can raise them."

"Ten thousand! Is it possible?"

Mordred flashed one of his rare smiles. "There is not a man in Britain, youth or graybeard, who would not drop everything to fight for Arthur. He is a legend. And he will win."

I faced him nervously. "Then why is Niniane here?"

He looked surprised. "I did not know she was."

"What! Was she not in Council?"

"No, my lady. I don't even know if the King knows. He said nothing to me about it."

Puzzled, I fell silent. Around us the March winds rose and sent the folds of Arthur's cloak flapping. I welcomed the cold rain on my face; it cleared my head and kept my fears at bay.

"How odd," I said suddenly, "that we should stand here speaking of these Romans with such horror. Nearly every man in the Council chamber is descended from a Roman; the King, you, and I are all descended from a Roman general, a Spaniard even, one of the conquerors themselves. Had Maximus left when Rome withdrew her troops, we would not be here."

"But Rome did leave," Mordred said quietly. "She cannot now think to take us back under her mantle, after having left us to fend for ourselves against barbarians! This is what so angers Arthur. The arrogance of the demand! That Rome thinks she can claim us at her will! She abandoned us when we were little more than a scattering of hill tribes; now we are one people, and now we are our own masters."

"Indeed. Now we are worth something. Tell me, will the King take Excalibur?"

"Since there may be fighting, I should think so," Mordred replied, watching me closely. "Why?"

I shrugged and, feeling uneasy, adjusted my hood about my face to hide it. "No reason. I just had a thought. The last time the Sword left Britain . . . you know the story. When Maximus himself raised it against the King of Rome, it availed him nothing, and he died."

Mordred gripped my arms and forced me to look into his eyes.

"Rome was not then Britain's enemy," he said firmly. "Rome had left. It was Maximus' folly to pursue her. This time she comes to us. She *is* our enemy. And the Sword was made to protect Britain from her enemies. The end will not be the same."

Tears sprang unbidden to my eyes. "Oh, Mordred, I pray not!"

"Fear not, Guinevere," he said gently. "We will protect him with our lives. Lancelot and I, and Bedwyr and Gereint, and every knight in that room, and in the Council. He is worth more than life to us. Trust that old fox Merlin. If it comes to battle, he will be victorious."

I nodded, drying my eyes on the King's cloak, and, taking his arm, headed back. "You are going with him, did you say? Tell me who else goes. And how many men?"

This diverted his thoughts from Merlin and his dreadful prophecies, and he named three-quarters of the kings of Britain and nearly every lord I knew.

"Why, Mordred, there is no one left," I said when he had finished. "Who will be regent?"

"You will, Guinevere," said Arthur's voice. I looked up, startled, to see him at the doorway, smiling.

"Whatever do you mean, my lord?" He held out his hand, and I took it. He led me back inside, where all the knights were gathered behind him, smiling at me.

"The Council has decided to leave you in charge," he announced, regarding me with pride. "Not a single voice dissented."

I stared at him.

"Long live the Queen!" Bedwyr cried, and they all shouted, raised their goblets, and drank. For a swift moment, I thought this the jest of drunken men, but the King's face told me otherwise. He, at least, was sober and was brimming with pride.

"My lord King," I said shakily, doing him a low reverence, "I do not know what to say. I thank you for the honor you do me, but do you think it wise? I cannot command troops, my lord."

He raised me and held both my hands. "I believe you could, you know," he said gently, and then smiled. "But you will not have to. I leave Ferron here as commander. The lords in your Council are all men you know: Kay, Lyonel, Gryfflet, Villers, Clegis, Dynas, and Bleoberys. With Ferron that makes eight. And Mordred will return before the battle to relieve you of the regent's duties, by your leave. I take him with me that he may meet Hoel and Childebert, and join our council of ally lords. It's more than time they got to know each other. But then he will return—I can't risk both of us—so you need not rule longer than you must, unless you choose to. I leave that decision to you."

There was no doubt any longer that he was serious. The weight of such responsibility set me trembling, and I gripped his hands hard, to stop it.

"If you have such faith in me, my lord, I dare not doubt myself. Tell me—tell me what dispositions you have made around Britain—who is left for defense?"

Arthur glanced swiftly, triumphantly, at the knights. By my question, it seemed I had confirmed his faith. He sat me in his great chair behind the work desk and began to pace.

"Drustan sends his sons with me, but stays to hold the east. Old Tydwyl will hold the north for Gawaine. Kay's son holds Galava, Hapgar's brother Pertolys holds Strathclyde, Maelgon's brother Peredur Gwynedd, Coel's brother Uwain is regent in Rheged." He ticked off the other kingdoms one by one, all of them held by old men or untried youths. Except for Cornwall. Constantine himself stayed in Cornwall.

"He has lately had a quarrel with Childebert," the King said carefully, "and I judged it best to leave him behind. A thousand of his men come with me, the best part of his army. But I have given him the guardianship of the West. It is an honor that I hope will heal his pride." Then his face softened. "It is thanks to you, Gwen, we can leave Britain so lightly defended. To the east sit the Saxons. Thanks to you, we have treaties with them and must consider them allies, at least at present. And thanks to you, the Irish have kept to their own coasts these twenty years."

"No thanks to me, my lord," I protested, "but to your own wise statesmanship!"

Arthur laughed. "Nonsense. Fion's been in love with you since he first set eyes on you. That's why he keeps peace with us." I blushed at this, and the men grinned. "Never mind," the King said in a kind voice. "Whether it is due to you or me or destiny, we have no threats from our neighbors. You will be safe here, Gwen. If I doubted it, I could not leave you."

"Thank you, my lord. How long until Mordred's return? And yours?"

"Hiberius requires his answer by the first of June. Mordred should be back shortly after. I hope I can be back by the solstice, having sent the Roman on his way. If not, by midsummer, surely. The more men we can muster, the less time it should take. Give me a month to gather the army; three weeks to make the crossings; by June we should be ready for battle."

I took a deep breath. "Very good, my lord. I can manage that, I think." Then I grinned. "But if I am gray when you return, it is your doing!"

Arthur laughed and raised a toast to me, and the men joined him. I caught Mordred looking at me unawares; he blushed when he caught my eye and turned away.

Niniane came to dinner, but sat where I could not get speech with her. Afterward, she sought an audience with the King, while Bedwyr, Kay, Mordred, Ferron, and I sat by the library fire and discussed plans. When Arthur joined us, he looked solemn but content, so I judged she had not brought him evil tidings.

Late that night when I had the King to myself, I asked him what she had said; it was none of my business, but I thought he would tell me. He demurred at first but, when he saw my fear, gave in to comfort me.

"It is nothing she has seen through her Power," he assured me. "Just what she calls a feeling in her bones. But, as with Merlin, her bones never lie. These are important matters we are facing; they matter to Britain's future. She came to see how seriously we took this summons."

"Did she predict nothing, then? Victory? Defeat? Stalemate?"

By starlight I saw his smile. "You should know by now, Gwen, it is ill luck to speak to a commander about defeat or victory on the eve of battle."

"This is not the eve of battle, Arthur. You are evading me. What did she say?"

He reached for me under the bearskins and pulled me close against his body. "Will you not be diverted, even for a moment?"

"How can I, when I fear for your life?"

"Do not fear it. What she told me was perhaps the best thing she could have said. She said my fate was in my own hands. It is something every king likes to hear . . . Why do you tremble, Gwen? This is not bad news."

"I do not like it when Niniane speaks of fate."

He shrugged and touched my hair. "It's the way enchanters talk. Think nothing of it."

"With your permission, Arthur, I will speak to her myself."

He laughed. "She warned me you would try to. You worry too much, Gwen. Remember Merlin's words: *Take what comes and*—"

I clapped a hand over his mouth and whispered furiously, "If you say that to me again I will scream aloud and wake the castle! Dear God, how tired I am of that stale advice!"

He began to laugh in earnest, with true delight, and it was impossible not to laugh with him. He was once again the warrior King of Britain, and the spirit of his youth had returned to him. I gave up my questions and joined him in his joy.

The truth is, Niniane avoided me. During the month it took to gather Britain's army at Caer Camel, she flitted between the Lady's shrine on Ynys Witrin, her husband's fortress in the River Isles, and Camelot. She saw to it no one ever knew exactly where she was, or when she was expected. In spite of all the preparations, I kept a constant eye out for her. And in spite of the constant planning and changing of plans, she was always there when her advice was needed and always gone by the time I got wind of it.

There was an immense amount to do. Couriers flew daily in and out of King's Gate; kings and dukes and earls and lords from every corner of Britain began arriving with their troops, on horses, on ponies, and on foot. Everyone rallied to the High King's call. He had given them twenty years of peace; now they were eager to fight under his Dragon standard. We did not bother to enlarge the stables; there were too many horses to accommodate them all. They were tethered to horse lines behind the soldiers' tents. The open meadows inside the fortress walls were soon filled; troops and tents spilled out down the hill itself, and onto the downs below. They gathered around their commanders and were grouped more or less by location; the wary Cornishmen together on this side, the boisterous Lothians on the other; the cheerful warriors from Rheged on the south slopes, the taciturn

Northumbrians on the east. The Welsh contingents disgraced themselves in my eyes, for the North Welsh condescended to the South Welsh, and fights broke out. They had to be separated from one another at the end, the men from Guent in one place, from Dyfed in another, the men from Powys yonder, and those from Gwynedd under my own watchful eye.

I saw my brother Gwarthgydd, older now than my father had been when he died. He was very glad to see me and said I had not changed a hair since my girlhood—this was his favorite refrain, but if he expected me to believe it, he was disappointed. He had left Gwillim to hold Northgallis, and had brought his brothers with him to fight for Arthur.

This huge army needed food, and water, and boots, and horseshoes and weapons. The street of smiths was busiest of all; they never slept; they worked in shifts; their forges were alight for a solid month. My women spun and wove and sewed: war cloaks, tunics, leggings, robes, and mantles; slippers, stockings, caps, belts, and gloves; and most important, banners with the High King's emblem, the Red Dragon on a field on gold, for every company wanted one to carry. I made the King a sash to wear across his tunic, a token from his lady of the finest, crimson-dyed silks in the storerooms. In tiny golden stitches I made a dragon, and a castle and a cross, and stitched the initials of his name over the breast—AR, "Arturus Rex." If Hiberius should meet him face to face, I thought, he would know with whom he had to deal. I worked long and intently on this project—I told myself it was for Arthur, but I knew it was to keep my mind from other things.

Nearly every evening after hall I went to the chapel and prayed. Some years before, Arthur had built a small chapel on the castle grounds to save me the walk to the church. Bishop Landrum always waited for me at the church, eager to help me in my devotions. He would leer at me and stare lewdly down my gown and sometimes even smack his lips when he came near to speak. He never bathed and smelled worse than the compost heap. He had aged unpleasantly, his lust growing with his years, until all my maids were terrified of him. He called himself a servant of God, yet had fathered over twenty bastards by girls in the town. I could tell he believed all the rumors about Lancelot and thought that if he could bring himself to approach me, he might have me. So I had begged Arthur for the chapel, and he built it for me.

Usually I was alone there and stayed long to enjoy the peace. But one night when I came in, a young soldier was there, head bent, back bowed in prayer. I took my accustomed place, some distance away, and began my prayers for Arthur's safety and the preservation of all he had built in Britain.

At length, when I had finished, I rose from my knees to find the young man beside me, although I had not heard a whisper of his approach. I looked up into the breathtakingly handsome face of Lancelot's son Galahad. At fourteen, with black hair shadowing his striking features, he was the image of how Lancelot must once have looked. But his sky-blue eyes, bold and merciless, were Elaine's. There was a light about him; in that setting it seemed like a holy aura, the touch of God.

"My lady Queen," he said solemnly, "there is no use praying to God unless your heart is pure."

"Good sir, God knows my heart. I hide nothing from Him."

He shook his head. "The bishop knows your sins, madam. Renounce my father, Guinevere, and be cleansed."

Alone of all the men in Camelot, including Arthur, he dared say this to me! But for Lancelot's sake, I treated him gently. "The bishop casts stones, my lord, yet he is not without sin."

His eyes flashed. "Your prayers will not be answered."

"Judge me not, Galahad. Look well into your own heart, before you seek to know mine. Good evening."

I left him and walked out with as much dignity as I could summon. He had been the bishop's favorite since he first came to Camelot. I was always astounded that he revered the man, that he was so very easily fooled about some things and so difficult to fool about others. I hoped fervently that Arthur was planning to take him to Less Britain and was much relieved when Ferron confirmed that this was so. Lancelot would be glad to see him again, at least for a little while, and I did not think I could bear him about much longer. Whenever I went to chapel, after that, he was there.

Finally, in the last week, Niniane came to Camelot to stay. Pelleas, her lord, was leaving, and she came with him. I sent for her; she sent back to say she was engaged and would speak with me on the morrow. I sent again; the page could not find her. I rode myself to Avalon, to find she had just left. Angrily I went to Arthur, who did not need to be bothered at such a time, and demanded that she grant me an audience. He heard me out with patience and told me she had just left him, saying she would meet me after hall in the orchard. She did not come to dinner, and I suspected another ruse. But when I came to the orchard, she was there. The apple blossoms were just out, dancing like white froth in the April breezes. Niniane sat on a stone bench in a pose of meditation, eyes closed. I signaled my two maids to wait and went forward to see her alone. She did not change her attitude when I came up; I stood before her and waited. At last she sighed and opened her eyes.

"Greetings, Queen Guinevere. You wish to see me."

"I do indeed, Lady Niniane. Why have you been avoiding me?"

She smiled, ever so slightly. "Perhaps because I do not wish to answer your question."

She was straight with me; I gave her that. She had always been so.

"And why would you not wish to answer it?"

She sighed again and faced me. There was no expression on her face at all. "I do not see into the future as you look into your bronze, my lady Queen. Great events, those that move history, throw portents ahead, for those who can read them. But most of life is as dark to me as it is to you."

I sat, suddenly weak in my knees. "And yet you came here. Unbidden, and on time. You must have seen some such portent. Did you not?"

The night was soft, and all around us the earth smelled sweet with new growth. But when I looked into Niniane's eyes, the air grew cold and rank. She looked away and showed me her profile. She drew a deep breath slowly and let it out. "Yes. The world is about to change. There are great events ahead. The wheel of time is turning. Things will not be as they were before." She stopped and closed her lips tightly.

"Niniane!" I cried, trying desperately to control my rising panic. "Niniane, tell me what you foresee!"

"No." Her voice was flat and empty. "I cannot. It is forbidden. But because you are dear to him, and fear for him, I will answer you one question. Choose it well."

I kissed her fingers. There was only one question to ask!

"Will he return?" I cried, as the tears slid down my face. "Will Arthur return to Britain?"

She turned to me slowly, and I thought for a fleeting moment she felt relief. "Yes," she said very softly, "he will return." Then she rose, made me a graceful reverence, and departed.

I sat alone for a long while in the spring twilight and let my tears flow unchecked. He would return; that mattered most. But a fear yet nagged at me. She had sat here, dreading something; yet she had not dreaded the answer she had to give. I began to fear that I had asked her the wrong question.

The night before they left, all the lords gathered for a great feast. The army numbered over twelve thousand men; not even Arthur had expected so many to answer his call. Hoel and Lancelot and even Childebert had sent ships across the Narrow Sea; ten ships lay in the Severn estuary, and a score more in the small harbors along the southern coasts. Even so, they would all make several trips; the crossing would take weeks to accomplish.

I could not partake of the meal; the wine was rich and unwatered, and the men grew rowdy, as they do on the eve of battle, to cheer themselves and banish fear. I led the women out early and went straight to my quarters. Usually the King stayed late, for the men needed his presence; but there was no battle on the morrow, only leave-taking. They let him go early, for they knew he had his good-byes to make.

I waited for him in his chamber. I had dismissed Bran and Varric for the evening, saying I would tend the King myself. They had understood. I dressed in his favorite gown of mine, a blue one, and brushed my hair and let it fall unbraided. I was determined not to weep. Niniane had promised he would return.

I heard him coming; in the antechamber he stopped and spoke to Bran in a low voice, then came up the stairs with a firm step and paused in the doorway. Meeting his eyes was like taking a blow to the chest; my heart began to pound, and tears sprang to my eyes.

"This is not good-bye, Gwen," he said gently.

"I know, my lord. But it is farewell." He came across to me, and I gripped his arms. "In spite of everything, Arthur, in spite of the great honor you have paid me, in spite of your obvious joy at leading the army again, in spite of the righteousness of the cause, my heart is heavy. I do not want you to go."

He wrapped his arms around me and hugged me tightly. "Come, come. We will not be parted for very long. Before you know it, it will be midsummer, and we will be idling around the fountain complaining of the heat."

I managed a smile and blinked away the tears. "And when did you ever complain of anything, my lord? You describe the rest of us, perhaps, but not yourself. Sometimes, Arthur, you are too sweet-tempered to bear."

"Your praises go to my head," he said lightly, "but I can be as angry as the next man. You have seen me so."

"Sloth and incompetence annoy you," I replied, "but little else. What a King you are, Arthur! Remember that Britain will not be Britain without you here, but a mere shell of herself, her innards gone. Every minute you are away will seem like days to me!"

He stood back and looked down into my face. "Why, Gwen, those are sweet words to carry with me. I will remember them."

He led me to the bed and sat down beside me. "Listen, now. This is how I regard it. What is the very worst that can happen? What do you fear most?"

I swallowed hard and tried to copy his calm speech. "That you will be slain on the battlefield and not return to me."

He smiled. "That is your woman's heart speaking. I can think of worse fates than death. So be it. Now, what is the best thing that can happen? What do you most desire?"

"That Hiberius should beg your pardon and withdraw before a single sword is drawn!" I whispered fervently.

He laughed. "Well, we are agreed on that. And now, what is likely? Surely it falls somewhere between the two. I believe Hiberius will test us and give us battle to see our strength. But, united, we will defeat him and come home the victors. How many men return with me depends upon his numbers and his determination. But I will be back, Gwen."

I nodded. "So Niniane has told me."

"*She has?*" He looked so startled, I knew he had been speaking more from his heart, to comfort me, than from belief. "Then she has told you more than she told me. Well, then, where is the cause for fear?"

I sighed and lifted my hand to his face. "I don't know, my lord, but I do fear for you." He took my hand and kissed my palm.

"Put fear away," he whispered. "Let there be nothing but joy between us tonight."

I yielded to him willingly and for a while forgot the darkening future. But later, as we lay spent from pleasure and waiting for sleep, my thoughts turned again to Niniane, and to Arthur, and to Mordred. The world would change, she had said—what could that mean? I thought Arthur was dozing, but then he spoke, in a voice so low I pressed closer to him to hear it.

"Guinevere, if the fates are cruel and part us forever, I would have you know this: In all my life I have loved no one more than you. Were we permitted to live our lives over, I would take you again to wife, and none other. I have been given many blessings, but the dearest one to me is you."

"Oh, Arthur," I whispered through tears, "this sounds like good-bye." He would not let me speak, but kissed me and held me close in his arms until the dawn.

They left at midmorning. The King rode out resplendent in a cloak of purple, with a circlet of gold on the brow of his helmet and the crimson sash across his chest. Above him flew the Red Dragon of Britain. On his belt hung his great Sword. His gray stallion was excited by the press of horses and soldiers and danced all the way to King's Gate, where a great shout was raised by the gathered armies beyond the walls. The stallion reared; laughing, Arthur brought him down and gave the command to march. Within an hour, all we could see of him was the dust he raised on the plains below.

46 ♛ THE QUEEN'S DILEMMA

God bless Arthur, he sent me a courier every day, and when he got to Less Britain, sent me one every week, to let me know how he fared. His crossing was easy; he made Kerrec in good time and was heartily welcomed there by Lancelot and Hoel. They met with King Childebert to plan their strategy and wait for the rest of the British forces to land.

Meanwhile, our little household at Camelot ran smoothly. We had only a hundred men left in the barracks, but Ferron drilled them daily. Niniane returned to Avalon and kept watch over King Melwas' young cousin, who held his fortress for him. We posted scouts along the Saxon borders, but Cerdic kept his word and gave us no cause for fear. It truly seemed that Britain lay quiet in peaceful slumber, hardly knowing her lord was away.

And then one night a courier arrived. Kay, white-faced, brought him to me as we sat in hall. He had not come from Arthur, which I guessed from the freshness of his clothing; he had come from Niniane. The message was short and to the point. Duke Constantine was lately come north from Cornwall with an army of four hundred men. She bade me take care, for he meant to take Caer Camel. I blanched as I heard this, then asked the messenger tell it again to all the knights who sat at table. To a man, they were furious and shouted out their protests. What did he think he was about, defying Arthur's orders the moment he was gone?

I thanked the courier for his speed and bade him sup with us. He gave me what little news there was: The last of the King's ships had left the estuary, and the Summer Country was quiet. But they kept good lookouts, I observed, to get news of Constantine so soon. The courier dropped his eyes. Melwas' cousin had not thought to post lookouts; the lady Niniane had seen it in the fire.

At that I rose and excused myself from the company, bidding the eight knights who formed the Council to meet me in the King's library after the meal. I went there immediately, to have a moment to think. Clearly, Constantine meant mutiny. As guardian of the west, he could move his troops through Cornwall, through Dumnonia and, skirting the Summer Country, even through Wales. But to approach Caer Camel defied Arthur's orders. And why patrol with four hundred men? No, he meant to take Arthur's fortress, whether to wrest it from him or to hold it for him made no difference. He was dealing with a woman now and saw his path to power clear.

Could we prevent him? That was the question. Could we hold Caer Camel, outnumbered four to one? And if we could, for how long? Six months? Three months? One? We were now halfway through May; this was not the time to send for Arthur, nor for Mordred, who was meeting for the first time the ally kings with whom he would one day have to deal. Could we hold out against the duke, or must we give him battle? Four to one were not odds I liked.

The knights hurried in a short time later, led by Ferron, all muttering their outrage and voicing threats. I got them settled and asked for their advice. They assured me, and Kay confirmed this, that the fortress could be held by a handful of trained men against an army of thousands. The walls could not be breached, King's Gate could not be forced; the battlements could be held by the archers forever. But the thought of a siege filled me with horror. Worse than the loss of freedom was the fear of leaving the rest of Britain on its own, with Camelot, its heart and soul, cut off by Cornish troops. I voiced my fear, and to a man, they were willing to fly out King's Gate and do battle, four to one. I shook my head.

"My lords," I said, "I will not be responsible for such slaughter. We cannot allow ourselves to be drawn into a battle. If he means us ill, that is to play into his hands. But we must be sure of his intentions. Until he declares himself our enemy, Constantine is Arthur's ally. If he knocks upon King's Gate and begs entrance of me, I must let him in."

I could see by their faces they thought me naive, or witless. Two of the younger men, Dynas and Clegis, scowled darkly.

"But, my lady!" Dynas objected. "You cannot let them in, not in such numbers! Once inside King's Gate, they will take us!"

"The man's a fox," Villers growled. "He's been waiting for the chance to get Mordred out of the country. He will give out that he comes to offer you support. He will say anything to get inside."

They all voiced their agreement; no one doubted that Constantine was our enemy, and a devious one at that.

"Then, my lords, we must devise a strategy. We cannot fight him; nor can we wait, cut off from Britain, for the High King to return. Once Constantine surrounds us, he will be High King in all but name."

They all looked at one another, nervous and unhappy, but no one spoke.

I glanced toward Ferron, who was frowning. "My lord, can you not think of some way to stall them?"

He cleared his throat. "Not with so few men, my lady. One hundred against four hundred are poor odds."

"Not fight them, Sir Ferron. Stall them. Slow them down."

Silence blanketed the room. Clegis and Dynas stared sullenly at the floor. I guessed that this was not the kind of talk the men were used to. Fighting was something they understood: good, clean fighting out in the open air. Not one of them, I was willing to wager, had ever tried to outwit his opponent. To a man, they lacked Arthur's patience for planning, talking, and waiting for the slow unfolding of events. I began to appreciate the skill it took to rule such men.

"Would my lords feel easier if I sent to Wales for troops to come up behind him?"

In relief they voiced their assent. But Sir Gryfflet shook his head. "Don't send to Gwynedd for troops, my lady. Maelgon's brother Peredur is lord there now, and Maelgon holds a grudge against you for banishing his sister to Less Britain. Where she died."

I stared open-mouthed at this nonsense. Before I could speak, Sir Clegis confirmed it. "Maelgon is loyal to the High King, my lady, but I would not count upon his loyalty to you."

"Banish his sister!" I cried. "This is fools' chatter! Her husband took her to Less Britain—the husband she alone chose out of all men—to bear his son, which she conceived of her own will. God knows—God *knows* I would have kept them both in Britain and unwed! I should have liked to send her back to Wales and her precious brother!" The men looked quickly at one another and shifted in their seats. I gripped the edge of Arthur's table and fought for calm. What these men had heard were only rumors. If Maelgon had indeed turned against me, it was because I had publicly opposed him in Gwynedd, when he accused Lancelot and I defended him. He was too much a coward to admit it openly. And these men, I wondered, could the same be said of them? Did their loyalty to Arthur extend to his person only, and not to me?

Just then the door behind them opened; they all looked round. Anna, a plain maiden of nineteen and the only one of my attendants with any sense, poked her head in.

"Not now, woman!" someone grumbled. "We're in Council!"

She looked straight at me, her brow puckered with worry. "My lady, I beg pardon for the interruption, but—"

"Unless it's a courier it can wait," Dynas cried. "Be gone, maiden!"

I raised my hand for silence. Since Linet had gone home to York, Anna was the only woman besides Ailsa I could talk to, and I relied upon her. "What is it, Anna?"

"It's Ailsa, my lady. She has fallen down and can't rise. Or speak, or move. I have sent for a physician but I judged you would want to know."

"Ailsa!"

"For pity's sake," Clegis murmured, "the King's Council interrupted for an old woman's fall!"

"You judged rightly, Anna." My voice shook, but whether with rage or sorrow I hardly knew. "I will come at once."

The men turned. "But, my lady!" It was Dynas and Clegis together. "What about Constantine?"

I paused at the door. "Fortify yourselves with wine and mead, send for the scribe, and await me. I will return directly."

I reached for Anna's arm, and we went out together.

"How they resent your power!" she whispered. "What fools men are!"

Kay's calm voice floated clearly down the corridor. "My lords, do as Arthur does and put your faith in the Queen. She will not disappoint you."

I squeezed Anna's arm as we hurried away. "Not all men, Anna. Thank God, not all men."

They had put Ailsa to bed. When I went in, the physician was bending over her, prying open her eyes, and shaking his head. He bowed to me and backed away. A sob welled in my throat as I looked down upon her face, so thin and old and gray, and so suddenly! I sat upon her coverlet and took her hand in mine. How soft and slack the wrinkled skin, how light the bones! I bent and kissed her pallid cheek. She slept, breathing noiselessly, but it was a deeper sleep than she was used to; neither sound nor touch awakened her.

"Ailsa," I whispered. "Dear Ailsa!" I pushed a lock of thin hair from her brow. "When did this happen? Where did she fall?"

"In your chamber, my lady," Anna said with a hand upon my shoulder. "She was folding a gown just come from the fuller's. I heard a noise—she did not call out—and ran up to find her lying on the floor. Her eyes were open then. She knew me, I'm sure of it, but she could not move or speak."

I turned to the physician, who bowed again. "What do you make of it, sir? Come, tell me the truth. I can see by your face how grave it is."

"I fear, my lady Queen, there is little that can be done. It's the sleeping sickness. If she awakens from it, she may live awhile longer. But she will not regain the use of her right arm. See the way her face is slackened. That is a sure sign of the sickness. And if she does not awaken, then death will follow."

I fought down the sob. "How long?"

He shrugged. "Two days. A week. It is hard to tell."

"And until then?"

"We will keep her warm with hot bricks at her feet and rub her chest with salve. If her breath stays quiet, she may recover. It is not unknown."

That slim hope was all that he could give me. I sat with her, holding her hand, until the bricks and hot water arrived. Then, as I was in the way of the physician's ministrations, I went out with Anna.

"Oh, Anna, I do not like the look of her. All the life is gone from her so suddenly! Only this morning she was chiding me about the state of my hair ... she always took such pains with it ... she always took such care ..."

I faltered; Anna held me tightly and, unable to bear it any longer, I wept in her arms. Ailsa was the only mother I had ever known, and no mother could ever, anywhere, love a child more than my dearest Ailsa had loved me. When I said I wished to arrange a pallet by Ailsa's bed and sleep by her through the night, Anna assured me she would see that it was done.

There was nothing else I could do. I wiped my eyes and returned to the library with Anna, hand in hand. We entered abruptly and found the men in heated argument. Kay, Ferron, Berys, and Lyonel were defending me to Dynas, Clegis, and Villers. Gryfflet stood between them, listening. They broke off of a sudden when they saw me, and some of their faces went red. Dynas and Clegis were young men, too young to have fought with Arthur in the Saxon wars, but Villers was an old friend—I looked at him in surprise, and he had the grace to color and look away. He had lately become a Christian; it crossed my mind that Bishop Landrum might have been busy with his tongue.

"Gentlemen." They were staring at the tear tracks on my cheeks. "My lords all, hear what I have decided. I will send first to Northgallis. Gwillim my kinsman will come to my aid. His wife is the King of Dyfed's daughter; between the two kingdoms, he can command a hundred men or so. And I will send to Drustan of Elmet. Since Arthur's generous recompense for Lamorak's murder, he has been a staunch supporter of the King. He might even come himself. Will that do?"

Relieved, they assured me that a hundred men on either side of Constantine's army could give him a battle he might not wish to chance.

"But," Gryfflet ventured, still sitting on the fence, "can they come in time? Even with swift couriers, and allowing time to muster what men are left"—he counted upon his fingers—"it will be a fortnight, at least, my lady. Constantine will be here long before that."

"Not," I said quietly, "if we can slow him down." They looked at one another and again went silent. "If you will, my lords, leave that part of it to me."

They agreed to this without much argument; no one asked me what I proposed to do. Kay got them settled drinking mead before the fire. I sat at Arthur's desk and beckoned to the scribe. He drew out his parchments and quills and mixed his ink, while from the pouch at my waist I took the regent's seal. With Ferron standing by, I dictated the letter to Gwillim, and below the scribe's neat Latin hand, I wrote it myself in Welsh, for I did not know if Gwillim kept a Latin scribe. My father certainly had not, but even Wales had grown more civilized since then. I sent the same message to Drustan. When the ink dried the scribe sealed the scrolls with wax.

Carefully I impressed the wax with the regent's seal. Ferron summoned couriers, and they went off at once, taking the northern road through Aquae Sulis to stay out of Constantine's way.

The scribe began to collect his things, but I bade him stay. "I have another message, good Julius. Bide a moment while I consider what to say."

Ferron looked at me hopefully, but said nothing. Any move of Constantine's was important. But this was treachery—Niniane had seen it through her Sight, so it was true—and clearly Arthur needed to be told. I did not wish to alarm him, for it might come to naught. I dared not ask for Mordred, or one of his top commanders, and yet he had to know the threat was real.

"Address this to Arthur, High King of Britain," I said slowly, and Ferron sighed in audible relief. I smiled up at him. "What did you fear, my lord? Did you think I would keep this from him and try to be King myself?"

"By the Light!" he swore softly. "It is not unknown!"

"Well, by the grace of God, I am not Pendragon and have not that ambition. I am his servant. How shall I tell him of this threat, without calling half his army back?"

In the end, we simply stated the facts as we knew them. I asked for a company of men on good horses to come as swiftly as they might, to help take Constantine from the rear in case he sat down in front of Caer Camel to besiege us. The message was sealed, and the courier sent.

I rose and turned to Ferron. "Thank you, Ferron, for your aid and for your defense of me. I know some of the younger men, especially the Christians, think it unseemly for a woman to govern men."

Ferron smiled. "Fools come in many colors, my lady. Pay them no mind. They have yet to learn that leadership wears different cloaks."

"Why, Ferron, I thank you for those words."

He bowed. "You raised the Sword of Britain, my lady. You are not like any other woman these men have known. Give them time to get better acquainted. They probably think"—and his eyes narrowed in laughter—"that you've done little else but weave Arthur his war cloaks. They will learn, my lady Queen, the lesson we all have learned. Give them time."

I said nothing, but made him a reverence to the floor. Once my foolish arrogance had endangered Ferron's future; now his forgiveness, so generous, so undeserved, touched my heart.

When we reached the women's quarters, I pulled Anna aside. "Anna, I must ask a service of you. It will require courage."

She straightened and dipped a quick curtsy. "Queen Guinevere, I am your servant. Command me."

"You must take a message to Niniane. To Avalon. Tonight."

I heard her indrawn breath, and her eyes widened, but she did not shrink from me. She was a brave girl. To every Christian woman, except perhaps to me, Avalon was a forbidden and frightening haunt of dark rites and pagan spirits. Girls her age could not remember, as I did, the days when the Good Goddess was worshipped throughout the land. Anna feared what dwelt behind the whitewashed pavilions of the Lady's shrine; but I recalled with fondness the clean, sweet-scented cells, the cool calm of the House of Healing, and the still beauty of the tended orchards encircled by the Lake. The only thing to fear at Avalon was Niniane herself, aloof and powerful as she was. She had served Arthur well these many years—would she now serve me?

"My lady, I will do it," Anna said firmly.

"Bless you, Anna. You will come to no harm, I promise you. I will give you a token to show the guards at the gates. You must ride alone—not secretly, but silently—I do not want the Council to know."

At once her interest quickened, and she nodded eagerly. She was nineteen and still unmarried; no one had yet offered for her, though she was a better woman than all of my pretty girls put together. Naturally enough, this had engendered in her a contempt for men's opinions; she was always eager to prove that she could do without a warrior's help.

"Say to Niniane—herself, mind you, no other—say to Niniane the High Queen begs her assistance—yes, begs—for the Kingdom's sake. Tell her we have sent for reinforcements, thanks to her warning, but we need a fortnight. For Arthur's sake, if not for mine, I beg she will call upon her powers and bring wind, storm, flood, or mists, or whatever catastrophe she can devise to bar Cornwall's way. Once he crosses the Camel, once he comes to the plain of Camlann, we are besieged and the heart is cut out of Britain! Then are we held captive, trapped and powerless, at the Duke of Cornwall's whim."

"Oh, my lady." I saw she trembled.

"Take heart, Anna. Niniane will heed my call. I am sure of it, else I would not ask her."

She swallowed. "It's not that, exactly."

"What is it, then?"

"Can she—my lady, can she really do such things?"

I smiled. "Oh, yes. Do not doubt her power. If she willed, she could raise mountains from the sea. But she has a fierce pride and must be cautiously approached. Take care to speak politely and hide your crucifix under your tunic. Plead for the Kingdom, Anna! I would go myself, in an instant—but Arthur would breathe flames if he knew I went without the Council's knowing."

"And they would never let you go. Never mind, my lady, I will do it. I will slip out now to the stables and be back before moonset."

I gave her the token. She curtsied, then paused on the verge of going. "My lady—"

"Yes, Anna?"

"Did you—did you really lift the High King's Sword?"

She stood perfectly still, but I could feel her fear across the space between us. She was barely nineteen, about to undertake a mission—alone and in secret—she had never dreamed of doing. I reached out and clasped her hand.

"It is one of the tales they tell," I said slowly, lowering my voice to a whisper, "and in truth, nothing is beyond a woman's strength if the need is great enough."

"My lady Queen," she breathed, "I believe it." She smiled shyly. "I will be back before moonset, and no one will know I've gone."

Four days passed. Ailsa slept and did not awaken. Every hour, it seemed to me, she grew smaller and thinner than the hour before. I saw that she had warmed bricks put to her throughout the day and night. By her bedside I kept a carafe of sweet water, for when she should awaken. Every few minutes I moistened a cloth and pressed it to her mouth. All it did was chap her lips. Without water, I knew, she could not live long. I did not sleep much. My heart was too heavy and would not allow me peace.

Ferron came by twice daily to report on Constantine's progress. We had sent scouts out at once and so learned of his quick march from the coast, his turning eastward well south of Ynys Witrin, and his steady approach from the southwest. But when Ferron came to summon me to Council, I waved him away.

"But, my lady"—he frowned—"the men are growing restless. Berys and I daily drill the troops, to keep them occupied and give Clegis and Dynas something to do, but time is running out. Something must be done. In three days Constantine will be at the banks of the Camel. We must devise a plan."

"Oh, Ferron! I cannot come now—I cannot even think—my thoughts are like dry leaves in a wind—"

"But the men are all gathered in the Round Hall."

I looked down at Ailsa's gray face. Anna sat in the corner, eyes averted, wrapping an herb-soaked cloth around a steaming brick. Slowly I shook my head. "I cannot leave her, Ferron. She is near death. I must be here."

"Guinevere, I pray you to attend us. The Council is divided, you must know that. Half of them want to take him on, face to face, if only because they are tired of waiting."

I looked up briefly. "Teach them patience, then. Set them an example.

Do what you can, Ferron. You must see that I cannot leave her. She is a mother to me. I would never forgive myself if I were not here . . ."

He hesitated, bowed low, and left.

"My lady!"

I jerked awake. It was very dark; the candle had gone out. A shadow darker than the rest, Anna leaned over the bed. "My lady!"

Too frightened to breathe, I jumped up from the pallet.

"Dear God, Anna—" I stopped. Ailsa's eyes were open and looking up at me. "Ailsa! Oh, Ailsa! My dear nurse! Bide a moment, pray, and take some water. Help me, Anna!" I lifted her head and shoulders—how light she was!—and put the cup to her lips. She could barely manage to swallow; most of it dribbled from her lips, but some of it went down. Anna placed a warm brick at her feet, then went for broth. I held Ailsa in my arms, and whispered to her and thanked God that she still lived. Her lips moved. I bent my ear close to her mouth and heard her breath, just on the edge of sound.

"Guinevere."

"Oh, Ailsa! I am here! Do not struggle yet with speech. You will be stronger soon. I am here, my dear love, I am here." I lit the candle and held her in my arms and told her what had happened and begged her take more water and assured her that everything would be all right in time; all the while she watched me with eyes full of fear.

She took a little broth when it came, a very little, then fell asleep as I sang to her and stroked her hair.

When she slept, her sleep was light and quiet, with little sighing breaths, the way she always used to sleep. Gratefully I kissed her brow and rose.

"Shall I send for the physician, my lady?"

"Later, Anna. Let her rest a little longer undisturbed."

"Will you be going back to your chamber, then?"

"No. No, I will stay here with her until she is quite recovered. And in the morning, I suppose I ought to show my face in Council."

"Would you like me to attend you?"

"Thank you, Anna, but not this time. Not in the Round Hall. To men, that is a sacred precinct. Stay by Ailsa and give her more broth if she awakens."

"Yes, my lady."

In the Round Hall the men sat with gloomy faces. They were a small gathering, eight sitting around a table built for thirty. Above the High King's chair Excalibur's hanger hung empty, and the great chamber, so often full of voices and the robust companionship of men, rang hollow like a gourd with its innards missing.

Kay looked glad to see me, and Ferron, relieved, asked kindly after Ailsa. But the others stirred in their seats and glared at one another. They had reached an impasse—some wanted war, some preferred to wait out the siege until our reinforcements came, and some wavered, undecided. Without Arthur, they were like nervous horses, pulling against one another with more passion than sense, and with little result. How they missed his steady, guiding hand!

In the middle of their arguments a scout arrived, still dusty from his ride, and fell to one knee at Ferron's feet.

"My lord! It is amazing—a miracle—they were bewitched, I think!"

"Speak sense, Aranor. Remember you are a soldier."

The youth gulped and twisted his hands together. "My lord! Duke Constantine has disappeared!"

"What!"

"Regis and I were watching from Berin's Hill, south of the Camelford—"

"I know your posting," Ferron said sharply. "Go on."

"We watched them camp, my lord, but—but in the morning, yesterday morning, they—they disappeared!"

Ferron scowled. "They got past you unseen, you mean, you young scamp. Sneaked past while you were sleeping."

"No!" the youth cried. "We checked the ground! They did not get by us! My lord, please believe me. I could follow the tracks of an army without getting down from the horse. We slept in shifts—they did not pass us!"

"Then where did they go?"

"My lord, we could not tell. A great mist crept in that night, all up and down the valley, encircling their campsite. It came down from the Lake. We saw it come. It did not lift in the morning, but seemed to draw strength from the sun and grow thicker. Toward midday it drifted back to the Lake, and—and the army was gone! We—we covered all the ground between where they had been and the river. My lord, they did not come this way, and they are not there. The tracks led toward the Lake." The boy gulped. "I don't know why they would change course, my lord. And I—I don't know where they went."

A couple of the men made the sign against enchantment, and the Christians crossed themselves. Ferron still scowled skeptically.

"Believe him, my lord," I said. "He is telling you the truth."

At that, they all turned to stare at me.

Kay cleared his throat. "My lady, do you know aught about this?"

"My lords, you agreed to leave that part of it to me." I looked around at all their startled faces. "Constantine has not disappeared, he has only been misled. Eventually he will find his way again. Thank you, Aranor, for your news. It could hardly please us more."

As soon as the scout was gone, Clegis spoke. "And when he comes, my lords, what will he find? An army of King's men too frightened to step outside the gates!"

"Too wise to step outside," Berys countered. "Don't be a fool, Clegis."

I raised my hand for silence. "I am the one who must answer to Arthur for the Council's action," I reminded them. "And I will not risk your slaughter. If we can even the odds, that's a different matter. But until help comes, I forbid the gates to open."

Several of them shifted in their seats; Dynas and Clegis scowled. These were strong words, and they resented hearing them from me. But my thoughts were with Ailsa, and I was almost out of patience.

"But, my lady," Clegis cried at last, "we cannot sit here and do nothing while the traitor approaches!"

"Certainly we will not," I said calmly. "We will do what we can. Sir Clegis, you are the finest archer in the High King's army. Pick thirty men—we can spare no more—and train them to hit their mark at a hundred paces. See that we have five times the arrows you would expect to need to kill four hundred men. I give you five days." His jaw dropped. "Can this not be done?" I asked innocently.

He colored. "It will be done, my lady Queen."

"Thank you, my lord. I am sure I may rely upon you. Dynas, I charge you with readying our defense against an attack of fire arrows. If it comes to confrontation, I don't expect Constantine has the stomach for a siege. Bid the coopers get busy. We'll need water vats and men to carry buckets. I can spare you five soldiers only, but you may organize a brigade from the pages and grooms and chamberlains. They will need drilling, of course. Take all the time you require. With so many gone from Camelot, they have little enough to do."

"I will do it!" Dynas cried eagerly. "I had not thought of fire arrows!"

Ferron of course was in charge of the fortress defense, and Kay of the castle's, but with these two young hotheads busy at other tasks, their own plans would run a smoother course, I thought. And I saw by the half-concealed amusement on their faces that they thought so, too.

They were all talking about siege defenses when I left. I smiled to myself. They had formed a plan, and hardly a man there knew how they had done it. Ahhhh, my dear Arthur, I thought as I walked quickly back to Ailsa, how they all must be as putty in your hands!

Three days later Constantine was discovered mired in the bogs at the southern reaches of the Lake of Avalon. How he had come there, no one knew. But everyone knows how easy it is to lose one's way in a fog.

For those three days, Ailsa was much the same, more sleeping than awake, unmoving, and saying nothing. I had hoped that, once she came out of her deep sleep and opened her eyes, she would come to herself again, but the physician told me not to expect it. When she was awake, she knew me. But although she listened to my voice and smiled a trifle when I sang to her, she could not respond, even with the lift of a finger. And when she slept, her breath rattled lightly in her chest. The physician frowned when he heard it, but said nothing beyond advising more salve.

Day and night I sat at her side; Anna and I took our meals in her little chamber. I found solace recalling events long past when Ailsa had helped me through one scrape or another, and I knew by her eyes that Ailsa enjoyed it, too. Anna, bless her, listened to my reminiscing without a word of complaint, laughed when I laughed, and once or twice was moved to tears.

"Oh, Anna!" I cried. "There never was such a guardian in all the world as Ailsa! She knows me better, even now, than I know myself. But for Ailsa, I should have betrayed—I should have yielded—always she held up before my eyes the honor of Gwynedd, the honor of Arthur, the honor of Britain, and bade me do what I knew was right! Ah, Ailsa, my mother in life, without you I should not now be Queen!"

I chanced to look down and found her awake and looking at me, thin tracks of tears sliding sideways down her cheeks. I fell to my knees and kissed her hands. "You know it's true, my darling Ailsa, don't you? You and Arthur, between you, have kept me on the straight path. Without you, I should long ago have yielded to temptation and betrayed the very things I hold most dear."

Half her mouth moved in a smile; her lips began to work. But as I bent down to listen, a knock came at the door, and Ferron burst in to tell me that Constantine was on his way again and fast approaching the Camel river.

"Come out of your fastness, my lady, I beg of you! The Council needs you!"

"Ferron, Ferron, I cannot come—"

Behind him came Kay's voice, stern and sad. "You must choose, Guinevere, between Ailsa and Britain. Remember Arthur once made such a choice."

"Oh, God!" I cried, pressing my hands against my face. "Surely that choice will not be asked of me!"

"But it is," Ferron pressed. "Clegis has roused Villers and Dynas and even Gryfflet almost to frenzy. They will not listen to a word we say— against orders, Sir Villers is rousing the army, even as we stand here!"

"Then give him an order he can obey!" I cried, my eyes on Ailsa's withered face. "Bid him take twenty men and cross the river. Set fire to the land on the other side, six leagues either way. We've had no rain for weeks and the land is mostly brush and meadow grasses. Let it burn toward Constantine; let him see a wall of flame. It will take him a day to get around it. A whole day of precious time."

For a long moment the men stood silent. Then Ferron grinned and bowed. "My lady Queen."

A hot afternoon, stuffy and still. Anna wiped my brow with a cool cloth, as I wiped Ailsa's. The sun beat down upon the castle walls and warmed the stones that encased us. Somewhere, I hoped, the flames were still burning around Constantine; in that little chamber we were roasting alive.

Ailsa was whispering, but it was mostly nonsense. She roamed a world where past and present mingled, and I could not follow half she said. Her breath came harder, no matter what we did to ease her, but she did not seem to know it. Arthur, Uther, my father Leodegrance, Alyse and Pellinore and a hundred others marched through her thoughts in a confused parade; she did not hear me when I spoke to her or listen when I sang.

Through the window we could see dark clouds building in the distance, slowly swelling and creeping toward us. Rain might bring us sweet relief, but it also signaled danger. It would put out the fires that had, for two days, kept Constantine at bay.

"Those men are fools!" Anna grumbled in my ear. "Sir Dynas is speaking treason! I overheard him with Sir Clegis when I went to fetch the water. He does not intend to obey you, my lady, even if you command him to his face. He says since women are not warriors, they cannot lead men!"

"Hush, Anna. I know what they are saying. It's even possible that it is true."

"But, my lady!"

"I should be with them. I know that; but I cannot go. I am not Arthur. Listen to her, my dear, sweet Ailsa. She is not in her right mind. I am so afraid, Anna—once, Arthur put his grief behind him, for Britain's sake. But I—I cannot seem to let go of mine."

When I closed my eyes I still saw Arthur, hands clasped in prayer, a shadow of himself, consumed with grief for Merlin's passing, consumed with the fear he had buried him alive in the stony ground. It was the Sword that had roused him and brought him to his senses; the great Sword, a gift of the god, which protected Britain from her enemies. But the Sword was not here now. He had taken it with him.

That night the skies opened. I lay on the pallet at the side of Ailsa's bed, listening to the wheeze and shudder of her breath. A silent seed of fear took root inside my heart and set me shaking. This could not happen, not now, not after so much. It was nearly summer; the sweet warmth of the afternoons and the sun on her face would bring her back to health, if I could move her outdoors! But moving her the physician flatly forbade. He said she would not survive it, and that was easy enough to believe, seeing what little nourishment she took. We were doing all that we could—what more could we do?

All that dark day her breath rattled loudly. We lit a coal fire in the grate and sprinkled herb water on it to steam the air and give her an easier breath. Anna brought me news that the Camel was in full flood, raging and impossible to ford. She crossed herself quickly and smiled.

Ailsa woke at dusk and looked at me beseechingly; her lips moved, but no sound came out; she was in need, and I did not know what she wanted! Anna and I brought her everything we could think of: blankets, bricks, tea, broth, water, wine, salve, soap, furs, and even ribbons. Then my glance happened to fall on the kerchief on the floor where we had collected all the charms and jewels the physician had taken off her.

"Her amulet!" I cried, lifting the soft, leather pouch full of lucky talismans. Something moved behind her eyes. I placed the amulet in her hand, and her spirit charms, too, and her prayer beads; her fingers, so long immobile, closed around them; her eyes fluttered shut, and she slept. I did not know whether to weep with joy that she could command her fingers or weep with sorrow at what her request betokened, but I wept.

Toward dawn I was awakened by a harsh, grating sound. I sat up; in the dimness I saw the glint of Ailsa's eyes. Her mouth was open; the horrible sound came from her throat!

"Lady Elen!" Her hard, rasping voice rang loud in the room. A thrill of fear raced up my spine. Elen was my mother, dead these five and thirty years. "It is done . . . You are delivered . . . of a daughter . . . A queen . . . like no other . . . One day she will make you proud." She gasped horribly, fighting for breath. I bent over her. Her eyes looked into mine. "So proud." The eyes rolled back, the racking noise faded to a sigh, Anna's hand came down upon my shoulder.

"No! Ailsa! Ailsa! Don't leave me! I need you still!"

Gently Anna's hand pulled me away. "Come, my lady. Let me cover her face."

"My lady, they have crossed the Camel! The floodwaters abated enough to let them through!"

"My lord Ferron, she takes no heed. Can you not let her grieve for the old woman? She loved her as a mother."

"But, Anna, she is regent. We cannot act without her."

"Have they sent a messenger?"

"Not yet."

"Are they shaping for attack?"

"Not yet."

"Then, I pray you, leave her awhile longer. She cannot attend you now. As you see."

"But how soon?"

"Ah, sir, that I do not know."

"My lady, Sir Ferron has come thrice to see you. Duke Constantine is camped upon the plain of Camlann and has sent a messenger begging entrance."

I stared at the shrouded figure on the pallet. "How dare he, when she is not even in the ground? Beg him say a prayer for her, my dearest Ailsa."

"I'm sorry, Sir Ferron, it must wait awhile longer."

On a gray morning in a warm rain we buried her. Bishop Landrum spoke the words that sealed her body in the earth and her soul in heaven. I blessed him in my heart, when he allowed my dear Ailsa Christian burial. In life, she had worshipped not only Christ but every god she knew.

47 👑 THE RESCUE

I opened the curtain to see Arthur standing by the window in a loincloth, his flesh shrunk to no more than a shroud upon his bones.

"Britain needs you, my lord! Take up your Sword and lead her."

"I am powerless to do it. Britain will have to wait."

"No!" I wept aloud. "I will lead the men myself, if you will not! Though a woman, I can die as easily as you!"

"Put down the Sword, Guinevere."

"I cannot! Oh, come and take it from me, my lord! It is so heavy!"

His hand gripped the hilt; light flashed from the living blade and burned my eyes.

I looked up. Sunlight streamed into my chamber, dazzlingly bright. I was in my own bed; I could not remember how I got there. But I remembered my dream.

"Anna, how long have I been here?"

She knelt nearby, head bowed against the coverlet, but when I spoke, she raised her head. "Oh, my lady! A day and a night!"

In irritation, I pushed the covers aside, sat up, and then stopped, dizzy. "What has passed? Where is Ferron?"

"Outside, my lady. Council has just ended." There was fear in her eyes, but also hope.

I paused. "How do we stand? Tell me, if you know."

"Elisane is below with a tray of food. I will tell you while you eat. I beg you not to argue with me, my lady, I can see you are dizzy. It's been over a week since you've had a proper meal."

While I ate she told me what she knew. Constantine had finally arrived and sat down at the foot of Caer Camel, blocking the Roman road and commanding the approaches to King's Gate. There he had sat for three days, every morning sending his second son, a youth named Markion, with a message begging an audience of the Queen.

"And what answer did the Council give him?"

Anna, as always, spoke straight. "None, at first. But as so long a silence demanded explanation, they finally told him you were ill and could not receive him."

"They should have told him it was grief. Constantine would delight to know they were all held helpless by a woman's weakness. It would have fed his pride and made him overconfident. I do not mind their scorn."

"My lady, their pride would not allow it. They would never admit to helplessness, not King's men."

I sighed. "Well, and what did Constantine say?"

"He laughed at them." Anna smiled. "He called them cowards and accused them of hiding behind a woman's skirts."

"How like him."

"But angry as they were, they took it and did nothing. Sir Kay made them obey, at swordpoint."

"Did it come to that? Bless Kay. It must have been hard for them."

I pushed aside the tray of food. Already I felt less lightheaded.

"He cannot be serious about war. He dare not make Arthur his enemy. His eldest son, his heir, Sir Meliodas, worships Arthur—he is with him in Brittany, leading the Cornish troops. I can't believe the duke truly wants a battle, unless he is using his sons to hedge his bets. Have we seen any sign of Wales or Elmet?"

"Not yet, my lady. They are daily expected."

"And where are the men now?"

Her smile faded. "On the practice grounds, my lady. Falling in, for battle. The horn sounded but half an hour ago."

"What! Are they mad? Who led them?"

"Sir Villers, my lady. And—"

"Dynas and Clegis, yes, I know."

"And Sir Gryfflet and Sir Bleoberys."

"Ahh, dear God, Berys gave in to them, did he? He swung the balance for war—well, what can you expect from rule by Council? The fools will kill themselves, and Arthur will hold me to account." I rose, and found my legs were steady.

"But—does not the Council always make decisions?"

I nearly laughed. "Don't you believe it, Anna. Arthur rules Britain. No one else. The Council is for consensus. And no one ever disagrees with Arthur. Long experience has taught them he knows well what he's about." I reached for my comb. "Quickly now, there is little time! Bring me my best gown, the blue one, while I put up my hair. And bring me my crown."

I stepped out into the bright June sun of the forecourt. The Council, on horseback, were mustering the troops, each commander giving his men instructions. Ferron and Kay had not yet mounted but stood with their backs to me, their very postures bespeaking their anger.

Someone called out and pointed. Several of the soldiers fell to one knee.

Kay and Ferron whirled. "My lady Queen!"

I strode down to where they stood, and they each bent a knee to the ground. "What goes on here, my lords? What is meant by this defiance?"

"My lady," Ferron began, glaring sideways at Villers, "in your absence, the Council has decided to give the blackguard fight."

Silence fell across the courtyard. Even the horses stood still.

"How dare they? Who gave the order?" No one moved. I turned to Villers. "Sir, you will follow me to King's Gate and bring the soldiers up behind me. Sir Clegis, I see your men are ready on the battlements. Bid them fit their arrows to their bows and when I go out the gate, aim them, every one, at Constantine."

Ferron gasped. "You are not going out!"

"My lady!" Kay cried in a strangled voice.

Villers slid from his horse and fell to both knees. "My lady Queen, do not take this risk on account of me!"

"You leave me no choice, sir. But it is not much of a risk, with Clegis' archers at the ready—if he so much as draws his sword, he will die."

I turned to face the troops, who stood gaping at me. "I know you men are loyal to King Arthur. Be patient yet awhile longer, I pray you. Together, we will protect Arthur's fortress and keep Britain whole. And I will spare your lives, if it is in my power. Now." I took a deep breath. "I will speak with Constantine."

They shouted protests, and Kay and Ferron begged me strenuously not to go, but I did not slow my pace, and no one laid a hand upon my arm to stop me. At King's Gate, Kay, near panic, forbade the guards to open the gates.

"I'm sorry, Kay, my old friend, to give you such trouble, but I must countermand the order. Guards. Open the gate." The poor guards shook, shrugged apologetically at Kay, and swung open the double gates. "Villers, stay here. If the archers let fly, you must needs attack. But until then, stay well out of sight."

"Guinevere!" Ferron cried. "You cannot go out alone! I am coming with you."

He shook from head to foot and had turned pale. I yielded; he would never be able to face Arthur, else.

"Very well, but leave your sword and dagger here. If you come, come naked."

He obeyed me without protest and followed me outside.

We took Constantine by surprise. We were well out into the sunlit meadow before his sentries saw us and sounded the alarm. I stopped within thirty paces of the gate. Above us, atop the length of the outer walls, Clegis' archers had their arrows ready. Clegis himself I saw, above the gates; he saluted smartly and bent his knee.

"Stay behind me, Ferron, and keep your eyes open. Don't shake so. It is too beautiful a day for death."

Ferron shook his head. "I have never faced a warrior without my weapons," he admitted. "Never mind an army."

I managed a smile for him. "Without fear, bravery is impossible."

He gave me a half smile back. "So Arthur has told his troops a hundred times."

The thunder of galloping horses turned our heads. Constantine and his commanders rode toward us at speed, with his army running up behind him. When they neared us, they slowed and formed a broad semicircle around us.

"They're in fighting position, my lady," Ferron murmured behind me.

I nodded. Duke Constantine himself was a man just past the prime of life, with gray flecks in his beard and lines around his dark, angry eyes. But he was as fit and lean as any warrior ten years his junior. He glared at me a long moment, then slid off his horse, signaling his commanders to stay on theirs. He walked toward me. Some whisper of sound made him look up, and he saw the long ridge of arrows aimed at his heart. He stopped.

"What sort of welcome is this?"

"Do you come as friend or foe, my lord duke?"

"As friend, of course."

"Then where is your greeting?"

Scowling, he bent his knee to the earth and bowed his head. His commanders glanced quickly at one another. I looked hard at them; one by one they saluted.

"Rise, Constantine, and be welcome to Camelot." Immediately he relaxed, and his hand no longer hovered near his swordhilt. "Forgive, if you will, the Council's stalling. It is my fault; I was abed."

"I am sorry to know my lady Queen was ill," he said gruffly. "And pleased to see you are now recovered."

"Tell me how you found the state of the country on your ride north from Cornwall."

He shrugged impatiently. This was talk that usually waited for a good seat at table, a pitcher of mead, and a leg of fowl. "Quiet. Not a whisper of discontent."

"And how was your journey?"

He looked at me sharply, but I kept my face straight. "Smooth, my lady, and swift. In spite of nasty weather."

"Ahhh. I am glad to hear it. But why swift, my lord? I thought perhaps you had had some news of unrest that we had missed, but you tell me it is not so."

I nearly laughed at his chagrin. How he wished he had thought of that before!

Instead, he came out with the excuse he had prepared. "I have brought you an army, Queen Guinevere, for your defense, since the High King left Camelot so lightly garrisoned. And as a warning to the Saxons," he added, as an afterthought.

I made him a deep curtsy, pleased to find him slow. "What a very generous gift. I thank you, my lord, on the High King's behalf."

His commanders relaxed, grinning at one another. The army, watching them, stood at ease. Constantine jerked his head toward the archers. "Why do they still threaten me, my lady? Call them off."

I smiled sweetly and spread out my hands. "They are my only weapon, my lord duke. You wear your sword, your men are armed. As you see, Sir Ferron and I are not. I will call them off when your men are well inside."

This suited him perfectly, and he smiled. "Very well. Let us go in."

"Of course," I added lightly, "you will come without your swords." He froze. "You are not our enemy, my lord; we are not yours. There is no need for weapons."

He took a long moment to control his rage enough to answer. "I have brought you an army, Queen Guinevere. But they cannot serve you without weapons!"

"Of a certainty," I replied pleasantly. "We shall return them. And I do not refer to your commanders, Duke Constantine. Only to your men. Have them stack their weapons outside King's Gate as they come in. Sir Ferron will collect them and give them back, when he has trained them and they have sworn allegiance to the High King Arthur. I thank you from my heart for this generous gift, my lord duke. How you will keep Cornwall without them is beyond my ability to imagine."

"They are not Arthur's men!" Constantine cried, reddening. "They are mine! And they do not move without their weapons!"

I feigned surprise. "Then they are not a gift, after all? My lord, what did you bring them for?"

"To keep you safe from Saxons! But they do not swear allegiance to Arthur. They are Cornishmen, and follow me!"

"Well, my lord, if they are yours and not Arthur's, you had better take them back to Cornwall. We are safe enough from Saxons now."

"This is tyranny!" Constantine shouted hoarsely. No woman had ever spoken to him thus, and it was more than his pride could bear. He took three sudden strides toward me; Ferron pulled me back as something whistled through the air and thudded into the turf a stride from Constantine's boots. A single arrow stood half buried in the ground, the shaft still quivering. Constantine stepped back, the color gone from his face.

"Another step," Ferron warned, "and you're a dead man."

On the rampart, Clegis saluted me and notched another arrow.

I shrugged off Ferron's arm. "I beg you, Sir Ferron, give the duke a chance to save his skin. My lord, I beg your pardon. In Arthur's absence, his men are anxious to protect me. Make no sudden move, I pray you. I cannot answer for their actions. You see how it is. I am sorry, but I'm no Arthur."

The duke glared, fighting for composure. "You don't fool me, you Welsh witch! You planned this insult! In all my life I've never been treated so! You will let me in the gates, and be polite about it, or—or—"

I waited calmly for him to speak the treason that would seal his fate forever, but suddenly the lookout sounded his horn and the archers on the wall pointed, shouting, to the plains beyond. From where we stood, we could see nothing, but the alarm could mean only one thing.

"My lord duke!" I called out, loud enough for all his commanders to hear. "Make your decision now! If you want war, you shall have it, but the contest will be more closely matched than you had planned. My reinforcements have arrived."

Constantine swore viciously under his breath, cursed me for a barren bitch, and swung on his heel. As he reached for his stallion's reins, we saw his scout ride up at a fast gallop.

"My lord duke! We are surrounded! They come from the west and from the east and from the south! Five hundred men or more! And a host of cavalry!"

"Damn all women!" Constantine shouted, leaping into the saddle and flinging his horse's head around. "I've been wronged, and I'll take what's due me! I'll be back!"

The last we saw of him, he was leading his troops down onto the plain as fast as they could go.

All we had to do the rest of that brilliant day was watch from the towers. Drustan from the east and Gwillim from the west met an army of horsemen riding fast from the south. The Dragon banner flew bright in the summer breeze, red on gold, unmistakable. The men from Elmet and from Wales gathered under the Dragon and took their battle stations. Villers led Camelot's forces out King's Gate to take the ground Constantine had yielded. Surrounded, Cornwall dug in his heels and waited. Arthur's commander, whoever he was, showed calm and sense, and sent to beg a parley. We watched from the towers as they met and spoke. Not until the shadows began to lengthen did Constantine turn and give the signal to retreat. The King's forces let them pass, then closed behind them and followed them on their way.

I drew a deep breath and sighed. "All is well. Thank God for Arthur's friends and allies! I wanted to avoid bloodshed at any cost." Beside me, Kay and Ferron smiled indulgently. "Whoever Arthur sent must be honored and commended. Will they be back by nightfall? Let us feast them well."

"Don't expect them until tomorrow," Ferron advised. "No doubt they'll see Constantine at least halfway back to Cornwall, just to be certain he goes."

Sure enough, four hundred men rode in King's Gate in the bright sun of midmorning. Drustan was there, and Gwillim my cousin; and leading them was Mordred.

"Oh, Mordred!" I cried with joy, hugging him in greeting. "How glad I am to see you! I am more thankful than you can know that he sent you! I asked only for one of his commanders."

"I know. I saw the letter," he said, smiling. "But he was angry he had misjudged Constantine and thought I should be here. You must tell me what happened."

I hugged Gwillim and thanked him most sincerely for coming to my aid. And Drustan, who was well past sixty but had come himself, I sat at my right hand at dinner. We celebrated a long time, and gave them food and wine and song and, finally, rest.

It was late in the evening before Mordred and I had time for talk. We strolled in the garden with Kay and Ferron, still discussing Constantine's bold move and Mordred's thwarting of his plans. Now that Arthur's declared heir was back in Camelot, Constantine had no excuse for leaving Cornwall.

"You will stay, won't you, now that you are here?" I asked, clasping his hand.

"Yes, my lady. I am to stay until the King returns, as regent, if you are willing to give up the post to me."

"Willing! Oh, yes, indeed I am willing! God knows I have had my fill of such responsibility; how he has borne it all these years, I cannot guess. I have aged a decade since his going!"

"Well," Mordred said, grinning, "you do not look it. You look but twenty, if you look a day."

I squeezed his hand, glad to feel laughter again. "Thank you, my lord. I will believe every word you tell me from now on!"

"I must send a report to Arthur tonight, for he is beside himself with worry. Only half his mind will be on Rome until he knows that you are safe."

"And how does my lord?" I asked him anxiously. "How do they treat him? Is he honored? Is his health good? Are they ready?"

"He is well and he is honored," Mordred said with pride. "He is a King among kings. He has become the arbiter of all their disputes; their battle leader; their judge. The Franks have a name for him: Riothamus. Beloved judge. It began among their soldiers, when he settled some impossible dispute to all their liking. They know his fairness now. His own troops have the hardest chores; it is seen he favors no one."

Kay and Ferron asked about the Romans and their dispositions. Mordred told them what he knew, although clearly he had left them before their final plans were set. Hiberius demanded the tribute by the first of June. The Franks and Britons proposed to send a party to treat with him and negotiate the demand; also, to get a look at his numbers and their equipment. Mordred was to have been the leader of this party, until my letter changed Arthur's plans.

"Who went in your stead?" Kay asked. "Bedwyr?"

"No," Mordred said slowly, frowning, "he was the obvious choice, of course. But Arthur wanted someone of royal blood. He sent Gawaine."

"Gawaine?" I gasped. "Send a hothead to negotiate with Romans? Is he mad?"

Mordred shifted and schooled his face. "He believes Gawaine has steadied and matured. He gave, as evidence for this, his treatment of Lancelot."

"What of Lancelot?" I whispered in panic. "Arthur said Gawaine had promised not to harm him!"

"So he has, my lady. That is what I mean—"

"He has forgiven him for Gareth?"

"No," Mordred said patiently, "but he has stood before Lancelot and promised not to kill him while they are both in the High King's service."

"What does that mean?" I asked blankly.

"It means Lancelot is safe while Arthur lives. To do him honor for that promise, the King sent him with the party to the Romans."

"But surely," I protested, "Gawaine could see that if he did not promise, Arthur could not keep him in Brittany!"

Mordred shrugged. "If he errs," he said quietly, "it is on the side of mercy."

I rose, clasping my hands in distress. "He knows himself he has always been blind to Morgause's wiles and has never seen her sons for what they are!" I gasped as I realized what I had said. "I beg your pardon, Mordred!"

He shook his head. "I do not," Mordred said solemnly, "think of myself as Morgause's son. No offense is taken."

I reached out a hand to him. "Thank you, Mordred. You are Arthur's son, indeed." He touched his lips to my fingers.

"How long have you been gone, Sir Mordred?" Ferron asked. "When was this mission to the Romans? Who else was in the party?"

"I have been traveling six days. They left soon after I did. They should have come to some conclusion by now." He named the knights who had accompanied Gawaine: Bedwyr and Gereint from Britain, Hoel's two sons, Galahantyn and Bors from Lanascol, and three of Childebert's best men. But to Gawaine of Orkney had gone the honor of leading them all.

I fell silent and worried over this while he talked awhile with Ferron and with Kay. They sent a message of reassurance to Arthur and made plans for the disposition of the troops he had brought home. But I fretted over Arthur. What was he about, trusting Gawaine? We should have war, for certain, if anything happened to spark Gawaine's quick temper.

At length Kay and Ferron left us, and Mordred and I sat alone in the dark garden, with a single cresset burning by the door.

"And how is Lancelot?" I asked quietly. When he did not reply, I placed my hand upon his arm and searched his face. "Do not begrudge me this, dear Mordred. Your father does not."

He opened his mouth to speak and then changed his mind. "He is well," he said at last. "He looks about the same. He had not been with the King five minutes before he asked 'How does the Queen?'"

I smiled. "And I will wager any amount that Arthur answered him without hesitation. Come, Mordred, you are a man now. Have you never loved a woman?" I knew he had two bastard sons; I had heard him speak of them to Arthur. But I did not know who their mother was, or if he loved her.

He lowered his eyes. "Oh, yes, madam. I have, indeed."

"Then you know its power; such a passion cannot be trifled with."

"I know it."

"A wise man recognizes this and accepts it."

He lifted his chin. "Are you asking me to condone it?"

"No. Just to accept it and forgive me for it."

Mordred remained very still. After a long while, he nodded. "Very well. But someday, Guinevere, I will remind you of these words."

I took his hand between my own; in shape and size and feel, his hand was so like Arthur's, even down to the calluses made by his stallion's reins. "So be it. Now tell me what I want to know— did he seem happy? Was he downcast? Do his sons delight him? Does Galahantyn's wife care for him well enough? Does he still miss Camelot? How did he greet Galahad?"

Mordred withdrew his hand and rose. He walked away some distance, staring up at the sky, then returned and stood before me. "Guinevere, I do not see him with your eyes. I cannot tell you everything you want to know. I am sure he would rather be back here in his old place than rule in Lanascol. But he seems content enough. I have not seen his younger sons. He greeted Arthur like a brother. There is nothing changed between them."

"Ahhhh. I am glad of that. And Galahad?"

Mordred began to pace back and forth. He had his father's stride.

"I would rather you did not ask me," he said finally.

"Why?" I cried. "What has happened?"

"They have had a falling out. It is not serious—I mean, not to Britain. For Arthur's sake, they have put their words behind them and are united in his service. But it was a close thing."

"Oh, Mordred, you distress me! How did this come about?"

"Must you ask me? Really, you would rather not know."

I rose, and he stopped his pacing to face me. "Mordred. You have gone too far not to go on. If you will not tell me, I must ask Arthur. Which of you can tell me with less distress?"

"I can," he said at once, and handed me back into my seat. "Very well, then. You know that Galahad has commissioned himself the High King's personal guard, ever since he first accompanied the King as a page, years ago? Well, he sleeps outside his tent at night—yes, right outside on the very ground, whatever the weather. He rejoices in personal discomfort. He follows the King everywhere; Arthur can go nowhere without him. How he bears it, I don't know. I could not."

"Does he not fight for the King? I thought he was skilled as a swordsman."

"Oh, yes, very skilled. He has Lancelot's quickness. But—I know this is hard to remember, because he is so tall and solemn—he is only fourteen and not old enough for the army. Even if he were"—and I heard a smile in his voice—"I don't know a single commander who would want him in his company. No one is good enough for Galahad, and he lets everyone know it."

"Mordred," I said suddenly, "do not take him lightly. I believe he is dangerous, and he bears you no love."

"I know that," he said. "And I know why. Don't worry. I watch him."

"He is feared by many, because he speaks with God."

"Or he says he does," Mordred replied with a smile. "That's a claim that cannot be disproved, and so has no value. Don't distress yourself with fear about Galahad; his vision is so single, he is blind to everything outside it. I have a plan for him. Arthur is going to send him on a quest."

"A quest for what?"

"For the grail and spear that lie hidden somewhere in Wales. The rest of Maximus' treasure, that his captain brought home to his wife. Excalibur she could not bear to keep, believing it the cause of her husband's death, and so sent it north to Caer Eden with the captain, but the grail and spear she kept. No doubt she buried them somewhere. We will tell Galahad it is holy and send him after the grail."

"Mordred," I whispered, shaken, "you are blaspheming!"

"No, my lady," he said gently. "I would not mock your Christian God. Merlin himself thought them sacred, saying they lay protected by the god, away from the eyes of men. And he should know." But then he smiled. "Galahad will dedicate his life to this if he thinks that only he is pure enough in heart to find it. It is a fit punishment for hubris, is it not?"

But I shivered with foreboding. "Only God punishes hubris."

"And so it will be. If his God loves him, he may find this treasure. I will not stand in his way. Only the lady Niniane knows where it is." He grinned. "And because she is a pagan, he will never ask her."

"Has Arthur agreed to this plan? It does not sound like him."

Mordred sobered instantly. "He was against it at first, but after what happened with Lancelot, he has changed his mind."

"Well, now you *must* tell me! Clearly, this is of importance. Tell me now."

He came reluctantly and sat beside me. "Remember that you asked twice for this."

"Go on, Mordred."

"When we first came across to Kerrec, we found old King Hoel in a terrible fury. His niece had been kidnapped by outlaws in the Perilous Forest. She was sixteen and was on her way home with her nurse and an escort of Hoel's men after a visit to Kerrec. She never arrived. Her father sent a message to Hoel asking what had become of his daughter, and Hoel was beside himself with rage. Arthur suggested that he and Lancelot gather a small force and find the girl, while they waited for the rest of the army to come across the Narrow Sea. You can imagine how readily Hoel assented to this offer!"

"With such powerful men for adversaries, I am almost sorry for the outlaws."

"Ahhh," Mordred said sadly, "you will not be. Only a handful of us went—Arthur, Lancelot, Bedwyr, Galahantyn, Gereint, Bors, and myself. And Galahad."

"Why did he go, if so many others did not?"

"You may find this difficult to credit, but it is like him. No one asked him to go. He just came. He showed up, mounted and ready, at the King's side as we set off, and because he was not in the army, Arthur felt sorry for him and let him come. We traveled the route the girl had taken and found clear signs of an ambush. These outlaws were not clever men, they left a trail a child could follow. We came to a lake, and in the center was an island. From the island came the sound of weeping."

I looked down in sorrow, remembering Melwas, a cold knot in my stomach. I had thought that terror was behind me, after all these years.

There was but one boat beached on the shore. As Mordred, the Orkney man, was the only seaman, he rowed them all across. When they came ashore they found the old nurse, dressed in torn scraps of clothing, covered with bleeding scratches and dirt and sand.

The tale the woman told horrified them all. Five outlaws had ambushed them and slaughtered their escort. The women were dragged to this place and raped by all five outlaws. The princess Elen had not lasted past the second day; they had stripped her and thrown her into a shallow pit and burned her bloodstained clothes. The old nurse was nearly out of her wits with terror; her age had been no protection. When the monsters had finally gone, the day before, she had used what remained of her strength to drag rocks and dirt over the pit to bury the poor girl. In Arthur's arms, the poor old woman died. They had buried them both well and placed crosses over the graves and said prayers over them.

Then they had gone in search of the murderers. The outlaws had divided, fearing pursuit, so the party divided as well, following the various trails. Arthur and Mordred had gone together, Bedwyr with Gereint, Galahantyn with Bors, and Lancelot had collared Galahad and led him away from the King. They each found their man and killed him. But Lancelot and Galahadhad found the last two together.

"When we gathered at the appointed meeting place," Mordred said slowly, staring hard at the garden walk, "Galahad's face was bruised and swollen, his lips were cut and crusted with blood, and he had lost two teeth. Everyone assumed he had been injured in the fight and so said nothing. But I noted that Lancelot was stiff with fury and that Galahad glowed with the joy of righteous suffering. He held his head high and was too proud to reply to anyone's solicitous remarks. When we got to Kerrec, neither father nor son could speak a word to each other; after ten days of this, Arthur finally summoned them to a meeting, and so discovered what had happened."

He stopped suddenly and passed his hand across his brow in a gesture so familiar I felt a stab of acute loneliness.

"Were you in the room?" I asked softly.

In the dark I saw his eyes flash. "At Arthur's request." He sighed. "Well, delaying the tale makes it no easier to tell. Here is what happened. They met the two outlaws; one of them, an old soldier gone to seed, drew his sword; the other, half his age and better armed, ran. Lancelot went in pursuit of the second and left Galahad to dispatch the first. When Lancelot had killed his man, he heard screams of terror coming from the spot where he had left Galahad. Racing back to rescue his son, he found—he found Galahad standing above the ruffian, unharmed, and with a bloody sword." Mordred stopped again. My hands twisted in my lap and I swallowed. My dear Lancelot!

"What had he done?" I whispered.

Mordred shrugged. "He had stripped the man and cut off his genitals and thrown them to the kites."

I pressed my fist against my mouth. Mordred went on in a flat voice devoid of feeling. "Galahad was raving. He would not kill the man, but shouted verses from the Scriptures about an eye for an eye, or some such thing. The outlaw, who had been a soldier once, begged Lancelot for death. Lancelot dispatched him with a stroke and gave him peace. But then— Galahad began shouting about the whore of Babylon, and the defilement of women—the rape had turned his wits, Guinevere, you must believe this. He had been unable to take his eyes from the naked body of the princess when we found her. It is time he lay with a woman." He paused and then said slowly, "The filth that came from his mouth made Lancelot ill. It was some minutes before he realized that when Galahad spoke of a whore who castrated men and stripped them of virtue, he was referring to you."

"To me?"

Mordred went on as if he had not heard me. "Lancelot strode up to him and struck him across the face with all the strength he had. And told him if your name ever passed his lips again, he would kill him and delight in doing so."

"Dear God!" I cried. "Oh, Lancelot! My poor Lancelot!" Weeping, I looked up at Mordred and found him watching me. "He said these things to Arthur? To his face?"

Mordred nodded. "What was worse, Galahad showed no regret. He admitted all this freely. He did not beg the King for forgiveness, although he knew Arthur has called men out to combat for smaller insults than that."

"Indeed!"

"Clearly the boy is mad. There is no question now of his ever serving Arthur with his sword. He can't be trusted. Arthur demanded that father and son swear their peace in his presence, and he will bring Galahad home when he returns, but something must be done with him to keep him out of the way. Hence the quest. That very night, Arthur assented to it."

"Oh, Mordred!" I whispered, covering my face with my hands. "How they are both wounded on account of me! In that, Galahad is right—I am a curse to both of them!"

He put his arm around me and comforted me while I wept upon his shoulder. "If it is indeed a curse, it is one neither of them would live without. You are not to blame for this, Guinevere. The boy has lost his wits."

"I am not thinking of Galahad," I cried. "But of Lancelot, who will never forgive himself for the fact that his own son spoke those words and wounded Arthur. And of Arthur, who will forgive it but will be unable to forget it. They cannot be as brothers now!"

"Their friendship is deep, and of long standing," Mordred said quietly. "They have weathered storms as bad as this. And they have a war to fight together. As time passes, these wounds will heal."

I fought to collect myself and be calm. What he said was true of Arthur, but I knew well that the wound Galahad had given Lancelot would never heal.

"Will there be war, then, do you think?"

"Of a certainty," he replied.

I searched his face in the scented darkness. "Are you sorry to have had to come home, and miss it?"

He faced me, but I could not read his expression.

"No, indeed," he said calmly. "I am well content to let Arthur, duke of battles, lead Britain's troops to war. I would rather be here at home, ruling as regent."

A pain struck my chest and I shivered, but I did not know why. I drew the regent's seal from my pouch and placed it in his hand. "Take this, then, and relieve me of my duties. I am glad it was you he sent, Mordred. Will you keep me informed of all that passes?"

He stood and raised me, and then bowed low. "I will treat you, dear Guinevere, with all the respect and honor my father pays you. Indeed, I will endeavor to make the difference between us, King and regent, as small as it may be."

Mordred was an excellent administrator. Under his hand, the Kingdom ran smoothly. He carried all the details of daily routine in his head and knew how to get his plans accomplished. He knew which men had power and how they stood with others and who was jealous or nursed a grievance, and who was loyal. He dealt deftly with the Council; never had their meetings been over so quickly and with so much decided. He seemed to know everything that was happening in every corner of Britain; he daily received and sent messengers, and I believe he had spies, as well. He knew how to treat men and he had their respect, if not their love.

Recognizing the threat that Constantine posed, he at once set about raising an army to replace in some measure the one that had gone with Arthur. He sent messages to every reigning ruler in the Kingdom and frankly explained his position. While Arthur was away, the stability of Britain was threatened by an ambitious lord. He requested men for the common defense. Where lords demurred, saying their numbers were depleted past bearing, Mordred paid them a visit, a courtesy call, he said. But afterward, he always got his men. Soon we were five hundred strong in Camelot. And I confess that I breathed easier with such strength at hand.

He kept his word to me and talked to me of all his plans and all his dispositions. He worked hard every morning and after Council at the King's desk in the library; he got quickly through the written work that Arthur so disliked. He kept two scribes busy at these times and could have used a third. The men drilled daily; when he had time, he liked to drill them himself, but usually it fell to Ferron. But almost every day, he made time to take his exercise with me and Ferron and Anna when we rode out. He was kind, attentive, and always courteous. Even so, without the daily running of the Kingdom to keep me occupied, and without Arthur, or Lancelot, or Bedwyr, I grew lonely.

I often found myself standing alone in Arthur's chamber. It was kept clean and swept and aired, just as when he was at home. I stood on the polished wood floor and let my gaze travel over the few pieces of simple furniture, the bare walls, and the old silk banner above the great bed. It impressed me now as it had on my first day in Camelot: a soldier's room, simple and direct, a place of stillness and of peace. I would stand there and feel my loneliness drain from me; he was still there, in that room. I felt his presence. And I came away with an easier heart.

Sometimes I went to the top of the northwest tower, for privacy and a chance to think. Arthur and I had often gone together, remembering our first time there, on our wedding night, and smiling at it. But sometimes I would go alone, and sometimes in the past had found him there, studying out some problem or simply surveying his dominion. Now that he was gone, I found it restful just to stand where he had stood and look at the fertile lands all about me, giving thanks for the peaceful beauty of the country. From this tower I could see the old Roman road that ran up from the river Camel and would watch the troops drill, or the men go forth to hunt, or a messenger ride in.

On the day of the solstice I went to the tower, feeling lonely and ill at ease. On this day of all days I wished Arthur were there. Twenty years ago we had been married. Sometimes it seemed like yesterday to me—except that at fifteen I had known nothing of men, had feared Arthur, and had thought I could not live without Lancelot. I smiled to myself, as I watched a dusty courier galloping along the causeway, heading for King's Gate. How I wished he was bringing the message that the High King's ships were in the estuary and that before nightfall he would be here! When I recalled his last night home and his great tenderness toward me, I was filled with the ache of longing. What I would not give to hold him in my arms again!

I put these thoughts aside, as they led only to weeping, and I wished to feel the joy that this day always brought me. I thought instead of Britain, and how she prospered, and how lucky I was to be alive in Arthur's time. He had been crowned at fourteen and had led Britain for twenty-six years! And for twenty years we had not had so much as a skirmish! Imagine, an entire generation growing up in a land at peace! It was almost beyond comprehension that such a miracle could happen in such a wartorn land as Britain. God must indeed love Arthur beyond all others.

I heard a soft tap at the tower door and turned to find Mordred behind me. I knew instantly it was not good news—not from his face, which was always well schooled and unreadable, but from the mere fact that he had come himself and not sent a page.

"My lady Guinevere," he said quietly, "please forgive the intrusion. But it is important."

My hand crept to my throat, then I straightened, stilling myself. "What is it, Mordred? You have had news from Less Britain?"

"Yes, my lady. Would you not prefer to come down to the library to hear it?"

"Certainly not. Tell me now. Is my lord well?"

He cleared his throat. I thought he looked uneasy. "Yes, my lady. This letter is from him." He handed me a scroll, and I recognized the flowing penmanship of Arthur's favorite scribe. "It is short, as you see, and dictated in haste. It is as we feared, Guinevere. Gawaine's embassy ended in disaster, and they are marching to war." I scanned the note, but it gave just bare details. Mordred would have the complete message from the courier's lips. I drew a deep breath and bade him tell me all he knew.

"It seems they had no sooner ridden into the Roman camp when trouble broke out. While the diplomats in the party were meeting, Gawaine accosted some Roman youth he thought showed him arrogance; an argument arose over a trifle; Gawaine ran him through on the spot."

I gasped. "He *killed* him? How did he dare? He was sent to talk, not to fight!"

Mordred's shrug was eloquent. "The youth turned out to be a nephew of Hiberius himself, so the insult is not likely to be forgiven."

"I should think not. Is Gawaine in disgrace?"

"Well," Mordred said slowly, "he has forced Arthur's hand. I should tell you, perhaps, of the conversation we had before I left." He paced back and forth a bit, then came to the parapet beside me and gazed across the rolling fields toward the Tor. "When you asked why Arthur sent Gawaine instead of someone more level-headed, I did not tell you all of Arthur's reasoning. He knew it would come to war. The embassy was only a stalling tactic, to get a look at their strength. But in his heart he felt that the sooner they met in battle, the better. The Burgundians were mustered, but Hiberius is lately come from Rome and probably does not have all the reinforcements he would like. Thus he agreed quickly to the proposal of an embassy. When Arthur chose Gawaine, he knew there was a chance there might be trouble. But if they fought the sooner for it, so much the better. Now it has come to pass. He says in the note they have gathered their forces and are marching to meet the Burgundians at Autun."

I shut my eyes and said a quick prayer to God for his safety.

"I knew it," I whispered. "I knew he would take the field himself. Oh, Mordred!"

He took my hands. "Do not fear, Gwen. He will not lose. You know Arthur."

"Yes," I cried, "and so do they! They will not come against him unless they outnumber him three to one—and even if he lives, what of those who fight with him? Mordred, if they meet in battle, so many will die!"

He nodded. "Perhaps. But fewer than if they waited until the Romans were ready. In a way, perhaps, Gawaine's hotheadedness has worked to advantage. It is unlikely they could outnumber him three to one."

I leaned upon his arm and tried to smile. "You would give me courage. Thank you, Mordred. But I think I will go to my chamber. When—when does this dreaded event take place?"

He looked at me with compassion; I remembered Arthur's words to me once when I had expressed horror at war: "How can war be evil? Fighting is as natural as breathing to men; and if your cause is just, where is the dishonor?" Mordred was Arthur's son, I saw. To him it was a matter of honor and glory, and certainly not a dreaded event.

"My dear Guinevere, it may be taking place even as we speak. The courier has been on the road a week."

"Dear God!" I whispered, feeling faint. Mordred bent toward me in concern, and I fought to collect my wits. "Then we may hear—within a week—all the world may change!"

He felt how I trembled and slipped an arm about me to support me. "Please, Guinevere, take courage. The King will be victorious. All that will change is that the Romans must leave Gaul, this time forever."

I straightened and stepped out of his embrace. "You will keep me informed, Mordred? Do not let this show of weakness make you fearful of sharing news with me. I will be braver next time."

His features softened. "You are brave enough now. I will indeed keep you informed of any messages I receive. Now, shall we go down together?" He offered me his arm.

"No. No, thank you. I have changed my mind. I would like to stay here awhile, and pray."

He bowed and left me.

Life went on unchanged. Daily Mordred sent for me and went over what news there was from around the Kingdom. Daily he rode out at my side. I had every chance to see him at work and see how Arthur's men took to his leadership. He was respected and admired. He was an able man, known to be clever and far-seeing. These weeks of being sole regent were the first chance he had ever had to rule. It had so long been his heart's desire, and he had had so many years of apprenticeship, it was as if a sleeping plant had at last turned its face to the sun and started to grow. It seemed to me he grew in stature daily.

At first I was elated—when he came to be High King, he would be a good one, as I had always known he would, and Britain would not suffer under his leadership. But then I grew uneasy, for an oak can never be put back into its acorn, or a falcon, once flown, go back into its egg. During these weeks, Mordred tasted power, and it agreed with him. When Arthur returned, he would find his son a king in all but name; he would have to find him some territory of his own to hold, for I doubted now that Mordred could go back to being merely his advisor and his heir. But what lands could Mordred, bastard prince of Orkney, call his own?

I pushed aside these thoughts, for no one could settle it but Arthur. I kept Anna by my side all the day long, and read to her, or sang to her, if I could bring myself to it, or rode with her and talked. She had more thoughts in her head than weddings and beddings and the catching of husbands. She was a great comfort to me.

It was Anna who told me that the young men of Britain, the sons and nephews of Arthur's friends and Companions, and even their grandsons, were growing restless under Arthur's rule. They thought the High King grew old and set in his ways, she said, and they were eager for a younger man to lead them. She knew this hurt me, and she told it to me gently, but I could hear the truth of it in her voice.

"All young men feel so, I believe," she said. "In your youth, my lady, young men had the Saxon wars to fight and a young King to lead them. But these young men thirst for power and are tired of peace and civilization."

"Tired of civilization? Anna, what can you mean?"

"I mean only that they want to be kings in their own lands and set their own laws and run their affairs as they see fit. They care nothing for Arthur's way of governing. They laugh at the notion of justice for common folk."

Was it possible? That young men raised in Arthur's Peace should wish to push us back into the violent dark? Why, we should be no better than the Saxons, with each kingdom at the other's throat!

"Oh, no, Anna, I cannot believe this! Simply because they are impatient for glory, they would tear down all the High King has built? It is wild oats, surely, and nothing more. And do they think that Mordred will be different from his father? He is a civilized man—none more so."

Anna was fond of Mordred; as fond as she had ever been of any man, although he had never so much as cast his glance her way. She could speak of him without blushing or growing shy, but she admired him and often followed him with her eyes and let affection warm her voice when she said his name.

"Sir Mordred is from Orkney, where ways are different," she replied. "These young men I speak of are all from the wild lands in the north and some from Wales. However Roman he behaves with Arthur, they think it only one of many cloaks he wears, and that in his heart Sir Mordred is of their blood. After all," she added softly, "he is a pagan."

"Do they accuse Arthur of being Roman? Why, at this very moment he risks his life to drive the Romans out! Can they not see this? Are they blind?"

Here she patted my hand and smiled. "Yes, indeed they are, my lady. Blind to anything they prefer not to see. Perhaps your assessment is the right one, and these are wild oats. In time they will settle down, as their fathers did, and be glad to be part of Britain."

I shuddered. What future was left for Britain without a strong King at

her center, giving her laws and granting justice, protecting her from enemies without and within? Why, without Roman civilization, we should be
back in the time my father used to speak of, when there were twelve kings
in Wales alone, each fighting with the other while the Saxons rowed their
longboats up our rivers!

"Dear Anna, keep your ears open, and tell me what you hear. It seems
the times are changing fast. Arthur will need to know this, when he
returns."

We had six days of rain; then the sun broke forth in splendor and the heat
of summer was upon us. A week went by, then two weeks, and still we heard
nothing from Less Britain. I began to sleep better. No news is good news was
a saying older than Merlin.

Between the stables and my gardens, I kept myself busy. And after hall,
when I went with Mordred and Anna and Ferron and some others to the
King's library, I would sit quietly in the scented cool of the summer night.
I'd let my thoughts wander and see the King's face in Mordred's features and
hear his voice in my ear.

One brilliant morning I walked in the library garden with Anna. Some
of the younger maids were learning the art of caring for roses, and they
laughed gaily together and chatted with the gardeners as they had their
lessons. Anna and I stood some way from the fountain and spoke quietly together. The door into the library was open, and we could see Mordred in the
dimness, at the High King's desk. Even as we watched, he rose and stood at
attention. A page backed away; a courier approached, filthy with the dirt of
travel, and went on one knee. I gripped Anna's hand—I dared not breathe.

"Victory is ours!" I heard him hoarsely cry. "My lord, the Romans are
defeated!"

I began to weep in silence. Anna gently led me away to the back of the
garden. I knelt where once I had knelt with Lancelot, and gave my thanks to
God for answering my prayers. So great was my relief, I could not rise, but
stayed leaning on the bench, hands clasped, for a long time. I never heard
Anna leave me. But when I heard Mordred's steps approaching, and I turned,
Anna was gone, and the maids and the gardeners, as well. We were alone.

I looked up smiling and had opened my mouth to speak, when I saw his
face and was struck dumb. There were tear tracks on his cheeks! Mordred,
who never showed but a fraction of what he felt, Mordred had wept.

My throat went dry; I could not find breath. Mordred sat slowly on the
bench and took my hands between his own. He himself was barely in control, and he trembled.

"Guinevere—"

"Victory," I whispered, "I heard him say it. We won the day. I came to give thanks."

Mordred nodded slowly, but his eyes were full of grief. "Yes," he managed. "The day was ours. Hiberius himself was killed, and his forces recalled to Rome. The Burgundians are defeated. The threat is—is past."

"Then why—no! Do not tell me!" I cried, as he opened his mouth to speak.

He held my hands hard. "The King is—Arthur is dead."

I simply stared at him. I felt nothing. Wrapped in numbness, I could neither weep nor speak. I shook my head.

Mordred sighed wearily. "I will tell you what the courier said. I have a—a dispatch from Lancelot, written in haste from a field dressing station, before he—while he could still speak. He is badly wounded," he went on quickly, "and not expected to live." I closed my eyes in pain and bowed my head. "They took the field ten days ago, with the High King leading the troops from the west; it took all day. It was a long and bloody fight. You were right, it seems, about their numbers. They dared not face Arthur of Britain without a force superior to his. But still he beat them. He broke them, Gwen, by midafternoon, and they retreated. The rest of the fighting was desperate skirmish only, with ragged bands of men putting up resistance here and there. Lancelot and Bedwyr were near him; Bedwyr was wounded, but is able to stand. At the end of the day, they could not find the High King. Lancelot lay gravely wounded on the field, and in the field hospital, after he had dispatched this message, he told the courier what he had seen. The High King was fighting with Gawaine near the banks of a small stream to Lancelot's left, when a small force of savage Burgundians burst out of ambush; one minute the King was there, and the next not. The Dragon was seen to fall. From the litter, Lancelot directed troops to the spot, and they searched but could not find him."

I found my voice. "Then he is alive. Somewhere."

Mordred looked pained. He swallowed. "It is possible, my lady, but not likely. You see—I don't think you know what happens after a battle. Men crawl out from nowhere, it seems, like ravens, to strip and rob the dead. Sometimes the troops, too, if they are not well led. Within an hour of falling, a man is cleaned of all his belongings, his weapons, his jewelry, his clothing. Sometimes they take his life, if his own men have not yet found him. When—when Lancelot sent men to search the place, scavengers had already been there." He reached inside his tunic and slowly drew forth a torn strip of crimson silk. It was the sash, hacked to ribbons and stiff with mud and dried blood. I took it in my hands. There at the ragged edge were the golden, interlocking letters, AR. "They found this by the stream," Mordred whispered, choking.

I seemed to feel a great cold grow inside me; my limbs were lifeless, my lips so stiff I could barely move them.

"Even naked, the King's body would be known," I whispered. "He lives, Mordred. He lives. The lady Niniane told me he would return."

His eyes flashed, then grew dull once more. "Did she? Did she say how?"

"What do you mean?"

"Did she say how he would return? Living? Or on a bier?"

I believe I screamed. Every day, every hour, I had comforted myself with this prophecy, and I had not thought of this! No wonder Niniane had shown relief!

"When Lancelot got to the field station," Mordred continued, "he sent this message. Rumors of Arthur's death are sure to flood Britain fast—he advises us to act as if the King were dead, to hold together. Soon—within a week—we will know for certain. There are search parties out every day. But as Lancelot points out, at the battle's ending, if he lived, he would have sent someone with a message. They waited hours, Gwen. They heard nothing."

I sat still, hearing his words, but unable to feel them. It could not be true; and yet, how could it be false? Of course Arthur would get word to his commanders, if he lived. The bitter irony of it ate at my heart: Lancelot on his deathbed telling Mordred he must be King! My dearest Lancelot! Lancelot and Arthur—both felled in one wicked day! It was too heavy a grief to bear; I could not bear it; I pushed it aside.

"You had better be King now, Mordred. When they find him—if he is—when they send you his ring and his Sword, we will crown you. But—but you had better take the title, for Britain's sake."

Mordred raised me from the ground and kissed my cheek. "What a noble Queen you are," he whispered, "to think of this amid your great grief. As you say, it must be done. But I want you to know that I would give anything not to have to do it."

He meant it; for once, his heart was in his eyes, and I read his love for Arthur there. "I will come," I said without a tremor. "I must. There may be some who would not accept you, else. We must be united."

So I went before the Council, grave men all, and after Mordred read aloud Lancelot's brief message and advice, I told them as clearly as I could that this was what King Arthur had desired, that his son Mordred be confirmed as High King after his death, and that all the kings of Britain swear allegiance and fealty to him as they had to Arthur. So it was done.

And after, I left them to their somber celebrations and let Anna guide me to my chamber. But there I bade her leave me. Alone, I stood before the leather curtain and gathered my courage. Slowly I lifted it and passed into his room. It was still and calm and clean, and I drew a deep breath. But my spirit did not lift; the place was empty; he was not there. From below his stairs I heard the sound of weeping. Gentle Bran, no doubt, had just heard the news.

"Oh, Arthur," I whispered to the air, "do not desert me! Who is left to bring me comfort and help me bear this grief? There must be something of you left here." I knelt by the trunk and threw up the lid, growing frantic to find something, anything, that bore his smell, his feel, any mark of his spirit. I lifted out his favorite winter robe of plain brown wool, trimmed with rabbit. I pressed it to my face; but of course Varric had sent it to the fuller's before packing it away, and it was clean, devoid of any trace of Arthur. I shook it out, and a moth flew free. Alarmed, I looked more closely. Over the left breast I found a hole made by the moth's tooth—and I burst into tears.

Bran flew up the stairs; Anna came running in. Between them, they got me into my own bed. I remember little of it. For days I lay unthinking, unseeing, unresponsive to entreaties, beyond grief and beyond hope.

When at last I arose, I began to accept the fact that Niniane was right: The world had changed. I forgave her for not forewarning me—had I known the truth, we could not have shared that last, sweet night together. As it was, Britain was still whole, and Arthur's son was King. Now it was time to give thought to where I should spend my future, for I had no doubt that, as soon as he could get the army home and see things settled, Mordred would get himself a wife. I must leave Camelot.

But when at length I went to talk with Mordred, I found he was not there. He had gone, with a troop of men, eastward to meet with Cerdic. The news of Arthur's death had indeed raced across the Narrow Sea and had reached the Saxons almost as soon as it reached us. They had sent an embassy, asking for a parley. I questioned Ferron, who had stayed as my Protector, and he said simply, "Cerdic has declared the treaties with Arthur void." Well, I thought, it was not surprising. Cerdic's treaties had been with Arthur, and now Arthur was gone. Mordred had gone to ratify the treaties in his own name, and it was right that he should. So I said nothing. I spent my days on the turret of the southwest tower, which overlooked the entrance to King's Gate, and all the lands between Caer Camel and the far woodlands, toward Brittany. Daily I watched couriers ride in, but none from Less Britain. We had no more news.

At last Mordred returned and sent for me. I went to him in the library and curtsied at the doorway.

"My lord King," I said quietly. He extended a hand, brown from the sun, and raised me. I looked up into his eyes and hardly knew him. He was tanned and relaxed, and happy and vibrantly alive.

"My dear Guinevere," he said softly, "you need do me no reverence—not you. Are you well enough to sit with me awhile? I would talk with you."

"Yes, my lord. And I would talk with you."

He dismissed the other courtiers and led me into the garden. He spoke very gently and watched me closely to see if I attended. When he saw I did, he gradually grew more natural and told me quietly all about his visit with Cerdic. He had been very successful. Cerdic had not only ratified the terms of the treaties he had had with Arthur, but he and Mordred had come to a new agreement. Cerdic's son Cynewulf was then in his Saxon homeland, organizing yet another "rescue" of his people to Britain's shores. Cerdic needed more land. Mordred, on the other hand, wanted landing rights in the harbors of the Saxon shores, for trade with the Saxons, with Bretons, Franks, and even the Alemans of northern Gaul. They had struck a deal. Cynewulf would be allowed to land his longboats unchallenged; British ships would have rights of passage along their shores. It was a giant step forward in friendship between the two peoples, a giant step along the road to making them one nation. I congratulated Mordred and wished that, for his sake, I could feel joy. But that part of me that looked forward had died when Arthur died.

Exultant though he was, Mordred was sensitive to my sorrow. "You are pale, Guinevere. How many days has it been since you have ridden out in the fresh air?"

I shook my head. "I do not feel like riding, Mordred."

"Not feel like riding? It is not the Guinevere I know who speaks! Is there aught that I can do to ease your sorrow?"

I managed a smile. "Indeed, I hope there is. I have come to ask for your advice."

He looked pleased and bowed low. "Any way that I can be of service— just name it, it shall be done."

I looked away. "You may think this foolish, Mordred. But then you are not a woman." I paused. "We women must depend upon men for our keeping. And now my protector has gone from me, I—I am adrift. It is a consequence of childlessness I had not considered, until now. I have thought of returning to Wales, but it is a long time since it has been my home. I cannot go to Gwynedd. Pellinore is dead; Alyse blames me for Elaine's early death; Maelgon despises me for other reasons. And even in Northgallis—Gwarth has four brothers, all with wives and children. Gwillim is still my friend, but he is married now, and I would only bring disruption to his household. I would go to Ynys Witrin and live with the ladies there, if Niniane would take a Christian, but it lies hard by Melwas' castle. And *nothing* will persuade me, loyal to Arthur as he has been, to set foot on his lands again." I shuddered, and Mordred touched my arm to interrupt me.

"Dear Guinevere," he whispered, "there is no need for you to go! Stay here in Camelot—it is your home. I will protect you. It will be my pleasure, for as long as you live."

I blushed under his gaze and looked down. "You are kind, Mordred. Very kind. I thank you for the offer. But you know well that someday soon, perhaps within the year, you will wed, and bring your own Queen to Camelot. I cannot stay here, like some worn-out gown still hung in the corner, because no one knows what to do with it."

"Guinevere!" Mordred looked aghast, and he went down on one knee before me. "Guinevere, do not speak so."

"Rise, Mordred! You are King now, you ought not to kneel before me."

"I will do as I please, my lady Queen. I will not have you think such thoughts! I beg you not to consider leaving! I have no plans to wed, nor will I make any—"

"What of the mother of your sons?" I asked gently, touching his face.

He trembled and shook his head. "They are by different mothers," he said quickly. "Those women matter not. They are content as they are. I have seen to that. My heart is—they have not my affection. Please, Guinevere, believe me. You matter much more than they."

He rose suddenly and paced back and forth before me. "The night before I left Brittany, the King spoke with me well into the night. About what should happen if—if he did not come back. The last thing he said, the last but most important, was about you. He bade me promise to protect you and care for you all the days of your life. I promised him, Guinevere, I promised willingly. So let me do it. It is Arthur's wish, as well as my own."

I bowed my head. "All right, Mordred. I thank you from my heart. In a year or so, you may feel differently, but—"

"Never!"

"—but for now, I will worry no longer about it. For this I thank you."

He raised me from my seat and kissed my hand. "Guinevere," he said fervently, "you are still Queen here. You need not ever bend a knee to me."

But I dipped him a curtsy as I left him. He was, after all, High King.

Time passed, and still no news came from Brittany. Mordred told me the reason.

"A summer storm assails the Narrow Sea," he said. "They say the wind blows out of the north, cold and strong, all day and night. Messengers going south may get across in record time, but no ship in Brittany can sail beyond the harbor. One good thing has come of it, though. Cynewulf is also held ashore. Some on the Council do not like this treaty, and I would win them over before he is here in fact."

"Then is our army stranded?"

"They are on Hoel's lands, and safe. The threat to them is past. This gives them time to reorganize and heal their wounds. We should know the truth of things as soon as the wind changes."

I looked at his face, Arthur's face, profiled against the sunlit garden. It was a strong, young face, full of authority and promise and the joy of wielding power, and doing it well.

"Mordred," I said softly. "What if—what if the courier brings the news that the King lives and has landed? What then?"

He turned to me, helplessly, beseechingly. "I—I will yield to him, of course. He is my father."

I drew a long breath of relief. "Will you, Mordred? Can you? Do you swear it?"

He nodded and swallowed hard. "I have thought of it every night since the news of his death. It would not be easy to give up kingship, even for a time. But he is Arthur. Even were he not my father, I could do no less."

I went to him and hugged him tightly, my eyes wet with tears. "You are a good man, Mordred. And I love you dearly. You grow daily more like him, do you know that?" I thought to please him by my words, but the joy had gone out of his face.

Eventually, the wind changed, then we had news. Not at first—I later learned that the army's ships had been caught in a squall and gone astray. The first ships that landed were trading vessels, and everyone on board had heard a different story. So the first things we heard were rumors—the King lived, the King was dead, the King lived but was mad. Lancelot had died of his wounds; Lancelot had recovered but could not yet walk. Gawaine lived and led the army, usurping Arthur's place. Gawaine lived and had vowed to kill Lancelot before he left Less Britain. Gawaine lived and supported the raving King, loyal to the end, while Bedwyr led the troops. Mordred and I looked at one another and knew not what to think. As we had heard no rumors of their deaths, we took Gawaine and Bedwyr to be living, and so knew that eventually we should have the truth.

But the first messenger to come was not from the British ships, but from the Saxons. The messenger, afraid for his life in Camelot, nevertheless braved the troops to give Mordred his report. Cerdic was furious and called Mordred to account. British ships had landed on his coasts, blown eastward by the fickle winds. This was allowed by the new treaty and so the local people had not panicked, but simply retreated inland to allow them passage. But the same ill wind had blown Cynewulf and his company ashore nearby. Most of those new immigrants were farmers, but some were thegns and fighters. They knew nothing of the treaty, of course, but saw in the presence of the British ships opposition to their landing. However, they had held back their attack, in case the Britons should prove peaceful. But no sooner had the Britons put ashore than they attacked, led by a wild young warrior who cried aloud for Saxon blood. And so battle had ensued, Cynewulf's men were defeated, and the land about laid waste as the Britons, ragged and weary but still a fighting force, moved north.

Nervously the counselors heard this news.

"What was landed first," Mordred asked, "horses or men?"

"Men," the Saxon replied, "and they had lifted the Dragon banner above a tall man with a great sword that shone like light. Everyone there thought it was Arthur."

Mordred went white. "Are you certain it was Arthur? Were there any there who knew him?"

The Saxon shrugged. It was not certain; nothing was certain, but that the Britons had landed on the Saxon shore and attacked, unprovoked.

Mordred shook his head. "Had it been Arthur, the cavalry would have landed first. If he meant war. Of course, it is possible that they were merely shipwrecked and felt themselves threatened by Cynewulf's armed force."

The Saxon nodded. "That is why King Cerdic sends to you, King Mordred. The fault may be on both sides. But the fact is, the Saxons and the Britons are once again at war. The treaty has been broken."

The knights around the Round Table looked at Mordred nervously. But Mordred had his father's calm. "Return to Cerdic with the message that I will come to his aid immediately with the army. I beg him to be patient. If this is Arthur, there should be no danger. Was it not Arthur himself who made the first treaty with your people? He would never break a promise he had made. If it is not Arthur but some remnants of the army, they are confused and afraid. I will show myself and bring them back home and make reparations to Cerdic for what damage they have in error caused."

With this the Saxon had to be content and took himself back to his territories. Mordred gave out orders to gather the troops and prepared himself to set out the next day. But first he came to find me.

I knew from his face he was beset. He looked both pleased and dismayed, relieved and frightened, angry and full of hope. He went on his knee at once and grasped my hand.

"Gwen, there is a chance he is alive!"

I sank into a chair. After all this! After the hard work of acceptance, to have hope given back! I did not trust myself to speak, but squeezed his hand.

"I've had a message from Cerdic." He gave me the report, and finished, "Some among them think it was the High King who led the Britons. I leave tomorrow to find out if this is true."

But here my courage left me. What I had been through, after hearing of Arthur's death, I could not go through twice. The scar upon my soul was deep and still bled. I dared not bare myself for another blow. I dared not hope. I turned away from Mordred and withdrew my hand.

"No," I whispered. "It is not he. It cannot be. He has stood face to face with Cynewulf; he knows the man. He would never have attacked."

"But Gawaine might have," Mordred persisted, surprised at my reaction. "From what the courier told us, it sounds just like him. And who else could it be, under the Dragon banner?"

"Bedwyr, perhaps." I sighed wearily. "Gereint? Who knows? But if it had been the King, they'd have known it. There would be no doubt."

Mordred chewed his lip, watching me. "Tomorrow I leave for Cerdic's side, and we move south together. The defense treaty binds me to this action. But I am not sure it is the best course—it will look as if we march against our own troops."

He was asking for my advice! With an effort, I met his eyes and gently touched his face, Arthur's face. "You are High King, Mordred. Of course you must go. Stay Cerdic's hand and bring our poor troops home."

He squared his shoulders. The gesture brought fresh tears to my eyes. "When we meet them," he said firmly, "we will parley. I will show them how misunderstanding has arisen. At all costs, I must avoid bloodshed. For all our sakes."

That night, after Anna had dressed me for sleep and brushed my hair, I knelt by the open terrace doorway and said my prayers. As I rose and turned toward the bed, I saw light creep under the leather curtain and heard soft voices in the King's room. Without stopping to think, I pulled aside the curtain and went in. Mordred stood there, just come from hall, and Bran stood trembling behind him, holding a night robe.

I met Mordred's eyes.

"No!" I whispered. "Not his chamber, Mordred. Not yet. Please."

"My lady," Mordred began, and then stopped. He waved his hand, and Bran fled down the stairs. Mordred came around the bed and stood before me.

"Guinevere, I would not alarm you. Have I misunderstood you?" His voice went very low. "Did you not this very day confirm me in my Kingship, while there is yet hope that—"

"Not his bed. No. Not yet." I twisted my hands together, my eyes on the familiar bearskins. "I still—I can't—I still remember—" I looked up at him and shook my head. "Then I must go, for I am not your Queen."

He took my hands and pressed them to his lips. Instinctively I drew back, but he pulled me closer and, before I knew it, held me in his arms and kissed my lips and my face with eager passion. Before I could even comprehend it, he was on his knees, his arms about my waist, his face buried in my skirt.

"I would make you my Queen, Guinevere," he cried, "if you would have me! I have loved you all these years, since my first day in Camelot—do not shrink from me, I pray you! I am not Arthur, I know it well, but I am his son. Can you not find some corner of your heart for me, or does he have it all?"

He looked up at me beseechingly, but I was speechless. There was nothing I could say. "Do you hate me?" he whispered. "Am I evil? You are so good, Guinevere, and I have loved you for so long! Tell me, please, that there is hope for me. You said yourself I was your King. You said it today, in spite of the news I brought you. Please—please, while I am away, consider my plea, and when I return let me know if there is hope for me. I see by your face you are affronted. Remember how you once spoke to me! Of the power of passion and how it overrules us! You begged me to accept it, in your case. Can you not accept it now in mine? You asked me once if I had ever loved a woman—you are that woman, Guinevere! By all that's holy, I do love you, as much as life. I intend no insult, my dearest love. I would only honor you as Arthur has always honored you, and I would love you as he always has."

As he spoke, his face revealed his soul. I recognized the blaze of passion in his eyes; I had seen it often enough in Arthur to know its meaning. In this, too, it seemed, he was Pendragon. Trembling, I freed myself from his embrace and stepped back.

"My lord," I breathed, "these words were better not spoken between us. How can I answer you, Mordred? I have always regarded you as my son."

Pain and anger flashed across his face, instantly suppressed. He rose, rather stiffly. "Regard me thus no longer. You are not my mother."

"Oh, Mordred, I would not hurt you for the world. I bear you naught but love. But—"

"But not that kind of love?" he asked gently, recovering his composure and guarding his face. "I tell you now, I will wed no other."

"Then Britain has no future!" I cried, clasping my hands to my throat. "Mordred, there is no sense in this! This is folly. You must marry, to keep his line alive. Let me go, my lord, and seek shelter where I may. While you are King, I cannot stay here!"

"You *must* stay." He reached out and held my shoulders firmly. "You *must* stay. I command you. If you are gone when I return, I shall seek you out and find you. You cannot hide from me. Be sure of that. We will settle this another time." He dropped his hands and looked about the room. "I will not sleep here tonight. Do not fear it. But when I come back—" He left it at that, bowed low, and left me.

I was still standing there, shaking, when Bran crept up the stairs.

"My lady?" he called anxiously. "Are you all right? Oh, please, my lady, do not look at me so! I would never betray the King! But the King is—and Sir Mordred bade me serve him, and he is—King."

"Be easy, Bran. I do not fault you. But I—I would ask a favor of you this night."

"Anything, my lady!"

"Will you sleep here, on this side of the curtain? Bring your own bedding, if you like, no one will mind. But I would have warning of—anyone's approach."

He understood and did not bat an eyelid. "Yes, my lady. With pleasure I will do it."

So I slept that night with Anna in my bed and Bran at the entrance to my chamber. I dared not look ahead. I prayed that wherever Arthur's spirit was, he had looked the other way. And not for the first time, I cursed my beauty, which had caused me so much more pain than pleasure in my life. Truly, it was a burden.

In the morning, Mordred left for the Saxon territories at the head of a great army. Not until he had been gone three hours did I draw an easy breath. Ferron, who was left in charge, was jubilant and, seeing me downcast, came to cheer me.

"Be easy, Queen Guinevere, the King will be home soon."

I looked at him in puzzlement, then shrugged. "How can he, when he has but left, and no one knows the end of his journey? But it matters not to me."

Ferron stood rooted to the ground, shocked. "I mean King Arthur, lady!" he cried.

I turned away. "No more of this, I pray you. I cannot bear it."

He grabbed my arm in anger and spun me around. Then his face softened. "Has no one told you? Arthur lives. The messenger minced his words in Council, seeing he was speaking to Mordred, but the Saxon grooms have told me what they overheard him saying to his servant." I met his eyes slowly. The world around me began to spin. "Cynewulf saw him and knew him and sent word to Cerdic. It is Arthur. He has returned."

I fainted.

49 ♛ THE WICKED DAY OF DESTINY

Two days later we received a courier from Mordred. He bore two messages, one for me and one for Ferron. Together we received him and heard his news. Mordred had met with Cerdic, and their forces rode south together to meet the men come from Brittany. Cerdic was angry. British troops had landed armed in his kingdom, a kingdom whose sovereignty Arthur himself had guaranteed, and had killed his people. As their king, he had no choice but to gather his thegns and foot soldiers and give them battle. But this Mordred, his ally, was determined to prevent. He wished to reassure Cerdic, but he also wished to protect his men. If it was true that Arthur led them, then this should be easily accomplished, he told Cerdic. If Gawaine or some other led them, as was likely from their warlike behavior, all would be well once Mordred met them.

"And did Mordred and Cerdic seem easy with one another?" I asked the courier.

He licked his lips nervously. "Passably easy, my lady. But the Saxons are very angry. The treaty has been broken, and someone must pay. They ride together as allies, but not in close friendship. It looks like a ticklish business to me."

"What did Cerdic have to say about Arthur?" Ferron asked, glancing at me sidelong. "He has had time to gather information. Were there any who could say with certainty whether the King is among these men, or no?"

The courier swallowed and met his eyes. "Yes, my lord. One of the thegns who had gone to greet Cynewulf's landing party was a veteran of the Battle of Agned. He saw the King and recognized him. He says it was Arthur."

I trembled and turned away to seek a chair. My eyes watered, and my knees would not support me.

Ferron spoke with him a moment, then dismissed him, turning his back to read his letter. I retired to a corner, afraid to open mine. I would have left Camelot within an hour of Mordred's going, if Ferron had not given me hope that the King was still alive. Trembling, I broke the seal and unrolled the scroll. It was not written in the scribe's hand, but in Mordred's own. The lettering was labored and took me a long time to read.

My lady Queen Guinevere, he wrote, *how can I ever beg your pardon? I have spoken the unspeakable and will regret it all my life. I apologize most abjectly for my rude and hasty words, and for the doubt and suffering I have caused you. I swear, on my life, that I will never again approach you in such a manner; you are safe from me, my lady, all the days of your life. I beg you will not flee your home on account of me; I do not wish to break my promise to Arthur, to keep you well and care for you, but I will not prevent your leaving, if you wish it. Should you stay, you will do me honor. I shall keep to the quarters I now occupy, for they are grand enough for such as me. You need never fear me. I am now, and will always be, if you will forgive me and show me the mercy for which you are well known, your loving son, Mordred.*

I stared blankly at this missive. Was this the same man who had embraced me in Arthur's chamber? I had never known Mordred humble before. I wished to believe him, but I could not discount the fact that he knew, when he wrote it, that Arthur was alive.

I looked up and saw Ferron watching me.

"What will Mordred do, my lady? Can you hazard a guess? He says here, it seems likely that the King lives, but he cannot understand why he comes home through the Saxon lands, swords drawn, instead of putting back out to sea, or crossing westward toward Potter's Bay and Britain. He says it has the appearance of deliberate provocation, and Cerdic is outraged. Thus far he has held his hand, but unless Mordred can get speech with the King beforehand, he fears there might be fighting. He assures me and asks me to assure you that he will not raise his hand against Arthur. But neither does he offer to abdicate his crown. What will he do, when faced with it?"

I shook my head. "I don't know, Ferron. Three days ago I would have said that he would yield to Arthur. He has promised me that. But now—I don't know. Indeed, I wonder if he knows himself."

Ferron cleared his throat. "You should know, my lady, that there are rumors everywhere. About you and Mordred."

I looked up swiftly. "Rumors of what?"

Ferron hesitated a moment only. "Bluntly, of marriage. That Sir Mordred has long loved you is well known. Lately, the gossip goes, you have shared his bed and agreed to be his Queen."

I gasped. "Do you believe this?"

"No," he said at once. "I know better. But while you stay here, it is a difficult rumor to disprove."

Tears sprang to my eyes. "What would you have me do? Fly from Camelot as my lord is nearing home at last? Oh, Ferron, he must be sick to death of fighting! I know why he presses onward, although Mordred does not! He is weary and looks forward to find the shortest way to his desire. A Saxon beach is not the place to take counsel and discuss the merits of various routes! Picture him! Stranded on a beach, shipwrecked perhaps, with a Saxon force approaching and the cruel sea at his back! Every instinct in him, every fiber of his being, would urge him onward, and through them, in a straight line to home. He knows, yes, he knows that the Saxons cannot stand against him. Once his men are back, and tended to, and given rest, there will be time to mend the fences he has broken. If only Mordred would let him be!" I stopped, fought back a sob, and continued in a whisper. "How will he feel, when at last he gets here, weary and grieving for all those he has lost in battle, and looks for comfort in my arms, to find that I am flown because of foolish, disgusting, ridiculous rumors about his own son!"

Ferron came to where I sat and knelt beside me. He was moved, I saw. "You are quite right," he said softly. "I understand it now. Forgive me, my lady, for the suggestion. You think only of the King. I should have, also."

"In my heart, I don't believe Mordred will stand against him. But you will know better how the soldiers feel. Are they Arthur's men, or Mordred's?"

Ferron frowned, considering the question. "Those that went to Brittany, all twelve thousand—every man was Arthur's. But those that Mordred raised here this summer, they are mostly young men, the sons and younger brothers of those who left with Arthur. They have sworn themselves to Mordred."

"Then there are two Briton armies?"

"I really do not know, my lady. Are there two Kings?"

Through tears I looked out to the garden, shimmering in the dry, late summer heat. "If they cannot speak, or reach terms—Mordred will not face him. He must fall back. But Cerdic cannot. I fear the Saxons will attack him, and Mordred will not be able to come to his aid, because he is Cerdic's ally."

"But, my lady, you said yourself the Saxons cannot stand against him. This is a prophecy of Merlin's, is it not?"

I nodded. "Yes. But he is weary, Ferron. I feel this in my soul. And Merlin—" As I spoke the name, I cried aloud, and my hands flew to my throat. I felt the blood drain from my face.

"Guinevere!" Ferron cried, catching me by the arms, and shaking me gently. "Guinevere, what's amiss? What is it?"

"Merlin!" I whispered in terror. "Dear God, I had forgotten! That deadly, fearful prophecy he made! Never in all these years could I envision how it could come to pass—and now I see! Oh, Ferron, all is lost! May God forgive them both!"

He did not understand me and begged me to tell him, but I could not. I could not lay that fearful burden on another. He took me to my quarters and gave me into Anna's care. I begged her to pack my trunk and make ready for departure.

"Are we leaving, my lady?" she asked in great surprise. "What has happened?"

"I am leaving, Anna. You need not come with me, unless you wish. I cannot stay and watch this. I cannot stay!"

She sat me in a chair and brought me water. "Where you go, my lady, there will I go, also. I will not leave you in these troubled times. Where are we off to?"

"I don't know, I don't know, Anna!" I cried in distress. "To Caerleon, perhaps? No, held by Mordred's men. Too near Maelgon. And not south—Duke Constantine will be upon them like ravens after a wolf fight. And not north—Drustan's sons lie dead in Gaul and Drustan himself is old enough to be my father. He cannot live much longer. And who will rule Elmet when he is gone? Hapgar was killed along with Coel of Rheged—their sons may be those lovers of the cold, north wind you spoke of. East then—but who will take me?"

"The Saxons lie east," Anna said sensibly.

I began to weep once more. "I am not afraid of Saxons." Anna tended me and comforted me, and at length I shared my fears with her. As always, she was calm and sensible and gave me good advice.

"You can know nothing until the Saxons meet the British. Then must King—Sir Mordred choose his fate. Wait and see what happens. And in the meanwhile, we can stealthily make arrangements for a sudden departure, should the necessity arise."

I yielded to her sound advice, and we talked long that evening, taking supper in our quarters and seeing no one. In the morning I went to the stables. Good Lyonel was overjoyed to see me and gladly consented to the favor I asked. He set two swift geldings aside for us and gave us saddle packs, the kind the soldiers used, and made a solemn oath never to reveal, except to Arthur, what he had done. I did not tell him when or where we were going; only that we were. His eyes misted, and he kissed me farewell in kindness, but he did not ask me why I left.

Anna and I packed well for the journey and hid the saddlebags in the straw and waited. Long days went by, dry and hot; nothing moved on the downs but dust devils, playing in the parched grasses. Ferron was worried about me and begged for my company.

"Call me when the courier comes," I said. "Until then, I would be alone."

He came on the day the weather broke and rode in drenched from rain. The skies lay low and black on the hills. Thunder rolled up the valleys and pounded on King's Gate. It sounded like a thousand evil spirits clamoring for entrance. I shivered and reminded myself I was a Christian.

Ferron summoned me to hear the courier's message. He had no letter, but had got his tale by heart. The High King—for it was he, indeed—had gathered his forces on a rise and saw below him the Saxon army and the Briton, marching together to meet him. He had not waited to greet them or send a messenger to beg a parley—veteran that he was, he had attacked.

In my mind's eye, I saw him, weary to death and sore of heart over his losses, confused by the Saxon hostilities after he had treated with them for peace, bewildered, perhaps, by the rumors of King Mordred coming in arms against his father. I saw him as he must have stood, looking down upon them, Mordred and Cerdic talking together even as they came in sight of him. I could imagine his grief, and his fatigue, and then his anger, as the old, cold hatred gripped his soul; and the Sword trembled in his hand, crying out for Saxon blood. No, to Arthur it must have seemed that the Saxons had turned against him, and he must have thought, if his son loved him, he would join his cause.

King Mordred, continued the courier, had recognized the High King and had withdrawn the Britons from the field. Ferron glanced at me swiftly and looked relieved. He would have parleyed, repeated the courier, but was given no chance. His host fell back and were returning to Camelot, for he refused to lead his troops against King Arthur. He would return home and wait for him here.

And Arthur, I thought, always cool and far-seeing in battle, had seen his son turn, not to come to his aid against the Saxons, but to desert the field altogether, leaving him alone to fight Cerdic with the ragged remnants of his strife-torn army.

By nightfall, the courier continued, Mordred's troops received word that Cerdic's forces were broken and had fled in disarray before the High King Arthur, who stopped only to regroup and bury his dead before pressing onward. Within three days Mordred's army would be here; within seven Arthur himself would come. Then, said the man, staring straight ahead, trancelike and unseeing, the Kings would parley and fences would be mended, misunderstandings cleared, and peace restored.

No, I thought sadly, none who knew them well could think so. Father and son they were, both proud men, each feeling betrayed by the other, whom he loved dearly, both Kings of the same land. Which one would bend the knee and say: I was wrong, my lord?

I shook myself out of my dark thoughts and found the courier had gone. Ferron tried to look cheerful, but I soon spared him the effort.

"I will retire, my lord. I am not well. I thank you for your care of me; we have had good times together; let us remember those days and not what is to come."

He let me go; perhaps he understood me better than I gave him credit for. I found my maids peacefully sewing, as unaware of the doom that threatened as they were of thunder on a dry day. But Anna was not there. I passed into my sitting room and thence to the stair to my chamber. I stopped, holding my breath. I heard voices above. One of them was Anna's, and the other was male. I went up silently and paused in the doorway. The room was dim, for the day was black, and Anna had lit no candles. The curtain across the terrace doors was partly drawn. Anna stood there, fastening the latch. Beside her in the dimness stood a tall, cloaked figure, dripping wet, and whispering his thanks.

"Anna!" I whispered, seeing by their quiet movements this was a secret thing. "What goes on here?"

She whirled to face me. "My lady!" The cloaked figure went down on one knee.

"Queen Guinevere."

I walked quickly to him. "I know your voice. Who are you?" His hood slipped back; he looked up, smiling. It was Galahad! I stepped back and caught my breath.

"Galahad! What means this? How did you come here?"

His smile was sly. "By the garden gate, my lady, and up the stairs. A family trick." Then he bit his lip and crossed himself. "My lord, forgive me," he said to no one.

I glanced at Anna. I had shared with her some of Mordred's story, enough for her to know this boy was not in his right mind. She backed quietly against the nightstand, where, since the night of Gareth's murder I kept a jeweled dagger, and surreptitiously opened the drawer. But Galahad bore no weapons, no scabbard, not even a knife tucked in his belt. What did he want?

I had not raised him. He still knelt before me. In the dimness, he looked beautiful, calm and serene; so must his father have looked, once, when his whole future lay before him. Lancelot had been his age at Caer Eden, when he first met Arthur.

"Have you news of my lord?" I asked him swiftly. "Fares he well?"

Galahad turned to me a guileless face. "Who is your lord, Queen Guinevere?"

"You know well who!" I retorted. "I ask after Arthur, and none other!"

He paused. "May I rise?"

"Will you behave?"

He smiled again, a smile that made me shiver. "I am tamed, lady. Your lord and husband has bound me round with oaths. I will not harm you. See? I come naked."

I raised him, and he thanked me. He was taller than I was by a head, and so handsome a youth, it took one's breath away. He had eyes that entrapped the gaze and mesmerized the mind, if one looked at him too long.

"Why are you here?" I asked him bluntly.

"I come from Arthur," he replied. "I have a message."

"You?" I gasped. "You travel with him? Were you aboard his ship?"

"Oh, yes," he said easily, brushing the water off his cloak. "I have been at his side this long while. I am his beloved, now that Gawaine is dead."

I swallowed hard. "Gawaine dead? How? Where did he die?"

"On a Saxon beach. He led the charge, and I was right behind him. I saw it happen. Cynewulf's ax got him. He died in Arthur's arms, when it was over."

"So—you have fought for the King, after all?"

"I have rid the earth of a hundred godless savages!" he cried, and then faltered suddenly. "I owe the King my life, twice over. Would I could be so cool in battle!"

I trembled and walked about the room to still my fear. "And how fares Arthur? Does he sleep? Eat? Is he weary?"

"He is angry. Fury drives him. His allies attacked him and bar his way." He shrugged. "That's what comes of making treaties with heathen bastards. Their oaths are soon forgotten."

I shook my head. "You don't understand it, Galahad. There is much more to this than you can see. But no matter. Has he his health?"

But again, he did not seem to understand me. "He is sick at heart, and weary. There is a knife in his back. The traitor kills him."

"Traitor! What traitor?" I gasped, fearing his answer.

"Mordred, of course," he replied calmly. "We saw him, plain as day, come take the field against us—against *us*—and beside Saxons!"

"Dear God!" I whispered, sinking to a chair. "It has come." I grasped at the last straw. "But Mordred never raised a sword against him!"

"No, the coward! The King attacked, and the coward turned and ran! It broke his heart."

I bowed my head. All was lost. It was time to be going. "One more thing. Does—does your father live?"

His eyes flamed, but he kept still. "I knew you would ask it—but I have promised the King politeness. Bedwyr lives and fights with us. Of my father, I say nothing."

"Please, Galahad."

"No."

I gave up. "Give me your message, then. Are you going back to Arthur? Will you take him a word from me?"

He reached in his tunic for a scroll as he shook his head. "I have a mission. I'm going on to Ynys Witrin to seek audience with a witch. The King would see her. Then I must purify myself at the monastery there. I have a Quest, you see."

He handed me the scroll, bowed low, fastened his cloak, and put his hand to the latch.

"Go with God, Galahad," I said softly.

He turned back and raised his hand in benediction, making the sign of the Cross in the air between us. Then, with a strange smile upon his lips, Lancelot's poor tortured son let himself out into the storm and crept out of Camelot by whatever way he had come.

"Anna, a light," I said softly, shivering from the encounter. With trembling fingers I broke the seal and slowly puzzled out the words. He had written it himself.

My dearest Gwen, I pray this finds you well and whole and free. I do not believe the rumors. I am beset on all sides and fear for your safety. Get you gone from the traitor Mordred and fly to Amesbury. I will take back what is mine and, when I am free, will come to you there. The abbot will take you without questions. He is beholden to me. Be quick and silent. The fox is sly. I hold you in my heart and trust you. Your once and future King, Arthur.

And at the bottom, hastily scrawled: *Forgive my sending Galahad. He has promised to treat you as his mother—there is no one else—I cannot spare Bedwyr. Lancelot lives. He will join me as soon as God gives him strength to walk. Pray for us both.—A*

My heart leaped with joy in the same moment it sank in despair.

"We are lost, Anna!" I whispered, rereading it with speed. *The traitor Mordred.* "Oh, Anna! We are lost!" *I will take back what is mine.* Oh, my dear Arthur, how take it back? Only by killing your son—and when we meet, what will you say to me then? "Come!" I said, thrusting the letter in my pouch. "My riding clothes. Quickly! It is time to go!"

"Now, my lady? But the storm!"

I laughed at her and saw her eyes widen in amazement. "Do you not know this about me, Anna? Why, I love riding in bad weather! Come."

It took us four days to make the journey, and for four days the skies were dark and leaden, cloaking our passage. Each night we spent in a peasant's cottage. The poor people of Britain gave us shelter, never asking who we were, but understanding the desire of women to seek shelter in the house of God. It was an omen of change.

The abbot took us in, good man, with tears at Arthur's letter. I did not want his finest rooms, but begged for a small cell. I needed no ornaments or furnishings beyond what the other women had; I needed only Anna nearby. He gave me what I asked for. My window looked out past willow trees to the river that wound slowly southward toward the great plain, and the Giants' Dance, where Ambrosius and Uther lay buried.

Ambrosius had been born here—hence the name of the place—and now it lay but a day's ride from Cerdic's lands. But this did not concern me. The Saxons might be entwined in Arthur's destiny, but I knew in my soul that they played no part in mine.

I could not think of Camelot without an ache in my throat. It had been my home for twenty years, and I knew every foot of it—chambers, towers, gardens, stables, and grounds. I thought of it as I had seen it for the first time, on that bright summer day: shining and golden upon its green hill, with flags flying gaily from its towers; a citadel of greatness and glory! The Kingdom was new then, and we had all been so young! I knew I should never see it again. Whatever the future held, I could not go back. I had but one room now; but it was more than enough for my needs.

I kept to my cell, apart from the others, joining them only for prayers in the little chapel. I knew from their sidelong looks and hushed whispers that they knew me, and I did not want their worship. Anna stayed by my side, and together we knelt and prayed for Arthur and Mordred, together we took our meals, together we took the air in the walled garden or in the grounds.

We often walked to the water's edge, arm in arm, saying nothing. It was a time of waiting. The weather cleared, and we had those calm, bright days that make September welcome, with cool breezes in the morning and the warmth of summer at noon. Leaves edged themselves with yellow, then gently fell and rustled underfoot. My heart was held by some unnatural calm; I did not weep or sigh, but found joy in the careful perusal of small things: a bird's feather, dropped upon the lawn, held soft and tickling between the fingers; the gleam of morning sun on the dewy grasses; the pleasant chuckle of the brook as it danced and frothed around the boulders in its way; the beauty of sunsets, the soft glow of chapel candles, the gentle, soothing strokes of Anna's brushes in my hair. I kept my thoughts to these, and so survived.

One lovely afternoon as we sat beneath the willows Anna told me stories of her childhood. I attended now and then, but my thoughts were on the tiny creatures that ran up and down along the rough willow bark. What heights they scaled, these mighty runners! What cliffs they overshot and valleys fell into, all unharmed! It amused me to watch their frantic efforts— did they have goals? I wondered, or did they scramble about undirected, for the sheer joy of running? And what end would they come to? A spider's web, most likely, or food for birds.

On the thought, I heard screaming in the sky above me and felt a cold horror grip my soul. I looked up—ravens in flight, no more, heading westward—but I felt the day grow dark behind the shadow of their passing.

"My lady Guinevere!" Anna cried. "Why do you shake so? Why do you weep?"

I rose unsteadily, and she took my arm. "Let us go in and pray."

"What is it? Oh, please tell me, what have you seen?"

"Nothing," I whispered, "nothing at all. Only ravens flying westward. Men believe—they can scent a battlefield fifty leagues away."

"Oh, no, my lady, these are old wives' tales. I am surprised that you believe them. It is the season for their movement, that is all."

But I knew, as we knelt in the chapel, that Arthur walked the earth no longer. He was gone from me forever. I knew it by the heaviness of my spirit and by the grief that shadowed me, a brooding thing, waiting upon a courier's word, waiting to engulf me. I would not recognize its presence and give it entry, but put on my white veil of mourning and prayed, day and night, for the salvation of Arthur's soul.

On the seventh day, the abbess came to me.

"My lady Queen," she said with a curtsy, "Father Albin wants you to know we have a soldier with us, convalescing, who would speak with you."

"A message?" I asked quickly. "From whom?"

"Not a message, my lady. The man is from the village and left with the King to fight in Brittany. He returned only yesterday, to recover from his wounds."

I clasped my hands together and held them hard. "Is he coherent? Does he wish to talk?"

She raised her eyes to me, and I saw compassion there. "Yes, my lady. When he learned the Queen was here, sent hither to await the King, he asked to see you. Will you come?"

"Indeed I will."

I dropped my veil and followed her. We passed Anna in the garden, and she left her task at my signal and came to me. Behind the convent cells was the house of healing. Avoiding the main chamber, which smelled, we were taken to a small, rude hut of wattle. On a dirt floor, strewn with straw, lay a pallet with the sick man wrapped in bloody rags. It was a far cry from Niniane's House of Healing, and I doubted anyone could recover here. A servant tended him and placed stools for us, then ducked out.

"Kerwas." The Mother addressed him gently. His face was gray, and his eyes dull. I did not know much about healing, but to me he looked beyond their help. "Kerwas, this is the Queen." She glanced at me. "A servant will be within call, if you need him."

I thanked her and turned to the dying soldier. He was about my age, at a guess, but ravaged by hard use and pain. He looked me over carefully.

"Are you truly the Queen?"

I was dressed in a plain gown of dull gray and wore no ornament of any sort. He had no way of knowing who I was.

"Yes, good sir. I am Guinevere of Britain, Arthur's wife."

"Let me see your face." Obediently I lifted my veil and drew it back. Anna loosed a pin and brought my hair forward. He sighed and closed his eyes.

"Good Kerwas, I would not tire you, but if you bear a message from my lord, or even news of him, good or ill, I would hear it."

"I have news."

"Does he live?" I blurted, not intending the question, and pressed my fingers against my lips, fearful of his answer.

He opened his eyes and looked into my face. "I do not know, my lady. But it is unlikely."

I nodded. "Go on," I whispered. "Tell me what you know." Anna gave me a clean cloth for my eyes.

"I was with him," he said slowly, "in the battle of Autun. I fought there in the company he led. We broke them. We broke the Burgundians and the Romans, and they outnumbering us five to one."

I smiled and slid off the stool to sit at his side. I took his rough hand in mine. It was cold, and I chafed it gently.

"My lord is the victor," I said softly, "in every field he takes."

He closed his eyes. "Aye," he said, "and the enemy knew it well. But near the end of the day, when we were mopping up and driving out the stragglers, we were ambushed."

"So we heard from Lancelot. He got a message home."

Kerwas grunted. "No doubt he meant well, but 'twould have been better for us all if he hadn't sent it!" He shifted in discomfort.

"Tell me about the ambush."

"Well, they came at us from behind, and we fought them across the stream. Savages they were—I will not tell you what they did. We were a handful only, thirty foot soldiers and only the King and Sir Gawaine on horseback. They must have been a hundred, easy. Maybe more. But the King has a cool head; he kept us in formation, and we repulsed them. Nay, we followed them into the wooded hills and killed every last man of them by nightfall."

"How many did you lose?"

"Half, my lady. But they lost all."

"You are a brave man, Kerwas. Were you injured?"

"No, my lady, not there. We had magic that day, God be praised."

"Why did not the King send a messenger back to the field headquarters, to report his whereabouts?"

The pale eyes opened, then, and met mine. "My lady, he did."

"He did? They—they never received it."

"We know this now. He sent young Dunstan, a fast runner, to Sir Lancelot. We were two days in the hills, scouting for stragglers and burying our dead. On the way back—"

"Two days! Why so long?"

He looked away and stared pensively at the thatched roof above his head. "Ahhh. The King was weary, my lady. And we thought, since we had sent Dunstan, there was no hurry. We would be at Autun a week, easy, just burying the dead. But on the way back, we came across Dunstan's body, locked in a death grip with a Roman youth, beside the stream. Then we hurried and found the troops in a panic because the King was lost. There was rejoicing when they saw his face, I can tell you!"

A glimmer of a smile crossed his lips. I called for the servant, but no one came, so I lifted his head myself and gave him a drink of the broth the servant had left.

"Everyone is always glad to see Arthur," I said gently, and pillowed his head on my lap.

"Aye, my lady. That's true enough." He looked better, and spoke stronger and kept his eyes on me. "But we held no celebrations, for Sir Lancelot was wounded and lay near death. For three days the High King sat at his bedside while he raged in fever. Sir Gawaine was always at the King's elbow and came out to give us news from time to time. The physicians were sure that Lancelot's suffering would end in death, but the King would not leave him. No one knew, until Lancelot passed the fever and opened his eyes and spoke, of the message he had sent home to Britain. Then was the King distressed and sent another courier off that instant, but in his joy at Lancelot's recovery, he did not think to double-check. We learned later, the man was thrown from his horse in the Perilous Forest and died of a broken neck."

"It seems, indeed," I said slowly, "as if God wished Britain to think him dead."

"Aye, lass. I mean, my lady. We stayed until Lancelot could be moved and our dead had been buried and their belongings gathered. The King made a list of all those killed and sent another messenger home."

"Another?" I cried. "But he never got here!"

"He left as the winds were rising on the Narrow Sea. Chances are he was drowned. We escorted Lancelot to his home in Benoic. We carried him on a litter. He vowed to follow us to Britain as soon as he was able, to fight the traitor Mordred."

"Mordred!" I gasped. "Dear Kerwas, you have left something out. Why did the High King think his son a traitor *in Brittany?*"

"Aye," Kerwas said slowly, with some reluctance. "I have indeed left something out. Constantine sent a letter."

I froze, staring at him. "Constantine? Duke Constantine of Cornwall?"

"Aye. The winds favored his courier, although they stymied ours."

"He sent a letter? To the King?"

Kerwas watched me carefully, and it seemed to me that he guarded his face, as much as was in his power.

"Why are you afraid, my lady?" His head lay in my lap, and he could feel my trembling.

"Duke Constantine is no friend of mine, nor of the King's. He bears me a grudge. I am surprised that he would send to Arthur, and surprised that my lord would read it."

"But he did read it," Kerwas said firmly. "And it brought him sorrow."

"And how," I asked, "do you know all this? Were you in his councils?"

"My lady, I stood guard upon the entrance to the tent. I was there when the courier brought the letter. Lancelot lay calling out in his fever. The King asked for quiet on his behalf, so he could hear his moaning and know that he still lived." I shut my eyes, and he went on. "The camp was quiet. The night was hot; the tent flap lay open. The King read the letter in silence, but Sir Gawaine, who was always with him, was not so skilled, and worked out the words aloud."

"And what did he say?" I asked, trembling, afraid that I knew already.

"I am no courier, my lady. I have not got it by heart. But the gist of it was this, if you will forgive me."

"I will forgive anything but falsehood, Kerwas. Tell me."

"He wrote to say that Sir Mordred had declared himself High King of Britain, without waiting for confirmation of Arthur's death, and was gathering a new army, loyal to himself alone. The duke predicted that when and if the King returned, he would stand against us. As he did."

"No," I said swiftly, "you judge too quickly. He did not. Not for that reason."

"He did," Kerwas said harshly. "I was there, and saw it."

"All right," I said to soothe him, for his color was not good. "But think back to Brittany, and how you felt then. Would you have opposed him, Kerwas, if Arthur were not with you?"

"If King Arthur were dead, my lady, then Sir Mordred would be King. Of course we would not oppose him."

I sighed. I had known the men were loyal Britons, all. I had known it. "Thank you, Kerwas. Go on with your tale. What did the King say?"

"Well, he understood it. He knew the message Lancelot had sent. It was to be expected, he told Gawaine. Mordred was only following his instructions. But Gawaine did not like to hear it. The duke wrote that Sir Mordred was meeting with the Saxons, all on his own authority, without even taking counsel."

"But of course. He had to. If the King was dead, the treaties were void. Cerdic sent for him."

"So Arthur said, my lady. But Gawaine accused Sir Mordred of rank ambition. I heard him cry that Mordred had not waited even a day to see if the rumors were true."

"He could not wait, for the Kingdom's sake," I protested. "And it wasn't a rumor. It was a written message from Lancelot. And in any event, waiting a day, even a week, would have gained us nothing."

Kerwas watched me with interest and with some fear, and I strove to calm myself.

"So the King said," he agreed. "But Gawaine said otherwise."

I looked away. My dear Arthur, with Lancelot fighting for life and Gawaine shouting in his ear that his son wished to betray him! Had no one loved him enough to stand by him in his need?

"Always, always the same story," I whispered. "The cold Orkney blast that destroys whatever he has labored to build! . . . Well, go on, Kerwas. I know Duke Constantine said more. I know his hatred for Mordred. I can even guess his next lie. He no doubt mentioned me."

That took Kerwas by surprise, and he looked at me intently. "It came last," he said, "but touched the King nearest, by his voice. The duke claimed that Mordred courted you, consorted with you, and planned to make you his Queen."

"And? Surely he did not content himself with such vague accusations?"

"All right, my lady, if you will have the truth, I will tell it. He claimed you had consented, and the wedding day was fixed."

I pressed the cloth to my face. "Oh, Arthur!" I whispered. "My dear husband and my friend! You were alone!"

At last Kerwas closed his eyes and sighed.

"I knew you kept faith," he said in some relief.

"But did the King know it, Kerwas?"

With an effort, he gripped my hand. "Indeed so, my lady," he said in a low voice. "It's my belief he never doubted you. I'm a married man myself, my lady. I'd have known, by his voice."

We sat silent a little while. Anna had left to fetch the servant. Now he came, bringing water and a blanket. Anna begged me to arise from the soiled and matted straw, offering to take my place herself. But I would not let her. His sickness did not offend me, nor his smell. I wanted only to sit with his head in my lap and hear him talk of Arthur.

"Well, then," I said, when he was comfortably settled and refreshed, and breathing easy. "Well, then, what happened next? If my lord did not believe the letter, how did he ever come to suspect his son of treachery?"

"You have Gawaine to thank for that—him and Lancelot."

"Lancelot! Why, they are sworn enemies! Are you going to tell me that they were one in this?"

"Gawaine was like a gadfly, always buzzing about the King, never leaving him in peace. Every word out of his mouth spoke ill for Mordred."

"I can easily believe it," I said sadly.

"It was Gawaine who told Lancelot about the letter, as we carried him back home. Most of it he took in silence." He stopped, and I touched his hand.

"You needn't tell me. I know well what part of it upset him. He believed it, then?"

"No. He never believed you had consented, my lady. He believed you trapped by circumstance. But he believed that Mordred was ambitious and looked to secure his title by taking you to wife."

"He always distrusted Mordred."

"Each of them pressed the King to hurry. When we left Sir Lancelot, he swore he would not be far behind us. But when we came to take ship for home, the winds were against us."

"So I have heard."

"And when we at last made land, we were blown off course."

"Were you shipwrecked, Kerwas? Were the vessels destroyed?"

"Ours was, my lady. Most were heavily damaged and could not put back out to sea. But ours and Sir Bedwyr's were destroyed."

"Ah, Bedwyr," I said, my eyes misting. "I am glad Bedwyr was with him." Kerwas cleared his throat, and I felt my heart sink within my breast. Was Bedwyr gone, too? "Go on, Kerwas. Finish your tale."

"It is easily finished. It is all killing. No sooner had we landed than we saw Saxon troops approaching. We were less than two hundred ashore and only twenty horses. Gawaine would not heed the King's call for patience. He saw we were outnumbered and rallied the forces under the banner. He had a young black-haired devil with him, who cried out for heathen blood."

I paled. "Galahad?"

"Aye, that's the name." He made to spit and then recollected my presence, and cleared his throat instead. "We attacked them and broke them. The King would have asked for parley, for he suspected some mischance. But Gawaine raised the war cry and led the young men forward. We veterans would have waited with the King, but our hand was forced. We broke them, but there Gawaine received his deathblow, and died later on the beach. With his last breath, he begged the King to send for Lancelot, to revenge his death."

I let out a long breath. "Then at the end, he forgave him. God be thanked for that."

Kerwas grunted, and I helped him to a more comfortable position.

"Kerwas," I said suddenly, "did you know you were on the Saxon Shore?"

He tried smiling, but could not bring himself to it. "No, indeed. We thought we were in Britain. Only the High King wondered, but even he was not sure."

"Ahhhh. That explains why you thought Cynewulf came to fight."

"Well, didn't he?"

"No, indeed. Never mind it now. What did Arthur do next? Organize the army and push for home?"

"You know him well, fair lady. That's exactly what we did. We knew soon enough we were in Saxon lands; we passed many villages, and the people there were sore afraid. But we let them be; King Arthur said they were our allies. He wished to move with speed, before news of the beachfront battle got to Cerdic and was misunderstood."

Too late, I thought sadly. How the fates had worked against him!

"But we fought several skirmishes along the way, my lady. It seems the news had spread, and though we left them in peace when they did not oppose us, when they gave us fight, we fought them."

I nodded. "How not? I see how this disaster came about. And I have heard from Galahad's own lips about the battle against Cerdic."

Kerwas trembled, and a tear fell from his eye. "Aye, that was a sad day. Until that day, the King had hope his son was not a traitor. But when he saw him, riding abreast of Cerdic, their forces coming upon him together"—he gulped—"he lost his patience. I have been a soldier these twenty years, my lady. I have never seen a man so angry. He rallied us for attack. 'Now,' he said, 'we will see which side he chooses!' But when we broke from the woods and came at them—Mordred turned and ran. That was what wounded the King so. He would rather have fought him, man to man, than see him run away."

"Did he see it thus?" I cried. "Or did you hear this from Galahad? He wanted peace! He had sworn in my presence he would never raise his hand against his father! And he kept that oath, that day. If my lord Arthur would not wait to speak with him, what choice had he?"

"We did not see it that way, my lady. The men didn't. I don't know what Arthur thought. He said little. But after we had buried our dead and set fire to the battlefield, we pressed on toward Camelot at double march. The King was heard to say he would be revenged."

I closed my eyes. Anna came forward and pressed her kerchief to my brow. "Take some water, my lady. Have some refreshment."

But I shook my head. "Thank you, Anna, but no. We are coming to it now. This brave man was with my lord to the end, it seems. Go on, dear Kerwas. Do not fear to tell me the worst. I have known already these seven days."

"Is that how long it's been?" He sighed and paused for breath. "We came to the Camel valley late one evening. We were only a league from home. But between us and Camelot lay Mordred's army. A lady rode into camp in the early morning, a fine lady upon a fine horse."

"A chestnut mare? A slender woman with dark hair? An air of authority and power?"

"I see you know her."

"It was the lady Niniane, Queen of the River Isles and Lady of the Lake. She is the King's enchantress."

"She stayed till dawning. When she left, she was fighting tears, and the King looked bitter. But he sent a knight as messenger to Sir Mordred, to request a parley."

"Thank God!" I breathed. "They spoke then? Face to face?"

"Yes, my lady. Around noon. With the armies all around them. They met in a tent near the river's edge. They talked for about an hour."

Even knowing the ending, I felt a great rush of relief. They were cool men, both, and possessed of patience. So they had sat and spoken together, father and son. I would be forever glad of that.

"You don't happen to know what was said?"

A bitter smile touched his lips. "No, my lady. I was close enough to see, but not to hear. We raised a cheer when they came from the tent, for they came out arm in arm, the King wearing his war helm, with the crown upon the brow. Mordred's head was bare. We thought—we all thought it was over, and all was well."

"And why wasn't it?" I asked softly, stroking the hair from his face. He closed his eyes, weary of talking.

"I don't know, my lady. Suddenly there was shouting; we looked up and saw soldiers fighting—how it came about, I will never know. But when have two armies faced each other, ready for battle, and not fought? Suddenly we were at war. Someone raised a paean—King Arthur saluted his son and turned back to his troops. Sir Mordred stood there, rooted to the ground, and watched him go. Then my captain called me, and we formed the phalanx. It had begun."

"He knew," I whispered, as the tears began flowing, "he knew, and chose the time. What a King he was!"

Kerwas lay still a long time and then at last drew breath. "Near midafternoon I was wounded, run through by a sword. I lay on the turf as the battle was waged around me. I lay unknowing for some of the time, and when I awoke, the sun threw shadows long. I heard someone calling 'The King has fallen! Look! The Dragon is down!' When I looked up, I saw Sir Lancelot, with tears on his muddy face. In his arms, he bore the High King Arthur." Kerwas coughed and spit out bloody froth; I hugged him close and wiped his lips with my sleeve. "He was awake, but groaning. There was blood in his hair, and a great wound—" He stopped. Gently I stroked his head, above his ear.

"It was here," I whispered.

He struggled to open his eyes but failed. "Yes," he breathed. "How could you know? It was—dreadful. They took him, I think, to Ynys Witrin, to the shores of Avalon. Lancelot carried him, although he was barely healed. I—I have come to the end, my lady. I know no more. They came with the litter and carried me back. No one speaks of it, except to say he is gone."

I kissed his forehead; his flesh was cold. "Yes," I managed, "I know he is gone. Thank you, Kerwas. There is only one thing more. What happened to Mordred?"

His breath came fast and shallow, and I bent low over his lips to hear his speech. "I know not," he whispered. "I heard nothing of him." He paused, and his body shuddered. "Now I have told it," he breathed. "Bless you." He went limp in my lap, and I hugged him tightly as my tears splashed down on his lifeless face.

"Stay, Kerwas," I whimpered, "oh, dear God, stay with me!"

It was Anna who drew me away, I think, and put me to bed. Black grief fell upon me when Kerwas died, the grief I had fought off so long, and for days I was senseless to all but pain. I wished for death; I prayed for it fervently—anything to be with my dear Arthur!

Nevermore would he hold me in his arms, or whisper sweetly in my ear in the still of night. I would never hear his voice again, or his laughter, or feel his lips against my hair. Gone forever were those loving eyes and the calm strength that supported me through every woe. He had become part of my own flesh, it seemed, part of my very soul, this man whose outstretched hand I had once feared to take.

Britain would miss him, certainly. But Britain would have other kings. It was I, Guinevere, who would not survive his passing, who would miss him a thousand times an hour in unmeasurable ways. He was more than a king to me, he was my world: my sweet spring, my rich summer, my brilliant winter dawning; he was my sleep, my rest, my peace, my joy, my very life—how could I go on without him? I closed my eyes and prayed to God to join my soul with his. I was unable to look back, dared not look forward, and could not bear the present. What was left for me, but death?

But death did not come.

Cruelly, the black grief passed and left me numbed and exhausted, without even the will for thought. When at last I rose from bed at Anna's begging, I sat alone in a chair, listening to the wind. The unbearable emptiness that was my future stretched out before me like a dead gray sea, flat, dull, and comfortless, without direction, without end.

"Oh, God," I whispered. " 'How I have wept, day and night, before you . . . How my soul is filled with trouble . . . Lover and friend you have taken from me, and all my acquaintance into darkness!' "

Anna, always at my side, took my hand and held it gently. "My lady, hold hard to faith. This is not the end."

"Without Arthur, it is the end."

"Ah, but 'A man's days are as grass, he flourishes as a flower in the field; the wind passes over and he is gone. But the mercy of the Lord is from everlasting to everlasting.' "

Everlasting! It had been Merlin's promise! I nodded suddenly as my heart lifted. "Yes."

Anna squeezed my hand, misunderstanding and withdrew.

I walked to the window. The wind, freshening, made the willows toss and dance. Beyond them the sky grew dark with storm. Everlasting! He would live forever, beyond this grief, beyond this life, beyond even my imagining. He was not gone; he would never leave me. He was everlasting, the once and future King.

I lifted my eyes to the wild, oncoming sky and listened to the thud of a horse's canter on the road outside the monastery walls.

THE END

♛ THE DESCENT OF PENDRAGON

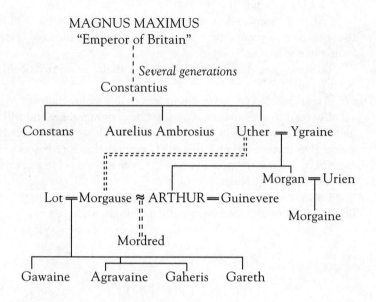

THE HOUSE OF GWYNEDD

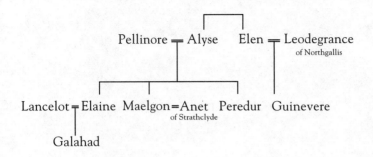